The KEY to CREATION

BY KEVIN J. ANDERSON

Terra Incognita

The Edge of the World

The Map of All Things

The Key to Creation

Kevin J. Anderson

The KEY to CREATION

Terra Incognita
Book Three

www.orbitbooks.net

ORBIT

First published in Great Britain in 2011 by Orbit

All characters and events in this publication, other than those clearly in the public domain, are fictitious and any resemblance to real persons, living or dead, is purely coincidental.

A CIP catalogue record for this book is available from the British Library.

ISBN 978-1-84149-661-0

Typeset in Baskerville by M Rules
Printed in the UK by CPI Mackays, Chatham ME5 8TD

Orbit
An imprint of
Little, Brown Book Group
100 Victoria Embankment
London EC4Y 0DY

An Hachette UK Company
www.hachette.co.uk

www.orbitbooks.net

To Shawn Gordon at ProgRock Records, who expanded the imaginary horizons in the Terra Incognita series by making possible the companion rock CDs, Beyond the Horizon *and* A Line in the Sand.
And thanks for being a cool friend, too.

Iboria
Soeland
Calavik
Farport
Calay
OCEAN SEA
Saedran Underwater City
Outer
Lahjar
Sen Rickcha na-Ware

rag
MIDDLE SEA
eholm
remurr Mines
Wahilir
Abilan
abar
Arikara
Desert Harbor
Missinia
NUNGHAL
LANDS
ABA
ERN SEA
ICEBERGS

The Story So Far

According to legend, ONDUN (the creator of all things) sent out His sons AIDEN and UREC in two Arkships to explore the world and also to find the mysterious Key to Creation, while His third son, JORON, remained in the Eden-like land of Terravitae. Leaving the world in the care of His sons, Ondun departed, leaving His creation behind.

Today, the known world has two continents, Tierra and Uraba, connected by a thin isthmus, on which stands the sacred city of Ishalem. The "Aidenist" people of Tierra are the descendants of Aiden's crew, while the "Urecari" people of Uraba believe that their ancestors originally sailed on Urec's ship. For all of history, the wreck of one ancient Arkship dominated a hill in Ishalem, and the Tierrans and Urabans dispute whether the ship originally belonged to Aiden or Urec. Likewise, each people has legends of a wandering hermit, the TRAVELER, whom Aidenists believe to be immortal Aiden watching over them, while the Urecari believe him to be Urec.

Despite their underlying rivalries, the followers of Aiden and Urec managed an uneasy peace for centuries, punctuated by occasional skirmishes. After long negotiations, KING KORASTINE of Tierra and SOLDAN-SHAH IMIR of Uraba agreed to divide the world into two parts, so that each land could have peace. Korastine traveled with his daughter ANJINE, the future queen of Tierra, and her childhood friend MATEO BORNAN, the son of a guard captain. Sadly, during the city-wide celebrations after the signing of the Edict, an accidental fire started and holy Ishalem burned to the ground. Thus began decades of furious fighting between the followers of Aiden and Urec.

During the fire in Ishalem, a fanatical Aidenist, PRESTER HANNES, who had been living as a spy among the Urabans, tried to desecrate a Urecari church, but was seriously burned and barely escaped with his life. One of the soldan-shah's wives rescued Hannes and nursed him back to health in the Uraban capital city of Olabar. However, sure that it was his sacred mission to wreak havoc on the hated Urecari, Hannes murdered the soldan-shah's wife and escaped from the palace. He spent years wandering the foreign land and took every opportunity to harm Urabans, poisoning wells, burning churches, causing mayhem.

Meanwhile, in the Tierran capital of Calay, the young sailor CRISTON VORA signed aboard the exploratory ship *Luminara*, under the command of CAPTAIN ANDON SHAY. King Korastine had commissioned the ship to discover new lands and find the lost continent of Terravitae, where Ondun's third son, Joron, would be waiting for them. Before sailing away, Criston said goodbye to his wife ADREA, took a lock of her hair, and promised to write her letters and throw them overboard in bottles. As the *Luminara* sailed, Criston did not know that Adrea was pregnant.

Adrea returned to her village of Windcatch, where she lived with her lame brother CIARLO and Criston's mother. They thought they were far from the war until a bloodthirsty Uraban raiding party struck, led by the soldan-shah's son OMRA. Ciarlo hid as the raiders burned the Aidenist kirk. Omra and his followers murdered Criston's mother and kidnapped Adrea, taking her off to Olabar.

During the amazing voyage of the *Luminara*, Criston grew close to Captain Shay and the ship's prester, who told stories about the Lighthouse at the End of the World. As storms approached and the waves grew rough, Criston took watch and saw a distant light on the horizon, perhaps the legendary lighthouse. But then the most horrific monster of the seas, the Leviathan, destroyed the *Luminara* and devoured Captain Shay. Floating among the wreckage, Criston made a crude raft and managed to catch a sea serpent with a grappling hook. The monster towed him to familiar waters, where he was eventually picked up by a fishing vessel. When he returned to Windcatch, however, he learned that his beloved Adrea had been taken away in a Urecari raid, and Ciarlo told him that she was pregnant at the time. Devastated, Criston turned his back on the sea and went to live alone in the high mountains. . . .

Another group of people are the Saedrans—scientists, craftsmen, philosophers—who believe their ancestors left Terravitae and settled on another continent, which sank beneath the waves. They have settled in both Uraba and Tierra but don't espouse either religion.

In Calay, one young Saedran, ALDO NA-CURIC, passed the rigorous tests to become a highly sought-after chartsman. In Aldo's youthful naïveté, he was duped by con man YAL DOLICAR, who told him a fanciful story and sold him a fake map. By the time Aldo learned he'd been tricked, the charlatan was gone. Nevertheless, Aldo established himself as a skilled navigator and served aboard several Tierran ships, until he was captured by Uraban pirates. The captive Aldo was taken to a Saedran woman in Olabar, SEN SHERUFA NA-OA; she was ordered to convince Aldo to serve Uraba as a chartsman. But Saedrans have their own priority—to complete the Map of All Things—and after Sherufa and Aldo shared their knowledge, she helped him escape and he made his way back home.

As the war continued, King Korastine and Soldan-Shah Imir expanded their armies. Anjine's dear friend Mateo began years of military training with DESTRAR BROECK in the frozen lands of Iboria, DESTRAR TAVISHEL in the islands of Soeland, DESTRAR UNSUL in the rangeland of Erietta, DESTRAR

SIESCU in the high mountains and mines of Corag, and glory-hungry DESTRAR SHENRO in the farmlands of Alamont.

Imir secretly established the Gremurr mines on the northern shore of the Middlesea, technically in Tierran territory but inaccessible due to the rugged mountains. From there, his miners (and Tierran slaves) extracted metals for swords and armor.

Both sides committed war atrocities. One of these acts included the slaughter of Aidenist settlers who came to rebuild the ruins of Ishalem.

Adrea worked as a household slave in Olabar. Because she refused to speak to anyone, many believed she was mute. She gave birth to Criston's son, SAAN, but when he reached the age of four, the sikaras (priestesses of the church of Urec) took him away. Over the years, the Urabans kidnapped Tierran children and, under the guidance of a sinister masked TEACHER, brainwashed them to become zealous saboteurs, called *ra'virs*. Saan was destined to become one of them.

Frantic, Adrea turned to an unlikely ally: Omra himself.

By eavesdropping, Adrea uncovered a scheme by VILLIKI (one of the soldan-shah's ambitious wives) and the ur-sikara (the head of the church) to assassinate Omra and pin the blame on Omra's equally unlikable wife CLIAPARIA—so that Omra's half brother TUKAR would become the next soldan-shah. Adrea revealed the plot to Omra, on the condition that her son be returned to her; Omra exposed the treachery, and Villiki was disgraced and banished. Though Tukar was a devoted, bumbling man who had no idea of his mother's schemes, Soldan-Shah Imir had no choice but to send him away to manage the Gremurr mines.

Impressed with Adrea, Omra promised that he would raise Saan as his own and protect her if she agreed to be his wife. Seeing no other way to ensure safety for her child and herself, Adrea consented and took a Uraban name, ISTAR, believing that her true husband was long gone. Meanwhile, Criston lived in isolation in the mountains. Once each year he made the trip to the seashore, where he cast another letter in a bottle into the sea, clinging to hope that somehow Adrea might receive one of them. . . .

Lonely and heartbroken by the war, King Korastine married the daughter of Destrar Broeck, ILRIDA, who gave birth to a son, TOMAS. Ilrida died when Tomas was young, and King Korastine was so paralyzed by grief that Anjine effectively became the ruler of Tierra. Korastine announced he would build another exploration ship to search for Terravitae. Anjine questioned the wisdom of this expense in a time of war until he showed her an ancient magical relic, Aiden's Compass, which would reveal the location of the lost land.

At the southern boundary of Uraba, a strange man named ASADDAN staggered in from the edge of the Great Desert. His people, the Nunghals, lived on the other side of the dunes. Asaddan convinced Omra to sponsor an expedition to the other side of the desert, via a balloon-borne sand coracle to ride the winds.

Over the years, Omra had grown fond of Saan and raised him as a true son, despite the boy's Tierran heritage. Saan, now twelve, and the retired soldan-shah Imir accompanied Asaddan across the desert, along with a reluctant Sen Sherufa. Among the Nunghal clans, as guests of KHAN JIKARIS, they traveled to the coast of the southern ocean. From maps used by seafaring Nunghals, Sherufa suspected that the southern ocean connected with the coastline of Uraba, far to the north. Sherufa, Imir, and Saan returned home with their exciting news, and Sherufa hired a courier—the ubiquitous con man Yal Dolicar—to deliver the details to Sen Aldo in Calay.

Korastine's new Arkship was constructed, and Aldo na-Curic was chosen as the Saedran chartsman for the voyage. Before the Arkship could sail, though, *ra'vir* saboteurs burned the great ship, dashing the king's dreams.

Prester Hannes continued his depredations against the followers of Urec until he was captured and sent to work in the Gremurr mines. He escaped into the rugged mountains and endured great tribulations until—frostbitten, starving, and near death—he stumbled upon the hermit Criston Vora. Criston nursed him to health and took the prester back to Calay. While all of Calay reeled from the destruction of the Arkship, Criston presented himself to King Korastine and offered to create and captain a new ship.

After many years, Soldan-Shah Omra set off with his armies and recaptured Ishalem just as Istar gave birth to his son and heir, whom she named CRISTON. Omra's third wife, a sweet woman named NAORI, was also pregnant, while his other wife, Cliaparia, grew murderously jealous of Istar. The baby Criston only increased her ire, and as soon as Naori gave birth to a son, Cliaparia murdered Istar's baby by having a deadly sand spider placed in his crib. Mad with grief and shock at the death of her child, Istar stabbed Cliaparia to death in broad daylight and staggered away into the market, where she found a merchant selling strange artifacts, including a letter in a bottle—a message from her dear Criston.

Over the next several years, as Omra consolidated his hold on Ishalem, his engineer soldier KEL UNWAR constructed a gigantic wall across the isthmus to bar Aidenists from the sacred ground. While excavating the rubble of the Aidenist church in Ishalem, Omra's builders discovered an ancient map in a deep underground vault: Urec's Map, a relic that could lead them to the mysterious Key to Creation.

The Tierran army tried to retake Ishalem before the wall was finished. Mateo, now a military leader, vowed to do this for Anjine, whom he had loved for many years. They had grown up together, and both had a very close connection that went beyond friendship, but they dared not show it. Now he was her adviser and went off with the armies to Ishalem. When the Tierrans prepared to attack, however, the masked Teacher appeared on the wall and issued a command. Suddenly, many young Aidenist soldiers revealed themselves to be *ra'virs*. They assassinated several army commanders, and Mateo barely escaped. The Tierran army stumbled home defeated.

In Olabar, Saan, now nineteen, fended off an assassination attempt; hating Saan and Istar because of their Tierran heritage, the sikaras used every opportunity to harm him and discredit his mother. When Omra returned from Ishalem after defeating the Tierran army at the wall, he was enraged to hear about the threats and disrespect. In order to keep Saan safe, Omra commissioned a fine vessel, the *Al-Orizin*, and sent the young man on a quest to find the Key to Creation. Saan gathered his crew, including con man Yal Dolicar, a reef diver named GRIGOVAR, Sen Sherufa, and the Urecari priestess FYIRI, who possessed a magic journal through which she could write instantaneous messages back to the main church in Olabar. The *Al-Orizin* sailed east into the uncharted waters of the Middlesea.

In Calay, Criston Vora prepared his new ship, the *Dyscovera*, for the voyage to find Terravitae. Among his crew were the Iborian shipwright KJELNAR, cabin boy JAVIAN, chartsman Aldo na-Curic, and the grim Prester Hannes. King Korastine saw the ship off with Anjine, Prince Tomas, and Destrar Broeck, Tomas's grandfather. Old Korastine longed to go on the voyage, but his failing health forced him to stay behind. Shortly after the ship sailed westward across the Oceansea, Korastine died in his sleep, leaving Anjine as queen of Tierra.

One of the *Dyscovera*'s sailors turned out to be a young woman in disguise, MIA. Furious at the deception, Prester Hannes wanted her marooned at the next landfall, but Criston refused. Two sailors, ENOCH DEY and SILAM HENNER, cooked up a scheme to rape the girl during a night watch, but Javian, who had taken a liking to Mia, and Hannes intervened. With no choice but to enforce the law of the sea, Criston sentenced Henner to twenty lashes, and Enoch Dey was cast overboard to his death. As they sailed onward, Aiden's ancient Compass awakened, and its needle pointed to Terravitae.

Meanwhile, the Nunghal adventurer Asaddan convinced a clan captain to sail around the southern coast in search of a new sea route. After a long and arduous voyage, they arrived at Ishalem. Pleased to have found a new trade route, the Nunghals returned home, promising to bring back many ships.

After Kel Unwar completed the great wall, Omra gave him an even greater task: digging a canal across the isthmus to connect the Oceansea and the Middlesea. Using explosive firepowder—a chemical recipe given to them by the Nunghals—and the manpower of Tierran slaves, Unwar began excavations. In anticipation of the canal's completion, Omra visited his exiled brother Tukar at the Gremurr mines. He instructed Tukar to armor a group of warships; these invincible ironclads would sail through the new waterway to destroy the Aidenist navy.

Incensed that the enemy was operating mines on Aidenist land at Gremurr, Destrar Broeck, his nephew IAROS, and Destrar Siescu of Corag proposed creating a road through the mountain passes so that the Aidenist army could ride a force of woolly mammoths over the mountains to seize the mines. Siescu's trusted scout RAGA VAR plotted the route, and work began for a full-scale assault.

Grieving for her father, Anjine accepted a marriage offer from JENIROD, whom she had never met. Because her dearest friend Mateo was just a soldier and not an appropriate husband for a queen, she decided to marry for politics, not love. Learning of Anjine's betrothal, and hiding his own feelings, Mateo impulsively married a blacksmith's daughter, VICKA SONNEN. Vicka was a lovely, strong woman, whose only flaw was that she wasn't Anjine.

When the queen finally met Jenirod, she was not impressed with the self-centered, chauvinistic man who treated her like a wilting flower. Anjine made her dissatisfaction with her husband-to-be plain, leaving the narrow-minded Jenirod baffled as to what he'd done wrong. In an attempt to impress her, Jenirod and Destrar Tavishel raided a Urecari shrine, Fashia's Fountain, and slaughtered the priestesses and pilgrims there. Although Tavishel's men called it a great victory, Jenirod was sickened at what they'd done.

After the desecration of Fashia's Fountain, the Urabans retaliated: Kel Unwar sent ships to intercept a royal cog carrying Prince Tomas. Urged on by the ominous masked Teacher (revealed to be Unwar's own sister ALISI, who was kidnapped and abused by Aidenist sailors when she was young), Unwar captured the boy, executed him, and sent the head back to Queen Anjine. To avenge her brother's death, Anjine ordered Mateo to decapitate one thousand Uraban prisoners of war and dump their heads before the Ishalem wall, in full view of the enemy. And the cycle of hatred escalated further. . . .

In the village of Windcatch, Ciarlo had persistent dreams that his sister Adrea was still alive. Though he suffered from a lame leg, Ciarlo set off overland to make his way to Uraba to find her, and to preach the word of Aiden to the Urecari. More often than not, he received a cold welcome, but he persisted. One night at camp, an old wanderer joined him, and they exchanged stories. When Ciarlo awoke the next day, the man was gone, leaving behind a thick journal of his travels. When Ciarlo discovered that his lame leg was miraculously healed, he realized he had encountered the legendary Traveler himself!

In Olabar, Istar/Adrea thwarted an assassination plot instigated from within the Urecari church by the banished Villiki. With Omra gone in Ishalem, former soldan-shah Imir responded to the treachery, purging the church; Villiki fled to the Gremurr mines, where her son Tukar lived with his wife SHETIA and their son ULAN. Tukar had nearly finished armoring the warships, per Omra's wishes, and he was not happy to see his disgraced, scheming mother.

When Anjine found out that Jenirod was responsible for the desecration of Fashia's Fountain—and by extension, the murder of Tomas—she broke their engagement and sent him away in disgust. Shamed, Jenirod rode to Corag to join Destrar Broeck in the military campaign to cross the mountains and strike the Gremurr mines. Mateo, scarred by being forced to decapitate a thousand prisoners, refused to face his wife Vicka or Queen Anjine with so much blood on his hands. He also rode into the mountains to join the attack on Gremurr.

On the far side of the world, the *Dyscovera* came upon an undersea city and a race of people descended from the lost branch of Saedrans. Aldo na-Curic was delighted to be reunited with his people, and their king, SONHIR, promised to help the Tierran ship. Hannes, however, led a mutiny and tried to force King Sonhir and his people to convert to Aidenism—by force, if necessary. The incensed mer-Saedrans fought back, and in the battle, Kjelnar was pulled overboard into the waves before Criston managed to quell the violence. But the damage was done; the mer-Saedrans abandoned the *Dyscovera*, refusing to offer further aid. Criston ordered Prester Hannes tied to the mast, where he awaited his sentence.

The *Al-Orizin* found a lush, isolated island surrounded by reefs and wrecked ships. Going ashore, Saan and his crew found an old crone, IYOMELKA, and her beautiful daughter, YSTYA, alone on the island. Sikara Fyiri took offense when Iyomelka claimed to be the wife of Ondun Himself and that Ystya was His daughter—the sister to Aiden, Urec, and Joron. The two women had lived on the island for countless centuries, and Ondun had drowned there in a magic spring that had now gone dry. If the spring could be restored, Iyomelka claimed, magic would return to the island, and she would regain her youth. She promised Saan any reward he wished if his crewmembers could repair the spring. Saan and Grigovar dove into the deep well and freed the blockage, making the waters flow. Underground, they discovered the preserved body of a mysterious old man, who rose to the surface in the resurgent spring. When Iyomelka bathed in the waters, her body shed many apparent years.

Saan claimed her daughter Ystya as his reward. He had grown very fond of the lovely and innocent girl, and she desperately wanted to get away. Infuriated by the demand, Iyomelka refused to let her daughter go, but Saan sneaked back to the island at night and slipped away with Ystya. The *Al-Orizin* set sail and fled. When Iyomelka discovered that she had been tricked, she resurrected a vessel from the sunken wrecks around the island and sailed in pursuit of Saan, carrying the preserved body of Ondun. Racing away, the *Al-Orizin* came upon an impassible barrier—the enormous sea serpent, BOURAS, that girdled the whole world, cursed by Ondun to bite its own tail for eternity. With Iyomelka closing in behind them, they had no way to get past Bouras.

With a great force of battle-armored mammoths, the Tierran army crossed the mountain pass to Gremurr. Reaching the Urecari mines, the shaggy beasts struck terror into the enemy soldiers. Tukar sent his wife and son to hide in the hills, while he tried to lead a defense but ultimately failed. Destrar Broeck declared a great Tierran victory, freed all of the Aidenist slaves, seized the nearly finished ironclad warships, and executed Tukar, sending the head back to Soldan-Shah Omra to show his hatred: after all, murdered Tomas had been Broeck's grandson.

Destrar Tavishel planned to get revenge for the killing of Prince Tomas in his own way. Without permission from the queen, Tavishel sailed to Ishalem, where he intended to launch kegs of burning oil into the holy city to destroy it again. However, a hundred Nunghal ships arrived, and the Nunghal cannons cut Tavishel's ships to ribbons. Furious at the unprovoked attack on Ishalem, Omra refused to rescue any survivors from the wrecked ships, letting the sharks feed instead. He didn't think his hatred for the Aidenists could grow worse . . . but he had not yet learned of the carnage at Gremurr.

To unlock the soul of mankind,
one must hold the key to creation.
—Urec's Log

Part I

1 *Outskirts of Calay*

As he rode across Tierra, the constant pounding hoofbeats echoed the pounding of his heart. After days of hard travel, Jenirod no longer heard the sound. He fought hunger, thirst, and exhaustion, keeping himself awake only through sheer determination, and pressed on. He had already crossed half a continent, but he had to reach Calay.

Queen Anjine needed to know what had happened at the Gremurr mines. After two decades of war, the Aidenists had finally secured a major victory against the evil Urecari.

Jenirod had pushed two of his three warhorses nearly to death before turning them loose and riding on. The animals could take care of themselves until some other traveler found them. Son of the Eriettan destrar, he had grown up with horses, won countless trophies and ribbons in Landing Day cavalcades; he couldn't believe he was abandoning such fine mounts. In fact, mere months ago, Jenirod's proud and shuttered mind would never have imagined that any mission could be so all-consuming. Now he rode long past the point where common sense told him he should sleep and let the horses rest.

If the queen pulled all her forces together, the Tierran army could ensure the final defeat of the soldan-shah. . . .

After the military triumph at Gremurr, fires had been extinguished, Uraban bodies dumped into the sea, and brave Aidenist fighters buried in graves marked by fishhook posts. But the queen needed to know of the victory as soon as possible, so she could plan for the next phase of the war. Jenirod had volunteered to make the long and crushing ride; no one was more qualified.

He had taken off as if demons were slashing at his horses' flanks, determined to go faster than anyone believed possible, needing to do something, anything, to blot out the stain of his foolish, immature actions. And after so many tragedies suffered, so many innocent Aidenists killed by the vengeful Urecari—including Prince Tomas—Jenirod longed to deliver unabashed *good* news for a change.

He had crossed the rugged new mountain path by which the Tierran military reached the undefended mines at Gremurr. At the Corag stronghold of Stoneholm, Jenirod paused for only a few hours to refill his waterskins and pack his saddlebags with food, then rode down through the foothills to the river and the well-traveled road that led to the Tierran capital.

All Tierra would celebrate the great Aidenist triumph, though cheers and applause no longer mattered to Jenirod. He would offer Queen Anjine whatever advice he could, but doubted she would accept it from *him*. Those scars would not heal soon . . . if ever.

These past few months had shown Jenirod that war bore little resemblance to the glorious depictions in pageantry, stories, and songs. During the interminable, exhausting ride across the land, he had time to ponder all the destruction that had flowed from his blind naïveté. How he regretted his earnest but juvenile suggestion to Destrar Tavishel that they attack a defenseless Urecari shrine, just to impress Anjine. Jenirod had never considered the consequences, never imagined what the Urecari retaliation might cost. Poor Tomas!

Now he felt shamed and soiled by what they had done. Jenirod had changed much in his heart, but the queen would never forgive him.

Still, his news would give hope to countless saddened families across Tierra. In the victory at Gremurr, the army had freed hundreds of slaves from the mines, innocent Aidenists who had been captured in raids or seized from fishing boats in the Oceansea. They were alive, and Jenirod carried a complete list rolled up in his saddlebags.

In the aftermath of the battle, Subcomdar Mateo Bornan had gathered the freed slaves and instructed scribes with paper and ink (confiscated from the Gremurr administrator's office) to take down all their information so their families could be notified. The scribes covered sheet after sheet with the names, homes, and occupations of the survivors. Those names would bring joy to so many in Calay. Their loved ones would be coming home as soon as possible. Subcomdar Bornan and the first group of freed prisoners would arrive within a few weeks.

But first, Jenirod had to see the queen.

It was sunset by the time his wobbly, weary horse reached the outskirts of the capital city. Jenirod didn't know what day it was. Ahead, rivers flowed into the harbor and buildings clustered around the waterfront, where long piers extended out past the tidal mud into deeper water. And, silhouetted by the low, blood-orange sun, he could discern the outline of Calay Castle in the distance.

Close . . . so close.

Half dead, he pulled his horse to a halt outside a warehouse at the harbor's edge and slid from his saddle as a curious merchant emerged, blinking at him. Jenirod knew he was filthy, wild-haired, and unshaven, but none of that mattered. He was intent on a thin bay mare tied to a fencepost. "A horse—I need your horse, in the name of the queen."

The merchant eyed Jenirod and his mount, noting the flecks of foam at the horse's mouth and flanks and seeing how it trembled just standing there, but he recognized fine horseflesh. "Have mine. It's a more than fair exchange."

Jenirod took the saddlebags, patted his mount on the neck. His legs could barely hold him up. "Take care of this horse. He's served me well." Jenirod didn't even ask for water or food. So close now. He staggered over to the spindly bay mare, climbed onto the horse's back—no time for a saddle—clutched the mane, and rode off into the city.

In less than an hour, he reached the castle gate and shouted in a ragged voice, "Guards, bring me to the queen! I must see the queen!"

Jenirod looked like a wild man, and the royal guardsmen were skeptical, but Guard-Marshall Vorannen recognized him immediately. "Jenirod? By the Fishhook, what's happened to you?"

"A great battle at Gremurr . . . we defeated the Curlies! Please, I have to tell Queen Anjine!" Guards helped him down from the mare, and Jenirod heaved, then reeled, nearly collapsing, but two men held him up. "All right . . . I think I'll take some water first." He didn't see who handed a cup to him.

"We've sent word to the queen," Vorannen said. "Maybe you'd like to change your clothes, wash up, rest?"

Jenirod realized that he stank of horse, sweat, and horse sweat, but he knew his priority. He shook his head, and Vorannen saw the unexpected ferocity in his eyes. "Follow me."

Jenirod knew that seeing him would remind Anjine of the Uraban emissary tossing her brother's severed head onto the throne room floor. When he stood before her, Jenirod swallowed hard and sketched a hurried bow. He had practiced his speech to the rhythm of thumping hoofbeats, and the words that had been running through his head during the endless ride now spilled out of him. "My Queen, your armies conquered Gremurr! We slew many followers of Urec and kept others alive to work the mines and foundries. It is the most crushing defeat of the enemy so far in this war."

As her eyes widened, he talked faster. "And we freed the Tierran prisoners who were forced to labor in the mines. Hundreds are alive and able to return home." He handed her the rolls of names. "Here is a list."

Astonished, Anjine unrolled the papers, scanned the names. A flush had come to her cheeks. "I didn't know you or Mateo had gone to Gremurr." She sat straight, entirely a queen now. "Give me a full report."

Wasting no words, Jenirod described the surprise attack led by armored mammoths from Iboria, how the Tierran army had captured the mines and foundries, as well as seven armored Uraban warships. "Destrar Broeck is eager to take those ironclads and strike undefended enemy cities on the Middlesea shore, but he sent me here so you can plan our final Tierran victory."

"And what of Mateo . . . Subcomdar Bornan? Is he well?"

"He was healthy and uninjured when I left him. Subcomdar Bornan will lead back as many of the prisoners as are able to make the trek. Ondun surely has smiled on us, my Queen."

Anjine sat back in her chair in silence. Waiting for her reaction, Jenirod began to feel even more weary, more hungry, more filthy. Finally, she gave him a cool, formal nod. "I will have this list copied and distributed as widely as possible. The people need to know." She looked down at the names, as if unable to comprehend so many. "This news has been a long time coming, Jenirod."

2 *Olabar Palace*

Soldan-Shah Omra sailed back to his capital city, eager to tell his people of the great Uraban victory at Ishalem. The remarkable cannons of his new Nunghal allies had utterly destroyed a Tierran fleet that had come to burn down the holy city. Every one of their Fishhook ships had been sunk, and Omra had left the mangled foreigners for the sharks to devour. His satisfaction was as clean and sharp as a fine steel blade: the followers of Aiden had gotten exactly what they deserved.

When the soldan-shah arrived in Olabar, however, he found his land being torn apart from within. The Urecari church was in an uproar, the ur-sikara dead, the palace reeling from an assassination plot against his First Wife Istar. Hearing the report from his palace guard captain, Kel Rovik, Omra felt blood pounding in his temples. "Is she safe?"

"Your family is unharmed, Soldan-Shah."

"Call for them! I need to see my wives and daughters, now. Let me look into their eyes and assure myself." He had fought in Ishalem to preserve his faith and his land, only to find that corrupt sikaras posed their own danger, right here in his capital. He had been at odds with the self-centered priestesses for some time. "Chain the doors of the main church until an investigation is completed. Question all the sikaras!"

Rovik gave a quick formal nod. The man had always been competent and reliable. "Your father issued exactly those orders, Soldan-Shah. We have already uncovered many participants in the plot."

Omra exhaled, barely containing his fury. Years ago, his father had resigned as soldan-shah because of the treachery of Villiki and the previous ur-sikara. When Imir had unshouldered those burdens, Omra accepted the challenge, vowing to be different . . . but apparently nothing had changed. "Where is my father? I need to speak with him."

When Rovik's face went ashen, Omra felt a deep chill. "He has sequestered himself, Soldan-Shah, in his grief."

"His . . . grief? What else happened?"

"A disaster at the Gremurr mines. A large Aidenist army crossed over the mountains on giant, shaggy monsters and struck Gremurr from the rear. They seized the mines and our ironclad warships, murdered our troops, enslaved others to work the mines."

Omra had to sit on a cushion to hide his sudden feeling of weakness. Across the open balcony, the curtains waved in the breeze. In the afternoon light, the red silk hangings gave an eerie crimson cast to his private rooms. Gremurr . . . lost! Those mines supplied metals, ships, armor, and swords for all of Uraba.

Rovik looked like a statue as he forced himself to stand straight, keep his voice flat, and deliver the rest of his report. "And there is more, Soldan-Shah."

Omra suddenly knew why his father was in mourning. "Tukar?"

Kel Rovik lowered his dark gaze. "The 'Hooks sent his head back as a message. That was a week ago."

Each breath chilled him like an icy wind in his chest. He knew exactly what sort of message the Tierrans intended to send. Queen Anjine had received a similar horrific gift after Kel Unwar impetuously executed her young brother. Just an innocent boy . . .

But Tukar was innocent too! He'd been exiled to the Gremurr mines through no fault of his own—a result of his mother Villiki's treachery—but he had served his soldan-shah faithfully.

Though Omra understood intellectually the pain Queen Anjine was trying to assuage with this barbaric retaliation, he shoved those thoughts from his mind, leaving no room for even the idea of sympathy. She had killed *Tukar*! Tukar . . .

Omra's hatred for Aidenists blazed like a bonfire built from bone-dry tinder. He tallied the appalling atrocities the 'Hooks had committed over the years. What pain and misery they had inflicted on his poor people. Omra's vision blurred, and he breathed faster and faster. There had to be a reckoning!

Istar's arrival at his doorway startled him. "My Lord, I am happy to see you back. I've missed you." Her tone carried clear relief.

But when Omra looked up at his wife of more than twenty years, he recoiled from the sight of her blond hair and blue eyes, her pale skin, her narrow features. Though she was the mother of his daughters, the mother of Saan, he momentarily saw only a *Tierran* woman. He loathed all Tierrans and everything to do with their hateful culture and religion. He covered his eyes. "Go away!" He drew another breath and calmed himself. "Please . . . just go away, Istar." He loved her, but he couldn't stand any more right now.

Whispering to her, Kel Rovik led Istar away, leaving Omra alone with swirling hatred. He clenched and unclenched his hands, squeezing the rings on his fingers. When Naori came with his two young sons, and then his three daughters arrived, he embraced them, but found his thoughts churning like a stormy sea.

Though he had come back to Olabar with hopes of winning this war, the soldan-shah now reached a harsh conclusion: total genocide of the Aidenists was the only acceptable victory. He was certain of that.

Trapped in the whirlwind of anger, Omra reached out for a moment of calm, thinking of Saan, who had sailed away aboard the *Al-Orizin* many months ago on a quest to find the mysterious Key to Creation. Such exciting adventure for a young man—to uncharted waters and new lands. Saan's ocean voyage must be peaceful, so far away from politics. . . .

3 *The* Al-Orizin

Iyomelka's resurrected ship chased after them, borne on storms and vengeance. From his own deck, Saan watched the island witch through the spyglass. He and his crew were in terrible danger, yet he did not regret his decision to rescue the intriguing and beautiful Ystya from her exile.

"I'm sorry I caused this, Saan. I wanted to be free, but Mother won't let me go."

Saan smiled at her. "I don't intend to let her have you back."

The young woman had delicate features so perfect that sculptors in Olabar would have lined up for the chance to reproduce her face in marble. Her hair was the color of ivory with a hint of honey, her green eyes shone with an innocent hunger to see and learn. Now Ystya looked pale and dizzy, but when she took Saan's arm she straightened like a wilting blossom given water. "I just wanted to see the world for myself."

"And that's what I promised you. I don't go back on my promises." He tried to look brave and confident, not only for her, but for his entire crew. The sailors looked to their captain for answers, sure he must have some kind of plan to save them. He would have to figure something out.

Iyomelka summoned ripples of sorcery and flung them at the ship. The *Al-Orizin* fled before the wind—away from the island witch's wrath and headlong toward another formidable obstacle: ahead, growing ever closer, towered the scaly body of Bouras, a sea serpent so huge that it was said to girdle the entire world, condemned to bite its own tail until Ondun's curse was lifted. The *Al-Orizin* had no way to get past it.

"I would feel better if I knew how we're going to get out of this, Captain," Yal Dolicar said. "Just a hint, perhaps?"

Ystya turned to stare at the racing, endless body of the Father of All Serpents, which blocked the sea from horizon to horizon. "My mother is no match for Bouras." The increasing howl of the winds snatched at the girl's quiet voice. "But she will not stop."

"Neither will we." Saan tried not to show how his mind was racing. "Don't you worry."

Dolicar, a man thoroughly familiar with half-truths and exaggerations, saw through the captain's cocky façade and turned pale.

Through the spyglass, Saan looked aft to study Iyomelka's jagged gray ship. Long ago, that old vessel had sunk in the reefs around her island, but the woman had used her sorcerous powers to raise it from the depths. Strands of seaweed held the tattered sails together, and the hull was encrusted with barnacles and starfish. A sharp, twisted extension of antler coral protruded from the prow. Iyomelka stood on deck beside a crystal coffin that held the preserved body of her husband. The witch's hair and garments whipped in the gale that she herself had summoned.

In front of them, the barrier of the gigantic sea serpent's body looked insurmountable, but at least the Father of All Serpents had no quarrel with them, as far as Saan knew.

Neither choice seemed particularly pleasant.

One of the *Al-Orizin*'s silken sails came loose and flapped wildly. The painted Eye of Urec folded, then stretched tight again, as if winking. The reef diver Grigovar grabbed the rope, using all his weight to pull it taut, then wrapped it around a stanchion until riggers could connect it properly.

From the bow of her ship, Iyomelka hurled black thunderclouds toward the *Al-Orizin* like missiles from an unseen catapult. Next, she summoned two waterspouts, whirling columns of water and air that marched across the waves.

The Saedran Sen Sherufa, her brown-and-gray hair whipping loose around her, shouted into the noise of the gale, "Captain, how will we get past the sea serpent?"

"I'm working on that."

They sailed ever closer to the enormous reptilian body of Bouras. The titanic thing reeled past with such speed that the armor scales—each the size of a mainsail—were a blur. The spray and ripple of Bouras's passage tossed the *Al-Orizin* about like one of the toy boats Saan's little brother played with. In minutes, their ship would ram into the reptile. "Turn south! Hard starboard!"

Grigovar used his considerable strength to turn the rudder hard over. The riggers set the sails to catch the wind, and the *Al-Orizin* heeled about until it cruised alongside the serpent, riding the swift currents drawn along in the wake of Bouras's unending circuit of the world.

Ystya stared hard at the infinite serpent. "My mother told me stories of great titans like this, and how only my father was powerful enough to impose order on them. He protected the seas by containing Bouras."

The wind increased as Iyomelka closed in, and Saan had to shout, "But he's in our way!"

Although the *Al-Orizin* sailed along at top speed, Iyomelka still closed the distance. Her sorcerous waterspouts swept closer, only to be caught in the turbulence that paralleled Bouras. They struck and rode over the serpent's body, then dissipated.

As increasing storms buffeted them, the island witch's voice boomed out, carried on the thunder, magnified by the gale. "You stole my daughter! Return her to me!"

A tall wave crashed against the *Al-Orizin*'s side, sloshing water across the deck and throwing Yal Dolicar and Sen Sherufa to their knees. A terrified Sikara Fyiri, pretending to be a bastion of strength, emerged from her cabin with a heavy unfurling-fern staff; she wobbled as she attempted to stand firm. "Captain Saan, you have no choice—give the girl back. Surrender the demon's daughter and save us all!"

Saan held Ystya's arm. "I will do no such thing."

As the crew muttered in fearful agreement, Yal Dolicar yelled out, "Don't be foolish, men—the only reason the witch hasn't sunk us yet is because she wants Ystya alive. That girl is our only bargaining chip!"

Ystya, no quaking flower, raised her chin. "We can't outrun my mother, Saan—she has powers you cannot imagine—so we have to find some other way."

"If we don't have weapons or powers to match Iyomelka's, then we'll just have to outsmart her." Saan held on as another wave rocked the ship from side to side. "I'd appreciate any suggestions."

Up in the lookout nest, a sailor had lashed himself to the mast to keep himself from being thrown overboard into the violent waters. "Captain, look at the serpent! Something big is coming our way!"

The crewmembers crowded to the side of the ship as lightning crackled around them. Bouras's scaly body seemed to be tapering off, until it abruptly changed to a huge angular shape with ridges, scales, flared horns, and a pair of golden, glaring eyes. Biting its own tail, the serpent's mountain-sized head split the waves and threw off sheets of water twice as tall as the *Al-Orizin*. As it plowed toward the ship, the reptilian eyes spotted them, and the pupil slits widened to drink in this unexpected sight. Scaled lips curled back to expose ivory fangs as long as mainmasts piercing the flesh of its tail.

Bouras came toward them like a battering ram.

4 *The* Dyscovera

It was a trial for mutiny. As captain of the *Dyscovera*, Criston Vora could not forgive what Prester Hannes and his followers had done.

Unresolved tensions weighed down the ship more heavily than any anchor. Criston was responsible for the lives of every sailor aboard, and had to ensure that their mission succeeded against all enemies . . . even those among his crew. The *Dyscovera* had sailed farther than any explorer had ever gone, well beyond the reach of Tierran courts or justice. The captain could rely on no one but himself, even for spiritual guidance.

Prester Hannes was the worst offender of all.

During the senseless uprising against the mer-Saedrans, their Captain's Compass had been smashed, so the *Dyscovera* could not find the way back to Calay. Fortunately, the ancient Aiden's Compass pointed the way to Terravitae. For the first time during their long voyage, the sailors were confident they would reach their holy destination—if they could survive the journey. . . .

In a hazy dawn, Criston summoned the crew to the foredeck for his pronouncement. His ship's boy Javian stood next to the young woman Mia; their support had been invaluable during the fight, helping to free the mer-king's daughters from the mutineers. The Saedran chartsman Sen Aldo na-Curic looked shaken and saddened.

The prester wore his dark Aidenist robe and stood straight, his gaze fiery, his expression unrepentant. He clasped his Fishhook pendant between his palms; Criston had agreed to that small concession when the sailors had bound Hannes's wrists with cords.

Everyone waited for the captain to speak. Criston felt a wave of disgust and disappointment as he faced the haggard mutineers. Some of the men were bruised and battered from the fight. Many looked cowed; only a few remained defiant. The prester looked up at him, unflinching and without anger.

Criston had meant to shout a thundering pronouncement. Instead, his voice dropped low. "I thought you were my friend, Hannes. I trusted you."

"That changed when you betrayed me and betrayed Aiden, Captain."

The crewmembers grumbled at the mutineers, Javian the loudest. Now Criston did shout. "I am the *Dyscovera*'s captain. I lead this ship! And you"—he jabbed a finger toward Hannes—"*you* cost me Kjelnar, our shipwright and first mate, a good man! You cost us our alliance with the mer-Saedrans, who could have been our allies against Uraba."

"Allies are not worth the price of our damnation, Captain," Hannes said, cold and calm. "Those people did not believe in Aiden and refused to hear the truth. You were too blind to see the dangerous course you were setting."

Sen Aldo added the edge of his voice to the captain's. "For centuries the mer-Saedrans studied the seas, the coastlines, the islands. They could have added to our knowledge of the Map of All Things. They could have taken us to Terravitae, but you turned them against us."

"I have all the knowledge I need," Hannes snapped back. "My loyalty is not to the Saedrans or to your map."

"Your loyalty should be to *Tierra,*" Criston said.

The prester chuckled. "No, my loyalty is to Ondun and to Aiden. That has always been the case."

"Our enemies are the followers of Urec—not everyone who seems strange to you." Hannes did not appear to see the difference.

The morning sun beat down on them all, and the *Dyscovera* sailed onward in calm waters. Javian looked nervous and restless. He reached out to squeeze Mia's hands, and she did not pull away. The cabin boy cleared his throat, making a nervous suggestion. "Captain, if these men give us their word that they'll follow only your orders, maybe you should give them another chance. They are our shipmates . . ." Several of the bound mutineers nodded, promising to do just that.

Even Aldo lowered his head. "I've had many philosophical disagreements with the prester, Captain, but I never wanted the man's death. The pull on Aiden's Compass is so strong that we must be near Terravitae. Perhaps it would be best if we let Holy Joron decide their fates?"

Hannes straightened. "In this matter, Joron is one of the only arbiters I would accept."

Criston was not in a forgiving mood. "The choice is not up to you, Prester." Though his heart was torn, he had to be strong. "You yourself advised me, Hannes: when Enoch Dey and Silam Henner tried to rape Mia, *you* were the one who insisted that a captain can show no mercy, that justice is absolute. *You* told me that for the sake of my command, I had to set a harsh example."

Dey had been thrown overboard to his death, while Henner suffered the lash. . . . Even the lash had been a mercy, and now Henner was among those who had turned against the captain. Criston narrowed his eyes. "Surely the crime of mutiny deserves an equally harsh example. By your own advice, I cannot spare you."

Hannes did not beg for mercy. His face was reddened from exposure to the sun and elements, though the burn scars on his cheek remained pale. He clenched the Fishhook in his hands, praying. He seemed to be daring Criston to make the decision.

Before Criston could pronounce the dreaded sentence, though, an excited shout rang from the lookout nest. "Land ho, Captain—coastline dead ahead!"

5 *Middlesea Coast, Near Sioara*

Holding his Book of Aiden, Ciarlo walked into the Uraban harbor town. He wore a calm smile; he whispered prayers. Despite the previous rejections, he kept believing these people would listen to a stranger.

Larger than a typical fishing village, this town boasted several long docks where Middlesea trading ships could tie up and unload. As he walked along the streets, Ciarlo passed crowded mud-brick homes, a small marketplace, a craftsworkers' district, and three Urecari churches built of wood and stone.

He didn't know the name of the town; in fact, he'd never even seen a map of Uraba. Making his way down the coast, he merely followed the roads that took him in the general direction of Olabar, where he hoped to find clues about his sister Adrea. During his travels, he had another calling: when he saw those poor, misguided followers of Urec, he had to preach to them.

Ciarlo went through the village, responding with a benevolent nod to anyone who glanced at him. His faith was a barricade against the resistance and hostility he had encountered so far. Very few of the stubborn Urecari were receptive to his message—in fact, they didn't want to hear him at all—yet he continued nevertheless. Now that he had met the fabled Traveler in person, he was more certain than ever.

The mysterious wandering hermit had appeared in camp one evening, told him stories, and left behind a new volume of handwritten tales. The Traveler had also healed Ciarlo's lame leg—a true miracle. Now Ciarlo felt he had to repay Aiden by preaching his word.

As the Uraban villagers stared at the stranger's pale skin and odd clothing, he raised his hand in blessing. When he showed his Fishhook, they recoiled as if a monster had just appeared in their midst. Women rushed children into their homes and closed the doors.

"I am glad to see you," he said in pidgin Uraban. He understood the language now and could communicate well enough, though his accent marked him as a foreigner. He held up his Tales of the Traveler, knowing these were safer stories, and even Urecari were more likely to listen (though these people erroneously believed that the Traveler was *Urec* rather than Aiden). "I have good news! Let me tell you about Aiden's voyage and his encounter with the Leviathan. Let me tell you—"

A woodworker stepped away from the bench he was building, still holding a hammer. "We don't want to hear it. Go away."

A potter came out of his shop and nudged his young apprentice down the dirt street. "Bring the sikara—now! Tell the mayor, too."

Ciarlo spread his open hand. "There is no need to be frightened. Ondun loved both of His sons. You should not cover your ears against the words of Aiden. We can learn much from the examples of his life." He lifted his book. "Aiden sent me a dream that led me here."

Someone threw a rock, which struck his shoulder with a stinging blow. Startled, he turned to them, his face plaintive. "Why are you afraid?"

Another rock grazed his cheek, though he raised the Traveler's tome to fend it off. More craftsmen emerged from their shops and began shouting, finding bravery in numbers.

Several guards marched down the streets, escorting a pompous-looking man who wore the maroon olba of a mayor. The official yelled such a rapid stream of Uraban that Ciarlo had difficulty understanding the words.

Ciarlo greeted him, offering explanations even before the man could ask. "I've come here to tell you of wonders."

The man's face flushed. He straightened the maroon olba on his head, tightened the silken sash that held his shirt closed over his potbelly. "You are not welcome here. Why do you come to this town?"

"Because Aiden guides me."

A woman in the red robe of a sikara strode down an intersecting street and said in a loud voice, "Cover your ears against his lies!"

In his travels, Ciarlo had received varied receptions from the sikaras; if not tolerant, at least they had not called for his death or imprisonment. Not yet. This one, though, looked very angry.

The woman's arrival gave the official all the impetus he needed, and he ordered the guards to grab Ciarlo. When he clung to his two books, the mayor yanked the volumes out of his hands. Squinting down at the pages, the mayor saw Tierran writing and looked as if he had swallowed a large insect. "What is this?"

"The Book of Aiden," Ciarlo said proudly. "I can read it to you. I will teach you, and all of your people."

The mayor threw the books to the dirt. "Gag him and bind his arms. Make him watch while we burn this blasphemy."

At first Ciarlo did not resist, but when the official tore pages from the books to make a pile for burning, he struggled to break free. A rag stuffed into his mouth by one of the guards prevented him from crying out. Without being asked, a lampmaker doused the torn pages with scented oil and set them ablaze. Ciarlo felt great sadness to see the Book of Aiden perish, but far more grievous was the loss of the unique Tales of the Traveler, each sentence in Aiden's own handwriting. Those stories were irreplaceable.

In only moments, the fire consumed the paper. Curls of ash drifted along the streets like funeral veils.

Ciarlo's shoulders sagged. He wanted to weep, but he was not weak, and he would not give up. He tried to convince himself this was merely another trial that Aiden had given him. The roads, and his beliefs, had brought him to this place, and he was here for a reason.

"Throw him down a well!" a shrill woman yelled.

"Why not stone him right here?"

"Or chain him out in the sun until he repents and accepts the word of Urec."

The sikara offered a hard smile. "I *could* instruct him. We have many implements to assist us."

Ciarlo struggled, more frightened by the thought of indoctrination than torture.

"No." The official turned to his guards with a flourish of one hand toward the sea. "The *Moray* came to port last night."

Some of the townspeople chuckled; quite a few seemed disappointed. The guards dragged Ciarlo along the street toward the docks. He tried to speak of Aiden on the way, but the gag muffled his words.

They approached a long galley tied up to the longest dock. Its silken sails were furled. Striding out onto the pier, the mayor whistled toward the ship. "Captain Belluc, are you still in the market for workers? You go through men quickly."

A bronzed man with a single earring came out on deck to greet them. He sized up Ciarlo. "I can always use new men at the oars."

"And you always pay gold." The mayor smiled. "Part of which goes to the church, of course." He extended his hand, and Belluc placed shining yellow coins in his palm. "This one's an Aidenist, so you won't need to pamper him."

"I don't pamper my men, Aidenist or not."

Through the galley's open hatch, Ciarlo could make out a dark, stuffy hold filled with long benches and shackles at the ends of long oars. When the guards finally took the gag from his mouth, he spluttered, "I came here to preach."

The bald captain raised his eyebrows and laughed. "You'll be too busy rowing to preach." He called to two other sailors aboard the galley. "Take him below and put him in chains with the others."

6 *Corag Mountains*

The rocky Gremurr coastline was no place to keep a herd of shaggy beasts that required tons of food each day. After defeating the Urecari at the mines, the battle mammoths were restless, unruly, and dangerous. Destrar Broeck dispatched his nephew Iaros to guide the big creatures back home to the high cold steppes.

Mateo joined him on the trek, along with two hundred freed Aidenist prisoners who desperately wanted to go home. Other Tierran captives were too weak to make the long journey, having been driven to exhaustion by their bloodthirsty Uraban workmasters, and so they remained behind to help defend the mines if necessary. Once they recovered, the prisoners of war would make the return journey to Tierra the following spring. Now that Gremurr was under Tierran control, the mines would not be such a hellish place—at least for Aidenists. For Urecari prisoners of war, it would be a different story. . . .

Mateo was glad to be going back to Calay at last, where his new wife Vicka was waiting for him. He had spent too little time with her since their wedding. After remaining aloof for decades through a succession of superficial relationships, he had chosen to settle down with the daughter of the blacksmith Ammur Sonnen. No woman could match Anjine, the standard by whom he measured all others, but Vicka Sonnen came close. . . .

He accompanied the lumbering monsters along the rough new road into the Corag mountains, still haunted by the things he had been forced to do in this war. He felt some reluctance to return home, since the guilt weighed so heavily on his shoulders.

But taking these refugees back to their families, who had surely thought their loved ones dead for so many years, would help heal his heart. Days ago, Jenirod had ridden off with his report for Anjine. Soon the queen would know that Mateo was alive and that he had helped secure a major triumph for Tierra. She would be waiting for him when he came home.

He and Iaros rode Eriettan horses, while a few of the men rode on the swaying mammoths. In a nervous habit, Iaros stroked his ridiculously long mustache. "That was a victory to be proud of, wasn't it, Mateo? We did a good thing."

"Don't ever doubt it. God was on our side." Mateo looked behind him at the hundreds of shuffling Tierran prisoners. "Ask any of those refugees—I think they'll agree."

The lead mammoth raised its long trunk and trumpeted, a sound so loud it echoed up the mountain canyons. Mateo was afraid the noise might trigger an avalanche from the snowy slopes, but Iaros didn't seem concerned.

When the group reached the top of the pass, Iaros looked north, beyond the gray mountains. "I'll be in charge of Iboria Reach for as long as my uncle stays in Gremurr." He dropped his voice. "But I must confess, the local problems of Iboria don't seem nearly so pressing, given the state of the war."

Mateo smiled wistfully, recalling his year of soldier training under Broeck. "The Iborian people are independent, Iaros. They can take care of themselves."

When they halted for a meal, Mateo distributed every bit of their remaining food, so the refugees would have full bellies for the march into Stoneholm. "Give someone else my share.

I can do without for now. These people have missed too many meals over the years."

A grin appeared between the tails of Iaros's long mustache. "Then I'll do without, too." His stomach suddenly growled, as if to challenge his resolve.

As the former captives ate, Mateo and Iaros strolled among them, offering encouragement about the long march ahead. They packed up and moved on. An early season snow dusted the path through the high meadow, but the mammoths trampled it down. Some of the prisoners from the northlands shared legends about ancient frost giants, who came with the winter cold and could freeze a man solid in between the words of a sentence, but the day was warm and they laughed at the stories.

Before nightfall, the group reached Stoneholm, the capital city of Corag, built into the mountain under an overhang. A rider came out to meet Mateo and Iaros. "Our scouts spotted you and rushed back to inform Destrar Siescu. He has prepared a victory feast, which awaits you when you arrive."

"A feast is well and good," Mateo said to the messenger, "but they've been on low rations for quite a while, so bland and wholesome food would be best. Also, make sure there are lodgings, or at least tents and campfires for everyone."

"It's already done. Destrar Siescu sent word throughout the Stoneholm warrens asking for families willing to share their homes. For any who need to sleep outside in tents, we have extra blankets."

The freed Gremurr slaves burst forward with increased energy as they reached the city built into the mountainside. Corag residents came out to welcome them, commemorating the victory, cheering the refugees and the soldiers. Mateo's heart warmed to see thirty of the haggard refugees reunited with their own families from Corag. He had come to know these tough, whip-thin men during the march along the mountain road, and he knew which ones had grown up in the rugged mountains. He watched the Corag men bound forward like gaunt antelopes, while women in woolen shawls and spun skirts came running out, calling names, searching the returning prisoners for familiar faces.

Laughing and weeping, women kissed their shaggy and dirty men. Children stared at unfamiliar fathers while the mothers spilled out a flood of words that had been pent up for years. Most of the returning Corag slaves just clung to their wives or sweethearts, rocking them back and forth. Warm tears filled Mateo's eyes, and he drew a deep breath, let it out slowly. He would be home soon, too. The palpable joy in the air heartened the others, who now looked forward to the long trek back to Calay.

The bald, pale-skinned Siescu came out to meet Mateo and Iaros with a grin wide enough to stretch the skin on his angular face. "This is cause for great celebration, gentlemen. We are glad to have you." The Corag destrar looked skeptically at the herd of large and restless russet beasts. "But your mammoths stripped the vegetation clean the last time they came through. They won't find much forage. You'll have to move along as soon as possible."

"My soldiers will guide them back to the steppes tomorrow," Iaros promised.

Siescu led them to his cavernous hall, where an ever-present fire blazed in the huge hearth. Tureens of hot soup and platters of steaming bread were laid out on the long table. He clicked his tongue against his teeth. "You must be frozen to the bone after that long journey. You can be warm in here."

Mateo ate his soup, a broth of some unknown meat enhanced by sliced root vegetables. The warmth and nourishment felt very good. "Destrar, can you send riders ahead to the river in the morning to secure one of Sazar's barges? That would make the journey easier for our returning friends."

"Consider it done," Siescu said. "We are all part of this war, and I sense it will soon be over."

Tearing into a chunk of bread, Iaros raised his chin. "I've decided that Iborians can take care of themselves, and I'll return to Gremurr after all. My uncle needs me more." When Mateo looked at him in surprise, the other man shrugged. "Capturing Gremurr was only the first part of the battle—now we have to hold it. They are already growing short of supplies."

Destrar Siescu considered for a long moment. "I've got a hundred soldiers to send with you—and I will go along, too. And a load of supplies. I don't much like to leave my hall this late in the season, but I want to see these mines before winter arrives. Raga Var can lead us safely over the pass."

"Winter will soon close the pass, Destrar." The mumbled voice came from someone not accustomed to speaking before a large group of people. Mateo spotted the shaggy-looking guide in tattered fur garments. "If we are going back to Gremurr, we'd better leave quickly."

7 Gremurr Mines

Destrar Broeck had never been much of a sailor, but now that he'd captured seven warships, he enjoyed hunting on the open Middlesea.

The ironclad vessels were quite different from the barges and carracks frequently used along the Tierran coastline, and the Uraban rigging style made the ships handle in unexpected ways, which was why Broeck insisted on so many shakedown voyages. Should there be open naval battles against the Curlies, he needed his fighters to be familiar with their commandeered ships.

Now, at the end of another successful patrol voyage, the ironclad sailed back to the docks at the mine complex. Behind it came two newly seized Uraban cargo ships, which would drop anchor with the other enemy vessels he had captured—seventeen so far.

Gremurr harbor was full of ships that Broeck's ironclads had seized in the Middlesea waters. While most were not suitable for naval warfare, at least they would no longer be delivering cargo to the Urabans. Sooner or later, as word spread, maritime traffic would avoid Gremurr entirely. Traders would be afraid to sail from port to port on their regular commercial runs. And that was a good thing, too.

Broeck smiled. Soldan-Shah Omra must be trying to figure out how to recapture the mines, but his minimal navy in the Middlesea could never stand against his own ironclad juggernauts. Isolated and protected by mountains, closed off by the isthmus of Ishalem, Uraban cities along the Middlesea coast had never faced an Aidenist attack and therefore had no defenses.

In the meantime, the destrar was eager to move. Regardless of how many enemies he had slain during the conquest of the mines, Broeck didn't feel he had avenged his grandson Tomas. Besides, although he needed to ensure that the mines continued producing vital metals for the Tierran war effort, he was a warrior, not a mine manager.

The high cliffs of the Gremurr shore were coated with a fresh layer of soot now that the smelters and refineries were operating again, and the air stank of sulfur and smoke. Standing on the ironclad's deck, Broeck regarded the bustle of activity with satisfaction. While he missed the cold, clean air of the north, even this tainted breeze had a heady quality that reminded him of a battle well fought and enemies crushed.

The armored warship tied up beside the other six ironclad vessels at the long pier, and sailors threw boarding ramps across to the dock boards. As Broeck tromped down the pier, his new mining chief, Firun—a former household slave of the defeated Uraban overlord—came out to greet him, knowing the destrar would want a report. From the smile on the old man's sunburned face, Broeck could see that the report was a good one.

"We are fully operational, Destrar. The damage has been repaired, the forges are relit, and the miners are back in the tunnels, pulling out iron and copper ore. As of today, our production is back at its prior capacity."

Firun had been captured fifteen years previously and put to work in the mines; when he grew too old to perform hard labor, he became a household servant for Tukar, the mine administrator. Having served here for so many years, Firun understood the workings of the mines, where the veins of metal ore were in the cliffsides, where the tunnels led, how the forges worked.

"A day sooner than expected—good! Were there any problems?"

Firun shook his head. "The Urabans spent years bullying Tierran slaves, and now they see what it's like to be on the other side of the whip. I don't think they like their reversed roles!"

Broeck was especially pleased to learn about the amazing chemical mixture called firepowder. During the Urecari administration, Aidenist slaves had been forced to mix batch after batch of the explosive for blasting mine tunnels, and thus knew the chemical recipe. Envisioning how Tierra could use firepowder in the war effort, Broeck had sent the secret back to Calay along with Subcomdar Bornan and the freed refugees.

Broeck walked with wobbly steps, getting used to solid ground again after a day aboard the sailing ship. Firun took him to the row of smelters that were producing new metal to be fashioned into armor and blades. The temperature was blisteringly hot inside the smelter building and the air nearly unbreathable with fumes. The defeated Urecari slaves looked sullen as they went about their labors. Theirs were the bloody backs now.

Firun was troubled by the aggressive punishment, however. "I know they are only followers of Urec, Destrar. Vengeance is one thing, but we do need those workers. If they are injured by harsh treatment, then they can't produce for us. Workmaster Zadar was a cruel man, but he understood how to enforce strict discipline without damaging his laborers."

Broeck brushed aside the concern. "It gives our men a much-needed sense of justice. For now, let them have their fun." He turned his attention to the crates stacked along the far wall. "Have you completed the inventory yet? I am anxious to know what sort of bounty we seized."

Firun lifted the lid of one crate to reveal packed, shining swords. "Nearly three hundred blades to arm three hundred Tierran soldiers."

Broeck ran his eyes along the piled crates and gave an appreciative nod. "I don't like the curved style of blades favored by the Curlies, but I suppose they'll chop through flesh and bone well enough."

8 *The* Al-Orizin

Overhead, thunder pounded like drumbeats from the angry clouds. From her spectral ship, Iyomelka's voice boomed out in a desperate scream: "Give me my daughter!" The island witch looked horrific, her dark hair blowing in the wild wind.

Yet she was a far lesser threat than the gigantic sea serpent. The fearsome head of Bouras split the water as it hurtled toward them. "Hang on!" Saan yelled, certain that no ship, no weapon could drive away the Father of All Serpents. As the first of the monster's bow waves slammed into the *Al-Orizin*, he held Ystya, trying to maintain a brave face.

The young woman shouted into the rising crash of waves, "This is not what my father would have wished, but what else can I do?" She tore free of Saan's grip and dashed for the stern, somehow keeping her balance on the lurching deck. "If Bouras has not learned his lesson, we are all in grave danger."

"That's nothing new," Yal Dolicar said. Sailors cried out to Ondun; the smart ones lashed themselves to any sturdy object.

Ystya reached the port rail and raised her face toward the oncoming dragon-like head. Great sheets of water sprayed up on either side of the massive serpent body.

Sure she would be cast over the side, Saan struggled to reach her in time.

The ethereal girl lifted both hands and began to *glow*. Ystya's skin, her hands, even her pale hair shimmered with a power that came from within. Saan had never seen anything like it, and for an instant amazement washed away his fear.

She called out, not in a titanic voice like her mother's, but in an eerie, compelling tone that nevertheless sliced through the storm. "Bouras, Father of Serpents!" Her voice seemed to resonate in Saan's very bones.

The monster's enormous eyes fixed on Ystya and *knew* her somehow. The slitted pupils widened in sudden recognition.

In a tone of absolute authority, she said, "You have endured this punishment long enough! Ondun condemned you—but now *I* release you. *Your curse is lifted.* Go, and cause no further harm!"

Ystya brought her hands together in a clap as loud as the shattering of a world.

Bouras's scaly lips curled back to reveal tusk-like fangs as large as trees, but flesh had grown around the yellowed teeth. The jaw strained, and with a great sucking sound the long fangs slid out, leaving scarred craters in the creature's tail. The Father of All Serpents opened his mouth for the first time in countless centuries.

Finally free, Bouras recoiled like a tight spring being released—the tail snapped downward loosely, the head reared back. The great body thrashed about, carving a huge canyon in the water, raising tsunamis on both sides and leaving a deep gulf between them. The tail struck the *Al-Orizin* and knocked the ship about like flotsam. The vessel careened out of control, rode high up on a mountain of waves, then crashed down into the valley between them.

Saan reached Ystya and pulled her down to the deck while he wrapped his other forearm around a stanchion. The *Al-Orizin* was airborne for a few seconds and crashed down with a splintering of hull boards and spars. Two crewmen were flung overboard into the churning sea.

Yal Dolicar flailed wildly as he flew past and managed to snag a post with the hook attachment tied to his wrist stump.

Dangling over the edge, he kicked and struggled. Grigovar hauled himself forward, muscles straining, until he grabbed the other man and heaved him back aboard.

Sikara Fyiri, her red robes flashing bright in Saan's peripheral vision, clung to the side, wailing. As the deck bucked like a wild stallion, Sen Sherufa slid toward her, and Fyiri clutched the Saedran woman's robe, refusing to let go. Sherufa instinctively helped the priestess back aboard, though Fyiri was not likely to thank her later.

Farther away, the moving mountains of water smashed Iyomelka's ship with the force of several tidal waves, flinging it toward the horizon.

The Father of All Serpents continued to unwrap itself from the world and sank back beneath the sea at last, while uncontrolled waves drove the *Al-Orizin* far away to the southeast. . . .

When the waters had calmed enough that Saan could regain his feet on the sloppy deck, he surveyed the ocean around them and knew they had been thrown a great distance. Far away, he could see Iyomelka's storm clouds dissipating. The *Al-Orizin* wobbled, battered but still seaworthy.

"We survived," Saan said, barely believing it himself. He hugged Ystya, confused by what he had witnessed, and more than a little intimidated. "How did you do that?"

She seemed utterly drained. "I just . . . did. My mother isn't the only one with powers." She smiled at him—and fainted. He caught her, then rested her gently on the deck.

With an increasing urgency, he watched the open sea around them, sure that Iyomelka's ship would come chasing after them again. He shouted to his crew, "Get the sails in place! We need to get moving—now! Bouras gave us a chance. Let's not waste it."

A drenched Sen Sherufa tried to wake Ystya. "Grigovar, help me. I'll get her some dry clothes. She needs to rest." The reef diver picked the girl up like a bolt of sailcloth and carried her to the Saedran's cabin.

Sikara Fyiri kept her distance, staring after Ystya with awe and fear.

9 Olabar, Main Urecari Church

The main church of Urec had never been so empty. The soldan-shah had commanded that the sikaras be evicted, and the main doors had been chained shut to keep the public out.

Entering through a guarded side door, Omra and his party walked toward the central worship chamber. The empty building felt as devoid of life as a tomb. After the recent appalling events, he had decided to demonstrate that *he* was the center of power in Uraba. He had let it be known throughout the city that he and his First Wife would be paying a visit to the main church. The sikaras had forgotten that the soldan-shah was the true descendant of Urec, and that by attempting to kill him or his family—not once, but several times—they had committed an unspeakable atrocity against Ondun Himself.

Not all the priestesses had been involved in the plot, but they had implicitly cooperated in the twisted system. Many sikaras had been imprisoned, and many more were humbled and sent off to serve in smaller houses of worship around Olabar. Meanwhile, the main church remained closed to the public. For now.

Istar followed Omra into the cold, empty worship hall, quiet and respectful. The soldan-shah knew he had been uncustomarily cool to his First Wife since returning home, and he struggled to separate his hatred for her people from his love for *her*. Istar was the mother of his two daughters, the mother of *Saan*; she had been his wife for two decades. Though he could not forget that she was of Tierran birth, he forced himself to remember all the good things she had done for him, and how he had allowed her into his heart.

The six guard escorts kept their distance so the soldan-shah and his First Wife could continue their inspection. Omra knew their entrance into the empty church today had resembled a victory procession: the soldan-shah reminding everyone who he was and flaunting a blond-haired foreigner as his wife. Just by bringing Istar, he showed everyone that she had survived the sikaras' plotting.

Omra maintained his silence as they walked across the polished floor tiles that formed the spiral pattern of the Unfurling Fern. When they were far enough ahead of the guards, he took a deep breath and pushed past his dark mood. He whispered, "It is not your fault, Istar. I am sorry for the way I've treated you. When I think of the heinous crimes the Aidenists committed, I just want to kill them all. But I do you a disservice by including you among those animals."

She regarded him with her sincere blue eyes, well aware that she herself had hated him for a long time after he burned her village and took her away from everything she'd known. But over the years, Istar had accepted her life, and now she looked on him with affection, even love. "I understand your pain, Omra." Her businesslike tone brushed aside the awkwardness. "The people don't care about internal politics. They want to go to their church and express their beliefs, but you've locked the doors. You know that can't go on. They'll need a new ur-sikara soon. Give them one, before the priestesses make their own choice."

Omra knew she was right. If he didn't heal the rift between himself and the church, there would be great turmoil, and the people would begin to feel they had to choose between their leader and their religion. And he didn't dare allow those scheming women to dictate his decisions.

He stepped up to the main altar from which the ur-sikara delivered her homilies. When Istar had been just a palace slave, Ur-Sikara Lukai had betrayed the church, scheming with Villiki to poison Omra. Now Ur-Sikara Erima had been manipulated into a similar betrayal and had taken her own life.

Omra would not trust the sikaras. "It has gone on far too long.

If I let the priestesses select their own successor, I'll be in the same predicament as before. I need an ur-sikara who is not politically insidious—a woman who has no ambitions or schemes beyond the church."

"Such a priestess might be difficult to find," Istar said, then added in a soft voice, "However, with your permission, I could suggest a name . . . someone I believe would be both pragmatic and loyal?"

He raised his eyebrows. "What do you know of sikaras?"

"I know that I was impressed by Kuari, your new emissary to Inner Wahilir. Soldan Huttan's First Wife."

"Huttan's wife? That would be asking for trouble. I am already annoyed with that man for his incursions into Yuarej soldanate. He's too ambitious."

"And his wife knows that full well. Kuari will never be her husband's puppet. I'm surprised he hasn't found a way to strangle her before now. The fact that she has survived also speaks in her favor."

Omra had met the woman and was also impressed with her. He had spoken to Kuari in her capacity as emissary, but would never have considered her as a potential ur-sikara. Istar explained that Kuari had been raised in the church and trained as a priestess, but chose to marry Huttan instead because she was frustrated with politics and power plays among the sikaras.

Hearing this, he nodded slowly. "That would indeed send an appropriate message to the church of Urec. The priestesses have to be reminded of their role, and their limitations. I am the secular ruler, while the sikaras guide the spiritual lives of the people. Will Kuari let herself be kept on a tight leash?"

Istar gave him a wry smile. "She'll view it as keeping the sikaras under control."

Omra drew a deep breath, wanting to close the gulf between them. "I do value your counsel, Istar. I will speak with Kuari and see if she can abide by my conditions. If so, I'll anoint her myself, and the church will have its new leader without further ado."

Without a body, it was difficult to give Tukar a proper funeral; nevertheless, Omra insisted on honoring his brother with a special ceremony.

Imir joined him, looking gray and wasted in his sorrow. The older man had surrendered his rule because he could no longer bear the weight of consequences, yet those consequences continued to dog him. Although the former soldan-shah attended the ceremony, he did not wish to participate in any speeches. Imir didn't trust his voice to deliver a eulogy for his fallen son.

Clad in formal olbas, sashes, and robes of state, the two stood in the main square outside the Olabar palace. On the worn flagstones, workers had set up a huge pyramid of kindling and logs. A scarlet banner with the Unfurling Fern fluttered like a battle flag from the top. Without a body, the funeral pyre was only symbolic, but the people of Uraba would understand the message.

Omra raised his voice and shouted to the crowd, "My brother has been murdered by the followers of Aiden." A reverent hush fell over the people. "Tukar's work at the Gremurr mines provided thousands of swords and shields for our war against the enemy, but the Tierrans killed him. They sent us his head, but refused to give us his body for these purging fires, and so our memories must be enough."

Omra carried a scimitar from the Gremurr mines—not an ornate one, just a soldier's blade, but it was appropriate. He placed the sword on the pile of dry wood and stepped back. "Let these flames shine so brightly that Ondun Himself knows our anger. I ask my faithful subjects not to forget Tukar, or the slain priestesses at Fashia's Fountain, or the thousand heads of innocent prisoners strewn along the Ishalem wall. The Aidenists want to weaken the heart of our beliefs, but we will not let them. We must hold Ishalem and show all the world our true faith."

He gave a small signal, and two guards cast lit torches onto the pyre. The flames caught in the kindling and the fire grew. Omra let the orange glow fill his vision, but Imir averted his eyes. His father spoke quietly. "Do not be so obsessed with Ishalem that you forget to rule the rest of Uraba. Olabar is your capital, not Ishalem."

"I have two capitals, Father. I must attend to them both."

"There is more to Uraba than just those two cities. You have five soldanates. When was the last time you traveled to Missinia to see your mother? Or visited the people of Abilan, or far Kiesh? When did you last go to Lahjar?"

Omra's nostrils flared as he heard his father's criticism. "But Ishalem is the heart of it all—our history, our heritage, our beliefs. If we lose Ishalem after so many years of struggle, then we lose everything." The pyre blazed higher and brighter.

The former soldan-shah simply shook his head. "We had Ishalem before, Omra, and even then we didn't have everything."

10 *Ishalem*

Despite a complete victory, the visiting Nunghals were appalled by their first experience with naval warfare. Memories of the horrors they had inflicted on the Tierran ships—the explosions, the blood and flames, the screams of the dying—shamed and sickened even the bravest Nunghals.

Asaddan was not surprised when all but seven of the hundred shipkhans decided to sail away in a large flotilla and head back to familiar coastlines. They would leave Ishalem behind. His friend Shipkhan Ruad and Kel Unwar joined him at the docks in the western harbor to say goodbye.

Unwar had built the impregnable wall above Ishalem, and was nearly finished excavating the canal across the isthmus, but losing these allies seemed to be a challenge he didn't know how to face. From his distraught expression, the city's provisional governor could not understand the Nunghal reluctance to stay and fight. "Your comrades know how much devastation the Aidenists meant to inflict on us. Do they not see we were right to use any means to crush them?"

Asaddan looked out at the ships in the harbor and tried to explain. "They don't understand war at all. Our clans have rivalries, but nothing that justifies outright slaughter. For the most part, we want to explore the world and make a profit." He shrugged by way of apology. "After that sea battle, the shipkhans and their crews just want to go home."

Since he couldn't speak the Uraban language, Shipkhan Ruad did not understand the conversation between the other two men. Impatient, he prepared to climb into the small boat that would ferry him from the docks out to his gray-sailed ship. He and Asaddan slapped each other on the back. "Are you certain you won't come with us, cousin?"

Asaddan shook his head. "The offer is tempting, but not yet. There are still parts of Uraba that I want to see. Khan Jikaris can rule well enough without me."

"You're just afraid of getting seasick again," Ruad said with teasing disappointment.

"I'll admit the voyage aboard your ships isn't a gentle one, but sailing with you was more comfortable than walking across the Great Desert. The new sea trade route will benefit all of our clans, but next time I think I'll go home aboard a sand coracle."

Surprisingly, tears sparkled in Ruad's eyes, and he turned his thin face away. "Thanks to you, Asaddan, I am no longer viewed as a joke among my people." He adjusted his sharkskin vest, brushed a hand across his eyes. "Long ago I made mistakes that cost me my ship and my crew, but I've redeemed myself. The khans will remember my name with honor now—and yours."

"Oh, they always would have remembered mine." Asaddan smiled, then noticed Kel Unwar fidgeting, not understanding a word they said. He lowered his voice and continued, "I wish you would stay, cousin. As soon as the new canal is open, you can sail through to the Middlesea! Think of all that coastline to explore."

Ruad shook his head. "It is tempting, but I'm looking forward to the next clan gathering. . . ." He broke into a grin. "Just imagine how many women will throw themselves on me, now that I am a famed explorer."

Asaddan whistled through the gap in his teeth. "Yes, I suppose they might even charge you less for their affections." Ruad winced and burst into laughter.

After a formal farewell to Unwar, with Asaddan serving as translator, the shipkhan climbed into the boat and rowed out to the clustered ships. Before long, the Nunghal vessels set their accordioned gray sails, weighed anchor, and caught the afternoon breezes to sail out into the deep Oceansea. From the dock, Asaddan and Unwar heard a loud succession of booms as the departing ships fired their cannons into the air in farewell.

At the very least, Asaddan was sure that Ruad's successful voyage had reawakened the spark of curiosity among the Nunghals. From now on, the clans would no longer be content to sail the familiar southern coastlines, but would strike out and expand their knowledge of the world.

When he did return home, Asaddan intended to speak to Khan Jikaris. The nomadic Nunghal-Ari wandered across the great plains, caring little where they were, so long as they had water and game. On the flat grasslands, the terrain was monotonous, but Asaddan suspected that ambitious riders might find wonders if they ventured beyond their familiar territories. Perhaps next season, when the winds changed, he would fly back to see his clans. . . .

As the Nunghal vessels sailed away, Kel Unwar was clearly troubled. "Losing all those warships is a great blow. I was able to buy four large cannons from your cousins—only *four*—but the other shipkhans would not part with them."

"They need them to defend against sea serpents on the long voyage."

Unwar blew out a slow breath. "Maybe so, but without the rest of the Nunghal cannons, Ishalem will be hard-pressed to defend itself. The Aidenists are sure to come again."

"Their war fleet was destroyed—they will think twice before they attack. You have some time."

"Time for what?"

The answer seemed obvious to Asaddan. "Time to install those four cannon in emplacements at the opening to the harbor." By now, most of the gray-sailed Nunghal ships had disappeared into the distance. "And time to complete your canal."

11 *The* Dyscovera

Aiden's Compass had guided the *Dyscovera* to this island. The ship eased close to the unknown shore where the hills were dark with evergreen groves and golden with dry grasses—but Criston could see that this was not Terravitae.

By now, however, they were sorely in need of fresh supplies. After dropping anchor, Criston dispatched the ship's boats to refill their casks with water and take on fruits, vegetables, and fresh game.

He had not yet delivered his verdict against Hannes and his fellow conspirators. When he instructed three of the accused mutineers to go ashore with the supply party, the men looked suspicious of what he might have in mind. Criston snapped, "There's hard work to be done and heavy barrels to fill and haul—or would you rather have the lash instead?" The mutineers decided they were eager to help. "Prester, you will accompany us as well."

Hannes had the look of a martyr about him and displayed no remorse whatsoever. "As you wish, Captain. Aiden's Compass directed us here. There must be a reason for it."

As Criston considered the island's hills and pine trees, he called to the Saedran chartsman, "Sen Aldo, I'm sure you'd like to look around?"

Aldo had been staring at the coastline, filing away in his mind the details of the land. "Yes, Captain. Everything I see is vital to my maps."

Javian joined him at the ship's rail, bright-eyed and eager.

"May I go with the shore party, sir?"

Criston glanced at him with a paternal smile. The cabin boy had seemed so young when they set off from Calay, but during the long voyage he'd matured into a solid and reliable young man. Criston could easily see that Javian's affection for Mia was progressing beyond boyish infatuation. "Yes, you and Mia will come with me in the first party."

The supply party used both of the ship's boats, and as they rowed toward the shore, Prester Hannes sat in the bow, intent on the uncharted island. When they were close, men from each boat, including Silam Henner and one other mutineer, slipped over the side and sloshed up onto the beach, pulling the boats along. Once ashore, Sen Aldo looked closely at the native plants and studied fruits that hung from scrubby trees. Javian and Mia bounded off along the coastline, heading into the hills to explore what the island might offer.

The three cowed mutineers shouldered empty barrels and

trudged off, following the sailors Criston had designated to watch them. The accused men were on their best behavior, eager to prove themselves to their captain, but Criston felt a knot in his chest, as the decision—the only decision—brewed in his mind. Silam Henner seemed convinced they were all going to be executed on shore.

Throughout the day, the men filled barrel after barrel with stream water and ferried loads back to the *Dyscovera*. Additional parties came ashore to help with the work, including the rest of the accused mutineers, who were eager to contribute their labor. Scavenging parties gathered sacks of exotic vegetables and fruits, and the cook was particularly happy when he found a patch of wild onions. The crew used hunting bows to bring down six dwarf antelope in the hills, and they all had a feast of roasted meat on the beach, after which they dug a smoking pit and lit a greenwood fire to preserve the rest of the meat.

They found no sign of human habitation, however—no ruins or any other indication that Aiden had ever set foot here on his journey. By late afternoon, when the *Dyscovera*'s hold was reprovisioned and most of the men returned to the ship, only a small group remained ashore. By design, Criston had made sure that Prester Hannes and the accused mutineers were among them, as well as some of his strongest sailors.

Having worked so hard on the island, the mutinous crewmen looked hopeful that they might be forgiven. Hannes merely raised his chin, as if he hoped that the captain would finally accept the rightness of what the prester had done.

But Criston's voice was hard and heartless as he announced his decision. He had rehearsed his words many times. "You all stand convicted of mutiny, and the law of the sea is clear. Had we continued to sail, I would have had no choice but to cast you overboard." The men groaned with fear; Hannes said nothing. "However, this island gives me an alternative. Maybe that's why Aiden's Compass directed us to this place." He looked at them all with steely eyes. "I will maroon you here. Call it mercy, if you like."

Hannes looked incensed. "We are nearly to Terravitae, Captain! What would Holy Joron say?"

"I hope I can ask him myself—and soon. In the meantime, you men can build shelters for yourselves, hunt food, remain alive—and that's a chance we did not offer Enoch Dey. You have an opportunity that he did not."

Now the prester was shaken. "You must not deny me the chance to see Joron!" His skin turned red, except for the pale patches of his burn scars.

The mutineers pleaded. "Please reconsider, Captain! We will be perfectly loyal."

Silam Henner fell to his knees in the sand. "Don't maroon us here!"

"My decision is made."

Turning his back on them, Criston saw Javian running down the hillside path, with Mia fast on his heels, yelling, "Captain, captain—don't leave yet!" They hurried up to the others, breathless, their excitement shattering the tense mood.

"It's a *monster*," Javian said, more astonished than terrified. "We found a monster!"

12 *Calay, Sapier's Lighthouse*

At the mouth of Calay harbor, the bright flames of Sapier's Lighthouse guided ships in the dark of night and symbolized the light of Aidenism, which guided the hearts of men. Now, in daylight, Queen Anjine met with her closest advisers in the open chamber atop the lighthouse; after Jenirod's news about Gremurr, they had to plan the next step in the war.

Anjine stood before the open windows, felt the chill breezes whipping in from the sea; far below, waves foamed against the rocks. Her heart remained hard since the murder of Tomas, and she would not allow her own counselors to forget all that was at stake. She had chosen this place for the discussion instead of the castle's war council chamber because she wanted them to look out at the city and the Oceansea and be reminded of the true scope of this conflict.

She turned back to the group of men who sat around a rustic plank table. "We have captured the mines at Gremurr, gentlemen, and it's time to launch our death blow while the Curlies are reeling. I've already studied our best approach, and I'd like your input on my plan."

Comdar Torin Rief, leader of the Tierran military, was prepared to offer advice if asked; on either side of Rief sat Subcomdars Hist and Ardan of the army and navy, who held their silence. The comdar pointed out, "Excuse me, Majesty. We might have taken the Gremurr mines, but we lost at Ishalem—*again*. Don't forget what happened to Destrar Tavishel's fleet. All of his ships were destroyed when he sailed to attack Ishalem. The Urecari possess a mysterious fleet we have never seen before, and a new kind of fiery weapon."

She shook her head. "We don't know how the Urabans destroyed the Soeland ships so easily, but Destrar Tavishel acted without my knowledge or my orders." She tried to keep the anger from her voice. "Because of his foolhardy actions, Tierra lost many ships. We are *better* than this!" Anjine paced the length of the table.

Destrar Shenro from Alamont fidgeted with impatience. "I am ready to ride with the army, Majesty, whenever you decide to move against the Curlies. I can go tomorrow." He seemed to expect applause for his eagerness.

Jenirod spoke up, "The *army* won't be ready tomorrow, Destrar."

He seemed a new man after his grueling ride across Tierra; he had shaved and bathed, eaten and rested—but Anjine sensed that the change went deeper than that. "And if we set off without proper preparation, they will massacre us—like the last time our army tried to breach the wall."

The knife edge of Anjine's voice cut off the angry mutters. "We've got to do everything right this time. We have to factor in the time it takes to gather all our forces, move them into place, and supply them while our plans take shape. The operation must be well coordinated. It could be our last chance to end this war, once and for all."

Destrar Unsul, Jenirod's father, was a man who liked everything planned to the last detail. "Excuse me, my Queen, but perhaps you could tell us more about this new strategy?" He and his son had not seen eye to eye for some time, since his son's priorities of horse shows and brawny bravado didn't match his own scholarly interests in agriculture and engineering.

She raised her eyes to the old Saedran scholar. "Sen Leo, shall we have a look at the world?"

Sen Leo na-Hadra began to unroll his largest chart, stretching out his arms until Subcomdar Ardan of the navy had to take the far edge so he could spread the whole map on the table. Anjine leaned over the chart, tracing her finger along the coastline from Calay to Ishalem on the thin isthmus that connected the two continents.

"Ishalem is vulnerable at several points. Even though the wall blocks us from the north, a large enough army could lay siege to it. Meanwhile, the Tierran navy could blockade the Ishalem harbor on the western side of the isthmus. And, if we can time it carefully enough"—she pointed to the rugged pass over the Corag mountains, the newly captured Gremurr mines, and Tierra's unexpected access to the Middlesea—"Destrar Broeck could sail with his ironclads and strike Ishalem from the unprotected eastern side. We will squeeze them from three sides *at the same time*, and by the Fishhook, Ishalem will be ours."

Khalig, the miserable Uraban messenger, sat on the floor against the wall of the lighthouse chamber, his wrists and ankles bound. He groaned out loud. "Why have you brought me here, Queen Anjine? I don't want to hear your battle plans. I am not part of this war—I'm just a merchant!"

Anjine rounded on him. "You brought my brother's head to me. You are definitely part of this war."

"I did only as I was commanded!"

The man had huddled in a dark cell ever since arriving in Calay with his grisly message from Kel Unwar. In her heart, Anjine understood that the messenger was merely a pawn, an innocent . . . but Tomas had been innocent as well. "Be silent, Khalig, or I will have you gagged."

The distraught man clamped his lips shut. He squirmed uncomfortably, and his haunted eyes were wide.

Comdar Rief spoke up, approving of the queen's plan. "This strategy will require a precise schedule. We've got to send a message to Gremurr so that Destrar Broeck knows how we expect him to assist the war effort. Our operation will take months to coordinate properly."

She smiled at them all. "The war has lasted two decades already—I'm willing to invest a few more months." Noting Destrar Shenro's eager bloodlust, Jenirod's unexpected new reticence, and Comdar Rief's businesslike determination, she added quietly, "The hearts and backs of the Tierran people cannot bear the weight of this war. We must finish it, and we must win. We will crush the followers of Urec, and when they beg for mercy, we will turn a deaf ear."

Khalig moaned. "I don't want to hear this! Why are you telling me?"

"So you understand that your people will be defeated." Anjine's voice was like a bludgeon. "I want to extinguish every spark of hope in your heart before you go to your grave."

The messenger cringed; the bindings at his wrists and ankles were bloody from his struggles.

"It is a small repayment on the debt of justice. You are indeed a messenger, Khalig, but you are not innocent. No Uraban can claim innocence after what your people have done. However, each drop of blood helps to balance the scales."

She called in Guard-Marshall Vorannen and another guard. The terrified Uraban messenger struggled, begging for mercy, but the guards went about their grim duty without sympathy.

"Alas, we have no prester-marshall to give you final prayers," Anjine said, "but I don't suppose the fish will mind."

She had hoped to feel satisfaction as the two men tossed Khalig off the lighthouse balcony. She didn't. Sen Leo looked sickened by what he witnessed, but Anjine refused to acknowledge the Saedran's expression. She turned back to her advisers. "Now then, on with the war."

13 *Corag River Port*

After resting for three days in their Stoneholm camp, the Gremurr refugees were eager to set off for home again. Thoughts of seeing Vicka after his long absence filled Mateo's mind, and these liberated slaves had similar dreams of their families. Free men needed little encouragement to march; all of Tierra lay before them, and the road was open.

Mateo led the refugees down the path into drainages that joined with the river network. He noted their energy and anticipation in sharp contrast to how weary and bedraggled they had looked back in Gremurr. Now they had a spring in their step—and hope.

And so did he.

He set an easy pace along the dirt road. The refugees talked with colorful cheer, reminiscing about their homes, their families, their once happy existences. After seeing the joyous reunions of some of the freed slaves at Corag, they all expected the same, imagining that they could seamlessly rejoin their old lives.

"I used to complain about working on my farm in Alamont, but now I can't wait to get the good, dark dirt under my fingernails."

"My family raised the best butter melons, as big as your head! Almost no seeds, and as sweet as a honeycomb."

"Ha, the sweet I want is the taste of my Jemma's lips!"

"I know, I've tasted them," another man quipped, which spurred a round of raucous laughter.

"A lover's kiss is sweet, but there's nothing like the excited hugs of your children. By the Fishhook, my two boys must be old enough to be apprentices now . . . or journeymen!"

"Kelpwine from Windcatch . . . have you ever tasted it?"

"I've heard about the Windcatch stench when all the seaweed rots and floats out to sea."

"My mother made the most delicious herb-rubbed lamb, with wild garlic and dandelions."

"One thing I'm not going to miss is the taste of Uraban food." In odd unison, several of the men spat on the ground.

Listening to the easy chatter, Mateo could not stop thinking about how long these men had been gone. He feared they might return home to wives who had remarried, children or parents who had died, or households that had simply moved away. . . .

Mateo was himself a different person from the man who had left to do the queen's bidding. An eternity ago, when he'd kissed Vicka goodbye and departed from Calay, his hands had not been stained with innocent blood. Now he shouldered the weight of a thousand severed heads.

When the group topped a hill and saw a small river town with wooden docks that served as a port for Destrar Sazar's boats, they let out a spontaneous cheer. With great relief, Mateo saw an empty barge tied up waiting for them. He faced the happy smiles and bright eyes of the refugees. "We can rest on the journey downriver—we'll be in Calay soon! Queen Anjine will host a feast and celebration for us when we arrive." He knew the return of these former slaves would be seen as a glorious victory for Aiden, a way to lift up a land full of battered hearts.

And Mateo just wanted to go home as well. Hadn't he earned it? He so longed to feel like a human being again, not just a soldier but a man with a loving wife and a warm house.

He had just married Vicka, and he could only imagine—not *know*—what a normal life would be like with her. She would be wondering why he had been gone for so long, but he had not been ready to face her, or Anjine, when the horror of the thousand heads was so deep and fresh.

Scarred and shamed by what he'd done, he had ridden off in search of some kind of cleansing. The victory at Gremurr gave him part of what he needed, and bringing these once hopeless men home would do the rest.

As the refugees came down the dirt road to the river, the townspeople emerged from their homes to welcome the crowds. Having received word from Destrar Siescu's riders, they had prepared large cookpots in the town square and were ready to serve a hot meal. The village prester came out to bestow Aiden's blessing on them all.

Aboard the waiting barge, rivermen and their families brought out flutes and fiddles and struck up a lively tune. Giddy refugees grabbed townspeople and began to dance. The joyful laughter sounded strange coming from the throats of the former slaves, and Mateo felt some of their hope rubbing off on him.

He spotted Sazar, the burly black-bearded man who led the river clans. He had helped Mateo ferry the thousand Uraban prisoners from their slave camp down to Ishalem for the slaughter.

Seeing Mateo now, the river destrar opened his arms in a gesture of welcome. "This is one human cargo I'll be most pleased to transport, Subcomdar."

"And I'm most pleased to deliver it to you. Let's take these men back home to balance some of the dark things we've done." He tried to swallow away the lump in his throat. "Maybe that's a victory we can hold on to."

14 *Mountain Road to Gremurr*

After Iaros relinquished the herd of mammoths to the Iborian soldiers, who took the beasts back to the cold northlands, Destrar Siescu and his scout set off over the mountain road with reinforcements and Uraban slaves for the mines.

Raga Var bounded along like a mountain goat on his moccasined feet, guiding the group into the windswept pass. Siescu pulled his furs tighter as the train of pack animals, soldiers, and Uraban slaves plodded along. Weather permitting, Siescu knew he would have to deliver engineers, professional miners, and metalsmiths to the former Uraban mines as well. Destrar Broeck had demonstrated his military prowess by capturing the outpost, but Siescu did not expect an Iborian to know how to operate mines or smelters. That required Corag expertise.

The path wasn't hard to find, considering that mammoths had trampled the route; he placed his complete trust in the scout to lead the way. Accompanying them on the mountain road, Broeck's nephew was impatient to get back to Gremurr. "We couldn't have taken the enemy stronghold without this new road, Destrar. Your Urecari prisoners did very useful work."

"They were human tools, nothing more. And now they can continue to serve." He glanced back at the line of roped-together captives shuffling along the path. If one of them were to slip off the cliff, the slave's nearest companions would be pulled down as well. To minimize losses, the Urabans were tied together in groups of no more than three.

Raga Var trotted back to them in his patchwork fur garments. "Part of the path ahead is covered with fresh snowfall. Treacherous going." The scout rubbed at a scrape on his elbow. "Even I slipped."

Siescu pressed his lips together. "We'd better send some slaves to break trail." The winds picked up as they passed along one of the steepest sections of the road. Sharp crystals of new-fallen snow swirled around them, sparkling in the sunlight.

Raga Var pointed ahead, sounding encouraged. "There's a wide patch once we get past these cliffs. Good place to make camp."

The wind blew around Siescu, cutting like a sharp knife through his furs, and he shivered. "Will we be able to have a fire?"

"I'll find enough firewood for you, Destrar."

"I don't know what I'd do without you."

Corag guards herded two roped trios of prisoners to the sloping, snow-covered path. Iaros stroked his long mustaches. "That dropoff would make me nervous even in good weather."

The reluctant slaves argued in their own language, which Siescu had never learned to speak. Impatient to set up camp and warm himself by a fire, he barked, "Go forward or die now! We need to make our way through." Afternoon shadows descended quickly in these canyons, and the temperature would drop further.

When the first group of slaves resisted, Siescu's guards prodded them forward with spears. The lead man stumbled into the snow, which covered a sheet of ice. Before he had gone three paces, he slipped and tumbled off the edge. The two behind him dug in their heels as best they could, but they slid over the side as well, falling in a rush of screams.

Fortunately, the commotion also knocked loose some of the snow on the path, which cleared the way somewhat. Behind them, the roped prisoners moaned and shivered; even Iaros looked ill, but Siescu knew it was necessary. "All right, send the next group forward. Maybe they'll make it through."

After more prodding, the second trio gingerly moved ahead, finding their footing, slipping, clutching at rough rocks on the cliff face until they made it across the narrow ledge. Once beyond the treacherous part, they hunkered down on rocks and sat shaking and shuddering on the other side.

"There, now you all see it can be done! Nothing to fear." Siescu was sure many of the captives spoke Tierran well enough to understand him. Terrified, the next trio moved gingerly along the path and also completed the passage without mishap. Next, one of Siescu's guards volunteered to cross so that he could watch the prisoners. Then more of the slaves.

When the path was well trampled, Iaros and Siescu made the passage, careful to keep their balance. The pack animals went across, one by one. Raga Var sprang back and forth with an agility that shamed them all. He was anxious to move along, watching the thickening gray clouds overhead that presaged a winter storm.

When the whole train of people and pack animals reached the stony clearing Raga Var had chosen as camp, they huddled for the night in the shelter of rocks. The winds picked up, funneled along the sheer cliff faces.

True to his word, the wiry scout gathered scrub bush and dry wood to make a campfire for his destrar, and Siescu sat close to the flames, shivering no matter how many furs he wrapped around himself. He offered to share the blaze with Iaros, but the Iborian seemed not to feel the cold at all.

The younger man turned uneasily, surveying the snow-capped mountains around them. He sucked in a long breath of the cold air. "Have you heard about the frost giants—powerful beings who look for unsuspecting travelers in the ice and snow?" He rubbed his hands briskly together. "They can bring winter with a breath."

"Never heard of them," Siescu said. The idea of such a being shrouded in cold was particularly unpleasant to him. "We don't have frost giants in Corag."

Iaros bobbed his head. "I heard they are even older than Ondun, titans that once tried to snuff out the Fires of Creation and freeze the whole world."

Siescu tried to hide his shudder. "How could any creature be older than Ondun?"

Iaros shrugged. "I don't know, but I wouldn't want to meet one."

Siescu called for more wood to build the fire higher.

Next morning, they awoke to find that a blanket of snow had settled on the road again—not enough to block passage, but sufficient to hide slippery patches of ice. Once again, Siescu ordered slaves to take point and trample the path clear.

When the road began to descend at a steep pace, Iaros looked ahead. "We're near the coast now, Destrar. Soon enough, we'll see the canyons and smell the mines."

Raga Var trotted up to them, concerned about the gloomy day. "There'll be another storm tonight, Destrar. Once winter sets in, the passes will be closed. We might not get back to Stoneholm this season."

"Oh, we will get back. I trust you to lead us," Siescu said. "For now, our destination is Gremurr."

In a side canyon above the mines, Shetia drew her young son deeper into the bushes as the party of Tierran soldiers and Uraban captives marched past. The boy's eyes were wide; he knew what terrible things they would face if the bloodthirsty Tierrans should capture them.

Shetia wished again that Tukar could be there to protect his family; she didn't think she would ever stop mourning his loss. Her husband had sent her and their son to hide in the hills when the enemy attacked on their monstrous hairy beasts. Shetia had never seen such violence. They were wildmen, barbarians, setting fire to the tents and buildings, slaughtering countless Uraban workers.

And dear, sweet Tukar had tried to defend Gremurr. She had not seen him since. Though she clung to hope for Ulan's sake, she knew in her heart that her husband was dead.

As the hated soldiers marched along the road, heading down toward the mines, Shetia told the boy to remain absolutely silent. Their greatest danger lay in the rambunctious puppy. Ulan clamped his hands around the dog's muzzle, holding him as still as possible. With the marching men so close, the puppy wanted to bark, but Shetia and Ulan dragged him deeper into the canyon.

When they were hidden behind the rocks, she forced herself to breathe. She had seen the haggard Uraban captives being herded like animals along the road, no doubt to be put to work in the mines. If she were captured, Shetia expected to be treated roughly, abused by the uncivilized men.

The Tierrans passing on the road looked foreign, their armor and weapons strange. One soldier carried a round shield that sported the Fishhook design. She couldn't imagine what heathen rituals they did in their worship services. Did they sacrifice Uraban children by impaling them on a large cast-iron hook?

Instinctively, she squeezed Ulan's arm. The puppy whimpered, but he sensed their terror. Somehow, they kept him from barking or breaking free as the last of the men filed past. Shetia let out a long slow sigh of relief. "We'll be safe now," she whispered.

The boy swallowed hard. "I'm hungry. We should go up the road and find their last camp. Maybe they left food behind."

Shetia's stomach clenched and growled; for more than a week

they had eaten only the scraps, berries, and plants they could forage. They had eluded discovery by Aidenist forces so far, but survival required much more than that. She didn't know how she and her son were going to live out here in the wilderness.

15 *Ishalem Canal*

When the final section of blasting was complete in the canal, water flowed freely across the isthmus like lifeblood, connecting the Middlesea and Oceansea for the first time since the creation of the world.

Standing at the western mouth of the new waterway, Kel Unwar admired the culmination of his work, and tears streaked his cheeks. This was a moment of unparalleled triumph for his soldan-shah, for Ondun, and (far less important) for himself. The feeling of joy—instead of hatred toward the Aidenist animals—seemed unnatural. Perhaps he could make improvements later, but for now, no one could deny the breathtaking accomplishment.

Unwar raised a shout to the crowd that had gathered to celebrate the inauguration of the waterway. "With this magnificent canal our ships can now sail from one end of Uraba to the other—from Lahjar to Kiesh." He meant to continue, but the cheers drowned him out.

Soldans Huttan and Vishkar were in attendance, for this canal was a symbolic joining of their two soldanates—Inner and Outer Wahilir—though the men had no great fondness for each other. The soldans had been commanded to build two giant churches on either side of Ishalem, as a contest. Huttan and Vishkar had brought their own engineers, workers, and resources to Ishalem. Huttan had vowed to finish first, and his church already towered higher than its counterpart; Soldan Vishkar, meanwhile, devoted himself to the details, planning meticulously, double-checking the work.

No matter how magnificent the two new churches might be, though, Unwar's accomplishments overshadowed both: the towering wall across the isthmus that kept out the Aidenists, and now this seven-mile-long canal that connected all of Uraba for trade and naval protection.

"It's a shame Soldan-Shah Omra could not be here in person for the celebration," Vishkar said with a wistful sigh. He was a pleasant and reliable man, the father of Omra's original First Wife.

"He would not have wanted us to wait," Huttan added sourly.

Unwar didn't want to hear the two men argue. "Uraban ships can now sail to all parts of the land, and I have completed my work ahead of schedule. The soldan-shah will be pleased, whether or not he is here."

As provisional governor of Ishalem, Unwar ordered casks of wine to be opened and a feast served to launch the day's celebration. Feeling generous, he even granted extra rations and a day of rest for the Aidenist slaves who had dug the channel. Then, while the people of Ishalem reveled, Kel Unwar slipped away from the noise and crowds.

Though the honor was rightfully the soldan-shah's, Unwar had decided to take the first boat through the canal. It was the only reward he wanted—he had no interest in greeting nobles or returning toasts that were made in his honor. He hurried down to the pier and chose a slender boat that he could row from west to east, from Oceansea to Middlesea, along the placid waters. He climbed into the boat, loosed the rope, and took up the oars.

As he paddled along the channel, the water was so peaceful, so smooth. Passing the city's bright new buildings, tiled roofs, silken awnings, and numerous churches brought both an ache and a warmth to his heart. Soon ships could sail through in both directions: cargo vessels carrying supplies for the city's defenses, war galleys filled with soldiers.

For now, though, Kel Unwar had the canal—*his* canal—all to himself. His mind was as placid as the water, and he let his thoughts wander, watching the landscape and skyline pass. He crossed the seven miles much more quickly than he'd expected.

People were also celebrating on the Middlesea terminus of the canal. Bustling crowds stood on the docks, though he had told no one of his plan to make the solo passage. When his boat approached, the people applauded. Most of them didn't even recognize him until they spotted his governor's sash and olba.

Unwar pulled up to the small pier and tossed the painter rope to a young man in the crowd, who grabbed it and tied up the boat. He climbed onto the pier, and suddenly Unwar's knees went weak as he realized what he had just accomplished. He had done the impossible. His canal had changed the world. Commerce throughout Uraba, and naval warfare against the Tierrans, would never be the same again. And now the Urecari could win the war and eradicate every living follower of the Fishhook.

Despite the applause and smiling faces, he felt a bittersweet emptiness instead of overwhelming triumph. He had dug the canal and been the first man ever to traverse it. He had also built the great wall, God's Barricade.

Unwar's smile faltered as he walked past a group of merchants who seemed delirious with the new opportunities before them. What more could he do in his life to compare to that? What else was left? He could retire, retreat to a private estate where he could relax and live well for his remaining years. It would drive him mad.

A hush fell across the joyous chatter, a creeping shadow of silence. Unwar spotted the Teacher walking through the crowd. People backed away from the ominous silver mask, the black-gloved hands. But Unwar knew who the dark figure was and what had driven her to become this enigmatic person. Aidenist barbarians.

Unwar stepped close to the mask, while everyone else moved away. The people must think him particularly brave as he extended his hand and grasped the Teacher's gloved one. He spoke in the barest of whispers. "It's done, Alisi—and now what am I supposed to do?"

Her voice was muffled through the small slit in the mask. "You will do whatever Ondun calls you to do. Defend Ishalem against the heretics. There is still much killing to be done." Though her body was concealed by voluminous dark robes, Unwar could tell she wanted to embrace him. That in itself was an odd thing, because after the crushing abuse she had suffered from Tierran sailors, his sister rarely wanted to touch anyone.

"I am proud of you, brother," she said. "Very proud."

16 *The* Al-Orizin

After the waves from the unleashed giant serpent drove them far from Iyomelka's vessel, they saw no sign of pursuit for two days, but Saan was sure their calm would not last.

He stood on deck, looking out at the waves and the empty sea. Sitting on a crate next to him, Sen Sherufa wrote in the sympathetic journal with tight, painstaking penmanship. Whatever the Saedran woman marked on these pages at sea was mirrored on the magically twinned volume on the other side of the world. She frowned as she reached the torn bottom of the half page. "I need to be brief, Captain. I am almost to the end of the journal's bound sheets, and our voyage may still last for many more months."

"Maybe the rest of the journey will be uneventful," Saan said in a joking voice, "if we can keep our distance from Iyomelka. Or maybe we'll discover the Key to Creation sooner than we expect."

Sherufa raised her eyebrows, gave a little snort, then wrote with even tinier letters, cramming words onto the torn paper.

Interrupting, Ystya ran up to them, flushed and obviously upset. "That priestess keeps teaching me the wrong things! Please tell her to leave me alone."

Saan automatically folded her into his arms to protect her. Ystya had collapsed after liberating Bouras from his curse, but she recovered quickly. When he'd pressed her for explanations about the power she had exhibited, she wouldn't discuss what she had done and seemed almost embarrassed by it. Nevertheless, he encouraged her, talked with her when he could, and hoped she would tell him more.

Now, before the young woman could explain herself, Sikara Fyiri barged up to them, equally incensed. "Captain, you must let me continue the girl's instruction! She lived alone on that island for a long time, and her education is woefully lacking. How can she follow the Map if she doesn't know what it is?"

Saan let out a sigh. They seemed like two sisters having a quarrel. "Ondun knows, *I* had to endure the sikaras' schooling, year after year. Why won't you listen to her lessons, Ystya?"

"Because she will not listen when I correct her," the girl said simply.

Saan chuckled, imagining Fyiri's expression when the impertinent young woman pointed out errors in the sikara's doctrine. "Maybe you should learn from each other."

Fyiri looked as if he had asked her to kiss a squid. "How can we engage in a debate if the girl doesn't have a basic education? One must begin from a foundation of truth."

"Why should I learn such things at all?" Ystya asked. "What do these old teachings of Urec matter to us now?"

Fyiri raised her hands in exasperation. "You see why she needs to be educated, Captain? If we don't save this girl from her ignorance, she might be corrupted by evil. We all saw the great powers she wields."

Sen Sherufa closed the twinned journal. "Captain, while I don't often agree with the sikara, we should have guessed that Iyomelka's daughter might possess remarkable skills like her mother's. We should understand them—*Ystya* should understand them, if she does not."

Saan was torn between his affection for the girl and the need to protect his ship, his crew, and his mission. "Whatever her magical abilities, I don't doubt that Ystya will be a great help against other problems the *Al-Orizin* is sure to encounter."

Fyiri remained adamant. "Knowing that she has such powers, Captain, we must make certain she does not fall prey to evil. That's why she needs to be given the most careful instruction."

Saan nodded and stood in front of the pale young woman, placing his hands on her shoulders. He glanced at the sikara. "You're right, we wouldn't want her to fall prey to evil. Ystya needs to be taught by someone we can trust." Saan smiled and turned her toward the Saedran woman. "From now on, Sen Sherufa will continue her education."

From the lookout nest, Yal Dolicar called, "Sea serpent, Captain! Off to port!" The sailors gathered to see the scaly shape atop the waves, but it did not rise up and attack them. In fact, it didn't move at all.

Saan extended his spyglass and studied the silvery serpent drifting on the water. As waves lapped it, the body slowly rolled over like a log to display ivory-colored belly plates. The serpent was dead, its eyes glassy, its mouth open.

Curious, Saan ordered the *Al-Orizin* to sail closer. When they were near it, they could see that the monster's carcass was covered with round welts. No one aboard had ever seen anything like it.

From the deck high above, Grigovar glowered down at the floating serpent. Sen Sherufa was at a loss to explain the inflamed wounds. Sikara Fyiri muttered a prayer and made a warding gesture, though the men took little comfort from it.

Saan scanned the waters uneasily. "Keep a close watch." The *Al-Orizin* continued across the open water.

Sitting on crates at the stern, Ystya listened as Sen Sherufa taught her about the geography of Uraba, sketching out maps of the Middlesea coast, the five soldanates, the Great Desert, and the recently discovered Nunghal lands beyond it.

When Saan approached them, Ystya glanced up, looking happy and engaged in the discussion. "I am learning about the world. It's much larger than I thought."

"Real cities are far more interesting than just dots on a map." He took a seat beside her. "I'll show it all to you when we get home. You should see the Olabar palace, and our harbor filled with hundreds of ships like this one."

"Hundreds? And they all sail to different places?"

"There are sand coracles, too, in the south. Baskets borne aloft by giant balloons that fly back and forth across the desert each year."

Ystya looked to Sen Sherufa to see if Saan was teasing her, but the Saedran nodded. "He's telling the truth. And we're discovering more places on this voyage."

"I will show you everything," Saan promised. "My father, Soldan-Shah Omra, commands all the soldans. He is rebuilding Ishalem, our holy city. My mother, his First Wife, will also tell you many stories. I have three sisters and two brothers—you'll meet them, too." He felt a pang of homesickness as he realized how long he had been gone. "I miss them all, but I'm partial to my little brother Omirr. He'll be the next soldan-shah someday."

Ystya stared out to sea, wearing a troubled expression. "I have brothers, too, though I've never met them: Joron, Aiden, and Urec.

When I was a little girl on the island, my father told me about them, even showed me images. They went out to search for me."

Saan brightened, hoping to ease the young woman's sadness. "It's a good thing they explored, since they found Tierra and Uraba. Urec planted golden ferns on his travels, because they reminded him of home. Do you think we'll find golden ferns on Terravitae?"

"My father talked about them when I was very young."

He stroked his chin. "In Olabar, it's tradition for boys and girls to hunt the golden fern in the surrounding forests. It was one of my favorite holidays when I was younger. One year I went deep into the forest alone, and assassins chased me while I was hunting the fern."

"Assassins?" Ystya blinked, again looked at Sen Sherufa for verification, who nodded. "But why would anyone want to kill you, Saan?"

Saan casually brushed aside her concerns. "Oh, I outwitted them easily enough by hiding deep inside a rotted log. When it was safe, I crawled out again . . . and there in the thick underbrush I discovered a single frond—a golden fern. It was supposed to bring luck to me, bless me in my life—and apparently it has."

Ystya laughed, and he seized the opportunity to give her a quick kiss on the cheek, which made them both flush.

By afternoon, the sea around them was dotted with strange gelatinous shapes, like large floating bubbles. The forms had a grayish translucence, with the blurs of mysterious organs and tiny sparkling lights within. The crew first spotted one, then several, and finally the water was crowded with the silent creatures.

"It's jellyfish!" Yal Dolicar said. "Jellyfish, each one the size of a fruit cart."

Sen Sherufa peered down into the water at the beautiful, ethereal creatures. "Now we know what killed that sea serpent."

A man bound to take ill-advised actions, Dolicar tossed a

harpoon down at a giant jellyfish that brushed up against the hull. The spear burst the gelatinous hemisphere, and ooze splattered out as the jellyfish shriveled. Ichor splashed the *Al-Orizin*'s hull boards and left a dark and smoking stain that ate into the wood.

Reacting with alarm, Saan shouted, "Pour buckets of water down the side! Wash away that slime before it eats through the hull!"

As the men scurried to slosh off the acidic ooze, Saan gazed around them. The *Al-Orizin* cut through the water at a brisk pace, propelled by the breeze. As the jellyfish infestation grew thicker, he feared that if the bow crushed too many of the creatures, the corrosive body fluids might eat through the hull. "Trim the sails—we'd better move gently through this."

The jellyfish made no aggressive moves, simply floated with the currents, drifted apart, then pulled together once more. Their body sacs seemed to store up sunlight during the day, and that night, as the ship sailed quietly onward, the swarm emitted a cold blue glow that lit the dark waters.

Ystya stood beside him, wearing a fascinated smile. Though the sailors remained uneasy, she seemed delighted with the phenomenon. "Another amazing thing you have shown me. Thank you, Saan—I don't regret leaving my island to come with you."

Even though Ystya didn't seem at all nervous about the jellyfish, he put his arm around her. "We'll be perfectly safe. Smooth sailing."

The ship drifted along with the giant jellyfish for another full day without mishap. When the winds picked up and the water became choppier, the group of translucent creatures broke up and drifted apart.

As soon as Saan saw clear passage through the waters, he called, "Set all sails! Let's get some distance from those things."

17 *The* Dyscovera

On the deserted island, Javian and Mia led Criston and Sen Aldo up to the headlands to see the monster they had found. An angry Prester Hannes took powerful strides with the group, like a general reconquering territory. "You would maroon us on an island infested with dangerous creatures, Captain?" His tone was accusing.

The sun hung low in the west and would set soon over the watery horizon, but they still had more than an hour of daylight remaining. The frightened mutineers kept an eye on the trees and underbrush, expecting predators to leap out at them.

"In the name of Aiden, Captain!" said Silam Henner. "If we are so close to Terravitae, give us another chance."

Criston remained resolute. "I have already granted greater mercy than you deserve. And that's *twice* for you, Mr. Henner."

The prester snapped at his comrades, "Captain Vora may be the judge of our lives for now, but Ondun will be the judge of our souls . . . and his."

"Up here, on this cliffside, right over the rise!" Javian called, running ahead. He and Mia trampled a path through waving grasses to the top of the hill overlooking the shore. Mia said, "It's a ferocious-looking beast, but it's been dead a long time."

One of the headland bluffs had sloughed away to expose a sheer cliff of sand and chalk, weathered by rains and high crashing waves. The skeleton of an enormous creature was fossilized in the raw rock. Its bullet-shaped skull was as large as a whale and held a mouth full of fangs. Criston saw the bowed ribs of the conical body, the thin central bones from a tangle of loose tentacles, each tipped with a set of jaws and jagged teeth. A hollowed socket in the center of its head had once held a single eye.

The sight of the sea monster's remains reawakened nightmares in his mind. Criston had watched a similar creature rise up out of a terrific storm. Those fanged tentacles had wrapped around the hull of the *Luminara*, broken her keel, torn away the masts. Jaws just like those had devoured Captain Shay and his shipmates, leaving only Criston and Prester Jerard alive in the wreckage.

"That is the Leviathan," he said.

Sen Aldo was studying the creature, sketching it into memory. "It closely resembles the beast that Captain Vora drew in his sea-monster journal aboard the *Dyscovera*. But that attack took place only twenty years ago. This skeleton is much older—it must have been embedded in that cliff for centuries or more. This can't possibly be the same monster."

"Yet it must be, for Ondun created only one Leviathan." Hannes's voice was breathy with surprise. "When God saw how fearsome the monster was, He chose to not make a mate for it, lest they reproduce and devour all life in the oceans. There is only one Leviathan, and it is lonely and angry. That is why it attacks ships."

"Well, it's dead now," Mia said.

Javian gave the prester a puzzled frown. "I thought the Leviathan lived forever, the horror of the seas. How could it die?"

Hannes glared at the white bones protruding from the cliff. "There cannot be more than one Leviathan, and the bones of the immortal Leviathan do not wash up on a shore to be buried in a cliffside. It cannot die." He shook his head. "None of this is possible."

"Nevertheless, that *is* the Leviathan," Criston said.

Sen Aldo interjected, "Maybe some details of the Leviathan story are not accurate."

Hannes looked angry enough to kill the chartsman right there. "The Book of Aiden is clear on the subject."

"The evidence before your own eyes is also clear," Aldo replied.

"I don't want to stay on this island if there are monsters here," mumbled Silam Henner.

"It's a monster of the *sea*, fool," one of the mutineers snapped. "We'll be safer here than aboard the ship."

Criston stared at the skeleton. The sinking of the *Luminara* was still vivid in his memory. Because of the Leviathan, he hadn't been in Windcatch to protect Adrea from the Urecari raiders who took her.

However, the fossilized remains proved that the beast could be killed—and he wondered how many more of the monsters were out there in the seas. Maybe he would have a second chance against it. Even after so many years, his desire for revenge had not faded.

If not for the Leviathan's attack, he could have had a different life, a happy life, a family. Ciarlo had told him that Adrea was pregnant at the time of the raid, and Criston could never be sure if his wife had lived long enough to give birth. If she'd had the baby, the child would be twenty years old now, a grown man or woman.

Oh yes, he looked forward to another opportunity to destroy the monster. He wanted a second chance for many things. The bones of the creature embedded in the cliffside symbolized the loss of those possibilities.

Hannes wrestled with the indisputable sight before him, trying to find an answer that fit with his inflexible beliefs. Watching the prester struggle with the irreconcilable, Criston could not forget that Hannes had turned part of the crew against their own captain. On the other hand, he could not forget how he himself had lived as a hermit for so many years, and how he had saved a starving and frostbitten Hannes. Wasn't that a sure sign from Aiden? The experience of nursing the prester back to health and returning him to Calay had also wakened the lost soul, Criston, from his years of haunted isolation.

If his life had been different, if he had chosen a new path, if he had seized a second chance. . . .

Turning away from the cliff, he spoke before he could change his mind. "Aiden advises that even the worst person can change, that a repentant man should be given a second chance."

"Yes, and in doing so, the giver is also blessed," Hannes said. "You know your Book of Aiden, Captain—but have you learned from it?"

Criston continued, "Rather than marooning you here, I will take you back aboard the *Dyscovera.* And when we reach the shores of Terravitae, I'll let Holy Joron decide your fates."

The mutineers caught their breath. "Yes, Captain! We promise to cause no trouble!"

"But first, you must swear your loyalty to me, all of you—on the Fishhook. When I give a command, you must obey it."

Hannes held up the Fishhook that hung around his neck, and Criston did not doubt his sincerity. "My destiny is to travel to Terravitae, where I can gaze upon the face of Joron. Therefore, I swear to follow your orders, even when I disagree with them." He wrapped his hands around the pendant and squeezed so tightly that his fingers bled. "I vow this to you, in the name of Aiden."

18 *The* Moray, *Middlesea Coast*

His palms were rubbed raw, his blisters bled, and his weary muscles screamed with pain, but Ciarlo continued to pull the oar to the ponderous drumbeat of the oarmaster. The shaft had been polished smooth by the sweat of countless hands.

Though the morning sky was bright and the breezes brisk, the air belowdecks was nearly unbreathable. Porthole coverings had been knocked open, yet the crosswinds did little to cool the slaves chained shoulder to shoulder on their benches.

Above on the deck, Captain Belluc stood at the open hatch, talking with the handful of travelers who had come aboard at various ports as the *Moray* worked its way toward Olabar. The passengers relaxed in comfort under private awnings, played games of chance, or picked out tunes on musical instruments without a thought for the galley slaves below.

The men did not groan or beg for mercy; they had learned to save their words. Despite his exhaustion, Ciarlo talked to them, whispering when he had no other breath. He saw a chance to tell his fellow wretches about better things, about hope. They were Urabans convicted of various crimes, and they had been taught nothing other than Urec's Log. Ciarlo knew that was why he'd been sent here.

"I met the Traveler in person," he said to no one in particular. "I spoke with him. He told me a story of the three brothers when they were back in Terravitae—Aiden, Urec, and Joron. He left me a new book of tales, but the people in that last town burned it."

The men clenched their jaws or squeezed their eyes shut as they pulled the oars against the water, then lifted, pushed forward, and dropped again. Upon hearing Ciarlo's fantastic claim, several slaves made scornful sounds, but they all listened.

"The Traveler is Aiden. He watches us. He knows all the things his children do."

"The Traveler is Urec," someone grumbled.

"That is not what I believe," Ciarlo said, as if that ended the matter. "He performed a miracle—healed my leg, took away my pain. An amazing demonstration of his powers."

"If the Traveler is your friend, then ask him to free us," another man said. "Now that's a demonstration I'd like to see."

"We are all here for a reason," Ciarlo said. "Maybe my reason is to tell you the things I know. And maybe the reason you're here is to listen. You were taught fanciful stories by the priestesses. Now let me tell you about Aiden's voyage." He rowed mechanically, but closed his eyes and traveled in his imagination, seeing the historical events as if he had been there himself. When he described how Aiden's Arkship was beached on a high hill in Ishalem, he wasn't surprised to hear grumbles and refutations, since Urabans had always insisted that the wreck was *Urec's* ship, not Aiden's.

But Ciarlo continued preaching without pause, talking about Aiden's grandson Sapier, who had sailed with a crew of disreputable men who cast him overboard with nothing but driftwood and a fishhook. Blessed by Ondun, Sapier had hooked a sea serpent, which towed him all the way back home. During his ordeal, Sapier had received revelations about Aiden's teachings.

In the midst of his talk, a fiery line stung like acid across his bent back, and Ciarlo heard the crack of a whip. "I'll have none of that garbage aboard my ship!" Captain Belluc's wide face was dark as he descended from the hatch into the slave hold. His earring glinted. He lashed his whip again.

Ciarlo braced himself against the pain, wondering how the captain could have heard him from above. The slaves chained next to him tried to squirm out of the way to avoid the lash, but one of them caught the tip nevertheless.

The oarmaster stopped drumming to let the confrontation play out, more interested than intimidated. With a sniff, the captain issued his pronouncement. "Since you have so much extra energy to talk, you won't need your rations today. You'll go without your bowl of food."

Ciarlo didn't argue, simply endured. Flustered that the Aidenist prisoner did not plead for mercy, the *Moray*'s captain glowered at them all, then climbed back up the wooden ladder to the main deck.

Later, after sunset, Belluc led a perfunctory prayer from Urec's Log for his passengers as the galley drifted in calm waters. The oarmaster shuffled forward with a heavy kettle, ladling out bowls of watery stew made from fish heads and guts.

Ciarlo went without, per the captain's orders. His stomach was tight with hunger, but he didn't complain. One of the nearby slaves looked at him with sad eyes and extended his own bowl so that Ciarlo could take a sip.

The oarmaster hurried back, yelling, and knocked the bowl from the other slave's hands. "You go without, too! Captain's orders!"

The kindly slave turned away from Ciarlo with an air of crushing disappointment. Ciarlo closed his eyes, breathed evenly, and recited his own prayers to Aiden.

Riding aboard the *Moray* allowed Asaddan to see parts of the land he had not yet visited on the Middlesea coast. He sat back on a wooden crate and watched as the dusk shadows cloaked the shore. Off in the distance, he could see the twinkling lights of lamps and cookfires in a coastal town.

If only Shipkhan Ruad had remained in Ishalem just another week or two, they could have passed through the new canal and voyaged together into the Middlesea, but that was not to be. Since he wanted to see other parts of Uraba, he didn't mind riding aboard this slave galley as it made slow progress toward Olabar, stopping at village after village.

Though the soldan-shah had given him a wardrobe of silken clothes, Asaddan preferred his traditional buffalo-skin vest that left his arms bare. He kept his thick black hair in an unruly mane, though he could have had it trimmed, oiled, and tied back in a ponytail. His hair and clothing marked him as an interesting foreigner among the Urabans.

He enjoyed being the center of attention. Asaddan liked to let eager bystanders buy him drinks in taverns, in exchange for outrageous stories. He could also charm daring women who were curious to know whether a Nunghal man had the same parts as a Uraban. "Oh, we do." He would quirk his lips in a grin to show off the mysterious gap in his front teeth. "Maybe more than you expect."

As he journeyed along the Middlesea coast, however, Asaddan was uneasy to see how poorly the captain treated the men chained to the oars. Captain Belluc insisted that every one of the rowers had committed heinous crimes, and now they were repaying their debt through blood and sweat.

Peering through the open hatches to scrutinize the downtrodden men, the Nunghal began to doubt that all these prisoners were unrepentant murderers or rapists, especially the meek and peaceable Aidenist who spoke Uraban even more clumsily than Asaddan did. He had heard terrible stories about bloodthirsty Aidenists, and had seen their hateful fleet attempt to burn Ishalem, but he began to gain a new perspective as he listened to that man's mumbled stories.

On deck, Captain Belluc often tried to engage Asaddan in conversation, eager to hear stories about the vast grazing Nunghal lands south of the Great Desert and how he had crossed the dry wastes to Missinia. "What would you say is the strangest thing you've seen among us?" Belluc was like a child, eager to hear adventure stories.

Asaddan scratched his shaggy black hair. "Strangest thing?" He gestured toward the open hatch and the slaves below. "I would say this practice." The echoing drumbeats wafted up, along with the clatter of chains and the groan of oars. "There are many beasts of burden—why treat men as animals?"

Belluc laughed as if he could hardly believe what the Nunghal had said. "But these *are* animals. They die content knowing they have served some use. Without slaves to work the oars, how would our ship get to Olabar on schedule?"

Asaddan shrugged. "Why not wait a few extra days for favorable breezes?"

Belluc laughed again. "You are a strange man, Asaddan."

As the galley quieted for the night, Asaddan remained awake on deck. Before long, in a low voice, the persistent Tierran slave began to speak again. Though he was chained to his bench, his dedication to his Aidenist beliefs remained undiminished. Asaddan was beginning to admire him.

19 *Arikara*

In his hilltop palace in the capital of Missinia soldanate, Xivir spent the afternoon with his abacus and registry rolls. He sat on silk cushions by a low mahogany table, making notations of taxes and goods kept in inventory. He did not hurry his letters and numbers: he could at least keep his penmanship neat, even when the ledgers showed losses instead of profits.

The bandit raid on Desert Harbor had destroyed the sand coracles, which ruined an entire season of trading with the Nunghals. Unable to cross the Great Desert, merchants reported plummeting profits, and the numbers on the soldan's tax ledgers showed a commensurate drop. Missinia Soldanate, and all of Uraba, had come to depend on the lucrative trade with the nomadic people.

But while Soldan Xivir might have lost tax revenue, the bandits had lost plenty of heads. His master carpenters had built special shelves to hold and display the heads of twenty-three executed bandit leaders, each gruesome trophy preserved in tar—far more impressive showpieces than any enameled vase or glazed pot, he thought.

The voice of his sister interrupted him. "I'm about finished with my letter to dear Imir. Do you have anything you'd like to add?"

Xivir slid his abacus to one side. Lithio often joined him in his afternoon ponderings, and now she lounged with a square of lacquered wood on her lap serving as a desk. She wrote pages of details that could not possibly interest the retired soldan-shah.

Lithio and Imir had been estranged for decades; though they were both proud of their son Omra, the two had little else to show for their union. They were content to live far apart, and Lithio persisted in writing Imir regular letters, although she never received any reply.

"Why do you spend so much time at your correspondence, sister? You know it merely annoys Imir."

"Precisely the reason." Lithio smiled teasingly. "And I find it amusing."

Xivir rearranged the beads on his abacus. "You should find another husband. Imir would certainly sanction it."

"Why do I need another husband? I'm quite content with my life as it is."

A servant entered carrying a tray with two glasses and a pot of steaming lemon tea. "Soldan, your son has arrived from Desert Harbor."

Xivir brightened, closed his ledgers, and set aside the abacus. "Send him in. He needs no permission to see me."

Lithio placed her wooden writing surface on the tiled floor and raised herself from her cushions with exaggerated grace. She embraced Burilo as soon as he entered, then wrinkled her nose. "You need a bath and some food."

"I would not disagree." Burilo pulled up a cushion in front of his father's low desk. "First, though, you should know the good news from Desert Harbor. After months of hard work, we've repaired the damage from the bandit attack—and completed the frameworks for ten new sand coracles. The improved design is even larger than before, so the coracles will be able to carry more cargo next season."

Xivir tapped a fingertip on the disappointing numbers on his sheet. "They'll need to make up for this disaster."

"By now, Khan Jikaris must be worried. Our merchants have come every year, and he will wait for months. I wish we could send him a message."

"And I wish the bandits would disappear." Xivir grimaced at the grisly display on his shelves. "But the winds are already changing for the season, and we'll just have to wait. Maybe next year Khan Jikaris will pay higher prices for trinkets and delicacies from Uraba."

"You could always walk across the dunes like Asaddan did," Lithio said. "Take the direct route."

"No, thank you. Even a trip by sand coracle sounds too rugged for me." Xivir sipped his lemon tea, then offered the rest of the cup to his son, who gulped it. "I am the soldan, and I enjoy my comforts of civilization."

As if to punish him for his smugness, a deep rumble shook the ground. The stone walls of the palace thrummed and vibrated, and heavy blocks fell from the top of a wall in the courtyard. Xivir's abacus fell over with a clatter of beads, and he sprang to his feet, looking in alarm at the cracks that raced along the plastered ceiling. "Outside—get outside, now!"

While Lithio stood openmouthed in confusion, Burilo grabbed her arm, and Xivir herded them both out into the wide corridor. Behind him, just as they rushed out of the chamber, the wooden display case creaked forward and toppled. The grotesque preserved heads tumbled onto the tiled floor like rotten fruit.

Lithio, Xivir, and Burilo rushed into the open courtyard, while portions of the palace began to collapse around them. Walls buckled and clay bricks fell inward; support pillars rocked and swayed drunkenly, and also collapsed. The roof crashed in.

From the rise on which his palace was built, Soldan Xivir gazed across Arikara, the marketplaces, the churches, the watchtowers. Bells clanged in a violent cacophony, and a roaring wave of sound seemed to press the very air itself. Swaths of rickety vendor stalls and tents collapsed; terracotta roof tiles became deadly missiles that smashed into the street. He could see the ground itself roll and heave as the earthquake went on and on.

Xivir watched his city fall.

20 *Olabar, Main Urecari Church*

At noon, Soldan-Shah Omra reopened the doors of Olabar's main church with great ceremony. His protocol advisers had staged the event carefully.

The applause of the crowd sounded like a sigh of relief after so much tension. Omra's father had sealed the entrance on that terrible night when Villiki had fled and Ur-Sikara Erima had taken her own life. For two weeks now, the towering main church had stood empty. Even though Omra directed his anger toward the corrupt priestesses, not the church of Urec itself, the people were unsettled.

After today, their stable course would be set once more and life would return to normal. . . .

In the past week, behind closed doors, Omra had given the cowed sikaras strict instructions to choose Kuari, former emissary from Inner Wahilir and wife of Soldan Huttan, as their new ur-sikara. He himself would install Kuari in her new office. Those concessions were the price of freedom for the priestesses.

Now, with both of his wives at his side, Omra stepped up to the fern-embossed doors with an air of authority. The people drew a hushed breath. The soldan-shah turned to the blacksmith he had chosen, speaking loudly enough that his words echoed back to the crowd. "Strike these chains away and open the church doors. Only fresh air and sunlight can cleanse the poisonous shadows from these halls."

With an iron mallet and chisel, the blacksmith snapped a link and pulled the chain away with a loud ringing rattle.

Two palace guards grasped the curved bronze handles and pulled open the massive doors. Light poured into the darkened church.

As arranged, Kuari stood just on the other side of the entrance, as if she had been waiting there for weeks. A matronly woman with broad hips and square shoulders, she wore the embroidered scarlet robes of her new office. Her neck and wrists were adorned with golden-fern jewelry, and her hair was pulled back and secured with a jeweled ringlet. Hers was not the exotic dark-skinned beauty of Erima from Lahjar, nor was she a seductress like the previous ur-sikara Lukai. Kuari was stern but fair, a powerhouse who looked capable of leading the church through this time of turmoil—in partnership with the soldan-shah.

"Our holy church welcomes you, Soldan-Shah Omra, descendant of Urec." Kuari emerged from the gloom of the entrance into the sunlight, holding a tall staff capped by a polished fern.

Omra stepped closer to the woman. "I searched for a wise and fair ur-sikara to replace those who inflicted so much damage upon the church. And I have found her."

During the preparation for his announcement, he had spoken with her at length, interviewing and then interrogating the woman to understand her attitude toward power, politics, and the church. Exactly as Istar had suggested, Omra found Kuari to be a sensible woman—more so than most of his own soldans. As the two had grown more comfortable in their private conversation, she told him chilling and unbelievable stories about her own training as a sikara. From her personal experiences, she understood the deep rot in the church of Urec; in fact, he suspected she might impose more substantive reforms than the ones Omra had requested.

She spoke in a clear, penetrating voice. "The corrupt ones have been rooted out, and my first act as ur-sikara is to excommunicate them from Urec's fold. They shall no longer be blessed by the light of the Golden Fern."

Hearing this, the people whispered with awe.

"Our church is pure again," Omra said. Kuari bowed her head as he completed the ceremony. "With the endorsement of your soldan-shah and the blessings of Urec, I hereby invest you in your office as the leader and mother of the church."

Istar and Naori waited on the step below the carved wooden door. Omra turned to his First Wife, who handed him the golden Amulet of Urec, which had always been the property of the ur-sikara. Kuari leaned forward so that he could slip the medallion over her head. "Help us all to follow the Map." The Amulet rested comfortably on her ample chest, gleaming in the sunlight.

After Tukar's funeral ceremony, when Imir had chastised him for worrying too much about Ishalem and not enough about the rest of Uraba, Omra had pondered much until he realized that he had a solution. When he offered the idea, Kuari had immediately endorsed it.

He spoke to the people now, "Because Ishalem is our holy city, Ur-Sikara Kuari will establish her residence in the new main church there. Ishalem will become the center of the religious world, while I will remain in Olabar to govern our secular realm." It would be an efficient balance and separation.

Kuari rapped the heel of her staff on the flagstones, giving the next announcement. "As the mother of the church, I am now forced to give up earthly comforts. I can no longer serve as the wife of Soldan Huttan. Instead, I will take up residence in Ishalem and fulfill my new role."

Omra did not let his smile show. Neither Kuari or Huttan had voiced any objections to severing their marriage ties.

"The ur-sikara and the soldan-shah must work together to defeat our enemy, who attacks us both in this world and in our faith." He raised his hand, and Kuari reached out to clasp it, presenting a unified front. "In a week's time I will sail with Ur-Sikara Kuari to Ishalem, where we will consecrate the new church. From her new home, she will guide us all."

Kuari was perfect, he thought. He would thank Istar again for her wisdom. After all the recent chaos, Omra felt that the internal politics of Uraba were finally stabilizing.

Now all he had to worry about was the Tierrans.

21 *Calay, Military District*

Tierran military experts fleshed out the queen's plan and set up schedules—when the army must be at full strength encamped at the Ishalem wall, when the navy could form its complete blockade of Ishalem's western harbor, and when Destrar Broeck needed to arrive with his armored ships on the opposite side of the isthmus. The Urabans would be caught in the middle of all three forces—but only with the proper timing.

Working with her personal scribe, Queen Anjine drew up a document that laid down the detailed schedule leading to the battle and beyond. The coordination and preparation for such a large operation would take months, but the onset of winter in the Corag mountains made it imperative that messengers head off immediately to guarantee at least one of them would get over the pass so that Destrar Broeck knew his part.

To keep the vital information from falling into Uraban hands, Anjine's lady-in-waiting Enifir translated each copy into an obscure Iborian dialect—which Broeck could read, but would be gibberish to anyone who wasn't from the northern reach. The riders raced off on fast horses, each separated by a day, heading up into the Corag mountains.

*

For most of his life, Jenirod and his father had not gotten along well, and he had only recently come to the bitter conclusion that *he* was mostly to blame. Destrar Unsul was a wise leader of Erietta Reach, tending to the tedious day-to-day matters that cocky Jenirod had always found boring. It shamed the young man to remember how he and his friends had snickered at Unsul's dull life. Now Jenirod had to admit that he'd been an annoying, immature ass. If the war ever ended, he would go back to Erietta and study his father's windmills and irrigation improvements with a new eye.

First, though, the Urabans had to be defeated.

Jenirod bunked in the barracks so he could help Comdar Rief plan the massive three-pronged assault on Ishalem. He wanted to be available at all hours, should any of the leaders ask his advice. To the best of his abilities, Jenirod had given a full accounting of the size and apparent capabilities of the seven captured ironclads. He estimated the production capacity of the Gremurr mines and smelters, and offered his best guess as to how many freed prisoners—and potential soldiers—Broeck could enlist for his own part of the operation. When Jenirod talked, his voice was bleak. The boyish thrill of war had been burned out of him. . . .

He ate a lunch of soup and fresh bread at the officers' table in the mess barracks, and Destrar Shenro joined him, grinning as he sat down. "Isn't it wonderful for Alamont and Erietta to have a true enemy after so many rivalries between our reaches?"

The Alamont destrar had let his hair grow long, perhaps because he thought it made him look more like a warrior. Jenirod, however, had learned that long hair merely gave enemy combatants something to grab, which was not a particularly good idea in real fighting.

"Rivalries are very different from warfare," Jenirod said. "I didn't understand the difference before, but now I certainly do."

Shenro made a habit of attending strategy sessions with

Comdar Rief and his advisers. He fancied himself a military historian, but he had no actual battlefield experience (though he longed for it). Alamont was Tierra's only landlocked reach, and most Urecari attacks came by sea. The more Shenro proposed audacious military advances on Uraba, the more Jenirod was reminded of himself only a few months earlier.

"We understand about war and suffering," Shenro said. "Ninety of my brave men rode off to seize Ishalem after the soldan-shah invaded it, and they were all slaughtered. Martyrs for Aiden." He sighed and shook his head. "Soon enough my people can avenge that sacrifice."

Jenirod gave a noncommittal nod. Now that he considered those ninety dead Alamont riders from a new perspective, he concluded that their lives had been wasted. Brash and poorly prepared, vastly outnumbered, without a plan. If the Urecari had *not* killed those riders, then they would have been the fools. But he didn't expect the people of Alamont to see it that way.

"I remember the old days," Shenro said wistfully, "when my father used to tell me about the beautiful women of Erietta."

"Yes, they are beautiful." Jenirod recalled how the ladies had swooned over him during Eriettan horse cavalcades.

Shenro recounted the story of how the brother of an Alamont destrar, many generations ago, had grown enamored of a beautiful Eriettan girl. "When she declined his marriage proposal—a political thing, I suppose—the smitten man rode to your reach, kidnapped the girl, and took her back to Alamont. One of our presters wed them in the middle of the night." Shenro chuckled at the tale. "That almost led to open war between our reaches until the king stepped in and forced the Alamont destrar to offer his own daughter in return as wife to an Eriettan nobleman."

Jenirod grunted, not amused by the story. "That deal still favored Alamont, since the Eriettan girl was much lovelier than your destrar's daughter."

Shenro answered with a good-natured laugh. Then with wolfish hunger he pressed for details of who had been slain at Gremurr and how they had died. "It must have been glorious! Our poets and minstrels have plenty of material for new works. This is a good reason to celebrate."

"Nobody felt much like celebrating." Jenirod continued to eat his soup and bread. "Let me tell you about my own battle experiences." He set his spoon aside, and Shenro listened eagerly. "When I was betrothed to Queen Anjine, I wanted to impress her by winning a great victory in her honor. Destrar Tavishel and I set off to desecrate one of the heathen shrines as a way to thumb our noses at the Curlies and show them that we're not afraid of their Urec."

Shenro nodded. "Yes, Fashia's Fountain—I've heard of it. You killed many of them."

"We killed many women and pilgrims—*none* of them fighters. I thought I would turn into a soldier that day. Instead, I just felt like an animal. They screamed for mercy, but we didn't grant it. Their blood fouled a pure spring. Fashia's Fountain was a beautiful place, a crystal pool with a waterfall." Jenirod blinked; his eyes burned, and his ears rang with the echoes of dying Urecari priestesses and pilgrims.

"And even after that," Shenro said, picking up the story and still oblivious, "the Curlies didn't surrender and leave us alone. They killed Prince Tomas. Obviously, they will never learn their lesson." He grinned. "I can't wait until our army marches."

Jenirod went back to eating his soup with a heavy heart. It seemed the Alamont destrar was also incapable of learning a lesson.

22 *Gremurr Foothills*

Though they faced another cold night, Shetia was too frightened to build a campfire. She and Ulan faced despair and starvation in the tangled trees of an enclosed canyon. The two huddled together, trying to keep warm, shivering as much from fear of being caught by Aidenists as from the chill in the air.

They were both woefully unskilled in making a rough camp. Being married to Tukar had not been full of extravagances, but she had never been forced to hunt her own food or build a fire out of dry brush. So far, she had kept the two of them alive, just barely, but they wouldn't last many more days.

Somehow, even without a telltale fire to draw his attention, their old household slave managed to track them down. "I brought blankets." Firun extended ragged swatches of cloth. "I'm sorry that I could find nothing better, my Lady. They are the same blankets given to slaves in the barracks."

Though they were thin, dirty, and probably lice-ridden, Shetia made no complaints. "Thank you, Firun. This will keep us alive for a while longer." She wrapped one around Ulan's shoulders and the boy pulled it close, crouching down.

Shetia swallowed a hard lump of fear in her throat, knowing that if Firun could find them, so might someone else, but he reassured her. "No one is searching for you. They believe they've rounded up all the Urabans at Gremurr, and Destrar Broeck does not suspect you're hiding in the hills."

The boy's puppy came forward, wagging its tail with such vigor that it seemed to be shivering. Scrawny now, it licked Firun's hand, obviously recognizing the old man.

He patted the dog and nudged it toward Ulan, who enfolded it in the blankets. "You always treated me well enough, my Lady. I know you weren't responsible for the wars of your people. And Tukar tried to do his best."

"Did you bring any food?" Ulan piped up. "I found berries this afternoon, and some flowers that Mother said we could eat, but they tasted bitter. I'm still hungry."

"I brought what little food I could smuggle out, young man."

The household servant looked sad. "Many storehouses were destroyed by the mammoths and the fires, and no more Uraban supply ships have arrived. We'll have a hard time of it when winter sets in. Destrar Siescu just delivered a load with his supply train, but even the Aidenist rations are still tight."

"I feel no sympathy for them," Shetia snapped. "They destroy whatever they touch, and they didn't care who they hurt. They took everything that was ours. They had no right!"

"Now, we don't want to argue about that, my Lady." Firun's tone was cool as he unwrapped lumps of hard bread, three scrawny carrots, some nuts, and a wedge of moldy goat's cheese. "I certainly don't blame you and the boy, but your people did build these mines on Tierran soil and forced Aidenist prisoners to work them. The queen is justified in taking back her own territory and freeing her subjects."

Shetia bit her tongue, remembering that despite his present kindness Firun was still a Tierran who believed in the Fishhook.

Ulan looked at the food eagerly. "What can we feed my dog?"

"A good dog can hunt his own dinner," Firun said. "This food is just for you, to keep you strong and healthy."

But the boy was adamant. "I need to feed my dog!" He broke off a chunk of bread and extended it to the thin puppy, who gulped it down. "Maybe I can sneak into their camp one night and take some food."

Firun and Shetia reacted with alarm. The old servant said, "Don't even talk like that, boy! Destrar Broeck has guards, and Siescu just brought more soldiers and workers from Corag along with his supplies. It's a very dangerous time."

Ulan continued to look defiant and pulled the thin blanket tighter around himself. He muttered in a surly voice, "Nobody wanted the Aidenists here anyway. My father would have driven them away, but the Aidenists brought monsters! Who can fight against monsters?"

While fleeing the villa, Shetia and her son had witnessed a little of the mayhem as the invaders swept through the camp. The two had run madly into the wooded hills and heard only the distance-faded din, but Shetia imagined what must have happened there.

"Do you have any word of my father?" Ulan pressed. "He was in the camp—they must have found him! He would have fought. I'll bet the Aidenist commander captured him."

Firun looked away, evading the direct answer. "There was great turmoil, young man."

"But he was in charge of the Gremurr mines! A very important man."

The old slave hesitated. "Yes, your father was a very important man. He was the brother of the soldan-shah. Even in the heat of war, there are certain expectations of civilized behavior among rival leaders. He . . . has been sent back to Olabar." He clamped his lips shut.

Ulan seemed to accept the answer and sat back, content, but Shetia heard something in the old man's voice. She clenched her fists, pressed her lips together, and sobbed quietly so that her son would not hear her.

23 *Calay*

After the recent hurricane in Calay, skilled carpenters and stonemasons were in great demand. Fortunately, Vicka and her father Ammur Sonnen had plenty of apprentices to help rebuild the battered forge and smithy. Outbuildings, sheds, and a charcoal storehouse had been blown over by the storm winds; part of the main house's roof had been torn off, and the chimney had fallen down.

Ammur was exasperated to be prevented from working at his

anvil or forge. He was not interested in household repairs, only in making swords and armor for the war. His entire life pivoted on his work as a blacksmith, and he just wanted the days to return to normal.

In the meantime, Vicka let her father stoke the fires and operate the bellows of their secondary forge, which kept him happy doing what he loved, while she took it upon herself to put the apprentices to work. First, she kept them busy clearing debris and putting up split-rail fences. Next, because of the late autumn chill, she had them rebuild the main-house chimney so that she and her father could have a fire to keep them warm at night. (She would rather Mateo were home to keep her warm, but she knew he was on his way.)

Perched on the slanted roof while Vicka stood in the yard below, the apprentices slathered mortar and cobblestones in a crude approximation of the previous chimney. The young men made up for their lack of skill with enthusiasm; the result wasn't particularly masterful craftsmanship, but it appeared to work, though with a bit more smoke and sparks than Vicka liked. Once they completed the chimney, the apprentices worked at reconstructing the main forge, so that her father could get the Sonnen smithy running again at its previous capacity.

Noting how badly the adjacent homes and businesses needed repairs, Vicka made the obvious decision. "We're going to loan some of our young men to the neighbors, Father. Too many other people need help getting their lives back together."

Her comment disoriented Ammur. He had carefully rearranged the tools on his repaired workbench next to the small anvil at the secondary forge. "But our apprentices have work to do here. The queen is depending on us to make all those swords, and I promised her a suit of armor made just for her. She'll need it when she rides off to war."

As soon as Queen Anjine had announced that she would

personally lead the final charge to recapture Ishalem, Ammur Sonnen promised to craft her custom-fitted armor himself, even though his smithy was barely functional. He was adamant that the queen's armor must be more than a costume, but a functional suit of finely worked plate to protect her against enemy assassins.

Vicka tossed her dark hair and put her hands on her hips. "Calay also needs you to fashion nails and hinges and bands to rebuild the city. You're not just a swordmaker, you're a blacksmith."

Ammur let out a sigh. "All right, the queen isn't marching to war just yet. We can help the neighbors."

Vicka yelled at two of the apprentices who had paused to drink a dipper of water from the rainbarrel. "You there, back to work!" She lowered her voice to her father. "I want everything back together by the time Mateo comes home in a few days. I don't want him to think I can't take care of myself when he's not around."

Vicka could not entirely keep the girlish anticipation from her voice. She missed her husband terribly . . . a brave soldier loyal to the queen and to Tierra. Not long after their wedding, he had gone off on a dark and terrible mission; no one would tell her exactly what it was, so she supposed it must be a military secret. But Vicka did know now that he'd been part of the recent victory at the coveted Gremurr mines. Mateo was a hero, no doubt about it. Even now, he was bringing back a group of freed Tierran captives. Naturally, Queen Anjine would praise him for his service, but Vicka had her own ideas about how to reward Mateo in the best possible way he could imagine. . . .

When she'd married him, Vicka had never expected Mateo Bornan to be a homebody. A subcomdar of the Tierran military had many duties besides simply being a husband. Vicka understood that; in fact, she didn't mind, since she was an independent woman with plenty of her own work managing the Sonnen forges. She let out a wistful sigh.

Seeing that Vicka wasn't paying attention, some of the journeymen stood around, and she brusquely pointed out things that needed to be done. "How can you not see it for yourselves? Clean up all this debris before we go to the memorial celebration tonight, or you'll stay here and keep working while the rest of us are lighting candles and singing at the kirk."

The young men jumped to obey.

At sunset, the residents of Calay gathered in the square outside the main kirk to mark the twenty-first anniversary of the Ishalem fire. Vicka and her father went every year, accompanied by their apprentices and journeymen.

The grim story put Calay's storm damage in perspective. Though the recent hurricane was the worst storm anyone could remember, the damage was trivial compared to what the world had lost that terrible night in Ishalem, when so many people, and so many dreams, had died.

No prester-marshall had yet been selected to replace Rudio, but five prominent presters stood outside the kirk by the cast-iron Fishhook. With cracking voices, two of the men told of seeing Ishalem in their youth and described the city's magnificent towers, whitewashed buildings, and ornate structures. And the sacred Arkship, the ruins of Aiden's vessel that had carried Aiden from Terravitae, left abandoned high on a hill—preserved for centuries, burned to ash in a single night . . .

When Queen Anjine emerged from the kirk, the crowd grew silent. "I was just a girl when I traveled to Ishalem with my father." Vicka listened with a smile because she knew that Mateo, Anjine's childhood friend, had accompanied her on that voyage. "I was there that last night . . . I saw the fire." Her voice hitched. "King Korastine had just signed the Edict with the soldan-shah, dividing the world to give us peace. But we should have known not to trust the followers of Urec."

The queen's anger was plain, and a hiss rippled through the crowd. "When the fire started, Aidenists rushed to extinguish the flames—and the Urecari rode our people down, hacked them with their scimitars, and threw torches to spread the fire. I saw it with my own eyes. *They* burned Ishalem."

As Vicka listened, tears sparkled in her eyes. She had never seen the holy city herself, but she had constructed vivid pictures in her mind. She wished Mateo could be here to tell her his own stories of that night. . . .

While courting her, Mateo had spent most of his time talking about the war, describing how he had sailed aboard Tierran patrol ships and fought Urecari raiders. Sometimes, he was reticent to provide details, and Vicka did not press him. If he didn't want to remember those events, then she didn't want to know. She loved him and knew he would come back to her. Soon.

Though Vicka wasn't an overly sentimental person, she did keep the ornate fishhook chains that were locked together to symbolize how their lives were joined. During their wedding in the main kirk, Mateo and Vicka had linked those hooks together to commemorate their bond of marriage, and she kept them locked in a drawer of her small wardrobe. She would have been embarrassed if her father, or any of the apprentices, knew how often she took out those hooks and chains, held them in her hands, and thought of Mateo, imagining him on some distant battlefield, and now traveling the long road back to Calay.

To finish the ceremony, the presters led the crowd in a somber but heartfelt hymn to Ishalem, after which they all took up the candles they had brought for the ceremony. After they touched wick to wick, each person held their small flame high. The candles were tiny sparks of hope for the future, glimmers of faith. No one in Tierra would ever forget the loss of Ishalem.

Afterward, Vicka returned home with her father. It had been a somber celebration, but necessary. "When Mateo comes back, we can be happy again."

"When he delivers those lost prisoners to their families, a lot of people are going to be happy," Ammur replied. "You married a good man, Vicka."

After nightfall, the air was chill even inside the large home. Ammur built up a blazing fire in the hearth, wrestling with the flue in the newly repaired chimney. Vicka kissed her father goodnight, then went to bed. Neither of them liked to stay up late; they rose each morning before dawn so Ammur could prepare the forge and Vicka could roust the apprentices for the day's work.

Before blowing out the candle, she took out the joined fishhooks one more time from her secret drawer, running her finger along the links. She put them back in her wardrobe and hurried across the cold floor to her bed.

With a woolen blanket keeping her warm, Vicka closed her eyes and thought of Mateo. She wondered where he was at that very moment—lying under the stars, perhaps, huddled in his own blanket in a camp along a road? On his way home to Calay, to her—

She awoke abruptly and opened her eyes to smoke; her vision was fuzzy, her lungs scratching and on fire. It hurt to breathe. In the other room, she heard her father coughing, retching, staggering about. She pulled herself off the bed, but was tangled in the blankets. Unable to clear her head, she tripped and fell to the hard floor, bruising her knee. She got to her feet, fumbling her way out of the bedroom.

Sparks spat out from the main fireplace. Rafts of black smoke filled the room with poisonous fog, and flames were licking up the walls next to the hearth. The smoke was so thick, she couldn't remember where the door was, but she found a wall, bumped a stool, kept blindly staggering forward.

The door's latch was flimsy, but it stalled her attempts to open it.

She was coughing; each lungful made her feel worse, not better. Finally, she undid the latch and dragged the door open so she could plunge out into the fresh night air, choking and gagging.

Smoke flooded out after her. Flames cavorted from the main house, poking through the closed window shutters, running along the roof. Some of the apprentices had emerged from the work barracks, yelling, "Fire! Fire!" Throughout the neighborhood, people came running. The apprentices grabbed buckets, filling them from the barrels of quench water near the forge.

Someone threw a blanket on top of Vicka, pounding her back and head, and she realized that her clothes and hair were smoldering. She didn't even feel the burning, and with a frantic, impatient gesture she yanked the blanket away.

In her mind she saw a clear picture of the joined fishhooks in her drawer—the symbol of her marriage, her bond with Mateo. The fire would turn the gold and silver into an unrecognizable lump, but she knew she couldn't go back in there to rescue an object, no matter how precious it might be. . . .

She reeled, hearing the crackle of flames, the shouts of people tossing buckets of water onto the burning roof. Inside, the ceiling beams groaned and cracked. One of the journeymen pressed a cup of water against her lips, which she tried to drink, but could not force it down her throat. Stunned, she needed to hold her father so they could comfort each other . . . but she didn't see him among the milling helpers.

Vicka wheezed out Ammur's name, but the smoke hurt her vocal cords so much she couldn't speak. Finally she grabbed the journeyman who had given her the water and managed to scratch out the words, "My father! Where is he?"

The young man's eyes went wide. "He didn't come out. He's still—"

Still fuzzy from the smoke, Vicka ran back through the open door, charging stubbornly into the main room. She couldn't see a thing, couldn't raise her voice to call for him. The smoke was thicker in here, and the air even hotter than when she worked over the coals of the smelter during the day's labors. Sparks flew about like angry stars, dotting the black smoke. Vicka swatted at her hair, felt her skin singe. Each footstep was heavier and more difficult.

A burning rafter beam collapsed behind her in a crash of sparks, barely missing her. Urgent voices called from outside, but she also heard her father coughing, crawling on the floor where the smoke was less dense.

She blundered into him by pure chance, nearly tripped, and grabbed his shoulder. The solid feel of him brought her back to reality, allowing her to focus once more. She pushed Ammur forward, and they lurched together across the room toward the open door through which smoke gushed like water down a waterfall.

Vicka fell to her knees and crawled after him. She felt a little better down here, knew where she had to go. Overhead, other ceiling beams groaned and began to crack. She no longer saw the fire, or the sparks, or the smoke, but at least she knew her father was safe. . . .

Ammur Sonnen vomited on the ground outside of his burning house, utterly exhausted. He rubbed his stinging eyes. Tears continued to flow, washing away the soot, but he still couldn't see. Vicka had been right behind him. Where was she?

He called out for her, but only incomprehensible sound scraped out of his throat. His neighbors and apprentices poured water on the fire. Men from nearby houses came with shovels and buckets.

Ammur rasped out her name. "Vicka . . . she's in there!"

The young apprentices and journeymen shouted her name—all of them had been smitten with beautiful Vicka—but no one dared go inside where the flames were too high, the smoke too thick.

Then with cracking sounds like repeated lightning strikes, the ceiling collapsed.

Ammur lurched to his feet and tried to charge into the house. Somebody had to save her! It took four young men just to hold him back. He shouted, and railed, and wept, but they wouldn't let him go. Even though his eyes finally cleared, he never saw Vicka emerge from the burning building.

24 *Calay Castle*

In the private eastern courtyard of Calay Castle, a previous king had created a contemplation garden surrounded by lilac shrubs (the king's favorite) as a peaceful spot where the Tierran ruler could think.

In the center of a marble platform stood the ornate prime Captain's Compass, the central instrument to which every Captain's Compass was twinned. Its needle had been drawn from the original block of iron and sympathetically magnetized; the needles in all other Captain's Compasses pointed back to it—an arrow home for every sailor who voyaged across the oceans.

Even as those twinned Compasses were drawn to this primary spot, their own sympathetic threads pulled *this* needle in random directions. While the queen sat in blessed isolation on a cool bench regarding the Compass, its needle wandered to and fro, indicating no clear direction. She would have to make her own decision.

Anjine sat in preoccupied silence by the lilac bushes whose flowers had long since faded away with summer and autumn. The fresh news weighed like an anvil in her chest: Mateo's wife Vicka had been killed in a fire at the Sonnen forge. Anjine had no one in whom she could confide, and she felt absolutely heartsick.

Sen Leo na-Hadra entered the courtyard with a determined gait, but when he saw her sober mood he hesitated. "My Queen? Guard-Marshall Vorannen told me I would find you here. Am I interrupting?" He took a cautious step forward.

"May I have a brief word with you?"

She answered automatically. "What is it?"

"We've received another bonded *rea* pigeon from the *Dyscovera.*"

Anjine raised her head as if lifting a heavy stone, trying to concentrate on business that mattered little to her right now. "And what news does Captain Vora send? Has he found Terravitae yet?" This was the fourth report from the *Dyscovera.*

Sen Leo took a seat beside Anjine on the stone bench. "The bird arrived at the coop exhausted, but the message tied to its leg was intact. Quite a tale, Majesty—not at all what we expected. I'm afraid there are heavy consequences."

Anjine couldn't bear much more bad news, but she had to listen. She was the queen of Tierra. "Tell me the full details."

Sen Leo gazed at the wandering needle of the prime compass as he told her about the discovery of the lost Saedran race and their sunken continent. Anger seemed to boil from him as he continued. "But the ship's prester led a mutiny against Captain Vora and attacked the king of the mer-Saedrans. Those people could have been great allies to Tierra, and could have helped the *Dyscovera* find Terravitae. But Prester Hannes ruined everything."

Anjine narrowed her eyes. "How did Captain Vora deal with it?"

"The mutineers were stopped, but too much damage had already been done. Several crewmembers were killed, including First Mate Kjelnar. The mer-Saedrans abandoned the *Dyscovera* and refused to offer any further help." His sinewy hands knotted. "I am greatly distressed by these tragic events."

A pounding pain echoed inside Anjine's head. "I am distressed as well, Sen Leo." From such a great distance, though, she was helpless to do anything to aid them. "But the *Dyscovera* remains intact? The ship can sail on?"

"Yes, Majesty. I visited the sympathetic model only this morning. Sen Burian na-Coway has seen no indication of damage to the ship." The old scholar paused, but he was not finished. She dreaded hearing what else he might reveal to her.

Sen Leo finally looked up. "This news emphasizes portents in our Saedran writings, in the prophecies we have kept over the centuries, and in the Tales of the Traveler. I can no longer deny that so many omens point to the same conclusion. For centuries, our people have laid the framework for the Final Days, and right now I see many uncomfortable similarities."

Anjine brushed this aside. "If Ondun wanted to bring the world to an end, what could I do to stop Him? I can only lead as best I can." She looked at the prime compass. "I've heard enough about the end of the world for now. My own sorrow is much closer to home. Thank you for the message, Sen Leo, but please leave me to my thoughts."

The Saedran scholar wanted to serve as a sounding board, as he had done many times for King Korastine, but Anjine needed to think. He rose from the stone bench and quietly exited the courtyard.

During her reign, Anjine had dealt with epic disasters, massacres, and unspeakable Urecari war crimes, but this was a deeply personal disaster. No one in all the world was as dear to her as Mateo Bornan, and this would devastate him. After all that Mateo had sacrificed in the name of Aiden, in the name of victory—in the name of *Anjine*—this would hurt him the most.

"Personal tragedies can be just as painful as great ones," she said aloud.

She knew she had to be the one to tell him. She could not send a messenger, would not shirk the responsibility. As queen, she had already forced Mateo to do unspeakable things. Her command to deliver a thousand Urecari heads to the Ishalem wall had burned his soul, and yet he had done it—for her.

She had so looked forward to his return, but now she dreaded his arrival. Mateo would be home soon.

25 *The* Dyscovera

Leaving the island and the fossilized Leviathan skeleton, the *Dyscovera* sailed off under a strong breeze, following Aiden's Compass. The needle pointed true now, sure in its guidance.

Prester Hannes and the contrite mutineers were back on board, though not quite forgiven; they behaved with delicate care, praying he wouldn't change his mind. Sen Aldo watched the prester wrestle with the contradiction to his beliefs posed by the dead sea monster. During his dawn sermons, Hannes spoke in a subdued tone of voice and never raised the issue of the Leviathan.

Adding to his leather-bound journal of sea monsters, Captain Vora sketched details of the embedded skeleton. Years earlier, he had meticulously drawn his version of the monster alongside the other naturalist sketches Captain Shay had made during his own voyages. The long-dead creature they had seen was clearly of the same species as the beast that had destroyed the *Luminara*. Logically, there must be more than one Leviathan, no matter what the Book of Aiden said.

Lulled by the gentle sway of the sea and the background creak of wooden planks, the captain finished his notes, then used one of his clean sheets of paper to write another letter to his long-lost wife. Aldo watched him, aware of the other man's persistent, hopeful correspondence, each letter sealed in a bottle along with a single strand of Adrea's hair.

As a Saedran, Aldo knew the captain had some reason to hope, but the bond of sympathetic magic was not likely strong enough to pull the letter all the way around the world. The chartsman had a more direct means of sending a message home to Calay, and he returned to his cabin to prepare another note.

Though Aldo had recently dispatched a *rea* pigeon to tell of the mer-Saedran debacle, he wrote a detailed account of the island, the fossil discovery, and the fact that Aiden's Compass was functioning again. In the bright yellow light of his lantern, Aldo hunched over with a sharpened stylus and free-flowing ink. He wrote in tight, coded letters, adding the coordinates of the island so that Sen Leo could mark it on their Mappa Mundi. With only six *rea* pigeons left, Aldo wanted to make sure each message counted for as much as possible.

His thoughts wandered to his lovely wife Lanni. He didn't regret his decision to sail away and see more of the world than any other living person had witnessed, but on a quiet night like this, with the ship gently rocking, he could not wait to return home. He missed his children; they would be almost four and five years old now—had the *Dyscovera* really been gone that long? Little boys and girls could grow like weeds.

Though Aldo was still a young man, he had crowded his life with adventures. Back in Tierra, he had seen the Corag mountains, traveled up and down the coast. He'd been captured in a raid and taken to the heart of Uraba, where he met Sen Sherufa na-Oa. However, once the *Dyscovera* came home from this voyage, Aldo planned to spend the rest of his days with the family and lead a quiet life.

Letting the ink dry overnight, he blew out the lantern and lay back on his narrow bed, rocked by the waves as the ship sailed onward into unknown waters.

The next morning, Aldo woke early and coiled the thin strip of paper, ready to tie it to the leg of one of the pigeons.

Since only Saedrans could read the message, he did not worry that someone might intercept the basic navigational knowledge. The *rea* pigeon would find its way across the seas to Tierra, following the sympathetic magic to its counterpart in Sen Leo's coop in Calay.

When Aldo emerged from his cabin, he heard Hannes gathering the faithful for sunrise service. While the prester spoke his terse morning message to the crew, Aldo went to the stern deck where he kept his birds in a cage.

He stared in horror.

All six of the birds were dead, their necks wrung, feathers strewn about. Some had been slit open with a knife, so that blood and entrails lay at the bottom of the cage. He bent over and retched on the deck. The thin strips of paper in his hand fluttered out of his numb fingers to be lost at sea, and he was finally able to utter a rough shout. "Captain!"

Crewmembers came running, their worship service interrupted. Javian and Mia were the first to arrive at the cage. Staring at the carcasses, Mia cried, "Who did this?"

Javian looked like a wide-eyed boy again. "Those pigeons were our only way to communicate with Tierra."

The prester strode forward with his preaching staff, a sturdy wooden stick topped with a metal fishhook. Aldo looked sharply at him, the answer obvious. "Maybe someone didn't want any messages to reach Tierra."

Yes, it made sense now. Hannes would try to censor the news about the Leviathan skeleton, because he couldn't tolerate any contradictions to Aidenist dogma.

Captain Vora was furious and dismayed. "First our Captain's Compass is destroyed, and now we can't send any more messages home." The captain looked at them all.

The sailors looked suspiciously at one another. Some naturally targeted Mia with their blame, but she simply glared at them;

others suspected that Aldo himself might have done it, since he was a Saedran and a stranger. Silam Henner shouted in a thin voice, “It wasn’t me, Captain! Why would we do anything to jeopardize our position here? You’ve only just agreed to let us stay aboard.”

“It is the guilty who point fingers and cast blame,” Hannes said.

“Well, *someone* did this.” Captain Vora closed his eyes, as if to summon strength from within himself. “We have a saboteur on board.”

26 *Iyomelka’s Ship*

Cold spray splashed over the bow, and the tattered sails stretched tight as Iyomelka lashed the storm winds like unbroken horses to drive her vessel. The moss-covered hull boards—held together by barnacles, starfish, and a weave of seaweed—groaned under the strain. The prow of antler coral stretched forward beneath an oblong sea-serpent skull she had recently incorporated as a figurehead. Reptilian vertebrae adorned the keel like a line of ivory bosses.

She did not sleep. Somewhere out on that open water she would find the *Al-Orizin* and the reckless interlopers who had stolen Ystya. Her foolish and naïve daughter had been sheltered all her life from the outside world. The girl did not fully understand what she represented, nor did Captain Saan, who had kidnapped her.

When they encountered the Father of All Serpents, she had never expected Ystya to discover her own powers, and the girl’s demonstration only reinforced Iyomelka’s determination to retrieve her. She had to use any means possible.

As her ship pounded through the waves without regard to natural currents or trade winds, she pressed her palms against the crystal coffin that held her husband's preserved body. "We will get her back, Ondun."

Immersed in magical water from the island spring, the old man looked serene and placid, his long gray hair and beard forming a corona about his head. He looked so different from the time when she had hated him, when he had drowned in the deep well. Immortals had so much time to change their minds and live with their regrets. . . .

After her disastrous indiscretion with Mailes, Iyomelka had gone through the motions, trying to repair her relationship with her husband. But when she found herself pregnant with Ondun's child—a wondrous occurrence for their dwindling race—she knew that her happiness would never be the same. Unable to remain in Terravitae with Ondun, especially after what he did to Mailes, she fled, seeking refuge far away on an uncharted island. But he sent their sons out to search the whole world, and eventually came after her himself, determined to find the daughter on whom so much hope rested. When Ondun finally reached the hidden island, Iyomelka begged him to stay with her and be happy, to let the world manage itself.

Isolated for centuries or millennia (she didn't even know which), they had lived as a contented family. Together, Ondun and Iyomelka always remained young, and Ystya never grew beyond a child. That had worked for a long, long time, but nothing—even love—could last as long as eternity.

Oh, Iyomelka had had plenty of time to regret her actions. It had been unwise for her to drown him. With Ondun gone, the island's spring dried up, and she and the girl began to age. Although Captain Saan and his men had indeed restored the flow of water and retrieved Ondun's preserved body, she could never be grateful to the *Al-Orizin* sailors.

Only if she retrieved her daughter, reunited her family, returned to the isolated island, and recreated their idyllic times would the fabric of destiny be repaired. Iyomelka could not ignore the romantic sop and his infatuation with the girl he did not understand at all. Captain Saan had to be punished, crushed, and brushed away like an annoying gnat. . . .

As the spectral ship sliced through the water, Iyomelka pressed herself against Ondun's coffin and stared down at his waxen face. In the faint reflection, she caught a glimpse of her own features, the years sloughed away, her vibrant youth restored from the old crone she had been. It reminded her of when her race on Terravitae had been so much stronger. . . .

"I will call upon all of my magic, my love—but you must help me. We need to stop that other ship."

Closing her eyes as tightly as she could, squeezing her thoughts into a loud summons, Iyomelka penetrated the cold dark waters and awakened things that had been asleep for eons.

She called the Kraken from the depths and sent it after the *Al-Orizin.*

27 *Olabar Palace*

Before the soldan-shah and the new ur-sikara departed for Ishalem, Omra agreed to consult with a driftwood reader. It was Naori's idea, and he knew it would make her happy.

Talented driftwood readers were well respected among the coastal folk, and this one came with impressive credentials and testimonials. Naori had met with the woman in her small harborside shack and been so impressed by the poignant observations and insightful advice that she begged Omra to let Aizara do a reading for him. Because he adored Naori, he agreed; his second wife asked for very little.

At the appointed hour, Imir joined him, casually taking a

cushion beside his son on the raised dais. The former soldan-shah was curious, but brought a healthy dose of skepticism as well. "I had a driftwood reading done when I was a brash and confident young man, when I was sure I could change the world." Imir's expression grew distant. "I insisted that I would never make the same mistakes my father did . . . then I learned that *he* had said the same thing about *his* father." He looked at Omra with an amused expression. "And no doubt you've made similar promises about following in my footsteps."

Sidestepping the comment, Omra said, "And what did the driftwood reader foretell of your future?"

"She made cryptic pronouncements that I considered unlikely at the time, but eventually they came true, much to my astonishment. After certain things happened, I would recall her prophecies, and I was absolutely convinced she had true magic." He blew out a long sigh. "Later, though, I realized that her words could be taken in many different ways, and because I was *looking* for a prophecy, I found it. I doubt she was endowed with special powers, but I do think she was a skilled manipulator."

Omra stroked his narrow beard. "Well, Naori was quite impressed with this driftwood reader, so I am honor-bound to hear what the woman has to say."

"I'm sure she'll say very important things, my son . . . though they may come from shrewd observation rather than magic."

Kel Rovik opened the doors to the audience chamber and presented the shaman. "Aizara from Kiesh." The guard captain made a brief bow and ushered the woman inside.

The driftwood reader did not wait for Omra to acknowledge her. "Not Kiesh exactly, Soldan-Shah. I was born in a tiny village in the sandy lands to the east of Kiesh, but my village has no name, and your guard seemed to want one."

Aizara's joints creaked as she moved. Her skin was whorled with wrinkles like the grain on a piece of wood. She was dark from years of exposure to the sun, and her brown hair was streaked with gray and tied back in a tight braid so that it looked like a knotted branch. Her skirt, blouse, and shawl were a ragged, fuzzy brown as if spun from frayed bark fibers.

"The name of your village doesn't matter to me," Omra said equably. "You are here to give me your driftwood predictions."

She kept her eyes averted out of respect, but when she came close enough, Aizara lifted her head. Her irises were an eerie hazel. "You have chosen a piece of driftwood, Soldan-Shah?"

"I selected one from the market stalls." From the cushion beside him, Omra lifted a gnarled branch that had been tortured into a whirlpool of wood.

Aizara reached out with her long-fingered hands. "I must feel it, touch it."

Next to him, Imir let out a quiet snort of amusement.

The driftwood reader explained the pattern of life and time woven into all things. "Ondun laid down His sketches of destiny in everything that lives. In trees, one can see the lines and paths clearly, depending on how the wood is cut. Driftwood is a special case—produced by a living tree with its own grains and designs, and then shaped by the forces of wind, weather, sea, and time." She stroked the smooth surface. "A piece of driftwood crystallizes destiny, keyed to the person who finds it." Aizara looked at him sharply. "You chose this piece yourself? You didn't have one of your men buy it?"

"It was my choice. The vendor had a great many of them, but this particular piece seemed the most interesting."

He caught a movement out of the corner of his eye—Naori watching from a curtained passage. She saw him looking at her and smiled.

Aizara cradled the driftwood he had given her, then closed her eyes and pressed the gnarled lump against her chest, folding her arms around it. She inhaled deeply, pressing her nose to the wood, breathing in the lingering iodine of seaweed, the dry dust of long exposure to the sun. She ran her fingertips along the thin cracks that split the surface. She touched the contorted branches and dug her nails into the wood so they left deep impressions.

Her hazel eyes flew open. "This is grave indeed, my Lord! The patterns are dire. The grain, the confluence of knots and branches . . . oh, this is very serious." Her arms trembled. She looked as though she wanted to drop the driftwood, but she didn't dare.

From the curtained alcove, Omra heard Naori draw in a sharp breath.

"Very serious? In what way?" He remembered what his father had said. "Please be specific. With the constant war against the Aidenists, it doesn't take a talented prophet to predict that hard times lie ahead."

"I mean the end of all things. Perhaps the destruction of the world, the loss of Uraba, and Tierra as well—everyone."

Omra sat back, glancing at his father. "I thought you said she was going to tell me what I *wanted* to hear."

"I doubt she gets much repeat business," Imir mused.

Aizara seemed angry. "This is not a trick, Soldan-Shah! I have never been so frightened." She held up the chunk of driftwood. "This speaks volumes for anyone who knows how to read it. The fate of the world hangs in the balance. Your actions have the gravest consequences. I promise you, great destruction will be upon us."

Incensed now, Omra leaned forward. "Did you come here with this act to frighten me?"

"I came to prepare you. And now, it seems, to warn you."

Imir just chuckled. "She does have an interesting manner. You should reward her for her bravery, if nothing else."

Kel Rovik shouted for the soldan-shah as he rushed a dusty man into the audience chamber. Pulling ahead of the guard, the newcomer gasped, "Cousin, I rode as fast as I could. It's a disaster!" Omra was shocked to recognize Burilo, the son of the Missinian soldan. "I rode across the land to get here! Arikara, my father's city, all the homes, the merchants—everything is laid waste by an earthquake! My father's palace collapsed."

Imir scrambled to his feet. "Is Lithio all right?"

"She is alive, but our homes are ruined, countless thousands are injured or killed. Please help us, Soldan-Shah! This is the worst catastrophe ever to happen in Missinia."

In front of the dais, Aizara dropped the driftwood to the tiled floor. "I am very sorry, Soldan-Shah. Please believe me—I did not wish to be right."

28 *Calay Harbor*

The riverboat pulled into the shallow eastern bay of Calay harbor, the deck crowded with waving and shouting men, some of them grinning, some weeping, some just staring in disbelief. The whole city celebrated the return of the Tierran refugees from Gremurr.

Queen Anjine had issued instructions that Jenirod's list of surviving prisoners be copied, then she commissioned Saedran printing presses to spread the list across Calay and dispatched messengers up and down the coast and across the reaches of Tierra. Joyful families began to gather in the harbor districts, waiting day by day for the freed slaves to arrive. They tied welcoming banners on poles. Now, as Destrar Sazar guided the flatboat to the cargo docks, curious spectators hurried to catch the ropes and lay down gangways.

By now, the Gremurr captives were well fed and rested, clad in garments given to them in Stoneholm or from the river clans. Men, women, and children pushed forward, calling out the names of loved ones. Merchants brought out food; tavern owners shared wine and ale. People in the crowd embraced the refugees, whether they knew one another or not.

The number of hopeful families was far greater than returning refugees, however. Even when they did not see the names of lost loved ones on the printed lists, still they clung to hope. Yes, some of the freed prisoners had stayed behind in Gremurr and would return later, but many families would feel the pain of disappointment. . . .

When Vorannen informed Queen Anjine, she threw on her ermine-lined royal cape, grabbed her ceremonial crown, and accompanied the guard-marshall down to the docks with more speed than decorum. Word spread quickly, and people flocked in from the city's districts to welcome the crowd of refugees. All work in the harbor had stopped for the day.

When the crowd noticed the queen's arrival, a spontaneous cheer erupted. Anjine shaded her eyes, searching the excited faces for the one she wanted to see more than any other. Despite the joyful celebration, she had a heavy heart because of her obligation—not as queen, but as friend—to tell Mateo. But she did not see him.

The buzz of conversation grew louder, and the people pressed around her. Vorannen leaned close and whispered, "They want you to address them, Majesty."

Caught in her role, Anjine tore her eyes away from her search, duty-bound to lead and inspire her people. "Yes, Guard-Marshall. I'll speak."

Vorannen clapped his hands for silence. The crowd quieted, except for a sporadic patter of conversation and laughter, like the last raindrops at the end of a downpour. Anjine drew herself erect and fashioned a smile, accepting their hopeful expressions, their relief. She was their queen, and they needed her too.

The words came naturally to her. "With indescribable joy I welcome you back to Tierra, back into the arms of Aiden. I'll assign my staff to take your names and help reunite you with your families. For those of you from other reaches, from any other town across Tierra, I will grant you passage home, where you belong. Presters will be available to say prayers for you."

Anjine swept her gaze over the crowd. The truth was hard, but necessary. "Some of you, sadly, will not find your missing fathers, husbands, brothers, or sons—at least not today. Some freed prisoners stayed behind at the Gremurr mines—those who could not make the journey before winter, or those who chose to stay and fight. Even so, many of our lost loved ones will never return."

Anjine's voice grew harder. "For too long the enemies of Aiden have enslaved or murdered loyal Tierrans. Let your grief become a weapon, your anger a shield! These returning prisoners are a sign from Ondun that we must continue the fight. We will crush the enemy and take back Ishalem."

She let the deafening cheer flow over her, but she was anxious to be finished. She still needed to find Mateo. With a final wave, she let them go back to their celebrations. Then she hurried across the pier to the riverboat, where bearded Sazar remained on the barge, ushering stragglers off the deck; the river clansmen were anxious to gather new goods and get back to the business of hauling freight up and down the riverways.

The burly man was pleased to greet her. "Majesty, this is likely the most satisfying cargo I have ever delivered, but all is not happiness. We've compiled another list, as painstaking as possible." He handed her a long roll of paper. "During the voyage, I had a Saedran clerk talk with the refugees, gathering as much information as possible about their fellow slaves who died over the years. Some of the names are sketchy, but they may help families to have answers."

Anjine took the roll, nodding absently, and interrupted him with urgency. "And Mateo—Subcomdar Bornan? I have a very important message for him. I understood that he was with you escorting the refugees."

Sazar's bushy brows curled like a pair of startled caterpillars. "Oh, he didn't want to stay for ceremonies, Majesty. As soon as we tied up at the docks, he was the first one ashore, heading for the Metalworkers' District. What a smile on his face! I've never seen a man so anxious to see his wife."

Anjine needed all of her strength to remain standing. She was too late.

As he hurried through the streets of Calay, Mateo was shocked to see how much damage the hurricane had done. Stacks of raw lumber were piled in the streets; many homes were partially rebuilt, while other cottages and shops had been abandoned and knocked down. He hoped Ammur Sonnen's smithies and forges had not suffered such damage.

Mateo knew his way through the district by heart, and he took shortcuts through alleys, splashed through muddy thoroughfares where carpenters had spread sawdust from lumber mills to stabilize the road surface. Only one thought dominated his mind, though.

Now that he was back, he intended to stay with Vicka and away from the army for some time. He could work in his father-in-law's smithy, help Ammur make swords and armor; though he didn't have any experience working at a forge, he supposed he could be taught. He and Vicka could have children, a normal family, a quiet and contented life. She could take him away from all the turmoil of the world and the pain of the war; she could help heal the scars. Mateo loved his queen and country, but he also loved his wife. Even Anjine would have to agree that he had earned time for himself.

He could see the black smoke of forges up ahead. The neighborhood held many smaller smithies, but the Sonnen forge was the largest, with the greatest number of apprentices and journeymen, anvils and grinding wheels. He remembered all the times he had shared dinner with Vicka and her father, and he grinned to think of how oblivious Ammur had been to the romance blossoming between the two of them.

Mateo arrived with a smile on his face, a spring in his step, and joy in his heart, but he stopped in shock to see that the main Sonnen house had burned to the ground. The young workers toiled in sullen silence, without the usual banter and happy challenges they called to one another at work. Only one of the fires had been lit.

He did not see Vicka or hear her lighthearted scolding as she shamed the young men into working harder. Ammur stood listless, like a stunned ox.

When Mateo stepped through the wooden gate, Ammur Sonnen looked slowly up, his soot-streaked face filled with sorrow. Mateo hurried forward, but before he could say a word, the older man began to sob.

Mateo couldn't speak, didn't want to ask. He already knew the answer.

Part II

29 *Gremurr Mines*

Destrar Broeck had made a serviceable home for himself at Gremurr in the villa of the former Uraban mine administrator.

The man (or more likely, his wife . . . did he even have a wife?) had decorated the home in traditional Uraban style, but Broeck's men pulled down the silk drapes and the Unfurling Fern tapestry. He replaced the furniture with blocky benches and plank tables so the house didn't look quite so foreign. Since he had no Iborian pine to work with, Broeck made do with scrap wood.

The destrar met daily with his lieutenants to discuss the defense of Gremurr, even though the soldan-shah had no warships left in the Middlesea. Omra didn't have the means to launch a retaliation, but Broeck kept the ironclads on constant patrol nevertheless.

In the rare evenings when he wasn't with Iaros or Destrar Siescu or one of the mine foremen, he liked to sit alone before a small fire. The local wood gave off a spicy resinous fragrance and too much smoke. Even though the nights were cool with the approach of winter, the climate was much milder than the destrar's home in frozen Iboria. He wanted the light more than warmth.

Since arriving in Gremurr with men and supplies, Destrar Siescu had taken up temporary residence in one of the other homes. Sooner or later Gremurr would become an established part of Corag Reach. Broeck certainly had no intention of staying here to carve out a new domain for himself. Miserable place!

Siescu spent most days with his expert metalworkers inside the smelter buildings; the Corag destrar liked to stand near the molten metal, and he built up blazes in all his fireplaces so that when

Broeck visited him he often had to step outside just to get away from the heat. It was a mystery to him how a man could be cold all the time. . . .

Now, alone and quiet, Broeck finished his dinner and pushed aside the chipped ceramic bowl. The camp cooks had produced another acceptable though odd-tasting meal with the supplies on hand, leaving only watery leftovers for the Curly captives. Unfortunately, the mammoths had smashed as many supply tents as military headquarters, and now the conquerors faced depleted food stores and diminished rations. Broeck also dispatched soldiers into the hills to hunt mountain goats, dwarf antelope, and grouse, so they could occasionally supplement their supplies with roast meat.

Whenever they seized Uraban cargo vessels or fishing boats, those stores were added to the camp supply tents. Urabans might have considered some of the odd items delicacies, but they all tasted strange to Broeck. But it was much-needed food. However, each time he brought a captured boat back to Gremurr to join the ever-growing cluster of ships at anchor, there were extra Uraban mouths to feed as well.

Many of his men didn't understand why he cluttered the small harbor with so many useless vessels. "What is the military value in such garbage?" Iaros had asked, not out of scorn but genuinely perplexed. "Why not just sink them out in deep water?"

Broeck responded, "I have an idea, but I haven't finished my plans yet."

The younger man stroked his long mustaches and nodded. "Ah." It was all he needed to know. He trusted his uncle.

Over the past several months, Broeck had grown rather proud of his nephew. Though clumsy in social matters, Iaros was hard-working and fervent, and he had benefited greatly from this adventure away from home. (Broeck did not shower the young man with too much praise, though; Iaros had a tendency to be vain.)

His quiet evening was soon interrupted when Iaros rushed inside accompanied by two camp guards. Broeck looked up from his scribbled tally sheets and complicated inventory lists. His nephew's face was flushed with excitement, although the young man did have a tendency to overestimate the urgency of most situations. "Uncle, we caught a young boy stealing food from one of the supply tents! The guards grabbed him before he could get away."

Broeck perked up. Now this was interesting. "What is a boy doing in this place?"

"I don't know, Uncle, but he's a wildcat—shouting and fighting. It took three guards just to hold him."

"My soldiers need more training if it takes three of them to capture a boy. Who is he? What does he say?"

"We can't understand him. He keeps spitting out Uraban words."

"That would be expected, if he's Uraban," Broeck said dryly. "Send for Firun. He can translate."

Iaros grinned as if his uncle had just complimented him. "He's already coming."

A pair of camp guards hauled a scrawny, dark-haired boy into the main room. He tried to yank his arms free from his captors, but they held him tight. Though the lad's clothes were well made, sewn from good fabric, they were dirty and worn. He looked as if he hadn't eaten in days. His face was thin, and his dark brown eyes flashed with anger. A soldier grunted as the boy jabbed an elbow into his stomach. Broeck noticed that another guard had a bruised and swollen lip.

Running his fingers along his bearded chin, Broeck regarded the boy with curious amusement. "Where in the world did you come from? This isn't a place for children."

The boy squirmed and kicked with undiminished energy and anger. He looked around at the room and seemed upset by what he saw there.

Finally old Firun came in. He took one glance at the young captive and his eyes widened.

Broeck said, "Firun, ask him what he wants. What is a child doing in this forsaken place?"

Instead of speaking to the captive, Firun addressed Broeck in a tired voice. "His name is Ulan, and he is the son of Tukar, the soldan-shah's brother." Seeing no recognition on the destrar's face, he clarified. "Tukar was the former administrator of the mines."

"The man I killed?" Broeck remembered cutting off Tukar's head and sending it back to Olabar on a battered ore barge. In all the chaos after seizing the mines, he hadn't talked much to the prisoner, simply convicted and executed him. Broeck did recall, though, that Tukar had gone to his death bravely, resigned to his fate. The man had not asked for mercy, nor had he mentioned a son who had escaped the mayhem. Tukar must have been hoping the boy would survive out in the hills.

"Ask him why he came here," Broeck said.

"Isn't it obvious? He's hungry. He wanted food."

"Ask him anyway."

The old servant spoke in Uraban, and the boy answered. They seemed to know each other. Then Broeck recalled that Firun had been the mine administrator's household servant. He should have thought to ask more questions earlier.

"Ulan says he was trying to feed his dog. He claims his father told them to escape into the wilds for their own safety as soon as the Tierran attack began. He says it's his obligation to take care of his mother. And . . . he wants to know what you did with the rugs on the floor, the red ones."

"The rugs?"

Firun's brows knitted. "When he and his parents lived in this house, they had two large red rugs from Olabar, prized possessions made by a famous weaver. I remember them well, Destrar. The family was proud of them . . . very little civilization out here at Gremurr."

"Oh, those." Broeck scratched his hair. "I got rid of them, and the hangings on the wall, the ones with the Unfurling Fern. I don't want my home looking like a church or a brothel." He leaned forward, glowering at the boy. "He's got more to worry about than my decorating tastes."

Iaros said with an edge of uncertainty, "Uncle, our war is not with children. Must we really punish this boy?"

Broeck's eyes flashed. "The Curlies started the war against children! Or have you forgotten how they chopped off my grandson's head? Tomas was only ten years old!"

Iaros swallowed hard.

Ulan obviously didn't understand what the men were saying, but he watched the conversation, flicking his eyes back and forth.

After another commotion outside the door, a woman entered, striding ahead of two Tierran soldiers who tried to hold her. Her face was dirty, her clothing in tatters, her hair bedraggled, but she was proud, her back straight. She stepped forward in cool surrender and spoke a musical rush of incomprehensible words, which Firun translated. "This is Shetia, Ulan's mother, the wife of Tukar. She says she surrenders herself and offers her life in exchange for her son's." She moved closer to Ulan, who also stood in quiet defiance.

Broeck frowned. "I never claimed this boy's life as mine to give *or* take."

"How many others are hiding out in the hills?" Iaros wanted to know. "We should send search parties out with the first light of day to scour the hills for any refugees or deserters."

"I request mercy for these two, Destrar," Firun said. "You've already executed Tukar. Shetia and Ulan treated me well, and they do not deserve to die for who they are."

"My grandson didn't deserve to die for who he was, either,"

Broeck said. The knife edge of that tragedy would never be dulled.

Shetia spoke again, and Firun translated. "She knows that you are the one who killed her husband, Destrar, and she says she is not afraid."

Ulan managed to free one of his hands and reached out to take his mother's.

Watching this boy, Broeck could not stop thinking about Tomas. Despite his anger, the destrar felt his heart begin to soften. "We are not animals. I do not murder women and children. Iaros, find a place for these two. Make sure they are comfortable, given fresh clothing and food—some of the Uraban stuff that no one else wants to eat."

Firun translated for Shetia and Ulan, and the boy made another demand. Firun chuckled as he turned to Broeck. "Ulan insists you take care of his dog as well. Apparently it's tied to a tree back at their camp."

Broeck surprised himself with a faint smile. "Yes, we'll take care of the dog as well."

30 *Olabar*

The earthquake tragedy in Arikara could not have come at a worse time. For years, Omra had drained Uraba's resources and used the bulk of his experienced laborers to rebuild Ishalem. Now he would have to withdraw workmen, tools, building supplies, and food from the holy city, and send them down to Missinia Soldanate. He would dig deeper into his treasury and raise taxes for merchants across Uraba—in the name of Urec.

In the main church in Olabar, new Ur-Sikara Kuari emptied most of the coffers to provide aid for the stricken city. She called on her faithful to help in any way they could. Listening to her speak, Omra's heart lifted. Perhaps there was hope in the aftermath of this tragedy, for healing the wound between himself and the church. As soon as possible, he would sail in the *Golden Fern* to deliver the ursikara to her new home in Ishalem; one of the two new churches was nearly completed and ready for her to take up residence.

But first he had to tend to the Arikara emergency.

Omra's father dove into the problem with a furious determination, possibly strengthened by concern for his estranged wife Lithio. The soldan-shah had never seen Imir so energized. He visited merchants, food storehouses, stablemasters, and caravan offices, collecting supplies and volunteers. He even went to the docks to recruit any able-bodied men he could find.

Imir entered the soldan-shah's private office, accompanied by Omra's First Wife Istar and daughter Adreala, who was nearly thirteen years old. Omra could see by their expressions that they had made up their minds about something.

Without formalities, Imir said, "I want to ride out with the next group of physicians and supplies to Arikara. Even those who survived the destruction face terrible hardship."

Istar spoke up. "Our daughter asks permission to accompany her grandfather on this errand of mercy."

The girl looked determined and ready for an argument. "I've been there before, Father," Adreala blurted. "Remember, you appointed me your special ambassador to the Nunghals. Now I am needed in Arikara—our primary trade center with the Nunghals. It was a beautiful city."

Omra was surprised. "It will be very difficult there—little food or shelter, many dead bodies, and conditions will grow worse as the bodies begin to rot and disease sets in."

"It is as you say, Father—so much work to do," Adreala countered. "Both of my sisters want to go, too. When I made my trip before, Cithara and Istala were being trained by the sikaras—

but they should see the world, too, and they want very much to help."

He frowned. "It does not sound like a fitting place for the daughters of the soldan-shah."

Istar was surprisingly stubborn. "The girls have been raised as princesses, Omra, but hard work will make them strong. It will not harm them to be without comforts for a while." At times, he forgot that his First Wife had been raised in a Tierran fishing village. Over the years, he had given her love, protection, wealth, and shelter here in the palace, but Istar's more humble upbringing had made her sensible, capable, and wise.

His father added his support. "Their presence will encourage the people of Arikara, and the work will do my granddaughters good. The princesses will bring honor to the soldan-shah."

Omra laughed as he looked at their expressions. "I have faced Tierran armies, but how can I stand against the three of you when you've made a decision?" He did not admit, however, that he was relieved to send the three girls far from the sikaras, who had so recently tried to use them in their schemes. "Go with my blessing. Just be careful."

31 *The* Moray

When the jeering crew brought out the rope for Ciarlo, he held out his arms, hands clasped together. Submission but not surrender. With the bright sun and cool breeze on his face, Ciarlo took a deep breath. The air smelled clean, salty, and rejuvenating. He did not give them the satisfaction of showing fear or begging for mercy. He said nothing, but his head was filled with silent prayers to Aiden.

The *Moray*'s first mate offered a large, wicked-looking fishhook used for catching grouper or tuna. Its barbed point had been filed sharp. Captain Belluc put on a cruel performance to amuse his crew. "Stick it through his palms and wrists, so we can drag him behind the boat like a fish."

Ciarlo didn't know how long his flesh would hold before the sharp metal ripped through his tendons and bones. He closed his eyes, ready to endure the crippling pain of the hook.

"Stop this!" bellowed a big man with shaggy black hair; a passenger, not a crewman. He had a gap between his front teeth, and he looked strange and exotic even for a Uraban. His expression was as dark as his weathered skin. "What crime has the man committed to deserve this punishment?"

The galley captain was offended by the interruption. "I wouldn't expect a Nunghal to understand. He believes in Aiden. That's crime enough." Ciarlo didn't know what a Nunghal was.

The large stranger stepped closer to Captain Belluc, intimidating him. "You said that was the reason he became a galley slave in the first place."

The captain shrugged. "He has been preaching to the other oarsmen, corrupting their souls."

The big stranger regarded Belluc with consternation. "You'll kill him if you use that hook and keelhaul him."

"He deserves to die."

Ciarlo spoke up with enough conviction that everyone heard him. "Thank you for your intervention, sir, but you can say nothing to stop the captain. He has made up his mind to inflict pain on another human being."

"I can report his behavior to my good friend, Soldan-Shah Omra," Asaddan said.

Belluc's eyes narrowed. "You are welcome to tell him whatever you like. The soldan-shah hates Aidenists."

With an abrupt move, the Nunghal man grabbed the fishhook from the first mate's hands and flung it over the *Moray*'s side. The wicked-looking hook spun in the air, glinting golden, then vanished into the waves.

The surprised crewmembers grumbled, wanting their captain to retaliate, but Asaddan broadened his shoulders and looked threatening. "Keelhaul the man if you must, but don't cripple or kill him. Where would you find a replacement oarsman out here?"

"I could always put you on the oars," Belluc snapped.

"You are welcome to try, Captain."

The captain did not choose to try.

Ciarlo still held his arms out, waiting, and the first mate wrapped the rope around his wrists, adding several coils, then pulled the rope through. Ciarlo would have liked to grasp the symbolic Fishhook of Sapier between his palms for comfort, but he no longer had his pendant. He clung to the knowledge that he was the only devout Aidenist in the whole expanse of Middlesea from horizon to horizon. No matter how far away He was, Ondun would see him and show mercy.

The galley captain didn't give him an opportunity to pray; the sailors simply threw him off the galley's stern. Ciarlo plunged into the water. He kicked his feet to try to keep up, but the taut rope nearly wrenched his arms out of their sockets. Spray filled his face, and he couldn't breathe. He choked, coughed. The oarmaster struck up a rapid beat so that the *Moray* moved at increased speed.

Over the stern rail, Belluc called down to him, "Don't you wish you'd stayed at home in Tierra by your little kirk?"

Ciarlo could barely think as he struggled to remain afloat, but this torture would never convince him to abandon his faith. With the rope burning his wrists and his joints in agony, he steeled himself by thinking of what Sapier himself had endured during his tribulations. He thought also of the agonies of Prester-Marshall Baine and his followers, all impaled on fishhooks because they had tried to rebuild Ishalem.

A commotion occurred on the deck of the *Moray*, crewmembers shouting and pointing. Ciarlo turned his head, saw a flash of jagged fin, a gleam of emerald scales as a sea serpent arced out of the water and then dove again. Dangling at the end of the rope, pulled along in the wake of the slave galley, Ciarlo was like bait on a fisherman's line.

The laughing men above seemed to be making wagers. Ciarlo was sure he would find himself in the belly of the serpent soon enough, and they would haul in the bloody end of the rope. But the Nunghal man was roaring now. "Pull him up—*pull him up*!"

Finally, the men hoisted Ciarlo out of the water. The pain in his shoulders was excruciating as he dangled there, dripping; his clothes weighed him down. Looking down to see the serpent's wedge-shaped head rising up, jaws wide open, he cried out. The men dragged him over the stern rail only inches ahead of the serpent.

Sprawled on the deck, he coughed and vomited water. Now that he was safe, the pain was so great that Ciarlo felt ready to die. Behind the *Moray*, the sea serpent drifted away.

"Let him rest for the day." Belluc sounded surly and dissatisfied. "Then put him back in chains at the oars tomorrow."

Asaddan watched the cruelty of the Urecari sailors with angry disgust. For days on their voyage, he had observed the devout Aidenist down in the stinking, stifling hold, heard the poor man tell stories with fervor, and listened to the heart of what he believed.

After witnessing the atrocities at Ishalem, he had not thought he could change his mind. He had seen evil Aidenist warships intent on setting the city ablaze. He had seen the line of rotting Uraban heads dumped along the great wall, victims of Aidenist hatred.

Which was the true reflection of Aiden's teachings? Asaddan didn't know. Maybe evil had two sides.

And after watching the behavior of these Urecari, he couldn't see that they were any better. He recalled that Istar, First Wife of Soldan-Shah Omra, had been taken from a Tierran fishing village. He knew that Urecari raiders had burned *her* town, killed *her* people, and dragged *her* away against her will. When Saan had told him his mother's story during their time in the Nunghal lands, the boy had colored the events with his own upbringing. Asaddan suspected that Istar might tell a different version of the story.

Ciarlo's courage affected him greatly. The Aidenist preacher steadfastly maintained that he meant no harm, that he simply wanted to spread the word. Admiring such devotion, Asaddan decided to listen with greater attention.

32 *Ishalem, Urecari Church*

Finally, after the many headaches, delays, and extraordinary expenses to build this damned church in Ishalem, Soldan Huttan felt satisfied, even victorious. For all the challenges and annoyances this grandiose project entailed, he was nearly finished with the task. The church was huge and ostentatious, a monument on the holy city's skyline. Exactly what the soldan-shah had wanted.

More important, he'd beaten his rival, Soldan Vishkar. On the other side of Ishalem, Vishkar's sturdy church was half completed, some of its minarets still only frameworks cocooned in bricklayers' scaffolds. Huttan's carpenters and stonemasons had far surpassed those accomplishments. He had ordered his crew leaders to use any means (even unethical ones) to get the job done with as much speed and as little expense as possible.

And it was only fitting, since his beloved wife Kuari—may she rot from within!—had just been named ur-sikara. Huttan couldn't believe the choice. How had she managed it? Surely the church of Urec had better candidates than that stubborn, abrasive woman?

Still, the selection granted him a great deal of political capital. Even though their marriage had been officially dissolved (alas), due to her new position Soldan Huttan would hold additional clout. Perhaps he'd finally be able to annex the weak territory of Yuarej and expand the soldanate of Inner Wahilir. Once his great church was dedicated as the new home of the ur-sikara, Huttan would be in an excellent position to ask the soldan-shah for such a boon.

By now, cautious and kindhearted Vishkar must regret wasting so much time developing blueprints and plans, consulting with Saedran architects (who didn't understand the first thing about the Urecari religion—how inappropriate!). Huttan had found it much more expeditious to spread a few bribes, and *his* church would be ready for the soldan-shah's arrival, in time for the revered ur-sikara to be installed in her new residence. . . .

As morning light softened the tiled window arches, Huttan walked through the church's cavernous main chamber, which was supported by dozens of pillars, all colorfully painted (rather than tiled, which took longer and cost much more). In his counterpart church, Soldan Vishkar had employed a veritable army of mosaic artists to assemble beautiful colored tiles, but Huttan convinced himself that the frescoes were more vibrant, and certainly less labor-intensive.

Hundreds of workers stood on scaffolds in the church's vault, painting events from Urec's Log. Up on the top platforms, the less skilled painters produced clumsier images; the colors had to be bright, the figures generally recognizable, but the details didn't matter, since worshipers far below would not be able to see them. High up on the great eggshell-domed ceiling, the soldan assigned the least skilled apprentice painters.

Huttan raised his voice so that his words echoed in the huge chamber. "The soldan-shah and the ur-sikara will be here soon. In the name of Urec, give me your best work—and your fastest! Ondun will surely punish you if we don't finish this church on time."

The other soldan would be forced to attend the celebration and eat his own shame, while Huttan smiled with superiority. He couldn't wait.

Servants swept the tiled floors. Each morning the workmen arrived to find that a layer of dust drifted down from above, trickling out of joints in the arches, cracks in the ceiling—more than just the hanging fog of construction dust and plasterers. His chief builder assured him that the enormous church was merely settling.

One of the apprentice painters, a harelipped young man from Sioara, hurried up to Huttan, chattering enthusiastically. Previously, the young artist had gushed his thanks, lisping all the while, for the opportunity to paint in this wondrous church. Now, however, the artist's earnestness was tinged with alarm. "Soldan, the dome has many new cracks this morning. Several are wider than my fingers!" He held up a splayed hand, as if Huttan didn't know how wide a finger was.

When he squinted upward, the soldan could see a spiderweb of black lines tracing the inside of the main eggshell dome. He grimaced. "It must be from those men pounding from above." Dozens of roofers had been crawling over the outer dome, applying lead sheets to protect the surface. For a while the lead plates would gleam like brushed silver in the sunlight.

"But we can't continue our painting," the young apprentice explained. "The cracks are too wide."

"Then take some plaster and fill them!" Huttan hated to be responsible for tiny decisions, but he realized this young man had no authority to do anything. "We can't let any flaws be visible for the soldan-shah when he arrives . . . or my dear wife, of course."

Workers scurried across the floor with hods of wet white muck, and the boy artist scrambled up the scaffolding like a monkey, as if he needed to supervise the plasterers. Men began to raise the first batch of plaster on ropes and pulleys suspended from the scaffolds. As he watched, Huttan pondered the cost of each load of plaster, each layer of bricks, each roofing sheet of lead. He would be relieved to have the spurting wound on his treasury plastered as well.

He crooked his index finger and raised it in the sign of the Unfurling Fern. "For the glory of Urec," he mumbled.

As if Ondun Himself heard the unintended mockery in Huttan's voice, a thrumming began in the spacious main chamber, a deep groan that emanated from the walls, the support pillars, and the dome overhead. Workers paused in their rushing about and began to mutter. A whisper of fear flew like a phantom around the chamber.

Two ceiling blocks dropped out of the dome and fell to the ground, shattering on the marble floors, wrecking the tiles and leaving widening cracks in the hemisphere above. Huttan looked up, furious at the damage. "Get crews up there and fix that gap right away! Now we need tilers to repair the floor."

Instead of obeying him, though, the workers fled. The high scaffolding shuddered, and the soldan realized that the church walls and support pillars were shaking. He suddenly wondered if an earthquake was striking Ishalem, like the one that had recently destroyed Arikara.

The jagged cracks in the dome grew like living things. The nearest scaffolding toppled forward and collapsed. The harelipped young artist fell, screaming; he landed on his head on the hard tiles, and the scaffolding crashed down onto his body. More painters dropped like overripe fruit from above.

Huttan turned to flee. An archway collapsed and blocked the church doorway. In a shrill voice, the soldan cursed his inept workers.

*

Kel Unwar had just climbed to the top of one of the new watchtowers erected at regular intervals along the seven-mile canal. The waterway was a landmark of Uraban engineering ability and strength, but it also created a defensive vulnerability: yes, Uraban warships could sail from the Middlesea—but enemy vessels might attempt to fight their way through from the opposite side.

Kel Unwar had to prepare for every eventuality, though he felt soiled whenever he tried to think like the enemy. There was no end to the evil and treachery in the hearts of Aidenists.

These watchtowers were only the first step in the defenses. They would be manned by archers and equipped with small catapults to attack any encroaching ships, but even that did not satisfy him. Unwar had many innovative ideas about how to keep the canal safe.

From the watchtower platform, where sentries would be stationed at all hours, day and night, he gazed along the silvery channel. Merchant ships entered from the Middlesea and cruised past the beautiful buildings. The functioning canal was a marvel.

What caught his attention now, however, was Soldan Huttan's church of Urec, in which the ur-sikara herself would soon preach. Unwar saw dust rising from it, saw the large walls *moving*. Tiny figures raced about like infuriated ants.

The dome fell inward. Minarets toppled like felled trees. Gouts of dust and smoke billowed up. Seconds later, an attenuated rumbling reached his ears, but he was much too far away to hear the screams as the entire church collapsed.

33 *Calay, Main Aidenist Kirk*

Mateo didn't eat, didn't even open his eyes. He knelt on the hard altar steps inside the main Aidenist kirk, praying and pondering long past the point at which his legs had turned as numb and dead as his heart. He refused to leave, wrapped in the dark blanket of his tragic private world. The Fishhook-tipped preaching staffs, the blue-and-green banners, the preserved ice-dragon horn etched with verses—nothing here gave him answers or hope.

But he stayed anyway.

He didn't react when other mourners came to share the kirk with him. After a while, even the presters left him alone. He huddled there for two days, not even marking the passage of time. He would have stayed there forever.

Mateo refused to think about the future. He wanted a reason to accept what he was asked to endure. No one could have shown greater loyalty to Tierra or to Queen Anjine, no soldier had ever served the land better, and yet Vicka—his bright spot, his wife, his hope for a normal life—was gone. Not the victim of an enemy attack or treachery, but killed in a simple, senseless house fire.

She died saving me, Ammur Sonnen had said, as if it were the most terrible confession he could make.

As the hours passed, and hunger, thirst, and weakness muddled his thoughts, he formulated the only conclusion that made sense. Vicka's death must be more than an accident of fate, more than a vagary of adverse circumstances. No, it was his punishment. Mateo had done terrible things; he had meted out the queen's justice, had overseen the slaughter of a thousand Urecari. That blood was on his hands. Even though Mateo had also done good for Tierra, Ondun had demanded Vicka's life as recompense. He could not plead for things to change, could ask for no mercy—what mercy was there? Vicka was already dead.

After a while, he gave up praying and simply knelt on the stone steps. He kept his thoughts and his heart blessedly empty.

Then Queen Anjine came to him.

He smelled the scent—not quite a perfume—that he had always associated with her. He heard the rustle of skirts behind him, and her soft compassionate voice. "Mateo, I've been trying to find you for days. I am so sorry."

He kept his eyes closed, sure that it was just a dream. In his disoriented state, he expected to hear *Vicka's* voice, but it was Anjine, always Anjine. Right now he wasn't sure he could even remember what his wife's voice sounded like. Vicka seemed an unreal memory to him, a brief flash of happiness that was gone, drowned out by more vivid memories of war.

When he didn't answer, Anjine knelt beside him on the altar steps where Prester-Marshall Rudio had given his sermons, where Mateo and Vicka had been united in marriage, linking fishhooks together as a symbol of their enduring bond . . . a bond that had ended in smoke and fire.

"I sent town guardsmen all over Calay to search for you. Ammur Sonnen is grieving, but he is also worried sick about you. So am I."

Mateo kept his head bowed, his eyes shut. He was incapable of forming words, though he longed to let his sorrow pour out. It would be so simple, but he couldn't allow himself that.

Anjine continued, close to him, her voice barely a whisper.

"I finally came here because Guard-Marshall Vorannen got a message from one of the presters, and he thought the grieving man in the kirk might be you. I came right away."

When he heard her, Mateo could think only of the sweet girl who had been his childhood friend forever. They were inseparable, Tycho and Tolli, Mateo and Anjine . . . without a care, blissfully ignorant of what the future might hold.

He felt the touch of her fingers like a gentle sparrow on his shoulder. Finally, he opened reddened eyes to see her, and caught his breath. Anjine looked like an angel that the presters might have described.

His voice was a faint rasp. "Vicka is dead."

"I know—I'm so sorry. I wanted to be there for you, to tell you myself." When she wrapped her arms around him, he tensed, struggling to bottle his sadness inside. She held him tighter. "You comforted me on the day that Tomas . . ." She swallowed her own words. "Let me do the same for you."

Mateo felt weak. He shuddered and forced himself to stand, pulling out of her grip, but she stood too and grasped his hand. "You can't go back to the Sonnen house—stay with me at the castle. I'll have your rooms reopened. It'll be like old times, happy times. You can finally feel at home, if not at peace."

Mateo let her lead him out of the kirk. "I don't have any other home."

34 *The* Al-Orizin

The sea monster attacked them in the mists of dawn. Gray-green tentacles rose out of the water, each one tapered to a barbed tip, like the stinger on a desert scorpion. Stubby brown suckers like flabby lips covered the pale undersides. The serpentine arms coiled and uncoiled in a menacing abomination reminiscent of the Unfurling Fern.

Sen Sherufa was the first to spot the creature as the sun shimmered through the morning fog. She had gone astern for quiet pondering while she munched on her hard breakfast biscuit, dipped in a bit of honey from a honeycomb she had hoarded throughout the journey.

The mass of tentacles twisted out of the calm water on both sides of the ship, questing for something. Sherufa yelled a warning, then dashed out of the way as a tentacle splintered the stern rail. A second one clasped a rigging rope tied to a stanchion and strained until the spar snapped in half; another slapped the deck, scattering the crew.

Ystya emerged from the cabin she shared with the Saedran woman. Her large eyes grew even rounder. "The Kraken! My mother summoned the *Kraken*!"

Saan called to her, "If your mother sent it, the monster will want to capture *you*, and I don't intend to let it succeed." Shouting for all crewmen to arm themselves, he picked up a harpoon himself. "Chartsman, get Ystya back in your cabin and bar the door so that she's safe!"

Grigovar picked up a scimitar and with a bellow put himself between the tentacles and Sen Sherufa, slashing so that she could escape. He pricked the tough flesh with the point of his scimitar. At first the rubbery appendage recoiled as if it had been burned, then it lashed back with its stinger. Although the reef diver jumped out of the way, the suckered appendage dealt him a grazing blow that sent him sprawling. Grigovar got to his feet again, wheezing but ready to fight.

Saan was close enough to the side of the *Al-Orizin* that he could see a shapeless mass just below the water's surface—the creature's main body, like a pus-filled bag that sprouted a nest of thrashing appendages. A tentacle curled toward him, and Saan chopped off the curved barb tip with the harpoon blade. Greenish slime spurted out, and Saan rolled out of the way as the tentacle stump still tried to find him. He got up and threw his harpoon into the shapeless body sac in the water. The sharpened tip penetrated deep into the bloated mass, but did no obvious damage.

An appendage seized one crewman and flung him like a stone far out to sea. Another tentacle wrapped itself around a second sailor's chest and lifted him up; though the man kicked, flailed, and stabbed with his dagger, the tentacle crushed his ribs and spine.

Sikara Fyiri charged out of her cabin, brandishing her staff and shouting defiant prayers. The Kraken released the crushed crewman, dropping his mangled body at her feet, dousing Fyiri with blood. The sucker-embossed arm smashed toward her, but she scrambled for shelter between two supply crates.

Yal Dolicar climbed out of a hatch from belowdecks, tugging on the leather laces that secured the artificial dagger hand to his wrist stump. "I'm ready to defend the ship, Captain Saan!" He slashed at the air with his dagger.

Grigovar crouched with his scimitar and gave the other man a snort. "With a puny blade like that? You'll have to get close enough to make love to the Kraken!"

"Hah, I'll kiss the thing with my steel." Together, Dolicar and the reef diver battled the nearest tentacle, jabbing and slicing as it tried to grab them.

Another tentacle rose from the opposite side of the deck, and Dolicar spun just in time to see the lashing appendage. He thrust his dagger attachment toward it, but the narrow end of the tentacle wrapped around his wrist and yanked him into the air. He dangled by his arm, kicking his feet and yelling.

Grigovar slashed at the line of suckers with the scimitar, but the Kraken refused to release its grip on his friend.

As the tentacle lifted him higher, Dolicar plucked at the leather laces that held his artificial hand in place. When he undid the bindings, his wrist stump popped free of the knife attachment, and he tumbled to the deck, while the tentacle snapped back, suddenly released from the weight it carried. Dolicar landed, rolled, and sprang to his feet, staying close to the big reef diver. "Now we have much in common, Grigovar! We've both survived being captured by a sea monster."

Grigovar wasn't impressed. "I killed mine from the inside. You just dropped to the deck."

Saan secured a second harpoon and went on the attack. The tentacles smashed another spar, and the hooked stinger-tip ripped a long gash through the silken sail.

From her cabin door, he heard Sen Sherufa's voice yelling for Ystya, but the ivory-haired young woman sprang back out of her cabin. "Kraken, I am here! You've found me." She ran to the port side, where the tentacles were writhing. "Though you were once an innocent beast, my mother has corrupted you."

Ystya seemed unafraid of the tentacles in front of her. She held up her hands in a warding gesture, and once again Saan saw the building of cold, bright power within and around her. Ystya spread her fingers, and her skin gave off an unearthly shimmer. "Ondun created you, but now that can no longer be."

She squeezed her hands into fists as if to concentrate her power. The tentacles towered over the fragile-looking girl, but did not move, as if the beast were intimidated by her. Ystya spoke with the force of an executioner's blade. "I choose to *un*create you."

The thick tentacles drooped and darkened with splotches of decay. The Kraken's rubbery hide sloughed off into gobbets of rotting flesh, and the cartilaginous bones collapsed like a jumble of reeds. The shapeless sac beneath the water burst and spread a stain of foul-smelling entrails. Chunks of the rotted monster dropped onto the deck, while the rest simply oozed down the *Al-Orizin*'s hull boards.

The crew were struck to silence by the monster's demise, as well as the strange power contained within the young woman. Ystya opened her clenched fists again. A moment later she reeled, disoriented and weak.

Saan ran to catch her before she could collapse. He hugged her close.

Sen Sherufa stared in amazement. Sikara Fyiri climbed out of her hiding place between the supply crates, and fear showed clearly on her face. Several sailors backed away from the girl.

Saan continued to hold Ystya, wanting to comfort her. He realized, though, that he needed some answers.

35 *The* Dyscovera

The waters around the ship grew murky and sluggish. Green seaweed appeared, woven like emerald strands of hair through the waves, then thickening into grassy clumps. The weed smelled sour and moist, like decaying moss in a swamp.

As the breezes pushed them ahead, the weed became a morass. Criston was concerned when sailors had to use boathooks to tear ropy tangles from the prow. He guided the ship through any channels that happened to appear in the dark water.

Though Prester Hannes vehemently denied any involvement in killing Sen Aldo's *rea* pigeons, Criston had his suspicions. How far would Hannes go to prevent the church from learning about the Leviathan skeleton? Still, the prester had sworn his loyalty on the Fishhook, a vow that would have brought down damnation if he reneged. And why would any of the mutineers commit such an appalling act so soon after receiving a reprieve? It made no sense.

Yet the birds were dead. The Captain's Compass was smashed, perhaps not accidentally. Suspicion hung like a cloud over the *Dyscovera.* Criston quietly asked Javian and Sen Aldo to remain alert and to report any unusual activity.

With the *Dyscovera* barely moving through the quagmire, the crew had little to do but peer over the sides and wonder how far the morass would extend. Criston stood on the open deck, inhaling the swampy odor of seaweed.

He took out the old sea-turtle shell on which some long-lost sailor had inscribed a few islands, an unfamiliar coastline, and weathered squiggles in the water. The squiggles might have been anything . . . this wasteland of seaweed, perhaps? Even if that were true, the sea-turtle map did not help him.

The lookout called down, "Captain, I see something dead ahead in the water—and it's moving." The sailor used his spyglass. "It's a *man*! There's a man adrift out there!"

Criston shaded his eyes. "How can a man be all the way out here?"

Hannes joined him. "It may be a demon in the waters to tempt us, Captain. Be careful."

Sen Aldo flashed a meaningful glance at the prester. "Or perhaps one of the mer-Saedrans came back to give us a second chance after they were so mortally offended."

Criston chose a more likely answer. "Better still, what if we're not so far from land as we thought? There could be other ships nearby. Maybe the man was only recently shipwrecked or thrown overboard. We'll rescue him and hear what he has to say."

The ship drew up alongside a bedraggled man in the water; he had draped himself over a weathered board from a ship's hull. He waved to them, but did not seem desperate or frantic. Long matted hair covered much of his face.

"Throw down a ladder and bring him aboard," Criston called.

As soon as it fell to the waterline, the castaway grasped the knotted ladder and pulled himself up. After the crewmembers helped to haul him over the ship's rail, the stranger collapsed to his knees, dripping wet. His clothes smelled of mildew and rot.

Curious sailors rushed forward, full of questions, and Mia brought the man a cup of fresh water from the nearest rain-barrel on deck. "You're safe now," Criston assured him. "You're aboard the *Dyscovera*."

The castaway looked up at them with a hollow, terrifying expression. "I know this is the *Dyscovera*." His skin was very pale, a grayish white. His eyes were sunken and dark after long privation at sea, but there seemed to be nothing behind them.

Mia was the first to recognize him, and she bit back an outcry. The stranger raised himself to his feet. "You don't know me, Captain Vora? After you threw me overboard to my death?" Still dripping, he clawed the clumps of weedy hair from his face. "I knew you'd find me here soon enough."

Thunderstruck, Criston realized it was Enoch Dey, the crewman who had tried to rape Mia. The captain had cast him into the open sea—months ago.

Javian put himself between Mia and the cadaverous man. "How did you get here? How are you still alive?"

"I am what you see," Dey said. "And if you sail farther, you'll discover other lost friends—I promise it."

Criston issued automatic orders, "Get this man to a cabin—give him food, dry clothes." Though deeply disturbed, he couldn't cast the man overboard again—not when there were so many questions to be answered.

Silhouetted on the horizon at sunset were the spires of masts, tattered sails, a group of skeletal ships caught in the trap of seaweed.

Criston had provided Enoch Dey with basic comforts, but ordered him kept in the small brig until they understood more. The *Dyscovera*'s crew was ensnared in superstitious fear, and the prester was particularly uneasy. Criston didn't blame them.

Dey remained in his cell, uncomplaining; he did not ask to come out, nor did he give any further explanations. He said only, "You'll see with your own eyes soon enough, Captain.

You wouldn't believe me if I told you." He gave a snort that rattled with mucus. "You never believed me before."

Now, upon seeing the graveyard of ships in the seaweed, Javian hurried up to Criston and asked, "If no one else has ever sailed this far, how can those vessels possibly be out here?"

Criston scanned the ships, trying to make out details. "They all look to be of Tierran design. I see no Uraban sails."

"Maybe they sank any Uraban ships," Hannes said. "A victory for Aiden."

As the dusk bloomed orange, Criston could discern shadowy figures on the decks, awaiting the arrival of the *Dyscovera.*

"Let Mr. Dey out of the brig. I want to speak with him."

The pallid man came across the deck. Though he had made some effort to clean himself, he still had an odd odor about him, like fermenting seaweed. "Now do you understand, Captain, what—and who—they are?"

Criston was losing patience. "Explain it to me, Mr. Dey."

The gray skin twitched on the man's face, and his lips curved, but it didn't seem to be a smile. "Everyone aboard the *Dyscovera* has lost friends to the sea. These are the remains of vessels and crew—you will each know someone here."

Prester Hannes held up his fishhook pendant and pushed it toward the undead castaway. "Our faith will drive away any demons."

Enoch Dey ignored him.

As the *Dyscovera* came closer, Criston studied the wrecks through his spyglass, and realized that he did recognize two of them. One was a fishing boat so familiar to him in his youth, a boat he had watched sail away from Windcatch nearly every day—carrying his father, Cindon Vora, who had been lost at sea.

The other, much larger ship was the *Luminara.*

36 *Ishalem*

The *Golden Fern,* a warship plated with armor from the Gremurr mines, was fit for the soldan-shah—one of his brother's last accomplishments. The *Fern* should have been the flagship of a powerful war fleet that would sail through Kel Unwar's new canal to crush Aidenist ships on the Oceansea.

How could Omra sail this ship without thinking of Tukar and

how the 'Hooks had murdered him? Yet another reason, of reasons long past counting, why he could never forgive or make peace with Tierra.

Nevertheless, the *Fern* was the soldan-shah's most magnificent vessel, and he sailed proudly to Ishalem with Ur-Sikara Kuari at his side.

Only days after learning of the earthquake in Arikara, the soldan-shah had dispatched a caravan with a military escort, four Saedran physicians, pack animals, food, medicines, and as many volunteers as could go on short notice. Kuari's donations from the church coffers provided additional food, as well as huge bolts of fabric for tents, clothing, and bandages. Omra included a written letter to Soldan Xivir promising more extensive aid soon, including building materials, engineers, carpenters, and other skilled workers. A few days later, Omra's daughters and father departed with a much larger caravan of supplies and laborers that Imir had managed to collect.

And now he could install the leader of the Urecari church in her new home in Ishalem.

From the Middlesea side of the isthmus, the ironclad entered the mouth of the straight new canal and glided serenely into the holy city. *His* city. Omra had rebuilt Ishalem from scratch on the charred scar of the old site, for the glory of Ondun. Though he wished he could have been here for the inaugural voyage through Kel Unwar's waterway, his satisfaction was not diminished.

Standing at the bow beside him, Kuari marveled at the canal and all the new buildings. "Back in Inner Wahilir, Huttan didn't allow me to travel much. Oh, I had great power and freedom in my own household, but I visited Ishalem only twice, and not recently." She drew in a deep breath. "What you've accomplished is breathtaking, Soldan-Shah."

"This is your city now, Ur-Sikara—where your church is." He

extended a hand to indicate the white buildings on the shore. "I hope we can establish a new relationship between us."

"We will, Soldan-Shah. We've already shown what we can do by sending so much aid to Arikara. The church and the palace should work together against the true enemies of Ondun, not against each other."

"Istar told me you were full of common sense."

She grinned. "I have always said a man should listen to his First Wife. I could never convince Huttan of that, though."

As the *Golden Fern* cruised along the canal, Omra scanned the buildings, seeing how many structures had been finished in the short time since his last visit. The completion of the canal had sparked a flurry of construction at the edge of the waterway—small docks, markets, taverns. However, as he looked toward where Huttan's church should have stood as a towering landmark, he saw only rubble, piles of debris, collapsed walls and roofs.

Only weeks earlier, Huttan's imposing church had been prominent among the other buildings . . . and now it was gone—entirely gone.

Kuari stood in stony silence for a long moment, staring from the ship toward the wreckage of the collapsed church. She composed herself with admirable alacrity. "Obviously I have much work to do here."

Omra convened an emergency meeting inside the incomplete but sturdy sister church being built by Soldan Vishkar. Kel Unwar met them there, looking upset, accompanied by the other soldan and his Saedran architect, Sen Bira na-Lanis.

"Only a few survived the collapse of Huttan's church," Vishkar reported, looking mournful. "All others perished."

Seeing the destruction, Omra had immediately suspected Aidenist treachery, but the barbarians were not to blame. Only with difficulty did Kel Unwar mask his scorn for Huttan, who had so utterly failed. His voice was cold and judgmental. "It is clear now that there were many architectural flaws, exacerbated by rushed workmanship and inferior materials. Gross mismanagement." He caught himself and flushed as he remembered who Kuari was. "I am sorry to tell you, Ur-Sikara, that your husband was among those killed inside the church. I believe he was inspecting the work in preparation for your visit."

Soldan Vishkar had sad, dark eyes and a subdued demeanor. "My deepest sympathies for the loss of your husband, Ur-Sikara."

Kuari surprised them all with her reaction. "Huttan was an ass. I have no doubt he caused the problem himself." In the stunned silence, she added, "He was no longer my husband, thanks to my new position, but I knew him well. He did not take the challenge to build the church as an honor, but as an onerous task that he could turn to his own benefit."

She appraised the sturdy structure of Vishkar's church, which had been erected on the foundations of the ancient Aidenist kirk. The roof and towers were not yet finished, but the whitewashed interior was ready for occupation. "There are formalities to observe, and the ur-sikara requires a suitable residence. I declare that this will be the new main Urecari church and my personal home."

Vishkar bowed his head. "I am honored, Ur-Sikara." He glanced at his pale Saedran architect, then back at her, deeply embarrassed. "But it is not yet complete. Much remains to be done."

Sen Bira added, "This is a large building, yes, but much too plain to be the central house of Urecari worship. My artisans have only just begun the ornamentation. The sculptors, the mosaic artists, the gilders—"

Kuari shook her head. "Come now, no more nonsense. *Building* a church is different from *ornamenting* a church. If the structure is sound, then we have a new main church. We should take a lesson in humility from the disaster Huttan caused. I will live here and take care of business. Meanwhile, your artisans can continue the paintings, mosaics, friezes, statues, and gold leaf. I don't think Urec would like to wait, do you?"

The scruffy Saedran architect bobbed his head. "Very well, I'll arrange the schedule of the workmen so they do not interfere with sunset services. If I have your indulgence, patience, and tolerance, Ur-Sikara, this church will be finished in due time, and we will all be pleased with it."

Omra wanted to end the discussion. "Ur-Sikara Kuari is the leader of the church. I support her decision. We have more important things to worry about." He looked at them all. "Kel Unwar has written me letters about Ishalem's weakened defenses. Now that most of the Nunghals have left, we must find a new way to enhance our navy before the bloodthirsty Tierrans send more ships to attack us. We've got to protect Ishalem harbor, as well as our coastal towns. The Aidenists may have been beaten badly, but they'll return soon enough. We must be ready for them."

Kel Unwar's expression darkened. "Only seven Nunghal ships remained behind, but they refuse to patrol the harbor. They want to be merchants and meet new customers, solidify new markets, establish new trade. They are selfish."

Omra, though, held no malice toward them. "This was never their war, Unwar, only ours. Be grateful for the service they provided when we needed it most."

"And they did leave four large cannon to guard the mouth of the harbor," Soldan Vishkar pointed out.

"I paid handsomely for those cannons," Kel Unwar said. "But they will not be enough."

"Agreed." The soldan-shah turned to Vishkar. The man's loyalty was genuine, and Omra trusted him completely. Through the original Istar, who had died in childbirth long ago, their bond of the heart went beyond any bonds of politics. "My friend, I want you to take a ship to all the coastal towns. Meet with sailors, harbormasters, and town leaders, and pull together all worthy vessels that can be refitted as warships. Commandeer them in my name, and rebuild our fleet to protect Ishalem before the Aidenists make their next move."

37 *Gremurr Mines*

Only one of the queen's three messengers made it safely over the Corag pass and rode a weary horse into the Gremurr complex; he was bedraggled and exhausted, his fingers frostbitten. "The snows are closing in. I fear my two companions will not get through, but we all knew the importance of our mission."

Destrars Broeck and Siescu gathered around the weary rider. "What news is so desperate? Has something happened to Calay?"

The courier caught his breath. "The fate of Tierra hangs in the balance—Queen Anjine needs you. I have an urgent message regarding plans for our attack on Ishalem."

"And about time, too!" Broeck laughed.

Siescu was more cautious. "What is the message? What does she need us to do?"

Flushed from his exertion, the man mopped his face and pushed his tangled hair out of the way. "I do not know the details, my Lords. Therefore, even Uraban torturers could not drag the information from me." He dug a packet wrapped in thin leather out of the sweaty folds of his shirt. "This is written in a coded language that the queen says Destrar Broeck will understand."

Broeck looked at Siescu, scratching his thick beard in puzzlement. "But I don't know any codes." He opened the packet, then laughed as he began to read. "Ha! Enifir used an old Iborian dialect! No Uraban spy would ever be able to translate this—even I can barely decipher it."

Meanwhile, Firun delivered a hastily assembled meal and hot tea, and the bedraggled courier fell upon the nourishment with renewed energy.

Siescu paced the room and groused as he waited. "Well, what does the message *say*?"

Iaros joined them. Filled with curiosity, he looked over his uncle's shoulder and moved his lips, struggling with the words in the letter. With a wide grin, he blurted out, "Ah, it seems our victory at Gremurr has inspired the queen! She's rallying the whole Tierran army and navy to Ishalem."

Broeck shot a silent, scolding glance at the young man for interrupting him, and Iaros clamped his lips shut, flushing red. The destrar sounded businesslike as he added, "Queen Anjine wants us to take our new ironclads and attack from the east in a coordinated strike. The timing will be critical since she plans to hammer the Curlies from three sides all at once."

Siescu's pale brow furrowed. "It will take the queen some time to gather all those forces."

"Three months," Broeck grumbled. "By the Fishhook, I'm ready now! But I suppose that'll give us plenty of time to cause some mayhem of our own. Call it practice." He already had plenty of ideas.

That evening, in front of a roaring fire in the house that had once belonged to the Uraban workmaster of the mines, Destrar Siescu treated the courier to a special dinner in order to ply him for information that had nothing to do with Tierra's military plans. Two fat grouse roasted on the fire, shot only that day by Raga Var in the nearby hills.

"The road over the mountains might be good in fair weather, Destrar, but it's treacherous now that winter is setting in," the messenger reported. "I hope my two comrades gave up and went home. If not, they'll be dead by now. Me, I'll stay here until spring."

Siescu had other plans. "I have no intention of spending winter in this place—I am the destrar of Corag Reach, and my people are well accustomed to snow and ice conditions in the mountains. Raga Var can lead us anywhere."

The scout removed a grouse from the roasting spit and served the two men before helping himself to the second grouse. "I can do it, Destrar, but I'd rather not." Though he had stripped off his furs and wore only a loincloth, Raga Var still perspired in the warm chamber.

Siescu would not be swayed from his decision. "The weather looks fine. We will depart in the morning."

"I advise against it," the courier replied, delicately licking grouse juices from his blistered, frostbitten fingertips.

Siescu responded with a pinched expression, since this was not what he wanted to hear. "Fortunately, you are not one of my advisers."

The other man fell silent with a respectful, chastised bow. . . .

Siescu spent the night bundled in blankets, comfortably warm, and in the morning the mine workers loaded two pack animals with a shipment of Gremurr swords for the Tierran army. The blue sky was full of sunshine, and Siescu was anxious to be on the road back to his sheltered cliff city.

He said farewell to the Iborian destrar, who had come to see the two men off. "Good luck with your naval attacks, Broeck. Make the Curlies hurt."

"Oh, we will," Iaros said.

Destrar Broeck made sure the sword bundles were lashed securely to the ponies. "Tell the queen this is merely the first shipment of many to come from these mines."

"When the road opens again in spring, the army may not need

any more swords," his nephew said. "The war will be over, and all of Uraba will be conquered territory."

Broeck clapped his nephew on the back. "Even I'm not that ambitious, but it is a pretty thought."

"We'll tell Queen Anjine that you received her message, and she can launch her battle plan with full confidence."

"The queen always has full confidence," Broeck said. "Farewell."

Siescu tugged on the lead rope of the first pony, while Raga Var sprang ahead. Leading the loaded ponies on foot, the two men headed into the mountains.

38 Calay Castle

Back in the castle, Anjine canceled her obligations for that day and the next in order to be with her devastated friend. She could not make Mateo feel happy or at peace, but she could make him feel welcome. Enifir had already opened and aired out his old rooms, adding fresh bedding, a washbasin, a pitcher of water.

Outside the castle, in the bustling Military District, the Tierran army prepared to depart for Ishalem. Per her orders, the first wave of footsoldiers, cavalry, and a supply train would march out the following morning, while other soldiers continued to arrive from the other reaches. As each group gathered in Calay over the next two months, they would be dispatched to reinforce the troops laying siege to the Ishalem wall, and the constantly swelling Tierran presence would make the Uraban enemy nervous.

The queen trusted her subcommanders to know their business; she didn't have to mother them. She *did* need to be with Mateo. She had willingly accepted her role as leader of the land; she had sacrificed her life, love, and happiness for Tierra, but she needed to do *this* for herself and for her dearest friend. Just for a little while, she would bar the door and keep the rest of the kingdom outside. For Mateo's sake. The heavy responsibility of the crown had enslaved her for too long.

Anjine sat beside him on the bed in his childhood room, offering her support and her love. His bleak expression tore at her heart. He looked like an empty husk of a man, a hollow sculpture of a handsome military commander who had lost his reasons to be a hero. She longed to heal his heart and give him strength, but she didn't know how. This was something she could neither command nor delegate.

"I need you, Mateo," she whispered, "and you need me. No one is closer to me than you are." She stopped herself from saying more. Over the years, Mateo had pursued other girlfriends because he felt he was supposed to, and Anjine had consented to marry Jenirod because it was her duty. Shortly after her own announcement, he had impulsively married Vicka Sonnen, as if he'd finally given up on Anjine. The two of them had denied each other so much for so long because of their respective roles. She squeezed his hand. "During all the battles and setbacks, tragedy after tragedy, you've always been there for me."

"I've been there for *Tierra*," Mateo said, but it sounded false. He drew a deep breath. "But mainly for you. You can always count on me."

Anjine looked around the room, the whitewashed stone walls, the wooden furniture, faded woolen blankets, and now-empty shelves that had held his keepsakes as a young man. The place was so familiar, because she and Mateo had spent much of their childhood here, playing games and pretending to be different people.

The future they had imagined in their youthful optimism and naïveté was not at all how their lives had turned out—Tycho and Tolli growing old together in a comfortable cottage somewhere in the woods. Even as children they both knew that would never happen, because Mateo was merely the son of a guard captain and she was a princess.

"I miss Vicka." His voice was small, and he seemed to tear the words out of himself. He sounded even more sorrowful when he added, "She was the first woman I could show my love to, but I don't think I ever really knew her. I never got the chance."

Anjine put her arm around his shoulder, and he put up no resistance as she drew him close. As the queen of Tierra, she was destined to have a marriage of politics, of convenience, of duty; she had never expected to love the man she ultimately chose as her husband. Her own voice was distant in her ears. "I don't think I have any love left inside me, after . . . after what happened to Tomas. Those damned Urecari! I have to be heartless, or I can't bear to do what I have to," she said. "I'm not just a woman—I'm the queen. The obligations of ruling Tierra make me wall myself off." She had personally given the order to behead a thousand Urecari prisoners, and Mateo had been forced to carry out that deed. Out of loyalty. Anjine bore the guilt of the decision, but he had the *memory* of actually doing it.

He raised his head and met her eyes. "Oh, you still have love within you, Anjine. I see it every time I look at your face, but you try to hide it from everyone else."

Mateo leaned toward her, but Anjine pulled back. "Sen Leo tells me that the Saedran prophecies are warning of the end of the world. Love is a weakness I can't afford to show. Romance is for swooning schoolgirls and handmaidens."

"Oh, Anjine—I know better than that. If the times are so terrible, then love is more important than ever." As if heaving himself out of a deep chasm, tearing loose from his fear and guilt, he turned and kissed her. He was shaking.

Anjine kissed him back, closing her eyes to shut out everything but the smell of him, the touch of him.

And then neither of them could stop.

39 *The* Al-Orizin

After the Kraken attack, Saan ordered his men to sail on. "We can make repairs while we're under way. Iyomelka sent that monster, so she's still after us." He paced up and down the deck to make sure his crew felt the same urgency. "You, stitch up that mainsail! Use whatever spare cloth you need from the lockers."

Grigovar and two other sailors took down the torn sail, spread the thick silk out on the deck, and sewed shut the gash that had cut across the Eye of Urec. Other men fashioned a replacement spar from spare wood in the hold, then lashed it tight. Carpenters repaired the smashed stern rail. Crewmembers holystoned the slime from the rotted Kraken off of the deckboards.

Clouds hovered on the horizon, a simmering storm that might have been a natural weather pattern, but Saan didn't think so. The island witch knew where they were.

Ystya seemed ashamed of what she had done. "My father trapped Bouras with a curse, and I released him. What will the consequences be? And today, I destroyed the Kraken. Those things cannot be made right again! I can't undo them." She hung her head. "What if my mother was right to try to keep me on the island?"

Saan tried to soothe her. "She was *not* right. You saved us, Ystya. I owe you my life, and I'm grateful—however you did it." He took her hands and looked into her strange eyes. "Can you tell me about your power? I want to understand."

The ivory-haired girl seemed at a loss. "The power is what I have. It's who I am—I . . . don't know what is normal for other people." She looked at Saan with both hope and reticence. "I *want* to protect you, Saan. You've shown me kindness, new experiences, the world itself. I love learning from you and Sen Sherufa. The way you care for me—it's wonderful."

Saan's heart warmed to hear her words. She was so beautiful and charming . . . and so incredibly innocent.

He wondered just how strong Ystya's powers were. After seeing the girl uncreate the Kraken, he could only imagine what would happen if she unleashed her magic against an enemy army. He pictured Tierran soldiers turning into corpses, the flesh falling from their bones until their skeletons dropped to the ground. . . .

Her pale skin flushed, as if she could sense his thoughts. "On the island, after the spring dried up and we began to age, my mother told me that I was born with magic, and when the time was right it would flow through me. I think she wished I would never grow up, and she would never grow old, but my powers were so strong that she couldn't just ignore them. Mother is a great sorceress herself, but I think I could be stronger if I practice, because of who I am."

Grigovar sat high on a mainmast spar, where he was hanging the repaired mainsail. His dark hair flew wild as he pointed toward the stern. "Captain, sea serpents are following the ship—dozens of small ones!"

Saan and Ystya looked over the side to see serpentine forms gliding along, flanking the *Al-Orizin.* He had never seen so many young serpents—silvers, blues, and leopard-spotted ones. They were the size of the giant pythons that Saan had once seen snake charmers use in a traveling circus from Lahjar.

Grigovar climbed down and took up a harpoon to spear a few of them, but Ystya stayed his hand. "They aren't harming us. They are the children of Bouras. Now that the Father of All Serpents has been freed, we will see many more serpents in the seas. But if Bouras has learned his lesson, maybe they won't pose a hazard to sailors."

Yal Dolicar made a disbelieving sound. "I would doubt that."

Sen Sherufa's brow furrowed as the serpents fell upon a small school of fish in a feeding frenzy. "But why are they following *us*?"

Ystya sounded surprised that Sherufa would ask. "Because I am aboard."

"Are they drawn to you in particular?"

Sikara Fyiri emerged to stand with them in her bright red robe. "Yes, explain it to us, young woman. We invoked your mother's wrath in order to bring you with us. Now you must confess your dark secrets."

"There are no dark secrets," Ystya said evenly. "Merely the truth. I joined you to see the wide world that Captain Saan told me about. I always knew there was more than my mother's island." She looked around at the curious sailors. "Didn't you all embark on a voyage to seek adventure?"

"Adventure, yes," Saan said, "but we are also on a quest for the Key to Creation, and possibly even Terravitae. As soon as I find what we seek, then we will sail home to Uraba."

"Why, I thought you knew." Ystya blinked at him in surprise. "Ondun is my father. Aiden, Urec, and Joron are my brothers." She looked at Sen Sherufa, but saw no understanding on the Saedran's face either. "*I* am the Key to Creation."

40 *The* Dyscovera

Drifting on the *Dyscovera* among the ships of the dead, Criston's crew found lost loved ones who had vanished at sea. They dropped anchor near the dark and tattered *Luminara*, and Criston stared with awe at her familiar lines. He recognized the figures standing at the rail.

The undead Enoch Dey waved a pallid hand at the *Luminara* and shouted, "Captain Shay, you were right. They were on their way."

A figure at the bow of the ghost ship called out in a voice that had never faded from Criston's memory, "I always saw the potential in you, Mr. Vora. I understand you're captain of your own ship now? A fine vessel!"

The *Luminara* wasn't the only relic from his past. Criston cupped his hands around his mouth and shouted in an uncertain voice, "I saw a fishing boat that belonged to my father, Cindon Vora. Is he . . . is he with you?"

Aboard the *Luminara*, another man appeared beside Captain Shay, and even in the dusk shadows Criston felt the stirring of long-blurred childhood memories. The man said, "We are all with you, Criston—all of your dead." The familiarity was heartbreaking, and mental images rushed back as tears flooded his eyes.

As sailors aboard the ghost ships lit their lanterns, Criston could discern his father in the eerie yellowish light. He seemed younger than Criston remembered, but Cindon Vora had perished at sea when he was even younger than Criston now was.

Criston's father shouted from the *Luminara*, "Come aboard, son!" He gave the chillingly familiar whistle he had always used to call his boy to supper. "I want to have a look at you after all these years."

Prester Hannes spotted no acquaintances who had drowned in storms or shipwrecks. "Beware of them, Captain. They are ghosts, maybe angry ghosts. We don't know what they want. What is this place? Heaven or hell? Some kind of purgatory? Why would your lost loved ones be drawn here?"

"Maybe they weren't drawn to these coordinates, Prester," Criston said. "Maybe something about this part of the sea drew them to *us*."

"I thought you didn't like to ask questions, Prester," Sen Aldo observed.

"I'm only doing my duty to provide spiritual guidance."

Though he felt uneasy, Criston could not turn down this chance to see his father or his beloved Captain Shay. "I intend to investigate further. Sen Aldo, you will accompany me. If that truly is the *Luminara*, there's a certain chartsman I want you to meet." He frowned at the castaway they had retrieved from the water. "Mr. Dey, you will remain behind with my crew. For now." The pallid man didn't seem to mind.

While the sailors prepared one of the ship's boats, Criston retrieved a few things from his cabin. Lightheaded with anxiety and wonder, he and Sen Aldo rowed across to the *Luminara*.

Aboard the spectral ship, Criston regarded the souls before him, feeling a prickle of gooseflesh. A dank smell hovered like low-hanging mist about the *Luminara*, but the smell was of saltwater and drenched sailcloth rather than rot. The ship felt solid, sturdy . . . and unsettling.

Captain Shay looked unchanged in his familiar bulky jacket, his dark hair bound in a ponytail. Though his skin had a cadaverous grayness, his smile was genuine, and the light in his eyes was not false. The lanterns on deck reflected a hint of a tear on his cheeks.

Criston had watched the Leviathan devour the captain, seen the ship sink. "But you are all dead . . . the shades of sailors lost at sea."

"We are what we are," Shay said. "Elsewhere in the uncharted oceans there may be Uraban ships like this, spirits captured by other titans. I know only that we found ourselves together, here, bound by ties that we cannot see."

Sen Aldo raised an unpleasant possibility as he gazed at the shadowy crewmembers. "If you were all lost at sea, then are we . . . dead too?"

"No, Chartsman, you are very much alive. But these waters are mysterious. The *Dyscovera* has sailed past the boundaries of the world and traveled far enough to find us."

Criston found himself speechless when his father came forward. Cindon Vora said, "I knew you were a sailor at heart, my son, so I had hoped to see you again . . . but not so soon, and not this way." He wrapped his arms around Criston in a tight and muscular hug. The man felt solid enough.

Among those crowded on the lost ship's deck, Criston recognized many faces. He was astonished to see Prester Jerard, who had drifted with Criston for days on a makeshift raft, only to be eaten by a sea serpent. "I see Aiden's blessing is upon you, Mr. Vora."

Words caught in Criston's throat. The kindly prester had made such an impact on him that when Criston lived in isolation up in the mountains, he had named his beloved dog after Jerard. . . .

The *Luminara*'s dark-haired and soberly intellectual chartsman, Sen Nikol na-Fenda, was curious to see Aldo. Captain Shay introduced the two. "The chartsmen will want to compare notes. For now, Mr. Vora, come to my cabin, and your father and I can have a good talk with you."

"Maybe we can help you on your journey," Cindon Vora added.

Criston turned to his chartsman. "Will you be all right with Sen Nikol?"

Aldo looked overwhelmed, but not fearful. "We have a great deal of information to share."

Leaving the two Saedrans to talk, Criston followed his father and Shay to the captain's cabin, which looked exactly as he remembered it. Though the Leviathan had smashed the ship to flotsam and splinters years ago, the ghost cabin was perfectly recreated. Flowerpots suspended from hooks in the rafters held herbs and green plants, though Criston noted that they had no smell. Narrow shelves were crowded with transparent bottles of preserved specimens that Captain Shay had studied—fish, plants, insects, shells. Meticulous sketches of places he had seen and creatures he had dissected were tacked to the walls.

Criston reached into his jacket and pulled out the water-stained leather-bound book that he had retrieved from his own cabin. “This is yours, Captain Shay. I rescued it from the wreckage of the *Luminara*, and I’ve kept it all these years.” Feeling young and excited again, he opened the yellowed pages to show the notations he had made.

The other captain was delighted. “No wonder I couldn’t find it among my things here. This is marvelous!” Shay flipped from one page to another. “I see you added your own sketches!” He stopped at the page where Criston had drawn the horrific Leviathan and glowered at the image. “Someday, I hope to have another chance at that monster.”

“So do I—especially now that I have evidence that it can be killed.” He told them of the Leviathan skeleton on the small island.

Criston’s father sat in a spare chair in the cluttered cabin, still beaming at his son. “You grew up well, Criston. For a long time, I’ve pondered what future you might have. Captain Shay couldn’t imagine how you got away from the Leviathan, but we didn’t see you here with the rest of the *Luminara*’s crew.”

“Prester Jerard told us part of the story,” Shay said. “You must have been rescued from the raft?”

Criston leaned back with a smile. “I’ll tell you that story, if you tell me yours, Father. We never knew what had happened to you. You sailed out from Windcatch one day and never came back.”

“I’m so sorry to have left you and your mother alone—it must have been hard for you.” Cindon Vora hung his head. “I went fishing as I always did. I set out my nets and hauled them in—a decent catch. But then something struck me from below, a giant beast with barnacles all over its back—a whale, I think. It was close to the surface and scraped my fishing boat, then swam away—probably didn’t even notice what it had done.

“With my hull cracked and leaking, I set sail for shore. I began listing badly, so I dumped my catch. I threw every spare item overboard just to stay afloat.

"Toward dusk, I spotted a distant fishing vessel, but their lookout didn't see me. When the clouds came in and the rains pounded down . . ." Cindon hesitated, struggling to face his own memories of the story. "I stayed alive as long as possible."

He spread his hands, looking forlorn. "I wanted to come back to you, Criston . . . but I couldn't."

Criston hugged his father again, but Cindon had questions, too. "And what of your mother? What of yourself? Captain Shay says you have a lovely wife. Any children?"

Saddened, Criston told them how the Urecari raiders had burned Windcatch, murdered his mother, kidnapped and possibly killed Adrea. "Because of the Leviathan and the shipwreck, I got home much too late to save anyone."

"Ah, that is a terrible thing, my son," said Cindon Vora. Even Captain Shay had tears in his eyes.

Criston didn't think he could face any more of the past. He drew a deep breath, and his voice was hoarse. "But those things happened long ago, to all of us. These ghost ships—why are you here?"

Captain Shay replied, "The last thing I remember is the Leviathan's jaws crushing me . . . and then I was here, aboard an intact *Luminara*, with other drowned or shipwrecked sailors. We've all felt the call of the sea, and we died in the water. Now these strange waters hold us. We're not going anywhere."

Criston felt a chill of fear. "But the *Dyscovera* has a mission to find Terravitae. We can't stay."

"Oh, you aren't trapped. You don't belong with us—not yet," his father insisted. "We'll help you get away from the seaweed."

In a strange and somber voice, Captain Shay added, "If *she* will let you go."

*

Aldo was curious to hear what his fellow chartsman had to say, and excited to reveal the progress their people had made. "Since the *Luminara* sailed, Sen Nikol, the Saedrans have filled in much of the Mappa Mundi. We have full details of the continent of Uraba, even a land beyond it and a vast southern ocean. This voyage has also greatly expanded our knowledge of the seas."

The other chartsman volunteered little, though. "During the voyage of the *Luminara* I saw a great deal of empty water, an island of skeletons, and not much else. Just before the Leviathan attacked and sank our ship, some sailors spotted a beacon in the distance . . . it might have been the Lighthouse at the End of the World." He gave Aldo a strange look. "But I can't be sure of the information, because I died before that."

Aldo couldn't contain his curiosity. "And how did you find yourself here? Does this place draw everyone who dies at sea?"

Sen Nikol's gaze was distant, chilling. "Even though you're my fellow chartsman, Sen Aldo na-Curic, I've gone to places that I cannot describe to you. You can only explore those dark landscapes for yourself when it is time."

Aldo realized that despite his lifelong curiosity, perhaps there were some things he did not want to know.

Aboard the *Dyscovera* in the dark of the night, Enoch Dey found his old partner, Silam Henner, who was terrified to be near him. "Don't wreak your vengeance on me, Enoch!"

The undead castaway laughed. "And why should I want to? You did me no harm."

The other crewman was flustered. "Because I survived, while you were thrown overboard. I had to endure lashes, but you . . ." Fumbling, Silam couldn't even find a way to speak his thoughts.

Enoch lowered his voice. "Your lashes were probably more painful than my death. Besides, I'm here again. No harm done."

Silam snuffled. "But *why* are you here? Did you come to haunt us?" His lips quirked uncertainly. "Did you come to torment that bitch Mia again?"

"I don't care about her. But I did come for you, Silam."

The other man paled. "No! I've already atoned for what I did."

"Truly? The captain can't punish me any more, as you see." Enoch spread his hands. "But do you believe he has just forgiven you and will never think again about your part in taking that girl by force?"

"But he knows I'm loyal! I promised."

Enoch's words dug deep into Silam's fears. "Do you really think that when the *Dyscovera* goes home to Tierra the captain won't change his mind and turn you over to Calay justice? You'll be hung when you get there, Silam Henner. Mark my words."

"That's not true!" His voice carried very little conviction.

"I can offer you another choice. Believe me, it's your best option."

"Wh—what?"

At the rail, Enoch gazed out at the shadowy vessels floating among the weeds. "Look at the ships anchored here. See how warm and welcoming the lights are. We have a community of sailors, all with a common bond. You would be welcome among us—and we both know Captain Vora would not miss you. He'd say good riddance."

"But I don't know any of them," Silam said.

"You know me, and I'd vouch for you. In fact, many of your crew have friends and loved ones aboard those ships. I wouldn't be surprised if at least a dozen joined us before the *Dyscovera* sails on."

Silam was deeply troubled as he weighed his options.

Enoch persisted. "Come with me, just for a little while. I'll let you meet my new shipmates, find you a bunk." He pointed to one of the dark hulks among the wrecks, outlined by the starlight.

"But how do we get over there? Do we take one of the ship's boats?"

"No need for that—the water's warm, and it's not far. We can swim." Enoch's eyes narrowed, and his voice took on a sharp edge. "I've spent enough time in that water."

Before Silam could reconsider, the pale man urged him over the side to scramble down the rope ladder. As the frightened sailor descended rung by rung, Enoch dropped into the water, stroked out among the seaweed. He trod water, whispering urgently for his friend. "Quickly, before someone stops you."

Silam hesitated on the last rung, then dropped into the water and swam toward Enoch.

Before he had gone more than a body's length from the *Dyscovera*, the seaweed began to move around him. One of the fronds grasped his ankle and drew tight. With a yelp, Silam tugged at the strand, trying to tear it free. Then more of the hairlike weed curled around his waist and grabbed his shoulders. "Enoch, help me!"

The other man floated, stroking gently. "It's perfectly natural."

Silam yanked a knife from his waist sheath and hacked at the weed, but more green strands coiled around him. One encircled his neck, choking him. He thrashed and screamed for help.

Above on deck, Javian, Mia, and other sailors rushed to see what was happening. They threw a rope to the struggling man in the water, but it was too late.

Silam Henner was cocooned in green webbing, and fleshy leaves dragged him under the surface. The seaweed gently stirred and closed over the opening he'd made.

Satisfied, Enoch Dey swam back to one of the ghost ships.

41 *The* Moray

When the Moray docked at another town, Captain Belluc and his crew were anxious to go ashore for a night of carousing. Asaddan's relationship with the galley captain had been strained since their clash over the Aidenist prisoner, but Belluc tried to make amends. He knew full well that the Nunghal was Soldan-Shah Omra's friend and a welcome guest at the Olabar court.

"They make a sweetwine here unlike anything you've ever tasted, my shaggy friend," the captain said with forced joviality. "Come with me for an enjoyable night. We'll find food, drink, and women—they have plenty of all three for sale."

Asaddan stood at the gangplank and peered out at the dock marketplace as the stalls closed for the evening. "The women look fat." He was not in the mood for celebrating.

"With enough sweetwine, they look more attractive."

The townspeople lit lanterns, and the inns and restaurants opened their doors to welcome customers from the newly arrived galley. These people knew the *Moray* well, as had other towns. As the passengers and crew disembarked, Asaddan pondered what he should do. He did not want to make Belluc suspicious.

"Very well, I'll dine with you and taste the sweetwine. I hope their inn serves something other than fish—how I long for a juicy buffalo steak."

"I have heard of those animals." Belluc worked hard to make light conversation. "Do they smell like the fur of your vest?"

Asaddan stroked his garment with pride. "All Nunghals wear buffalo hides."

The bald captain's scalp furrowed. "Maybe someday I'll have a chance to taste the meat . . . but I don't exactly look forward to it."

Asaddan forced himself not to look back at the galley as they walked down the creaking pier. The hatch was open, leading to the slave holds where the rowers remained shackled to their benches while the crew went ashore. Belluc clearly suspected nothing, and Asaddan had to pretend an interest in the captain's company.

He had been in a foul mood ever since watching Ciarlo keel-hauled. The poor man's wrists were bloody from the rope, his shoulders nearly torn from their sockets. Asaddan had gone below to tend the man, brushing aside the surly crew, and used brute strength to wrench the injured Aidenist's dislocated joint back into place. He shared his own rations with the Tierran, used strips of cloth to bind the wounds, applied field healing techniques that any Nunghal rider knew.

Exhausted and in pain, Ciarlo had thanked him, but did not ask why a stranger would care about him. Instead, he gave Asaddan a sincere blessing (one that would have offended a devout follower of Urec, though it pleased the Nunghal).

Despite his swollen arms and bruised muscles, Ciarlo was ordered back to work the following day; Asaddan noticed that the man's companions worked harder so his weakness would not be apparent. Despite his physical pain, Ciarlo told more stories from the Book of Aiden, again recounting how the Traveler had healed his lame leg. Some of the men found the tale dubious, while others were awed to hear of the miracle. Asaddan didn't know what to think, since he had no proof that Ciarlo had ever been lame in the first place. Still, the man's voice and demeanor had the ring of truth to them.

Meanwhile, Captain Belluc was baffled by his interest in the prisoner. "Why would you bother?"

"Because I'm not convinced the man did anything to deserve his punishment."

"Then you don't know what Aidenists have done to our people. He deserves to die either way. The only difference is how much work I can squeeze out of him before he perishes."

Asaddan shook his head. "I know very well what the Aidenists have done, and I've seen how cruel they can be."

"Then you understand."

"I have seen more than enough cruelty."

Now, in port, the two men ate dinner at an inn that Belluc recommended (the meal was fish, as Asaddan had feared, though spiced heavily enough that the flavor was not quite as offensive). The galley captain was cheerful, especially after Asaddan insisted on paying for three of his companions' glasses of sweetwine to every one that he consumed himself.

With increasingly slurred words, Belluc talked about his travels on the *Moray* along the Middlesea coast. He described women he liked at each port of call, brawls he'd gotten into. But for all his talk, Belluc really had not traveled very far. His route was set, from Sioara to Kiesh and back; he never varied his destinations, nor did he intend to, even now that the Ishalem canal was open and the whole Oceansea coast was waiting for direct trade.

The innkeeper sent two women with false smiles who offered to service them. Although the women were not quite as unattractive as Asaddan had feared, he had little interest in them. When Belluc tottered away with the taller of the two, and the second led Asaddan to her room, he simply paid her and slipped out through a back door, knowing that Belluc would be occupied for some time. This would have to be his chance.

Asaddan sprinted through the town to the docks, where he slipped aboard the *Moray*. Only two unhappy crewmembers remained aboard, both in a foul temper because they were forced to stay behind on watch. To spite their captain, they had fallen soundly asleep, unconcerned about the ship in a familiar port.

Asaddan crept down into the hold, where chained prisoners dozed upright on their benches, hunched over the oar shafts. Though he was injured and should have been sleeping, Ciarlo was awake, his eyes bright in the shadows when he saw Asaddan's arrival.

The Nunghal kept his voice low. "I suspect you've had enough of this ship. I've come to take you out of here."

"How can you free me?" Ciarlo asked.

Other prisoners began to whisper, but Asaddan hushed them. He held up a small iron pry bar and grinned. "Simple enough."

He wrenched down on the bolt that held the shackles and snapped it free. The sound was too loud, and all the tense galley slaves held their breath, but they heard no response from above.

"Will you free my companions as well?"

"I hadn't intended to."

"Don't they deserve a chance?"

Asaddan set the metal pry bar down on the bench where the next man could reach it. "That's up to them. You're the one I came for."

While the slave frantically began to work on his chains, Asaddan led the injured Aidenist up the ladder through the hatch. Ciarlo winced every time he had to bend his arms, but he asked for no help. On deck, he stared into the starry night sky and breathed the clean open air.

The guards remained sleeping. Asaddan had little trouble binding and gagging them before they could make a sound. It would give them the extra time he and Ciarlo needed.

Before he led the Aidenist off the ship, Asaddan went to the captain's cabin and set a stack of gold coins outside the locked door, a fair price for the purchase of a galley slave. Then he hurried Ciarlo down the gangplank and onto the dock. They slipped into the night streets of the town.

Behind them, other escaped slaves began to emerge, and Asaddan wanted to be long gone before anyone raised an alarm. "We'll make our own way to Olabar, my friend. I know someone there who might be able to help you."

42 *Desert Harbor*

Blown by the hot winds, five bright sand coracles drifted over the expanse of blond dunes. Even the sparse brown grass of the hills looked like paradise to the travelers after their long passage across the Great Desert.

The coracles were not the same as the typical airborne vessels flown by Uraban merchants each season. Instead of wickerwork, tanned buffalo hides were stretched tight over the wooden basket frames.

For their first attempts, the Nunghal travelers had filled the braziers with dried buffalo dung, which was in great supply across the plains; those attempts, though, generated barely enough heat to lift the coracles into the air, and the baskets had crashed without going very far. So Khan Jikaris dispatched riders to explore the land until they found exposed veins of black coal—the same stuff the Uraban merchants used—which proved to be an appropriate fuel.

Finally, the first Nunghal expedition set off. Khan Jikaris had never been so far from his open grassland, his tent city, or his wives. The women, who did not often agree, were unanimous in considering him foolish to embark on such a ridiculous adventure. He hadn't listened to them (in fact, he rarely did). He felt enthralled, and a bit nauseated, as the heat from the coal fire lifted the balloon and carried them out into the desert.

Queasy, he leaned over the side of the basket and vomited out into the open air. Two of his companions laughed at his discomfort, and he forced them to push fingers down their own throats until they too vomited in a gesture of solidarity.

The khan had grown quite fond of the annual visitors from the strange lands to the north. Each year, they brought fascinating and desirable items and told remarkable stories. He anticipated the arrival of the sand coracles as much as he looked forward to the Nunghal clan gatherings on the southern sea.

Several times in the past, Imir had encouraged Jikaris to visit Uraba, but since he was the khan, he had always let the strangers come to him. But this year there was no sign of any strangers from across the desert. Week after week, the khan waited for the colorful

Uraban coracles to arrive, and eager anticipation faded into disappointment, until the watchers simply wandered off and went about their own business.

Some, however, encouraged the khan to go investigate himself. It began as a joke, but to his annoyance the pressure mounted, and Jikaris felt pushed into a corner. It wouldn't do for some blustering young rider to label his reluctance as *cowardice*, which would force Jikaris to defend his leadership of the clans. Though he was old, no one had yet demanded that he surrender his title to someone younger and stronger. In point of fact, few Nunghals particularly cared to become khan, since the independent clans weren't easily led.

But Jikaris did want to know why the foreigners hadn't come on their usual journey. Perhaps some great disaster had occurred, a plague or a storm that had killed everyone in their land. (He had no real concept of how large Uraba was.) Or, worse, had the Nunghals committed some offense that caused his friends and trading partners to turn their backs on him?

Honor-bound to investigate, Khan Jikaris commanded his people to build coracles and prepare for departure. Many of his clansmen understood the sand coracles, since they helped repair and rebuild the battered vessels each season before the Urabans sailed back across the Great Desert.

Once up in the air, however, even the khan of the Nunghal-Ari could not command or guide the floating ships. They were at the mercy of the winds. After many days of forlorn drifting and grumbling among his crowded companions—no doubt this grumbling was reflected in the other four coracles—they spotted the end of the desert and a small Uraban encampment.

"We'll soon be on the ground again, where we can stretch our legs and run!" Jikaris was happy to take credit for the success of their voyage. He could hear the loud Nunghals in the other craft cheering.

However, the settlement they approached was almost empty. With all the stories Asaddan and Imir had told, he'd imagined that the Uraban capital would be much more extensive. He spotted only a dozen or so structures, some of which were tents. Two surprised young men ran out of a dusty shed, shouting in excitement when they saw the coracles.

As the Nunghals banked the coal fires in the braziers, the coracles settled toward the ground. Two of the craft crashed heavily, tumbling the occupants onto the grassy ground. Jikaris got up, brushed off his breeches, and stood tall as a handful of Uraban people ran forward to greet them. The khan tried not to show his disappointment, though he had expected a more extravagant celebration of his arrival.

Jikaris knew a few words of their language, but he had always pretended to not speak it in order to force his guests to use the Nunghal tongue. One of his companions had made two prior coracle voyages to Uraba and was more fluent in Uraban, so he served as translator. Jikaris nodded when his name was spoken, and the locals talked with one another, hurriedly discussing what to do. Apparently, their village was named Desert Harbor.

"Where is Imir?" Jikaris finally asked. "My friend Imir?"

After one of the Urabans responded at length, the Nunghal translated for his khan. "This is merely a place for the coracles to arrive. Their nearest capital city, Arikara, was recently destroyed in an earthquake. Their buildings collapsed. Many people are dead. I think he said Imir is there."

Though distressed to hear this, Jikaris swelled his chest and struck his buffalo-hide vest. "Then it's a good thing we have arrived. Have them take us to this Arikara. We will show them the way Nunghals help in a disaster."

Khan Jikaris knew little about living in buildings, but he knew everything about living without them.

43 *Ishalem, Main Urecari Church*

Now that she was the ur-sikara, it was unseemly for Kuari to spend time grieving over the death of her husband. Even before the great building collapsed, she had been technically married to the church instead of the leader of Inner Wahilir. Besides, Huttan had been a pompous blowhard. Her followers understood implicitly that while the loss of the soldan was a sad thing, the far greater blow was the collapse of Urec's church so close to completion.

Meanwhile, Kuari had work to do, much of it cleaning up the messes her husband had created. As ur-sikara, she considered it her duty, both in the name of Urec and the soldan-shah, to make Uraba strong again where cracks of weakness showed.

Leaving the defense of Ishalem in the hands of Kel Unwar, Omra had already sailed the *Golden Fern* back to his capital. Soldan Vishkar had departed on his mission to round up a makeshift navy to patrol the coast and protect the sacred city. When they arrived, their priority would be to guard the Oceansea mouth of the canal, so that the enemy could not penetrate into the Middlesea.

Kuari had her own ideas to set in motion here—ideas that would help consolidate Uraba. She assumed the soldan-shah would approve.

She had already sent word to Sharique, the official emissary to Yuarej and the First Wife of Soldan Andouk. Even during the endless war against the Aidenists, the five soldanates of Uraba squabbled with one another, annexing territories, sniping at their respective leaders. Kuari thought it was about time the female emissaries demonstrated a new way of solving problems—relying on wisdom rather than stupidity.

Kuari had chosen adequate quarters in the large, incomplete church: a spacious, well-lit set of chambers and an anteroom behind the main worship hall. The perennially exhausted Saedran architect was happy with Kuari's easygoing manner, and quite accommodating to her ideas and needs. Sen Bira na-Lanis sent teams to refurbish the chambers according to her specific requests.

Kuari had never been overly fond of the trappings and treasures so often coveted by sikaras and soldans alike (the ambition never seemed to make anyone happier, as far as she could see). Her husband had always wanted more, even though he was the soldan of Inner Wahilir; the sikaras always wanted more, even though they commanded the faithful. Kuari had always put up with the foolish attitude—until now. As ur-sikara, she was as rich as she could imagine, and she could do as she wanted.

After receiving the ur-sikara's summons, Sharique rushed to Ishalem. The lovely woman had a thin face and slight figure, her dark hair tied behind her head in an intricate braid in the style of Yuarej. She wore the finest silks, since her husband's soldanate was the sole provider of the material across Uraba. Though quiet and intelligent, Sharique was a bit too meek to be a force in the government. She was also Soldan Andouk's first and only wife. Their only daughter, Cliaparia, had married Omra with disastrous results, and they had never truly recovered from the shame.

Sharique performed an appropriate obeisance. "Ur-Sikara Kuari, I am honored to meet with you." She seated herself on the cushions at the other woman's invitation.

Kuari brushed aside the formality. "We need to talk, you and I. Our husbands have made a mess of things between their soldanates, and this is simply not acceptable. Uraba is at war with *Tierra*, not with herself. Soldans cannot be squabbling children." She made herself comfortable, while her guest paled to hear her tone. "Let us fix it together and provide a good example for our people."

The other woman looked down and away. "My husband sent

repeated complaints to the soldan-shah about the illegal new settlements on our borders. I don't know what else to do. Andouk doesn't want to go to war with Inner Wahilir."

"And thus you look weak! Doesn't your husband understand that?" Sharique was surprised by the rebuke, and the ur-sikara continued. "Yuarej must *appear* to be willing to defend its territory. Huttan moved retired soldiers to your frontier where they built homes and took your land, since you didn't care enough to fight for it."

"We wouldn't spill the blood of other Urabans!"

"Then we'll have to find another solution." Kuari sat back, flushed. "The recent disaster in Arikara provides a tremendous challenge for us—and a way to resolve our difficulties."

Sharique was curious now. "How so?"

"The people of Arikara have a great need, with so many injured, so many buildings destroyed. They require food, shelter, and workers to rebuild the devastated city." Kuari tapped her fingers on the low table that held pastries topped with jellied fruit; not bothering with ceremony, the ur-sikara picked up a pot of steaming coffee and poured for both. "We must hurry, though—and not only because of Arikara's desperate circumstances."

Sharique sipped the bitter coffee. "Is there another reason to hurry?"

"Soldan Huttan is only recently dead, and his replacement has not yet been chosen. We need to do something before politics can get in the way. As ur-sikara, I will announce a call to action. All the soldanates must help our brothers and sisters in need."

Sharique understood immediately. "My husband is gathering a shipment of fresh silks to be used for tents and garments. He is ready to contribute."

"Not good enough. *Everyone* should contribute. Let me give you a list of silk merchants who have been taking bribes from Soldan Huttan while also paying taxes to Soldan Andouk. By playing both sides, they mean to place themselves in a favorable position, whichever way the conflict is resolved."

Sharique scowled, not knowing how to answer, but Kuari smiled. "Your husband should confiscate their silk and use *that* as his donation. How can the merchants complain when it's going for such a good cause? I'll write a formal letter expressing my personal gratitude to the merchants, and then how can they say no? While they are whining about the expense, your husband can quietly inform them that he knows of their duplicity. They'll realize that they are getting away with a rather light punishment. That is the way politics is played."

Sharique laughed. "Andouk would never have schemed like that. What about the new settlers who have built their homes on our lands? That is the sore point."

"Hmm, think about it. Delivering all those supplies to the refugees in Arikara will require a long and difficult journey. Your husband can assign the expedition to those new colonists, have them carry the silk packets all the way down to Arikara. If they serve Urec and Ondun properly, I will grant them the special blessings of the church. And when they return from their journey, Soldan Andouk can welcome them as new citizens of Yuarej, and they will of course pay taxes to Yuarej. After all, with Huttan dead, they have no loyalty one way or another."

"Won't Inner Wahilir feel cheated?"

Kuari had considered this, and she let out a long sigh. "It's too bad you have no other daughters that could be married to the new soldan."

Sharique hung her head, still stinging from the fallout of Cliaparia's marriage to Omra. "I'm not certain anyone would *want* one of our daughters, if Cliaparia was any example."

"Then there's another solution. Maybe your husband should take one of Huttan's remaining wives as his second wife, just to seal the alliance, create stronger ties between the soldanates."

Sharique swallowed hard and looked dismayed, but forced herself to give a stoic answer. "I will . . . make the request."

Kuari wondered why the other woman would look so distressed, until she remembered that Soldan Andouk's preference was to be monogamous. She had thought it an odd affectation for a soldan, but now seeing Sharique's hurt and jealousy, she realized that he truly loved this woman! Given the history of her own marriage, Kuari hadn't even considered the possibility. Nevertheless, the need was greater than a bit of infatuation.

She gave Sharique a reassuring smile. "Now, don't look so heart-broken. Just because he marries her doesn't mean Soldan Andouk has to love her—or even *make* love to her. Huttan and I certainly did not share a bed for years. This would just be a political formality. Now that I think of it, I doubt any of my former husband's wives will complain about the arrangement."

Sharique let out an uncomfortable sigh that might have been relief. "As I said, I will raise the matter with Andouk and try to convince him. If that is the way to ensure peace, he will accept it."

The ur-sikara was happy to put the matter to rest. "I'm glad that's settled. We have plenty of Aidenists to kill. Why shed good Uraban blood?"

44 *Calay Castle*

After his night with Anjine, Mateo slipped away, moving as silently as he could. He wasn't sure if he should stay, if he *could* stay. His thoughts were a whirlwind, and he searched for some moment of calm.

Anjine was the calm, the center. She was also the hurricane.

Mateo couldn't remain here in Calay. It was not fair to him, to her, or to Tierra.

The room was still dim when he left Anjine sleeping. Her maidservant would notice that the queen hadn't returned to her royal chamber during the night, but right now Anjine looked so peaceful, so happy. As she pulled the pillow up against her head, rumpling her hair, the expression on her face was innocent and free of care . . . just like the young girl with whom Mateo had spent so much time, loving her unconditionally as only childhood friends could. Even back then, he had never thought of her as a sister, but as a part of himself. He knew that Anjine felt the same way.

But now it had brought them to this. The experience seemed as unreal and dreamlike as any of the blinding tragedies he had endured.

In a separate room down the hall, in the dimness of approaching dawn, Mateo put on the light, fitted body armor that Vicka had given him from the Sonnen forge. *Vicka* . . . the very thought of her stung him with grief and guilt. Her loss made him feel as if he had stepped off the edge of a roof and never stopped falling.

The armor felt cold in his hands. Each time he returned from his battles, even before they were married, she had helped repair the damage. "Don't worry about a few nicks and dings," she would say. "That shows the armor is doing its job. I'd be embarrassed if you suffered a fatal wound due to some flaw in the armor."

Driving away thoughts of her, and of Anjine, Mateo took his sword, grabbed his cloak, and crept out of the castle into the first streaks of dawn light. He left by one of the castle's obscure side entrances that he and Anjine had used for slipping away from their teachers in order to roam the streets of Calay as normal children. Carefree days . . .

He felt confused and distraught, shamed and elated. He needed to escape these dangerous emotions, and to free Anjine from inappropriate concerns. If he stayed here, they would both be harmed, and the queen wouldn't be able to rule as she needed to. Mateo was a loyal soldier and brave enough to do what he must. He could not let himself become a liability to the queen in this time of war.

Yes, he had loved Vicka deeply—and he had always loved Anjine in ways that he didn't know how to measure. But right now Aiden had placed an overriding responsibility upon them all. Mateo had no time for longing thoughts or soft caresses. He would throw his energy into winning the war, putting so much concentration into that one duty that he hoped he could forget about his feelings.

Reaching the Military District amid the bustle of soldiers gathering for departure, Mateo presented himself to Subcomdar Hist. The leader of the Tierran army directed the cavalry to saddle their horses for riding out at daybreak. "Good to see you joining us, Subcomdar Bornan," Hist said, red-faced and sweaty. "We're already an hour behind the schedule I had in mind."

"I'll do what I can to help you move out as soon as possible." Mateo joined an intense-looking Jenirod and an exuberant Destrar Shenro, both of whom would join the vanguard on the march.

Surprised to see him, Jenirod broke into a wide grin. "I never expected you, Subcomdar Bornan, but you always seem to arrive where you're most needed."

"I needed to go," Mateo said, meaning his statement in two different ways. He felt awkward standing before Jenirod, the man who had once been betrothed to Anjine.

Within an hour, the first group set off on the road heading south. Mateo risked one last glance back at Calay Castle high on its hill before facing forward once more and focusing his thoughts, and his heart, on the enemy ahead.

*

When Anjine awoke, she felt both wonderful and adrift. She found herself still in Mateo's old quarters, but she didn't see him. She whispered his name, hoping he would respond, but the room was silent. She was alone.

Sunlight seeped through the windows as the sun rose, and Anjine climbed out of bed. Her heart ached and thrummed with joy at the same time. She clung to her memories of the night, reliving each touch, every time Mateo had stroked her hair, kissed her lips. She could not imagine any sensation so wonderful, and she knew it would not have been the same with any other man she chose as her consort.

But he was gone.

She understood exactly why.

Though Anjine longed for him, she swiftly rebuilt the tumbled wall around her emotions. Yes, Mateo had understood, and done without question the correct thing—as always. She went to the narrow window, from which she could see the Military District where soldiers were mounting their horses in preparation for departure.

Yes, today the army was scheduled to head south for the siege of Ishalem. She knew Mateo would be among the many small figures there, riding alongside his comrades bound for the holy city . . . and away from her.

Anjine knew he wouldn't be gone forever. They would be together again soon, with a different and just as singular goal. As the queen of Tierra, she intended to join the massed army for the final battle that would destroy the followers of Urec.

With a wan smile on her lips, Anjine straightened her hair. Maybe she could slip back to her quarters before Enifir noticed. In any case, she would never speak of this, and she would command her lady-in-waiting to keep her silence as well.

She and Mateo would meet in Ishalem in a few months.

45 *Middlesea*

Sailing two of the ironclads south, Broeck and his nephew prowled the open Middlesea. He had no intention of just kicking pebbles on the shore for months while Queen Anjine moved the rest of the Tierran army and navy into position. A warrior didn't bide his time. While he waited, he continued his Aidenist reign of terror upon the luckless Urabans. By now the Curlies feared these armored warships more than any sea monster.

Since neither Broeck nor Iaros could read the tangled loops of Uraban writing, they didn't know (or care) what the foreigners had originally named these ironclads. Iaros had selected a traditional Iborian name for his vessel—*Raathgir*, after the famous ice dragon. For himself, Broeck had named his flagship *Wilka* as a memorial to his wife, lost but not forgotten. Years ago, Wilka had frozen to death in an unexpected Iborian snowstorm while out picking frost-berries. This ironclad was hard and strong, yet graceful, as Wilka had been.

Though he would not strike the eastern side of Ishalem until the appropriate date, the Middlesea coast offered plenty of alternative targets. Since Soldan-Shah Omra must be planning some kind of attempt to recapture the mines, Broeck intended to make the first move and keep the Curlies reeling. With the *Wilka*, the *Raathgir*, and his five other armored vessels, he would soon launch a strike the enemy would never forget.

He and Iaros sailed along, their ships within shouting distance of each other. The Middlesea was uncharted territory for them. By simple geographical logic, if they continued far enough south, they would find the opposite coast. Within two days, they spotted the Middlesea shore—a sight not seen by free Tierran eyes for a generation.

Standing at the *Wilka*'s bow, Broeck peered through his spyglass.

As he adjusted the cylinder's focus, he saw waves striking a milk-sand shore, and the colorful sails of many ships that pulled into a bustling harbor. Broeck could make out the city's buildings, the tall minarets of huge Urecari churches, and a shining palace that he'd seen only in fanciful pictures. He felt a flush of heat on his cheeks. Olabar, the capital of Uraba, the seat of the soldan-shah.

The waters were calm, and in the still air Iaros's voice rang out as he called across the gap between ships. "Uncle, are we going to attack?"

Broeck took a long moment to answer. How he longed to sail into Olabar harbor and strike the unsuspecting Urecari. That would teach the Curlies a lesson after all the harm they had caused. But it would be a futile gesture, no matter how glorious it might seem. Even unprepared, Olabar had enough fighters and ships to drive back the *Wilka* and the *Raathgir*. And Broeck had to keep his fleet intact for the attack on Ishalem.

"Not today," he shouted back. "But soon." He clenched his jaw and whispered, too low for Iaros to hear, "Not soon enough."

Within a week, Broeck planned to deal Uraba a crippling blow. He would make the soldan-shah and his followers reel with pain and despair before the Aidenists delivered the coup de grâce at Ishalem. That, at last, would make Broeck happy.

"Come about," he told his navigator with great reluctance. "We sail back to Gremurr."

"So soon, Destrar? We still have much scouting to do."

"I don't want to be seen—it's broad daylight. Our sails have no doubt been spotted, but they probably don't know who we are. Let's not give them an inkling of their danger."

On the voyage back to their stronghold on the northern coast, the ironclads encountered three wide-ranging Uraban fishing boats. Broeck ordered them seized, their crew trussed up like cargo sacks on the deck after a brief and ineffective struggle. Tierran soldiers boarded the small boats and piloted them back toward Gremurr, where they would join the other captured vessels.

Iaros came aboard the *Wilka*, impatient and full of questions. He gave a disparaging look to the small craft. "Uncle, what good will those fishing boats do for our war effort? The captives won't even be much help working in the mines."

Broeck assessed the three sturdy boats. True, they were not large, not powerful, not swift. "With those little boats, Iaros, we may just win our most important battle. I have a plan."

46 *Corag Mountains*

After departing from Gremurr, Destrar Siescu and his scout toiled into the isolated mountains, following the icy trail. Raga Var bounded ahead of the two pack ponies to study the path conditions, while Siescu shivered and walked along.

The cliffs around them were steep and slick with snow. Picking his way, Siescu could not imagine how armored mammoths had made the passage, but the shaggy army had not been hindered by snows as they crossed over the passes.

Storms occurred with increasing frequency this time of year, and conditions worsened with each snowfall. Calendars down in Calay would not mark the turning of the season for another month yet, but winter set in much earlier in the high mountains.

In normal times, Siescu would have ensconced himself in Stoneholm with stockpiled firewood and full storerooms so he wouldn't have to emerge again until spring. Though he had insisted on delivering this load of swords to the Tierran army before the battle at Ishalem, in truth he just wanted to get home and warm himself in the comfort of familiar surroundings.

Siescu kept his head down as the biting wind numbed his

cheeks. It had been warmer back at the mines. He locked his gaze on the rocky trail in front of him, on Raga Var's widely spaced footprints in the snow. He daydreamed about the throbbing heat in the forges back at Gremurr, then he thought of his giant cheery fireplace in the main hall at Stoneholm. He looked up from his woolgathering, startled to see the scruffy scout standing before him. "Destrar, I don't like this weather."

Siescu shivered. "It's damned cold, that's for sure." When he saw genuine concern on Raga Var's face, the fact gave him pause. He had never seen the scout worried about anything.

Mountain weather patterns changed swiftly. Even so, Siescu was surprised to see how quickly the sky had turned a cottony gray. Icy fog settled into the canyons, followed by a veil of snow. Behind him, the nervous mountain ponies snorted and stomped.

"We need to pick up the pace, Destrar. Move as quickly as you can." Raga Var looked from side to side. "This will be a bad spot for weathering a blizzard."

"It might blow over quickly," Siescu said.

"No. It's a blizzard. We need to get off this pass. Half a mile beyond, there's an elbow of rock where we can take shelter. I might even be able to find enough wood for a fire."

"A fire! That sounds nice. Let's go, then."

The footing was treacherous; snow and ice packed the trail. The sky now had an angry opacity, and a thick whiteness flurried down. The wind skirled feathers of snow along the ground, and before long Siescu could barely see the path in front of him.

Raga Var came back to grab his arm and pull him along. Behind them, the pack animals snorted, trying to find their footing. One of the ponies stopped and refused to go farther. When Siescu tugged on the lead rope, the pony backed away, resisting. One of its hooves slipped as a rush of snow cascaded from the cliff.

Raga Var grabbed Siescu. "Let go of the rope!" He pulled the destrar to shelter as the shower of ice and snow came down, scaring the ponies, which turned and bolted. Rocks tumbled down with more snow, and he could no longer see what had happened to the animals. Both were gone.

Siescu stared in shock, but the scout drew him on, urgently trying to keep him moving. "This way, Destrar. We still have to go over this defile, and then we'll find shelter, I promise."

Raga Var seemed frightened now, and Siescu was so cold he couldn't even feel distressed at the loss of the ponies. "Freezing . . . Do you think it's getting colder?"

The wind howled, and the snow was thicker than before. Raga Var trudged several steps ahead, waited for Siescu to catch up, then trudged a little farther. Finally, the path widened, and large gray rocks jutted out. The scout pulled him around a corner, where the wind became blessedly quieter, although the cold seemed even more bone-chilling than before.

"This is the most sheltered place I can find, Destrar. You can sit here." The scout found two large boulders and guided Siescu to them, brushing away the snow with his bare hands. The rock shelter trapped and circulated the wind, blowing the snow around in endlessly changing patterns. Though he moved with clear anxiety, Raga Var didn't even seem cold. "We'll be protected from the worst of the storm." He gazed into the thick, blinding whiteness. "Though after the snow passes, we will have difficult going the rest of the way along the road."

"We must be close to Stoneholm," Siescu said. "It'll be warm there."

"We're still two days' journey out, Destrar."

"Oh. That is . . . unfortunate." He huddled down, pulling his cloak and furs closed against the chill, then looked around, dazed. "I had another blanket, but it was with the ponies."

Raga Var's face showed genuine concern for him. "Would you like a fire, Destrar? I'll try to find wood, some scrub brush, kindling."

Siescu's teeth chattered. He looked up, saw only swirling snow. "You'll never find wood in this whiteout."

"I'll find wood, Destrar. Just stay here and wait for me. I'll bring you a fire."

"Yes, then . . . a fire would be nice." He hunched over, pulling his warm garments close, but he couldn't stop shivering. Raga Var bounded off and within seconds vanished in the swirl of snowflakes.

Raga Var was gone less than an hour, searching in cracks where hardy mountain vegetation would grow. He returned to the sheltered place where he had left Destrar Siescu, worried that he'd been away too long. In his arms he carried dry scrub, twigs, grasses—enough to start a small campfire, he was sure, though it wouldn't burn long. Regardless, the destrar would be pleased to have the fire. Raga Var hoped it would be enough.

When he came back to the clearing, he saw Siescu still sitting hunched in his cloak and furs. Always cold, the man had never stopped digging deep mines in hopes of finding the last spark of the cooling Fires of Creation. Raga Var had never understood the obsession.

After living most of his life in the wilds, the scout knew how to endure shifting temperatures and could make himself comfortable no matter what situation he was in—although now, he had to admit, it was bone-chillingly cold. The blizzard intimidated him, and he doubted even he could find the narrow mountain road after such a snowfall. They were in a very bad situation.

He dropped the pile of twigs and kindling in front of Siescu, pleased with himself. "See, Destrar? I told you I'd find enough for a fire." He bent over, took out his flint and steel, and shielded the pile of combustible material with his own body. He struck three times until a strong spark leaped out, catching the grasses. "This will warm you, Destrar. Just a moment more."

Though Siescu didn't answer him, the scout continued to nurse the fire until the blaze caught and flames rose bright and golden in the swirling blizzard. "Here, Destrar, lean forward, and warm yourself."

But Siescu didn't answer. When Raga Var investigated, he found that the Corag destrar would never move again. The man had frozen entirely solid. Even his eyes, though wide open, were solid ice.

It was not possible in such a short time, yet Raga Var could not doubt what he saw. The blizzard had stolen all the heat from Destrar Siescu's body, leaving only this icy statue, frozen through to the marrow. Siescu's pale, hairless face was lined with frost.

Raga Var sat back heavily, but kept adding twigs to the fire, building it brighter. He looked into the petrified face of the man who had been so kind to him. "I'll just sit here awhile, Destrar," he said. "I'll feed the fire for you until I run out of wood, so it can keep you warm."

Outside of the small sheltered area, the storm continued to worsen, and impenetrable winter settled in over the Corag mountains. In the wind's voice, Raja Var thought he heard a frost giant laughing.

47 *Arikara*

Arikara, the capital of Missinia, had once been a magnificent city of clay-brick towers and arched gateways, open courtyards and busy marketplaces. But when the former soldan-shah arrived with his three granddaughters, he saw only wreckage and death.

Even the driftwood reader's dire predictions and Burilo's report had not prepared Imir for such devastation. Swaths of Arikara's buildings had fallen into piles of rubble; thick walls were shattered, support beams broken, roofs collapsed. It was as if an angry Ondun had smashed the city flat.

When the traveling party rode up, Adreala cried out in dismay. Cithara looked surprised and saddened; Istala began to pray aloud.

Imir pulled up his horse. "The whole city will have to be rebuilt."

Burilo's face was drawn into a sketch of grim lines. "We will rebuild later. The injured are still in dire need of medical attention. We'll need to provide shelter and supplies to the survivors. After all that is done, we can think about Arikara's future." He nodded toward Adreala and her sisters. "Welcome, cousins, but I'm afraid we have little hospitality to offer."

Conversation swelled among the volunteers who had accompanied the group from Olabar. Before the sight of the ruined city discouraged them, Imir called out in a loud and confident voice, "God challenges us, and we do not turn from a challenge."

Their response was dutifully determined, though with forced enthusiasm.

He nudged his horse forward. "Come, Burilo, we should let your father know that more help has arrived. Girls, follow me." They rode toward the shambles on the hill where Soldan Xivir's palace had stood. Only two of the walls remained now; the rest of the structure had collapsed into a pile of tan bricks, terracotta tiles, and splintered timbers. A cluster of temporary tents had been erected in what remained of the courtyard.

When Burilo shouted, the Missinia soldan emerged from the largest tent. Xivir looked drawn and haggard, and beside him came Lithio. The matronly woman saw the former soldan-shah and ran forward, grinning. "My husband, I knew you would come to save us!" She kissed him on the mouth, making Imir feel awkward until she added a typical barbed comment: "Although you should have come sooner. You aren't the first to arrive, you know."

"We came as fast as we could, Grandmother Lithio," Adreala said, swinging down off her horse.

Lithio gasped and released Imir. "You brought our granddaughters into this mess?" She clucked and gave each of the girls a hug.

Imir sighed. There was no pleasing the woman. "Our party left Olabar within days of learning Burilo's terrible news." He turned to address Xivir. "We brought carpenters and engineers, diggers and stonemasons, not to mention food, fabric, and tools. And more will come in the next caravan."

An older, leathery-skinned man clad in gray-brown furs emerged from the tent and squinted into the sunlight. Most of his hair was gone, and large hoop earrings dangled from both ears. He chattered in heavily accented Uraban. "Imir, old friend! I finally came to see your lands, and look what I find."

Imir sputtered. "Khan Jikaris! When did you arrive? How—"

"We built our own sand coracles." Jikaris was obviously proud. "I came to visit you, since your merchants did not come to trade this year. Now that you are here, you can help translate."

"Me? I don't speak your language well." Imir watched other Nunghals emerge from the smaller tents, attracted by the commotion. "But I suppose I do well enough to pass along instructions. There's plenty of work to do."

The Nunghals had arrived from Desert Harbor only the day before, and after assessing the huge task at hand, Khan Jikaris and his companions offered many interesting ideas. "Your buildings are hard and stiff, so they fall when the ground shakes. You could be more flexible if you moved from place to place and lived in large tents."

"We don't have either tents or buildings right now," Xivir pointed out.

The khan continued, "You must treat your city as a large camp—we show you. Nunghals know how. You forgot how to dig latrines, how to store water, how to bank cookfires in the open, and how to set up a tent against the wind and rain. Let my people remind you."

The former soldan-shah nodded. "He's right, Xivir. With so many dead, the rotting corpses will draw flies and may cause sickness."

"We should let the collapsed buildings become their tombs." Burilo sounded sad. "The world has already buried them."

Soldan Xivir drew himself up. "I have no intention of letting Arikara become a cemetery city. We must take the corpses away in carts, and build giant funeral pyres outside the city."

"Not funeral pyres. We will need the wood for rebuilding," Imir said. "Better to make mass graves, pile stones atop them."

The khan added, "Far from the city. As far as possible." Jikaris fell back into his own language when he didn't find what he wanted to say, and Imir helped translate.

"The gray fever struck a Nunghal clan gathering seven years ago. Hundreds died. The Nunghal-Su believed the sickness was carried on the buffalo hides the plainsmen brought to trade. The Nunghal-Ari claimed the fever came from the ships, from some foul wind out at sea. Either way, they had to destroy the entire camp. They burned the tents with the bodies inside and moved on."

Soldan Xivir said, "We've got to take care of the living as well as the dead. Many of our storehouses were destroyed in the quake. Granaries collapsed, silos crumbled, casks shattered. The food from the first caravan is nearly gone, and what you brought will not last long with a whole city to feed. I'm afraid my people will be hungry until we get relief from the other soldanates."

Imir nodded. "Soldan-Shah Omra is gathering supplies as quickly as he can, but it will take some time for them to arrive from all across Uraba. With the defense of Ishalem, the army has already drained the surplus from other soldanates."

Jikaris hunkered down outside the tent. "Combine your supplies, bake the bread, and cook large pots of stew and soup. Serve everyone. Your people work harder and sleep better if they know their khan takes care of them. And my men will help build large tents. Fortunately, your climate is warm."

Xivir said, "Yes, my people will feel safer with a roof over their heads."

The Nunghal khan let out a dark chuckle. "I would not feel safe. Many people just died because roofs fell on their heads. Better to be out in the open."

Adreala spoke up. "We're ready to do our part—whatever you need most. I'll even crawl into the rubble and pull out bodies, if you ask me to."

Cithara said, "Istala and I would like to help with the injured. Where should we go?"

Soldan Xivir regarded the earnest young girls with consternation. "Our local haulers and the Saedran surgeons have set up a pavilion not far from here, but I'm afraid it's no place for children."

"*Arikara* is no place for children right now—or anyone else, for that matter—yet your people have no choice but to be here," Imir pointed out. "The whole city is in desperate need."

"Which is why we came all the way from Olabar to help," Istala said.

Adreala raised her chin. "And if this is no place for children, then it's time my sisters and I grew up."

"Shall we share a meal first?" Lithio suggested, apparently anxious to spend time with Imir and her granddaughters.

Imir patted his stomach, which had grown rounded over the years of his retirement. "I can do without a meal or two, if so many people in Arikara are hungry. There is work to do."

"I'd like to get started now," Adreala agreed. "I think I should learn how to set up tents and dig latrines."

"My men are ready," Khan Jikaris announced. "Nunghals will show you how to run a camp."

48 *The* Dyscovera

As dawn spread a flush of colors across the weed-choked sea, the living crewmembers of the *Dyscovera* and the shades of drowned loved ones gathered with a somber purpose.

On the shadowy *Luminara*, Captain Shay gave a stern reproach to his spectral companions, and then called across to the *Dyscovera*. "It is dangerous for the living to stay among us. One of your crew is already lost to you, Mr. Vora—how many others might soon be tempted?"

Aboard a two-masted carrack that floated alongside the *Luminara*, Enoch Dey now stood with the revenant of Silam Henner. After being lured overboard into the deadly seaweed, Henner looked disconsolate, forever bound to the ghost ships and separated from the *Dyscovera*.

Criston raised his voice in answer from the bow of his own ship. "We do not belong here. We must continue our voyage. Lead the way."

The night before, in the watery lantern-light of Captain Shay's cabin, Criston, his father, and Shay had talked for hours, discussing memories and lost possibilities. At the same time, the ghosts of forlorn seamen had approached the *Dyscovera*, beseeching Tierran crewmembers to jump overboard. The undead sailors were aloof and carefree, no longer bound to the land or their families. Having already paid the price, they had nothing left to fear from the sea . . .

yet their voices were lonely. After seeing the fate of Silam Henner, however, even those tempted by the offer were frightened.

Before Criston left the ghost ship in the dead of night, Captain Shay had warned in a quiet voice, "Leave now, Mr. Vora. Set your sails, hoist anchor, and be under way by the time the sun rises. The longer you stay among us, the more dangerous it will be for you. Once your ship gets trapped, there is nothing even in life or death I can do to help you."

Cindon Vora was heartbroken. "I want to stay with you, my son, but I can't accompany the *Dyscovera*, and I don't want to condemn you to stay with us for eternity." He embraced Criston. "I wish I could have watched you grow up, worked with you aboard my ship. We could have sailed the uncharted seas together." He swallowed hard. "But wishes are like whitecaps. They fade quickly and leave nothing behind."

Criston gave him a bittersweet smile. "I had thirteen years with you, Father. You trained me, and now I am captain of the finest ship in all Tierra. You need have no regrets."

Before dawn, Criston and Sen Aldo had rowed back to the *Dyscovera* and met with the frightened crew. After they told him about the man lured overboard only to be killed by the seaweed, he felt angry and disappointed. "Prepare to sail," Criston ordered. "Unless you'd like to stay behind, as Mr. Henner did."

That was enough to put a chill into them, and the crewmembers went about their tasks, tugging ropes, stretching sails to catch the faint breeze. The *Luminara* would clear a channel through the unnatural seaweed and lead them out of the morass.

As the ships prepared to depart, Captain Shay's shout could be heard by all the spectral seamen. "The living cannot stay among us. We simply have to wait for their company. If they are true sailors, they will join us here eventually."

The ghostly *Luminara* moved ahead, her sharp prow cutting through the green strands to open a passage, and the *Dyscovera* threaded the needle behind her. All around them, Criston could smell the fermented stink of rotting vegetation, like the lingering odor of death. Somehow, it did not remind him of the stench of his own town during the annual seaweed die-off.

The *Luminara* guided them out to where the vegetation thinned. At the prow, Captain Shay looked anxious, as if racing to keep the *Dyscovera* safe. When the water finally opened up enough that Criston could turn to port and add more sail, the *Luminara* came about and tied up her sails.

Criston's father waved from the deck. "May the Compass guide you, son. We are always here. We are part of the sea now."

Captain Shay whistled. "Safe travels to Terravitae, Mr. Vora—I know you'll find that land, even though we did not. If you need us, simply call. We are bound to you by magical ties much stronger than sympathetic magic."

Prester Hannes maintained his stern composure, while other crewmembers wept to leave their loved ones behind. At the stern, Sen Aldo peered down at the *Dyscovera*'s wake, puzzled. "Captain, the seaweed is . . . twitching."

Javian and Mia ran to look overboard. The young woman said, "That weed grabbed Silam Henner and dragged him under."

"Best possible speed," Criston called with rising concern.

As the *Luminara* rejoined the other ghost ships, the green fronds thrashed with more vigor. The tangled surface undulated, as if something were generating the waves from below. More and more strands of weed lifted into the air, like hair flailing in a violent breeze. Mysterious currents began to draw the *Dyscovera* back toward the seaweed morass.

Criston watched the seaweed clear beneath the water . . . and saw a huge pale shape just under the surface, so large that his imagination could barely encompass it. As it rose, the underwater blur became an enormous oval that resolved itself into a *face*, a titanic female face far larger than the *Dyscovera*.

The seaweed squirmed and twitched around the ship and Criston realized that the strands were her hair. This gigantic woman had lain submerged, drawing all the ghost ships to her and keeping them there as a strange collection.

As the *Dyscovera* kept sailing, breaking the strands of weedy hair, Criston yelled, "Add all possible sail—stretch every scrap of canvas!" He ordered them to use daggers and swords to cut the strands. The *Dyscovera* strained against the grasping weed, pulling free by the time the giant demon, or goddess, breached the surface. Her head was the size of a small island, and her eyes locked upon them like a cat's upon its prey.

The crew screamed, and Prester Hannes prayed at the top of his lungs. "In the name of Ondun and Aiden, leave us in peace!"

Rather than rising farther out of the seawater, the titanic woman laughed, a huge sound like rolling thunder. "I am older than your Ondun or his sailor sons. I am patient. I can smell you. I see you. I know you are lifelong sailors. I have other collections of souls, just like these." She smiled as the *Dyscovera* continued its frantic flight. "Most of you will come back to me, sooner or later. I will wait for you."

She closed her eyes and lay back, submerging herself again as she continued laughing. She stirred up large waves that struck the *Dyscovera*'s hull, making the ship rock and sway like a dinghy in a rainstorm. The last strands of seaweed released them, and the vessel lurched ahead with new speed.

Criston's throat was dry as he said, "What was that woman, Prester?"

Hannes stood close to the captain and shook his head, visibly terrified; his hands trembled as he grasped the wooden rail. "Nothing in the Book of Aiden ever prepared me for such a thing."

49 *The* Al-Orizin

Under full sail, the *Al-Orizin* continued southeast, and the weather turned bitter cold. The choppy water became gray instead of blue. They had not sighted land in some time, and even the ancient Map of Urec could not help Saan or Sen Sherufa figure out where they were without any landmarks or navigational points. At night the constellations were entirely unfamiliar.

After Ystya revealed that she was the Key to Creation, Saan had to redraw his own maps of understanding. How could the innocent, ethereal girl be the mysterious treasure sought by Urec, the powerful object that Soldan-Shah Omra had asked the *Al-Orizin* to find? Yet Saan believed her.

He hoped Sikara Fyiri would accept the girl's amazing story, though he did not actually expect it. Shouldn't a devout priestess of Urec leap at the chance to speak with the actual daughter of Ondun? But Fyiri denounced Ystya's claim. Even though she had witnessed the girl's astonishing power—twice now—the sikara was more wedded to her teachings than to miracles. Beneath her façade of skepticism, she seemed genuinely intimidated by Ystya.

Sen Sherufa, on the other hand, asked the mysterious girl many questions, trying to learn more about her abilities, but Ystya did not have all of the answers. "I was on the island for many centuries, but still just a child. Apparently, my mother was pregnant with me when she left Terravitae because of some conflict with Ondun, a scandal or dark secret. I was little more than an infant when my father joined us on the island."

"How can the creator of all things have a scandal?" Fyiri scoffed.

Ystya shrugged. "You've told me how Ondun is portrayed in your church, but to me my parents seem more like people than the omnipotent deities you claim to worship."

"I do not *claim* to worship them!"

Another shrug. "I can only say that if they were so benevolent and omnipotent, my mother would never have drowned my father in the well."

Emphatically denying this, the sikara retreated from Sen Sherufa's cabin, leaving the wooden door swinging open to the cold breeze outside.

Now that they had found the Key to Creation, Saan could have run home along their previous course, but he felt they must be close to Terravitae. He hoped to find the lost, sacred land. There was even a chance Holy Joron could keep them safe from Iyomelka.

Yal Dolicar gave a shrill whistle from the lookout nest. "Captain, you need to see this. There are mountains in the water—white mountains!"

Saan pulled a woolen blanket around himself before stepping out onto the deck with Ystya at his side. Even Grigovar had wrapped himself in extra shirts, no longer leaving his arms bare. Though the air crackled with deep cold, the young woman did not seem uncomfortable in the biting chill, despite her thin garments and slight body.

Ahead, jagged white islands protruded like molars from the water gleaming in the sun. The mounds were entirely covered by glistening snow and ice, and Saan gradually realized the frozen islands were floating.

The icebergs became a maze, forcing the *Al-Orizin* to pick a tortuous path. When they drifted close to a frozen wall, the men came out with their picks, hammers, and shovels and hacked off large chunks, which they stacked in barrels to melt for drinking water.

One of the frozen mountains scraped the bottom of the hull, and Saan yelled out a course correction. "Careful! Hitting one of those would be like running aground on a reef!"

"These are dangerous waters," Sherufa said. "Maybe we should turn back."

Saan gestured behind them. "Iyomelka's still after us somewhere back there. We go forward."

Then as they rounded a particularly large berg, Yal Dolicar let out another startled cry from the lookout nest. "A ship, Captain—a ship, frozen into the ice!"

Ahead, a strange squat craft with tall masts was caught in the flowing embrace of an ice mountain. Its tattered, frost-rimed sails hinted that the vessel had been there for some time. The ship's design was unlike anything Saan had ever seen.

"How can another ship be here, Captain?" Grigovar called. "Who else has ever sailed this far?"

"No one . . . that we know about," Saan said. "Bring us close. I want to go across and see just what that ship has to offer."

"There may be demons aboard," Fyiri admonished, "ready to trap unwary travelers."

"I'll join you," Ystya said, unafraid.

The priestess quickly responded, "Then I will come along as well, to grant Urec's protection, if necessary." Saan didn't comment.

Slow-flowing ice locked the mysterious ship in place against the frozen mountain, but her deck and masts remained clear. Crewmembers threw hooks to grapple the vessels together. Saan was the first to spring across, careful to maintain his footing on the slippery deck, then he helped Ystya over. Grigovar and Fyiri came next, followed by the Saedran chartsman and Yal Dolicar. All open surfaces were glazed with ice—every rope, every spar, every plank. They walked along the eerie deck, their voices hushed.

They soon found the crew. The ancient sailors were in position, their hair shaggy and dark, their clothes thick and lined with fur for a cold voyage. But now they were motionless, frozen instantaneously in place while in the midst of their normal activities.

Saan tried to read the expression of the nearest man. The

sailor's eyes showed neither terror nor pain. Saan rapped the man's cheek with his knuckle, but he was frozen solid, encased in ice.

50 *Gremurr Mines*

In a moment of compassion, Destrar Broeck surprised himself by suggesting that the female prisoner Shetia and her son Ulan move into the villa, since it had once been their home. Though the two remained under heavy guard, some part of him felt better about having them there. He even let the dog be tied up outside, so long as it didn't bark too much. The soldiers in camp had already grown fond of it.

Broeck could have gloated and made the two prisoners suffer by sleeping in drafty tents with the other enemy captives who now served as mine slaves. He could have flaunted the fact that he had seized their home; he could have taunted them because he had executed Tukar.

At one time, he might have done so. Though he still felt the white-hot pain of his grandson Tomas's murder, he found that he didn't want to take his revenge on these two. Maybe someday Broeck would come to believe in innocence again.

The Uraban boy walked into the main room, attracted by the fire in the hearth. Ulan was more subdued now, perhaps because living in the villa reminded him of all he had lost. By now Ulan understood some phrases in Tierran, and Broeck had picked up a few of the foreign words. Firun was there to translate when necessary.

Tonight the boy carried a game board composed of alternating squares of polished wood and jet. With a set expression, not a smile, Ulan set the game board down on the writing desk and emptied a small sheepskin sack of oddly shaped playing pieces onto it.

Broeck was amused. "What are you doing here, boy? I don't know how to play that game."

Persistent, Ulan arranged one set of the pieces on the board. He then looked at the second jumble and nodded toward Broeck.

"I don't have time for games."

With a sigh, Ulan set up the other pieces for the destrar and waited.

Broeck was about to call for his guards when Firun bustled in. "Ulan—there you are! You must not disturb the destrar." He looked up. "Apologies, sir. I'll have him go play with his dog instead." He spoke in Uraban, and the boy answered quickly. When the old servant shook his head, Ulan insisted.

"What's he saying, Firun?" Broeck asked.

"He wants to play *xaries* with you. The boy claims to be quite good at it. He even beat his father several times."

"He wants to beat me, too, I'd wager," Broeck grumbled. "No surprise there. I'm a novice. I don't even know the rules."

Ulan looked disappointed, but he refused to go away. The boy spoke imperiously in Uraban, and Firun relayed with a sigh, "He wants me to explain the rules to you, Destrar. This is *xaries*, a traditional game among Urabans. Perhaps if you learned it, you might have insight into Uraban strategy. All of their leaders play this game. Tukar and Workmaster Zadar had become masters of it."

Broeck stroked his gray beard, appraising the game board and its exotic pieces. He saw hope and eagerness light up the boy's face. "Oh, very well. One game."

Ulan made the first move, and Firun explained the strategy. Broeck moved a piece, not sure what he was doing, but he demonstrated confidence nevertheless. With a chuckle, the boy moved another piece, though Broeck couldn't discern any plan to what he was doing. The destrar narrowed his eyes and studied the board. Obviously Ulan saw *something*.

Broeck sniffed and looked up at the former servant. "Do you have any advice for me? How shall I respond to this?"

The old man seemed amused. "I would not deign to dictate strategy to you, Destrar."

Wearing a faint scowl, Broeck moved another piece, and the boy pounced, taking one of the carved objects. Broeck didn't even know what the piece was called or what its shape was meant to represent, but somehow he had left that piece vulnerable. He glared at Firun again. "Can he do that?"

"Oh, it is a perfectly legal move. I would suggest you guard your flank more carefully, sir."

Firun continued to coach him on the rules, but gave no advice on specific moves. Regardless, the Iborian destrar grasped the general outline of the game. It reminded him of a similar gambling and strategy game that he, Iaros, and other men would play in the cold of winter. In less than an hour, he and Ulan did not need to speak, but let the game communicate for them. Firun's own duties called him away, so he left Ulan and the destrar together.

Ulan did win the first match, but Broeck wasn't disappointed; he actually found it amusing. "Go away now, boy. I have work to do," he said, a little softer this time, but Ulan set up the board again. "I said I don't have time." The boy was undeterred, and when the board was ready he waited patiently. "Oh, all right! But you won't trick me this game. I know how to play now."

Broeck got into the challenge more intently, playing better, and it was a close match. The destrar did win the second game, but Ulan won the third. They were setting up for a fourth when Shetia came in, bleary-eyed and tired. She looked worried and said something to her son that Broeck did not need to have translated. The boy's crestfallen expression—that of any young man who did not want his mother to send him to bed—spoke for itself. With a glance at the game board, Shetia said in broken Tierran, "His father play *xaries* with Ulan." Then she led her son away.

Broeck's heart felt heavy as he imagined this boy sitting across from his father. Maybe he shouldn't have killed Tukar, just kept him as a prisoner, so that Ulan and Shetia could have had their family intact.

And that thought led him to wonder about the last moments of Prince Tomas . . . how the young prince had met the sharpened scimitar that bit down on his neck. Broeck's sense of calm melted away, but at least he didn't need to take his revenge on this Uraban child and his mother.

51 *Calay Castle*

Shouldering emotions he did not know how to express, Ammur Sonnen came to Calay Castle and insisted on seeing Queen Anjine. The army, and Mateo, had been gone for two weeks now, advancing toward Ishalem.

At first she was surprised by the blacksmith's visit, then she felt a sharp stab of guilt: in their shared dark freefall of grief, Anjine and Mateo had reached out to each other, like finally touching a flame to the tinder they had built up for most of their lives. But she felt shamed by it. It had been her own weakness, and she knew Ammur Sonnen would see their actions as an insult to his beloved daughter.

Her skin grew cold. How had he known? Somehow the blacksmith must have heard a whispered rumor, maybe something from a maid who had noticed the queen's absence that night. Why else would he come to the castle, asking to see her? Though she was the queen of Tierra, Anjine didn't know how she could face the accusations of a grieving father.

But when the burly man was escorted into her private wing of the castle, Ammur bowed and averted his eyes. "I have finished my task, Majesty. I brought the fine suit of armor I promised to make for you. It's about time you donned it, if you intend to lead the army in a few months." Two of his apprentices followed him in from the entry hall, carrying components that rattled together. They pulled aside draping cloths to reveal their work.

Anjine, who had forgotten all about the blacksmith's offer, caught her breath as she saw polished steel inlaid with ornate bronze work. The bright metal glinted in sunlight that streamed through the windows of her chamber. Words caught in her throat, and she felt a sudden dizziness of guilty relief. He had not come to accuse her of betraying Vicka's memory, of taking advantage of Mateo's grief. Ammur knew nothing about her love for Mateo; he'd come to honor her, to give her this special gift.

"The cuirass is thin but strong, Majesty, formed to cover your chest and back, yet granting you movement. It is more lightweight than the plate mail for your soldiers who will be in the thick of battle, fighting against Uraban scimitars."

"I intend to be in the thick of things," she said.

His brow furrowed. "Oh, this is more than a costume, Majesty. The suit will protect you from enemy arrows and blades. I would not want so much as a scratch to harm your skin." He showed her the greaves, gauntlets, vambraces, and the airy helmet with its well-oiled visor. The Fishhook symbol had been inset in bronze in the proper places.

He had crafted the suit with great care. After Vicka's death, Ammur must have buried himself in his work, intent on completing the armor, but she could see his unbounded sadness. She held up the helmet and felt proud. "Thank you, Ammur Sonnen."

After the apprentices had spread out the components, the blacksmith said, "We must fit it, Majesty . . . if now is a convenient time?"

She picked up the breastplate, looked at the thin, flexible gauntlet. "Yes, now is a good time." She felt a *need* to wear it, to be a warrior, protected by the blessings of Aiden as well as the love and care of her finest craftsman.

Enifir hurried in. "I will assist in dressing the queen."

Ammur was flustered. "We are not *dressing* the queen, we are *armoring* her." He retrieved a satchel of tools from his apprentices and took up his tongs, pliers, and hammer as if each were a surgeon's implement. He and his young helpers worked to fit the queen's armor, strapping on the cuirass, buckling the greaves, sliding the gauntlets into place over her hands.

With each piece that covered part of her body, Anjine felt more protected, more sheltered . . . and more walled off. That was how she needed to be, as the queen. She had to think of the big picture, of Tierra, of Ishalem, of the enemy. When the hard plate covered her chest, shielding her heart, she allowed herself to think of Mateo and how he had gone off alone. Soon, he and the army would reach the Ishalem wall.

Only yesterday, Anjine had dispatched Comdar Rief with the full Tierran navy. By now, one of her couriers should have gotten through the Corag mountains to deliver her message to Destrar Broeck. One of the three riders had returned, disheveled and disappointed that he had been unable to get through the snowy passes, but she had heard nothing from the two that were sent ahead of him.

She vowed that this would not be a disorganized strike, no matter how energetic her warriors might be. A few years ago, ninety foolhardy riders from Alamont Reach had dashed off on horseback to reclaim Ishalem, only to be slaughtered. And the more recent humiliating rout of the Tierran army at the wall, betrayed by *ra'virs* in their midst, had been another lesson. Anjine did not intend to fail again.

Not until she had won this war and crushed the Urecari enemy would she let herself think of Mateo. The human part of her missed him and longed to be with him, but the queen within chastised her for pondering personal happiness rather than the survival of her land and people. . . .

When the armor was fully fitted and in place, Anjine moved her arms and legs, then turned about. Ammur Sonnen regarded her movements with a critical eye, and added a finishing touch by attaching an embroidered cape displaying the green and blue colors of Tierra.

Enifir brought a looking glass, and Anjine performed a slow rotation, feeling comfortable and strong inside her carapace. "I am a formidable queen, a soldier for Aiden."

"Yes, Majesty, you are," said Ammur.

She would command her army to knock down the Uraban barricade that blocked the Aidenists from the holy city. Though the blacksmith's eyes were still red and his cheeks gaunt, he gave her a faint hard smile, a satisfied smile. The apprentices stared at her with undisguised awe.

Enifir let out a long sigh. "Majesty, you have never looked so beautiful—or so terrifying. You will strike awe and fear into the hearts of the Urecari."

"Good, that is how it should be."

52 *The Road to Ishalem*

The Tierran vanguard had been marching south for weeks, and Ishalem was directly ahead. Though weary, the soldiers were well provisioned, and more supply trains would follow as the army camp swelled at the wall. The initial enthusiasm upon leaving Calay—loud fanfares, waving banners, cheers of townspeople, and the easily given promises of young women—had fallen behind them now, and they settled into a routine of travel. As they approached their destination, however, the marching men picked up the pace.

Mateo rode in the lead between Destrar Shenro and Jenirod. Each day put him miles farther from Anjine, but no closer to contentment. He concentrated on his duty; that, at least, was a thing he could hold on to.

At the southern boundary of Tierra, the terrain became scrubby and rocky, the dry air full of dust. The old Pilgrims' Road was rutted and overgrown because little traffic went to the wall anymore. Though the army was still too far away from God's Barricade for the enemy to see them, Mateo was sure that outriding Uraban scouts had spotted their arrival. The Curlies would be gathering their defenses, preparing to meet another impulsive Tierran attack . . . but Queen Anjine had a plan much more ambitious than the Urabans had seen before.

Mateo looked around as he rode, squinting in the bright sun. Not so many months ago, he had come down here to set up a squalid camp for a thousand doomed Urecari prisoners.

He told himself over and over that this time it would be different. . . .

The presters accompanying the troops held their Fishhook banners high. The marching soldiers came to a halt in the late afternoon to set up their last camp, which would be the army's main base for the next several months. They moved about in a well-practiced flurry of activity, pitching tents, making fire rings, gathering scrub brush, lighting campfires, and digging latrines. Itinerant presters moved from one group to another, offering blessings and sharing the camp food.

Engineers and scouts had ridden into the nearby hills to scavenge trees for the lumber with which to build catapults and siege engines. Supply wagons rolled in, and would continue to do so as more food and material came by boat or by road. Destrar Sazar had set up dropoff points for deliveries along the river routes. This was one of the largest-scale operations Tierra had ever attempted.

Meanwhile, in nearby Ishalem, the followers of Urec would be heading to their sunset church services.

Sooner or later, if Anjine was true to her promise—and she

would be—the queen would join the army for the final campaign, after all of her pieces were in place. He longed to see her, and he dreaded seeing her. Every time Mateo thought of Anjine and the love he could no longer hide, he was reminded of Vicka, too. The two of them hadn't even had a chance. . . .

But Mateo couldn't afford to think of either woman right now. Though the actual fight wouldn't begin for some time yet, defeating the enemy consumed his attention and energy.

As the soldiers set up camp, Destrar Shenro tossed his long brown hair and wandered among his men. After talking to a pair of tired, dusty Alamont riders who had joined the march only that day, Shenro came to Mateo with a gleam in his eye that suggested secrets. "Subcomdar, come with me before the light fades. I have something to show you."

Mateo was ready to set up his headquarters tent, eat his evening meal (preferably alone, but he knew Jenirod would likely join him), then rest. He generally spent little time among the men at night, avoiding their campfire stories and evening songs. He did not want to dampen the unabashed enthusiasm of the mostly untried soldiers. "Is it important?"

Shenro smiled. "It'll show you how to take Ishalem and win the war. It's going to make a great deal of difference to our plans for storming the wall."

Mateo did not have any immediate plans for storming the wall; their multi-pronged assault was not scheduled for more than two months yet.

Jenirod came up to the officers' tents just in time to hear the comment. "That's a bold statement, Destrar. You've found a way to bring Ondun back and sweep the enemy from the world?"

"Oh, nothing so extreme—but it should impress even an Eriettan."

Jenirod raised his eyebrows. "Then it must be impressive indeed."

Like an excited boy, Shenro led the two men out of the camp and into the grassy hills. The two dusty riders also joined him, each carrying a standard bow slung over his shoulders, as well as a long, thin package wrapped in canvas. The small group trudged through knee-high rustling grasses, circled a hillside, then emerged in a broad meadow studded with gray boulders.

Shenro whispered to the two riders, who answered with confident nods. They laid their long canvas packages on the ground, while Mateo and Jenirod exchanged curious looks.

Like a showmaster beginning a performance, Shenro placed his hands on his narrow hips. "These fellows are skilled archers from Bora's Bastion. Everyone knows that Alamont archers are the finest in the Tierran military." The destrar scanned the meadow, then pointed to a clump of lichen-spattered rocks overgrown with grasses. "You see those boulders? Would you agree that's about the typical range of a bow shot?"

When he was younger, Mateo had trained under Destrar Shenro and practiced for many months shooting arrows out on the Alamont prairies. "A bit far, but I could probably make that shot, depending on the wind." He didn't see why the man was so excited.

"These two men will demonstrate." Shenro rubbed his palms together. "And then we'll move to the interesting part."

Each rider removed his traditional bow, drew an arrow from his quiver, nocked it, and pulled back the string. Without taking careful aim, they loosed their shots. Mateo shaded his eyes in the low light. The arrows flew upward, then plunged down to clatter on the target rocks.

"I've seen Alamont archers many times," Mateo said. "This is nothing new."

Unable to restrain either his smile or his excitement, Shenro motioned for the men to unroll the canvas packages, each of which contained a new longbow made of laminated strips of hardwood, curved and then recurved.

Mateo bent forward to inspect them. "I've never seen a bow like this before."

"It's a new design we developed in Alamont, a carefully guarded secret. Anyone who saw or worked on the project was held in closed quarters and remains under house arrest."

Jenirod was startled. "House arrest? Isn't that a bit extreme?"

"As security, not punishment. Too many *ra'virs* have already harmed us, and we dare not let the enemy discover these new bows. You'll see why."

When the two riders took up the new longbows, stringing them required all of their strength. With their odd, doubly curved profiles, the bows stood nearly as tall as the strong men who carried them. Once strung, they thrummed with energy.

"Now watch," Shenro said, his eyes gleaming. "Men, please impress my guests."

Without saying a word, the archers each nocked an arrow and drew the string back, straining as they did so, then released. The arrows soared out, flying high—and kept going. The shafts had barely begun their downward arc by the time they passed the target boulders. The arrows dwindled in the distance and landed well past the rocks at the far edge of the prairie. They went so far Mateo could barely see where they struck.

"That's twice the range of a normal bow!" Jenirod exclaimed.

Shenro was smug and happy. "Now you see why we can't let *ra'virs* discover these? My archers are well practiced, and can hit a target so far away you can barely see it. Won't that be a nice surprise to spring on the enemy at the wall?"

"Yes, it will," Mateo said. "We'll have to factor this into our plans. How many of those bows do you have?"

"I've had craftsmen working without rest for the past month, ever since we tested and proved the new bow design. These men just came from Bora's Bastion with their report. A hundred specially trained archers with a hundred new longbows will join us in camp within the next week or so."

Even Jenirod was pleased. "And you've kept it a secret all this time?"

"I didn't want the men to travel with the rest of the army. There's always the chance that someone might talk."

Shenro told his men to unstring the bows and wrap them in the canvas before anyone could see. In the deepening dusk, no hidden observer could have made out the details anyway. "Ah, Subcomdar, I tell you this is going to be a glorious campaign."

"I hope you're right." They returned to camp. Tomorrow, the Tierran military would begin the siege of Ishalem.

53 Sapier's Glory

Aboard the flagship of the Tierran naval fleet—seventy-three vessels ranging from large carracks to heavy cogs to swift patrol caravels—Comdar Torin Rief studied the waters of the Oceansea. According to the charts, his warships would reach the holy city in three days. The warm sea looked peaceful, but blood had stained this water red many times over the past two decades.

According to the plan, the Aidenist navy would blockade Ishalem's western harbor, perhaps capture some of the foreign merchant ships. Rief's primary goal was to close off the harbor so that the Uraban occupiers would have no ready supply of weapons, food, and other cargo. The siege couldn't be entirely effective, though, since the Curlies still had overland routes as well as the port on the Middlesea side of the isthmus. Nevertheless, Rief's blockade would cause hardship, wreak havoc, strike fear—and send a message to the soldan-shah. With Queen Anjine's army encamped along the wall and swelling in numbers, the Urecari would sense Ondun's anger gathering against them like a summer thunderstorm.

However, as the ships sailed south, the crew were worried about what the Curlies might unleash against them. Everyone knew that Destrar Tavishel and his Soeland warships had been annihilated by some terrible Urecari weapon. Tavishel's sturdy whaling vessels should not have been easy targets, but every one had been splintered and burned. None of Tavishel's crew had survived, as far as Rief knew.

Information about the disaster was sparse, but the comdar suspected the Urecari had a weapon fueled by explosive firepowder. The recipe for the incredible substance had only just been brought back to Calay with the Gremurr refugees; while firepowder was too new for him to grasp its full possibilities for war, Queen Anjine had already made plans. . . .

From *Sapier's Glory*, his flagship, Rief stared across the sunlit water. The dapples of golden light had a hypnotic effect. He was a tall and thin man with unusually black hair for a Tierran; his narrow face sported a scar from a previous battle. Once appointed comdar of the Tierran military, Rief had maintained a crisp, professional demeanor, and never let himself be seen out of his formal uniform.

Torin Rief was a quiet man who liked to plan his conversation rather than let words just spill from his mouth. From an early age he had studied warfare, and his fascination had rapidly become practical instead of theoretical. He'd fought against the Curlies in several engagements, one on land, two aboard patrol ships. The enemy had wounded him and cut off two of his fingers, but he had killed many of them to make up for it.

Rief rarely saw his wife and three children—of late, he didn't want to. She had gotten pregnant and given birth to a son, their first, but Rief had been out on campaign, sleeping in military camps, when the child was conceived. He knew how to count months as well as any other person.

She tried to tell him that the baby was a miraculous blessing from Aiden, insisting that she had not been unfaithful to him, but he rebuked her for embarrassing him with such silliness. Rief did not publicly call her an adulteress, or denounce the son as a bastard; he merely went off on a new campaign, knowing he would be at Ishalem for many months.

He could not stop wondering whether the other two children were his. He let her keep his name and her counterfeit honor, knowing that he had made far worse sacrifices in the name of the war. She might have her lovers and her shame, but he would have Ishalem and history. . . .

The crews went about their familiar daily work, exchanging and embellishing stories about their previous engagements against the Curlies. The recountings grew more extravagant and more unbelievable as the days passed. Comdar Rief listened with a wry smile that he kept to himself: if such tales were true, then he had a crew of titans who would surely sweep away the enemy with a mere glance.

Every Tierran mainsail in the fleet was painted with the Fishhook, a sinuous curve tipped with a deadly barb. He liked to think that the hook's point was sharp enough to gouge out the Eye of Urec that all Uraban sails displayed.

During the voyage, Rief thought of happier days when merchant ships had sailed back and forth, trading with exotic foreigners, when pilgrims went freely to Ishalem. Even in those good times, though, the Urecari had been hiding their hatred; they did not want a life of peace and harmony with their rivals, never believed in showing tolerance toward the followers of Aiden. . . .

When the fleet reached the Edict Line marked on their navigation charts, Rief gave orders to tack eastward toward Ishalem, and announced to the crew, "We're in enemy waters now." The men peered over the side into the blue Oceansea, as if expecting to see an obvious change.

From the lookout nest, the young man called down, "There's a ship on the port horizon, sir. A colored sail—the Eye of Urec!" His voice cracked, not with excitement but with the embarrassing changes of puberty.

Rief shaded his eyes, trying to spot the vessel. "Change course. Let's do a little hunting before we reach Ishalem."

The seventy-three Tierran ships struck out toward the lone foreign vessel. The men gathered their swords and knives, sharpening the edges for a heated battle, though it became obvious that the target was merely a fishing boat, not any kind of military threat. "Capture it anyway," Rief said.

Standing next to him, the first mate mumbled, "And what if that vessel carries one of the fiery Urecari weapons, sir? The thing that destroyed Destrar Tavishel's fleet?" Damnably, his voice was loud enough for others to hear.

Rief made a scornful sound, but already a chill had gone down his spine. "Why would a fishing boat carry such a devastating thing?"

"Could be a decoy, sir. Maybe they mean to lure us close to a ship that looks helpless."

As he heard the sailors mumble, Rief realized that others had formed the same speculation. He was a cautious man, and he did not forget Tavishel's hubris. If nothing else, the Soeland destrar's disastrous failure provided a warning, an example, for the comdar. "Proceed with caution. Look sharp."

As the Tierran vessels closed in on the Uraban fishing boat, the foreigners aboard waved their hands. They looked panicked, obviously unable to get away.

The first mate considered. "They seem to be surrendering, Comdar."

"Yes, they *seem* to be, but it could just be a ruse. I'm not going to take the chance. Archers, light your arrows!"

Five of his men strung their bows and dipped their arrows in pitch, while bowmen aboard adjacent warships scrambled to get their own weapons, anxious to participate. "Loose your arrows when ready."

Two of the archers were so eager that their smoking arrows fell short and plunged into the water, but most of the shafts struck the foreign boat.

Although the panicked Uraban fishermen flailed colored rags in an attempt to signal, the rain of arrows hammered into the sails, the deck, the rigging. As the fire caught and spread, another wave of arrows peppered the boat. Either through intent or by happy accident, dozens of shafts skewered the pitiful Uraban fishermen, pinning them to the deck as smoke began to rise.

"Enough—stop wasting arrows!" Rief called. The fishing boat was already ablaze. There would be no taking of prisoners or confiscating cargo.

The first mate pursed his lips. "It seems they don't have the weapon that destroyed Destrar Tavishel."

"I suppose not. But it was a good exercise anyway."

The Tierran fleet sailed away as flames consumed the fishing boat, leaving a tall smoky stain in the sky. Though they were still far out at sea, lookouts in the high lighthouses on the Ishalem coast could probably see it. The Curlies would know that something bad had happened.

Rief ordered the ships forward, closing in on Ishalem.

54 *Off the Coast of Khenara*

Soldan Vishkar had never considered himself much of a sailor, and certainly not a commodore to lead a fleet of ships, whether designed for battle or for hauling cargo. In fact, he still had difficulties imagining himself as soldan of Outer Wahilir, though he understood why Omra had selected him for the role.

And now the soldan-shah had given him another mission, one even more important than building the new church in Ishalem.

Vishkar would do the best possible job, not out of ambition, but because Omra had asked it.

After weeks of sailing down the coast, Vishkar was impressed with the number of ships he had gathered. The ragtag fleet was a motley assortment of large fishing vessels, cargo ships, and military patrol craft. When he stopped at coastal towns and spoke with the harbormasters and the captains of any ships in port, Vishkar was not aggressive or pompous. He merely brought out Omra's decree and informed them in a businesslike manner that he was commandeering their vessels in the name of the soldan-shah.

He hoped this imposing fleet would be sufficient to scare off further Aidenist attacks and protect the vulnerable canal across the isthmus. He didn't really want to face a major naval battle, since his swordfighting skills were rather rusty.

Accompanying him, more for their own amusement than out of military necessity, were the seven remaining Nunghal ships. More than ninety of the foreign vessels had sailed home with their powerful cannon and firepowder, leaving only these adventurous few behind.

Even the adventurers, however, had little interest in Uraba's war preparations or the growing defensive fleet. Now that Vishkar had reached far Lahjar, the southernmost city in the land, the seven shipkhans told him they would catch the seasonal winds and sail home.

As the Uraban fleet turned about for the long voyage north to Ishalem, the shipkhans came aboard his flagship to say farewell. Crowded around his table, they ate fresh fruits and skewers of spiced lamb (which Vishkar preferred to fish). He laughed when the Nunghals laughed. They presented him with ivory carvings and a sharkskin vest that barely fit him (and also made him look silly, though the Nunghals gave approving whistles).

Because they had given him gifts, he was required to reciprocate. He ransacked his bureau and found two bronze armbands, a medallion, a bottle of pungent perfume (which made him sneeze anyway), an orange scarf with silver bangles, and a leather-bound book with blank pages that he had always meant to use as a journal. He had no idea what the Nunghals would do with the book, but they seemed to admire it. Though the shipkhans kept ledgers, he wasn't certain they had a written language.

Most of the Nunghals were not hampered by their inability to speak the local tongue. They had adopted the Uraban system of numbers quickly enough, which let them haggle prices. They used hand gestures and signs, offered objects for trade, and picked up a few key words to get their points across. They learned how to request food items, women, and general services, doggedly repeating mispronounced words until someone understood and gave them what they wanted. The seven shipkhans made no attempt at proper grammar or expanding their vocabulary.

Vishkar valued words, however, and saw the beauty in the Uraban language. He was proud of several long-form poems he'd written, though he would never read them aloud to the foreign visitors. He doubted the Nunghal clans even had such things as poets. . . .

"We say farewell," one of the shaggy captains stated, then bowed.

"I am very sorry to see you go," Vishkar said. "Very sorry. We will miss your ships and your cannon."

"You have ships." A second shipkhan gestured vaguely, indicating the numerous vessels around them, outside the captain's cabin. "We sold Ishalem four cannon."

"We could always use more. Of both."

"Want sailing home," said the third captain. "We again trade next year." He scratched his head, searching for words. "Not come for . . . war."

And then it was time for them to go. Vishkar reached out to shake their callused hands formally, but the Nunghal shipkhans enveloped him in vigorous bear hugs, one after another after another. He waved farewell as the Nunghals climbed into boats and rowed back to their gray-sailed ships.

When they were gone, Vishkar stood alone on the deck of his flagship for a long time, watching as the seven exotic vessels raised their spars and stretched the accordioned sails.

Antos, the captain of the flagship, stood beside Vishkar. The man was short with enormously muscled arms. He shook his head as he watched the Nunghals go. "We don't need them, Soldan. They were undisciplined anyway, and this navy must be a fighting force that can defeat the 'Hooks."

Vishkar grunted. "When battle plans are reinforced by a hundred Nunghal cannons, ship movements require little finesse." He didn't have the tactical background to be a good naval commander, but he would have to learn. "But we will follow the Map and fight our own battles."

Captain Antos was satisfied with the reply.

55 *Olabar*

Whenever he visited the Uraban capital, Asaddan marveled at the whitewashed buildings and tiled roofs, the bustling bazaars and the church minarets. He was pleased to return to the familiar marketplace and the stalls where vendors sold olives, lemons, and honey pastries.

"So this is fabled Olabar." Ciarlo adjusted the hood that covered his face. He looked with interest at the market stalls: candlemakers, rug weavers, potters, food merchants with sizzling skewers, fabric dyers, tanners, spice merchants, thread-makers. "This is also the home of the church of Urec, where the sikaras preach their hatred."

"It is, but not everyone listens. There are many good people here."

"Then those are the ones who need to hear my message."

Ciarlo touched his chest to draw out the fishhook pendant he had fashioned from scraps of material, but Asaddan put out a large hand to prevent him. "Remember what I told you! Have a care, unless you want to end up being stoned, or hung from a hook, or whatever these people do to heretics."

"I am not the heretic. They are."

"That depends upon your point of view. Now be quiet and follow me. I have many friends in the city—including the soldan-shah. We will be safe here."

After helping Ciarlo escape from the *Moray* during the night, Asaddan had hidden him in an alley near a tailor's shop several streets up from the harbor. He pounded on the door until a red-eyed proprietor appeared, wondering what sort of clothing emergency might occur at such a late hour. Asaddan asked to purchase several sets of clothes, and though the shopkeeper was puzzled, his questions vanished when the Nunghal gave him gold coins.

Weary and sore, Ciarlo had huddled in the alley shadows wearing the filthy clothes of a galley slave, still injured from his harsh treatment. Asaddan pushed the pile of new garments into his hands, and the Aidenist changed into traditional clothes, wrapping himself up and pulling a hood over his light hair and pale skin. Asaddan gave him a quick inspection. "Good enough. We have to get out of here as soon as we can. Lean on me, and we'll move at your pace."

Hurrying was problematic, though. Ciarlo's arms were stiff, his hands and wrists swollen and abraded, his legs weak. He had spent weeks, perhaps months, chained to a bench and prevented from walking. As Asaddan guided his companion through the streets, he expected to hear shouts and alarms. Once the *Moray* sailors discovered that their captives were gone, the search would spread out in all different directions.

Asaddan needed to find some other solution. He led Ciarlo inland along a rutted dirt road and came upon a small cottage set back from the path. Inside a rickety corral stood an old gray mare, hoof cocked, half asleep. She was not a sturdy beast, obviously not accustomed to carrying riders, but the mare would do. With Ciarlo off his feet, they could travel faster.

Asaddan knew that if he roused the family and offered them money for the horse, they might raise an alarm. Instead, as quietly as he could, he helped his companion up onto the placid horse, then crept to the closed cottage door and left several *cuar* coins on the step, more than enough to pay for a replacement horse.

Holding the halter rope, Asaddan hurried into the night with the mare jogging alongside him. Hunched over, Ciarlo threaded his fingers through the mane and hung on.

They headed off on the main coastal road toward Olabar. Since he was accustomed to running across the Nunghal plains, Asaddan did not tire easily. They covered many miles before dawn, but during daylight they hid in the nearby olive groves. The next night, they covered many more miles.

Eventually, Asaddan began to relax. No matter how angry Captain Belluc might be, searchers wouldn't come this far in pursuit of a mere galley slave. Besides, they would expect any freed Aidenist to head west toward Tierra instead of in the opposite direction, toward the Uraban capital and the heart of the Urecari church. Ciarlo had insisted on going there.

The man wanted to preach the Book of Aiden to anyone who would listen; he was also desperate for news about his sister, who had been kidnapped so long ago. After more than two decades, it seemed impossible that Adrea could still be alive, but the man clung to hope.

Asaddan knew that Saan's mother, Istar, was also a captured Aidenist from long ago, and *she* had survived in Uraba. He thought perhaps she could help.

Now, as they moved through the press of people in the streets of Olabar, Ciarlo kept trying to brush back his hood so he could see, but Asaddan tugged the covering back in place. "People will stare at *me* enough, but you should not call attention to yourself."

"They will have to see me if they are to hear my words when I preach."

"Not now! I have no idea how these people will react when you start telling them things they don't want to hear."

In the shadows of his hood, Ciarlo wore a benign smile. "I spent all that time chained to the oars. I was keelhauled. I watched them burn the Tales of the Traveler. I think I understand how Urabans might react." He picked up the pace. "But I can't abandon what I must do. Once they know the truth, they will realize Aiden was good. Their Urec did similar things, and he was also a son of Ondun. The people cannot hear only one side of the story."

Asaddan spoke in a gruff voice out of the corner of his mouth. "Nunghals have a different version of the tale, too, but when I tried to explain our beliefs to the sikaras, they ridiculed my religion and called it unbelievable."

Ciarlo would not be deterred. "A farmer has to plant many seeds before a fruitful crop will grow. If I tell enough people, *someone* will believe."

"Maybe so, but not right now." Asaddan tugged the hood farther down over the man's fair face. "Be patient. Let me talk to Soldan-Shah Omra first."

Asaddan had sold the gray mare as soon as they arrived in the city, and now he found a bustling inn near the harbor. He decided against quieter lodgings on a side street, because this busy one received sailors, merchants, and caravan drivers from Lahjar to Kiesh. The innkeeper saw enough strangers from far-flung lands that he wouldn't be overly interested in Asaddan or his quiet companion.

After securing a dinner of stringy mutton and root vegetables with the last of his coins, the Nunghal carried the platter up to their room. Asaddan wolfed down his meal while Ciarlo picked at his. The Aidenist seemed restless, but Asaddan cautioned, "Wait here until I have news for you." He finished his food, set the platter aside, and turned to go. "Promise me you'll stay in the room while I go to the Olabar palace. If I can convince the soldan-shah to speak with you, you might have a chance. In the meantime, don't talk to anyone."

Ciarlo touched his fishhook pendant. "I have waited so long already, but I can endure another afternoon." Implicit in his tone, however, was that if Asaddan did not achieve his purpose, Ciarlo would go down to the inn's common room and preach the Book of Aiden there. Even the big Nunghal wasn't sure he could protect Ciarlo then.

When Asaddan arrived at the palace and asked to speak with the soldan-shah, Kel Rovik lowered his voice. "He is in a foul mood—we just learned of two more merchant ships captured in the Middlesea by those pirates from Gremurr. The son of the Abilan soldan was aboard one of them." He shook his head. "Maybe you should wait until later."

Asaddan made light of the warning. "Omra should be happy to see me. I have news to share."

"Alas, the soldan-shah avoids news these days," Rovik said. "Too many bad reports."

With feigned casualness, Asaddan entered the throne room where Omra sat alone on the dais, studying documents. The leader's face wore a dark expression, but when he saw the guest his demeanor softened. "I'm glad to see you again, my friend, though these are not good times."

Asaddan noted that the weight of responsibilities had aged the soldan-shah greatly in just the past few years. "When are times ever good? I don't know why anyone would want to be khan or soldan-shah. You face one problem after another."

"These days I am consumed with thoughts of how to destroy the Aidenists. Again and again they hurt us. Why doesn't Ondun just make the world open up and swallow them, the way Arikara was leveled by a quake?" He clenched his fists.

Asaddan was taken aback by the intensity of his tone. "Not all Aidenists are so hateful, Omra. Perhaps you just haven't met the right ones."

The soldan-shah glowered as he looked down at the documents. "Countless reports of fishing boats, cargo vessels, ore barges seized in the Middlesea! Those waters were always safe, but Aidenist pirates now cruise the coast, attacking us with my own ironclad ships. They prey on our defenseless fishermen and traders, and none of my warships can fight them."

Omra's rising anger startled him. "I thought you had your own ironclad, Soldan-Shah."

"The *Golden Fern* alone is not enough for the battle I need to wage. We have to retaliate somehow, but I have no force that would be sufficient for the task. How I wish your Nunghal fleet had stayed behind. Those hundred ships could have sailed through Unwar's canal and recaptured Gremurr."

Asaddan swallowed, lowered his eyes. "I'm sorry, Soldan-Shah. They were eager to voyage home instead of involving themselves in this war. Maybe as a neutral party they could have talked with Tierra and tried to broker a peace—"

"The Aidenists are *monsters*, Asaddan!" Omra looked up, his eyes blazing. "They piled a thousand severed heads at the Ishalem wall as revenge for the death of their boy prince, and now I vow that even *ten thousand* Aidenist heads will not be enough to avenge the murder of Tukar."

"And then won't the queen want a hundred thousand heads for her revenge? Can you see any end to this?"

The soldan-shah's voice was quiet. "No, Asaddan. No, I can't."

Asaddan, who had never seen such violence in Omra, decided that this might not be the best time to tell him about Ciarlo after all. He took a step backward. "When the days are quieter, Soldan-Shah, maybe we can dine together or play a game of *xaries*?"

"I would like that—if the days ever grow quieter." Omra seemed distracted, and Asaddan left quickly, greatly alarmed by the conversation. Ciarlo would be in great danger indeed if he ever revealed himself.

The Nunghal decided to find a more sympathetic listener.

It was unusual to request a private audience with Omra's First Wife, but Asaddan didn't care about stepping on the toes of protocol ministers. He had grown very close to Istar's son during the first sand coracle journey across the desert to the Nunghal lands, and Saan had told him the heartwrenching story of how his mother had come to be in Uraba.

Glad to have the Nunghal's company, she served him tea, pistachio pastries, and dates. Though he had his own reasons for wanting to talk to her, he listened with interest as she described what she knew of Saan's current adventures, as conveyed by Sen Sherufa via the sympathetic journal. After she had brought Asaddan up to date, he leaned forward, clasped his hands together. "My Lady, I brought someone to Olabar—someone I think you should meet. He is a stranger to Uraba, but the two of you have much in common."

Istar was curious. "Well then, bring him here and introduce me. It's lonely with my three daughters gone to Arikara."

Asaddan shifted uncomfortably. "You'll soon understand why his identity must remain secret, my Lady. It would be best if you quietly came to our inn at dusk. After you've met him, you can decide what to do."

Istar laughed. "You're being very mysterious. But I'll accept your recommendation. I'll meet him, as you ask."

56 *The* Al-Orizin

Surrounded by icebergs in air that was breathtakingly cold, Saan stepped gingerly across the deck of the ancient frozen ship. The petrified sailors were entirely coated with ice, as if caught in a terrible spell in the middle of their daily activities, frozen solid before they even suspected their danger. One man had a finger raised, pointing at something that was no longer there; another had been solidified in the middle of a sneeze; a third had become one with the icy rope he pulled, his frozen arms bulging with the strain. Even now, the cold was so intense that each breath felt like inhaling sharp needles.

Sen Sherufa was both intrigued and frightened. "What could do this? It must have happened in an instant."

Saan whispered to Ystya. "Is this your mother's work?"

But the ivory-haired girl was mystified. "I don't recognize the power." She sniffed the air. "I doubt there is any danger now, though—this magic is old . . . very old."

"The men look so alive," Grigovar said, with a hint of intimidation in his voice. He didn't go close enough to touch any of the figures.

"Careful, they'll jump out at you!" Yal Dolicar teased, darting his flattened hand in front of the other man's face. The big reef diver did not appreciate it.

Tentatively, Saan asked Ystya, "Can you awaken these strangers? As the Key to Creation . . ."

The girl shook her head. "They may look lifelike, but these men are long dead. For many centuries, I would guess." She looked around the icebergs, heard a distant crack and crash as a chunk of white ice calved off and fell into the water.

Sen Sherufa studied the details of the frozen crew, their clothing and facial features. "Note the tattoos, Captain. I've seen symbols like that before." She indicated a thorny pattern on each man's left cheek, and a diamond mark clearly visible through the frozen film on the back of their hands.

"Didn't the Nunghals have patterns like that?" Saan frowned, trying to remember designs he had seen on some of the nomadic clansmen.

"Similar . . . but details can change over the years and distance. Given enough time and miles, things that started out the same become unrecognizable." The Saedran woman regarded the ship's rigging style, the trapezoidal sails, the curve of the hull. "Nunghals have legends of two sailor brothers and how their main clans were stranded on uncharted shores . . ."

As a breeze gusted, some frost from the rigging ropes broke free and tinkled down like crystal chimes. In her scramble to get out of the way, Sikara Fyiri slipped on the icy deck and came down on her backside; her body was only bruised, but her dignity was severely injured. Yal Dolicar bent over laughing at her, until a piece of falling ice struck the back of his head.

Grigovar brushed a frozen chunk from his shoulder, unruffled. "I don't like the looks of this ship, Captain, and I don't like where the *Al-Orizin* is, either. Beware we don't find ourselves frozen into one of these ice mountains, too. Whatever sorcery did this might come back."

"We'll stay just long enough to look around. There might be something belowdecks. Let's see if this vessel has anything we can use."

"Or anything of value," Dolicar added.

Saan found a closed-off cabin—the captain's quarters, he hoped—but the wooden door was cemented shut with ice. He hammered it with his shoulder, and the door shattered into frozen planks. Shrugging gamely, Saan entered the room.

The cabin's frost-covered windows allowed only an eerie gray light to filter in. As Saan's eyes adjusted, he spotted a broad-shouldered, bald man with a thick dark beard seated at his table. He wore an insulated tunic made from the reddish fur of some animal. His arm rested on a rime-encrusted tabletop, his fingers clasping a brittle quill in the act of writing. Nearby, a clay ink bottle had shattered, spilling crumbly black crystals of ink.

Under heavy eyebrows, the frozen man's gaze was directed toward several charts spread out on a navigation table. The papers were glazed onto the table with a varnish of rippled ice as thick as a pane of glass that distorted the lines and letters on the ancient chart, making it illegible.

Saan said aloud, "So, my fellow captain, what do you have to tell me? Where have we sailed? And how can we find Terravitae?"

Not surprisingly, the petrified man did not answer.

Yal Dolicar considered the thick wooden beams across the cabin ceiling and running down the wall; each was carved with a series of blocky totems. "I saw designs like this long ago, when I went to Iboria. Now that's a cold and miserable place . . . but then, so are these seas." He pointed to the crude carving of a bearded, angry-looking man. "This looks like a frost giant. Why would these sailors on the other side of the world have the same legends as northern Tierrans?"

Hovering at the cabin's doorway, shivering with cold and reluctant to enter the small room, Fyiri made a skeptical noise. "Who can say what causes fearful people to make up silly stories?"

"Maybe frost giants truly exist," Ystya said. "Ondun didn't create everything. There are older and more powerful beings in the world."

Fyiri responded with a rude snort.

Sen Sherufa was interested in the charts on the table. "We need these maps, whether or not we understand the notations. I might be able to read common root words."

With his dagger Saan pried the man's fur sleeves free of the table's coating of ice. "Sorry to disturb you, my fellow captain." When he tried to lift the stiff arm, though, the limb broke away with a sharp, hollow snap at the elbow. Red and tan crystals fell from the jagged stump. Saan was more embarrassed than horrified.

"That doesn't solve our problem," Sherufa said. "How can we chip away the ice without damaging those charts?"

As a solution, Grigovar simply smashed the legs of the table, picked up the entire tabletop—wood, ice, and charts—and tucked it under his arm. "We can worry about that back on the *Al-Orizin*."

On a thin wooden shelf, Yal Dolicar discovered four gold coins imprinted with an unusual design. He pried the coins free with the tip of his dagger and pocketed them with a crooked smile and a shrug; Saan indulged him.

"We've disturbed these sailors enough," Ystya said. "Can we go back to the ship now?"

Outside, the cloudy sky grew grayer, and the icebergs seemed to have crowded closer. Tied up to the strange ship, the *Al-Orizin*'s hull creaked. "Best to sail on, before we all freeze," Grigovar said.

"Or before the frost giants come back." Yal Dolicar's teasing tone fell flat.

Saan scanned the floating white mountains, half expecting to see a giant bearded figure emerge from the ice crags.

When he heard his lookout shout, he couldn't make out the words, but he saw his crew pointing at the icebergs, at the water. Rather than a frost giant, though, he saw a sinuous blue-and-silver form that undulated through the gray waves.

The cold waters parted, and a scaly metallic blue head rose up. A graceful knurled horn protruded from its snout. A whirlpool of frost curled from its blowhole as the monster let out a loud hoot, then dove again and circled the two trapped ships.

"It is Raathgir," Ystya said.

57 *Ishalem*

From the high lighthouse tower on the Ishalem headlands, Kel Unwar used a spyglass to peer out at the waters beyond the harbor.

For nearly a week he had been expecting the arrival of Soldan Vishkar and his warships. Without the hundred Nunghal vessels, Unwar felt vulnerable, and he needed guardians to protect the canal mouth. His men had finished mounting the four bronze cannons in stone emplacements at the mouth of the harbor, their barrels pointed out to sea. The weapons would not be enough to stop a concerted attack, however.

Unwar had already sent word to Olabar to inform the soldan-shah about the Aidenist army camped to the north of God's Barricade, but he was not overly concerned. Even though they were assembling catapults, the Tierrans could not penetrate the towering stone wall; Unwar had built it to be eternal.

Still, these Aidenist soldiers seemed far more determined than before. And every time he saw their army, their Fishhook banners, their hateful faces, he was reminded of what they had done to Alisi. . . .

Clad in silver mask, dark cloak, and black gloves, the Teacher—his sister—joined him in the breezy tower room. Alisi peered through the thin slits in her mask. "We lost an important weapon when the Aidenists rooted out my *ra'virs*. If any still remain hidden among the Tierran soldiers camped at the wall, I have no way to contact them."

"The 'Hooks will be suspicious of any unusual behavior, especially now," Unwar said. "But they can't have discovered all of our *ra'virs*."

"My students know their mission, and we will have to trust them. The Tierran army clearly plans to stay for some time."

Alisi spotted the ships on the horizon before he did. She pointed, and he turned the spyglass. "Vessels coming—a great many sails."

He let out a satisfied sigh upon seeing the impressive fleet, running calculations in his mind. "Vishkar has done well. This is better than I had hoped. We may even have enough vessels to sail through to the Middlesea and strike Gremurr." He knew the soldan-shah would be pleased at that.

But Alisi kept staring. Sunlight reflected off her burnished mask, and her voice had a razor's edge. "Those are not Vishkar's ships."

Unwar jerked up his spyglass again, twisted the barrel to sharpen the focus, and realized that the sails had been painted with a barbed curve—a Fishhook. The sight sizzled into his eye like a hot nail.

The Aidenist warships dispersed to form a cordon along the mouth of the Ishalem harbor, leaving themselves room to hunt down any vessels that ventured too close. Over the next hour, they encircled and seized four outbound ships and chased off three military patrol craft.

As soon as he saw the ships arrive, Unwar sounded the alarm and had his soldiers launch war galleys to go fight the Tierrans, but they were greatly outnumbered and broke off without engaging the enemy. Instead, Unwar stationed his forces at the mouth of the canal, to prevent the invaders from penetrating the waterway at all costs; he sent anxious archers to man all of the watchtowers along the length of the canal, should the Tierrans succeed in breaking through.

But the Aidenist fleet was content to stay out of cannon range, far from the war galleys, like vultures waiting to feed on a carcass.

"Why won't they come in and attack? They are cowards." Unwar paced around the upper lighthouse room.

"They might attack, but they would never hold Ishalem. We would overthrow them within a week, a month." She watched the ships out at sea. "No, they are blockading us, which is just as bad. We can't sail in or out. They've cut us off."

Unwar couldn't understand the strategy. "Do they think the great city of Ishalem can be harmed by a siege like that? We can still get supplies by other routes." He wrestled with the unanswerable questions. Though he was a kel, a military leader, by vocation he was an engineer, a planner. He understood how things worked, but this behavior had no logical explanation. "What are they trying to accomplish, Alisi? And what does the army camped outside the wall intend to do?"

He remembered the foolhardy Alamont horsemen who had ridden to Ishalem thinking that a mere ninety brigands could take the holy city from the entire Uraban army. Perhaps Queen Anjine and her military didn't understand the geography of the isthmus and of Uraba. Could she truly be so ignorant? He didn't think so.

With a whistle and a smash, several huge boulders hammered into the high wall at the northern end of the city; he could see the puffs of white rock powder from the impact. The Aidenist army had begun using their catapults.

Shrill horn blasts, made tinny by the distance, sounded an alarm, and soldiers rushed to God's Barricade. Unwar drew in a long breath to quell his surge of anger. He said through gritted teeth, "They are like vermin, attacking any weak spot of exposed flesh."

Alisi stepped away from the window so that her ominous form fell into shadow again. "They are not stupid, Unwar. The fact that you do not understand their tactics does not mean they won't surprise you. Be vigilant. You can be certain they're planning something terrible."

"In that, I never underestimate them."

58 *The* Dyscovera

The next island they encountered was small and relatively featureless, its hills covered with golden grasses and hunchbacked shrubs whose branches pointed along the direction of the prevailing winds.

With every landfall, Prester Hannes hoped they would at last find a sign that proved to everyone the correctness of his convictions. Hannes had not deserved his initial punishment and never felt guilty, never experienced doubts. His faith was his anchor, and his vision was crystal clear. He pitied those who did not possess his absolute certainty. The world would be a better place if all people had such clarity and conviction. When one carried the word of Ondun, there was no room for doubt and indecision.

He could only hope the captain would come around as soon as he saw the proof for himself. He could sense that Captain Vora *wanted* to resolve their differences so they could stand united when they reached Terravitae.

Now, as the two ship's boats ground ashore on the rocky beach, Hannes set foot on the solid land like a conqueror. "I claim this land, whether inhabited or not, in the name of Aiden." He regarded the captain with stiff formality. He noted the rustling brown grasses, felt the cool wind that moaned over the hills. "If you have decided to maroon me, after all, Captain, the previous island seemed much more pleasant."

"I'll not maroon you unless you give me cause. Stay true to your promise and you have nothing to worry about."

"I take my vows seriously, Captain. I swore on the Fishhook."

The captain had chosen six strong sailors to accompany him, and the men trudged off in two groups with empty water casks in search of island springs. Hannes dreaded that the men might discover another abomination like the misleading Leviathan skeleton. . . .

Javian accompanied the small party ashore, and Captain Vora asked the young man to join him and the prester as they scouted the island. He gestured toward a high point on the headlands. "Let's walk up there to get the lay of the land."

"We'll be able to see the whole island from there." Javian set off ahead of them with his usual energy. From the *Dyscovera*'s lookout nest, they could tell this was just a small swatch of land, but Ondun had asked His sons to discover the world. Hannes dutifully joined in the exploration. He was also glad for the opportunity to spend time with Javian, who showed signs of becoming a devoted follower.

They hiked uphill through the grasses, saying little, which was fine with Hannes; Javian called back for them to hurry. At the summit of the hill, the breeze increased to a shrill, relentless gust. Hannes's hair whipped about his face.

Javian called, "Look what I found! Someone's been here before us."

Hannes shaded his eyes and saw a stone obelisk, a four-sided pillar as tall as a man, propped up by a cairn of rocks. "Maybe they came from Terravitae. We could be very close."

With his hand, Javian scraped away thick moss and dust. "It's covered with writing, but I can't read it."

Symbols had been chiseled into the flat stone surfaces, now pitted and weathered nearly to indecipherability. Hannes ran his fingers over the writing in search of the Fishhook or, with uneasiness, the Unfurling Fern. But if this obelisk dated from before Ondun left the world, it had been here before Aiden's

Arkship landed at Ishalem—long before his grandson Sapier had formed the church with the Fishhook as its symbol.

The captain stood beside the obelisk. "Can you translate it for me, Prester?"

"Give me a moment, I think I can make out some of the letters." Hannes traced them with his fingers, interpolating the designs, trying to match the symbols with what he knew from the most ancient pages in early editions of the Book of Aiden. "This is very old."

As he studied the marks, the prester struggled to hide his surprise and confusion. He was glad the Saedran chartsman hadn't joined them, for Sen Aldo might have been able to decipher the message as well. While waiting for the prester, Javian kicked around in the grasses, looking for other artifacts.

When he was ready, Hannes spoke the lie with great conviction. "It's cause for great hope, Captain. See the writing here? It says this marker was left by Aiden himself on his voyage from Terravitae. He placed the obelisk as a sign of his passage!"

Captain Vora's eyes shone. "A marker left by Aiden . . . I'll call the men, and they can uproot this pillar and carry it back to the *Dyscovera*."

"No!" Hannes had to quash that idea at all costs. The captain was startled by the vehement reaction, but Hannes made up a believable explanation. "Captain, if Aiden himself left this marker, then it's a sacred object. Who are we to disturb it? Leave it here as a sign for others who come searching."

The captain pondered, then nodded. "If that's your wish, Prester. Maybe we shouldn't disturb it. I'm glad we stopped, but now I'm even more eager to move on."

Javian peered out to sea from the high point. "Does that mean we're close to Terravitae?"

"I believe so. Let's gather the men and set off by nightfall."

Hannes ran his fingers over the stone, afraid that the sacrilege would burn his hands. But he had to know more. "Please,

Captain . . . I'd like an extra hour here to myself, while they finish. I wish to contemplate and pray. This is very important."

The other man studied him, trying to read falsehood in the prester's eyes, but Hannes remained firm. Finally, the captain nodded. "Don't tarry too long. If you're not there when we're ready to push off, I'll leave you behind."

"I have no intention of being marooned, Captain—especially when we're so close." He knelt to study the obelisk in an aspect of prayer and meditation.

The captain said, "Javian, run ahead and tell the men to get the water barrels loaded aboard the boats." The young man hurried off in front of Captain Vora, who took his time following the grassy slope back down to the shore.

When he was alone at the site, Hannes scowled and reread the markings, hoping he had been wrong in his initial translation, but there could be no doubt. The stone pillar stated that Aiden *and* Urec had sailed here together, that they had stopped at this island for supplies and left this marker as a sign of their passage. *Together.* Then the two Arkships had continued their joint search for the Key to Creation.

But that was impossible. The two brothers could not have sailed together, could not have had the same quest, could not have *cooperated.* Aiden and Urec would never have camped in these hills as companions rather than as rivals.

At first, Hannes had felt a thrill of fear to touch the ancient stone, sure that the letters had been carved by Aiden himself, but now the truth began to dawn on him—the only possible explanation. *Someone else* had placed this marker to deceive faithful travelers. It was a counterfeit, a lie.

This must be a test Aiden had left for him, a trick that only a devout believer could see through. Since few of the *Dyscovera*'s crew had strong faith, he had no intention of letting others be deceived, and he would not confuse them with muddled facts.

He tore away the rocks that supported the pillar and pressed his shoulder against the stone face, straining until the obelisk loosened in the dirt that had held it for so long. He pushed and rocked, and at last toppled the pillar to the ground. Soon, grasses would grow up and over it, and no one would notice it again.

But even that wasn't enough. Hannes had to be sure. He picked up a rock from the pile and hammered at the hateful letters, eradicating the symbols so that no other human eyes could ever read the falsehoods.

Sweating and exhausted—yet satisfied by the good thing he had just done—Hannes ran down the hill to the beach where the captain and his sailors were loading the last water barrel into the boats.

Captain Vora seemed impatient. "So you decided to join us after all, Prester? We're ready to go."

"I finished my prayers, Captain, and I'm ready to travel to our destination." He climbed into the boat. "Let's be on our way—we don't want to keep Holy Joron waiting."

59 *Olabar*

The Nunghal's invitation had made her very curious. Istar dressed in nondescript clothes and slipped away when the Urecari went to sunset church services. No one noticed her; no one knew where she was going.

On a busy street near the harbor, she found the inn that Asaddan had described. Inside, sailors and servers filled the common room; the air was heavy with conversation, laughter, shouts, and the smells of sweat, beer, and woodsmoke. She slipped past the crowds and went up the stairs to the Nunghal's room. He had given her precise instructions.

When she knocked, Asaddan opened the door, but hesitated before leading her inside. "Thank you for coming discreetly, my Lady. My companion has good reason to keep his presence secret, but we hope you can use your influence to arrange a meeting with the soldan-shah."

Istar pulled aside her veil as Asaddan closed the door behind her. She saw a man sitting quietly on a stool, wearing a fishhook pendant at his throat. He had light brown hair, blue eyes . . . and impossibly familiar features. Her world collapsed around her.

Twenty years. Twenty years now spooled backward and out of control like a snapped fishing line. She sucked in a gasp, and with it came the only thing she could say. "*Ciarlo!*"

Her brother recognized her in the same instant, bolting upright and toppling the stool. His mouth hung open as if someone had struck him with a club. Though she was decades older and dressed in Uraban clothes with touches of face paint and fine jewelry, speaking the language of a foreign land, she was still his sister. "*Adrea!* . . . Adrea, this is a miracle!"

Ciarlo flung himself at her and they embraced, rocking back and forth. He began sobbing into her shoulder, and she realized she was weeping as well. *Adrea.* She hadn't heard that name in so long. "I knew you weren't dead, Adrea! I had dreams, and I came to find out what had become of you!"

A gulf of empty years stretched out behind her like a blank sea on a sailor's chart. She had last seen her brother during the Urecari raid on Windcatch. Ciarlo had been at the kirk on the hill, ringing the bell to alert the town. The raiders had ransacked the houses, burned the piers. When they dragged her to one of their ships, she had caught a final glimpse of the small kirk in flames. So many people of Windcatch had been slaughtered that day. Istar—*Adrea*—had never dared believe that Ciarlo might have lived through it. With his lame leg he could not outrun the raiders, and Urecari scimitars could easily have cut him down.

The two began talking at once, spilling words over the top of each other; Adrea realized that for the first time in ages she was speaking *Tierran.*

Unable to understand what they were saying, Asaddan said in rough Uraban, "What is this? How do you two know each other?"

Ciarlo rubbed at the tears in his eyes and refused to let go of her. "This is my sister, Asaddan! The one I was searching for. She's the reason I came to Olabar! Aiden has blessed us both—can there be any doubt?"

An avalanche of questions fell into Istar's mind, and she didn't know which one to ask first. Then she realized that Ciarlo had jumped to his feet and run across the room to her. She had never seen him move without pain, not since his leg had been broken. She stood back and regarded her brother. "Your limp, Ciarlo! What happened?"

Though reluctant to release his hold on her, he was eager to show off. "I am healed." He hopped from one foot to the other, sprang up onto the bed, then back down to the floor. "I can walk and run as well as any man."

"But how?" Not even the most skilled Saedran physician could have healed an old injury like that.

"The Traveler, Adrea! I met him, and he performed a miracle. He gave me his book of new tales, took away my pain, and made me see my mission clearly—to come here and preach the word of Aiden. And also to find you. I've been blessed by two miracles now."

She was stunned, and each inquiry came with both eagerness and a commensurate weight of dread. "And . . . Criston? Did he ever return from the *Luminara*? Is he . . ." She couldn't even finish her question. Is he alive? Is he married? *Has he found a family and happiness for himself?*

"The *Luminara* was sunk by the Leviathan." Adrea reeled, but her brother was not finished. "Criston was the only survivor. He came back to Windcatch, but too late—you were already gone. Yet he never stopped hoping for you. He still writes you letters. He seals each one in a bottle and trusts it to the sea."

Tears began pouring down Adrea's face. "I received one of them, a long time ago. He still . . . remembers me?"

"He still loves you. Criston never married again, never found another woman, but he sailed away on a new ship, the *Dyscovera.* He'll be home—I know it. *We* have to return!" Ciarlo was so full of happiness he could barely speak.

Adrea hesitated, feeling tightness in her throat and an aching in her chest. She couldn't simply leave Olabar and sneak off to Tierra. She was the soldan-shah's First Wife; she and Omra had three daughters—one adopted, just as Omra had adopted and loved Saan.

Criston's son. The child that Criston wasn't even aware he had.

"You knew I was pregnant when . . . when the raid happened. I had a son, a strong son. Saan is now twenty years old—a sailor like his father. Omra raised him to be a fine young man, and he even looks like Criston." She hadn't thought of that in a long time.

"The *soldan-shah* raised Criston's son? How can that—" Ciarlo blinked, then his eyes widened as he realized what Asaddan had told him. "*You're* the wife of the soldan-shah?" He was aghast, and Adrea didn't know how to respond.

The Nunghal, meanwhile, watched them both, trying to decipher their conversation.

Adrea squeezed her eyes shut and wiped her face. "So much has changed. There's so much we need to decide." She turned to Asaddan and spoke in Uraban again so he could understand. "How can we reveal this to Omra? After the loss of Gremurr, he wants to kill any Aidenist he sees."

"There'll be time enough for all the explanations we need," Ciarlo said. "Right now, by the Fishhook, I won't let anything overshadow my joy at finding you still alive!"

Outside, a bell from one of the small harbor churches began to ring, then more bells set up a brassy clamor that echoed up and down the streets. Istar knew it should have been well past time for the summoning to sunset services. Below in the inn's common room, the buzz of conversation grew louder, and people rushed out into the streets. Asaddan went to the second-story window and threw open the shutters, trying to see the harbor in the dusk. The bells grew louder and louder.

With her mind struggling to absorb all that she had just learned, Adrea joined the two men at the high window, glad for the distraction. They could see seven ominous vessels sailing into the harbor accompanied by dozens of smaller ships, fifty or more, all closing in toward the docks.

A man shouted as he ran up the street from the nearby docks, "Olabar is under attack from the sea!"

60 *Olabar Harbor*

Broeck had timed his sunset arrival at Olabar with great care, when all the Curlies would be at their heathen church ceremonies—probably sacrificing Aidenist captives, slashing throats and collecting innocent blood in bowls. The Iborian destrar would show them how a true Aidenist fought for his beliefs.

Aboard the *Wilka*, a flagship as beautiful as his lost wife, he led the ironclads to the harbor along with fifty small ships he had captured over the past several months—fishing boats, patrol ships, ore carriers, and more. It had been a challenge to keep the flotilla together on the voyage across the Middlesea; a big storm would have brought disaster, but Ondun was on their side, and they'd had smooth sailing all the way.

By now, he was sure that at least half of Queen Anjine's army should be camped at the Ishalem wall, preparing for the full attack in another month. But tonight Broeck's ships might well cripple the entire Uraban empire.

As they closed in, he could hear the city's alarm bells ring out. The arrival of so many unexpected ships could not be hidden—but the Curlies could do nothing about it. His confidence was undiminished. Ahead, Uraban vessels of all sizes were tied up at the extended docks. He wished he had enough men to seize those ships, but he would have to satisfy himself with destruction, if not plunder.

He called across the water to Iaros, who stood excited at the bow of the *Raathgir*. "Send word down the line, nephew—tell the men in the small ships to tie down their rudders and set course for the harbor. Once they're ready, have them light the kindling, then get back to the ironclads!" Iaros bellowed to the nearest craft, and the message echoed from ship to ship as they proceeded toward the harbor.

The captured small boats were filled with dry brush, oil-soaked rags, crates of tinder. Now his men struck sparks and jumped overboard to swim to the nearby ironclads. The flames blossomed bright and raced up the rigging and masts, devouring the sails and intensifying the blaze.

The fireships reminded Broeck of funeral barges, like the pyre for his dead daughter Ilrida, who had died from the scratch of a rusty nail, or for King Korastine, who had died of a broken heart. Somehow, Broeck found it easy to blame the Curlies for those tragedies, too. The placid harbor waters would soon reflect many fires, an orange blaze to overwhelm the sunset. . . .

While his ironclads remained behind, the sacrificial boats drifted without guidance among the Uraban vessels tied up to the docks. Olabar residents scrambled to rescue their ships by untying them and setting sail, but they had little room to maneuver among the fireships. Broeck watched one small merchant ship try to pick its way through the tangle of vessels, but a burning fishing boat drifted against it as if driven by the vengeance of Aiden. The fire spread, the merchant's silken sails caught fire, and soon all of her crew were jumping overboard. Joined with the fireship in a deadly embrace, the merchant ship collided with another dock and smashed into a two-masted dromond, which also caught fire.

Though the ironclads held back for now, the destrar wished he could ram the docks and jump onto land, using his heavy Iborian sword to hack and slash at the terrified enemy. But he kept his armored ships just outside the harbor, happy to destroy Olabar without shedding a single drop of Tierran blood.

As more burning boats crashed into the docks, the fire intensified and consumed more vessels, even spreading ashore to the shacks and warehouses that backed up to the docks.

Shouting orders, Uraban soldiers rushed aboard five sleek war galleys tied up to the military pier. In rhythm with loud drumbeats, their oars extended as soldiers pulled at the shafts, and the galleys struck out like sharks, heading straight toward the ironclads.

Broeck crossed his arms over his chest. "Come right ahead. Let's see what you can do against us."

From the *Raathgir*, Iaros gesticulated toward the oncoming galleys, but Broeck gave a dismissive wave. Soon all the Tierran sailors aboard the ironclads were jeering and hooting, adding insults that the Urabans would not understand. Broeck laughed. "The galleys can try to ram us, but they'll never damage these hulls. Archers, prepare to fire as soon as the enemy gets in range."

Iaros was still calling out, but now he wasn't pointing at the war galleys. "Uncle, look!"

In a separate part of the harbor, Broeck spotted a sturdy ironclad that was larger than any of his own ships, and he knew immediately what it was: the *Golden Fern*, the first armored vessel Soldan-Shah Omra had commissioned from Gremurr.

Her sails had been set, and the soldan-shah's ironclad moved out to engage the invaders. Broeck let out a loud laugh and called, "Come and face me! I am ready for you!"

61 *Olabar Harbor*

Omra had faced Aidenist attackers before, but he had never dared contemplate a night like this. This was Olabar—*Olabar!*

Only an hour earlier, he had dutifully attended sunset services with Naori and their two young sons, but upon hearing the first alarms he rushed to the docks. He still wore his formal clothes, a clean olba, robe, and sash, but he also carried his scimitar; though ceremonial, it did have a wicked edge.

By the time the soldan-shah reached the naval piers, his war galleys had moved out into the water, their captains shouting orders as soldiers rowed toward the invaders. "Faster! Pull for Urec!"

Without delay, Omra leaped aboard the *Golden Fern* and commanded its launch. He had barely enough crewmembers aboard to set off, but they used the full complement of oars to propel the ironclad forward. Leaving the spreading harbor fires behind, the *Golden Fern* advanced on the armored ships. Omra hoped to catch up with the war galleys and block any further attack.

"I want to see that 'Hook commander's head on a spike!" he yelled. "All of their heads on spikes!" The men responded with angry shouts of approval.

Behind him, the devastation caused by the fireships was already appalling. Olabar's population had turned out to help stop the spread of the flames, throwing buckets of water, stamping out fires, cutting ropes to push smoldering ships away from the docks. Kel Rovik was at the docks trying to manage the rush of disorganized helpers.

The war galleys fanned out as they drove in toward the enemy ironclads, each captain choosing his own target. Each galley had a jagged prow, capped with a cast-iron beak; they were made to smash into enemy vessels, rip open hulls, and sink them . . . but they were not designed to defeat the thick armor cladding.

As the *Golden Fern* struggled to catch up, the first war galley collided with the nearest Tierran ironclad. Omra heard shouts in two different languages, both crews bracing for impact, a resounding blow louder than a thousand church bells, followed by the grinding of metal against metal. The war galley's metal beak slammed into the armored hull and scraped aside, ripping a bright silvery scar of clean metal, but did little actual damage. A shower of sparks looked like the spray from a blacksmith's grinding wheel.

While the galley shouldered against the Aidenist ship, enemy sailors rained arrows across onto the Uraban crew, slaughtering Omra's soldiers. Waving their scimitars, the greatly outnumbered Urecari swarmed onto the ironclad's deck.

As the other galleys closed with their targets, Tierran arrows arced up and struck down like lightning bolts, killing countless Urecari before their ships could come together. The second galley slid past its target entirely, the captain and helmsman both dead and too many rowers wounded to maintain the ramming course.

The third Uraban war galley had better luck as it charged into the Aidenist flagship. Its metal beak struck a seam between armor plates and wedged there, splitting the sheets of metal apart. Uraban soldiers threw ropes, grappling hooks, and a wooden ladder so they could swarm across. Omra saw a bearded Tierran man standing on the deck waving a great sword and hacking at Uraban fighters who rushed aboard.

The galley remained stuck into the flagship's broken armor plates. In the furious battle on deck, Aidenists outnumbered the

Uraban soldiers ten to one—until Omra could bring more fighters into the fray. He pointed. "That is our target! We will ram the flagship and break open her hull." With the enemy's armor already damaged, perhaps the *Golden Fern* could strike a mortal blow.

The oarsmen pulled harder, driving the *Fern* to greater speed. At the approach of the soldan-shah's ironclad, someone from the Tierran flagship shouted wildly, but it was too late. Omra embraced the foremast, planting his feet for the impact. His crew shouted a war cry.

The two ironclads collided, sparks flying. The heavy *Fern*'s momentum pushed the jagged maul on its prow through the flagship's armor plates, gutting the Aidenist ship like a fish. But the crash also crumpled the *Golden Fern*'s keel, and many of her own armor plates split off as the hull planks burst beneath them—a death blow for the soldan-shah's ship.

Omra didn't care; the two armored vessels were locked in a death dance now. His men threw ropes and hooks and charged aboard. "We're at too close quarters for them to use arrows now!" He raised his scimitar. "For the glory of Urec!"

Omra had held back his hatred for so long that he leaped in among the enemy like a tightly wound spring being released. Having just come from the church service, he wore no body armor, but he didn't feel naked. Urec would protect him. He slashed with his blade, striking off arms and heads indiscriminately.

Around him, the soldiers who had come aboard from the war galley were fighting and dying, and even the influx of fighters from the *Golden Fern* did not change the tide of battle. The Aidenists simply hacked and killed, and Omra's men did the same.

A screech and groan of metal filled the air: not the clash of blades, but the ironclads themselves, taking on water, foundering. Locked in a tangle of metal, both vessels were sinking. Omra knew the *Fern* was lost—as was the enemy flagship—and he meant to take as many 'Hooks down with him as he could.

He fought his way forward, nearly slipped on the bloody deck, then ducked just in time to avoid the thrust of a Tierran sword. His olba had come unwound, his sash severed, and he yanked the scraps of cloth away. His fine garments were drenched with blood and sweat.

The damaged Aidenist ship listed to one side. The *Golden Fern* was also sinking rapidly, taking on water through her burst hull and dragging the other ironclad down with her.

Nearby, he heard guttural Tierran words, and in the flame-lit darkness Omra watched a second stolen ironclad draw alongside the flagship, their crew also joining the battle. A Tierran man shouted orders at the helm; long red mustaches drooped down his cheeks like a rooster's tail feathers.

With this new flood of enemy fighters joining the fight, Omra's men had no chance. They had left plenty of Aidenist corpses strewn on the deck, but he saw that more than half of his fighters were already dead. The bearded Tierran commander fought like a berserker, slashing in one direction and another, killing anyone clad in Uraban silk.

As the locked ironclads shifted and sank, the embedded war galley sprang free with a lurch. More water rushed into the wide hull breach with a loud gurgle, pulling the Aidenist flagship down.

In his heart, Omra wanted to stay aboard until the very end to kill as many Aidenists as possible. While that would bring him joy—and it was the brave thing to do—he had a much greater obligation to his people.

He couldn't just sacrifice himself here, no matter how great his hatred for the followers of Aiden. His harbor was in flames, and the blaze could well spread into the city. He had a war to fight and win—and if he died here, now, he would leave young Zarif Omirr to rule, a boy who had not yet been trained in the basics of government.

No, the soldan-shah could not abandon his land and leave his people without a leader. He called to his surviving fighters, "The ship is lost! We must go. Quickly, overboard—swim to our war galleys and save yourselves."

With a last glare at the bearded Tierran commander, Omra dove over the side of the sinking ship, avoiding the floating debris and flames. Weighted down by sodden robes, he stroked toward the nearest war galley. A few arrows slashed into the water nearby, but none struck him.

As the two death-locked ships went down, the bearded Aidenist commander and his crew abandoned ship and climbed aboard the adjacent ironclad, where they were welcomed by the redheaded captain with long mustaches.

Shaking with exhaustion and only now realizing how spent he was from the fight, Omra dragged himself aboard the nearest galley. He breathed heavily and did not say a word despite the activity around him. He merely stared as the majestic *Golden Fern* finally slipped beneath the surface, taking the enemy ironclad with her.

62 *The* Al-Orizin

As if made of quicksilver and ice, Raathgir rose out of the frigid water, breathing frosty steam and regarding the two vessels.

Saan and his companions scrambled back aboard the *Al-Orizin* while the horned ice dragon circled, looking for any chance to lunge forward and snatch them in its jaws. Its long fangs were translucent, like icicles.

From the deck, two sailors threw a boathook and a harpoon at Raathgir, yelling challenges. The creature flinched when the spear points struck its polished scales, and it let out an ominous hoot from its blowhole. Still, it seemed more curious than ferocious as it darted away then immediately circled back, keeping out of range of the projectiles.

"Sea monsters just don't learn their lessons," Yal Dolicar said with false bravado.

"I don't fancy diving into that cold water to wrestle with the beast," Grigovar replied. "I'd throw you overboard first."

"Maybe it thinks we invaded its territory," Saan said. "Ystya, can you uncreate that monster, as you did the Kraken?"

Alarmed by his question, she vigorously shook her head. "There is no call to destroy him—Raathgir hasn't harmed us. These are his waters."

"But it's . . . a monster!" Fyiri cried. "You won't use your powers to protect us against it?"

"Raathgir is one of Ondun's creations—as you should well know." She looked pointedly at Fyiri. "I won't simply destroy a creature because you call it a 'monster.'"

"What if it attacks?" Saan asked.

"It won't attack."

The sailors hurled more curses, followed by another round of harpoons. One iron point struck Raathgir's jagged dorsal fin with a clang and ricocheted off to splash in the water.

"Stop wasting our harpoons!" Saan snapped. He turned to Ystya, shaking his head. "How can we get out of here with that beast guarding the waters?"

Raathgir let out a shrill blast of frosty steam, recoiled, and raced away from the two ships. The ice dragon darted to a cave opening in the blue walls of a nearby iceberg and slithered into the passage like a worm burrowing into dirt to evade a hungry bird. Its pointed tail vanished into the ice mountain.

Grigovar shifted his grip on the frozen tabletop he had taken from the ice-locked ship, which was still tucked under his arm. "That was easier than I expected."

"Ha! The beast knew we wouldn't back down." Yal Dolicar swelled his chest. He raised the stump of his right wrist.

Sen Sherufa remained unsettled. "We should get out of here now, Captain. Something powerful froze that ship . . . something we don't understand."

Saan felt as uneasy as the Saedran woman. "You're right, Chartsman. We don't know what frightened the ice dragon. Prepare to set sail!"

Beside him, Ystya suddenly looked around in dismay. Her face paled to the color of chalk. "Raathgir sensed it before I did—my mother is coming."

Saan shouted to the crew, "Quickly, hoist those sails and strike the ropes!" The *Al-Orizin*'s crew detached the hooks and ropes that tied them to the ancient ice ship.

Shivering on the lookout nest above the mainsail, a man called out, "Captain, I see that ship again—the island witch!

She's entering the field of ice mountains!" The encroaching icebergs blocked the pursuing vessel from view.

"These frozen islands are going to be a maze to navigate, Captain," said Sen Sherufa. "It'll be dangerous."

"That's to our advantage. We'll be like a buck taking refuge in the forest from hunting dogs. Iyomelka might have our scent, but we can hide among these ice mountains, like thick underbrush."

Long ago, when the *Al-Orizin* had sailed away from Olabar amid cheers and celebrations, Saan had been proud of his colorful sails, but now he wished he had plain white or gray ones, like a Nunghal ship, which would blend into this pale oceanscape.

Saan whispered to Ystya with more confidence than he felt, "Don't worry, we'll keep you safe from her."

The young woman was too filled with apprehension to smile. "And I'll protect you, too."

Moving again, the *Al-Orizin* sailed into the cold gray channels between icebergs, leaving the ancient vessel behind. Though his hands were stiff with cold, Saan climbed the mainmast to join the lookout high above. The man pointed around a blue-white wall of ice. "She's back there, Captain. I don't think she saw us."

From the high vantage, he caught a glimpse of Iyomelka's resurrected ship, like a flash of detail illuminated by a lightning strike. The masts were dark and sharp, like the branches of a dead tree on an autumn's night; the ragged sailcloth was stitched together with seaweed.

"Hard to port!" Saan cried. "Stay out of sight." The ship turned swiftly, scraping close to a floating berg. The *Al-Orizin* deftly threaded its way through the frigid labyrinth.

63 *Olabar Harbor*

All in all, Destrar Broeck considered it a successful night. Drenched, bloody, and exhausted—but happy—he joined Iaros aboard the *Raathgir.* A surgeon now worked to sew up deep sword cuts on his left arm, right side, and right thigh. He hadn't even noticed the injuries during the fight aboard the foundering *Wilka,* but they continued to bleed, and the surgeon was concerned, so Broeck let the man poke him with needles and sew the wide wounds shut with tough gut string. All the while, the destrar sat on a barrel on deck, where he could watch the glorious flames spread in Olabar harbor.

Three of the soldan-shah's war galleys were adrift, their decks a hedgehog of arrows and strewn with dead bodies. Some of the Curly soldiers remained alive, wounded and groaning, too injured to pull the oars. Broeck was saddened to lose the *Wilka,* but it was a price he was willing to pay. He may have lost one ironclad, but the soldan-shah had lost *all* of his.

Fifteen of Broeck's men had been killed in the fighting aboard the *Wilka*, and several more of the injured went down with the ship, unable to swim to safety. The destrar took heart from knowing, however, that his fighters had killed many more Curlies than that. Ondun could count the bodies Himself and sort them out.

Iaros stood at his side, no longer so young and foolish, and his long mustaches looked dramatic rather than absurd now. Broeck gave an approving nod. "You did well, nephew."

Instead of puffing his chest with pride, Iaros mumbled in response, "We still have six ironclads and plenty of eager fighting men. If we press forward into Olabar harbor, we could cause much more damage."

"That we could, Iaros." Broeck winced as the surgeon tugged a suture tight. "But the cost would be too high. We dare not lose any more armored ships or soldiers. Remember, Queen Anjine expects us at Ishalem. This was just . . . practice."

Though disappointed, his nephew agreed. "Time to turn about and head back to Gremurr."

Broeck cursed under his breath as the surgeon tied off the thread. He changed the subject. "Are the woman and her son aboard your ship, as I asked?"

"Yes, they've been held below where they could cause no trouble."

"Bring them up. And find someone who speaks their language—I need to tell them something."

Iaros smiled at the burning ships in the harbor. "You don't need a translator—that sight will explain more than words!"

Broeck's voice was harsh. "Maybe I want to tell them something else."

Abashed by the sudden rebuke, Iaros turned quickly. "I'll get them, Uncle."

Shetia and Ulan were brought on deck to where the destrar sat on his barrel. The woman wept at the sight of the fiery skyline, and the boy looked horrified and awed. He turned to the bearded destrar, his ghostly face backlit by the fire. "Olabar?" Ulan pointed. "Olabar?"

Broeck doubted the boy had ever seen the Uraban capital before. What a way to remember it now! "Yes, that's Olabar, lad—your soldan-shah's city."

Shetia wiped her tears and faced Broeck, her face ruddy with anger. It was the first time he had seen such passion in her. "You kill us now?" The woman drew Ulan closer to her, ready for whatever fate awaited them.

One of the sailors accompanying them, a former mine slave, looked back and forth, not sure what he was expected to translate.

"No, I won't kill you," the destrar replied. The interpreter repeated the words, but Shetia brushed him aside. Broeck said to the translator, "Tell her this: I didn't bring you here to gloat, either. It would be shameful to rub your nose in this, not befitting of a fighter. This is war, and a victory for our side. It had to be done. But . . . you don't belong in the middle of it. I wouldn't want you hurt."

Shetia and Ulan glanced at each other in surprise at the translation.

He added, "I'm setting you free."

Surprise animated his nephew's face. "But Uncle, those are valuable hostages!"

"They are a woman and a child, and I'm going to turn them loose. Prepare one of the ship's boats. They can make their own way back to the city."

"Aye . . . Destrar." Iaros hurried to do Broeck's bidding.

Shetia shook her head in surprise. She spoke, and the interpreter relayed, "She says she thought you would torture them."

Broeck's brows knitted together, and he lowered his voice.

"We've all been tortured enough." He cupped Ulan's chin in his broad palm. "You'll need to find someone else to play *xaries* with, young man."

Whenever he looked at this boy, the aching loss of Tomas filled his chest. He closed his eyes and drove away the image of his blond grandson. He had gotten to know Ulan and his mother, and as the course of honor he refused to take the revenge that would have been his right. He had at last discovered a line that even he did not want to cross.

"Go now, the boat is ready. Row into the harbor and find someone to help you. These are your people."

His cut leg hurt too much for him to stand up, and it would have been awkward and inappropriate for him to embrace the boy and his mother. He simply watched as Shetia and Ulan climbed into the ship's boat and were lowered over the side into the water. With all the ships and the soldan-shah's sailors, someone would find them soon enough. Broeck had no intention of staying there to make sure.

"We're done, here. Turn the fleet and head north across the Middlesea. We still have work to do before we join the queen at Ishalem."

64 *Ishalem Wall*

Anjine had not been to Ishalem since the conflagration destroyed not only the holy city, but all their hopes as well. The Edict had been an ill-advised gesture of peace based on the naïve belief that the followers of Urec could be trusted. *Twenty years.*

This time, Queen Anjine took the land route, accompanying the third wave of soldiers marching south. Most of this group came from training camps in Iboria and Soeland, rushing to answer her call for fighters. These thousands of additional troops would join the thousands already camped at the Ishalem wall, building up a breathtaking force that would bring down the barricade once and for all.

The journey from Calay was long and arduous, the camps rough. Since she was queen, a detachment of men pitched her tent for her, but she refused to ride in a wagon like a packet of goods. She was the queen of Tierra, an example to these soldiers who had sworn their lives in the service of the Crown and Fishhook. She would not let them think she was some vapid and pampered princess who sent them off to die without understanding the consequences of her decisions.

Instead, she rode a seasoned Eriettan warhorse or walked beside her fighters, letting them know that she understood both their fervor and weariness. She assured them that she wanted the war to end as much as any of them did—not in peace, but in victory.

She ate the same camp food as the soldiers did, accepting whatever supplies the army shared, though she often felt nauseated. Hard traveling did not suit her, but she told no one about her queasiness and hid how difficult the march was for her.

At the halfway point of the journey, the road ran along a river where the marching troops met up with a barge captained by Destrar Sazar himself; the flatboat was so laden with supplies that it rode low in the water. Anjine was glad to see him. "If you miss a dropoff, Destrar, then my army doesn't eat."

"I have the full schedule, Majesty. Keep sending your supply carts to the cache points, and I will deliver sacks of grain, baskets of vegetables, sausages, and anything else my boats can gather from the other reaches."

Anjine had met with her destrars, ordering them to maintain a constant flow of supplies so that the troops at the Ishalem wall would not go hungry. Destrar Sazar promised that his river clans would deliver all necessary goods to prearranged supply stops, as far south as his boats could go before the rivers drained into the Oceansea. Additional cargo ships sailed down the coast, stopping to unload crates of food on shore, which were then transported to the ever-growing army camp.

It was an intricate and tedious plan, fitting together like the components of a Saedran machine. She had to time the waves of her troop movements to coincide with the availability of supplies. Her battle commanders, destrars, and advisers helped with the carefully balanced arrangements, but Anjine oversaw it all.

Even so, her heart distracted her. On the long journey, Anjine couldn't stop thinking of Mateo. She forced her thoughts back to happier days in their youth when they'd taken care of each other and laughed at hardships and embarrassments. Now, when she arrived with these soldiers at the Ishalem wall, Mateo would be waiting for her. A flurry of hard-to-quell emotions filled her, and during the three-week trek to the border she thought much about seeing him again.

Anjine hadn't said a word to Mateo since the night they had made love. He'd vanished with the dawn, marching off without pledging his love, without bidding her farewell. Anjine pondered again and again what she would have said to him, given the chance. She didn't even know if he thought of that night with joy or regret, with weighty guilt or wistful pleasure. The prospect of seeing him again frightened her more than the thought of facing a city full of angry Urecari.

Anjine hoped his feelings were the same as hers.

Finally, the marching army arrived at the Ishalem camp at midafternoon. Scouts had ridden ahead to announce the queen, and Anjine could hear the occasional crash as the catapult bombardment of the wall continued with renewed vigor in her honor.

Anjine donned her crown and fur-lined cape and tried to put all thoughts of Mateo from her mind. She was the ruler of Tierra now, the commander of this army, the woman who would defeat Soldan-Shah Omra and punish the Urabans for their crimes against God. The catapults had done only cosmetic damage to the thick wall so far, but at least the hammering boulders would keep the Curlies awake.

As she rode up, Destrar Shenro came to meet her, looking like an excited boy on Landing Day. He led her to a large headquarters tent, while a group of soldiers set up her personal camp. She ducked into the command tent and was immediately struck by the odors of sweat, paper, and candle wax. The army's officers met here nightly for long discussions about the final assault due to take place in several weeks. To her disappointment, she did not see Mateo. "Where is Subcomdar Bornan?"

"On patrol, Majesty," Shenro said. "But we will see him by nightfall."

The news disoriented her. He should have known of her impending arrival—had Mateo intentionally chosen to be out of camp? Was he avoiding her? She pushed the thought aside, telling herself that Mateo wasn't her concern right now; Ishalem had to be her focus. "I would like to see my enemy. Is the soldan-shah in residence?"

"Oh, there are enough enemies on the wall, Majesty," replied Hist, "but we aren't sure Omra is among them. We've seen men in formal clothes strutting up and down the barricade, clearly officers or noblemen of some importance, but they all wear those cloths wrapped around their heads, and we don't know what the colors mean."

Anjine drew a long breath. "Well, I don't want the Urecari to have any doubt that Queen Anjine of Tierra has come to defeat them. I'm not going to hide. Fetch my suit of armor from my pack train. I will don it myself." An entire army of men had accompanied her south, but now Anjine discovered to her consternation that she needed Enifir or her ladies-in-waiting, who had remained behind at the castle. She had not wanted to drag them off to a battlefield, expecting they might get in the way. Now, though, she would make do. "Also, find a competent page who can help me secure the components when I'm finished."

As soon as her tent was ready, Anjine had her armor brought in and unwrapped from the canvas that protected the polished metal pieces from rain. She sorted the components on her cot, donned her woolen underlayers and padding, and pulled on the pieces as Ammur Sonnen had shown her: cuirass, greaves, helmet, gauntlets.

Though the armor was light and delicate by the blacksmith's standards, it felt heavy. Anjine was strong, though, and she wore it proudly. When she called the page in to help, he seemed in awe of her, nervous about touching the queen, but she said, "Young man, I need your help . . . and you can't be very helpful if you fawn over me so much." Fumbling, the boy finished adjusting the straps and buckles.

As Anjine stepped out to approving gazes, the page draped her cape over her shoulders. Destrar Shenro laughed and pronounced her magnificent. With the sun lowering in the sky, she said, "Ready our flags. I want to stand before the great gates while there's still enough daylight for those cowards to see me. Standard-bearers!"

Jenirod, Shenro, and Hist brought the camp's highest-ranking prester to bear the Fishhook standard. Shenro held two flags, one for Alamont Reach and one for all Tierra; Jenirod bore the flags of Erietta and another Tierran standard; Hist carried the Crown and Fishhook.

After several men helped Anjine mount her horse and balance in the saddle, she gazed through her open visor and announced, "I have brought along something very important." Two presters from Calay came forward with the pearlescent ice-dragon horn, which had formerly resided in the main Aidenist kirk. "Raathgir protected our city, and now he will bless our soldiers and grant us a victory at Ishalem."

Their procession left camp and headed for the no-man's-land outside the Ishalem gate. Clad in fine armor that glowed in the dying sun and surrounded by standard-bearers and military commanders, Anjine truly felt like a queen.

At the sight of the formal honor guard, the banners, and the queen in her full kit, Uraban sentries jeered from atop the wall. The Curlies summoned other men who wore olbas and sashes of various colors, presumably higher-ranking officers. Anjine had hoped the ice-dragon horn might glow with power, as when she'd driven away the sea serpents in Calay harbor, but the relic did not respond. No matter, her faith and determination would have to serve.

Though well out of arrow range, she could hear the Urabans, so she knew they could hear her as well.

"You should fear us!" Her voice was blade-sharp and clear, though she wasn't sure any of them could understand her. "You should fear us, because Ondun is on our side. And I, Queen Anjine of Tierra, have come to defeat you."

65 *Olabar Harbor*

After the loss of the *Golden Fern*, Soldan-Shah Omra quickly changed into dry clothes provided by the war galley's captain, but his ordeal was not finished. Before the last of the waterlogged fighters had been pulled onto the deck, he commanded the oarmaster to strike a sharp, swift beat to return to the piers. Though he longed to pursue the enemy ironclads as they sailed away, his overriding responsibility was to defend his city against the flames. He would not let Olabar burn to the ground as Ishalem had!

Omra had sunk the Tierran flagship, but the Aidenists were not fleeing to Gremurr in humiliation and defeat. No, the enemy had caused unspeakable damage, and they knew it. This sneak attack had decimated Uraba's naval capability—not just warships, but *all* shipping in the Middlesea. His land would be decades recovering from this loss.

"How many more reasons do I need to hate them?" he said quietly to the galley captain.

The other man shook his head. "We've long had more reasons than we could possibly need."

Half of the war galley's crew had been killed or wounded by the rain of Tierran arrows, which left the oars sparsely manned, but the drumbeat set a rapid pace nevertheless. The rowers groaned and sweated as they pulled the ship into the harbor, dodging obstacles. The jagged metal prow crashed into the smoldering wreck of a small fishing boat, knocking it aside so the galley could reach a section of docks not yet touched by flames.

The rest of the harbor was an inferno, and many vessels still tied to the piers were ablaze and foundering. Greedy fires spread from ship to ship, and burning tatters of sails, borne on the firestorm winds, drifted to new targets, setting new blazes.

The random courses of the unmanned fireships were wreaking havoc, spreading fire indiscriminately from one pier to another. The flames ate the pilings and dock boards, and would-be rescuers couldn't get close enough to the water to fill buckets for dousing the blaze.

The churches of Olabar rang their bells in a constant, deafening alarm. People flooded from every quarter of the city, responding to the orange glow in the night. Guards mingled with soldiers and craftsmen, fishwives and old men, all desperate to stamp out the spreading blaze. The fire was everywhere, as was the noxious smoke. Coughing men called out conflicting instructions.

As soon as he came ashore, Omra took over, ordering his people to form a line and stop the fire from advancing into the city. Though Uraban architecture typically used stucco, stone, and tile, there were enough wood structures and fabric awnings to maintain the blaze. Fortunately, the evening wind was quiet, blowing out to sea. Maybe something could be saved, he thought.

Omra shouted orders until he was hoarse. Throughout the night, he worked beyond exhaustion, but even as the fires died, his fury blazed brighter. His face was covered with soot, his hands raw and blistered. His clothes were dirty and blood-spattered; without his olba, his dark hair hung free and dripped with sweat. The smoke stung his eyes, making them burn so that he wasn't sure whether or not he wept.

By dawn, the people had contained the blaze, but the marketplace, the shoreline warehouses, and the wooden piers were a disaster. Out in the harbor, many ships still smoldered, but they were isolated now and would burn out on their own. It would take months or years to remove all of the blackened hulks and make the bay's draught safe for shipping. Until then, merchant ships could not tie up close to shore, and even the handful of intact vessels would not be able to sail away anytime soon.

There was so much work ahead—so many blazes to extinguish, so much damage to repair, so much loss to assess in goods and ships and *lives*—that Omra didn't know how he could deal with it all. He was already fighting a war, they had lost the ironclads and the mines at Gremurr, Tukar had been murdered, Arikara had been leveled, and now this. . . .The challenge seemed even greater than building a great wall across the isthmus.

He looked at the skeletal wrecks of ships and recalled the driftwood reader's prediction. His heart ached, for he now believed that the gnarled woman had somehow read Uraba's grim future in the whorls and rings of the piece of wood. No one could have prevented the destruction of Arikara, but Omra knew exactly whom to blame for this attack on the harbor.

Kel Rovik came up to him, his face soot-blackened, his hair disheveled, his cheek marked with blisters from a blast of fire. He led a woman and a young boy who wore drab clothes and appeared gaunt and frightened. "Soldan-Shah, we found these two in a small boat in the harbor."

Omra narrowed his eyes, recognizing them. "Shetia—and Ulan! We thought you were prisoners at Gremurr, or dead."

Shetia bowed. "When the Aidenists came to conquer the mines, Tukar sent us away into the hills to hide, while he remained to fight. But it was no use. We were eventually captured and held prisoner by their leader, Destrar Broeck."

Omra growled. "Did he harm you? What has he done?"

"He didn't harm us, but he has done enough. I believe—" she began, and her voice hitched. "I believe he killed Tukar."

A storm crossed Omra's face at the reminder. "Yes, Tukar is dead. I'm sorry. I loved my brother and wanted him to come home."

The boy had a distant look in his dark eyes. "My father was very brave. He didn't surrender the mines, but the Aidenists took them from him."

"How did you escape, then? How did you get here?"

"The destrar let us go," she said. "I think he felt guilty."

Omra didn't believe that. "I would not show compassion for him, or any 'Hook."

"And yet he set us free. He fed us, gave us shelter, kept us alive. We would have starved to death out in the wilderness."

"He played *xaries* with me," Ulan said. "And he took care of my puppy."

Omra was troubled. "Why would he burn so many of our ships, kill hundreds of people, and yet save you?"

"Only Urec knows."

Omra turned to Kel Rovik. "Have them taken to the palace, give them whatever they need. Their long nightmare is finally over." As Rovik led them away, the soldan-shah knew his own nightmare would continue for some time.

Causing a commotion along the shoreline path, a rider tried to force his way toward the soldan-shah, and Omra irritably waved at his guards to let him pass. Due to the confusion and milling people, the rider had taken some time to find Omra. He now presented himself with a quick bow. "Soldan-Shah, I come from Ishalem with news from Kel Unwar."

Omra just stared at him. After this night, he didn't want to hear any more news, but the rider spoke anyway. "The Tierran army has laid siege to the Ishalem wall—thousands of soldiers."

"Their actions insult me." After the sneak attack on the harbor, this seemed even more appalling. "What do they hope to accomplish? Does Kel Unwar believe they can smash down God's Barricade?"

"The provisional governor believes Ishalem is safe, Soldan-Shah, but the size of the enemy army suggests they intend a major strike. And their navy has arrived to blockade the harbor."

Omra fought down his fury. "After last night, I'll never underestimate the Aidenists' penchant for destruction. I'll leave now and go directly to Ishalem." His instinct was to take a fast ship and head west across the Middlesea, but one look at the smoke-filled harbor reminded him that the *Golden Fern* had sunk, and most of these vessels would never sail again.

"Get me a horse!" he shouted at Rovik. "I'll ride to the next town and commandeer a ship there."

Rovik was startled. "But Soldan-Shah—how can you leave Olabar now?"

Omra's heart was torn between his capitals. "You're in charge of recovery operations. I must go back to Ishalem. If we lose there, we lose the world."

Part III

66 *Calay, Saedran District*

With the bulk of the Tierran army gone to Ishalem along with large numbers of camp followers and support workers, the city of Calay seemed empty. Since most seaworthy vessels had been conscripted into the Tierran navy, few ships sailed into the harbor with marketable goods.

The Saedran District remained busy, however. Though the Saedrans were loyal citizens of Tierra, they had never been asked to fight this holy war against the followers of Urec. While Sen Leo na-Hadra was happy to assist the queen in every way possible, he was a scholar, not a warrior. Few of his people were. They were painters, instrument-makers, apothecaries, doctors, architects, and chartsmen. Thinking of his son-in-law Aldo far away aboard the *Dyscovera*, Sen Leo couldn't imagine the young man raising a sword in a battlefield charge. Aldo had many talents, but butchery was not among them.

The old scholar went to the na-Curic household for their traditional midweek family dinner. Leo's wife was already there, having helped to cook the meal while the grandchildren played underfoot. Biento welcomed him into the house, while Aldo's wife Lanni came forward to hug her father. Lanni's eyes were bright and eager. "Do you have any news of Aldo? Has there been another *rea* pigeon?"

"Sorry, nothing for some time."

"Do you think they're all right?" Yura na-Curic wiped flour from her cheek. "It's a mother's job to worry."

Aldo's brother Wen chimed in with a snort of bravado. "Of course they're all right—they have the best Saedran chartsman in the world."

Sen Leo put as much reassurance into his voice as he could, not wanting to admit that he was concerned. "Since they have only a limited number of *rea* pigeons, Aldo wouldn't waste a bird unless they have adventures worth writing about. They must have quiet sailing for now."

Lanni rounded up her young children and herded them toward the table. "The message *I* want to hear is that Aldo has found Terravitae and the *Dyscovera* is following their Captain's Compass back home."

After a satisfying meal, Sen Leo made his way through dark streets to the warehouse that held the sympathetic model of the exploration ship. Because the intricate replica remained intact, Sen Leo had good reason to believe the *Dyscovera* was undamaged.

Queen Anjine had stationed guards to protect the replica, but with the army gone and the city guard stretched thin, the Saedran model-maker Sen Burian na-Coway spent most of his time there, sleeping nights inside the warehouse so that no one could harm the model.

As Sen Leo approached the building, he heard gruff shouts, followed by a chatter of feral laughter. He hurried around the corner to find burly Sen Burian balling his fists and fending off three teenaged boys who threw debris at him. One soft tomato splashed against the model-maker's chest, and he roared at them. "Come back here so I can wring your necks—or go far away so I never have to smell you again!"

When the boys saw Sen Leo running toward them, they laughed and darted into the shadowy alleys. The old scholar caught his breath as he stopped at Burian's side. "What did they do?"

"They made me angry is what they did." Burian wiped a big hand down his chest, smearing tomato seeds, then wiped the wet hand on his trousers. "Troublemakers and hooligans—they've come around here before. I wish *they'd* been conscripted into the army."

Sen Leo was worried. "Did they harm the model?"

Burian brushed aside the thought. "No, they aren't that imaginative." He pointed to the warehouse's shuttered windows, which had been bombarded with spoiled fruit and smeared with fish offal. "I'd rather they threw garbage at the Ishalem wall. Damned vandals."

"Even if they're not *ra'virs*, vandals can cause great harm," Sen Leo said. "Do you know who they are?"

"No, but they've been coming around here more often, getting bolder. I suspect their fathers went off to the war and their mothers can't control them."

The Saedran scholar pressed his lips together. "I'll tell Guard-Marshall Vorannen to keep a close watch on this place. If that model is destroyed, the *Dyscovera* may not survive."

"Oh, I can handle them for now," Sen Burian said. "I will sleep with one eye open and a cudgel beside my cot. A good bruise and a cracked rib will teach those boys a lesson."

The two men entered the warehouse, which was lit by lanterns. Sen Leo looked at the impressive work of the large ship model, marveled at its sturdy hull and masts, the delicate webwork of rigging, the detailed painting. The actual *Dyscovera* was a wonder, and this replica was an equal achievement of Saedran skill and sympathetic magic.

The sight made him think of Aldo sailing across the unexplored seas, farther than any chartsman had ever gone. "I'll stay with you here for the rest of the night, Sen Burian—if you'd like the company."

"That would be good." The model-maker reached out to shake his hand, then noticed the tomato smear on his palm. "I'd better get cleaned up."

67 *The* Dyscovera

In the dark of night, Criston came out on deck carrying another sealed bottle containing a letter to his beloved Adrea. He slapped the cork tight against his palm and tossed the bottle overboard, hoping it would follow the sympathetic magic contained in the strand of her hair. She had given the lock to him a lifetime ago, and by now the strands were almost gone.

Though decades had passed, he did not give up believing that there was some way he could be with Adrea again . . . *some way*. He drew a deep breath and pictured her face, which remained so clear in his mind, though half of his life had passed since he had last seen her.

Javian approached him quietly. "Do you think your wife has ever received one of your letters, Captain?" Since the killing of the *rea* pigeons, Criston had doubled the night watch. Crewmembers patrolled the deck in pairs, watching for trouble—watching each other. There had been no further incidents.

"That isn't up to me. The currents and tides have to do their part as well."

He looked up toward the horizon, where he saw a sudden flash of light that shone out, then faded. Sure that his eyes had fooled him, he stared into the crowded starfield of a moonless night. The flash came again, a yellow-white beacon at the edge of the horizon.

From atop the mainmast, the lookout shouted, "Captain, I see a light!"

Javian pointed, and the other night watchmen crowded forward to see. The beacon came and went, flashing at regular intervals—far away, but definitely there. A signal . . . a sign of life.

An eerie shiver went down Criston's back as the flash of light brought back memories from twenty years earlier. He spoke in barely a whisper. "I've seen something like this before."

He would never forget that storm-swept night when tumultuous waves had battered the *Luminara.* Clinging to the lookout nest, thrown about by the storm, Criston had seen the flash of a bright beacon far away—just before the Leviathan came. . . .

Prester Hannes emerged from his cabin, without even a hint of sleep in his eyes. The prester remained awake most nights, poring over his books, studying each word. After finding the stone obelisk on the unnamed, windswept island, and seeing the inexplicable undersea titan with seaweed hair, he had been even more intent in his devotions.

Hour by hour, the beacon brightened as the *Dyscovera* sailed closer. By the time dawn broke, Criston could make out a rocky mound not large enough to be called an island. The rocks were topped by a monumental white brick tower built on a succession of stepped stone platforms. The spire stretched impossibly high into the sky.

"Who built that?" Mia said. "And how? Where could they have gotten the materials? Why would anyone put it out here?"

"It's the Lighthouse at the End of the World," Criston said, barely whispering.

Prester Hannes, though, had no questions. "Ondun did this, and His reasons are His own." His gaze ran up and down the gigantic tower. "One does not ask God how He does things."

Though it was daylight, a dazzling beacon shone from the apex of the lighthouse tower. Lines of foamy water around the rocky mound indicated barrier reefs. Criston wondered whether it was a signal, or a warning. . . .

He ordered the sails furled, the anchor dropped. "We'll take one of the ship's boats over."

"I will go with you, Captain." Hannes seemed to consider it a foregone conclusion.

"I intended to take you along, Prester. You too, Sen Aldo—and Javian. If there is a man living in the lighthouse, the man in the legend, maybe he can tell us how close we are to Terravitae."

Criston felt both excited and wary as they rowed the ship's boat over to the rock outcropping and the tower; he noted that the prester did not offer to take a turn at the oars. Javian and Aldo found a place among the rocks to secure the small boat, and the four men climbed out onto the mossy water-washed stones and ascended the stone platforms.

A wooden door opened at the base of the huge tower and a man waved, as if he had been expecting them all along. "You arrive at last, Captain Criston Vora!" The tall, majestic stranger had carefully combed silver hair and a neat silver-gray beard. His clothes were of a style that Criston had never seen, and his expression held a weight of impossible age, although he seemed healthy and energetic. "I have watched your *Dyscovera* for months."

Criston blinked. "Who are you? How do you know my name?"

The man smiled from the doorway. "I know all of you, quite well in fact. Prester Hannes"—he nodded—"the well-traveled Saedran chartsman Sen Aldo na-Curic . . . and young Javian. I could list every person aboard your ship, if you like. I watch. I make note of what I see." He shrugged. "I have nothing else to do, and it eases the boredom of the centuries. I am Mailes."

"And this is the Lighthouse at the End of the World." Prester Hannes was visibly shaken. "I have read the Book of Aiden."

The man seemed charmed by the idea. "Ah, young Aiden! I wonder what he has to say about me."

Hannes looked awed and perhaps a bit disgusted by this man, and his voice had a biting, judgmental undertone. "We already know your story, sir—how you offended Ondun and were exiled here."

The lighthouse keeper was amused. "Do not be convinced of what you know, Prester. Stories have a tendency to change as they are told and retold." He stepped back through the doorway and gestured them inside. "Come, I have plenty of bread, wine, and fish."

He sighed and mumbled, "Always plenty of bread, wine, and fish . . . I am happy to share it with you."

As they climbed an endlessly spiraling series of flagstone steps, Hannes raised his voice, a bit out of breath. "If you did know Ondun in the flesh, then I can't help but show you respect. But you also angered Ondun so much that He sent you away from Terravitae and imprisoned you in this lighthouse forever."

"Oh, not forever—just until Ondun returns. And I wish he'd stop dallying. He can be very stubborn." Mailes sounded flippant.

On their way up the dizzying staircase, they passed shelves of books on the walls, packed with volume after volume after volume. Aldo looked longingly at the unread tomes, but even with his perfect memory it would take him decades to absorb and memorize such a vast library.

Noticing the Saedran's intense interest, the old man commented, "I have all the time in the world to write down my thoughts. Some good work in there, if I might be so immodest, though I have no expectation anyone will ever read them."

Halfway up the stone tower Mailes stopped at a main chamber, which contained even more impressive bookshelves. Without addressing the prester's accusations, the lighthouse keeper invited them to a table that was set with loaves of bread, roasted fish, and a jug of wine, as promised. He took a seat in a sturdy driftwood chair and gestured for them all to eat.

Javian tasted the food. "Not much flavor," he observed.

"Ondun promised that I would be nourished and cared for in my exile," Mailes explained. "But he didn't want me to enjoy it."

Criston asked in spite of himself, "And what did you do to offend Him so greatly?"

Mailes looked wistful rather than guilty. "I had an affair with his wife. I loved her, Ondun didn't . . . but he refused to admit it. As I said, he can be very stubborn." The stranger's gaze grew distant. "Iyomelka . . . a fine woman, lovely and strong, opinionated, passionate, and absolutely fascinating. Ondun grew bored with her over the centuries, and she didn't deserve that. I loved her, truly I did."

Aldo raised his eyebrows in surprise, while Hannes sputtered in the middle of a draught of wine. He lurched up from his chair and shoved aside the plates of fish and bread. "You are a liar! That is not what the scripture says!"

Mailes was surprised by the rude outburst, but his voice remained mild. "I believe I know what I did and did not do, Prester."

Hannes turned his gaze toward Criston and Javian, ignoring the Saedran chartsman as irrelevant. "He is a deceiver! Ondun exiled him. We can't trust anything he says."

Mailes gave a bittersweet chuckle. "Oh, Ondun exiled me, all right. He demanded that I stay here and watch for him to return. What an arrogant, petulant person! After he managed to rid himself of me, Ondun tried to patch up his relationship with Iyomelka, even got her pregnant, but she fled Terravitae. That was when Ondun sent his sons after her . . . but they couldn't find the girl either, so he left."

Hannes was filled with disgust. "That is not why Ondun departed from Terravitae!"

Mailes gave him a curious frown. "Why are you so frightened of the truth, Prester? I knew Ondun. I have been here in this tower for all the centuries your civilization has existed. I might be the only true witness left alive in the whole world—there were very few of our people remaining, even that long ago. Do you not welcome a chance to correct your misunderstandings?"

"I have no misunderstandings," Hannes said.

"That is your greatest misunderstanding!" With a chuckle, Mailes began to eat his fish, chewing mechanically, and tore a chunk of bread from the nearest loaf.

Hannes was so angry he was rendered speechless. Criston was also at a loss. Aldo asked, "How do you know so much about us?"

Instead of looking at the Saedran, Mailes fixed the prester with his gaze. "I have watched all of you, all your lives. I *know* you, Prester Hannes. I know where you have been, and what you have done. I watched you burn Urecari churches in Uraba. I watched you poison kegs of wine at the feast of the soldan of Inner Wahilir. I saw you strangle Asha, the wife of Soldan-Shah Imir—a woman who had only tried to help you."

"They were Urecari!"

"They were still people."

"I was improving the world, in the name of Ondun." He crossed his arms over his chest, and Mailes simply raised his eyebrows at the defense.

Javian and Sen Aldo looked stunned by the revelations, though Criston already knew about the mayhem the prester had caused in his years of wandering Uraba. Hannes had been rather proud of what he had accomplished. After learning what the Urecari raiders did to Windcatch, to Adrea, to his unborn child, Criston felt little sympathy for them. He couldn't blame the prester for his hatred.

Mailes continued, drawing satisfaction from his recitation. "I saw you in the church of Urec during the Ishalem fire, I saw you escape from the Gremurr mines and struggle over the mountains. I saw Criston Vora save you. I saw you stir up violence against King Sonhir and his people, leading a mutiny aboard the *Dyscovera*. I saw what you did to the obelisk on the island. Need I go on?"

Despite his anger, the prester refuted none of Mailes's statements. "How can you know these things?"

"As I said, I am here in my lighthouse. I observe the world." The old man turned his smile to Criston. "And you, Captain Criston Vora—I watched you kiss your Adrea goodbye when you sailed away on the *Luminara*. I saw you floating on your raft of wreckage and cheered when you hooked a sea serpent that towed you to rescue. I saw you become a hermit in the mountains. I cried along with you when your beloved dog died."

Criston swallowed hard. All the memories of his life pressed down upon him like a heavy snowfall.

"And Sen Aldo na-Curic—let me tell you that your wife and children are doing well. Your sister remains unmarried, finding fault with every suitor who comes. Your brother still does not know what profession to choose. I must say that the Mappa Mundi your father has been painting is most impressive."

Tears sparkled in the chartsman's dark eyes.

Javian blanched in superstitious terror. "Captain, who is this man? Does he mean us harm? How does he know all these secrets? A man's life is his own, not a puppet show to share with everyone else."

Mailes just chuckled. "It is the only diversion I have, and not all secrets are bad, young man." He rose from his chair and went to the curving staircase again. "Let me show you, if you will have a look. Come to the top of my tower." Leaving their flavorless banquet, he led the four men up another winding staircase to the top of the dizzying tower.

In the center of the turret chamber, a thick crucible held a ball of magical flame that blazed but consumed no fuel. The yellow-white fire danced against the dish of a large mirror that rotated slowly, directing the beacon along a circuit of the horizon.

More volume-filled shelves covered the walls of the room. On a small table, a tome lay open, its pages covered with line after line of tiny words. Sen Aldo hurried over to gaze down at the letters and drawings.

Mailes explained, "I write down what I see—and I see everything." He walked to a brass stand that held a large circular lens on a swivel. He grasped the handles on either side and peered through. "I watch every land, all the people. I witness them going about their lives, since I no longer have a life of my own. Some parts of the world are forbidden to me, such as Terravitae and my own people—Ondun being petulant again. I am condemned only to observe, but I can see anyone, anywhere. Would you like to have a look?"

He turned the lens from side to side, pressing his eye closer. Then he glanced back at Criston. His lips quirked in a smile. "In fact, Captain, I know you will be most pleased to learn that your wife Adrea still lives."

68 *The* Al-Orizin

The *Al-Orizin* sailed through the sea of icebergs for two more days, barely managing to stay out of sight of Iyomelka's ship.

Ystya followed Saan whenever he went out on deck. "If I can sense my mother, then she must know I am here as well. She will never give up."

Saan looked into her eyes and gave her a reassuring smile. "And I promise *I* won't give up either."

He climbed up to sit with Yal Dolicar, who was taking his turn in the lookout nest. Both men wrapped themselves in blankets and stared out at the waters. Dolicar's teeth chattered. "I've traveled throughout Uraba and Tierra, and once I went all the way to miserable Iboria Reach, but I have never been as cold as this." When Saan reached out to take the spyglass with his cloth-wrapped hand, Dolicar warned, "Take care, Captain. It's so cold the metal will freeze to your eyelid. I doubt you want a spyglass attached permanently to your face."

Saan cautiously peered through the eyepiece, sweeping the sea around them. Large sections of ice calved off from the nearest berg and splashed into the water. Spray drenched the shivering crew on deck, who shouted in dismay.

Dolicar rubbed his hands together under the white steam of his exhalation. "I have a proposal for you, Captain—if you finish my shift for me, I'll pay you one of the coins I took from the ice-locked ship."

Saan's lips quirked in a smile. "I never said you could keep those coins in the first place."

Yal Dolicar shrugged. "Then I'll split them with you. You're the captain."

Saan laughed. "Yes, I'm the captain. I have other duties besides chatting." He took his leave and climbed down from the lookout nest.

By the time he got back to his cabin, his fingers were numb. When he closed the door behind him, relieved to feel the warmth, he was happy to find Sen Sherufa and Ystya huddled there, studying charts.

Over the past two days, the Saedran woman had carefully thawed the ice that covered the chart table salvaged from the ancient ship. Slowly and gently, she removed the frozen layer until she could peel away the chart underneath. After flattening and drying it, she spread the chart beside the ancient Map of Urec that Saan had brought along.

Ystya stood up, excited. "We've figured out something important—the maps match up."

Sen Sherufa was not one to speculate, but she also seemed convinced. "I can't decipher the frozen captain's language after all, but his drawings are careful and detailed." She pointed at the rough chart. "Look here, a sea of floating ice mountains. And they're on Urec's Map, too."

Saan bent closer to look. On the fringe of Urec's Map next to stylized drawings of curved waves, illustrations depicted white mountains floating in the sea. From studying this relic before, Saan had always thought those drawings were a chain of islands, assuming that either the ink color had faded or that they represented snow-capped peaks. Now that Sherufa compared them with the frozen captain's charts, he realized that the white mountains were indeed the icebergs in this frozen sea. "That's the connection we've been waiting for! Now we can mark *our* ship's position on Urec's Map and follow it all the way to Terravitae."

"Oh, we are close," Ystya said. "We will be in open water again soon, and then we can chart a straight course to Terravitae."

He hugged Ystya, wrapped himself in a blanket, and wrapped his hands in warm cloths. "You two continue your work and keep my cabin warm. We have a course to set."

That afternoon, they sailed between two large icebergs and discovered open waters beyond—the end of the frozen sea, and Saan meant to get a good head start on Iyomelka. At last they could proceed as fast as the wind and sail could take them.

Somewhere far behind, Iyomelka's ship remained lost in the ice. "This is a race," Saan said, "and I plan to reach Terravitae before she catches us."

69 *Tierran Military Camp, Ishalem Wall*

Now that Queen Anjine had joined the encamped army at the wall, the Tierrans cheered, sang Aidenist hymns at the top of their raucous voices, and swore to tear the barricade down, brick by brick. As darkness fell, the soldiers built their campfires brighter, banged on their shields, and yelled out defiant insults to ensure that the cowering Curlies could hear them. The catapults continued their bombardment.

Though Mateo had known that Anjine and her party would arrive before day's end, he didn't rush forward like an eager puppy (though he very much wanted to do so). For nearly three months now he had clung to the wistful recollection of the night they had finally let down their walls and admitted their love in the darkness. But he had left her without speaking a word. She must think *he* was ashamed, guilty. He had run from her as if embarrassed—how that must have hurt her! For all that time, he had wrestled with the uncertainties in his heart, but he hadn't been able to resolve his doubts.

Anjine might be pining for him as much as he pined for her . . . or, being left alone to think about the night they had spent together, she might have developed an entirely different mindset. She was the queen of Tierra, responsible for five reaches, hundreds of cities and towns, taxes and laws and decisions. She might have decided to protect herself by creating a larger gulf between them, and they would have to go back to pretending. He just didn't know.

So, even though Anjine was on her way to the camp, Mateo saddled a bay gelding and rode out on patrol, following the Ishalem wall. Out of arrow range, sometimes out of sight, he paralleled the hateful barrier that sprawled across the isthmus. He surprised two Urecari scouts and thundered after them, but they ducked through a small gate in the wall before realizing that he was only a single soldier. Mateo turned the bay about and galloped away before the Urecari could summon reinforcements.

Most important, as he followed the hills inland he discovered a possible vulnerability where intrepid fighters might be able to scale the wall. The stone barricade followed the landscape, but at one point the crest of a hill came close enough to the wall that he guessed soldiers with ropes and ladders might be able to swarm over the top. But it was a mile from the army's main encampment, and if he embarked with a full fighting force, the enemy would spot them and easily mount a defense. A small party might get over the wall . . . but what would they accomplish?

Mateo arrived back at camp by nightfall with this new information. His heart beat harder when he saw the new banners and an additional large tent erected near the headquarters. Yes, Queen Anjine had arrived and was already meeting with her officers and field commanders.

He handed off his mount to a horsemaster, straightened his uniform, and wiped off as much mud and dust as possible in an effort to resemble an impressive subcomdar rather than a trail-weary scout. He had to deliver his report like a good soldier. From inside the headquarters tent, he heard voices, *her* voice, and a thrill of anticipation ran through him at the thought of seeing her again at last. Mateo hesitated, braced himself, and pushed aside the flap.

Anjine saw him, and her eyes widened just a fraction, but she schooled her expression not to let any joy show through. His own words caught in his throat. She looked so beautiful, but so tired, her face unusually pale. He wanted to hold her, but he could not, especially now.

"Majesty," he said. The formality sounded foreign.

"Subcomdar Bornan," Anjine said. "Just in time to give your report. We've had good news from Comdar Rief." She gestured, and another man at the table acknowledged him.

Mateo forced himself to tear his eyes away from Anjine. Rief gave a cool smile of acknowledgment. "A small dinghy took me ashore north of the wall so I could make my way here to the camp. Our navy has blockaded the Ishalem harbor, and Uraban ships won't be going in or out if I have anything to say about it. They are cut off." The comdar indicated a chart on Anjine's table—a detailed drawing of the western harbor and the rebuilt docks. Rief looked at the other officers with clear satisfaction. "Our ships are ready to fight whenever the army is."

"The army is ready to fight," Shenro said. "We've just been waiting . . . and waiting."

"Another supply train just arrived," Subcomdar Hist reported. "We are well provisioned."

Rief had brought additional sketches. "South of the wall and below the city, the Urabans have excavated a large canal. There have been rumors of this waterway for some time, and now we have confirmed it. I sent spies ashore, several of whom were killed, but others returned to report that they had seen the canal extending miles inland. From our fleet, we studied the western mouth from afar, approached it with three of our warships, but the bulk of the enemy navy is arrayed there. Because they defend it so heavily, I am convinced the canal has great strategic importance."

He paused, as if worried the queen wouldn't believe him.

"We have seen ships emerge, Majesty—large sailing vessels that seem to have come all the way from the Middlesea. Apparently the canal does indeed span the isthmus, from one sea to another."

"If we could capture that waterway, our warships could sail through and attack Olabar!" said Subcomdar Hist.

"Ishalem first," Anjine said. She was entirely businesslike and did not look at Mateo. "Patience, all of you. We've still got three weeks before Destrar Broeck is due to arrive. You know the plan. We must strike at once from all sides, or the Curlies will fight us off one by one."

"I don't mind letting them sweat on their cots each night," Jenirod said. "It will only build their dread of what we intend to do."

Destrar Shenro fidgeted with excitement. "I have news as well. My men have been watching the wall and taking notes in great detail. From some of the high points, we can even see parts of the city." He sounded breathless. "Based on what my scouts reported, I am now convinced the *soldan-shah himself*—or some person of great importance—has come to Ishalem. I believe his residence is very near the wall, if only we can get to him." He looked around, waiting for the others to see the implications. "It gives us a way to end this war immediately. Think of it, Majesty. If we kidnap Soldan-Shah Omra, hold him hostage, we could force the Curlies to surrender. They would have to pay the ransom and sue for peace!"

A dark flush crossed Anjine's face. "I was willing to pay the ransom for Tomas, but they killed him even so."

Comdar Rief seemed intrigued by the possibility. "Capturing the Uraban leader would fundamentally change our situation, Majesty."

Jenirod kept his tone carefully neutral as he summarized the faulty plan. "So, if only we could get through a wall we haven't been able to breach, and run through a city we don't know, that's full of enemies who want to kill us, in search of the soldan-shah—whom we aren't even certain is there, nor do we know what he looks like—and if we could somehow bring him back to our side, *then* we'd have a quick and easy way to win the war." His sigh sounded like a disappointed horse.

Shenro was annoyed. "It wouldn't be as difficult as that . . ."

Anjine turned to Mateo. "Subcomdar Bornan, you spent the day out on patrol yourself." He heard no warmth in her voice. "I thought we had trained scouts for that, but I trust your eye. What did you find? Any sign of the soldan-shah?"

He forced himself to participate in the discussion as if this were any other strategy meeting. "No, but I discovered a possible vulnerability, Majesty." He moved Comdar Rief's sketches to reveal a map of the Ishalem wall and pointed to the area he'd scouted. He glanced at her, and her eyes briefly met his.

Mateo explained about the barricade's low point with respect to the adjacent hill, and his theory that a team of dedicated Tierran soldiers might be able to scale the wall at that spot under cover of darkness. "Once there, we could open the gates from inside and let the rest of our soldiers charge in."

Destrar Shenro seemed particularly excited by the prospect, but Anjine cut off further discussion. Mateo could see that she wasn't feeling well. "We should revisit the idea, but only if we have better intelligence." She let out a long sigh. "Gentlemen, I have had a long trip. I need time to consider what we've discussed, and I'd like to retire to my tent alone."

As the queen and officers stood to leave, Mateo remained at attention, hoping that Anjine would see the longing in his eyes, but she kept her face averted. Perhaps she was trying to find a way that they could meet alone. He finally found his voice. "My Queen, if I may have a . . . private consultation with you? There is a matter we should discuss."

Anjine's cool response, however, surprised him. "Another time, Subcomdar. Your scouting today was sufficiently enlightening. We'll speak later."

Though she spoke without any obvious emotion, her words struck Mateo like a slap. He had waited so long to see her, and she was pushing him away. He saw it clearly now: she hadn't forgiven him for riding off like a coward, for fleeing with the army rather than facing her in the light of day.

Though it devastated him after months of wondering, at least now Mateo had his answer. She had dismissed him. Maybe Anjine didn't want to take the chance of opening her heart once more. Or maybe she didn't want to see him at all.

Queen Anjine might well be ashamed of the weakness she had shown when she'd made love to him. She obviously didn't want to be with him.

"As you wish, Majesty." Mateo was sure he would never be able to break through her icy façade again. He bowed and followed the other men out into the dark night.

70 *Tierran Military Camp, Ishalem Wall*

When most of the soldiers had bedded down and the campfires died to embers, Anjine waited for the Saedran physician in her tent. Outside, everyone but the night watch and perimeter patrols had gone to sleep.

After waiting for months, how she longed to speak with Mateo. He must be hurt because she had brushed him aside, but this was crucial. She had to *know*. It wasn't fair to him until she had an answer; the question would change everything.

In Calay, Sen Ola na-Ten had treated Anjine's occasional illnesses over the years. One of a handful of Saedran doctors qualified to tend battlefield injuries, Sen Ola had joined the siege camp; the wise and cautious woman served the army not because the crown paid her well, but because she felt obligated to help the inevitable wounded.

From prior conversations, the Saedran physician knew of the unsettled stomach and general malaise that had afflicted the queen for several weeks. Those who noticed probably blamed her nausea on a delicate stomach, on camp food, on travel, or on mental turmoil over the impending battle. But Anjine had other suspicions, so she requested that Sen Ola examine her—in secret, at an hour when the visit would go unnoticed. After careful consideration, Anjine decided that even Mateo could not know . . . not yet.

The Saedran doctor entered her tent without ceremony. Sen Ola normally kept her gray-brown hair in long braids while in Calay, but had recently cropped it short so it would not get in the way on the battlefield. Her brown robes were clean, her hands rough and red from frequent washings with strong soap. The curt woman had never been overly compassionate with her patients, but she was also nonjudgmental. She had once said to Anjine, "Infirmities of all sorts are part of being human. If we didn't have them, we would be tempted to consider ourselves gods, and then why would anyone need Ondun?"

Sen Ola set her leather satchel on the plank table where Anjine had spread out strategy charts and diagrams of naval positions to review. The physician opened the case and removed beakers, herbs, chemical jars, and treated papers. "How are your symptoms today, Majesty?"

"Unchanged for the most part. Continued nausea. My head aches." Anjine sat back on a wooden chair, but no matter how many pillows and blankets she used for padding, the seat remained uncomfortable. "I feel tired and weak at a time when I cannot afford to be either. My army is here, and we're due to end this war."

The Saedran looked up at her. "I ran the chemical tests you requested, and I have an answer." Anjine realized she was holding her breath. "Mind you, these tests are not infallible. They provide a point of reference, to be interpreted along with your symptoms, but they could be wrong."

"They are usually right," Anjine added in a dull voice.

"Yes, they are usually right."

The queen wished the woman would just hurry up and answer. Sen Ola looked at her with a penetrating gaze. "It is the result I'm sure you've been expecting. A woman tends to know, without other tests or explanations."

The strength drained out of her in a rush, like water from a sprung barrel.

"You are pregnant, Majesty—as far as I can tell." Sen Ola paused delicately, then continued, as if merely asking about how often the queen slept, "And what is . . ." She paused again. "What is the time frame?"

Anjine knew exactly how long it had been since the Tierran army had departed from Calay, how long it had been since Mateo had left her at dawn to march off. For weeks now Anjine had feared that she carried his child, and she also feared what she might have to do about it. That was why she'd been so cold and distant to Mateo, until she had a real answer. She needed all of her strength to face her own fears, and Mateo frightened her; her feelings for him frightened her. He could not know about it until she decided what to do. And perhaps not even then.

The physician looked uncharacteristically happy. "In times like these, this is good news. Your people will rejoice that Tierra is going to have an heir at last. They were so excited when you announced your betrothal to Jenirod, and dismayed when the engagement was broken. But this . . . this is cause for hope."

Anjine's voice was as hard as her armor. "I forbid you to tell anyone!"

Sen Ola was startled. "But they must know, Majesty. Another few months and it will be obvious to anyone who looks at you."

"*No one.* Not now."

The physician gave a brusque bow. "I will not speak, if you ask me not to. It is the oath of my profession." Then Sen Ola seemed to put the pieces together. "And who is the father?"

Anjine wanted to rebuff the woman for daring to ask, but there was no purpose in hiding the answer from her. Since the physician couldn't tell Mateo, Anjine decided to unburden herself of the secret she had carried for months. "Mateo Bornan," she said quietly, as if making a confession to the prester-marshall.

"A fine man," Sen Ola said.

"He has been my friend most of my life. And he . . . we needed each other." Anjine looked up, her eyes filling with tears so that the other woman's image swam in her vision.

Sen Ola did not scold her or look disappointed, which somehow made things worse. "You've created new life, Majesty. There is no shame in that."

"But this is not the time!" Anjine tore the words out of her throat as uncertainties rose to the forefront of her mind. "Even my daily bouts of illness make it difficult for me to do my important duties."

"I have herbs for that. Taken as tea or chewed, they will lessen the effects."

It wasn't enough. "This is a crucial time for the war! We could win the climactic battle, or the conflict might drag on for months or years yet! As my pregnancy progresses, how could I lead a battle charge? My body's changes will build my emotions into a storm so that I can't think straight—how can I allow that at a time when it's vital that I make wise decisions?"

Sen Ola nodded, but offered no advice.

The words poured out of Anjine. "And what if we are here in camp for months yet? I can't give birth to a baby on the battlefield! I can't be distracted by taking care of an infant when I must dedicate myself to the needs of my army."

"You exaggerate the difficulties, Majesty," Sen Ola said. "Women have done this very thing since the beginning of history. They managed somehow."

"That may be, Sen Ola—but those women were not the queen of Tierra."

Sitting in her chair, Anjine looked over at the trim suit of armor Ammur Sonnen had made for her. The breastplate was sleek, its polished metal fitted to her slender body. Anjine had vowed to wear that armor while leading her troops in battle.

She heaved a great sigh, still wondering what to do. "Sen Ola, I may request that you give me one of your other chemical potions. I might not have any other choice."

71 *Arikara*

As the recovery work continued in Arikara, Imir was constantly exhausted in mind and body. He labored as hard as any galley slave, and he could see the progress. The impossible disaster now seemed to be merely an unspeakable one.

Istala and Cithara spent every waking hour at the healer's tents. Adreala, true to her word, took on any assigned task without complaint. She spent much of her time among the Nunghals, learning their work methods and picking up their language. Imir saw little of his granddaughters except when they came to evening meals on the citadel hill.

For the first weeks after the quake, dust from freshly dug grave pits billowed outside the city, but by now most of the corpses had been pulled from the ruins and transported to the burial sites, placed in mass graves, and covered with stones. Sikaras had sung funeral rites hour after hour until Soldan Xivir made them stop because their constant keening distressed the survivors.

When a caravan arrived bearing extensive supplies of Yuarej silk all the way from Inner Wahilir, along with a written proclamation of blessings from Ur-Sikara Kuari, the people celebrated. While the Nunghal khan placed little stock in the priestess's blessings, he did say the fabric would make good tent material—cause for rejoicing, since the cloth from the first emergency supplies had already been used up.

In the late morning, Imir and Khan Jikaris rode on sturdy Missinian ponies through the streets, passing work crews that excavated bricks and fallen timbers. Now that much of the rubble had been carted away into huge piles of debris, from which rebuilding materials would be salvaged, Arikara was a skeleton of its former self. What had been marketplaces and living quarters, schools and trade shops, were now a motley carnival of tents and canopies. Floppy roofs covered collapsed ceilings.

As they rode, Imir appraised the city's new appearance. "Did you mean to make this look like your own tent city back in the grasslands?"

Jikaris shrugged. "The Nunghal ways are superior."

"Superior? Those primitive tents would collapse in the first hard wind."

The khan sniffed. "When tents collapse, they don't kill thousands." He glanced around. "By the way, where is that Saedran woman you brought to Nunghal lands on your first visit? She was quite beautiful—for one of your people."

The thought of Sen Sherufa made Imir smile. "Yes, she was beautiful—*is* beautiful. But she's gone on a long voyage."

The khan frowned. "So the Nunghal lands did not provide enough excitement for her—and neither did you? Ha!"

A troubled expression crossed Imir's face. "She accepted an important mission. I don't know when she'll be home again."

"I hope she comes back soon. I can stay awhile, but not forever."

"She wasn't all that eager to go in the first place." Imir had been the one who wanted to undertake the sand coracle voyage across the Great Desert; he had put her forward as the Saedran chartsman for the voyage of the *Al-Orizin*, but now that she'd sailed off, he missed Sherufa, her stories and wit . . . just *her*. "I will pass along your greetings when I see her next."

Jikaris was impatient. "That will not be good enough. I want to ask her to be one of my wives. My other ones have grown old and fat, and they bicker too much. That woman could make them behave."

Imir felt a flash of jealousy, but he calmed himself. "I don't think she'd accept your marriage proposal." He gave a dubious chuckle. "Or anyone's."

Jikaris found this hard to believe. "How could she turn down the great khan of the Nunghal-Ari? I would make her a very rich woman."

Imir shrugged. "She turned down the former soldan-shah of Uraba."

"At least she is a woman with a mind of her own." The khan urged his pony forward through the streets.

The two men tied their mounts to a makeshift picket line. Dusty workers stood in line at the central cook tent for a plate of food, which they ate quickly before shuffling back to their worksites. Cooks served grain porridge, soup, and rice. To avert unrest and starvation, Soldan Xivir had commandeered all private stores and stockpiled the food here in guarded supply tents. The meal was not appetizing, but Imir was so tired he had little appetite anyway.

Lithio served from one of the large cauldrons with her hair tied back and her fine dress covered by a dirty apron. Imir barely recognized her. She lifted her wooden spoon and signaled the two men as they arrived. "Have you done enough work to earn your food today? Supplies are dwindling, but there are chickpeas for the stew today."

Jikaris said, "Seeing your beauty always restores my strength."

Lithio wiped her dirty face and smiled. "You are such a gentleman, Khan Jikaris, and handsome too. No wonder you have so many wives." She served him a large portion, then a much smaller one to the former soldan-shah. "You could stand to lose weight, Imir."

He knew she was trying to make him jealous. "You're delightful as always, Lithio."

"I can be completely delightful, when I wish to be."

The khan hovered beside Lithio, eating from his plate while she served other workers. "Nunghal women have their own beauty, and they need no adornments or perfumes. A Nunghal man can see the true loveliness in their eyes." He made a point of staring into Lithio's eyes. Gruel dripped from her spoon back into the cauldron.

"You're holding up the line," Imir said.

As he followed the former soldan-shah to a place where they could eat, Jikaris mumbled, "I know she is your First Wife, Imir, but Lithio says you never visit her. You leave her here in exile. How can you stand to be apart from a woman like that?"

"Better than when I'm *not* apart from her."

Jikaris shook his head. "Well, if that Saedran woman won't have me, why don't you release Lithio as your wife? I'll take her back to my own tent."

"A tempting offer, Jikaris, but let us rebuild the city first. One disaster at a time."

Soldan Xivir and his special guests gathered on the palace hill for the nightly "banquet" of food brought from the central cooksites. Imir and Jikaris sat by Xivir, while Lithio and his granddaughters sat at a table near them. Despite the meager fare, the sikara blessed the meal with great ceremony. When she finished, the Nunghal khan raised his goblet. "And now I add the blessing of my people and my church." He spoke in his own language, rattling off a benediction. "Normally we would celebrate with fireworks, but I understand you use firepowder for other purposes."

After the Nunghal men at the table finished their own prayers, Jikaris spoke up, as if the idea had just struck him, though it was obvious he had been planning for hours. "We need to construct many new buildings. Since so much of this city is ruined, my companions and I wish to erect a tent and an altar, establish a Nunghal place of worship, so we can feel more at home."

Conversation around the banquet tent quieted. Xivir was obviously unprepared for the request. "Is that necessary? There are so few Nunghals here."

The khan's expression darkened. "Your priestesses often come to Nunghal lands to preach Urec's Log to us. Are we not allowed to have our own place of worship here? You tell us about your gods—why should you not want to hear about ours?"

"That would not be acceptable," said the priestess who had prayed over the meal. Her face was as withered as a dried date. "We cannot allow it."

The khan looked baffled and offended. "I did not expect this after the help we give you. You think you have the only true belief? Ondun watches us all." After he relayed to his men what the sikara had said, the Nunghals grew restless.

Imir didn't want the matter to sour the evening. Worse, he feared that the Nunghals were on the verge of riding away and leaving Arikara to fend for itself. He said to the soldan in a warning tone, "They're not being unreasonable, Xivir. We should not make a rash decision."

Adreala, as independent as ever, said, "Hasn't their selfless work here earned them the right to build their own church?"

To Imir's surprise, Istala piped up; she was the most devout of Omra's daughters, and she had wanted to join the priestesses at Fashia's Fountain. "I think so. We can disagree without needing to disrespect. The words of the sikaras teach valuable lessons, but only a person's *actions* show the contents of the heart."

"The Nunghals are good people," Cithara agreed.

Xivir gave a shrug of mock helplessness to the priestesses at the banquet table. "I bow to the will of the soldan-shah's daughters."

"And as a matter of courtesy," Imir added, "I think the sikaras should attend the first Nunghal services. It seems only fair, if they expect the Nunghals to listen to *them*."

72 Olabar

Olabar harbor smoldered for days. The water was crowded with charred wooden hulks, drooping masts, hulls burned to the waterline, and dead fish, all of which only added to the misery of the place. Dismayed merchants rowed about, looking for any salvageable items in the water.

Worst of all, their soldan-shah had raced off to Ishalem, which was under siege by the Tierrans. Even Imir was far away in Arikara, tending to the earthquake disaster. Commerce ministers, guard officers, palace functionaries, and city bureaucrats had their own designated tasks. Kel Rovik organized all the recovery efforts, and the rest of the city's citizens went about their lives trying to return to normal. But they needed a leader.

Istar remained disoriented by her brother's surprise return. Any day, she expected to wake up and find that it was all a dream. She had unrolled the crumbling sheets of Criston's old water-stained letter, scanned his handwriting again and again. Now she knew that he was out there alive and that he still remembered her. Ciarlo had seen him less than a year ago!

Throughout the time she was held captive here, and even after she married the soldan-shah, bore him daughters, and helped raise his sons, *Criston* had refused to marry anyone else, tied to his hope and memories. But Adrea had simply moved on. . . .

She was ashamed, though she could not have made any other decision. Knowing what she knew now, however, she doubted she could look Omra in the eye. Would he sense the difference? What would he think? How could she make love to that man again, hold him and touch him as she had done countless times over the past twenty years? Omra had been her husband, her lover, for far longer than Criston ever had. And yet. . . .

Omra hadn't said goodbye before he galloped away to Ishalem . . . perhaps that was a relief.

Aidenist armies besieged the holy city. Maybe the Tierran queen was there—*Adrea's* queen. She vaguely remembered King Korastine from her days in Windcatch, and she knew that the old man had died. His daughter Anjine—who'd been just a little girl when the raiders kidnapped Adrea—now ruled Tierra.

Tierra.

Adrea didn't know whether to call herself Tierran or Uraban now. Her heart and her life tied her to both lands.

While Olabar reeled from the fire, Adrea had taken her brother to the palace, still disguised in Uraban clothes. The big Nunghal had followed her into the second wife's wing, where they joined Naori, who accepted the stranger despite his Tierran features. When she learned that Ciarlo was Adrea's brother, that he came from the same fishing village she often talked about, Naori greeted him warmly, oblivious to the problems or uncomfortable consequences.

Seated at a low table in Naori's quarters, Ciarlo ate food and drank tea, looking intently at the mother of the soldan-shah's sons. "Let me tell you the story of Aiden and the story of Sapier," he said. "You may find it interesting."

Naori was at first uneasy, but curiosity got the better of her. Ciarlo spun his tale with great passion, and his eyes were intense. Adrea had never heard her brother talk with such fervor before. Back in Windcatch, Ciarlo had apprenticed at the kirk only because his lame leg prevented him from doing other work. But now he had changed as much as she had.

As he talked, his hands worked with strings of twine he had secured from Adrea's rooms, and his nimble fingers created intricate webwork figures, much to Naori's delight. When he finished his story, Ciarlo smiled, as if expecting Omra's second wife to rise up and embrace Aidenism with all her heart. Instead, she just chuckled. "What a silly story! But it is amusing."

"It is more than a story," Ciarlo said.

"We all have our stories," Asaddan interjected. He leaned forward, looking far too big to fit on the small cushion Naori had offered him. "And since we are telling them, you should know about the two brothers, Ari and Su, who established the Nunghal clans. They sailed away from the land of Paradise—probably what you would call Terravitae—because God told them to wander. It's in the blood of mankind to see what there is to be seen, to explore what remains unexplored.

"But the brothers sailed for so long that they could not find a place to land, and they could not find their way back home. Lost, hungry, and disheartened, they cursed God for sending them on a foolish errand. Then a great storm whipped up and drove the two ships apart. The winds and waves flung them along for many days, until the ships crashed on an unknown shore.

"Each captain and crew struggled to survive in the wild land. The descendants of Ari's crew—the ancestors of my clan—moved inland to live off the grassy plains. Those from Su's vessel built new ships and explored the oceans. We are two separate people, but all Nunghals. We believe that someday God will send ships from the land of Paradise to find us."

"That's what you wait for?" Adrea asked. "Is it what you pray for?"

"When it happens, it will happen." Asaddan shrugged his broad shoulders. "In the meantime, we live our lives as best we can."

"What imaginative people you are," Naori said with a sparkling laugh.

Ciarlo looked troubled. "Nunghals must have garbled the telling over the generations. I told you the story of Aiden and Urec, so now you know the truth about the sailing brothers."

Asaddan raised his bushy eyebrows. "Oh, I agree that something has changed in the retelling. Maybe my people got it wrong, maybe yours did. Or maybe the followers of Urec did." He looked over at

Naori. "What do the details matter? Are we not all of God? Aren't the core truths the same? Do you honestly believe Ondun would be pleased by this bloodshed on all sides?"

"But I have seen the Traveler with my own eyes," Ciarlo said. "I felt the love of Aiden—I know in my heart what is true."

"You're confusing devotion with facts," Asaddan said. "No one can know the *facts* of the stories. Too many centuries have passed. But I do know your heart, Ciarlo. Your cause is just and passionate, and I believe you. You could teach these people much if they will listen—and if *you* will listen to *them*."

Adrea shook her head. "After so many years of war, so many unforgivable acts—on both sides, I admit—we've come too far for peace and reconciliation."

Omra would never listen to Aidenists, but she hoped that Kuari could be practical and sensible. Maybe if she took Ciarlo to see the ur-sikara, let the two of them talk . . .

When Adrea explained her idea, Ciarlo swallowed hard, as if Aiden himself had placed a burden on his shoulders. "I am willing to return to Ishalem and speak to the leader of your church."

Asaddan let out a loud laugh. "I just came from there, but I will turn and lead you back. I may need to twist a few arms and knock a few heads to let you have your say."

Adrea looked from her brother to the big Nunghal. "All right, then. We go to Ishalem."

73 Gremurr Harbor

Though he was exhausted and bruised, Destrar Broeck did not sleep much during the voyage back north. The sword cut on his thigh made his leg stiff, and if he turned too quickly, the stitched gashes in his side made him wince. He hoped the injuries healed quickly, so he could fight at full strength once the ironclads reached Ishalem. He decided he would yank out the sutures if they bothered him too much.

The recent attack wasn't the first time Broeck had shed Urecari blood. He had heard their screams as his mammoths stampeded through Gremurr. But torching all those ships in Olabar harbor, a direct blow to the soldan-shah's capital—ah, that victory tasted incredibly sweet.

Aboard the *Raathgir*, which had been designated as the new flagship, the destrar was acutely conscious of the calendar. Queen Anjine had a schedule for the main war, and regardless of how much destruction he had caused at Olabar, the real goal was to conquer the holy city. No longer burdened by the slow captured boats that had served as fireships, his six remaining ironclads sailed swiftly. All of his men were restless and excited, ready for their rendezvous at Gremurr and then onward to Ishalem.

Hobbling across the deck to loosen the muscles in his healing leg, Broeck thought about how much Iaros had matured. When he first brought his nephew to King Korastine not so long ago, Iaros had been gawky, socially clumsy, and full of himself. Now, though, he called out commands and guided his sailors with skill and confidence. Normally the young man would have looked to his uncle for advice, second-guessing his own decisions, but he did not hesitate now. He might even be a worthy successor as Iboria's next destrar.

Broeck grinned as he devised a way to honor his nephew. He limped into his cabin, closed the door, and poured a basin of water. He used a cake of pale soap to lather his chin and cheeks and took up his razor-sharp dagger. He scraped his chin with the blade, smiling to think of the look on Iaros's face as soon as he saw.

Broeck toweled off his face and went out into the open air. Iaros was holding on to the rigging ropes at the ship's side, pointing toward the smoke of the smelters and the coastline of Gremurr.

"Nephew, I have a gift for you!"

Iaros turned, and his mouth dropped open. He began to laugh. "You look like a fine, handsome man, Uncle!"

Broeck stroked his two long mustaches that matched his nephew's. "You always wanted to start a new style. I think it may catch on."

The other sailors looked at their destrar and guffawed, and Broeck singled out those who laughed loudest. "You, you, and you—I command you to shave your chins! Let's see if you think it so ridiculous on your own faces."

The men balked, but they had to do as the destrar commanded. Soon enough, every man aboard had scraped away whiskers and beards, leaving only mustaches. Broeck considered it a gesture of solidarity.

When the six ironclads tied up to the Gremurr docks, old Firun came to greet them. He counted the ships. "What happened to the *Wilka*?"

"Sunk," Broeck said, "but she took the soldan-shah's personal warship with her! A fair exchange, I'd say."

The old servant hesitated, then asked in a quiet voice, "And the boy and his mother—Ulan and Shetia?"

"Set free. They should be safe enough." Broeck cleared his throat awkwardly. "They're back home."

Weary fighters disembarked onto the docks, and the conversation swelled to a loud buzz as they told tales about the fireships and the victory over the Curlies. The dog that had belonged to Ulan, now adopted as the camp mascot, barked happily, running up and down the shore.

Broeck would allow the men only a short rest before they resupplied the ships. He shouted from the end of the pier, "No time to waste! Eat, rest, clean yourselves, for tomorrow we overhaul all six ironclads. Every able-bodied fighter will go aboard this time—to Ishalem!"

The soldiers had unloaded Urecari swords from the storehouses to practice fighting, and by now even the former slaves were skilled at slashing and stabbing. With snows closing the mountain road through Corag, no one could make it back to Tierra along that route until spring, but if these men were victorious at Ishalem, they could have passage home whenever they liked.

By now Queen Anjine and the whole Tierran army must be at the wall, and Comdar Rief's navy would have blocked the western harbor. It was time for his armored warships to complete the trap.

74 *Tierran Military Camp, Ishalem Wall*

Anjine's cool response told Mateo all he needed to know about any future they might have together. His hopes had been delusions, his dreams foolish. Having been close to Anjine most of his life, he could read her mood from the slightest flicker of expression. He had always understood her troubled thoughts when no one else even noticed that she was bothered. Something was definitely, terribly wrong. And her distant message was completely clear.

In his camp tent, Mateo lay awake, heartbroken but determined. He had lost Anjine, and it was his own fault; their one night together had cost them a lifetime of friendship and closeness. He had been weak, grieving for Vicka, and clumsy with his emotions, giving no thought to consequences. How many more blunders could he make? He had lost his wife to fire, a capricious slap of fate that punished him for daring to hope for a normal life . . . and before that, he had lost his soul by murdering so many innocent Urecari.

Now he had lost Anjine.

All he had left was his loyalty, and despite the cold downpour of tragedies, Mateo refused to surrender. He couldn't just wallow in misery: he needed to do something, make plans, take action. He would count down the days until he could race into battle at the head of the army. Victory was the only thing that remained. . . .

Two hours after midnight, Jenirod came to his tent and whispered loudly at the flap, "Subcomdar, I felt you should know. I wasn't sure who else to inform, but the destrar's made up his mind. I think it's a bad idea."

Mateo had been awake, and now he swung off his cot and pushed open the flap to let the other man inside. "What is it? Who?"

"Destrar Shenro—he's pulled together all the men and horses he needs, and they're saddling up now."

Mateo automatically began pulling on his boots. "To what purpose?"

"He thinks he can kidnap the soldan-shah. He's going to lead a raid, scale the wall at the vulnerable spot you found." Jenirod looked awkward. "I . . . I don't think it's a well-thought-out plan."

Mateo tugged on his other boot as a rush of thoughts swirled in his mind. Now that he no longer had to shield himself for Anjine's sake, he felt liberated. So many more possibilities were open to him. Shenro's idea was audacious, daring, and a chance to make an indelible *difference*. "If he's correct, Jenirod—if we do capture the soldan-shah—it would bring the war to an immediate end. And without further Tierran bloodshed."

Jenirod was taken aback. "But he can't be sure the soldan-shah is even in the city, or where to find him. We don't know what goes on behind the wall."

Mateo buckled his sword belt around his waist and pushed past Jenirod, keeping his voice low. "Then he needs all the help he can get. Maybe we can make a difference tonight—take me to him." A nagging voice at the back of his mind questioned the wisdom of the strategy, but he didn't want to think about it.

They came upon Shenro and his armed men as they were quietly saddling their horses. The destrar glanced at Mateo, flushed with excitement. "Subcomdar, I hope you're not going to tell me to stay here. Now that you and I have made our reports, I fear that some *ra'vir* spy will spread the word. We could lose the element of surprise. We have to go *tonight*, or we forfeit our best chance."

Mateo regarded the men who were ready to ride off. "I won't stop you. This is a risk worth taking and a fight worth having. I intend to come along. What better way to demonstrate our loyalty to Tierra?"

Jenirod straightened after seeing the force of Mateo's resolve. "I'll saddle horses for both of us, then, Subcomdar. Maybe we can salvage an ill-advised plan if it's swiftly executed. At the very least, I'll watch your back."

The waxing moon rode high in the sky, shedding enough light for the horsemen to ride westward over grassy hills, parallel to the stone wall. Seventy-five riders had received the hushed summons, Shenro's best warriors.

After weeks of restless waiting, the Tierran army had accomplished little beyond hammering the wall with catapults and killing a few sentries with well-placed arrow shots. It amounted to little more than harassment. The queen was saving the full force of the attack for her main strike.

The Alamont destrar was giddy with anticipation. "We'll be victorious by morning! We can be over the wall, find the soldan-shah's residence, and have him bound and gagged by the time the presters begin their sunrise prayers—if all goes as planned."

"Battles rarely go as planned," Mateo said.

Jenirod rode out with them, still not convinced. "With one extra day of preparation, we could be better supplied, bring two hundred riders instead of seventy-five."

Shenro said, "That only gives some damned *ra'vir* spy extra time to report what we intend to do."

Mateo agreed. "Besides, the moon will be brighter tomorrow. This is the best way to leverage our surprise." The real reason he refused to delay, though, was that he didn't want the queen to forbid him from acting. It had to be now, before he came to his senses. "I do wish we had spies inside the city, though. I'd prefer to have better intelligence."

"If we had spies in the city, we could bribe one of them to open a gate." Shenro shook his head. "And who could trust a Curly to tell the truth anyway? Our army has been camped at the wall for more than two months. By now, the Curlies probably think we'll just sit on our thumbs for the rest of the year and lob catapult missiles at them every day."

The riders slipped out of the main camp, telling no one where they were going lest some soldier unexpectedly spread the word. The sentries assumed they were off on some secret mission for the queen.

The horses ambled along at a quiet walk, rustling the grasses in the starlight. The soldiers kept silent so that enemy sentries would not hear their approach. They could see the glow of Ishalem's lights on the other side of the hill.

Jenirod was still skeptical. "Even with the element of surprise, are seventy-five of us enough? The Curlies are all armed. This won't be like—" He swallowed hard. "This won't be like killing priestesses at a sacred temple."

"You're welcome to turn back if you like," Shenro said in a biting tone. "We'll make do with seventy-four."

Jenirod was not offended. "Oh, I'll fight with you, and I'll die beside you if need be. I just want to know that Queen Anjine supports this plan."

"The queen trusts me more than any other. She lets me lead the army as I see fit," Mateo said. "And I support this operation. Destrar, tell me what you know about the soldan-shah and his location."

Even though he had already made up his mind to participate in this bold venture, Mateo doubted the reliability of the scouts' reports. There were conflicting sightings of a man in a scarlet olba and a fine sash—an important or wealthy man, certainly, but not necessarily Omra himself. Mateo had seen the Uraban soldan-shah during the abortive earlier battle at the wall, when the *ra'virs* had struck down so many Tierrans. Despite the chaos of that bloody day, Mateo vividly remembered Omra's face. He would recognize the soldan-shah again, if their raiding party should find him.

Taking the lead, Mateo guided them to where the slope made for easier access to the sinuous stone wall. The soldiers dismounted, taking the knotted ropes and iron grappling hooks they had brought from camp. Though occasional watchtowers punctuated the length of the wall, they saw no silhouettes of sentries immediately above.

Mateo tightened his belt, secured his sword and dagger. "Let's be quick about it. Up and over, before anyone spots us."

Shenro wore a broad grin. "My sword has been waiting for this a long time."

Mateo had a brief thought of Anjine but brushed it aside. He couldn't think of her right now, only victory. He had no idea what was on the other side of that wall, but he would fight it, follow Destrar Shenro to the soldan-shah. He could open one of the small gates and gallop away with their priceless captive. Uneasy questions clamored in his mind, but he pushed them away. If they did indeed seize Omra, then all risks would be justified . . . even to Anjine.

Jenirod held one of the ropes and twirled the grappling hook before casting it high into the air, as if he were roping a stray

Eriettan calf. The hook arced over the thick stone barricade, and even before it struck, seven other soldiers followed suit with their own grappling hooks. As swiftly as if they had practiced the operation down to the last detail, they began scaling the knotted ropes.

Unfortunately, the thrown iron hooks and the fighters' metal armor made plenty of noise, and before the first Tierran reached the top of the wall, Uraban sentries began to shout an alarm. One man used a brass horn to blast loud notes.

Mateo grasped his rope, dug his heels into the knots, and hauled himself up the stone wall. He had no intention of stopping now.

Within minutes after being awakened by the trumpets, Kel Unwar was dressed in his scarlet olba and sash, carrying his scimitar, and riding a horse along the cobblestone streets adjacent to God's Barricade. He had been waiting for this. He had known the 'Hooks were up to something.

The lookouts by the main gates reported that the Tierran army hadn't stirred; their fires still burned low and the tents remained in place, with the usual number of sleeping men visible. But the assault was taking place a mile away. Some of the vermin had penetrated into the city! Were they here to kidnap and rape young Uraban girls, as they had done to poor Alisi all those years ago? How he hated them!

He rode faster, wondering what sort of vulnerability he had left in the wall. After building God's Barricade and digging the great canal, Unwar did not intend to let failure leave a dark blot on his legacy. The wall was perfect and secure, yet somehow these Aidenists felt they could breach it. Despite constant bombardment, their catapults had done little damage, and his archers would never allow them close enough to use battering rams against the gate.

Criers roused troops from their barracks, and some of Ishalem's citizens gathered makeshift weapons. Kel Unwar knew these people would fight tooth and nail to defend the holy city if necessary. History had already showed them what sort of horrific damage the Aidenists could cause.

Finally he heard a commotion ahead, saw armored forms atop the torchlit wall, the flash of swords, and Urecari soldiers defending the barricade. One man tumbled down the inside of the wall, sliding on the stone blocks and leaving a red smear before he struck the bottom.

Ahead, Unwar saw the Tierran invaders furiously stabbing and chopping. He was surprised at how small the force was. There couldn't be more than a hundred men, yet they had scaled the wall! He frowned. What could their plan possibly be? What were they after? And how did they expect so few fighters, however determined, to defeat all the defenders of Ishalem? He would mount their heads on stakes above the main gate.

More of his men rushed up wooden scaffolding or stone access stairs to reinforce the defense on the wall. He dispatched ten soldiers to ride the length of the barricade and check for further Tierran treachery. Perhaps this advance was just a decoy. It made no sense otherwise.

75 *The Lighthouse at the End of the World*

Criston had never been so thunderstruck. "Adrea is . . . alive? All this time I hoped, I prayed, I believed—"

For a moment his heart stopped; all other thoughts and concerns in his mind blew away like dry leaves in a wind. For years he had clung to the idea of her: the young face that had stared at him from the dock in Calay, slender hands waving as the *Luminara* sailed away.

Criston whispered, "I wrote her countless letters, never forgot her." Tears began streaming down his face. "Where is she? Is she well? How can I find her?" A thousand questions whirled around him, but they were all basically the same. He wanted to know everything about her in the intervening years. *Adrea is alive!*

Mailes was delighted by his reaction, ignoring the others now. "Here, let me show you." The old man turned the round lens on its brass stand, and the glass brought faraway sights into amazing focus. Adjusting the view with dizzying speed, Mailes found the city of Calay on the other side of the world, then the town of Windcatch. As the images whirled past, Criston saw the Aidenist army camped at the Ishalem wall, saw Tierran naval vessels blockading the western harbor of Ishalem. Moving inland with jerky speed, across another expanse of water—the Middlesea?—another view showed him a large Uraban city with its harbor burned, the waters crowded with blackened ships. "That is Olabar," Mailes said. "Looks like they've had some trouble."

He moved back eastward, focused the lens on three figures on horseback, who were riding a wide road on the coast of a calm, blue sea. A big foreign-looking man with thick black hair was riding beside a smaller man in the brown robes of a traveler or pilgrim—Ciarlo!

And a woman. She was dressed in Uraban traveling clothes, her hair bound in colorful scarves, but he could see a flash of blond hair exactly like the lock she had given him twenty years before. He could see her blue eyes, a face that had been rounded by the years, now a middle-aged woman instead of the girl he had married . . . but she was still beautiful. Still Adrea. And still alive.

Criston began to sob, weak with joy, transfixed by what he saw. He wanted to stare at her image for hours more.

Mailes swiveled the lens away. "That was just to give you a taste, Criston Vora. I don't want to be cruel, but Ondun would not want you to see and know too much. I'm sorry, but I'm forbidden to reveal any more."

Criston was trembling. At least he knew that she was alive and safe, and that Ciarlo had found her somewhere. "You have given me the greatest gift, Mailes. I thank you with all my heart." He was tempted to turn the *Dyscovera* around and head directly back for Tierra, abandoning his quest. But he could not do that. By now they must be quite close to Terravitae. He felt lightheaded, determined. "Mailes, I would be grateful for any assistance you grant us, so that we can finish this with the greatest possible speed. How can we find Terravitae?"

The lighthouse keeper stroked his lush silvery beard. "After sailing for the better part of a year, it would be a shame if you didn't reach that majestic shore. I myself can't look to see what's been happening there, or who is left of our race, but I can give you charts to help you find your way."

While Sen Aldo skimmed the tomes left open on the tables, the old man searched his shelves, studying the unmarked spines of his books. A restless and unsettled Prester Hannes paced the room, scrutinizing the magical fire. The dazzling flames glanced off the rotating mirror, and the flash of light cast its bright beacon across the seas.

Finding what he wanted, Mailes pulled out a heavy volume and flipped past pages full of dense writing until he stopped at sketches of coastlines and islands. "Captain, these charts show exactly how to find Terravitae, and how close you are." He gave a secretive, wistful smile. "It shouldn't take long."

Criston studied the maps with a heightened urgency. Now he knew reaching Terravitae was possible—and that Adrea was waiting for him somewhere in Tierra or Uraba. He couldn't stop repeating the thought in his mind. It was like a hypnotic chant. *Adrea is alive!*

While Aldo and Criston compared details from the charts,

Javian went to the open window of the high turret and stuck his head out into the brisk breeze. Not far away, the *Dyscovera* lay at anchor, waiting for them. He gazed up at the sky, where fluffy white clouds had tightened into gray clumps. "Bad weather coming, Captain. We should leave soon, or rough waves might smash the ship onto the rocks."

Appraising the storm, Mailes nodded. "Such furious seas usually mean the Leviathan is coming." He raised his eyebrows. "And *you* know the monster all too well, Captain Vora."

Cold dread and anticipation flooded through Criston's veins, nearly countering the giddy thrill of seeing Adrea again. He clenched his hands as if wrestling with an eel, though his emotions were much more slippery. "I would dearly love a second chance to throw a harpoon down the Leviathan's gullet."

"No, no, a harpoon wouldn't be enough to kill it." Mailes stepped over to take up his position behind the broad swivel lens and peered into the heart of the oncoming storm. "The beast often circles here—attracted by the bright beacon, I suspect . . . or maybe it senses my presence."

"Why would the Leviathan be interested in you?" Hannes asked, sounding argumentative.

The lighthouse keeper turned to him mildly. "I understand the monster's heartbreak and loneliness. The Leviathan was denied its mate, just as I was. We've both been spurned by Ondun." He heaved a deep sigh. "Perhaps it sees me as a kindred spirit."

He adjusted the round glass and the distant seas expanded before his view, showing a glimpse of a nightmare creature awash in storms and whitecaps. It had a gigantic body, yawning mouth, and thrashing fang-tipped tentacles. Even the glimpse of the monster was enough to chill Criston to his core.

Mailes talked as if he saw nothing more than a group of boisterous dolphins. "Yes, that is definitely the Leviathan."

Hannes was pleased rather than terrified. "You see, Captain?

The Leviathan is not dead! That skeleton we found must have been some trick."

Criston could not dispute that the beast was still alive, nor could he deny the fossilized sea monster he had seen on the cliff. He tried to peer at his nemesis through the old man's lens, but Mailes nudged the brass stand and continued to scan the ocean in the vicinity. With a startled gasp, the old man froze, entirely uninterested in the gigantic monster. "Even I never imagined it could happen!"

Criston wondered what could possibly surprise a man who had seen the whole world for generation after generation.

Mailes looked youthful and exuberant, his face beaming with joy. He nearly danced in front of his lens. "My exile must be at an end! I was cursed to wait here until Ondun returns . . . and *he is returning*!" He continued in a whisper. "Along with Iyomelka."

In the lens's field of view, Criston saw a fearsome-looking ship with tattered sails and a barnacled hull, the vertebrae and skull of a sea serpent forming its keel and figurehead. A long sharp prow of antler coral protruded from beneath the skull. A woman stood at the helm, her hair flying in the breeze. Iyomelka? On the deck rested a crystalline coffin that held a motionless old man.

In his astonishment Mailes nudged the lens just a hair, widening the field, and saw that the spectral ship was in swift pursuit of another vessel whose bright sail was emblazoned with the Eye of Urec. "That's a Uraban ship!"

Hannes growled, "Captain, we are so close to Terravitae, we dare not let any follower of Urec arrive first! We need to go immediately—this is a race we must win. The heretics cannot be allowed to befoul the sacred land."

Javian tugged on Criston's sleeve. "He's right, sir. Back to the ship, as fast as we can . . . this man and his spying make me nervous. The storm is coming, and we've got to sail away before the Leviathan arrives."

Sen Aldo gathered the chart that marked the islands and the coast of Terravitae, though he plainly wished he could take dozens of the other books as well.

Criston turned to the old man, still stunned by all the revelations he had just received. "Mailes, will you come with us?"

Hannes lashed out, "And break the commandment of Ondun? Captain, we dare not!"

Mailes no longer looked forlorn, though. "I was going to ask you to take me from this cursed place, but now I will wait.

I have endured centuries of punishment, but it's at an end. When Ondun returns, he will forgive me."

Criston was anxious to set sail and take the *Dyscovera* away from here. He had to reach Terravitae before the Urecari ship did, or Iyomelka, or even the Leviathan. "This man's fate is not for us to determine. It's a moot point now."

"As your religion says, Captain Vora, may the Compass guide you," Mailes said by way of benediction as he followed them down the stone stairs.

"Thank you, I believe it will. We have the actual Compass, and it's brought us this far."

76 *The* Al-Orizin

Not long after the *Al-Orizin* left the iceberg sea behind, Iyomelka's spell-driven ship caught up with them again. The island witch's weed-stitched sails belled outward with a roar of cold winds, closing the distance in a flurry of storms. Saan knew that despite his best navigational prowess, Iyomelka would be upon them soon.

Angry winds came at them from all directions, and the desperate crew scurried to set and reset the sails. The *Al-Orizin* was forced to tack back and forth, while Iyomelka's vessel came straight on toward them.

Overhead, the sky turned gray and bruised. As Grigovar winched down a rigging rope, he kept his gaze on the clouds. "That's not a normal storm, Captain."

"I wouldn't expect it to be normal. We've seen how Iyomelka can use the weather. We have to try to outrun it."

"There's more to the storm." Sen Sherufa pointed to an even darker set of thunderheads and a splash of intermittent lightning ahead to port, apart from what Iyomelka was driving ahead of her. "*That* doesn't look like her doing."

The ominous knots ahead comprised a separate rogue storm. With the fury of the island witch behind them and the strange tumultuous weather ahead, the *Al-Orizin* was being trapped between the prongs of hurricane pincers.

A burst of lightning illuminated the sky like a thousand Nunghal fireworks, accompanied by an explosion of thunder that rattled the masts. Behind them, Iyomelka's ship closed in, and the serpent-skull figurehead stared at them as if regarding prey.

The whitecap waves became huge swells that heaved them up and pitched them back down again. Gale-force winds drove sheets of cold rain nearly horizontal to the deck. Sikara Fyiri locked herself in her cabin, vomiting into a basin or all over the floor, and Saan didn't blame her.

He fought his way to the bow, and Sherufa staggered out to join him. Her thick Saedran robes were quickly drenched. He searched for any safe haven ahead, but could barely see through the downpour. Far away, an unexpected flash of light sliced through the sheeting rain and spray. The dazzling beacon brightened then faded, like the eye of a demon slowly opening and closing.

"Look there—a light!" The insistent light came again, and Saan made up his mind. "I don't know what that is, but I don't see much other chance out here." He shouted into the gale, "Change course, two points to starboard! Head for the beacon!"

"Aye, Captain!" The helmsman wrestled with the rudder. The sailors staggering about on deck pulled on the ropes, trying to turn the sails, though the storm fought back.

Ystya came to him. The downpour had plastered her ivory hair to her head; even so, she looked achingly beautiful. Droplets streamed down her pale face, but she didn't seem cold or frightened. "I've come to help you."

Saan took her hand. Her fingers were cold, and he squeezed them, repeating his promise. "I'll defend you against your mother if I can. She may well strike me dead within seconds, but I'll do my best."

Ystya gave a slight laugh that the wind snatched away. "No need for that—it's time for me to teach her how much I've learned from being with you, how strong I've become. I'm no longer an infant she can tuck under her arm and carry away against my will." As he gripped her, he felt Ystya's skin tingle with static electricity. She released his hand and stepped to one side as she began to exude a faint glow. "Remember, I'm the Key to Creation."

As Ystya's power shielded them, the winds died, the rain stopped, and an eerie calm descended over the *Al-Orizin*, yet her silken sails remained stretched, filled by an unfelt breeze. Ystya looked at Saan with an enigmatic gaze. "My mother isn't the only one who can control storms."

The young woman gathered energy and struck her own blow. A spiderweb of lightning danced in the clouds, then lanced back toward the spectral ship. The whitecap waves surged back toward the witch's patchwork vessel. Ystya clenched her hands, and a roar of thunder boomed out, one powerful force challenging another.

With her feet firmly planted on the moss-smeared deck, hands grasping the barnacle-encrusted rail, Iyomelka hung on. She called upon the magic that suffused her and also borrowed from the ever-increasing reservoir of power that emanated from her husband's crystal-encased body.

Though Ondun had drowned long ago after an unfortunate set of circumstances, even in death he had not entirely lost his power. As she sailed nearer to the magical shores of Terravitae, Iyomelka sensed the spark brightening in the crystal coffin. Though she spent his power calling storms in pursuit of their daughter, Ondun seemed to be growing stronger. It would be just like her husband to reawaken and bother her again, precisely when he was least needed.

Her ship sliced through the water, helped along by the streaming waves. Not far ahead, she could see the *Al-Orizin*'s colored sails and sense her daughter's presence aboard. Close . . . so close.

But Iyomelka felt other powerful storms approaching—a knotted, self-contained hurricane that was not of her making. That other unnatural storm pressed against her spells, an independent force. Though she was about to collide with it, she refused to alter course, intent upon Saan's ship and her kidnapped child.

Iyomelka was taken aback, and gasped aloud as a bright white beacon stabbed through the whipping rain. She knew instantly what it was: *Mailes!* A place in her heart opened again, exposing memories she had buried under centuries of dust. She reeled.

So long ago, at the end of an era, Ondun had forced her to stand at that isolated rocky outcropping—sad and contrite—while he exiled Mailes to the Lighthouse at the End of the World. In her shame at betraying her husband, Iyomelka had turned away from her lover, unable to bid him farewell, leaving Mailes abandoned for all time on that lonely speck of land.

Ondun hadn't loved Iyomelka for some time, though his pride wouldn't let him admit it. Everything was falling apart in Terravitae, their people weakening, their race dwindling away. His severe punishment of Mailes had more to do with refusing to accept failure than wanting to win his wife's heart again. For a while afterward, she and Ondun had tried to rekindle their love, but even he couldn't just command such a thing, no matter how great his powers might be. It hadn't worked, even though she had conceived his child—an extreme rarity among their long-lived race. If timing and circumstances had been different, Ystya could have been the child of Mailes, a daughter born out of real love.

Now, as she spotted the lighthouse beacon, Iyomelka realized that her own journey had come full circle—fleeing Terravitae, hiding on her island for so many centuries, and then sailing in pursuit of her daughter. She wondered what Mailes would think to see omnipotent Ondun sealed in a transparent box, drowned and helpless.

Iyomelka looked down at the old man's placid face beneath the sparkling water. "We've come back here after all, husband, even though you never wished to return. It must be our destiny."

She longed to see Mailes, but rescuing her daughter was the most important thing. The Key to Creation. The girl was already at risk of learning too much about herself.

The opposing storm buffeted her ship and actually pushed the vessel backward. The petrified masts creaked, and the wind blew in Iyomelka's face with enough force to make her stagger on the deck. Startled at the strength, she realized that Ystya was doing this!

Impressed, but not deterred, she summoned more storms of her own and pressed on toward the *Al-Orizin* and the Lighthouse at the End of the World.

77 *Ishalem Wall*

The furious battle atop the Ishalem wall was everything Mateo needed, and he lost himself in the sheer unfettered violence, the unencumbered goal of attacking the enemy. As soon as he and his men scaled the ropes and surmounted the stone barricade, they ran along the top of the wall toward the nearest Uraban sentries who were just beginning to respond to the threat. Here, a mile from the Tierran army's main camp, the sentries seemed less prepared for a fight.

Shenro ran ahead, breathless. "We'll have to be quick. I thought we might have a little more time to search."

The first Uraban they met let out a thin yelp as he died with a sword in his stomach. The next sentry shouted an alarm before Destrar Shenro slashed sideways so viciously that not only did he cut the man's throat, he nearly decapitated him. Shenro looked down at the crumpling body with disgust. "I'd hoped one of these men could tell us where to find the soldan-shah."

"Do you speak Uraban?" Mateo asked.

"I would have made my point, somehow."

With clamoring alarms, more sentries rushed from the watchtowers. Urecari soldiers emerged from their barracks, still not sure what was happening. Mateo urged the Tierran fighters forward, and they raced in a group along the top of the wall. Destrar Shenro seemed enraptured, as if energized by the sight of blood on his blade.

Jenirod followed close behind them. "They'll be mustering reinforcements from all across the city. Even if we do find the soldan-shah, how are we going to get out of here with him?"

"Maybe we should just kill him in his bed, then," Shenro said, undaunted.

"That wouldn't put an end to the war!"

Shenro shrugged. "Still . . ."

Instead of adding his own comment, Mateo swung his sword at a Uraban soldier in front of him. Jenirod shoulder-blocked another enemy fighter with enough force to knock him off the wall. The man plummeted to the ground with an audible snap of bone.

Uraban horses galloped through the streets below. Dark-haired men raced up the steps to the top of the wall, carrying naked scimitars.

The Tierran soldiers charged with enough enthusiasm to drive back the larger numbers of Urabans. They called Omra's name, as if that would magically bring him to face them. Destrar Shenro threw himself into the fray without regard for his own safety, and Mateo understood exactly how the destrar felt. He drove back the nagging whisper in his head that Jenirod had warned them this was not a good plan. It was too late to change course now. Instead, he concentrated only on fighting the enemy—for Anjine.

Mateo fought hard enough that he didn't have to pay attention to the odds rising against them. Anjine had already walled herself off from him, and he felt helpless to do anything else. Perhaps this way he could leave his mark and prove to her that she needed him, that he was valuable to her . . . and to Tierra.

Although he had a well-defined objective, he didn't have a clear path to reach it, and that was a poor example for a military subcomdar to set. He *reacted*, driven by emotion and anger, pursuing an idea he had not considered logically. And now he was dragging these other men off the cliff with him.

He shouted at the top of his lungs, "For the queen!" and pressed forward with greater vehemence.

Shenro leapt ahead like a dancer, striking down two Urecari and facing a group of armed men who surged up the stone steps. "For Aiden!"

"If we don't retreat soon, Subcomdar, we'll be overwhelmed!" Jenirod cried.

"We haven't captured the soldan-shah yet."

"We haven't *found* the soldan-shah!"

Accompanying the rush of soldiers up the steps came a man dressed in fine clothes, wearing the scarlet olba and sash of a commander. Recognizing the man's rank, Shenro threw himself forward, sliced open the arm of another Uraban who got in the way, and knocked him aside. "There he is—the soldan-shah! Seize him." The Uraban in the red olba coolly brandished his scimitar, staring down the edge of the blade. Shenro lifted his sword and let out a yell. "Take him, and we can leave!"

Mateo was confused. "That's not the soldan-shah."

From behind, the man Shenro had knocked aside struck back, hitting him on the head with the flat of his scimitar. The destrar reeled from the blow, tried to hold up his sword.

The man with the scarlet olba thrust with his curved blade, and Shenro barely managed to squirm out of the way. Jenirod grabbed the destrar and pulled him to safety before he even realized his danger. When one of the Alamont soldiers engaged the enemy leader, the Uraban ran him through with his curved blade. The Tierran coughed in disbelief, held upright by the scimitar that skewered his chest. His own blade slipped from his fingers to clatter on the stone steps, and it slid, bumping on one step after the next, until it dropped off the edge to the ground. The man flailed with his empty hand, still trying to hit the Uraban commander, but the light faded from his eyes. The Ishalem commander yanked his bloody scimitar out of the body.

The Tierrans fought with increased vigor, and Shenro seemed disoriented. "That's the soldan-shah! We have to take him."

Mateo pulled him away. "I've *seen* Soldan-Shah Omra, and that isn't him."

Shenro was crestfallen. "Then we still need to find him in the city."

More enemy soldiers ascended the access stairways. Though he had already known it at the back of his mind, Mateo finally realized the folly of their raid. "We can't do it, Destrar." He raised his voice to sound the retreat. "Back to the ropes!"

Four enemy soldiers engaged him, their scimitars dancing in the dim light. Mateo held a dagger in one hand, sword in the other as he backed away, defending himself against the scimitars. But when he tried to block two thrusts at the same time, another Uraban darted into the opening. His long slim knife plunged into Mateo's side.

The blow made him stagger. It felt as if someone had poured ice down his throat. He used his knife to fend off a killing thrust, cut deeply into a Uraban arm, then slashed weakly with his sword as he scrambled away.

Taking charge, Jenirod bellowed for the soldiers to get to the ropes and climb back down to their horses. Several more Tierrans died as they withdrew, and their bravado faded as the tide of battle shifted in their minds. Instead of feeling invincible, they saw the surge of enemy soldiers and a thousand blades waiting to kill them. They carved their way through the handful of defenders to their rear, retreating along the top of the wall.

The Ishalem commander shouted an order, and through the haze of pain from the knife wound in his side, Mateo watched a line of enemy archers take a stance, nocking arrows. Urecari swordsmen dropped back to leave an open field of targets.

"Run!" Jenirod shouted. Somehow, Destrar Shenro had gotten ahead of him, leading the surviving fighters to the ropes and grappling hooks. The first three Tierran soldiers scrambled down to the ground and ran to the horses.

Mateo staggered along, holding his side, which was slick with hot blood.

Arrows sang through the air, and five Tierrans fell at once. Mateo was dropping behind, limping and reeling. He felt lightheaded, as if the pain were far away, no more than a nagging shout drowned out by the storm of adrenaline. The archers loosed their next round, and a Uraban arrow struck him squarely between his shoulder blades. It felt as if someone had hit him with a hammer, a blow that Vicka's father would have admired. He couldn't run. His legs gave way, pitching him forward. He found himself sprawling. He struggled to get up.

Mateo knew he was dead. He couldn't move, couldn't reach the ropes, much less climb down. He was going to die here, after all, atop the Ishalem wall.

Jenirod grabbed him by the arms, pulled him up, and carried him over his shoulder like a rolled rug. The clash of swords, the shouts and screams of men, the defiant roars all faded to a blur in his head.

Jenirod faced the oncoming enemy on the wall and let out an animal snarl that drove them back. He slung a rope around his waist, tightened his grip on the limp Mateo, and lowered himself as fast as he could. He dropped to the ground as the Urabans reached the edge of the wall, hurling curses.

The enemy soldiers found the ropes and cut them. A few Tierrans fell; one man broke his ankle, but his boot kept the joint together enough that his companions could help him to the horses.

More archers appeared silhouetted against the top of the barricade, pulling their bows. Jenirod ran, zigzagging to foil the archers' aim, hardly even winded despite his heavy burden. Mateo was only marginally aware of what was happening.

"*Go!*" Jenirod bellowed to the men ahead of him. "Mount up and ride for your lives back to camp!"

Arrows whispered around them in the tall grasses, reminding a groggy Mateo of fish leaping in a pond.

Somehow Jenirod reached his horse and heaved Mateo across the saddle before he swung up himself. He bent forward and galloped off into the night. "We'll get you to the Saedrans, Subcomdar—just hold on. You'll be all right."

Mateo didn't believe him. He gasped for breath, trying to cling to a memory of Anjine until he finally lost consciousness.

78 *The* Dyscovera

As they sailed from the Lighthouse at the End of the World, caught in the fringes of colliding storms, Criston felt as if all the strands of his life had knotted together in this place, at this moment. Spray flooded over the deck, thunder and lightning clashed in the angry clouds overhead. The beacon from the ancient tower pierced the thickening squall even as the *Dyscovera* pulled away.

As he willed his ship to greater speed, Criston's cold anticipation was stronger than his dread. The storm seemed familiar, and this time he understood what it meant. The Leviathan! Now that he knew Adrea was still alive, he vowed that this monster would not take her away from him again.

He called over the storm noise, "I would ask you to pray for us, Prester, but I doubt it would do any good."

Hannes stood in the cold rain as if he had something to prove to himself, wrestling with his internal fury after leaving Mailes. "Prayer always helps, Captain—in one fashion or another." But it was an automatic answer; the man's doubts were inscribed on his troubled face as clearly as words in a journal.

As worsening winds drove the *Dyscovera* onward, one of the canvas sails tore, and a rope whipped free, flailing about like a wild animal trying to escape. Together, Javian and Mia struggled to pull it down and fastened it to a stanchion. An unexpected swell curled over the side, knocking Mia off her feet. Javian yelled after her as she fought for any sort of hand-hold. She clutched a loose crate. It tumbled and rolled, so she grabbed on to the capstan instead. The crate flew overboard and was lost in the wild sea. Javian recklessly sloshed forward to grab Mia's arm, and they huddled together on the capstan. The wave passed, and as the waters drained from the deck, the two held each other, panting and frightened.

Lightning struck again. Criston saw a shadow moving through

the water—a dangerous form, like a nightmare embodied. "All hands on deck!" he bellowed, though many crewmembers would be reluctant to emerge from shelter. "I need every man here!"

The word was passed, and a dozen bedraggled men fought their way into the storm. Criston urged them along. "Break out the harpoons and spears—I need every man armed and ready! This will be the fight of our lives."

Since Adrea was alive out there, he *had* to survive. Criston tried to penetrate the driving rain with his gaze. The pearlescent ice-dragon horn attached to the bow did not glow. Perhaps Raathgir's protection drove away sea serpents . . . but not the Leviathan.

Soaking wet and still shaky, Javian and Mia got back to their feet and armed themselves. The crew took up harpoons and spears, shielding themselves from the downpour, looking for a target.

"Our faith will protect us, Captain!" Hannes shouted. "Do not be afraid."

Criston narrowed his eyes. "Even Ondun regretted creating the Leviathan, Prester. We should all be afraid."

As if it had merely been waiting for the *Dyscovera*'s crew to gather their laughable weapons, the dark monster of the deep breached the frothing waves. The Leviathan's body was cylindrical, its snout tapered to a point at the end of a mouth as large as a sea cave. From the middle of its brow a single milky eye stared out with a cold and demonic glow completely unlike the bright gleam of the lighthouse beacon. A line of spines surrounded its head and gills, like the frill of a poisonous lizard.

Criston's sailors threw their harpoons against the armored gray hide, and the sharpened iron tips struck sparks off the scales, but they barely made the Leviathan twitch. The beast let out a sound like a deep, lonely groan, exhaling a cold wind that stank of rotted fish guts and deadly plague.

The creature lifted sets of tentacles, each like a writhing cobra tipped with another fanged mouth and bright eyes in search of prey. The tentacles clasped the *Dyscovera*'s deck rails, splintering the wood, chewing through the hull.

Like a man caught up in a spell, Criston strode toward his nemesis. This monster had destroyed the *Luminara*, ruined his life, killed Captain Shay and all of his shipmates. He remembered that last night as clearly as any Saedran chartsman could recall the details of a map: Captain Shay had run forward to hurl a spear into the monster's eye . . . and when he missed, the Leviathan lurched onto the *Luminara*'s bow and devoured the captain in a single gulp.

Now Criston threw the first harpoon at hand, which plunged into the monster's gaping maw, piercing the soft pink flesh. "Tonight, one of us will die!"

The fanged appendages grabbed the masts and snapped spars like twigs. Two of the tentacles seized sailors, while another one tore off great chunks of flesh and tossed the morsels overboard to be eaten later.

While the storm continued to rage, the monster let out another slow, rumbling groan and opened its mouth wider. Panicked, sailors threw their spears, and a few wobbly archers loosed a volley of arrows. Sen Aldo dove to the deck as a tentacle swooped overhead. Criston grabbed another harpoon and did not flinch from where he stood.

The Leviathan drew back, intent on destroying the ship. From beneath the water, it rammed the *Dyscovera* with its bullet-shaped snout. The sailing ship heeled to port, nearly capsizing, and a long crack shivered down the side. The fanged tentacles reached out to snap the mainmast in half and tore away the mainsail.

Prester Hannes leaned against the foremast, gripping his fishhook pendant. His eyes were closed in fervent prayer, and the expression on his scarred face was oddly peaceful.

Criston shut out the sounds of cracking wood and screaming men. Time seemed to stop for him as he gathered his courage and determination. He called for help, summoning allies who hated the Leviathan as much as he did, if not more. He prayed they would arrive before it was too late.

79 Calay

His wife told him he was being foolish, but Sen Leo knew that his fears were justified. Guard-Marshall Vorannen had promised to increase patrols in the dockside area, but the city guard didn't have enough remaining members to watch the *Dyscovera* model properly.

The old scholar was anxious because it had been so long since Aldo had sent a *rea* pigeon, but he didn't want Lanni to suspect that her husband might be in danger. Now Sen Leo tossed and turned in his bed. If the last days of the world were indeed upon them, according to Saedran prophecies, then he could not change the fate of humanity. Yet it was necessary as a human being, as an intelligent man, to *do something*. He could not simply give up.

In bed, his wife gave a loud sigh. "Go there, if it worries you so much. When you're restless like this, you flop about like a fish on a dock. If you're not going to sleep, then spend the night watching over the ship model with Sen Burian. At least I'll have peace here, and one of us can rest."

Sen Leo did not need to be asked twice. He pushed himself out of bed and pulled on his clothes, while his wife mumbled teasingly into her pillow, "If you think this means you can nap all day tomorrow when there's work to be done, you'd better reconsider."

"I always get my work done, dear."

In minutes, he was out the door and making his way through the quiet streets of the Saedran District. His anxiety increased as he approached the dockside warehouses, where the silence seemed tense and ominous instead of restful. He saw none of the promised guards stationed outside the warehouse building, which meant the *Dyscovera* model was unguarded! What was Vorannen thinking?

Leo hurried forward and was shocked to find the warehouse door unlocked and ajar. Something was not right here.

He heard voices inside, people stirring. Indignant, sure they were up to no good, he marched through the door, ready to protect the model. Just inside the threshold, he stumbled over a body. He fell to his knees and let out a loud gasp, which made the voices fall silent. His hand landed on the chest of the corpse on the floor and came away wet with the blood that had soaked the man's tunic. Sen Burian na-Coway.

Sen Leo struggled to his feet, shouting. "Who are you? What are you doing here?" Three forms sprang toward him.

Several candles shed enough light inside the storehouse for him to discern that the figures carried mallets, cudgels, axes, and long knives. Leo recognized the hooligans who had harassed Sen Burian several days earlier. Before, the vandals had seemed intent on annoying the model-maker, but this was different from throwing rotten fruit or breaking windows—they had murdered Burian!

"Stay away from that model!" Sen Leo shouted. "Help! *Help!*"

But the neighborhood streets were empty.

"And you're going to stop us, old man?" said one of the young men.

Leo saw the glint in their eyes in the dim light. These were not just restless, irresponsible teenagers. "You are *ra'virs,*" he said.

"And good ones, too." The teens snickered and moved closer.

Leo grabbed a broomstick and brandished it as a weapon. With a deep ache in his chest, he saw that they had already smashed part of the model and severed the rigging ropes. One of the masts was down.

Not only did that majestic ship symbolize the hopes of Tierra, it was also the best chance for the Saedrans to complete the Mappa

Mundi. If these young men destroyed the model, then the ship herself might be irreparably damaged due to sympathetic magic.

And Aldo was aboard the *Dyscovera*!

Though he had little chance of defeating these *ra'virs*, Leo charged, swinging the broomstick. The young men had the gall to laugh at him. Two of them closed in, while the third went back to hatcheting the model with wild abandon.

"Stop!" Sen Leo swung again, but one of the *ra'virs* grabbed the broomstick and yanked it from his hands.

The second vandal moved close and with an odd, impatient casualness plunged his long dagger into Sen Leo's chest, driving it deep. He withdrew the knife and let the old man fall to the sawdust-covered floor.

The rattle emanating from Leo's throat was as much despair as agonal pain. "Stop," he whispered.

The *ra'virs* ignored him. All three took up their tools and weapons and fell upon the model once more. They no longer seemed interested in the old man, or in keeping quiet.

The scholar feebly reached out a hand, still trying to stop them. He stared upward as they smashed and pummeled the model. They had nearly finished by the time the life faded from his eyes.

80 *Tierran Military Camp, Ishalem Wall*

A pasty-faced Subcomdar Hist roused the queen, urgently reporting something about a raid, Mateo, Destrar Shenro, and other soldiers. Barely able to process what the man was saying, Anjine threw on a robe and emerged from her tent.

"Subcomdar Bornan is seriously injured, Majesty," Hist said. "He's with the Saedran physicians."

The camp was beginning to stir like a bashed hornets' nest. Riders returned, groaning and blood-spattered, many of them wounded. Her mind racing, she absorbed the chaos in an instant. "We're going to the medical tent—now!" She pushed past him into the cold morning and the smell of campfires. "How great are his injuries?"

"He is alive, Majesty. Beyond that, I have no details."

Two steps ahead of the army leader, Anjine hurried through the milling soldiers, past the corral where the patrol horses were kept at night. Most of them were gone.

Because the Tierran army had not yet engaged in major battles, the canvas tents erected as field hospitals were being used primarily for temporary storage. So far during the months of siege, the doctors had tended illnesses, sprains, broken bones from misadventure, and cuts and contusions the soldier-trainees received during daily sparring practice.

With the unexpected flood of wounded, army workers moved supply crates out of the medical tents and set up cots and tables. Saedran physicians hurried to the hospital tents as the injured soldiers were brought in; they grabbed their instruments and called for rags and suture strings to be boiled, cauterizing irons heated.

As Anjine raced toward the medical tents, Hist added as many details as he knew, although the information was sparse and contradictory. She barely heard him through the fears swirling in her head. "How could this happen? You're the subcomdar of the army! Why wasn't I informed of this foolish assault?"

"I was not informed myself, Majesty. This was an impulsive act concocted by Subcomdar Bornan and Destrar Shenro. Jenirod was apparently involved as well. We're still debriefing the returning soldiers as to what this was all about."

Anjine swore under her breath. "What were they *thinking*? How many did we lose?"

"At least ten—maybe more. It's hard to tell. There's still a great deal of confusion."

They reached the hospital area just as a shaken Jenirod stepped out of the main tent. His shirt was soaked with blood, his face ashen. When Anjine saw him, she lashed out, unable to stop herself. This man's stupid bravado had already inflamed the Urecari once and led directly to the murder of Tomas. She slapped Jenirod with all her strength. "Now what have you done?"

He lowered his gaze, devastated. "This was not my doing, Majesty, but I did bring the subcomdar back alive." He plucked at his shirt, frowning. "This is his blood. He lost a lot of it."

"Was this your idea?"

"No, Majesty." Jenirod continued reluctantly, "Destrar Shenro and his men planned to kidnap Soldan-Shah Omra, but were unable to find him. Apparently they had mistaken another man for the soldan-shah. Fortunately, the Alamont destrar didn't suffer a scratch."

She couldn't believe what she was hearing. "They went without preparation? Without support troops?" The Alamont destrar had always been far too eager to throw himself into battle, having studied so much military history. Jenirod had once been much like him, and she'd had enough of that sort of idiocy.

Anjine tried to move past him into the tent, but Jenirod blocked her. He chose his words carefully, after a discreet glance at the others moving around them. "Majesty, when I learned of the plan, I reported it to Subcomdar Bornan, expecting him to stop the destrar, but he wanted to join the fight. It wasn't clear whether anyone had a . . . fully developed tactical plan. The subcomdar seemed quite distressed about something and said he needed to demonstrate his loyalty to you. Though I counseled him against the mission, I could not question his orders. I had no choice but to go with him." Jenirod let out a sigh. "I tried to keep him safe."

Anjine felt a flash of anger. "I'll speak with you later, Jenirod—

you're dismissed. Subcomdar Hist, talk to the soldiers. I want to know exactly what happened, every detail."

Both men bowed and left. Despite their import, the words were just distractions to her. She'd had enough of being the queen for now; at this moment, she needed to be a woman, worried about her dear friend . . . her *lover*. Mateo was all that mattered. He might die.

She drew a deep breath, forcing herself to be calm and prepared. Then she entered the hospital tent.

Her senses were instantly assaulted by groans of pain, the stench of blood and burnt flesh, a cacophony of shouted instructions. Her head reeled, and she had to steady herself. Six soldiers lay on cots or plank tables, tended by Saedran camp doctors and shell-shocked young helpers. One man let out a raw scream as two doctors used hot irons to cauterize a wound.

The Saedrans looked up at her arrival. Two offered brief respectful bows, but the rest just continued their work. One of the wounded men died, and the attending physician stood in regretful silence for a moment, before bracing himself and turning to the next patient.

Trying to control her urgency, Anjine looked around until her attention was drawn—by instinct—to Mateo. He lay facedown on a bloodstained wooden table. The physicians had cut away his uniform vest and shirt, and now operated with sharp, thin blades—like fish-gutting knives, she thought—to extricate an arrow shaft that protruded from the center of his back. The cut was delicate, and the surgeon worked like a patient clockmaker, worrying away the flesh and muscle until he could extract the barbed arrowhead from Mateo's back.

A second doctor carefully packed a knife wound in Mateo's side. Though the gash looked small, it was deep and continued to ooze dark blood. Mateo flinched under their ministrations, his face contorted in pain, his eyes shut.

Anjine wanted to clasp his hand and whisper soothing words, but he was mercifully unconscious. Instead, she hovered beside him and peppered the physicians with questions as they operated. "How serious is it? Will he recover?"

"You can see that it is bad, Majesty." The doctor barely glanced up at her. "But we stopped the blood loss in time—I think."

The second physician finished packing the knife wound. "Tending the immediate injuries is only the first hurdle, Majesty. Infection could set in. The loss of blood itself might be enough to kill him."

She knew what she had to do. "I'll stay here and give him strength." When she touched Mateo's hand, his fingers twitched.

The physicians glanced at each other, flustered. The elder of the two spoke with firm respect. "He is unconscious, Majesty. You can do nothing for him by waiting here—and, truthfully, you are in the way. Let us do our work."

"You *are* doing your work," Anjine replied stubbornly, but she stepped away from the table. "But . . . I would not want to distract you. Please, do whatever you can to save him." The physicians continued their care, now using sizzling irons to cauterize the arrow wound.

Anjine remembered all too clearly that years ago the Saedran physicians had been completely helpless to save her father's wife from the scratch of a rusty nail. Ilrida had writhed and thrashed in her royal bed.

Anjine ground her teeth, vowing that such a thing would not happen to Mateo . . . but she had no power to prevent it. She wanted to cry out to him and demand why he had done such a stupid thing, why he had practically thrown his life away. But those were empty questions, for she already knew the answers. Afraid that she might be pregnant, Anjine had pushed Mateo away to protect herself, though she had not meant to hurt him. How could she not have opened herself up to *him*? Of all people in the world, whom did she trust more? She had kept herself cool and distant because of what she feared Sen Ola na-Ten's tests would reveal—and he had interpreted the signals as a rejection of him. She had been so stupid!

But Mateo had given his own signals: within hours after they'd made love, he had fled the castle without saying goodbye. Rather than face her, he had escaped with the army. Wasn't it obvious that he regretted what he'd done? If he was ashamed of loving her, so soon after the death of Vicka, how would he react if he found out that Anjine was carrying his child? What would he say when she told him that, as a queen with an army to command and a war to win, she didn't dare let the pregnancy come to term?

Thinking it the safest course, Anjine had walled off her emotions to protect Mateo and herself. She wanted to make it easier for him to stay away. But now in the thick-smelling hospital tent, as she observed the pain on his face, the blood from his wounds, and the stark expressions of the Saedran physicians, Anjine knew that her own rebuff had driven Mateo to this.

No matter how much she tried to hide it, Anjine loved him, and she had no doubt that he loved her in turn. But their unwillingness to admit it only caused more tragedy. Mateo had cared a great deal for his wife, and Vicka's death had devastated him, but Anjine suspected deep inside that he had married Vicka Sonnen because he could not have *her*.

It was time to stop hiding. Anjine's love and support would give Mateo the strength he needed to recover, and in turn, he would do the same for her: He would help Anjine to be the leader that Tierra deserved and demanded.

But first, he had to live.

Careful not to interfere with the doctors' ministrations, Anjine took his hand and held it. She bent down and whispered, certain that at some level he could understand her. "I need you, Mateo."

She repeated it many times over the next several hours and refused to leave his side. "I need you."

81 *The* Dyscovera

As another resounding boom of thunder pealed across the sky, and lightning flashed from cloud to cloud, the Leviathan attacked the *Dyscovera*. The creature heaved its bulk onto the deck, crushing two of Criston's sailors. The other crewmen scrambled away in a wash of slime and foam, screaming as they grabbed for ropes, open hatches, anything to hold on to.

The splintered deck groaned and foul-smelling water swirled over the boards. Criston lurched to his feet again, still gripping the harpoon. The *Dyscovera* was mortally wounded, doomed to sink. Her deck, hull, masts, and keel were shattered beyond repair. He felt a pang in his chest. Now he would never reach Terravitae, never make it home to Adrea. . . .

The monster's fang-tipped tentacles thrashed in all directions, and a low, rock-grinding growl thrummed out of the Leviathan's chest. A sickly pale glow emanated from the beast's milky eye, as if it recognized Criston Vora as the one victim who should never have gotten away years ago.

Then suddenly the waters around them were full of ships—dark vessels with ghostly silhouettes, including the unforgettable form of the *Luminara*. The specter of Captain Andon Shay stood at the prow, shouting into the storm, "Leviathan, your time has come!"

The haunted vessels had escaped from the seaweed morass. Criston had no idea how they had slipped away from the titanic woman to respond to his call. Many of these crewmembers had also been killed by the Leviathan, their ships smashed and sunk by the beast's unreasoning anger. Now they had returned from the grave. Countless angry sailors issued challenges from aboard the ghost ships, demanding revenge. And tonight they would get it.

Sensing this new threat, the monster released its tentacled grip on the *Dyscovera* and slid back off the deck like a beached whale retreating to sea with the outgoing tide. Opening its maw, the Leviathan let out a curious, booming growl.

Though far away now, the lighthouse beacon still shone bright enough to penetrate the black, whipping clouds. The storm came at them from all directions now, drawn to the vortex that was the Leviathan.

Criston gripped his harpoon and ascended the wet, canted deck like a man climbing a mountain slope. Below, the Leviathan loomed in the water, tentacles thrashing. With the *Luminara* and the host of ghost ships closing in, he felt emboldened. At the very least, if he died here, he would rejoin those ghostly sailors and spend eternity with his father and Captain Shay. But he remained alive, for now.

Standing at the wrecked bow, barely holding on as broken boards fell into the churning sea, Criston saw the Leviathan turn its staring eye back toward him. He hefted the harpoon, cocked back his arm, and hurled it, releasing two decades of rage for all that this monster had cost him.

His aim was true.

The sharp point sank into the milky eye, burying itself halfway up the shaft. Translucent ooze spurted out, and the Leviathan reeled and clawed at the harpoon with its numerous tentacles, ripping away the spear and tossing it out to sea. But the light in the mangled eye had gone out.

As the blind creature reached for the *Dyscovera*, the ghost ships closed in. The *Luminara* drove forward with such ferocity that her hull groaned as she rammed the Leviathan. The undead crew hurled their own spectral spears and harpoons, and two struck the open wet flaps of the monster's gill slits.

Wounded now, leaking black oily blood into the water, the beast lurched and writhed away, leaving the *Dyscovera*. But the *Luminara* and the other ghost ships hounded it, propelled by ghostly force. The Leviathan swam off in blind rage, pulling clouds and thunderstorms with it.

Criston swayed, nearly losing consciousness. His legs trembled. Mingled tears and rainwater streamed down his face, and he held fast to one of the last intact ropes.

But before he could dare think they might be safe, he saw something as ominous as the Leviathan—the dark ship of Iyomelka, bearing down on them.

82 *The* Al-Orizin

The *Al-Orizin*'s silk mainsail was torn and tattered, despite Ystya's best efforts to protect the ship from winds, waves, and lightning. As the young woman struggled to unleash and control her magic, the storms returned. A jagged bolt shattered the foremast, hurling splinters in all directions. The deck rocked and heaved from the huge swells that Iyomelka threw at them.

Saan shouted orders to steer clear of the hazardous reefs. Rogue waves hammered the ship, spinning the *Al-Orizin* until Saan couldn't even tell which direction they were heading. At least three of his crew were swept overboard.

Iyomelka's ship continued to close on them. "She wants to drive us onto the rocks by the lighthouse," Saan called.

Her skin aglow from within, Ystya continued to exert her powers, calling up winds, so that the hull of the *Al-Orizin* screamed with the strain of being pulled in different directions at once. She wavered on her feet. "I've never fought like this before."

Saan saw no way they could outrun Iyomelka in the storm, but even as he refused to give up, flashes of lightning illuminated another ship halfway to the horizon—a large sailing vessel of Tierran design.

Before he could comprehend what he was seeing, many more vessels crowded the waters—a shadowy fleet that appeared from nowhere, as if summoned from the depths.

The mysterious lighthouse beacon cut through the storm, calling them. Saan didn't understand how a lighthouse could be so far out here, nor did he know what these other ships were. Most of all, he could not comprehend the horrific monster that suddenly careened through the water toward them. Maddened with pain, thrashing as it fled from the spectral ships, this beast made even the Kraken seem a mere annoyance by comparison.

The ghost ships hounded the monster, and haunted men crowded their decks, hurling countless spears and harpoons. Unable to see where it was going, the wounded monster plunged directly toward the *Al-Orizin*.

Ystya cried out with genuine fear, "It is the Leviathan!"

"Pull your sails! Turn the rudder—hard to port!" Though he saw a line of foaming water that warned of nearby reefs, Saan had to evade the chaos coming toward them. The deck tilted as the helmsman pulled the ship hard over.

The Leviathan's eye was a horror of mangled jelly and film. Somehow, it was drawn not to the *Al-Orizin*, but toward Iyomelka's ship. Though the island witch screamed from the deck of her vessel, Saan saw that they would all collide in moments.

"I think the Leviathan knows my mother." Ystya drew a quick breath. "She is the wife of Ondun—who denied the Leviathan its mate. It wants revenge."

"As long as it keeps her away from us," Saan said. "But I don't know how much longer this ship will hold together."

Aboard her resurrected ship, Iyomelka splayed her fingers into claws as she drew upon her power to call down the lightning.

Jagged bolts scored long black marks on the Leviathan's body, but instead of being driven away the creature merely roared and spasmed in pain. Seeing the danger, the island witch turned her ship to point the sharp antler-coral spar toward the sea creature in hopes that the blinded beast might impale itself.

But the ghost ships surrounded the monster now, and another dark vessel rammed it. Fighting for its life, the Leviathan crashed forward into Iyomelka's ship. The coral spar tore a long wet wound in its side before the spike snapped. One sharp prong dug into the monster's gill slits and forced them open.

Saan tried to sail the *Al-Orizin* away from the battle, but his ship was swamped, barely afloat and taking on water. They were trapped and forced to watch as the storm drove them farther away. Saan held Ystya, who was transfixed with terror by what was happening to her mother. Despite the dangers they had faced and the harm Iyomelka had wrought, the woman was still her mother—and the Leviathan was intent on killing her.

The creature hurled itself at Iyomelka's ship. She called down more lightning, wringing it out of the clouds, but the sea monster seemed not to feel the pain. The Leviathan rammed her ship, shattering the coral and barnacles that held the rotted hull boards together.

Even Iyomelka's wrath could not match the monster's. Though the beast's central eye was blinded, its numerous tentacle heads could see or sense their surroundings. A writhing knot of fang-tipped tentacles lashed out at Iyomelka where she stood on the deck. She flailed her hands and called spells to drive them away, but tentacles grabbed her with fluid movements, sinking sharp fangs into her arms, her legs. They wrapped around the witch's waist and lifted her into the air. The storm continued to rage while Iyomelka fought for her life, but this was the Leviathan's storm, not hers.

The tentacles drew back and whipped forward to skewer

Iyomelka on one of the sharp-ended spars of her mainmast. The long wooden spear protruded from her chest, and she dangled grotesquely, impaled and twitching, before she went still.

With a mighty heave, the Leviathan surged onto the deck of her dark ship, tearing down the masts, shattering the hull, and pulling the pieces into the water. The sea-serpent skull mounted to the prow broke loose and drifted away. Iyomelka's rotted ship sank quickly, leaving a field of debris and foam on the stormy waters.

Though it had killed Iyomelka, the monster was also grievously wounded, its single eye destroyed, its gills mangled by the sharp prongs of antler coral, its body abristle with harpoons and spears from the ghost ships.

The Leviathan let out a subsonic cry of pain and despair, reminding Saan of a dying shark caught in a fisherman's net. Ystya clung to him, sobbing.

Studded with spears, the monster's great bulk rolled. Its huge open maw filled with water. The gill slits stopped flapping and hung lax. The Leviathan floated belly up amid the wreckage of Iyomelka's ship, leaking blood and slime in a wide, foul-smelling stain.

On the deck of the *Al-Orizin*, Ystya shook, while Saan just stared. His sailors were cheering or weeping. Sikara Fyiri staggered forward, and Saan expected the priestess to hurl curses at the Leviathan. Instead, she doubled over and vomited onto the deck.

The greatest monster of the sea was dead.

83 *Tierran Military Camp, Ishalem Wall*

For much of the next week, Anjine remained in the Saedran medical tent, praying at Mateo's side. He hovered between life and death, his skin chalky, his respiration fluttery and weak. Field commanders came to deliver their reports to her, and she forced herself to listen, despite her preoccupation; the main attack would begin in less than two weeks.

The intermittent bouts of nausea from her pregnancy often grew severe enough that she vomited into a basin. Sometimes she gave the excuse that the blood and stench made her queasy, or she mentioned a slight fever she had picked up from the rugged conditions in the camp. Observers construed her illness as signs of grief and worry.

Surrounded by patients, the other Saedran physicians had more serious concerns, but they were not fools, and she was sure that the truth would eventually dawn on them. She couldn't believe soldiers hadn't already started rumors . . . or maybe they had.

Sen Ola offered strong herbal remedies from her pharmacopeia and urged Anjine to retire to her tent and rest, but the queen refused to leave Mateo's side. Her symptoms seemed to be getting worse day by day, and she knew the difficulties were just beginning.

Subcomdar Hist presented his cool summary to her, standing at Mateo's bedside. "Majesty, of the seventy-five soldiers who rode out to strike the Ishalem wall, twenty-one were killed in the raid. Another sixteen were wounded but made it back to camp. Three of those later died."

Around them the physicians continued to change dressings, feed broth to the wounded, bathe feverish foreheads with cool cloths. "And all to what purpose, Mateo?" She stared down at him and whispered, "You didn't need to do this for me."

The subcomdar cleared his throat delicately. "Also, the Urabans have sent scouts in increasing numbers, and several have clashed with our soldiers. The raid on the wall threw them into turmoil."

"Why? Did our men kill an inordinate number of the enemy?"

"Possibly, but it's more likely the Curlies are baffled and suspect there was more to our plan. They don't know what we intended to accomplish."

Anjine inhaled deeply. "*I* don't know what they intended to accomplish. Increase the catapult bombardment on the wall, keep them busy. Unfortunately, the enemy is now alerted."

Hist heaved a sigh, but his anger was clear. "Destrar Shenro is uninjured, Majesty. In fact, he seems rather embarrassed that he returned home without a scratch. Would you like me to send for him?"

"Yes, send him to me," Anjine said fiercely. "Let him explain himself to his queen." She would find it easy to blame the Alamont destrar for Mateo's injury, make him responsible for her own pain right now . . . but she knew she was as much at fault as he. Her reluctance to admit the truth had driven Mateo to such a desperate, foolish act.

"I will take care of it, my Queen." Hist bowed briefly and left.

Anjine could not defend Mateo or his ill-advised raid, but Hist's words brought her back to a reality that she needed to hear. As queen of Tierra, her absolute priority was to win this war, to defeat the followers of Urec and drive them from the holy city. She had to punish them in the name of Ondun, break the back of their army, defeat them so utterly that her own people would be safe from their attacks. She had gambled everything on this.

Anjine realized that she could no longer afford to expend all of her time and emotions on Mateo. He would live or he would die. Her frailties as a woman, as a *human*, were subordinate to her duty as a ruler. She had to be the queen of Tierra now, with no other distractions. There would be time enough for love later—*if* she succeeded here. Everything came down to the next few weeks.

Destrar Shenro appeared before her, stepping gingerly into the medical tent. He wore leather breeches and a clean linen shirt; his brown hair was disheveled, and he kept his gaze down. Unlike all the other soldiers in the tent, Shenro had no wound dressings, no bruises, no scrapes. "You called for me, my Queen?"

She stiffened and held his gaze without speaking a word for a long moment, as if he were a fish caught on a hook. He squirmed, but remained at attention. "I see you are well, Destrar. Unfortunately, many of your soldiers are not. Subcomdar Bornan is not. They were injured or killed because of your impetuous action!" Her voice rose at the end.

When she paused to take a breath, he said, "I offer my apologies, Majesty—but only an apology for our failure to capture the soldan-shah. If we had seized him as planned, we would have ended the war without further bloodshed. I told no one of our plans because I am convinced that many *ra'virs* still hide among our soldiers, and I didn't want to give them the chance to betray us."

He looked down at Mateo. "I am sorry for those injuries, truly I am. But I'm not sorry for wanting to kill the Curlies. All of the men wounded or killed during that raid were soldiers loyal to Aiden. They fought the enemy, and took down as many as they could." He sniffed. "You can blame me for brash planning, Majesty, but *Urecari* blades caused those cuts, *Urecari* arrows made those wounds, and *Urecari* fighters tried to kill us." He blinked at her, his eyes blazing. "I know that you haven't forgotten who our real enemy is, and I—along with all your loyal subjects—will fight them until our dying breath."

"But at what cost?" she said in a whisper. "Until we are all dead?"

"Or until we are victorious. If we don't win this battle, maybe we'll win the next one. Or the next. It may take a year, ten years, a hundred! But we will not back down."

Anjine felt deflated rather than galvanized by his anger. "Leave me," she said, and Shenro turned smartly and left the tent. She did not get up.

Her thoughts seemed to be on fire. Her responses were volatile, and her decisions were no longer so clear to her. A baby grew inside her, an unexpected complication to Tierra's plans, a trick that love had played on her. She could never be a mere woman with a happy life—Anjine had to be mother to all of Tierra, not to one child. The queen could not be seen as weak, not now. The soldan-shah and his armies would laugh if an enormously pregnant woman challenged them on the battlefield.

King Korastine had left too much weight on his daughter's shoulders, and she had been asked to be many things. Back in Calay, in a time of relative peace, her mother had numerous nursemaids, teachers, and castle staff to help her raise Anjine, only one child. How could Anjine do that herself in a rugged military camp? What if this war lasted another twenty years? She could not be a nurturing mother; all she wanted was to slaughter the enemy. If Mateo recovered, she could not make him a babysitter while she sat on the throne. And if he should die . . .

No. This was the worst possible time for the queen of Tierra to have a child—especially an illegitimate one. She must not even consider it. Anjine couldn't afford to be sick, or distracted, or weak. Tierra itself was at stake. She had to make her decision—and quickly, before anyone else knew. Every day of delay only posed an increased risk to her own health.

Anjine summoned Sen Ola na-Ten and told the doctor to meet her in the royal tent.

The Saedran physician was a long time coming, and Anjine knotted her hands together. Her anxiety had nothing to do with the nausea of her pregnancy. When the gruff old woman finally entered her tent, her expression told Anjine that Sen Ola already knew what she would ask.

The Saedran spoke first, as if trying to prevent Anjine's unutterable words. "I have talked with Subcomdar Bornan's physicians, looked at his wounds myself. He has survived, though he is still weak. The next few days will decide. Any change could send him down, or he could rally and recover. They say your bloodline is directly descended from Aiden, my Queen. Now would be a good time to pray—and not make rash decisions."

"I have already prayed, and pondered much. But the decision is mine alone."

Sen Ola nodded slowly. Anjine sat heavily on a stool and looked at her for a long moment. "I will require your chemical draught. I must take it now, before anyone else knows, so that I can recover before the final assault. In less than two weeks I need to be healthy and . . . undistracted. If we defeat the enemy, there will be time for children later."

The Saedran's expression fell. "But not for this child."

Another wave of nausea washed over Anjine, and she fought it down with difficulty. "No, not for this child. But who can count one unborn child among the countless parents and children who have already been slain in this war?"

Anjine had seen the look of joy on the Gremurr refugees when they were reunited with their families, and she had also seen the crushing despair in those who did not, and never would, find their loved ones. Such bright hope followed by such crushing disappointment seemed more cruel than the news itself.

"It's for the best," she said. "I cannot be a mere woman now. I need to be Tierra's ruler."

84 *The* Dyscovera

With both the Leviathan and Iyomelka dead, the unnatural storms began to dissipate. But although the thunder faded and the cauldron of angry waves simmered back to sleep, the damage was done. The battered *Dyscovera* was like a man robbed and beaten by thugs, left to die in an alley.

Criston stood among the debris on the deck, feeling more empty than triumphant. He couldn't tear his eyes from the huge carcass that drifted in the wreckage of Iyomelka's ship. "My whole life has been shaped by that monster." Even though he now knew that Adrea was alive, the Leviathan had stolen decades from the two of them. "And now it's dead."

Javian stood next to Mia with his mouth agape. "Why would even Ondun create such a beast?"

In despair, Prester Hannes looked around at the wrecked ship. "How will we ever reach Terravitae? We were so close."

Criston's victory was tempered by the cold reality of their situation. They had survived the night and the storms, but the ship might not last much longer. The *Dyscovera* was adrift, barely navigable, and could well sink if the weather worsened again. He faced the brisk cool breeze. Many years ago, after the sinking of the *Luminara*, he had survived by building a makeshift raft from the debris. This time he had more to work with, a whole ship that could be repaired.

The morning after the storm, thick mist rose from the sea like an exhausted exhalation. The ghost ships sailed closer, and Criston wondered how long they could remain separated from the female titan that held their souls in her seaweed net.

He didn't understand how they had escaped her hold in the first place, except that Captain Shay had promised. . . .

Going to the broken bow, where the ice dragon's horn protruded from its splintered socket, he could discern the other captain aboard the spectral *Luminara*. From his long-lost fishing boat, his father gave him a melancholy wave.

Criston called out into the mist, "Thank you for saving us."

"I wish we could help you more, Mr. Vora," Shay shouted back, "but we have limitations."

His father added sadly, "And now we must return, for She calls us."

Several pallid-looking men joined Captain Shay on the deck of the *Luminara*, and Criston recognized them with a start: they were members of his own crew who had been lost overboard during the storm. "Fifteen of your sailors are now among us, Mr. Vora. Don't worry—we'll take care of them."

Cindon Vora added, "Try not to join us too soon, my son."

"I won't, I promise." And he meant it, now that the thought of Adrea could pull him back to Tierra.

The fleet of ghost ships faded into the fog until they became shadows, then nothing.

Struggling for some kind of normal activity, Javian and Mia helped clear debris from the tilted deck. Below, the hold was taking on water, and six crewmembers had already climbed down the hatches to man the pumps.

"Javian, gather anyone who can wield a hammer to patch the leaks below. Mia, try to determine what's been washed overboard. I want to know what supplies we have left. Can we make repairs? Can we sail again?" He wished he still had Kjelnar aboard; the Iborian shipwright had built the vessel in the first place and would know how to fix the worst damage.

Criston did not ignore the seriousness of the situation. All three masts were shattered, the sails torn and many of them blown away, the spare bolts of canvas were mostly spoiled. The men could do very little rigging with the rope they still possessed. While a simple cloth sail might catch enough wind for a small raft, a hulk the size of the *Dyscovera* was another thing entirely.

"We're still afloat, Captain," Javian pointed out, as if that alone was good news. "It's a start."

Over the course of the storm, the raging wind and waves had driven the ship far from the Lighthouse at the End of the World. Perhaps when the dense fog cleared his lookouts might spot the beacon, which would give them a sense of direction. But Criston realized that the ocean currents were drawing them away, like a swift river.

When the fog burned off by midday and offered a clear view of open water, the lookout at the top of the splintered mainmast shouted, "Another vessel nearby, Captain! It's the Urecari ship!"

Criston rushed to the starboard side, recalling the vessel he had seen from the lighthouse. The foreign ship seemed to be in as bad shape as the *Dyscovera*: her silken sail shredded, spars shattered, hull and masts splintered. The two damaged vessels were drifting closer to each other. Across the water he could hear echoing voices shouting in a foreign language.

Prester Hannes joined him at the side of the ship, his face suffused with anger. "They are followers of Urec, Captain. You know they will want to kill us, so we've got to attack them first." He lowered his voice to a stage whisper. "Trick them into coming closer."

With a wry laugh, Criston indicated the *Dyscovera*'s condition. "There will be no trickery. They can plainly see who we are."

Javian was also deeply troubled. "We can barely move, Captain, and this was never a warship. How would we attack them?"

"With our own swords and bare hands!" Hannes said, as if the answer were obvious.

Sen Aldo shaded his eyes to study the other damaged ship. "This ship won't survive as it is, Captain. Maybe they have supplies or tools we can use to keep the *Dyscovera* afloat."

Hannes quirked his lips in a smile. "Yes! We can kill or capture them, and seize their supplies."

Flustered, Aldo stared at him. "Actually, I was suggesting cooperation. You can see they're in no better shape than we are."

The ships were very close now, and the wary Uraban sailors hefted their scimitars and harpoons. Criston's crew took up whatever clubs, sticks, or knives they could find and crowded the *Dyscovera*'s side, each group searching for the slightest excuse to engage in the free-for-all they had long anticipated.

As the two battered craft wallowed closer, a woman's voice called across the water. Her words were heavily accented but understandable. "Ho, Tierran ship! We are the *Al-Orizin*, in search of Terravitae!"

Criston shouted back. "We are the *Dyscovera*, out of Calay—and we have the same quest."

Wearing a look of complete astonishment, Aldo pushed past Criston, yelling at the top of his voice, "Sen Sherufa na-Oa, is that you? I recognize your voice!"

Criston could hear a flurry of discussion aboard the other ship, and he spotted a woman in Saedran garments standing on the tilted deck. "Aldo na-Curic?"

"It's *Sen* Aldo, now!" He laughed.

"A much-needed voice of reason! We both seek Terravitae, and we have nearly reached our destination. Neither of our vessels is seaworthy, but if we joined the two hulls, our ships could continue the voyage."

Aldo turned to Criston, his expression bright. "She's right, Captain. We could lash the ships together, keep the hulls afloat, pool our resources and rig some sails."

Hannes drew himself up. "We will not work with the followers of Urec." He eyed a dour-faced, red-robed woman who stood next to the Saedran on the other ship. Hannes lowered his voice, like rustling dry weeds. "They have a priestess aboard."

Aldo ignored him and turned back to the rail. "Sen Sherufa! We can also share our charts. I think we are very close to completing the Mappa Mundi."

Criston grabbed his arm. "What are you doing, Chartsman? This is a *Tierran* ship. We do not give our discoveries to the enemy."

Aldo pulled away and spoke coolly. "I am a Saedran as well as Tierran, sir. We can learn more from this woman than we could ever find out on our own."

Sherufa called back, "My captain Saan agrees that we might

join our ships and sail the rest of the way to Terravitae. He says he will let Holy Joron punish the heretics, if He wishes."

Hannes grumbled, eyeing the sikara. "Yes, I would like to witness exactly that."

Aldo turned to Criston again. "Sherufa and I can act as translators, Captain. I speak Uraban, and she obviously speaks Tierran. The Leviathan has dealt all of us a terrible blow, and surely none of us will survive without helping each other." When the crew looked angry and skeptical, he scolded them impatiently: "What is more important, killing the enemy, or reaching Terravitae?" He raised his voice and shouted the question again so that those aboard the *Al-Orizin* heard him as well. He could hear Sen Sherufa translating.

Both crews grumbled, neither giving an immediate answer. Criston wrestled with his decision, then finally nodded to Sen Aldo. "Very well, Chartsman. We'll remain on guard, but I tentatively agree to work with our enemies."

85 *The Lighthouse at the End of the World*

After the skies cleared to reveal a bright, mocking sun, Mailes was still alone.

Throughout the clashing storms, he had been trapped and transfixed in his tower, watching the Leviathan, the ghost ships, and Iyomelka. The sight filled him with simultaneous hope and horror. Even amid the churning waves and winds, with sorcery being hurled back and forth, he felt his heart split open like a chrysalis. *Iyomelka!* A flood of sweet memories came back to him.

She had returned, but she was in terrible danger. And he was cursed to do nothing but observe.

From the top of the turret, the magical lighthouse beacon continued to shine out into the water. Even through the downpour, Iyomelka must have seen the lighthouse and remembered him. Mailes had not forgotten a moment of their time together, even after so many centuries.

So few of their people remained . . . so few choices to love. Passionate and imaginative, Iyomelka had been the perfect consort for Ondun, leader of them all. His was the most powerful magic, but mastery of the powers innate in the world was not the same thing as love; Ondun had taken Iyomelka for granted, taken the world for granted . . . and Mailes had truly loved her. How could the two of them possibly hide their romance from one who claimed to be all-seeing?

A disaster, a tragedy . . . and they had expected nothing less. A jealous Ondun had forced Iyomelka to watch as he imposed eternal exile on the other man who had dared to love his wife. And after doing that to Iyomelka, Ondun expected her to forgive him. How could he understand so little?

In the centuries since then, Mailes had written countless volumes of love poems pining for the woman he had lost. Though no one would ever read the stanzas, Mailes wrote, and wrote, and wrote. What did it matter if anyone—even Ondun—ever found them?

During the night, he had peered through the magical lens, staring at the face he had loved so much and so long ago. He hoped she might look up at the lighthouse, but even with her powers, Iyomelka couldn't possibly see him waiting for her in his distant tower. . . .

And then he had watched her die.

The awful monster, maddened by loneliness, had attacked Ondun's wife, taken out its anger on *her*. Mailes had been helpless to do anything. . . .

Now her ship was destroyed, her body lost amid the wreckage—

and Ondun's crystal coffin, no doubt, gone with her. Now the earlier pain of heartache seemed as nothing. Mailes would never be freed of his curse. He would never leave this lighthouse island, and most agonizing of all, he would never have Iyomelka back.

It was too much pain for even a demigod to bear. . . .

When the waters calmed, Mailes managed to scrape enough strength from the bottom of his despair. He emerged from his tower, went down to the rocks at the waterline where he kept a small boat—even though he had nowhere to go. He took up the oars and pushed away from the islet.

It didn't matter how long it would take. Mailes rowed and rowed until he reached the flinders of Iyomelka's ship. Flotsam and jetsam drifted about, rotted wood from a sunken vessel she had resurrected from beneath the waves.

Her journey had brought her back here after all, but not to happiness.

The carcass of the Leviathan floated atop the water like an enormous dead whale. Its body was scored with numerous wounds; the tough hide had been ripped apart by weapons and lightning strikes. The creature drifted, its eye gouged out, its lax tentacles hanging like strands of seaweed. Seagulls wheeled above, already attracted by the foul-smelling feast. They landed and fed, then flew again, shrieking insults to one another before returning to tear off more strips of pale flesh.

Mailes didn't care about the Leviathan. This monster had killed the woman that he once—and still—loved. He rowed and searched through the debris, his heart aching, until he finally located what he sought. He trapped the moan of despair in his throat.

Iyomelka floated facedown, her skin pale, her hair drifting in the water. He pulled his small boat closer and leaned over the side to touch her, remembering all the times he had touched her when she was warm and alive. But she was cold now and unresponsive.

He pulled her body close, tore away the remaining splinters from the spar that had impaled her. With tears pouring down his cheeks, Mailes hauled her out of the water and placed her carefully in the boat.

Unable to express his grief, he rowed Iyomelka back to the lighthouse.

86 *Tierran Military Camp, Ishalem Wall*

At first, darkness washed away the pain, and then the pain washed away the memories, but gradually it came back, one step at a time. Mateo remembered the fight on the Ishalem wall, the knife wound in his side, the arrow in his back, and the blood.

Sharper still, he remembered how he had longed to see Anjine for months, and how she had rebuffed him, showing that she did not want to be close to him. Her reaction to seeing him again was worse than facing an enemy charge, and now the recollection made Mateo want to fall back into the cycle of pain and darkness.

But he'd hidden in that place long enough already. No matter what he had lost, Mateo was still a soldier, and a soldier should never surrender.

He opened his eyes, unable to see where he was. The first thing that filled his bleary view was a woman's face. He wanted it to be Anjine smiling over him, but this was an older woman with closely cropped hair and Saedran robes.

"I was right," she said with a cluck of her tongue. "The other doctors said you wouldn't awaken until tomorrow, if ever, but I could feel your strength."

"How . . . long?"

"Long enough . . . two weeks. I've given you the best medicines we have, fresh and potent herbs to prevent infection, and a few secret ingredients of my own to keep up your strength." Her frown lines deepened. "If you are the man I thought you were, you'll understand how much you are needed right now. There is very little time."

When Mateo tried to speak, only a rough sound came from his throat. She gave him tepid water, which he drank gratefully. "Anjine?" he finally said.

"Yes, it's about Anjine. I am Sen Ola na-Ten, her personal doctor. I know things that others do not. She has had me quietly monitoring her condition, and I am oath-bound to maintain the queen's secrets . . . but it can't be a secret to you." She raised her eyebrows and looked at him meaningfully. "Can it?"

He couldn't fathom what she was saying. From the doctor's expression, she seemed to expect an answer. Sen Ola helped Mateo sit up, and he felt unfathomably weak, worse than when he'd suffered from the gray fever as a child. Back then, he had needed months to regain his strength, but he couldn't afford that now. He tried to turn, but pain ripped through his side and back. He nearly passed out, but Sen Ola caught him.

Two physicians hurried over, chattering excitedly. "Subcomdar Bornan, please lie back down! You must rest and regain your strength."

Fussing over him, one of the physicians said, "I'll give him a potion to make him sleep for many hours. His body is healing itself."

Sen Ola shooed away the other two doctors and called for simple broth. "I'm tending him. Don't you have your own patients?"

"Subcomdar Bornan *is* my patient," said the first doctor.

"Well, he's mine, now. He and I have matters to discuss. Now go away."

The men were surprised and puzzled, but when a soldier cried out on his cot, thrashing and pulling at his bandages, they ran to him.

When the broth came, Sen Ola removed two packets from a deerskin pouch tied to her waist. "The writings of Saedran apothecaries in Uraba describe the benefits of certain local flowers." She crumbled the dry petals of pink blossoms into the broth and added a sprinkle of hard, dark seeds. "And a hint of innat seeds for the pain and to sharpen your thoughts. You need to *think* right now."

Sen Ola fed him spoonful by spoonful. Mateo sipped, and the broth tasted salty, hot, and nourishing.

She whispered, "The queen commanded me to give her an abortive potion, though I strongly advised against it. The . . . process will be hard for her, but she's convinced herself that she can't be troubled by *human* responsibilities in such a time of war." She lowered her chin, shook her head. "It is a terrible thing."

"What terrible thing?" Mateo asked, trying to clear the fog from his thoughts. He could feel the broth restoring him, the innat seeds giving him energy, focusing his thoughts. Had she said something about a secret?

"Shouldn't it be your decision as well as hers, Subcomdar? She should consult with you, at least. The queen clings to the odd notion that she can't be a ruler and a mother at the same time, but I believe she feels she doesn't deserve any such happiness. In punishing herself, she's truly punishing an innocent child."

Mateo reeled, sure that this was some fever hallucination brought on by pain and loss of blood, but when the Saedran woman grabbed his arm, she felt solid enough.

"A child?" He kept his voice low, and his throat was dry again. Then another thought clicked into place, a sharp and solid answer like the tooth of a gear in a Saedran machine. No wonder Anjine had been avoiding him! Her reaction to him wasn't just cold and formal—it was *protective*. She was trying to prevent him from sharing her pain. It was his child, *their* child. His heart pounded harder in his chest, and strength flowed through him—strength and urgency. "I need to see her."

"Yes, Subcomdar, you do. After she drinks the chemical draught I gave her, her body will reject the baby. She believes that is the only way she can keep fighting the Urecari."

Mateo breathed heavily. "No . . . not yet. I must see her." His body had barely grasped the idea that he was still alive, and this was more than his mind could handle. He felt dizzy. "Let me talk to her first."

He and Vicka had once talked breezily about the children they would have, but he went off to war so soon after their wedding that they never had a chance for a family. Having lost Vicka forever, he'd assumed that children would never be possible.

Sen Ola stood up and thrust the bowl back into his trembling hands so he could finish. "I will talk to her. Once she knows you are awake, she will come to see you."

"Hurry," Mateo said. The Saedran woman ran off.

A guard prevented her from entering Anjine's tent, despite Sen Ola's loud protests. The man wouldn't budge. "The queen has commanded that no one disturb her."

The Saedran knew exactly why Queen Anjine insisted on being alone, what she was contemplating . . . if it wasn't already too late. She raised her voice. "Tell her that Subcomdar Bornan is awake."

The guards shook their heads. "Her instructions were specific and very strict." Sen Ola tried to push past them. Again the guard blocked her.

She shouted for several minutes more, without result, until a commotion occurred near the medical tent. Ola looked over to see a bandaged figure stagger out, followed by insistent physicians who fluttered around him like gulls on a fishing boat. Barely able to move, Mateo shuffled forward, swaying with each step. He pushed himself along by sheer force of will. The Saedran doctors tried to drag him back into the tent, but he yanked his arm away, his face tightening into a grimace of pain. A blossom of blood appeared on the bandage at his side; his left arm hung limp.

Sen Ola whirled on the guards. "If you don't bring the queen out *now*, Subcomdar Bornan will die. Look at him—he'll kill himself to get to her!" She intercepted Mateo and, recognizing Sen Ola, he slumped against her.

Anjine emerged from her tent, looking pale and shaky, her eyes wide. Mateo looked up to see her, and their eyes locked. She stopped short, seemingly as disoriented as he was. "Mateo, what are you doing?" She ran forward. "Don't hurt yourself any more—you've already lost so much blood!"

"I've lost so *much*, Anjine!" Mateo let out a rasping shout. It took the queen and Sen Ola in concert to hold him up. "Please don't, don't do it . . ." He sounded delirious, but Sen Ola and the queen knew what he meant.

Anjine's expression hardened, and she shot an accusing glance at the Saedran physician. Sen Ola remained unruffled. "It is his child too," she whispered harshly.

"Take him to my tent, now!" Anjine barked. "He'll rest there, and I'll watch over him."

"He needs his physicians, Majesty," protested one of the doctors.

"I have Sen Ola. That's enough." The two women managed to get Mateo to her tent and gently laid him on her fur-covered camp bed. He seemed to melt onto the cot like fading mist. His eyes were glazed but open, staring at Anjine.

Sen Ola worked at his dressings, examined the sutures, and prodded with exaggerated concern at his cuts and the renewed bleeding. Saying nothing, she applied fresh dressings to his wounds, while Mateo and Anjine studied each other, as if the physician were not there.

"We have a child," Mateo said.

Anjine looked both stony and despondent. "I have to lead the army, Mateo. I have to be queen. You and I aren't married. And . . ." She let her voice trail off.

Sen Ola noticed the small glass vial of green liquid, the draught she had provided. For now, it remained sealed.

"It wasn't an accident," Mateo said. "It's a blessing from Aiden."

"Or a burden and a curse. When I think of Tomas . . ." The words caught in her throat. "This could open us up to so many more tragedies. I don't dare—I couldn't stand it! I don't deserve—"

With a flash of anger, Mateo interrupted her. "I've had enough tragedies too. I no longer have Vicka, and I gave up hope for children, a family . . . any kind of happiness."

"I didn't want you to know, Mateo. It was my decision. I can't think only of my own heart. *I'm the queen of Tierra.*"

Mateo reached out to clasp her hand. "This war has already demanded too many bloody sacrifices—don't make another one. If the queen has no heart, then Tierra is lost." He slumped back, having expended all of his energy.

Sen Ola finished bandaging the side wound, then attended to the deep cut on his back, which was also bleeding. "Just coming to see you has cost him a great deal, Majesty. It is obvious what this means to him."

Anjine drew a hitching breath, and clear realization washed over her face. "If . . . if he should die, then I would have nothing of him but memories." She took the glass vial from her tabletop and handed it back to the Saedran physician. "Take this away, before I change my mind."

Part IV

87 *The* Dyscovera

Now that they had come together in an unknown ocean, the two Saedran chartsmen had a whole world to share. Aldo and Sherufa were colleagues from long ago, and over the years they had secretly traded knowledge about newly discovered lands, helping to complete the ever-expanding Mappa Mundi.

Earlier that afternoon, when the uneasy crewmembers mingled aboard the joined ships, Aldo recognized one of the *Al-Orizin* sailors with a start. "You! I know you." The man looked startled; he pretended not to understand the Tierran language, but Aldo pressed him. "You delivered a message to me in Calay. Sen Sherufa gave you a package with her notes about the Great Desert and the Nunghal lands, and she sent you all the way from Olabar."

Yal Dolicar flushed, feigning a heavy Uraban accent (which he had not used before). "You must be mistaken."

Sen Sherufa frowned at him. "You know it's true, Yal Dolicar. You are only aboard this ship because I vouched for your story before the soldan-shah. Chartsmen have perfect memories. You can't expect him to have forgotten."

Dolicar seemed nonplussed and embarrassed. "Oh yes! Now I remember. What a surprise to see you here."

Aldo narrowed his eyes and continued with an edge in his voice, "You're also the same man who sold me a fake map on the day I became a chartsman. At the Calay docks, you told a fantastic tale about coastlines you'd seen, and I paid for a chart of those foreign lands—but of course it was a scam."

Yal Dolicar looked as if he very much wanted to be somewhere else. "I am certain that's not true. I would never cheat a young man, and it was so many years ago you couldn't possibly—"

"Chartsmen have perfect memories," he and Sherufa reminded him in unison.

Dolicar flushed a deeper red and let out a long sigh. "How can I argue with you? My recollection is much fuzzier than that, but if I did something foolish and impetuous all those years ago, you'll have to forgive me. I can repay you the money you lost—I have some very interesting coins I found on a mysterious ice-locked ship. . . ."

Aldo laughed. "Still telling ridiculous stories!"

"That one, Aldo, is actually true," Sherufa said.

While the two separate crews continued repairs to the vessels, reluctantly sharing their sparse materials and tools, the two chartsmen engaged in hours of excited conversation. "Since we parted in Olabar, my life has changed." Aldo smiled as he let the thoughts run back through his mind. "I'm married now, with two beautiful children, whom I miss very much . . . as well as my parents, my brother and sister. I used to long for adventure, but I have a new appreciation for home now. I miss Calay, too. And Landing Day festivities, and there's a special kind of fruit pastry made in Alamont Reach. I liked to walk across town to one particular bakery, just so I could bring fresh pastries home for the whole family." With the perfect recall of a chartsman, Aldo could crystallize every face, every memory. But it wasn't the same as being there.

Sherufa sighed. "Ah, to sit at home, to cook my own meals . . . to relax on a spring evening during a rainstorm, with water running off the gutters and into the streets." She smiled at him. "Imir would often join me for dinner so that he could listen to my stories. I think that's why he wanted me to travel so much—just to give me more tales to amuse him."

Aldo also told Sherufa about the mer-Saedrans and their lost continent, and she described how the Nunghal-Su had sailed around the southern continent up to Lahjar, proving that such a passage was possible. When the five reaches of Tierra were included, along with the five soldanates of Uraba, the Great Desert, and the southern ocean, their patchwork map sprawled across the entire tabletop.

Sen Sherufa laced her fingers together, as if to cage her excitement. "Significant pieces of the Mappa Mundi are falling into place."

"We would know much more about the seas and the continents if Prester Hannes hadn't offended the mer-Saedrans." Aldo scowled at the memory. "Their undersea libraries have records of every place they've explored—coastlines, islands, open waters." He sighed. "I doubt we'll see them again."

Working in concert, they compiled an extensive chart of the known world, piecing together details from their voyages and all the maps they possessed, the sights they had seen and the landfalls they had recorded. It was intricate and time-consuming work, but enjoyable.

As they compared the routes the two ships had taken, an obvious—and astonishing—realization came to both chartsmen at once. The *Dyscovera* had sailed west across the Oceansea, heading past the islands of Soeland Reach, then south . . . and the *Al-Orizin* had voyaged *east*, crossing the Middlesea, yet the ships had both arrived at the far side of the world.

Aldo blinked at the implication. "How did we both end up here?"

"How, indeed? We have long known the world is round, and this is proof that the great seas are connected." She drew in a sharp breath. "Continent after continent—the world is vaster and more amazing than I could imagine. Such a marvelous creation. Why would Ondun have left it?"

Aldo wasn't sure how to accept Ystya's stories about Iyomelka and her island, or what Mailes had explained to them in the Lighthouse at the End of the World, but his pulse quickened as he looked at the compiled map. "Do you think the Mappa Mundi is nearly finished? Is there more to explore, or are we merely adding fine details from this point onward?"

Sherufa ran her palm along the edge of the last piece of paper. "Or maybe Ondun created something greater than we could understand in a hundred more generations. All that we have seen might just be one grain of sand on a vast beach."

"We still have to find Terravitae," Aldo said. "From the charts Mailes gave us, and with Aiden's Compass pointing true, we know we're close . . . if our ships can survive long enough to get there."

Sherufa gave a wistful sigh. "The only thing that matters is that *someone* describes the world . . . the whole world."

The prophecy known to all Saedrans, the very creed by which chartsmen memorized the knowledge collected over the centuries, was clear enough. Aldo recited it. "Ondun will return when the Map of All Things is complete."

88 *Ishalem*

Using a standard letter of passage from the soldan-shah, which Istar obtained from the palace commerce minister, along with sufficient funds to pay for travel and necessities, she set off across Uraba with Ciarlo and Asaddan.

Once Istar had convinced her brother that Ur-Sikara Kuari was not a scheming fanatic like so many other sikaras, Ciarlo was enthused by the idea of speaking to the woman. "If we heal the hatred between our religions, then we can stop this war. If she is reasonable, perhaps I can make the ur-sikara listen to us."

"And will you listen to her as well, friend Ciarlo?" Asaddan asked. "Are you interested in the worthy points of her religion?"

Ciarlo wrestled with his answer, knowing how he needed to respond. "I will . . . listen. Aiden and Urec—and Joron—were brothers. They must have loved one another. We should start from there."

As they traveled along the coastal road toward Ishalem, Istar found Ciarlo's sincere passion heartwarming. Her brother had no violence in him, did not seek to eradicate anyone who followed the Fern instead of the Fishhook. She was surprised at how brave (some would say foolish) he had been to travel to Uraba without even speaking the language and knowing almost nothing about Urec's Log. He had been naïve, unprepared, and full of faith.

As they rode east, Istar said, "I had to learn about a whole new world when I was brought to Uraba. I spent my first years as a household slave, absorbing the language, learning about their religion. It is very strange for an Aidenist to hear what they believe."

In all her years in the soldan-shah's palace, Istar had never fully embraced the Urecari faith, although she was familiar with the scriptures and rituals. When she agreed to become Omra's wife in order to protect her son, she had convinced herself that it would never be a true marriage, since their religion was a lie. In the eyes of Aiden and Ondun, Criston Vora would always be her true husband.

But over the course of two decades, as her son was raised in Olabar, as she bore Omra two daughters, as he took care of Istar and gave her prominence, listened to her advice and treated her as a true partner rather than a spoil of war, her attitude had slowly changed. Istar could not have endured if she had spent every day believing that her life was a lie, that her *daughters themselves* were the result of a crime.

"My feelings became blurred over the years. There is some good in what the Urecari believe, just as there is good in the Book of Aiden. In fact, presters and sikaras teach the same things, but too few people on either side truly practice what they claim to believe."

Asaddan said, "I respect Ciarlo because he lives by his beliefs—I have seen it for myself."

Ciarlo gave a solemn nod. "I still remember the raid on Windcatch . . . the fires, the murders, poor Prester Fennan. Since coming to Uraba, I've seen terrible things, and had terrible things done to me." He visibly steeled himself and then told her again how angry followers of Urec had burned his irreplaceable Tales of the Traveler, how he'd been chained to a galley bench aboard the *Moray*, whipped for speaking the word of Aiden, then keelhauled. "I have also met a few kind sikaras."

Though she cringed, Istar said, "Aidenists aren't entirely innocent either, Ciarlo." With great pain, she described the beautiful hanging lake of Fashia's Fountain. "Istala wanted to join the priestesses there. But Aidenist attackers defiled the shrine and slaughtered every one of the pilgrims and priestesses. If it had happened a few months later, my own daughter would have been murdered along with the rest of them."

Shocked to hear this, Ciarlo rode on in silence, deep in thought.

Riding ever westward, they reached Ishalem five days after Omra had arrived in the city. A huge Tierran army had besieged the wall, commencing a constant catapult bombardment, and the Aidenist navy had blockaded the Oceansea harbor.

According to the news they received in the streets, Omra had increased defenses on the wall and stationed numerous guards at the gates and watchtowers, preparing for the large military assault that was sure to come. After the fiery attack on Olabar harbor and now the threat to Ishalem, he was understandably outraged—and Istar was afraid of how the soldan-shah would react to Ciarlo, even if he was her brother. Omra might not be in any mood to talk about peace and understanding.

"I'll speak with the ur-sikara first," Ciarlo said. "We may understand each other after all. Can you get us an audience with her?" He blinked his blue eyes at Istar, so innocent, so earnest—and entirely without fear. With unsettling calm, Ciarlo had told her he was willing to die a death similar to Prester-Marshall Baine's—strung up on a post with a fishhook through his throat—if it provided an example that would open the hearts and minds of the Urecari to the light of Aidenism.

Istar did not intend to let it come to that.

They passed the rubble of Soldan Huttan's collapsed church, where dusty laborers picked over the piles of debris to salvage metal and stone. Carts rattled away, piled with broken blocks, either to be used in construction projects or hurled as missiles should the Tierran army breach the Ishalem gates.

Asaddan secured lodgings so their party could rest before Istar requested an audience with the ur-sikara. Omra would be preoccupied with the city's defenses, but she was confident Kuari would at least receive her and give her brother a fair hearing. Beyond that . . .

When the three unpacked their belongings and changed out of dusty traveling clothes, Istar was distracted by nostalgic thoughts of her brother, of Criston Vora . . . and Saan. And that made her want to open up the sympathetic journal she carried in her pack.

For several months now, Istar and Sen Sherufa had carried on a correspondence, writing messages back and forth on the book's ever-diminishing pages. The long-distance conversation allowed Istar to feel close to her son, to know what Saan was doing and how far he had sailed. But most of the twinned half-pages were already covered with writing, and Istar worried that every scrap of paper would be used up before Saan could come home safely.

Opening the book, she flipped to the last pages and saw fresh lines of Sen Sherufa's tight handwriting, shorthand sentences that used as little paper as possible. The message was devastating, unbelievable.

At first, Istar read a recounting of the icebergs and the ancient frozen ship, Iyomelka's continued pursuit, the destructive storm, and the Leviathan attack—which sent a chill down her back, for Ciarlo had told her how the very same monster had sunk the *Luminara* and nearly killed Criston. Sherufa provided only bald facts: Iyomelka was dead, killed by the Leviathan, which had in turn been slain by the mysterious ghost ships. The *Al-Orizin* was badly damaged, barely able to make sail.

Istar squinted down at the last sentences Sen Sherufa managed to fit at the bottom of the torn page. The *Al-Orizin* had joined forces with an equally battered Tierran vessel, the *Dyscovera.* Istar recognized the name from her brother. Criston Vora had sailed away aboard that ship on his quest to find Terravitae.

The implications made her reel. Saan was with his father, and didn't even know it!

Though her heart was torn, she felt a great and unexpected joy. Saan needed to be told. Choosing her words carefully, but writing as fast as she could, Istar—Adrea—picked up a pen.

89 *The* Al-Orizin

The Urabans on board, especially Sikara Fyiri, were unsettled to be so close to the Aidenist vessel. Ropes and grappling hooks tied the wrecks together, and the ships held on like two drunken men supporting each other as they staggered away from a tavern fight.

Tierran and Uraban sailors eyed one another across the decks; Sikara Fyiri glowered at the Aidenist prester as if he were a murderer of children, and he regarded the sikara with equal hatred. The man had waxy burn scars on his face and hands, but the greater scars seemed to be behind his narrowed eyes. Sen

Sherufa and the other Saedran chartsman were the only two people unabashedly pleased with the encounter.

Saltwater continued to leak through gaps in the *Al-Orizin*'s hull, despite the best efforts of the crew to patch the damage. At Saan's urging, and to test her powers, Ystya attempted to draw upon the magic in the water and wood, to recreate her mother's spell in resurrecting her sunken ship.

The young woman did spark enough magic to regrow the wood of shattered planks, knit the threads of the sails, twist and bind some of the frayed ropes, but when she finished she looked gray and weak. "I used up too much strength when I fought against my mother and called the storms." Ystya shook her head. "I'll have more power when we reach Terravitae. That land is a wellspring for my people, just as the island spring was a source for my mother."

The storm had smashed the window of Saan's cabin, and flooding saltwater had ruined the ancient chart from the frozen ship; fortunately, he kept the Map of Urec in its leather case, where it remained protected.

The sympathetic journal had also gotten wet so that some of the ink in the older entries ran, but he rescued it and left it out to dry. Now, as Saan gingerly turned the soggy pages, he knew his mother would be worried, so he decided to tell her that he was alive, at least for now.

New words had appeared there in his mother's hand, and he read with widening eyes. None of Saan's adventures or discoveries during his voyage prepared him for what she revealed.

He knew most of his mother's story, of course. She had been taken from a Tierran fishing village, and his blond hair and blue eyes proclaimed his foreign heritage like an insult every time he peered into a gazing glass. He knew that his true father was a fisherman or sailor who had been away when the raiders struck Windcatch.

But now she wrote to tell him that the captain—the Aidenist sailor who had guided his vessel all the way around the world—was that man. Criston Vora. His father. It was impossible . . . but she would never lie to him.

Criston. With a lurch in his chest, Saan felt the resonance. Though he hadn't made the connection before, now he understood why his mother had chosen that name for her other baby boy . . . *Criston*, the son of the soldan-shah who was murdered by Cliaparia.

This was more unbelievable than learning that Ystya was the Key to Creation, more unbelievable than finding Ondun's drowned body deep in a well on the island. The other captain, right there across the deck, was his father.

Saan stared at the handwritten page, afraid to tell anyone. Even though the sympathetic journal was nearly used up, Istar had devoted an entire sheet to explain everything in full detail. He took a long time to absorb the fact that his own quest had been on an unwitting collision course with his father's. Criston Vora.

If Istar declared that the bearded man on the damaged Tierran vessel was truly his father, Saan would not dishonor his mother by refusing to accept it as fact. But he found it very difficult.

Saan pondered what to do, trying to loosen the knot in his stomach. He had not crossed over to the *Dyscovera* as yet, had not spoken directly with the other captain, the prester, or any of the Aidenist crew. Sen Sherufa and Aldo na-Curic had worked out the terms of cooperation.

How would the Tierran captain receive this news? Saan hoped he would be happy. Would he even believe it? Saan wasn't sure how he felt about it himself.

On unsteady legs, he went to the door of his cabin where the lashed-together boards barely hung in place on one intact hinge. When he signaled for Sen Sherufa, she saw his troubled expression. "What is it, Captain?"

"Please ask the captain of the *Dyscovera* to come aboard. I would like to meet with him in my cabin. There is . . . something important I've got to tell him. A private matter, but I want you and the other chartsman here to act as translators—both of you, but no one else."

Intrigued, she went off to find Sen Aldo and arrange the meeting. Saan withdrew into his cabin and sat down, wrestling with what he was going to say.

Before long, the other captain arrived, looking wary. When Criston Vora entered, Saan searched the man's face, and could not deny the familiarity he saw there . . . the same features, the blue eyes, the Tierran nose and chin line. When Captain Vora saw Saan's light complexion for the first time, he too was thrown off balance, and even more surprised when Saan unwrapped the olba from his head to reveal his blond hair.

Saan looked at the two Saedrans and held out the sympathetic journal that contained his mother's words. He cleared his throat. "I have a story to tell you, Captain Criston Vora." Saan spoke so quickly that Sen Sherufa and Aldo had difficulty keeping up with their translation.

Listening, the other captain sat back heavily in the chair, as if Saan had dealt him a hard blow to the chest. "I only just learned that my Adrea was still alive . . . and now this."

Saan talked about the soldan-shah's palace, Istar's two daughters, even the baby boy she had named Criston. "Look at me, Tierran," Saan said. "Look at my eyes and study my face, as I have studied yours. The truth is there. You know it now, just as I do. Your wife—my mother—is still alive. And I am your son."

90 *Desert Harbor*

After months of constant labor, Arikara began to recover. The dead were buried, the wounded healed or healing, shelters rebuilt after the earthquake. By now, regular caravans went back and forth, businesses were reopened. Soldan Xivir even remarked that his people were thinking about normal lives again.

Many of the survivors in Arikara considered their new awnings and tents to be homes, not just emergency shelters. The people were not in any particular hurry to rebuild brick-and-wood structures again, especially after a sharp aftershock struck the city three weeks earlier.

Khan Jikaris and his Nunghal adventurers grew restless in the crowded city, even though it would still be months before the seasonal winds shifted and their sand coracles could cross the Great Desert again. At the khan's insistence, Arikara now boasted a small Nunghal church, where the nomads could commemorate the two sailing brothers who had discovered their land. The place of worship was a matter of pride for Jikaris, though he wasn't overly religious; he simply wanted to show the sikaras that his people's beliefs were important, too.

For his own part, Imir was also anxious to move. Since his retirement, he felt footloose and didn't like to stay in the same place for long. He had intended to sail across the dunes to see the Nunghal lands and the southern sea again, but the bandit raid had crushed those hopes for this year. Imir considered riding up to Kiesh, the easternmost city of all the Uraban soldanates, just to see it. He did not doubt that his granddaughters would want to come with him.

Khan Jikaris, though, wanted to ride south to the edge of the desert, "if only to look at the dunes, and to make certain our coracles are being taken care of at Desert Harbor."

Imir offered to join them. "I'd like to see how repairs on our Uraban coracles are coming along. At least ten should be ready to take flight."

Adreala, Cithara, and Istala rode their own horses for the journey down to Desert Harbor. By now, the three girls had learned how to catch, saddle, and bridle their mounts, and their

Nunghal companions showed them tricks each night in camp. Adreala was particularly proficient with knots and ropes.

Upon reaching the outpost at the edge of the desert, Imir was glad to see that the buildings had been rebuilt after the bandit raid. The coracle baskets were repaired, the colorful silken balloon sacks carefully folded and protected from the weather. The five Nunghal coracles had also been patched and readied for the voyage home.

Jikaris shaded his eyes and gazed at the blistering sand dunes. "I would not want to walk across that. Asaddan did it once. That is enough."

"I want to see the Nunghal lands someday, Grandfather," Adreala said. "I won't let you forget your promise to take me there."

"I had a good excuse each time our plans changed," Imir said, and tousled the girl's hair. "If you can avoid being kidnapped by bandits, and if another severe earthquake doesn't strike, maybe we'll go when the time is right."

A sweaty, dust-encrusted rider came pounding into Desert Harbor, letting out a shrill whistle for attention. The people in the camp closed in to hear the urgent news that had brought him here at such a breakneck pace. "Soldan Xivir commanded me to find the former soldan-shah with all due haste!"

Imir came forward. "I am here. What is it?"

"Olabar harbor has been attacked by Aidenists from Gremurr! Many ships burned, hundreds killed. I've been riding for more than a week."

Imir felt as if a lead weight had dropped into the pit of his stomach. "Was the enemy driven off? Is the city safe?"

"The enemy retreated and the fires are put out, sir, but there are worse tidings. Even as the flames were raging, Soldan-Shah Omra received word that a massive Tierran army has laid siege to the Ishalem wall, and their navy has blockaded the harbor."

Khan Jikaris, who had understood most of the report, flushed red. "Then we must go and help in the fight. You are our friend, Imir. We have heard your terrible stories about these Aidenists. Do you have any weapons?"

Imir felt cold inside. He had been away from that conflict for a long time. "I wish I could be there to support my son, but here I am, on the farthest edge of Uraba. There is no way I can go there."

Jikaris snorted. "We will use the sand coracles. Fifteen of them are ready to depart as soon as we pack them."

The former soldan-shah sadly shook his head. "The coracles go where the breezes blow, and Ishalem is west and then north."

The khan scratched a few strands of gray hair that stuck up from his tanned bald scalp. "Have you not discovered how to change course by raising or lowering the balloon?"

"What are you saying?"

"Air currents flow in different directions, depending on altitude. They are like rivers, crisscrossing in the sky. Change your height until you find a stream blowing in the direction you want to go." Jikaris looked to his companions to make certain he was explaining it correctly, and they nodded. "How can you not have discovered this in all your voyages?"

The former soldan-shah was taken aback. "We . . . simply caught the strongest current, and it blew us south, or north, depending on the time of year."

"We have to go," Adreala said, and her sisters agreed. "Bring archers and arrows, and anything else you used when you fought the bandits."

"If it is possible," Imir said, still unsettled, "then we are off to Ishalem." He raised his voice and shouted to the people of Desert Harbor.

91 *The* Dyscovera *and the* Al-Orizin

The two ships combined their materials and stretched swatches of repaired sail to catch the breeze. The currents of the sea drew them onward in the right direction, according to Aiden's Compass. Prester Hannes wasn't surprised: Ondun would want to bring them to Terravitae.

The waters were gray and the temperatures cool, but he felt warm anticipation. Before long, he would stand before Holy Joron. He braced himself with a preaching staff, which was tipped with a hard bronze fishhook. The emblem made him feel strong enough to deflect Sikara Fyiri's questions. She understood so little! He looked forward to seeing the last son of Ondun smite the obnoxious Urecari priestess and scoff at her silly beliefs.

Javian stood with him at Aiden's Compass, looking out at the water in search of a misty horizon. The young man had been an excellent addition to the crew, and he'd been spending more and more time asking insightful questions. Since the beginning of their voyage, Hannes had secretly hoped to convert the cabin boy into one of his devotees. Javian had not yet embraced Aidenism with ardent faith. Still, the prester maintained hope. Some evenings, the two would read the Book of Aiden together, and Javian listened with apparent interest when Hannes pointed out the foolish contradictions in Urec's Log.

Hannes still wasn't sure he liked Javian's easy friendship with the female sailor, and it appeared that his romantic interest was reciprocated. Though Mia had deceived them by hiding her gender, at least she did not speak out against Aiden or openly question the church's teachings. The Uraban sikara was a far more worrisome enemy.

Though they tended to stay aboard their respective ships, the crews could cross back and forth at will via a plank bridge that had been laid over the intact portions of the ships' rails. Hannes looked for an appropriate chance to lecture the crew of the *Al-Orizin*, to point out the errors of their beliefs. After all, he spoke the language perfectly, having lived in Uraba for so many years.

That time had been a special and important part of his life. Prester-Marshall Baine had sent him to Ishalem in disguise to learn Urecari ways, and Hannes had undertaken the assignment with great fervor, living a double life. He acted like one of them, infiltrated their church services, understood their weaknesses. When Ishalem had caught fire, however, he had been burned trying to steal the sacred Amulet of Urec from their main church. After recovering in Olabar, and murdering the soldan-shah's wife, he had spent years wreaking as much havoc as possible. A warrior for Aiden. He was proud of his success. . . .

But Sikara Fyiri refused to let her people listen. Instead, the red-robed priestess delighted in debating Hannes face-to-face, challenging him and twisting his words. Now she walked across the deck of the *Dyscovera* as if claiming the ship in the name of Urec. "Are you filling this boy's head with more lies, Prester Hannes?"

"Javian's mind and heart are filled with the truth of Aiden," Hannes said. "There is no room left for lies."

Fyiri pouted at the prester's rebuff, but she enjoyed the debate and challenge, mocking every point Hannes brought up. Though impressed by his intimate knowledge of Urecari scriptures, she offered only glib responses when Hannes pointed out irreconcilable contradictions in her beliefs. The woman's inflexibility was maddening.

Incensed by her, he had spent hours in his cabin over the past several days, annotating his copy of Urec's Log, highlighting discordant verses, falsehoods, impossibilities. He intended to show petulant Fyiri, line by line, everything that was wrong with her holy text. On the other hand, he thought, it might be more effective if he simply burned the volume in front of her. . . .

*

As the two ships sailed on, Criston allowed wistful personal thoughts to overshadow his larger worries. He still didn't know if the two ships would ever make it home, or even reach Terravitae. But he was here, with a young man whom he now knew was his son.

Neither he nor Saan had revealed the secret to their crews, although many aboard the *Dyscovera* marveled to see that the captain of the Uraban ship had blond hair and blue eyes, like a Tierran, like Captain Vora. If anyone noticed a resemblance in their features—and it was definitely there—they had not remarked on it aloud.

But it was undeniable that he and Saan were already close and spent a great deal of time together. They exchanged stories of their voyages, but Criston was most interested in hearing about Adrea. Mailes had revealed that she was alive, but gave him no details.

The longing was plain in his voice when he asked Saan to tell him more about his mother. The young man smiled, struggling to use the rusty Tierran language that she had taught him long ago. "If you'll tell me about her as well. All my life, I didn't want to hear about her early years in Tierra.

I was embarrassed by the color of my hair and eyes. I tried to hide my Aidenist heritage . . . and still the priestesses wanted to kill me for who I was."

Criston ached to hear that Adrea had become one of the soldan-shah's wives, that she had given birth to a son—who was murdered—and two daughters, who were now young women. But so much time had passed, how could he have expected her to stay alone for her entire life? He had waited for Adrea, pined for her, blocked off so many chances to let himself be happy, clinging to a slender thread of hope that was as thin as a strand of golden hair. Marrying the Uraban soldan-shah had never been her choice.

Criston wistfully told Saan how he had courted Adrea, saved

her from a broken family . . . how they had been wed by Prester Fennan in the old kirk on the hill above Windcatch, how they had lived with his old mother and her brother Ciarlo, a contented family. But he had followed his dreams by sailing off on the *Luminara*, leaving her behind, sure he would come home safe.

"I survived a shipwreck for her. When I had nothing else, not even a drop of water to drink, I clung to the thought of her, just to come home and see her again . . ." His voice hardened as his heart grew heavy. "But when I did find my way back to Windcatch, Soldan-Shah Omra and his raiders had burned the kirk, killed my mother, and taken Adrea with him."

Saan looked stung, even though he knew the story. "He is not a bad man. He was my father for most of my life, kept us safe, gave me opportunities a slave would never have had. I understand how you feel—no, on second thought I really can't imagine it. But Omra does care for her very much, and he relies on her for many of his decisions."

Criston was not so quick to forgive, however. "Omra killed my mother. He took my wife."

"And he raised me. I realize that you won't simply forgive him, but please try to balance the good he has done with the bad." Saan was clearly troubled. "I can't just forget him because I've found you."

"Then we'll have to stand together," Criston said. "Many things are going to change if we ever get back home."

92 *Ishalem Wall*

The time had come. Queen Anjine marked the days on her calendar, issued orders to her field commanders, rallied the soldiers. She was ready—they all were. They had waited decades for this. The imminent attack would be a thousand times more furious than the recent hurricane that had struck the Tierran coast.

Every man in the army camp kept close watch for any potential *ra'vir* activity, which created unfortunate tension among soldiers who would have to fight shoulder to shoulder in the upcoming battle. Realistically, Anjine couldn't imagine how *ra'virs* could remain undetected among these brave soldiers who trained together, ate together, worshiped the Fishhook, and attended dawn services each day. But she knew not to underestimate the Urecari.

For the past three months, each step of the operation had moved forward, unwavering, like the moon passing through its cycle of phases. Anjine had no way of knowing where Destrar Broeck was out in the Middlesea, but she counted on him to come with his ironclad warships. And if he didn't arrive, they would crush the Urecari anyway.

She dispatched a messenger to row out to the naval ships blockading the harbor, telling Comdar Rief to be ready to move in. After restless weeks and months, the Tierran sailors were anxious to storm Ishalem; Rief had promised to light a victorious fire atop Aiden's Lighthouse before the end of the day.

Destrar Shenro was agitated and eager, sleeping little, practicing on the sparring field, bragging to anyone in earshot about how many Curlies he intended to kill. He seemed intent on making up for his embarrassment after the raid on the wall.

On the day before the final march, Anjine ordered her army to increase the catapult bombardment, concentrating their missiles in a relentless and dizzying stone-storm that lasted from dawn until nearly midnight. Boulder after boulder smashed against the thick stone blocks, leaving white starbursts of powder. Some of the crenellations were chipped and battered, and a handful of enemy soldiers atop the wall were killed by well-placed strikes, but the wall remained strong.

When the Tierran army used up all the missiles they had harvested from the rocky countryside, the Curlies jeered from the wall. *Good*, she thought. Let them believe *that* was the major attack Tierra intended to mount.

She also had her men carry two immense battering rams and drop them out of bowshot from the wall. The intimidating rams would make the enemy nervous, though they would feel safe behind the reinforced wooden gate. Anjine knew the battering rams were merely decoys. The Urabans would expect the ineffective attack to continue, but Anjine had a secret weapon that would turn the great gates into splinters and sawdust. Let them feel confident. . . .

On the final morning, the queen rose in the cold darkness, ate a small breakfast (although anxiety, and her pregnancy, left her with little appetite), and then went to visit Mateo in the Saedran medical tent. After dragging himself through the camp several days ago, he had suffered a relapse, falling into a deep, restorative sleep. But he was strong, and Anjine had given him even more reason to live.

Mateo rested while Sen Ola hovered over him, dispensing medicines, changing dressings, applying poultices, and feeding him nourishing food. At last, after two weeks, he rallied and began recovering his strength. Sen Ola had just rewrapped his bandages and reported that the injuries were healing nicely when the queen entered the tent.

Mateo sat up on his cot to greet Anjine. "I would stand and bow to you, but my physician says I am not allowed."

"You need never bow to me in private, Mateo." She looked at him with a furrowed brow. "Today we launch our attack against the Ishalem wall, and within days the holy city will be ours. I wish you could be at my side."

"I am gaining strength, my Queen. Perhaps I could ride as an observer." He looked at the Saedran doctor. "I'll stay away from the fighting, I promise. I—"

"I forbid it!" Sen Ola interjected.

Anjine agreed. "And if the physician's command is not sufficient, then your queen forbids it as well. You will stay here and rest."

Mateo lay back on his cot with a sigh. "But I am feeling stronger." His voice was petulant but defeated. "Stay safe, my Queen—for me."

"I will stay safe for you . . . and for Tierra." Anjine kissed him on the cheek and left to make preparations. She donned the armor Ammur Sonnen had made, took the sword that had been given to her originally as a ceremonial weapon, though she had since learned how to use it. The edge was so sharp that it would easily slice through Urecari flesh and bone.

As she emerged from the tent, she felt like a shining angel in the dawn light. She called her presters, assembled the archers, footsoldiers, and cavalrymen. Drumbeats rang out, calling the garrisons to order. The increased activity would attract the attention of Uraban sentries, but the Tierran army could no longer hide their intent.

The presters sang hymns: "Ishalem, Ishalem, Ishalem!" Joining the chant, soldiers formed ranks on what had once been the wide and well-traveled Pilgrims' Road. Now the road was cut off by the stone barricade. The immense gates remained closed against them, and against Aiden. Queen Anjine could no longer stand for that. After today, the wall itself must fall. She had many surprises for the Curlies.

Anjine sat tall in the saddle on a gray Eriettan mare. Destrar Shenro rode back and forth on his antsy horse, shouting about their coming triumph and raising repeated cheers from the soldiers. Jenirod and Subcomdar Hist positioned their mounts at the front of the cavalry lines, behind which came the archers and footsoldiers. Loaded carts rolled along beside them.

The queen called in a strong voice that rang out above the shuffle and din of moving soldiers, "May the Compass guide us."

A resounding response to the benediction roared from thousands of Tierran throats. "May the Compass guide us all!"

Anjine urged her mare forward to where she could see the Uraban watchers who rushed to the top of the barricade. Enemy archers were crowded shoulder to shoulder on the wall, anxious to massacre the Tierran footsoldiers. Anjine's troops knew not to get too close, too soon.

Advancing toward the wall, her forces encountered row upon row of ivory skulls on the ground, empty eye sockets staring sightlessly into the brightening day. A thousand heads—*the* thousand heads.

For a moment, before she drove all thoughts away, she was glad Mateo wasn't there to see the grim reminder of what she had ordered, what he had done. The Urecari had left the skulls there as vengeful sentinels, perhaps hoping to evoke guilt and shame from the Tierrans. But Anjine felt only a dark satisfaction; those victims had been a necessary and sufficient payment for the death of one young prince. And today Tierra's enemies would pay a much heavier price.

Shenro rode up beside her and sneered at the skulls. "After today, Majesty, we'll dump ten times as many here—for a start. We need to keep some of the Curlies alive, though, so they can scrub their filth from the streets."

Anjine issued a challenge, and her soldiers bellowed a response loud enough to make the stones of the wall vibrate. They pushed forward, the horses' hooves and soldiers' boots crushing the dry skulls as they approached the gate. The queen raised her sword before her and vowed that by the end of the day she would see the steel covered with lovely Urecari blood.

93 *Ishalem, Main Urecari Church*

Even using her personal and political leverage, it took Istar two days to arrange a meeting with the new ur-sikara, due to the turmoil in the besieged city. Just after daybreak, Kuari received her, the big Nunghal, and a cloaked man in her anteroom behind the vaulted primary worship chamber.

"This is my brother," Istar said. "And as you can see, he is an Aidenist."

Ciarlo shrugged back his hood to reveal the Fishhook symbol that hung at his throat.

Kuari's eyes widened in surprise. Fortunately she did not respond with superstitious horror, but showed skepticism and dismay. "I didn't think you were the type of woman to play a joke on me, Istar . . ." She shook her head. "The Tierran queen is pressing against God's Barricade and the enemy navy has blockaded the western harbor. This is *not* a good time for a Fishhook worshiper to be in Ishalem."

"On the contrary, Ur-Sikara, now may be the best time of all." Istar still had hope, and possibly even faith.

Ciarlo stood beatifically before the head priestess. "I think that you and I should talk." He laid two fingers on the fishhook pendant, all he needed in the world.

The ur-sikara paced around him, completing a full inspection as if he were some strange sort of animal. "If you think you can convert me, sir, you are sadly mistaken." She seemed amused by the very idea.

"Not convert you, my Lady, but perhaps convince you to listen."

Asaddan laughed. "I haven't seen a lot of listening going on for quite some time. Neither Aidenists nor Urecari can claim to be the innocent ones."

Kuari was surprised by the comment. "Haven't you seen? Queen Anjine is outside our gates with the full Aidenist army!"

Istar stepped forward. "Yes, and what better time for the leader of the Urecari church to speak with her? What if I can convince the soldan-shah to do the same?"

Her heart had changed since learning that Saan and Criston had found each other. On the far side of the world, her son and his long-lost father had discovered a way to work together. Was it so impossible that the soldan-shah and the queen could *speak*? However, with Omra's attention so focused on the enemy, Istar had not yet informed him of her arrival.

Istar began, "When I was a young woman, King Korastine and Soldan-Shah Imir came to Ishalem to sign the Edict, to forge a peace. But because of some careless spark and people too ready to cast blame, we were thrown into decades of war. We have been going in the same bloody spiral for more than twenty years." Istar hadn't realized how much this meant to her until she was reunited with Ciarlo; seeing her brother reawakened all those old memories. "Is that the course we want to set for ourselves, or should we take this opportunity to change? With your voice, and Ciarlo's, and mine, maybe we can *stop this*."

"We can look for common ground in the Book of Aiden and Urec's Log, instead of battling over differences," her brother suggested. "Aiden and Urec were both sons of Ondun, they both came from Terravitae, they both set off to explore the world, and they both landed on these shores. We are all their children, and Ondun created us all."

Istar knew Kuari had a logical rather than fanatical mind-set. That was why she liked the woman so much and had championed her as the new ur-sikara. But Kuari remained skeptical now. "Yes, and each side has inflicted bloody wounds on the other, year after year. Ships captured or sunk, villages raided and massacred, one murder in revenge for another, and then another one after that. Do you suggest we all take an apothecary's potion to make us forget?"

"Perhaps to forgive," Ciarlo said. "Ur-Sikara, you and I could spend the afternoon trading stories of atrocities, tit for tat, like colored marbles on a game board. Are we keeping score? Is *Ondun* keeping score?" He raised his eyebrows. "A better way, I think, would be to find verses in the scripture that tell us about forgiveness. I know there are many in the Book of Aiden."

Kuari pondered for a moment. "And also in Urec's Log. Lately, however, the sikaras do not include those lines in their homilies." The head priestess ran a fingertip along her lips. "Despite what all the other sikaras say about our holy cause, I have not seen Ondun Himself showing any particular support for our side. Or yours."

Istar clung to hope. Ciarlo smiled at the ur-sikara.

Just then alarms sounded throughout the city. After months of tension and troop build-up, the Aidenist army was marching toward the wall.

94 *Ishalem Wall*

Upon hearing that the Aidenists were on the move, Omra rushed to meet Kel Unwar on top of the wall near the gate. The rising sun had not yet driven away the morning dampness, and the air still smelled of rock dust from the previous day's harrowing catapult bombardment.

"Do you actually sleep here, Kel Unwar?" Omra asked. He wore his pristine white uniform, maroon olba, and sash.

"This is no time for sleep, Soldan-Shah—and *that* is not a practice drill. It feels different to me." Unwar stared to the north where the Tierran military milled about with more commotion than usual, obviously intending to advance. "If they have found their balls at last, I am ready to castrate them."

Omra stroked his dark beard and watched the enemy army. "I

don't believe they were hesitating out of uncertainty or fear—it's part of a plan. This is no impulse, but a carefully orchestrated operation. They have moved too many soldiers, brought in too many ships."

Unwar let a small smile curve his lips. "No matter, Soldan-Shah. They can't breach God's Barricade. It has stood firm against a thousand boulders hurled at it. It can stand up against a cavalry charge."

Omra knew Unwar was right, but his heart wasn't convinced. He had called reinforcements to the wall as a show of force, and they crowded together in an impressive force, waiting to see what the Tierrans were up to. Thousands more Urabans were massed behind the main gate, ready to move against the Aidenists if the gate happened to be breached. In such great numbers, the soldiers were laughing and boisterous.

As the 'Hook soldiers lined up and marched forward, the kel shouted orders down the line. "Bring forth our archers to mow them down as soon as they're in range. Queen Anjine will lose half of her fighters before they even touch the gate."

The soldan-shah continued to study the army's approach, deep in thought. Could that be Anjine's plan? To sacrifice all those soldiers, hoping that enough would survive to reach the wall itself? And then what? "Who can understand these mad Tierrans?"

Unwar's personal anger seemed to dwarf Omra's. "If they come close enough for us to kill them, I'll be happy to decorate the wall with their heads. God's Barricade extends seven miles—room for plenty of victims." He looked eager for it. "I built this wall, Soldan-Shah, and I dug our canal . . . but if we exterminate the Aidenists, *that* will be my greatest achievement."

Uraban archers rushed up ladders and staircases to the top of the wide wall; they strung their bows and took up positions, propping full quivers beside them.

Below, the Tierran army tramped over the grim line of

weathered skulls that waited for them. Omra whispered to himself, "Let's leave a line of their skeletons that far outnumbers all the innocent Urabans they have slain."

He recognized the Aidenist queen riding at the fore, resplendent in new armor; a standard bearer at her side carried the Crown-and-Fishhook banner. Though he had never met Anjine in person, Omra loathed her for the things her people had done. She ruled Tierra, and thus the responsibility for all Tierran atrocities rested on her shoulders. The queen symbolized the terror and harm that had been inflicted upon devout Urecari. He prayed for the chance to face her himself. He didn't care that she was a woman; he would cut off her head just the same. She would bleed like any other victim.

Though the Tierran soldiers were nearly in arrow range of the wall, they did not slow. The cavalry horses whinnied, the footsoldiers' armor clanked, their swords flashed under the bright sun. He found himself holding his breath.

Unexpected trumpets and alarm bells sounded from deep within Ishalem. Unwar and Omra whirled to see a bright flare shining from a watchtower far to the east. More signals passed; messengers used mirrors to flash an urgent message, according to the routine Kel Unwar had put in place. "Unwar, what is it?"

The kel shaded his eyes, trying to identify the source of the disturbance. "It's coming from the guard posts along the canal, Soldan-Shah. Something seems to be happening at the Middlesea harbor."

"But the Tierran army is right in front of us." Omra frowned. "What new treachery is this?"

Together they hurried to the nearest sentry tower. The watchmen on the top platform were looking south and east, engrossed in something other than the advancing Tierran army. Omra brusquely took a spyglass from one of the sentries and stared along the straight new canal that flowed from one sea to the other.

A messenger came running up then, having translated the coded mirror flashes, but Omra saw the heartwrenching truth in the spyglass before the man could deliver his report. "It's the ironclads," he said, feeling a hot weight in his heart. "*My* ironclads." He should have expected it.

The tall sailing juggernauts, designed to be the most powerful ships in his own navy, were now commanded by Tierran invaders. The six armored vessels had wrought breathtaking havoc in Olabar harbor. Now they cruised majestically into the Ishalem canal.

95 *The* Dyscovera *and the* Al-Orizin

As the ocean current dragged them along, Aldo and Sen Sherufa went out on deck, facing the brisk wind that whispered around them. Sherufa leaned far over the rail, peering into the sea, where a flash of movement caught her eye. "Was that a dolphin? In these cold waters?"

Aldo spotted another shape, then two more streaking through the water. "Those aren't just dolphins." He turned with a joyful grin, calling out, "Captain! Captain Vora!"

The aquatic forms transformed with a blur and a splash to become shapely human figures, men and women who circled the battered ships like playful creatures. The sailors set up a great hue and cry.

Aldo impulsively embraced Sherufa. "Those are the mer-Saedrans!"

Several of King Sonhir's daughters surfaced, waving slender arms at the ship. Aldo shouted to them, "You came back—I can't believe you came back! We never meant to hurt you. Please, help us."

Captain Vora spoke sharply to two sailors. "Confine Prester Hannes to his cabin, *now*! I won't let him interfere as he did last time. We need them."

As he was led toward his cabin, Hannes tried to pull his arm free. "I will cause no trouble, Captain—I swear. You need my guidance." The prester looked so earnest that Captain Vora believed him.

"Very well, but the moment you go against me, I'll have you thrown overboard." He shook his head. "You damaged our relationship with King Sonhir's people last time, but maybe they've come to offer us a second chance."

While the mer-Saedrans circled the wallowing ships, King Sonhir's daughters tried to coax Aldo to jump into the sea and swim with them, but he shivered at the very thought of the chill gray water. "Will your father speak with us again? I promise he will be safe. Please give us a chance."

With a splash, Sonhir surfaced among the swimming mer-Saedrans. "We will hear your explanations. My daughters speak highly of Sen Aldo na-Curic—and I have a man here who vouches for Captain Criston Vora on his very life."

Another broad-shouldered form swam up from beneath the water and rose next to the king. Captain Vora let out a shout. "Kjelnar . . . you're alive!"

"Yes, I'm here, Captain! They pulled me overboard during the fight, but never meant to harm me." The shipwright cast his gaze along the splintered hulks of the two ships. "I don't know what you've done to my *Dyscovera*, but it looks like you could use our assistance. The king and I would like to come aboard, with permission?"

Men threw a rope ladder over the side of the ship, while the Urecari watched from the adjoining hull with uneasy curiosity.

King Sonhir and Kjelnar stood dripping on the deck; they did not shiver, despite the cold breeze. When Aldo introduced Sen

Sherufa, the mer-king was thrilled to meet another Saedran. Sherufa found only halting words as the often-repeated legend of her people became real around her. "I never wanted to leave Olabar at all, but I wouldn't trade this for anything."

Kjelnar was bursting with energy and excitement. "Oh, Captain, the things I have seen, the places these Saedrans have shown me! They worked some kind of spell or transformation on me, so that I have the ability to breathe underwater. I can swim and explore just like they do."

Aldo felt a pang upon hearing this, for the mer-king's daughters had extended the same invitation to him, but he had refused to give up his life and family back in Calay.

"We have had time to ponder our unfortunate last meeting." The mer-king turned to Captain Vora. "We seized Kjelnar in anger, but he has been a good instructor. The Saedrans understand you better now."

Aldo asked, "But how did you find us? We've sailed so far from where we met."

"But I knew where the *Dyscovera* was going," Kjelnar explained, "and I convinced Sonhir and his people to search for you. Good thing, too—your ship looks half-wrecked, and these Urabans . . ." He looked at the foreign crewmembers with deep suspicion. Hatred was shockingly plain on his face, and Aldo remembered that Kjelnar was one of the only survivors of Prester-Marshall Baine's volunteers, who had been slaughtered by Urecari at Ishalem.

The captain shook his head ruefully. "We have stories to tell, Kjelnar. Much to catch up on." He turned to the leader of the mer-Saedrans, who had taken a seat on a bleached and cracked barrel. "I'm very grateful, King Sonhir—for giving us a second chance."

"Our races share a common history that leads back to Terravitae—Saedrans, Tierrans, and Urabans. It's fitting that we are drawn there together. I can guide you the rest of the way."

*

True to his promise to Captain Vora, Hannes kept his feelings to himself, refusing even to speak of the undersea people, but he still loathed them for what they represented. He felt beset on all sides, his ship infested with heretical followers of Urec, guided to their goal by mer-Saedrans—Ondun's Stepchildren. It was a backbreaking set of tribulations that God asked him to face.

The prester had given up hope that Sonhir's people would accept the Fishhook, but if they led the *Dyscovera* to Terravitae, he would forgive them some things. Maybe he could convince them to turn against the Urecari, whom Hannes would never forgive. . . .

Sikara Fyiri persisted in taunting Hannes, though he kept his dignity and did not rise to her bait. He had irrefutable answers for every one of her ridiculous questions, but the priestess would not budge when he explained the truth to her, and he grew more and more strident as they approached the promised land. After clinging to his faith for so long, surviving the fire in Ishalem and dutifully wreaking destruction across Uraba, Hannes would not surrender now.

Fyiri found his intractable attitude amusing. Hannes wanted to throw her overboard, but even if he did, the annoying mer-Saedrans would probably rescue her. . . .

At sunset, the sailors spotted a dark haze on the horizon and a blur of low clouds—a coastline that stretched as far as they could see. "Land ahead! There's a shoreline!" Tierran and Uraban sailors shaded their eyes and stared.

Sen Aldo said, "That's much too large to be an island."

Hannes knew exactly where they were, and his eyes filled with tears. Fyiri was silent for once as she stood too close to him, her perfumed auburn hair blowing about in the breeze. The landscape ahead appeared rugged, but the prester painted a picture with his own expectations.

Javian approached him, ignoring the priestess. "Prester, is that truly Terravitae? Have we finally arrived?"

"Yes, Javian. I told you to have faith."

Fyiri smiled at them and spoke in Uraban. "Tomorrow, Prester Hannes, we shall see who is right."

She moved off to administer sunset services on the *Al-Orizin*, telling her people to rejoice. Hannes gritted his teeth when he heard her ululating voice crying the blasphemous untruths about Terravitae.

At dusk, the two captains called for a halt to their progress, much to the dismay of the crews, though they knew the shores might be treacherous. The joined ships dropped anchor and the mer-Saedrans swam away, promising to guide them in the morning. The ships remained motionless on a quiet sea, tantalizingly within reach of Terravitae.

"Yes," Hannes muttered to himself, "tomorrow we see who is right."

96 *Ishalem Canal*

The six ironclads sailed straight toward the mouth of the new canal, and Destrar Broeck did not know whether to trust his eyes. Back at Gremurr, the freed Tierran slaves had talked about the soldan-shah's absurd scheme to excavate a waterway across the isthmus from the Middlesea to the Oceansea. Now, with Ishalem before him, Broeck could only stare. "It's true. By the Fishhook, they have done it!"

Broeck saw the dawning opportunity, a change of plans that would allow his men to inflict even greater mayhem: instead of just striking the eastern harbor, miles from where the Tierran army was attacking the wall, he could lead his warships into *the very heart of Ishalem*! He raised a fist high. "Let's show these Urabans how much damage their own warships can cause."

Since returning to Gremurr, Broeck had taken command of one of the remaining vessels and designated it the flagship, since his noble *Wilka* now lay at the bottom of Olabar harbor along with the wreck of the *Golden Fern*. Although some claimed it was bad luck to reuse the name of a sunken ship, Broeck wasn't superstitious. He insisted on also christening the second flagship after his lost wife; he had no interest in other names.

The sails of all six ironclads displayed a defiant Fishhook as they cruised into the canal. Because the channel was narrow, the *Wilka* led the fleet in single file, with Iaros captaining the *Raathgir* behind it. They would push as far as they could go into the city, and they would fight all the way.

"Call out the archers," he shouted. "Flaming arrows where needed, but if you're just shooting at people, plain arrows will do well enough."

When the ships entered the waterway, Urecari citizens sounded the alarm and pointed in horror. Intermittent wooden watchtowers lined the banks of the canal, and silhouetted sentries lit torches or flashed messages with signal mirrors. Broeck laughed deep in his chest—what a surprise this must be! Battle horns rallied the citizens, but he didn't care. Unless the soldan-shah possessed another juggernaut like the *Golden Fern*, these warships were unstoppable. In fact, he hoped the Curlies would raise alarms loud enough to let Queen Anjine know that he and his warships had arrived.

He heard a commotion rippling from the rearmost ironclads, and sailors relayed a message by shouting along the line. Broeck went to the stern of the *Wilka* and saw Iaros waving from the bow of his ship. "Destrar! They're blocking us off!"

Ahead of him, Uraban men in rowboats left stubby piers and pulled across the waterway to cut in front of the *Wilka*—towing a line of kegs chained together, like floats to hold up a fishing net. Some kind of barrier?

Broeck chuckled, knowing his ships could cruise right over the top of the obstruction. Then he realized what the kegs must contain. "Archers! Stop those rowers at all costs!"

Without asking the reason for the destrar's sudden alarm, his sailors shot volley after volley of arrows. They killed the man in the first rowboat, but the Urabans were laying down three lines of casks, and the third one was farthest away and hardest to hit. When the first rowboat failed to draw its line across the canal, two more Uraban men dove into the water from shore, recklessly swam out to the boat, climbed aboard, and finished rowing to the opposite pier. The chained barrels now connected one side of the waterway to the other.

"Strike down our sails!" Broeck shouted. "Drop anchor before we ride up on those kegs. It's firepowder!" The crew scrambled to furl the sails, and chains rattled as anchors plunged to the bottom of the shallow canal. The *Raathgir* stopped so abruptly that the following ironclad rammed her stern.

Broeck scrambled up the *Wilka*'s mainmast so he could look down the line of his armored warships. Chains of firepowder kegs lay both before and behind them. His fleet was neatly bottled up in the middle of the enemy city.

97 *The* Dyscovera

Next morning, setting their makeshift sails and raising the anchors, the lumbering vessels drifted toward the mysterious coastline with the mer-Saedrans swimming ahead in the turbulent waves. A low fog rolled in, softening the sharp edges of the shore, but the coast looked rocky and bleak, with high cliffs that offered no place to land—a far cry from the lush paradise they had hoped for.

"A continent is a large place," Criston said, as if by way of apology. "And we'll have much to explore."

Closer to the rugged shore, Criston was stunned by what he saw: cast high on the rocks was the skeletal wreck of an enormous ship. Its keel and ribs, toppled mast, and few intact hull boards reminded him very much of another wreck that had rested on a hill in Ishalem. An Arkship.

Sikara Fyiri's cry was as sharp as a scimitar. "It must be Aiden's ship, which he sailed home after leaving Urec's vessel in Ishalem."

"*Aiden's* vessel was the one in Ishalem," Hannes snapped. "I was in Ishalem. I made the pilgrimage. I lived there for years. I—"

The sikara chuckled. "Delusions do not become true just because you speak them loudly. *Aiden* is the one who turned and ran home, while Urec remained."

"You have no proof of that."

"Of course I have proof," Fyiri said sweetly. "Urec stayed behind, because Urec is the Traveler. His tales and adventures are part of our history."

"Aiden is the Traveler," Hannes said with exasperated patience. "Not Urec."

Criston and his son consulted each other about the wreck, both longing to see it close up. But frothing waters curled around the cliffs, and jagged teeth of rock protruded from underwater outcroppings. "We can barely maneuver our ships as it is," Saan said. "I don't think we should go closer."

Kjelnar warned, "This is not a good landfall, Captain. Dangerous and not worth the risk."

Criston knew the shipwright was correct. "If even Kjelnar is uneasy, then I don't dare take the *Dyscovera* close to that shore. We'd be dashed upon the rocks. We'll have to find a safe landing and come back overland."

King Sonhir had emerged from the choppy waters and climbed up onto the deck. He looked at the weathered skeleton of the intriguing ship with a smile. "We have something far more compelling to show you farther down the coast—we can be there tomorrow. I promise, it will change your entire understanding of the world."

With the guidance of the mer-Saedrans, the two ships made excellent progress down the Terravitae coast in search of a safe landing, dodging treacherous rocks and foamy whirlpools. They dropped anchor at a safe distance from a bulwark of stone dotted with patches of moss and weeds, where seabirds flitted about the cliffs. Criston could see several prominent caves at the waterline, like secret tunnels leading into the heart of the continent.

As evening fell, Kjelnar trod water at the bow of the *Dyscovera*, undeterred by the cold sea. "This is as close as these big ships can go, Captain Vora! Drop anchor, and tomorrow we'll lead the small boats from here." He tossed his long, reddish-gold hair out of his face. "Believe me, there's something in those grottoes you'll all want to see."

Chains rattled, and the heavy anchors dropped into the water, catching on the rocky sea floor.

Terravitae.

In his private cabin Hannes lit two large candles for reading, knowing he wouldn't sleep this night. He could smell and taste the majestic new land just off the *Dyscovera*'s bow. Tomorrow, he would set foot on sacred Terravitae.

Inflamed with passion, he hunched over the Book of Aiden. He sharpened his pen's writing tip with his dagger and scribbled copious notes in the margins of Urec's blasphemous Log, cross-referencing verses from the Book of Aiden that refuted the lies in the rival text. Even if he showed all this to Fyiri, of course it would do no good. Fuming at the thought of her stubbornness, he jabbed the dagger point down into the wooden top of his writing desk.

It was the dead of night, still four hours until dawn, when Hannes's cabin door creaked open. Indignant at the intrusion, he turned to see Fyiri standing there in her red robes, a demon come to haunt his dreams. He rose from his writing chair, ready to cast her out like an impure thought, but she smiled and held up her hand. "Prester, you and I need to talk before tomorrow."

"I've talked a great deal with you already, Sikara, but you refuse to listen."

Impatient with him, she stepped inside and closed the cabin door behind her without a sound. "Nevertheless, a new time is upon us. Once we stand on Terravitae, there will no longer be any doubt."

"I have never had doubts."

Fyiri stepped closer to him. Very close. *Too* close. He noticed that she was dressed differently. She had sashed her immaculate red robe tight and low to accentuate her hips, her breasts. Her rich hair had been brushed back and caught up in jeweled pins; several thick, gaudy rings adorned her fingers, and a gold pendant danced into her cleavage, drawing his gaze. The scent of exotic perfume wafted about her.

"Why are you here?" he asked. "I did not invite you."

"Prester Hannes, I understand you better than any person aboard these two vessels. Whichever book we study and serve"—she indicated the two texts on his writing desk—"you and I are the true representatives of Ondun aboard these ships. When we find Holy Joron on Terravitae, should we not stand together? Be partners and show our strength?"

"Holy Joron would only think less of me if I were partner to a heretic."

Fyiri let out a tinkling, seductive chuckle. "Is that how you think Joron will see us? As Aidenist and Urecari? Tierran and Uraban? We are two sides of the coin struck by Ondun. Man and woman. We are parts of each other." She stepped even closer.

Hannes realized with astonishment that Fyiri was trying to seduce him! Did the sikara think him so weak? Were the Urecari so malleable and shiftless that they could surrender their core beliefs just for pleasures of the flesh?

"Come, Hannes, let me show you how we can be compatible." She stroked the waxy burn scars on the side of his face without fear or revulsion. But the nerves there were deadened, and he pulled back sharply, finding her touch abhorrent.

A flash of anger crossed her face. Fyiri drew her hand back as if to slap him, and he instinctively lifted his left arm to protect himself. It was exactly what she wanted. With a lightning stroke, she scratched his forearm with a barb that protruded from one of her rings.

She stood back and laughed as he looked down at the long red welt. "And now you are a dead man. That poison will act soon enough. There is no antidote."

She had come here with a complex scheme to kill him, but Prester Hannes preferred a more straightforward approach. He rarely resorted to tricks to get what he wanted—he simply acted. That was his nature. Grabbing the dagger from his writing desk, he plunged it deep into Fyiri's chest.

He found her heart with the first blow, precise and efficient, and Sikara Fyiri couldn't even scream. She gasped, her mouth and eyes wide open; blood welled from her chest as she fell to the floor.

Hannes yanked the dagger from her body, knowing that every beat of his heart drew the poison further into his bloodstream; he could not delay. He held out his arm where the scratch was reddening as he watched, and without even bothering to clean the woman's blood from the blade, he stuck the dagger tip into his skin. Starting above the poisoned scratch, he drew a long, deep cut all the way down the forearm. His hand did not shake; his grip on the hilt did not falter. Blood welled up from the gash, streaming out and washing away the poison.

He let the blood flow for several minutes, spilling red droplets onto the priestess's scarlet dress rather than on the deck. The sikara's last gurgles and twitches acted like a metronome.

When he began to grow dizzy and lightheaded—from loss of blood surely, not from the effects of the poison—Hannes picked up one of his candles and tipped the molten wax into his wound, filling the long cut. He did not cry out, barely even winced. He had suffered much worse, and was accustomed to the pain of burns. The wound should be well enough cauterized.

One-handed, using clean but ragged kerchiefs from his wardrobe chest, he bound up the wound, tying it as tightly as he could, using his teeth to yank the knots. When he was finished, he looked down at the dead woman sprawled like a squashed bug on his cabin floor. "Another victory for Aiden."

Hannes knew, however, that the sikara's murder would infuriate the Urecari crew, which would cause problems for the faithful Aidenists aboard the *Dyscovera*. The holy destination was at hand. After they reached Terravitae, Hannes could abase himself before Holy Joron and ask for forgiveness—and then it wouldn't matter what he had done to Fyiri. For now, he needed to buy time and stall their questions. Captain Vora must not be allowed to delay the exploration of the new land, and dawn was only a few hours away.

The night was quiet, and the sentries prowling the *Dyscovera*'s deck were intent on spotting Urecari treachery rather than watching their own prester.

Seeing no one nearby, Hannes slipped from his cabin, dragging the woman's body, hiding in shadows when necessary. He took great care not to let her spill blood on the deck as he brought Fyiri to the side of the ship, tied one of the ship's weight-stones to her ankle, and slipped the body overboard into the cold water.

He looked around and waited a few moments, but no one reacted to the splash. He returned to his cabin and there, with a satisfied smile, he closed Urec's Log.

98 *Ishalem Wall*

Even as the Tierran army trampled the line of skulls on their way to the wall, Kel Unwar reassured Omra about the ironclads in the Ishalem canal. "We have defenses in place, Soldan-Shah—do not fear. They'll be trapped like rats, and they will drown in their own folly."

Omra locked his hands behind his back, looking down at the invading army. "The Aidenists are making their most ambitious assault, but that only means their failure will be greater."

With silent suddenness, the Teacher arrived to stand beside Unwar and the soldan-shah, in plain view, knowing the black robes and silver mask were sure to strike fear into the hearts of the enemy. "If any of my *ra'virs* are still hiding among those soldiers, Soldan-Shah, they will act. But you should not count on them to help you win the battle. Many of my students have been rooted out by now."

"We have other ways to defeat the 'Hooks," Unwar said.

Omra studied the Tierran army. "Their catapults barely scratched the wall. Maybe they mean to push it down through sheer force of numbers." He was only half joking.

"Vermin," Unwar whispered under his breath.

The Uraban archers lined up along the wall, setting up for the best shot as they waited for the enemy to come into range. "The Aidenists are wearing armor," Omra called down the line. "Better if you target the horses, and once you've struck them down, aim for the footsoldiers. Infantrymen will have less shielding. But don't fire too soon—no need to waste arrows."

The Urabans were keyed up, their blood running hot. They had seen the Tierran army camped outside the wall for months, making only halfhearted skirmishes, and the soldiers of Ishalem were anxious to fight. Behind the main gate, reinforcements milled about, ready if the Tierrans should somehow break through, or if the soldan-shah threw open the wooden doors and unleashed his howling forces.

The Aidenists marched closer, step by step, in the same formations they drilled every day. On top of the wall, two tense archers loosed arrows, shooting recklessly at the front lines, and then like a flock of startled pigeons a flurry of archers fired, despite Omra's orders to hold. All the arrows fell short, pattering into the ground some thirty feet ahead of the front ranks of the enemy.

The armored queen raised a gloved hand. Standard-bearers waved their banners, calling a halt. The cavalry stopped their advance.

Unwar gave a gruff nod, as if that had been his intent. "Now they'll think twice about coming closer."

Omra was not pleased, though. "I'd rather we lured them into range so our arrows could strike Aidenist hearts instead of just the ground."

A few more Uraban archers took heroic shots, but didn't achieve enough range. The rest of Omra's bowmen jeered at the cowardly enemy that hovered just out of reach.

When Anjine halted her advancing army, the helmet visor hid her satisfied smile. She studied the neat line of feather-tipped arrows spread out on the ground and mentioned to Destrar Shenro beside her, "If any of the Curlies survive this battle, I'll have to thank them for so thoughtfully delineating their range."

"My archers have what they need, Majesty," Shenro said.

Her soldiers made rough noises, and the horses snorted; armor and swords clanked as the men shuffled and held their places. Even so, she could hear the distant insults hurled by the Uraban soldiers high on their wall.

With a predatory grin to Shenro, she said, "Call out your archers, Destrar."

Shenro echoed the order. Ninety specially trained bowmen had come down from Alamont, where they had practiced in the grassy hills—one archer for each Alamont horseman slain at Ishalem. The destrar's archers spread out in a line and strung their long recurved bows. They had more arrows than they could possibly require—and Anjine wanted the bowmen to use them all.

Destrar Shenro signaled to the queen, "My bowmen are ready, Majesty."

"They'll never have a better target than this," Subcomdar Hist said, indicating the line of men silhouetted atop the pockmarked stone wall.

She called over her shoulder, "Archers, loose your arrows swiftly and *keep shooting*. Don't let them run and hide under rocks like the cockroaches they are!"

Well outside the demonstrated range of the Urecari bows, the Alamont men pulled back their strings and with a whistling twang loosed the first volley. In perfect coordination, ninety arrows flew into the air, arcing high and far, then dropped upon the surprised enemy soldiers massed on the wall. Most of the shafts flew even farther, pelting the crowded fighters who waited on the other side.

The Alamont archers shot a second volley, and a third, even before the first arrow storm struck. Nearly three hundred deadly shafts hammered the Uraban forces who had felt safe behind their wall.

With unwavering grim expressions, the Alamont archers fired swarm after swarm of arrows, as quickly as they could. Some of them pinpointed their range and mowed down the ranks standing atop the barricade, while other arrows rained down into the city itself, massacring random civilians in the streets. A wave of shock and fear swept over the enemy.

"They aren't jeering at us anymore, my Queen," observed Shenro.

The tiny figures atop the wall fell like dropped stones.

*

The hail of arrows came from out of nowhere. Soldiers sprouted shafts from their backs or shoulders, and collapsed on top of one another; others clutched arrows in their throats or chests. More shafts fell, and then more, with an eerie hum like buzzing bees.

The Tierran archers did not let up.

Amid the screams and chaos, Kel Unwar pulled Omra to shelter behind the battlements. One shaft sliced through the soldan-shah's silken tunic to clatter on the stones at his feet, missing him by only a miracle. The Teacher did not move quickly enough, and one of the shafts plunged through the black robe and into the upper chest. The black gloves flailed and clutched at the arrow.

Unwar yelled in dismay and grabbed the Teacher, holding the figure up. "Don't pull out the arrow! We've got to get you away from here." Looking up to see Omra safe, he yelled, "Soldan-Shah, get to shelter! Run!" Then he began to drag the Teacher, whose silver mask somehow remained in place.

But Omra helped Unwar pull the Teacher to the steps. Arrows showered past the wall and clattered into the streets, skewering people who fled in panic. The Uraban soldiers crowded behind the main gate dropped by the dozens.

As Unwar wrestled with the Teacher, he called a sharp command: "Soldiers—bring shields! Protect the soldan-shah!" Several men responded, holding their shields up to cover Omra's head. Two arrows thunked into the raised shields, and the men hustled the soldan-shah swiftly through the streets.

The Tierran arrows continued to fall.

99 *The* Dyscovera *and the* Al-Orizin

With the first breath of dawn light, the swimming mer-Saedrans called to the crews that it was time to take boats to the tantalizing shore. Criston felt energized by faith and anticipation, ready to go see what King Sonhir believed would change their lives—though simply reaching the sacred land would do that.

Prester Hannes emerged from his cabin, wearing long sleeves against the chill. He held one of his preaching staffs as he called out the morning Aidenist prayers. On deck, the sailors had flushed faces as they watched the cliffs and crashing waves.

Criston barked orders, anxious to go, feeling caught up in another skein of unreality. So many unbelievable things had happened already. . . .

The quest to find this place had drawn him for most of his life, since his dreams as a young sailor. The thought of Terravitae had led him to make his worst decision ever: leaving Adrea behind. And though Mailes had now informed him that she was alive after all, Criston could not turn back the calendar.

Saan was his son.

Adrea was still alive.

She was married to the soldan-shah of Uraba.

And now, at last, Criston Vora had come to Terravitae.

He faced ahead, resolved to see Holy Joron and the sacred land, hoping it was worth the pain he had suffered to get here. "Prester Hannes, you'll accompany me, and Sen Aldo and Javian as well. Captain Saan will make his own choices and bring one of the *Al-Orizin*'s boats. We'll see this together."

Out of a sense of obligation, Saan felt he had to include Sikara Fyiri, but she had not yet emerged from her cabin, despite the commotion outside. How could she not be clamoring to be the first ashore? He wondered if she might be reluctant to see Terravitae, now that it was time to face the reality of her beliefs.

Grigovar pounded on her cabin door but received no answer. Finally, more impatient than concerned, Saan told him, "Pull it open. Let's see what's wrong with her now."

The sikara's cabin was empty. She had not slept in her bed, and she'd left no indication of where she had gone. The crew of the *Al-Orizin* raced about, calling out for the priestess, but the battered ship offered few places she could—or would—hide. Neither Sen Sherufa nor Ystya knew where the priestess might have gone.

"Maybe she swam ashore herself in the middle of the night," Yal Dolicar suggested. "Just so she could get there before the rest of us."

Saan fumed, fearing that she was up to some kind of trouble. "I'm not waiting any longer. If Sikara Fyiri doesn't care to join us, we'll just have to tell her what we find. Grigovar, Yal Dolicar, Sen Sherufa—you will join me in the ship's boat." He smiled. "You too, Ystya. You belong with us."

While Captain Vora lowered the *Dyscovera*'s boat, Grigovar asked Saan in a low voice, "Shall we bring the banner of Uraba, Captain? Plant our flag on the new continent and claim it in the name of Urec?"

"I think not. If we do that, then Captain Vora will want to bring the Tierran standard, and we'd have a race to see who can jump off the boat first and plunge a stick into the dirt. I will not have us looking like ill-behaved children if Joron is watching. Besides"—he looked over at the ethereal Ystya—"if Terravitae is the land of Ondun, then it isn't ours to take or give."

After they crowded into the two boats, Kjelnar surprised them by hauling himself out of the water and into the *Dyscovera*'s boat so that he could row, while burly Grigovar took up the oars in the other boat. The mer-Saedrans swam off in the lead.

Saan looked over at his father, communicating with the flash of an eager smile. His mother had taught him the Tierran language, though Saan had few opportunities to practice. Now, speaking that foreign tongue seemed natural in a strange way. Ystya sat in the prow of the *Al-Orizin*'s boat, admiring the cliffs of Terravitae, a home that she had never seen.

Prester Hannes rode like a statue in the stern of the *Dyscovera*'s boat, his back ramrod straight, his eyes glittering and hard. He clasped his fishhook-tipped preaching staff, as if determination alone could transform anything they were about to see into what he wished were true.

The two boats dodged frothing waves and rocks to slip into the mouth of the nearest sea cave. A surge of water swept them farther inside, so that Grigovar and Kjelnar rowed backward to stabilize the boats, then pulled them forward again.

Between the two groups, the conversation was excited and tense. When Hannes grudgingly began to translate for the Urabans, Yal Dolicar corrected some of the prester's misrepresentations, much to the man's annoyance.

As soon as they entered the sea cave, the temperature dropped precipitously. Saan blew out a steam of breath, but this was a different kind of chill than the raw and bitter cold of the iceberg sea. Ystya wrapped her arms around her narrow chest. On the other boat, Javian looked around in silent astonishment. Around them, the rock walls sparkled with diamond-like ice crystals. Seawater lapped and echoed, making sounds like phantoms whispering.

Saan's father gave him a wistful glance. "I set out for Terravitae when I was little older than you are now. I'm finally here, older, wiser, and scarred. But I never could have dreamed I would be doing this with you."

Saan heard the uncertainty and determination in Criston's voice. "It hasn't been easy for any of us, but at least we are *here*."

"I'm very happy with what I've found," he said, and only Saan understood his true meaning.

Icicles dripped down from the ceiling like sharp stalactites in a cave. As he pulled the oars, Kjelnar said, "It's just ahead—the main grotto."

With the swimming mer-Saedrans leading the way, the rowboats approached a large chamber where thick ice stood in great frozen columns at the entrance, like the gateway to a temple. They drifted into an amazing vault with a dome overhead of pure, transparent ice. The water ended at a flat rocky platform, like a stage, beneath the curved ceiling.

As if waiting for them, two ancient bearded men sat on blocky chairs of petrified wood in the center of the frozen floor, like a pair of powerful lords holding court. They were regal-looking, practically giants—and motionless, encrusted in a shell of clear ice. Frost sparkled in their long beards. Their eyes were closed, their expressions peaceful. One of the two men had brown hair dusted with gray, while the other's dark locks were intertwined with silver.

A cold wind of awe slipped into Saan's chest and wrapped around his heart. "Is that . . . is that Aiden? And Urec?" When he saw their features, he could indeed see echoes of Ystya there, a definite resemblance.

"Both together?" Criston said. "Here?"

Ystya raised her chin, and her eyes shone. "Those are my brothers—I know they are. Back on the island, when he was alive, my father used his magic to show us images of their travels, though he was too weak to communicate with them. When Aiden and Urec couldn't find me, as Ondun asked, they sailed back home. To Terravitae. And now we have found them."

Javian let out a trembling breath, like a sigh. "They're dead . . . aren't they?"

"No!" Hannes stood abruptly from the bench and lifted his staff. The boat rocked from side to side, nearly capsizing. "No, they never would have sailed home together!"

"Sit down, you fool!" shouted Criston.

Yal Dolicar gave a delighted laugh. "We saw the Arkship crashed farther up the coastline. Isn't it obvious? The brothers left one ship behind in Ishalem on the hill and traveled home together in the second."

Hannes was appalled. "This is not what the scriptures say!"

Aldo explained in a patient voice, "Prester, if they wrote the Book of Aiden and Urec's Log before they sailed home, then their stories would not have been complete. The tale wasn't finished."

"But Aiden remained behind," Hannes insisted. "Aiden is the Traveler!"

"Or Urec," Saan said with a shrug.

Sen Sherufa added, "Or, since we see both brothers here, the Traveler is someone else—if he exists at all. Either way, it's obvious that the stories told by the presters and the sikaras are flawed."

Prester Hannes gazed with a mixture of amazement and horror, as if he could just *will* the unexpected sights away. Yal Dolicar laughed to see the shocked look on the prester's face. "Oh, I only wish Sikara Fyiri were here. I am sure her expression would be as funny as yours!"

They climbed out of the boats and stepped onto the flat, cold surface, standing there in awe. The grotto was silent and eerie, as if the air held as much reverence as cold. The motionless men seemed to exude power, waiting . . . but they were certainly dead. No one ventured close enough to touch the preserved figures.

"Someone—or something—entombed them here," Criston said, "possibly even Holy Joron."

"We should not disturb them," Ystya said, "until we know more."

The brown-haired man—Aiden?—wore gray robes tied at his waist with a bright yellow sash. The threads sparkled; the fabric seemed to be spun out of crystalline fibers. His dark-haired companion wore a purple shirt and brown leather breeches. The men had similar boots, and both wore a silver ring on the left hand, but no other jewels or ornamentation. The two preserved bodies were so lifelike that Saan expected their eyes to snap open and awaken them to a new world.

Some relics had been carefully placed around the pair: two navigational instruments that were more complex than anything Saedran chartsmen used. An ornate spyglass rested beside Aiden's chair, its barrel partially extended. A sturdy wooden chest formed a table between them, the lid sealed with a complex-looking lock. On top of the trunk rested a thick tome whose cover was inscribed with archaic scrolled letters, stating merely *Captain's Log.*

"These are all ancient and sacred relics," King Sonhir said.

"Valuable, too," Dolicar added. He was fascinated by the lock on the petrified wooden trunk. "I could possibly pick that lock. Let's see what's inside the chest—there might be a message for whoever finds these two men."

"We should not damage or disturb any of these objects," said Sen Aldo. "Anything we do here could have grave repercussions. We must be very careful."

Criston was the first to step forward, fascinated by the bound book resting on top of the chest. He touched the cover, smudged away a tiny film of frost, then picked up the tome. When Criston opened the cover, the leather binding creaked and snapped, stiff with cold. "It's an account of their voyage back. This is the Book of Aiden and Urec."

"Sikaras and presters need to read this," Saan said. "It will tell us what really happened. This is proof."

"It's just a book," Hannes said. "Anyone could have put it there . . . just like the obelisk on that island."

"It is a priceless record. We have to study it," Sen Sherufa said. She glanced over at Hannes. "You can read it as well, Prester."

"I have already read the Book." He turned his attention to Criston. "How can you so easily change your own beliefs, Captain?" He looked around, his expression now beseeching. "This is not what we were supposed to find in Terravitae. These discoveries will shatter the beliefs of all Aidenists—and Urecari as well. We can't allow that."

"There's no need to rush," said Criston. "Each of our ships has sailed a year to get to this place. Let's study the relics and learn more before we take drastic action."

"More importantly," Saan said, holding Ystya's hand, "we've got all of Terravitae to explore. We just landed, and we need to find Joron, perhaps some evidence of Ondun's home. There's a whole continent to see."

100 *Ishalem Canal*

Though the ironclads were trapped in the Ishalem canal, Destrar Broeck had no intention of failing in his mission. Ishalem was his target, and his armored warships had already penetrated to the heart of the holy city. He wasn't going to let rows of chained powderkegs stop his assault.

"Iborians have never needed ironclads to win a battle. We'll go ashore and storm the city on foot!" While the Uraban army faced Queen Anjine's main force at the wall, his hundreds of soldiers would surprise the enemy from behind.

His orders spread down the line of ironclads, and the men cheered as they lowered boats down into the narrow canal. Some of the eager men simply dove overboard and swam toward the nearby docks.

The ironclads were invaluable military assets, and Broeck disliked simply abandoning these giant warships in the canal. But where could the Urecari take them? In fact, he had half a mind to ignite the line of powderkegs himself, sink the heavy vessels, and clog the strategic waterway just to spite the Curlies.

But the destrar was more optimistic than that, and he wanted to keep the Ishalem canal open for when the Tierrans conquered the city. Comdar Rief could lead the full Tierran navy into the Middlesea and devastate all those enemy ports that had never before faced an outside attack.

However, the trapped ironclads were directly within range of the watchtowers on either side of the canal. From the top of the towers, sentries creaked small catapults forward and turned winches to pull down throwing arms. Iaros yelped a warning as Urabans filled the catapult baskets with large stones and debris.

The first boulder crashed down on the deck of the *Wilka*, sending shattered boards and crewmembers flying. From the opposite bank of the canal, a second watchtower catapult launched its load with a loud *thwack* and whistling cry. A stone block crashed through the *Raathgir*'s mainmast and into the water, narrowly missing some of the Aidenist fighters who were splashing their way to the canal's edge.

A few of Broeck's men shot arrows at the watchtowers, but the Urabans took cover on the battlements while they continued to load their catapults. The canal waters were clogged with swimming men and crowded boats. Many Tierran soldiers reached the docks, where they climbed out of the water and turned back to watch the continued catapult bombardment.

Next, the Urabans hurled burning tar-covered timbers that crashed into the ironclads' sails, setting them aflame. Within moments, a stray spark was sure to catch on one of the floating powderkegs in the line. Broeck shouted for all of his men to jump overboard and make their way to shore by any means possible. "Abandon ship!"

Giant boulders struck three of the ironclads, projectiles large enough to crack even the reinforced hulls. As water rushed in and the flames rose high, the armored ships wallowed and sank in the shallow canal. Another thump sounded, then a buzzing sound rolled overhead just before a block smashed the stern of the *Raathgir*. Iaros was still waving his hands, shouting orders for his men to leave the ship.

Broeck bellowed to his nephew, "Go! Get off of there!"

He saw a flash of light from behind the line of ships, followed by a rumbling roar. Someone had lit the rear lines of powderkegs.

Explosions erupted in a steady, deadly succession, one keg igniting after another. The rearmost vessel, and possibly two beyond that, sank. Flames were everywhere. Smoke curled into the sky.

Looking ahead, the destrar spotted two Uraban men swimming along the forward line of chained kegs, holding firebrands up out of the water. The destrar grabbed a bow that someone had dropped on the deck, found a loose arrow, and made his shot.

The arrow knifed into the water near the kegs like a leaping fish, making the Uraban man jump. With greater urgency, the man worked a bung free, pushed a wadded cloth fuse into the top of the keg, and pressed his burning brand against it. Broeck shot three more arrows and received momentary satisfaction when he saw one strike the Uraban in the back. The man floated next to the smoldering fuse of the powder keg.

When the small barrel exploded, it ignited the second, which exploded and caught the next along the chain, and the next. When the other lines detonated as well, the firepowder hurled flames and shards into the air, ripping out the *Wilka*'s bow. Broeck was thrown to the deck, his skin sliced in a thousand places, his hair singed, maybe even on fire. He forced himself back up to his hands and knees.

The watchtower catapults launched a renewed storm of huge stone projectiles.

Iaros barely knew how to swim—the waters of Iboria Reach were too cold to consider such a thing—but now he thrashed across the canal to the shore. Though his heavy leather armor, shield, and sword dragged him down, he gasped and paddled and kept going.

The firepowder explosions deafened him, and he ducked his head under the water to avoid the rain of debris. He pulled himself up again, coughing, and swam forward. A stubby pier was close at hand, and when he grasped the wet piling, he felt safe again.

Around him, many fellow soldiers climbed out of the canal, their bloodthirsty mood sodden as they looked back at the smashed and burning warships. Iaros climbed up onto the dock, panting, dripping—and turned to see the *Wilka* a flaming wreck, her bow destroyed. The sails were an inferno, and she canted to port as her hull filled with water through a ragged dark hole in the side.

Iaros stared in dismay, as if someone had wrenched his heart from his chest. He could still discern a figure on the deck—his uncle!—struggling as the warship heeled over. The flames were high, and the ship was collapsing like a wounded mammoth. He could do nothing to help Broeck. Another catapult projectile—a giant block of whitewashed stone, colorfully decorated with . . . frescoes?—crashed into the *Wilka*'s deck, sending up a geyser of sparks and splinters.

On shore, the men roared in anger and prepared to run through the streets intent on revenge. Iaros stood in nauseated shock, but he knew that if he did not lead the soldiers now, they would run off without a plan and divide into smaller groups, which would be slaughtered one by one. He had to rally them into a single charge. Yes, that was what Destrar Broeck would want him to do.

The burning hulk of the *Wilka* continued to sink, and he watched the destrar go down with his ship. Iaros swallowed hard to realize that *he* was the Iborian destrar now. He had never expected this day to come so soon.

And as the new destrar, Iaros would not let his first act be the loss of his men! He shook dripping water from his hair, brandished his sword, and shouted to the hundreds of Tierran soldiers who were already ashore. It was time to lead them deep into Ishalem.

101 *Ishalem Wall*

A constant whicker of arrows flew from the long-range Alamont bows, and Uraban soldiers fell from the stone wall like rows of harvested wheat.

"I don't think they much care for our surprise, my Queen," Shenro said in a smug tone. Jenirod sat on his saddle, his face pale but satisfied.

As she watched, Anjine could not help smiling. The horse shifted restlessly beneath her, uneasy from the commotion, but she squeezed her thighs and yanked the reins, bringing the mare under control. "Two more volleys, then move forward."

"Get those wagons ready!" Subcomdar Hist shouted.

Field commanders repeated the queen's orders, and foot-soldiers cleared the way for overloaded horse carts to come forward. The large battering rams lay on the road, untouched. The Alamont archers shot more arrows, continuing the mayhem, though all of the Urabans on the wall had already fallen or fled. The far-flung arrows passed over the barrier and pattered indiscriminately into the streets of Ishalem, where they were no doubt taking a great toll.

The queen watched, her jaw set, her eyes bright. The blue-and-green Tierran banner flapped behind her. Dray horses strained against the traces, and the heavily laden carts rumbled forward.

Despite the enemy army hammering God's Barricade, Kel Unwar could think only of Alisi. He had seen to it that Soldan-Shah Omra was safe, and now he had to concentrate on his sister. No one else knew the Teacher's secret.

"Don't take me to a surgeon." She clutched at his arm with a gloved hand. "Don't let them take my mask . . . or see me."

Even if he managed to convince a Uraban surgeon to leave the polished silver mask in place despite her choking on blood, her garments would have to be cut away in order to remove the arrow. With one look at her body, her breasts, the surgeon would know the truth. Alisi could never allow that.

During the panicked retreat from the hailstorm of arrows and the chaos of screaming wounded, Unwar dragged the Teacher's limp body to a small storage building nearby. He kicked in the door, pulled her inside.

Though the arrow protruded from her chest, Alisi said she did not think it had pierced her lung. Working intently, his expression grave, Unwar used his dagger to slice the fabric of her dark robe and expose the arrow shaft.

"It's not bad—the bone stopped it. I can cut it out." He wasn't lying to her. Unwar had been a battlefield commander, and he knew about emergency medicine. He looked down at the knife, and his voice became quiet as he braced himself. "This is sharp. I'll be as quick as I can."

"I am used to pain. I've had enough of it, and what you do can't possibly be worse than the abuse I suffered from the Aidenists. Do it."

"I hate that they've hurt you again," he said through clenched teeth.

Unwar cut with the dagger tip, extending the wound just enough that he could work the arrow back and forth; he finally tugged it free with a grating, sucking sound. Alisi nearly fainted, but she uttered only a quiet whimper and kept the rest of the pain within, as she always did.

She bled, but not as much as Unwar had expected. He unwrapped his olba, cut the cloth into strips, and bound her wound around her shoulders and chest; the olba soaked up the blood and kept her arms immobile.

"I'll live, brother—but not if the Aidenists break through. You have your duty. Go, and defend Ishalem."

Unwar knew well enough not to argue with her. Understanding his obligations, he raced back to the wall.

In the lull after the Uraban defenders died or fled from the storm of arrows, Anjine's soldiers seized the opportunity. Jenirod grabbed the lead. "Hurry, men—get those wagons to the wall and the gate!" The seven carts creaked forward on the weed-overgrown road, and the dray horses snorted.

Behind the high wall, moans rose from the wounded and dying. A few surviving soldiers poked their heads out from the parapets to see what the Aidenists were doing. Spotting the barrel-loaded wagons, a young Uraban soldier waved his hands and shouted, "Soldan-Shah! Soldan-Shah!" Ten arrows peppered his body and drove him backward before he could give any details.

Anjine's sword felt light in her hand. The carts seemed to go so slowly! The wooden wheels bumped over rocks, and the horses strained until the large wagons were up against the stone wall and towering gate. "In the name of Aiden," she whispered, "this barricade must fall."

On the wall, a group of Urecari soldiers struggled to shoot arrows and throw rocks down at the vulnerable drovers, but the Urabans were wounded, and their aim was poor. Several arrows stuck into the piled barrels, and one grazed Jenirod's mount, leaving a red wound on its flank. He wrestled with the reins to control the horse. "Hurry! Unhitch the horses and light the fuses!"

While Aidenist soldiers held shields over their heads as best they could, the wagonmasters worked at the quick-release Eriettan harnesses. The wagonmasters jumped onto the freed horses and rode away, while the huddled soldiers struck sparks to the fuses with flint and steel.

"Light only one on each wagon—the rest will take care of themselves!" Jenirod shouted.

Finally the fuses caught, and the soldiers ran away as if pursued by monsters, holding their shields behind them to protect against Uraban arrows. Jenirod turned his mare about, scooped up a young soldier who had fallen behind his comrades, and pulled him across his saddle. Uraban sentries clamored for help, and Jenirod smiled as he galloped back toward Anjine and the front line of waiting troops.

He was still riding hard when the first barrel detonated with a roar like all of Ondun's anger unleashed at once; his mare stumbled from the shock wave, and the soldier he held nearly slipped off the saddle. The explosion spread across the seven firepowder wagons, hammering through the stone blocks and the wooden gate. Boulders, shattered rock, and splintered wood flew in all directions, carried high by the fire and smoke.

From her front line, Queen Anjine watched with awe. The explosions were far more spectacular than she had dared hope. Around her, cavalrymen and Tierran footsoldiers fell silent, drawing a simultaneous breath. Moments later, they exhaled in a wild and frantic cheer.

The explosions had smashed a large hole in the barricade, and the titanic wooden doors groaned with slow thunder as they collapsed inward to crush many of the enemy soldiers waiting there.

"To Ishalem!" Anjine shouted, and a resounding cry from the troops echoed her words. The queen watched from her position as thousands of faithful Aidenists poured through the wall and into the holy city.

102 *The* Dyscovera

When the boats reached the *Dyscovera* and *Al-Orizin*, the two captains didn't know how their crews would accept such changes in the very foundations of their history, their beliefs. The two holy brothers had sailed home, *side by side.* Aiden and Urec hadn't hated each other. There had been no betrayal, no abandonment, and neither brother had remained behind in Tierra or Uraba.

Criston had brought the ancient Captains' Log back from the frozen grotto. The Saedrans would study the pages, learn the stories that had never been told. Whenever Sikara Fyiri was found, she would also want to see it (and no doubt argue endlessly with Prester Hannes over its content).

As word spread about the discoveries inside the grotto, the crewmembers were as confused as they were jubilant. Standing together, both captains called for calm and caution, while even the most devout followers of Aiden and Urec wrestled with the contradictions.

"We have to decide what Ondun would want us to do. We need to learn more," Criston said. "Tomorrow, we take parties ashore to explore the new continent. At last, we will see Terravitae."

Prester Hannes could not comprehend why the two captains were so cordial with each other. After the massacre of his hometown, Captain Vora knew full well the violence and treachery that the Urecari held in their hearts.

Meanwhile, no one had found Sikara Fyiri, and the *Al-Orizin* sailors were growing concerned. Hannes hid his satisfaction, but he was particularly annoyed when he heard a silly rumor suggesting that Ondun Himself had translated her off to Paradise, leaving the rest of them behind as unworthy. The followers of Urec were such gullible fools! Even if the vile priestess had lived long enough to see the grotto, she would have found some way to delude herself into thinking that the two frozen brothers proved the *Urecari* version of the story. Lies, of course.

In his own cabin—which he had scrubbed clean of Fyiri's blood—Hannes stared at the Book of Aiden. How had he misinterpreted the lines of scripture? What other explanation could there be? The things he had seen on the voyage—the Leviathan skeleton, the stone obelisk, a young woman who claimed to be the daughter of Ondun—challenged *everything* he knew to be true. The secret grotto with the preserved bodies of two demigods, side by side, was such a fundamental paradox that it could not be tolerated. Weak-willed members of the church would be confused; they might come to the wrong conclusion, or begin to doubt.

Hannes knew exactly what he had to do.

The following day, boats full of sailors—half of them Urecari—would go ashore and explore the land; other parties might return to the sacred grotto and continue to poke around, where they would probably find more lies. Hannes had to act before then.

After midnight, he came out on deck, passed a sailor on night watch. "I have come out to gaze upon Terravitae and pray."

"Pray for us all, Prester. Our long voyage is finally at an end." Hannes performed a perfunctory blessing, and the man went about his rounds.

He could have tried to enlist the watchman's aid, but he had decided to take Javian instead. Safer that way. The intelligent, respectful young man had always been interested in Aidenism, and Hannes was confident that Javian would understand what needed to be done.

When Hannes roused him and led him to a quiet place at the stern, he spoke in a whisper. "I need you to go with me back to the ice cave. I have a task to do—a task for Aiden and Ondun—which cannot be done with a crowd of people looking on." He glanced meaningfully toward the battered *Al-Orizin*. "And I want to be away from the eyes of those followers of Urec."

The prester had brought two of his sturdy preaching staffs, each one tipped with a bronze fishhook. Javian's eyes were wide and dark in the starlight. "Are we going to set up a shrine beside the preserved bodies?"

The prester smiled. That seemed a good enough explanation.

"Yes, and we must do it before Sikara Fyiri tries to defile it with her Golden Fern."

Javian looked troubled. "We should ask Captain Vora first."

Hannes fought to contain his anger, making sure the young man couldn't see it. "*I* am the captain of the church, and this is unquestionably a religious matter." Later, he would find some way to dispose of the Captains' Log as well.

Javian pondered this for a moment, then agreed. After the two managed to lower the boat quietly into the water, the young man began to row, while Prester Hannes sat motionless. He gripped the two preaching staffs—one for him and one for the young man—as if they were spears to fight against heretics. The prester stared ahead, listening to the night, wrapped up in his own thoughts.

The rushing waves were loud, scouring the rocks. He closed his eyes as they approached the cliffs, but he could not forget the lie of what he had seen.

He could only imagine what Prester-Marshall Baine would have said about this conundrum. The fiery church leader had picked him to live among the Urecari and study their falsehoods, to expose the enemy's weaknesses. Hannes's whole life had shaped him into a soldier for God, with the mission to improve the world in the name of Ondun. And now, on the far side of the world, he found himself alone again with his faith, called upon to save the Aidenist church and its sacred beliefs.

"Tonight, Javian, we will do a deed to help all future generations, whether or not they applaud us for it, or even know what we have done."

Hannes never questioned whether the young man could maneuver them safely through the surf or thread his way to the icy grotto. He removed the two pitch-wrapped torches he had brought along and lit them to guide their way. Javian pulled the oars, taking them into the gullet-like passage, where ice crystals reflected orange gleams of torchlight in all directions.

Reaching the large grotto, the young man pulled the boat up to where the stone platform met the still water. Icicle stalactites and stalagmites formed the pillars of a mythical temple.

Stepping out of the boat and onto the stone floor of the vault, Hannes wedged the torches into cracks in the stone and handed Javian one of the heavy preaching staffs. "You have been educated in the ways of Aiden, young man. You know the truth, for I have told it to you."

Javian looked uncertainly at the staff in his hands. "I've heard your sermons, Prester."

"Then you know that the fundamental power of Aidenism is *faith*. No believer who hopes for salvation can question his beliefs, because that would be questioning Ondun Himself."

Hannes was convinced that the revelations in this tomb would destroy the church. The tableau raised too many unanswerable blasphemous questions, and he could never allow that, no matter the cost. Because the prester's faith was so strong, he was even willing to strand the two exploration ships, and himself, on this unknown shore in order to preserve the secret. It was the only safe course.

He did his best to explain the obvious to Javian, but the young man turned white, appalled. "So you're saying our entire voyage, everything we found, every struggle we survived, was just a test for us to discover a . . . a *trick*? That none of this is real? I can't believe that, Prester!"

"Nevertheless, you must believe it," Hannes said. "And this is what we have to do." He stepped toward the two frozen men seated in their petrified chairs as if positioned to be the judges of mankind. Hannes raised the Fishhook staff back over his shoulder and brought it down hard against the side of Urec's chair, smashing away the ice. He pounded again, the blow echoing through the grotto as Javian cried out in dismay. A third swing and he smashed one of the navigational instruments.

Panting, he said, "Help me destroy the evidence and cast it into the sea."

103 *The* Dyscovera *and the* Al-Orizin

In the dark hours before dawn, Kjelnar came to Criston's cabin, dripping wet. He didn't look cold, but his expression was grim. "We've found something, Captain . . . something you must see."

Criston felt a dread in his chest. He stepped out into the starlit air, fully awake, to see other mer-Saedrans climbing up the side of the ship and gathering on deck. The undersea people carried something with them.

King Sonhir crossed his arms over his bare chest as two mer-Saedrans spread a body on the deck—a woman's body, still wrapped in bright red robes. "We found the missing priestess, Captain," Kjelnar said. "The body was weighted down."

"Did she . . . kill herself?" Criston knew that Prester Hannes's faith had been disturbed by recent events; had the Urecari priestess been unable to cope with the revelations?

Sonhir let out a humorless snort. "Not unless she found some way to plunge a dagger into her own heart, then tie the weight-stone around her ankles and jump overboard."

The mer-Saedrans pulled aside the red robes to expose the knife wound over her heart. Fyiri's skin was gray and puckered, her face bloated and ugly. Parts of her fingers, lips, and nose were already missing from where undersea creatures had fed.

The slowly awakening truth was far uglier than the corpse. "Go to the *Al-Orizin* and send for Captain Saan immediately." He clenched his fists, then released them. "And somebody bring Prester Hannes out here, now. I have questions for him."

*

Saan wore a tense, contradictory expression; Criston knew that his son had clashed with the Urecari priestess, just as he himself had often disagreed with Prester Hannes. "My crew is not going to like this," Saan muttered.

Mia came running back to them, her expression curdled. "The prester isn't in his cabin, Captain—and I can't find Javian, either. What if he's done something to *Javian*?" She looked down at the sikara's corpse. "It's obvious he killed that woman."

Ystya was distraught. "I did not think you came to Terravitae for murder."

Criston wanted to stop the situation from growing into a deadly clash. "If Hannes did this, I will not defend his actions. We have to find him."

Another crewman ran up. "Captain, one of the ship's boats is gone."

Criston swore out loud, immediately knowing the answer. "Hannes must have gone back to the grotto himself, and he took Javian with him."

Saan gave a grim nod. "We'd better put a stop to whatever your prester is doing."

When King Sonhir looked from the sikara's body to Criston, he spoke no accusations, though his thoughts were clearly judgmental. Kjelnar said, "The mer-Saedrans will pull you along—that'll be fastest. Take one boat from each ship. No telling how long the prester has been about his mischief."

Criston indicated Fyiri's body. "Get some canvas to wrap her up and take her below until we get this solved."

The captains climbed into the pair of boats at water level, followed by Ystya and the two Saedrans, as well as Grigovar and Yal Dolicar. Mia insisted on going along, concerned for Javian, and Criston didn't have the time or inclination to argue with her. "Javian isn't part of it," she said.

"That remains to be seen." King Sonhir dove into the water in front of the two boats. When everyone was situated, a group of mer-Saedrans grasped the tow lines and took off, pulling the boats at a fast pace toward the sacred grotto on Terravitae.

104 *Ishalem Wall*

The Teacher struggled to remain conscious after her brother left. Though her arrow wound ached, Alisi could not let herself be found like this, wounded and weak. With Unwar gone, she pulled the bloodstained robe around her and fought to gather her strength. The ominous figure of the Teacher needed to be visible to trigger any *ra'virs* who might still be among the Aidenist invaders. This was their last chance.

She fixed the silver mask in place and pulled the hood over her close-cropped dark hair. Walking slowly to hide her faltering steps, the Teacher made her way through the chaos of running soldiers, past numerous dead and dying men who lay akimbo with long arrows sprouting from their bodies. She spotted her brother standing just above the wooden gate, calling for his soldiers to stand firm regardless of the Aidenist archers.

And then the wall exploded.

The blast knocked her backward and she fell sprawling. It was agony to regain her feet, but she paid no attention to the pain. Through the rock dust and smoke, she watched the stone barrier collapse, burying—burying!—her brother. The Teacher scrambled forward, screaming his name through the silver mask.

God's Barricade came tumbling down. Broken stone blocks, powder, and smoke accompanied the roar, and the Aidenist army flooded through the breach. They trampled the shattered gate, their cavalry horses screaming and rearing as riders urged them into Ishalem.

But Alisi stumbled into the rubble with nothing but the dagger at her side. She was deaf to the premature Tierran victory cries and the defiant shouts as the Urecari fighters rallied. Though she hated the Aidenists, her only concern was for her brother. She knew where he had been standing, and Alisi pulled at broken rocks with her gloved hands. She had begun bleeding again; her bandage was soaked, but she didn't care. Many Uraban soldiers had been buried under the blocks; she could hear them moaning, dying.

Finally, she spied a swatch of cream cloth, the shirt her brother had been wearing. She called his name and saw his finger twitch, then bent closer to hear a weak groan in response. She pulled some stones away, but could not move the immense blocks that covered him. His legs were crushed; large boulders pressed down on his chest. Unwar was still alive, though blood seeped from his mouth, nose, and ears. She could not free him from the rubble.

The Teacher had long ago given up hopeful dreams, and she could not fool herself that Unwar would be all right, that there was any chance he might survive these terrible injuries. She could not lie to her brother, either; he had never lied to her.

Unwar's eyes flickered open, and he looked up, saw the silver mask. A faint smile curled his lips. "Alisi . . . if I'm going to say goodbye . . . let me see you. Take off the mask."

Alisi froze, leaning over him. "I don't dare." There were too many others around, all fighting or scrambling to help the wounded.

"*Dare*," Unwar said. And she had no choice. She removed the silver mask, and his expression changed. "Ah . . . I had almost forgotten what you look like." He sighed. "It's done, now. God's Barricade has fallen."

"No! We will still win." But the cheers of the Aidenists and the sounds of the dying all around them belied her confidence.

"Our fight is over . . . for now." Each word was an obvious struggle for him. "But I need *you* to survive."

"I will fight and die to defend us."

"No!" Something stirred in the rocks, and he freed his right arm. His fingers twitched. She took them in her hand, then yanked off her gloves so she could touch his skin once more.

"They will find the Teacher, punish the Teacher," Unwar said. "So you can no longer *be* the Teacher."

"It's who I am!"

"It's who you *were*. Do this for me. Find your own life . . . happiness, or at least peace. I am so proud of you, but the Teacher is dead. Become Alisi again, please." His bloody lips smiled. "It's the best way for you to win against them."

Her thoughts spun, and she tried to grasp what he meant, not sure it was even possible. How could she stop being the Teacher? She had burned the identity of Alisi on a funeral pyre long ago. That tormented girl was dead.

"Promise me." He gripped her hand with surprising strength.

"I promise." Her voice was steadier than she thought it would be, and Unwar believed her. She didn't say the words merely to comfort him, though, and now she was bound by her word. Already her mind was working out how she might hide her identity. No one could know who the Teacher really was. No one could ask the questions.

In giving him her promise, it was as if Alisi had dismissed him. Unwar let out a long bubbling sigh, and his fingers went slack, releasing hers. He died in the rubble of his great ruined wall.

Alisi knelt like a statue, but she allowed herself only a precious minute to grieve. With the barbaric Aidenists swarming into the holy city, she closed her brother's eyes. She had made her promise, and now she wrestled with how to keep it.

Though it was difficult to move, and her wound continued to bleed, Alisi shrugged back the hood and struggled out of her signature dark robe. She stood with her chest bandaged, wearing only a simple chalwar. Holding the Teacher's mask, gloves, and robe, she knew the best way to remove any lingering questions.

Alisi thought back to how she had recreated herself after slitting the throat of Captain Quanas aboard the *Sacred Scroll*, killing several Aidenist crewmembers, and jumping overboard. After swimming ashore, she had pretended to be a Tierran woman and lived among them for years, learning their ways. Now she would have to learn how to be—or pretend to be—a normal Uraban woman once again. She hoped she had sufficient skill.

Alisi discovered the dead body of a middle-aged soldier in the rubble of the wall. That would do.

While people were fleeing and the Aidenist army flooded into the streets, Alisi moved with painstaking thoroughness. She pulled the loose robes of the Teacher onto the dead soldier's body, adjusted the hood around his head, pulled the gloves onto his limp hands. As a last gesture, she firmly placed the mask over his face.

She had no idea who this soldier was. He had died in the service of Urec, and now he could serve in one final way.

She took a cloak from the body of another soldier and wrapped herself in it. Ducking down, calling no attention to herself amid the fury of fighting, Alisi—*just Alisi*—staggered off again. The makeshift bandage on her chest was soaked with blood, but her loose clothing covered it. She slipped away, hiding within the battle itself.

105 *Ishalem Canal*

Drenched and exhausted, Iaros slogged along the canal bank. The wet armor was heavy, but adrenaline kept him moving.

From behind, he heard loud booms as the last casks of fire-powder exploded. Each one felt like a personal blow to him. The masts and spars of the remaining ironclads were crooked like the clutching fingers of a man thrown alive onto a funeral pyre. The *Wilka* was nearly sunk, heeled over, engulfed in flames.

Iaros took one last glance back at the canal that was now clogged with burning wrecks. Oily tumbles of black smoke curled into the sky. He saw no sign of Destrar Broeck. The hollowness in the pit of his stomach wasn't what Iaros expected victory would feel like, but *he* was the Iborian destrar now, and he would not tarnish his uncle's memory. He pushed aside his sadness.

Most of the Tierran fighters had escaped from the ironclads and made their way to shore. They were drenched, singed, and stunned, many of them deafened by the firepowder explosions. Now they held their swords aloft, shook water from sodden leather armor, and looked at one another.

Iaros yelled out in a ragged and raw voice, "This is *Ishalem*, men! The holy city will be ours, but only if you fight—fight for Aiden!" He jabbed the air with his sword, but the responding cheer had little enthusiasm. "What was that? Aiden is frowning at you! Can't you summon more energy to defeat the Curlies who did this to us?"

The second cheer was louder. Iaros stroked his dripping mustaches and nodded. That would do.

Shouts drew him back to the reality at hand. Now that the ironclads were destroyed, Urecari soldiers abandoned their catapults and climbed down from the watchtowers to defend the canal bank. Their scimitars gleamed like razor-edged silver smiles as they ran toward Iaros and his waterlogged men. "Stand ready to defend yourselves, men. Look at them—they're the ones who destroyed our ships! By the Fishhook, they are the ones who *killed Destrar Broeck*!"

With a wild yell, the Tierrans rushed forward to meet the Curly soldiers, stunning them with their ferocity. As Iaros threw himself into the fray, he felt detached and a bit surprised. Fighting had always been a theoretical thing to him. He had practiced and tried to fashion himself as an Iborian warrior, but now he had to put his learning to good use, and found, to his relief, that he was quite proficient at it.

Iaros cut down the first two enemy soldiers before he realized exactly what he was doing. The pure exhilaration of swordfighting—the slashes, the parries, the thrusts, and the sensation of steel sinking into flesh swept through him like a fever. The cries of the dying inspired rather than revolted him. When another Curly fell to his sword, Iaros noticed that he himself was bleeding from a gash high on his left arm. He hadn't even felt the wound, and he decided he had no time to do so now.

From the streets where he and his men fought, Iaros could see a high point in the center of the city, the largest strategic summit in Ishalem—Arkship Hill, where the wreck of Aiden's vessel had rested for so many centuries. *That,* he decided, was where they must go.

Like floodwaters bursting a dam, the Tierran fighters cut through the Urecari soldiers and pressed forward. Swinging their bloodstained swords, they rushed into the heart of the holy city.

106 *The Ice Grotto of Terravitae*

The prester's fury seemed heated enough to melt the frigid air of the grotto. Hannes swung his Fishhook staff to smash the sacred relics around the two preserved ancients. He hammered on the locked wooden chest, chipping pale gouges from the lid, denting the complicated padlock, though he did not succeed in smashing through.

The mummified corpses did not stir, but fragments of ice tinkled away like broken glass.

With a shocked cry, Javian lurched forward. "Stop!"

Hannes flashed a frenzied glance toward him. "Don't be tricked! This can't be real, and we dare not let anyone else see it, for the good of the church!"

But Javian grabbed his sleeve and held his arm to prevent him from swinging the preaching staff. Hannes glared at the young man in confusion. "You know the truth! You *know* that faithful Aidenists can't be allowed to see this. It's wrong—it's blasphemy!"

"It's the evidence of your own eyes!"

The prester said, "My faith gives me eyes."

He pulled himself free and threw his weight against Aiden's chair, pushing. The icy throne creaked, overbalanced, and crashed into Urec's chair. Both frozen bodies tumbled onto the ground. Standing before the figure of Urec, who looked helpless lying there, Hannes raised his preaching staff high.

Javian sprang between him and the frozen figure. "I said *stop*!" His voice had changed to a growl. "I know more about faith than you ever will."

Hannes was startled and confused by this persistent defiance, but Javian continued. "I've watched you and listened to you, Prester, just as I watched Sikara Fyiri. You accused each other of lying, but you were both saying the same thing."

"I would never speak the same lies as a follower of Urec."

Javian gave a derisive laugh. "Considering what I was taught, it's a good thing you weren't the only Aidenist I met. Captain Vora and the *Dyscovera* crew welcomed me as one of them. And Mia . . ." The young man shook his head. "It's not the followers of Urec, or Aiden, who should be hated—it's *bad people* like you and Fyiri, who inflame the passions of those who would otherwise live together in peace."

"How dare you say such things?" Hannes cried. "I showed you the truth. Where would you learn that hateful nonsense?"

"In the *ra'vir* camp." By now, Javian realized that what he had been taught—what had been *burned* into him—was all false. The Teacher had lied to him.

His comment rendered Hannes atypically speechless. Javian had held this confession back for half of his life, muzzled by his years of training and dammed up by his own fear and conviction. After keeping a secret for so long, though, the disguise had become as real as the truth, making Javian wonder which part was the lie.

He forced the words out of his mouth. "When I was a child, raiders kidnapped me from the village of Reefspur and took me to Uraba, where I was raised and trained to fight against wicked Aidenists." It was like a memorized speech. He had heard the vitriolic words so many times as they flowed from behind the Teacher's polished silver mask.

Javian had lived his mission without wavering. Convinced of his own righteousness, he had held to the course set for all *ra'virs*. He'd been warned (and often beaten to enforce the lesson) that Aidenists lied, that they were evil, that their beliefs were offensive to God . . . that they must all be exterminated.

After returning to Tierra, Javian established an identity in Calay, glad to have found such an easy way to get close to Captain Vora during the construction of the *Dyscovera*. He felt smug and strong that he had not let himself be deluded by the evidence he saw, the kind people he met, the strong families, the love, the charity, the teamwork they demonstrated. Those were things that the Teacher counted among the blessings of *Urec*'s followers.

Tierrans and Urabans had much in common. They were all people, with generous hearts or scheming souls. Javian saw no reason why Ondun would choose to love one race over the other just because of the symbols on their flags or which son of Ondun they revered.

Hannes looked at him with horror and revulsion, and Javian pressed his advantage. "Yes, I am a *ra'vir*, sent here to sabotage the voyage and make sure the *Dyscovera* did not reach Terravitae."

Now, though, the idea of who and what he was nauseated him. But in front of this obsessive prester, and in the presence of the final truth of Aiden and Urec, he continued his confession. "*I* sabotaged the Captain's Compass so we couldn't find our way back home. *I* killed the Saedran's pigeons, so that Tierra wouldn't receive any more messages from us. I also listened to your words of mutiny, Prester. I watched how you spurned the aid of the mer-Saedrans, because your hatred of them was greater than your desire to find Terravitae and Holy Joron."

"That's a lie!" Hannes spat. But it was true, and they both knew it.

"Beyond that, you murdered as many Urabans as you could. You killed Ondun's children and took pride in it. When Mailes told us, you did not deny it."

"Why should I deny doing a good thing? Improving the world, by the grace of Ondun."

"The Teacher used the same rationale." Javian's grip was white on the preaching staff. "Yet even though I did all those things, I was wrong. Have *you* ever said that, Prester Hannes? 'I was wrong'? It wasn't the ship that needed to be destroyed, it wasn't the *Dyscovera*'s mission that needed to be stopped. It's fanatics like you and Sikara Fyiri. *You* are the blight and the danger. *You* are the ones from whom Ondun turns His face and His light."

Infuriated beyond reason, Hannes gripped his Fishhook staff. "You are an abomination, *ra'vir*! I curse you with all the power that Ondun has granted me!" The prester pointed an accusing finger and continued with increasing vitriol, hurling damnation. "I call upon Aiden to destroy you! In the name—"

Javian swung his Fishhook cudgel and struck the center of the prester's forehead, caving in his skull and leaving a crater of bone fragments and brain. Hannes fell to the floor of the ice cave, dead before he could even finish his prayer.

107 *Ishalem*

After the wall fell, the Tierran army plunged into Ishalem like a hunting knife gutting a fresh kill. Battle horns sounded.

"Victory is ours!" Anjine shouted above the tumult. "*Ishalem* is ours!"

The battle would continue for days, but she had no doubt as to the outcome.

The energized soldiers roared in response. Riding high on their horses, Jenirod and Subcomdar Hist led the initial cavalry surge, and the horses barely slowed as they picked their way through the rubble. The footsoldiers ran to keep up with the mounted men. Since Alamont's long-range archers had already wiped out the Urabans clustered behind the gate, and the firepowder explosions at the wall had knocked the enemy reeling, they met with little resistance.

Anjine had wanted to lead the charge into Ishalem, but Subcomdar Hist and all of her advisers vehemently argued against it. Hist was firm, almost to the point of insubordination. "It is not *necessary*, Majesty. You must stay here. We will batter down their defenses and clear the way for your triumphant entry—that's what we are for."

Jenirod had always been a man full of bravado, but now he was completely serious. "You lead and inspire us by your presence, not by your sword arm, my Queen. We'll clear out the last of the enemy and secure the city. Ishalem belongs to us now. There's no need to hurry."

Anjine knew the two men were right. It would be arrogant for her to believe that she could outfight a seasoned Uraban warrior. That wasn't her role to play. And she dared not put her unborn baby at risk.

"We'll be quick about it, Majesty," Hist promised, then rode forward. Destrar Shenro had already led the first group into the city.

She sat her horse with her visor raised, a hard smile flickering on her lips. From behind the main battle lines, Anjine received reports throughout the day as the furious fighting continued. She looked longingly at the holy city.

Beyond the wall, Tierran soldiers continued to fall upon the enemy like a wolfpack on a flock of sheep. They would pave the road for her with spilled Urecari blood. She watched dust and smoke rise into the air, counting the hours until she could ride through Ishalem victorious. . . .

Hours later, as fresh groups of footsoldiers jogged past, and the rear ranks called out impatient encouragement, anxious to get to the plundering, a lone, slow horseman rode toward her from the near-deserted army camp—a familiar figure. Though he had donned his uniform again, Mateo looked pallid. He sat his mount unsteadily, holding the pommel to keep himself upright.

She reined her horse about to intercept him. "You should be resting! I told you to stay behind in the Saedran tent."

"Yes, my Queen, and I disobeyed you." His grin was so familiar. "I wanted to make sure someone was here to defend you. Just in case."

"My entire army can defend me. I don't need you here."

"You need me, Anjine."

She sighed. "Yes, I need you. But I need you *alive.*"

"I could say the same. Let's make sure both of us stay that way."

Anjine couldn't imagine how he had managed to bind his wounds and gain enough strength to dress, much less saddle and mount a horse. He must have had assistance. The Saedran doctors would have argued, but Mateo could be very insistent. Besides, most of the battlefield physicians were with the army, following the charge so they could tend the wounded; Mateo would have been left virtually alone, and Anjine knew he would never just sit quietly.

Despite how weak and tired he appeared, Anjine was glad to have him there. His presence inspired her as much as seeing the wall fall down. "This is a very foolish thing you're doing, Mateo."

He gave her the mischievous smile she knew so well. "Yes, it is, but how could I miss this final battle, this glorious victory? I need to be at your side during the greatest triumph of your life." He lowered his voice, though few soldiers remained close enough to hear him. "And I would rather die at your side than live without you."

"I should never have told you I loved you," Anjine said in a tone that was partly cross, partly teasing. "Now you're going to distract me at a critical moment."

"I shall do my best not to be a hindrance, Majesty." He raised his head, listening to the sounds of continued mayhem in the streets. His expression was pensive.

She cocked her eyebrows. "You don't look very joyous and triumphant, Mateo."

"Oh, I want to see the enemy defeated for the terrible things they've done, but we are partly responsible for this as well. I cut off a thousand heads for you, because you commanded it." His voice wavered. "When will it stop?"

"Tomorrow. This is the day we win the war." She realized she sounded glib. "Let's go see what the army has accomplished so far. Ride forward with me?" She nudged her horse, and together they made their way along the trampled road toward the holy city.

Anjine remembered when they had sailed to the holy city aboard the royal cog with King Korastine, when they were just innocent children. "You were with me the last time I entered this city, Mateo. It is only right that you should be here now."

A wistful expression crossed his face. "Let us hope it turns out differently this time."

Anjine heard the shouts of soldiers, the continuing clash of weapons up ahead. "It will."

108 *Ishalem, Main Urecari Church*

Panic spread through the city as Tierran invaders swarmed into the streets. Ishalem was an anthill of confusion. Some people fled, while others rallied and fought back. Enemy soldiers came not just from the blasted wall, but also from the ironclad ships in the canal.

Ur-Sikara Kuari ordered the sturdy wooden doors of the main Urecari church thrown open so that refugees could take sanctuary. Soldan Vishkar had built the great structure as a place of worship with fortress-thick walls, and the people believed Urec would protect them. In the meantime, Asaddan took a ceremonial pike used to hold the Unfurling Fern banner, yanked off the fabric, and positioned himself at the church's main doors as if he alone could guard against the Tierran army.

Anxious people crowded in to fill the huge worship chamber, babbling and wailing. Their voices spontaneously broke into familiar hymns, and the ur-sikara led prayer chants every hour. Kuari presented a particularly brave and strong face for them, letting her followers draw hope, although she was not convinced that even the massive building would save them.

Withdrawing to her anteroom where Istar and Ciarlo sat listening to the tumult outside, the ur-sikara said in a low voice, "When the Tierrans take over the city, they will defile this place first. Remember, the church stands on the former site of the main Aidenist kirk. This ground was sacred to them."

Though he could hear the mayhem in the streets, Ciarlo insisted that the ur-sikara's worries were unfounded. "Followers of the Fishhook know the word of Aiden. No true believer would cause the kind of carnage that you're afraid of. We don't harm innocents."

Ur-Sikara Kuari let out a snort of derision. "How do you expect me to take you seriously, when you speak such foolishness? After all the monstrous things your people have done?"

Ciarlo let out a frustrated sigh. "Adrea, tell her it will be all right. They are *Aidenists.*"

Istar placed a hand on each of her brother's shoulders, as if lecturing a child. "That may be what the Book of Aiden *says*, Ciarlo, but that isn't the way all Aidenists behave. The same is true for the Urecari. Both Aiden and Urec must have turned from us in disgust by now."

Kuari paced the anteroom. "I don't expect Aiden or Urec to magically solve our problems. We created this mess ourselves. It is our responsibility."

Istar looked at her brother and the ur-sikara, knowing that Omra was out there somewhere, fighting against her own former people. She realized that she might have to do something herself.

Scattered contingents of the Tierran army spread into neighborhoods, setting fires and attacking anyone who stood against them. When the first line of troops rushed the main church, Ur-Sikara Kuari shouted for the panicked stragglers to hurry inside. Asaddan barricaded the sturdy doors as the Aidenist invaders ran up, swords drawn; he slammed the crossbar home moments before sword hilts and gauntleted fists pounded on the door.

"See that all the other doors are secured," Kuari called out.

The big Nunghal prowled the perimeter of the chamber, carrying the long pike. A broken roof tile hurtled through one of the windows from the outside, and when a zealous Aidenist soldier tried to crawl through the broken window, Asaddan jabbed at him with the blunt end of the staff, smashing the man in the teeth. The soldier screamed and dropped away.

Ciarlo still wore nondescript robes and a hood to hide his pale hair and blue eyes, but many Urecari refugees looked askance at him. Others glanced suspiciously at Istar and her Tierran features.

She stared back at them, confronting their silent accusations. There wasn't much she could say.

Soon the hammering on the main wooden doors became a heavy pounding that made the hinges rattle.

"They're using a battering ram," Istar said.

Ten blows, and then twenty. Finally, a pale crack splintered down one of the thick planks like a streak of lightning.

"They'll be inside before long." Asaddan stood with his pike ready. "I suggest the rest of you find someplace to hide, or a way to defend yourselves."

Another heavy blow from the battering ram, loud shouts from the soldiers outside, and the crack in the door widened. Ur-Sikara Kuari stepped forward, looking fearsome. "I will stand and defend my church." The refugees scrambled to the back of the main worship chamber, hoping to remain unseen, while some crowded around the ur-sikara, ready to give their lives.

Ciarlo placed himself between Kuari and the door. "Let me talk to them—I can make them leave us alone, if they are true Aidenists."

"Ciarlo, they'll kill you," Istar said.

He gave his sister a beatific smile. "My faith is an anchor." The battering ram smashed again, and the crossbar fell out of its cradle. The planks split apart, and Aidenist soldiers began to hack at the debris with their swords. Someone thrust a staff and colorful flag through the gap; Istar recognized the banner of Alamont Reach.

Looking annoyed rather than frightened, Asaddan seized the staff and yanked it out of the man's hands, tossing it with a clatter into the worship chamber. The soldiers howled, redoubled their efforts against the door, and pushed their way through the broken planks.

The leader of the small fighting group was thin and haughty, his eyes shining, his hair wild. He spoke in Tierran, although he couldn't have expected the refugees to understand him. "I am

Destrar Shenro of Alamont Reach. I claim this church in the name of Aiden."

Ciarlo surprised them by planting himself in front of the soldiers, holding out both of his hands. "By the Fishhook, I command you not to harm these people! I speak on their behalf, in the name of Aiden." He fumbled for the pendant at his throat and yanked back his hood to reveal his blond hair.

Shenro didn't pause. He ran forward, swung his sword without even looking at his target. Ciarlo stumbled backward, too close to get out of the way. But the downsweep of Shenro's blade was blocked with a loud clang as Asaddan brought the pike into the sword's arc. The Alamont destrar staggered, his arms jarred by the impact of the counterblow.

Asaddan swung his pike to smash the side of the destrar's head, then skewered Shenro through the chest, driving him to the ground. He ripped the weapon back out and held it before him to face the oncoming charge.

The other Alamont soldiers pushed their way inside the church, but the crowded refugees battered them with poles and heavy candlesticks. The Nunghal was a tornado, sweeping his pike from side to side, stabbing them and pushing the bodies back through the door. It was over quickly, and four Tierran men lay dead. The other six—and only six, for it had been a small contingent—fled.

Ciarlo was on his knees, praying over the Alamont destrar. He touched the Fishhook pendant to the dying man's lips. The ur-sikara stood behind him. She did not look smug. "You aren't even a follower of Urec, and he tried to kill you."

"I'm not a follower of Urec either," Asaddan said, propping the bloody pike upright. "But I defended my friends." He was barely even winded.

Kuari pointed to the crowds in the church. "We need to barricade that door again and protect all the windows. They will be back."

109 *The Ice Grotto of Terravitae*

As the searchers entered the sea caves, the chill in Criston's heart felt colder than the ice encrusting the tunnels. Swimming in the frigid water, King Sonhir and Kjelnar drew the ships' boats along. Saan and the strange girl Ystya rode next to Criston in the lead boat.

Mia hunched forward, her hands grasping the gunwales. "Do you think Prester Hannes would harm Javian?"

Criston's answer was terse and grim. "I don't know what the prester is capable of doing."

Saan's Tierran words were halting. "We know he murdered a priestess of Urec."

From the other boat, Yal Dolicar made a rude noise. "Come now, Captain—Sikara Fyiri was an infuriating woman, and she would not have hesitated to kill the Aidenist prester, given half a chance."

The two Saedran chartsmen did not comment, but King Sonhir gave a snort as he splashed along. "Now you see why my people sank our continent and retreated beneath the shelter of the waves."

Ystya sat with her thin arms wrapped around her knees. "I don't understand any of this. Why would either of them think bloodshed is what my brothers, or Ondun, wanted?"

Dolicar shook his head with a sad smile. "Not to point out the obvious, Ystya, but you told us that Iyomelka drowned your father. And that Ondun exiled Mailes forever because he had an affair with your mother. It seems there isn't peace among the gods either."

Instead of reacting with anger, Ystya closed her eyes in shame.

When the two boats reached the frosty grotto, which was lit by flickering torchlight, they came upon Javian. He stood on the smooth rock floor not far from the two toppled thrones; he held a heavy Fishhook staff that was splashed with crimson, as was his shirt. Specks of red dotted his face.

Prester Hannes lay sprawled on the floor, obviously dead, his skull smashed open. Javian simply stared at what he had done.

"*Javian!*" Mia sprang from the boat as soon as the mer-Saedrans pulled it close, and she ran over to the young man, shaking him, but he could not tear his eyes from the corpse.

"He tried to destroy them," Javian whispered. "Both of them . . . everything."

Criston and Saan disembarked, gazing in horror at the smashed instruments and artifacts, the damaged chest, the two dethroned demigods. "Prester Hannes hated both of them," Criston said.

"I think he hated what they represented," Saan replied.

Ystya looked upon the scene and wept. "I never met Aiden or Urec, but they were my brothers. They spent most of their lives searching for me. Terravitae should have been our home. I hoped for a new beginning, and all we brought here was more hate."

Javian's shoulders slumped, and he enfolded Mia in an embrace. "You saved me . . . you truly saved me."

Mia stared into his eyes. "What do you mean? I wasn't even here."

"It doesn't matter. You still saved me."

Criston stepped up to him. "Tell me what happened."

With hitching words, Javian explained how Hannes had come here. The young man was trembling. "I thought he meant to pray, to study Aiden and Urec in private . . . but he came only to destroy. And he wanted me to help him. When I refused, he went wild and—" The young man stared at the prester's body on the ground, the face that had been scarred by the Ishalem fire, and the staring blue eyes that even in death seemed filled with conviction. "I killed him."

Criston wavered, appalled by the murder, but he did not deny what Hannes meant to do. He crouched beside the prester's body, pushed to his knees by a great weight of conscience. He remembered saving this man in a high meadow of the Corag mountains. The two men had a great deal in common, but Criston had never shared the prester's fervor or hatred. Hannes happily *bragged* about how he had poisoned entire households in Uraba, how he set ablaze Urecari churches full of innocent worshipers.

"I should have marooned him on an island after all," Criston said. "What more did he want? We reached the shores of Terravitae. We found answers. I had hoped that would put an end to his hate. But it wasn't enough for him."

The mer-king regarded the body and turned to Kjelnar. "Is this the way your world is, shipwright? If so, I would not want to go back to it."

"This is the way some people are," said Kjelnar. "And good people don't do enough to control men like this."

"I killed him," Javian said again. "I stopped him."

Saan was pale as he spoke to his father. "Back in Olabar, the sikaras were responsible for murders, too . . . and your prester murdered Fyiri. Do you think sikaras and presters will ever stop arguing, even when they have proof in front of them?"

Looking outraged, Ystya blurted, "They don't *want* proof!" She turned her back to the scene of destruction and bloodshed and threw a last troubled glance at the desecrated mummies of her brothers. "We must leave here. Now."

The mer-Saedrans guided all three boats out of the ice caves. Saan tried to comfort Ystya, but she would not be comforted. The daughter of Ondun, the Key to Creation, insisted that they touch nothing else in what should have been a sacred grotto. They even left the body of Prester Hannes behind.

Criston gazed with bittersweet wistfulness at the looming cliffs as they left pulled away. "Our ships have reached Terravitae. This should be a wondrous moment."

Saan's mind and heart were a tangle of questions and disappointments. Terravitae, the entombed brothers, the wrecked Arkship . . . the Leviathan, the Key to Creation, the island of Ondun's exile—so much about this voyage had changed him, changed the very foundations of the world.

He had been indoctrinated in the teachings of the sikaras. He was familiar with Urec's Log, and Omra (his adopted father, not his real one) had taught him to despise all Tierrans, for political reasons rather than religious differences.

But Saan was also aware of the ruthlessness of the priestesses, for they had made repeated attempts on his life since his childhood. He wondered whether Sikara Fyiri had truly believed in the *blessings* of Ondun and in her own salvation, or if she merely acted as a mouthpiece for the church.

For her own part, Saan's mother had been raised with the Book of Aiden and a prester's sermons at her local kirk. In Uraba, forced to keep her true beliefs hidden, Istar had dutifully attended Urecari services, but she held her spiritual thoughts close to her heart.

Now that he'd met Criston Vora, his real father, the knowledge affected him deeply. Before then, devoted to Omra, Saan had never cared to know much about the man, but he understood that his mother had loved her original husband very much. Saan found it disorienting to realize that if the raid on Windcatch hadn't occurred, or if Criston Vora had returned home a little earlier from his shipwreck, then Saan himself would have been raised in the Tierran village, given a different name. He would have been brought up to believe in the Fishhook, and his whole life would have followed another course.

Yet he was the same person. It bothered him to think that the beliefs that shaped a person's soul were more a result of geographical circumstance than proof or truth. Shouldn't devotion to the Book of Aiden, or Urec's Log, be based on the value of the teachings themselves, and not whether a baby happened to be born in Tierra or Uraba?

As the three boats returned to the open, gray sea, Saan spoke in a troubled voice. "Captain Vora, when we return to the *Dyscovera* and the *Al-Orizin*, there will be an uproar. Prester Hannes killed Sikara Fyiri—no one disputes that—and now your ship's boy has killed the prester. But the crews will still find reasons to be at each other's throats."

"Only if we let them," Criston said.

"We can already see what will happen." Ystya stared back at the rugged shore. Her head seemed too heavy to hold up. "Someone from the *Al-Orizin*'s crew, or the *Dyscovera*'s crew, will want to go back and steal a holy relic as proof for his own church. And if not that, then other ships will eventually come to Terravitae, crowded with devout followers of Aiden or Urec, and they will fight over this holy site—in my brothers' names."

"But this is one of the greatest discoveries in recorded history," Saan said. "We can't keep it a secret."

"You all know the truth because you saw it." Ystya's voice was bleak now. "You proved your determination by sailing around the world to come here. No one can fault you for that. But both the prester and the sikara demonstrated how eager your religions are to exploit and distort beliefs. Maybe the new Captains' Log we found here will make it possible for your churches to reconcile. But I'll believe that when I see it for myself."

Saan did not argue with her. How could he?

Tears were streaming down her face. "These are my brothers, the sons of Ondun, and I am still their sister. I am obligated to protect them." She squared her shoulders, and her ivory hair began to glow in a wind that she created. "I'm sorry, Saan, but I have to do this. If faith is enough, then that is all you should need for now."

Her eyelids dropped closed, and she spread her fingers, then curled them slowly into a fist. Her skin shimmered, as if a sunrise had occurred inside her flesh. The water around the cave opening roiled and foamed; the sheer cliff walls that were studded with moss, weeds, and vines began to writhe with a surge of new growth.

The mer-Saedrans released the rowboats and swam into the open sea. "What is happening?" Sonhir called.

"She is the Key to Creation," Saan said. He couldn't even say that he disagreed with Ystya's decision. "Creation and destruction are two sides of the same coin."

Long strands of kelp drifted in from the ocean; tangled seaweed rose up from the sea floor, forming a mat. The strands reached higher, whipping and questing. At the same time, vines and plants from the cliff edge reached downward—thick trunks, thorny stems, and fleshy leaves all combined, like fingers clasping, growing together, twisting. The verdant explosion rapidly formed an impenetrable barrier across the cave opening.

When she was done, Ystya's shoulders slumped. She let out a long sigh and opened her eyes again. "Now they are safe and protected, and so are we. They will wait for us until it's time."

"There's so much for us to see and learn," Sen Sherufa said. "We haven't even set foot yet on Terravitae."

Criston sat up straight in his boat. "Yes, let's go discover a new land."

Part V

110 *Ishalem*

In the convoluted streets of Ishalem, the new Uraban buildings all looked the same, with similar architecture, whitewashed walls, and tiled roofs. Colorful silk awnings were stretched out above placards written in incomprehensible foreign characters.

Iaros hadn't the slightest idea how to get to Arkship Hill, but he led his men vaguely upward on the principle that so long as they kept moving, they were making progress. Sooner or later, if Queen Anjine had managed to break through the wall, he was sure his fighters would meet up with the main Aidenist army.

Uraban shopkeepers and families fled screaming as the disheveled Tierrans pushed through the streets, shouting and waving their swords. They snarled at carpenters and coopers; they smashed a glassblower's shop and hurled the shards of colored bottles onto the cobblestoned streets.

When a portly man with a bushy beard tried to defend his wickerwork shop, Iaros commanded his fighters to leave the man alone. "No need to prove your manhood by slaying a craftsman. There'll be enough Curly soldiers to kill." Iaros barked for the disappointed soldiers to follow him as he ran ahead.

They paused long enough to ransack a food stall displaying bowls of dates, grapes, and pomegranates (though the latter proved much too messy and difficult to eat on the run). After drinking from a public water fountain, they charged onward.

They were closer now to the central hill that had once held the wreck of Aiden's Arkship. Once the Tierrans conquered that landmark, they would truly hold the heart of Ishalem. Iaros extended his arm. "To Arkship Hill!"

He led his group in the right general direction, chasing chickens and cats out of their way, only to be brought up short when the street hit a dead end. So they reversed direction, clattering swords and shields against the brick walls, and rushed back out, down another street, through a marketplace, and past several small Urecari churches, until finally they could see a clear path up the hill.

Running toward the path, they collided with a mass of Uraban guards, who did not expect the encounter either. With undiminished momentum and enthusiasm, the Tierran soldiers engaged the guards. Iaros immediately saw that they had overestimated themselves. Enemy fighters outnumbered them two to one, and they were fresh, while his own men were already worn out from battling their way through the streets for many hours.

But there was no stopping them now. Iaros raised his sword and yelled like a bull mammoth during mating season. The sound startled the Urabans so much that he was able to dispatch one and wound another before they rallied.

When the enemy guards regrouped, Iaros and his men found themselves surrounded and battling for their lives. The Tierrans fought with a reckless fury that startled the enemy; they killed two more Urabans, but after several Aidenist soldiers fell, their morale began to turn.

Iaros stabbed, thrust, and slashed repeatedly, though his limbs felt leaden. "Keep fighting!" It was all they could do, but he felt a growing dread that none of them would survive to reach Arkship Hill.

As he was being driven back by a particularly burly Uraban fighter, Iaros realized he would soon collapse. His responses were sluggish, and he barely avoided a fatal mistake. Panting heavily, he flicked perspiration from his red hair and raised his sword to ward off another blow. Suddenly his attacker reeled backward with a grunt of surprise.

With a feral roar, a big soot-streaked man appeared among them. "Need some help, nephew?" Destrar Broeck grinned savagely and rammed a Urecari fighter with a body blow that knocked the man off balance. When the opponent fell, Broeck thrust his sword into his chest and yanked it back out. "Next time, pick your fights more wisely."

"Uncle, you're alive!" Iaros cried.

"A few explosions and a sinking ship aren't enough to stop me." Though burned and blood-streaked, with a wild look in his eyes, Broeck laughed and fought with increasing frenzy. The destrar's berserker energy turned the tide, and the Uraban guards scattered into the marketplace. A few Tierran soldiers laughed and tried to give chase, but Broeck and Iaros called them back.

Iaros gave his uncle a quick embrace. "I wasn't ready to be destrar yet."

"Are you ready to conquer Ishalem?"

The younger man gave a vigorous nod. "We're heading up the hill!"

The two Iborians led the charge.

111 *Terravitae*

As the boats pulled away from the now-covered sea cave in the cliffs, Criston gazed toward the shore. The clouds had begun to clear, leaving a bright blue sky. "Both our crews endured months of difficult sailing to reach this place. We owe it to them to finish our quest."

Saan agreed. "I am ready to set foot on Terravitae."

"It seems impossible that we're really here," said Aldo with an undertone of awe in his voice.

"If the legends are true, Holy Joron is here as well," Sen Sherufa said. "He can enforce peace."

Guided by the mer-Saedrans, the boats moved along the coast in search of a spot where they could beach the three boats. After an hour, they came upon a sheltered cove and pulled up to the shore. By unspoken agreement, the two captains set foot simultaneously on the fabled continent.

As he planted his feet on the long-anticipated soil, Criston expected some magical response, a tingling through the soles of his boots, but this land felt like any other that was wild and unexplored by mere mortals.

Leaving the beach, the group filed up a narrow game path to a plateau above the ocean. When they reached the top of the headlands, Criston peered across an expanse of blue ocean down to where the two battered ships were anchored at a safe distance from the cliffs and rocks. Saan touched his arm, and instead of looking out to sea where they had been for so long, the men directed their gazes across the virgin plain with tufts of grasses, low cypress trees, and orange lilies in full bloom.

Caught up in the beauty of the land, the travelers explored—two captains, both chartsmen, Javian and Mia, Kjelnar and King Sonhir, Grigovar and Yal Dolicar . . . as well as Ystya, who traced her origin back to this land. They found bushes laden with sweet berries, bubbling streams of clear water. Rabbits and antelope bounded away, startled by the strangers.

Sen Sherufa said, "Every step we take is on untouched land that no one from Tierra or Uraba has ever seen."

Sen Aldo's dark eyes drank in the details. "This may be the final piece of the Mappa Mundi."

"My people might still be here," Ystya said, taking Saan's hand. "Even if they aren't, it's *Terravitae,* and that's enough for me."

Still shaken by the act of violence he had committed, Javian leaned on Mia and drew on her solid support. "It feels so strange not to have Prester Hannes here with us," he murmured.

Overhearing, Criston put a hand on Javian's shoulder. "He

made it to Terravitae. If Hannes couldn't accept what we found in the cave, he might have murdered all of us to keep the secret."

"The prester saw more of Terravitae than he deserved," Ystya said. "He *rejected* it."

Mia took Javian's hand. "We're *here*. We're together. Hold on to that."

Yal Dolicar looked around. "Somehow I was expecting Holy Joron to greet us as soon as we arrived."

Ystya's very presence seemed to have a magical effect on the already lush terrain. Wherever she passed, new blooms burst forth like applause. Streams seemed to swell, and waterfalls appeared, tumbling over bluffs that had been dry only moments before. The grasses grew thicker, as if Ystya's arrival had reawakened the entire continent.

They walked for miles along the coastal cliffs. Eventually, the hills began descending toward an expanse of open beach where a line of reefs formed a calm lagoon. The group passed through a lush dell filled with shimmering ferns—*golden* ferns that stood tall, unfurling to display burnished fanlike fronds.

Laughing, Sherufa walked among the ferns, running her fingertips through the fronds. "According to legend, whoever finds a golden fern is supposed to be blessed."

Grigovar chuckled. "It seems we're all blessed, then."

"Just like the fern I found when I was just a child." Saan looked up with a smile of wonder. "I suppose I have accomplished great things—I'm in *Terravitae*. And I'm only just getting started."

Yal Dolicar surreptitiously plucked some of the smaller fern fronds and tucked them inside his shirt.

From the fern grove they continued downward, following the sounds of seabirds crying and the whoosh of water. They came upon a stretch of beautiful white sand, and Saan stopped short. "Well, I never expected this. I thought we were done with the island witch."

Cast up on the beach was an oblong crystal case, like a coffin. Knocked askew, the lid lay gleaming in the bright sunlight.

Saan explained to Criston, "That coffin held Ystya's father, the man they say was Ondun."

"But it's empty," Sen Aldo said.

A chill shivered up Criston's spine, and his skin prickled, but he also felt a sense of wonder. "Whoever was inside the case must have been washed away in the storm."

Ystya looked up with a bright smile. "Not washed away." She turned from the beach and gazed toward the hills farther along the shore. "My father is here."

Against the bright sky, they saw the silhouette of a man walking toward them. Light shone from the stranger's white robes, white hair, and thick beard. Criston, Saan, and all of the shore party stared, awestruck. King Sonhir bowed his head to the man, averting his gaze.

As the man approached, Criston had to lean back because he was very tall. Despite the stranger's age, the power that radiated from his form gave him the appearance of a giant.

"Terravitae has reawakened him." Ystya smiled. "The land brought him back." Letting go of Saan's hand, she ran forward as the old man strode up to the group.

He regarded them all with kindness and recognition. "I am Ondun, and I am pleased that my children have returned to Terravitae."

112 *Ishalem Harbor*

On the deck of *Sapier's Glory*, Comdar Rief raised the colorful blue-and-green battle flag to the top of the mast. For weeks, the navy had waited for the signal that it was time to go to war, and now the Tierran ships sailed forward to take the piers and destroy or seize any vessel that remained in the harbor. His sailors whistled and cheered. He expected the holy city would fall within days.

As the Tierran warships closed on the harbor, the lookout on *Sapier's Glory* shouted and pointed out to sea. Rief turned his spyglass to study the distant Uraban fleet that waited in open water far beyond the harbor.

The hodgepodge group of Uraban vessels kept station far away out to sea, obviously unwilling to come closer. The large collection of enemy vessels had arrived in the past weeks, but Rief judged that his own vessels could defeat them in a straight-up fight. The Uraban ships protected the mouth of the canal leading inland, concentrating their efforts there, rather than trying to repel the Aidenist fleet. Their commander must be very cautious, Rief decided.

"They've set sail and are racing in, sir," said his first mate. "I think their commander is trying to stop us."

Rief just smiled as he gazed through his spyglass. "He won't be able to intercept us in time." Strategically, the enemy might plan to bottle them up in the harbor, but the comdar didn't particularly care: once the seventy-three ships reached the piers, his fighters would swarm onto the docks and race through the streets to join the Tierran army. They would hold the holy city, and Comdar Rief could deal with the enemy warships as part of routine mopping-up operations.

Tied up in the harbor, the blockaded Uraban ships were caught unawares by the sudden move after two months of waiting. The siege-weary Uraban sailors scrambled up onto the decks, and a ragtag group of Curly soldiers ran to the ends of the piers. But they wouldn't get their ships ready in time, even if they had a place to go. This was going to be easier than he thought.

As the Tierran navy approached, sails swollen with wind,

Fishhook banners and pennants flying, Rief noticed two pairs of black cylinders mounted in emplacements at either side of the harbor mouth. Soldiers wearing white olbas busied themselves at the tubes, fumbling with . . . kegs of firepowder? He saw a wisp of smoke. Before he could point them out to his first mate, loud explosions split the air, followed by a whizzing sound.

A black projectile hurtled toward them, smashed one of the spars, tore the rigging, and hammered into the deck of the adjacent ship. Rief was dumbfounded to see a gaping hole torn through his mainsail.

The second metal cylinder belched fire and smoke and hurled another iron projectile; the third and fourth weapons also fired. Monstrous and destructive firepowder weapons. With a sudden chill in his gut, Rief wondered if this was what had wrecked all of Destrar Tavishel's ships.

The Tierran sailors were in a panic, but Comdar Rief could not change course now. "Straight ahead! Stay on course—and put out those fires!" The men rushed to follow their orders, and Rief wondered how long it would take the men at the emplacements to reload those monstrous weapons.

Aboard his own ship, Soldan Vishkar was preoccupied in his cabin, writing a few more lines of poetry inspired by the fresh sunny day. Now he dropped his pen as the cabin boy hollered for him. "The 'Hooks are moving, Soldan!"

"Not the canal again?" His orders had been explicit, to guard the waterway at all costs. The Tierrans could blockade Ishalem harbor, but they must be prevented from sailing into the Middlesea. Vishkar simply did not have enough ships to break the blockade *and* guard the canal.

"No, Soldan—their ships are pressing Ishalem."

Vishkar felt a surge of adrenaline. "Set our sails, then." His breathing came faster, and he realized that all the planning in the world had not prepared him enough, now that the time had come. Fortunately, his captains had discussed numerous strategies and maneuvers at gatherings aboard his flagship. He hoped that his powerful fleet itself would be enough to do the job.

Vishkar had always been a merchant, and he preferred delivering exotic cargo to embarking on adventures himself. But Omra had put him in command of a defensive fleet that consisted of ships he had scrounged. He hoped his crew and the other captains knew what they were doing.

Several weeks ago, when he proudly brought his fleet to Ishalem harbor, Vishkar had been dismayed to find Aidenist warships already there. He was too late! His ragtag fleet might have looked intimidating, but the ships weren't built for war. Even with his numerous vessels, he would be unable to crash through the Aidenist blockade (and he was sure that the Tierran commander must have far more naval experience than he did). For days, then weeks, Vishkar hoped that the size of his impressive fleet would intimidate the Tierrans and drive them away. Instead, the two fleets had remained at a standoff—until now.

Racing out on deck, he was half blinded by the sunshine. Antos, the captain of his flagship, watched the Tierran ships close in on the harbor. "It'll be crowded in there, Soldan. Close quarters for fighting."

Vishkar pursed his lips. "You are all seasoned swordfighters, aren't you?"

Captain Antos patted the hilt of his scimitar. "We've had training, and we've had some experience. So has everyone. Never can tell when 'Hook raiders are going to strike one of our seaside towns."

"Good, good. Tell everyone to prepare. We're moving into the fray." Yes, that was what the soldan-shah expected from him. The Uraban vessels sailed toward the 'Hooks.

His crew laughed and cheered when the four harbor cannons

opened up. The Nunghal weapons took the enemy navy completely by surprise, belching fire. The hot projectiles pounded the foremost vessels, wrecked the sails and rigging, started fires.

"They didn't expect that," Antos said with a grin wide enough to show that one of his back teeth was missing.

"Too bad we have only four cannons. It's enough to surprise them, but not enough to stop them."

"*We'll* be enough to stop them, Soldan."

"Good, good. I hope you're right."

Soldan Vishkar carried a scimitar, though he wasn't accustomed to using it. He supposed he was going to get some practice very soon. As the two fleets closed, the cannons fired again, smashing another Tierran ship.

This would be a very bloody day.

113 Ishalem

Omra watched the Aidenist army swarm through Ishalem like plague rats erupting from a sewer. For more than a day, thousands upon thousands of mounted cavalrymen and armed footsoldiers clashed with loyal Uraban fighters, who laid down their lives to stop the monsters from desecrating the holy city.

Years ago, Aidenists had started the fire that burned down Ishalem. Omra had reclaimed the barren land in the name of Urec, rebuilt the glorious city . . . and now these heretics fouled it with every footstep. Aidenists had massacred the innocent priestesses and pilgrims at Fashia's Fountain, dumped a thousand severed heads at the Ishalem wall, invaded Gremurr, beheaded his brother Tukar, set fire to Olabar harbor. They had used firepowder to blast through the wall—*firepowder*, which his own father had brought back from the Nunghals. The Aidenists had stolen even that! The list of atrocities was endless. The most sophisticated Saedran instruments could not measure the level of hatred and contempt he held for them. Why didn't Ondun just strike them down and rid the world of their stain? The Fishhook army cut down his brave defenders and trampled their bodies as they pushed into the city.

Astride a horse he had commandeered from a guard captain, Omra rode back and forth, shouting, "Defend Ishalem! Its fate is in your hands!" Recognizing their soldan-shah, many of his men regained their courage and stood together. "Where is Kel Unwar?" Bodies lay in a tangle at the base of God's Barricade, shot down by Aidenist arrows or killed in the explosion. It looked like a massacre. "Unwar! Where is Unwar?"

Finally, one of the soldiers looked up at him; the right side of his face was marked by a smear of blood. "The kel is dead, Soldan-Shah. Buried in the collapse of the wall."

The news came like a blow to his stomach. The kel had been so proud of his masterpieces, the barricade and canal, but those defenses hadn't been enough. Ishalem was breached.

Hearing cannon fire out in the harbor, Omra saw tall ships pushing toward the docks. The Gremurr ironclads had also entered the canal from the Middlesea side, where they were no doubt wreaking havoc. And Tierran soldiers swarmed into the city, killing anyone they encountered, whether soldier or civilian.

The agonizing truth became clear: as matters stood, Omra could not save Ishalem. Again, he remembered the biting truth of the driftwood reader's words, telling him that the fate of the world hung in the balance. *Your actions have the gravest consequences.* At first he had thought her a charlatan, but he could no longer deny that she had predicted what he saw all around him now. *I promise you, great destruction will be upon us.*

And so he made his dark decision, knowing he could not win, and knowing he couldn't simply surrender either. He faced the high ground, the holiest land in Ishalem. "We need to make a stand, hold a defensible area. Fall back to Arkship Hill—we must save what we can." He wheeled his horse around. One of his soldiers held a battle standard rescued from a watchtower on the wall, and Omra seized the staff from him. Holding the Fern banner high, he rode toward the hill. "To me! In the name of Urec!"

The barbarians raged through the streets, hacking at Uraban defenders. Omra led his men past the fortress-like church of Urec, whose thick walls and heavy doors would protect the people inside . . . for a time. If he didn't succeed today, however, the 'Hooks would torture and slay the faithful, just as they had killed the priestesses at Fashia's Fountain—of that he was certain.

From Arkship Hill, though, Omra hoped to organize a defense, regroup, and drive them back out of Ishalem.

As he rode up the Pilgrim's Path, he reminded himself that this was the site where his father had signed a supposed peace treaty with old King Korastine, thinking a new era had dawned. Now, Omra thought, it was a fitting place for the war to end.

On the first day that her army surged into Ishalem, Queen Anjine watched all semblance of strict military order fall apart. Jenirod and Subcomdar Hist tried to form organized prongs, as planned, but in the tangled alleys and streets the soldiers encountered small knots of defenders.

Even after they crushed the Urecari resistance, Anjine knew the ransacking would continue for days—and deservedly so. Her soldiers had bottled up their thirst for revenge for too long, not just during the recent siege but for years before that. Some of these men had waited all their lives for a chance to strike back at the monsters who had inflicted so much pain on Tierra.

By the time she and Mateo followed the army into the city, the advancing ranks had spread out. Her armor gleamed in the sunlight, showing the bronze filigree of the Fishhook. Mateo rode close to her, sitting his horse with difficulty; she could tell how much he was hurting, though his countenance was a façade of grim strength. He should not be here, but she felt very glad he was. They rode into the city together.

Through her helm Anjine looked toward the hill in the center of the city. She and Mateo had climbed its path as children to stand before the ancient shipwreck while King Korastine and Soldan-Shah Imir pricked their fingers and imprinted their promises in blood . . . for all the good that had done.

Now Urecari horsemen and soldiers converged on the defensible ground to make a last stand. She saw crimson banners fluttering, as if the wind itself were stained with blood. The soldan-shah's banners. "There, Mateo."

He nodded. "I see it, Majesty. The soldan-shah is there—I expect he'll surrender soon. He's got no choice."

Anjine wasn't so sure. "Omra will not give up that easily." She clenched her jaw and added quietly, "I hope he doesn't."

She whistled to Jenirod, who in turn attracted the attention of Subcomdar Hist. While some battle groups continued to spread out and secure neighborhood after neighborhood, the bulk of the Tierran army advanced toward Arkship Hill.

114 *Ishalem, Arkship Hill*

After the fighting started, Istar didn't know how long the church of Urec would remain a safe refuge. So far, the troops rushing through Ishalem had taken advantage of the less defensible places first, but she knew the queen's soldiers would come back to the fortified church, break into it, and ransack the chambers.

It would not be so different from when Omra and the Urecari raiders had attacked Windcatch, killed Prester Fennan, and burned down the town's Aidenist kirk. . . .

After placing the body of Destrar Shenro and the other dead soldiers outside, the ur-sikara's followers rebarricaded the doors and windows and drove off two other groups of roving pillagers. Now they waited.

From a high window, Istar, Ciarlo, and Kuari watched Omra's armies retreat up the Pilgrim's Path to the high ground, where they could protect themselves against Aidenist fighters. She guessed that was where the main clash would take place—unless they could do something to stop it.

Istar pointed to the crimson banners of the retreating army. "I need to find Omra and speak with him—he'll be out of options. Maybe now he'll listen. Maybe Ciarlo and I can even talk to Queen Anjine."

"It's our best chance to stop a wholesale slaughter," Ciarlo said, "in the name of both Aiden and Urec."

"There has been slaughter enough," Kuari said quietly. "Let's do our best to stop it."

"I'll get you there," Asaddan said. "I'll smash skulls to clear a path if I have to."

After giving a perfunctory blessing to the priestesses and worshipers crowded in the main sanctuary, Kuari closed the door to her anteroom. "It's better if they don't know I'm leaving. They're frightened, and I don't want them to think I've abandoned them." Together, they slipped out one of the service doors and into a silent alley.

Asaddan guided them through the back streets at a brisk pace, circling buildings and taking narrow side streets until they reached the base of the hill. Up there, Istar saw some of Omra's defenders gathering their spears to form a picket line, while others stood with scimitars ready. The Tierran army would be upon them soon.

Asaddan trudged up the steep hill with Istar, Ciarlo, and Kuari behind him. Below them in the city, Istar heard cheering fighters and screaming civilians. She watched, sickened, as pockets of Ishalem's defenders were surrounded and cut down. In a determined, organized charge, Queen Anjine's army reached the base of the Pilgrim's Path and began ascending.

Omra's soldiers saw Istar and her companions and recognized the ur-sikara and the soldan-shah's First Wife. When their group reached the end of the path, where the ancient Arkship had stood, the Uraban soldiers bowed and stepped back deferentially, letting them pass through the defenses.

Sweating, blood-streaked, and incredulous, Omra came forward to meet his wife. "You should not be here, Istar! Why did you come to Ishalem? I wanted you safe in Olabar."

"Olabar isn't safe, either. The only safety lies in ending this war."

Despite the circumstances, Omra seemed defiant rather than defeated. "I will not surrender Ishalem."

With Asaddan beside them like a bodyguard, the ur-sikara and Ciarlo approached the soldan-shah. Omra frowned at the man who was obviously an Aidenist. "Who is this, Istar? An important hostage?"

"We are all important," Ciarlo replied in accented Uraban. "We are all children of Ondun."

Istar drew a deep breath. "He is my brother, Omra." Her answer stunned him. "His name is Ciarlo, and he came from Tierra to find me. Listen to what he and the ur-sikara have to say. Ishalem needs people like them to speak on our behalf."

Before Omra could respond, sentries around the perimeter shouted to draw his attention. "Soldan-Shah, they are coming!"

He looked sadly at Istar, but the interruption had reminded him of why he was here. He rallied his confidence and raised his voice. "We must defend this hill at all costs. Do not let them reach the high ground. Give me a spear!" He held out his hand, and someone thrust one into his grip. "We'll slaughter as many Aidenist animals as we can, and let Ondun judge us afterward."

Istar intentionally stepped in front of him, blocking his charge. "Omra, stop and listen to me! I know you want to kill the Tierran queen, but we're all on the edge of annihilation. What happens next will determine the fate of Uraba *and* Tierra."

Anger transformed his face so that she barely recognized him. "Look around you! See what they've done to my Ishalem. The streets can only be cleansed with their blood. Death to all Tierrans!"

"*All* Tierrans?" Istar placed herself directly in front of the spearpoint and stared him down. "If you want to kill all Tierrans, then begin with me."

He was startled momentarily out of his wrath. She continued, "If you truly hate them all, if you truly believe not a single one is worth saving, why not finish what you started in Windcatch when you raided my village? You meant to kill me then. Only a brief hesitation stayed your hand—and look how your life changed." The spearpoint touched her chest, biting into her silk wrap, her skin. She paid no attention to the tiny trickle of blood. "Do you regret that decision? Do you truly wish you had killed me twenty years ago? Then go ahead."

She showed no flicker of fear. The gamble was too great. "And what of Saan? He is Tierran too, born of myself and a Tierran father."

Omra flinched. "Saan is *my* son. I raised him. He is as loyal a Uraban as any man here."

"He was *raised* Uraban, but his true father is a Tierran sailor and explorer. Criston Vora. And Saan is with his father now. I read it in the sympathetic journal. The *Al-Orizin* encountered a Tierran sailing ship on the far side of the world. Their ships were damaged in a storm, and the crews are helping each other to survive. By now, they have surely reached Terravitae."

Omra stared at her in disbelief. "You cannot know this for certain."

She looked at Kuari, who produced the twinned journal and held it up. "She speaks the truth, Soldan-Shah. I've read his words myself." The ur-sikara showed the journal to everyone around them.

"Urabans and Tierrans *can* work together. Saan is proving it right now. He loves you and wants more than anything to make you proud of him, no matter what blood runs through his veins." Swept away with her plea, Istar reached a hand toward him. "Omra, you can die here for nothing, or you can live for Saan—for *all* of your children—and for Uraba."

The soldan-shah could not escape the truth on her face, or in Kuari's hand.

Just then the first Aidenist soldiers made it up the hill, and the Uraban defenders blocked the end of the path with their weapons, ready to die. Omra looked at his wife in dismay. "Istar, get out of the way!"

"I will not."

Her brother Ciarlo stepped closer. "Let me help you broker peace, sir. With the help of the ur-sikara, we can do what your father and King Korastine started—what Aiden and Urec would have wanted."

But before Omra could respond, the Aidenist army broke through the Uraban defenders with battle cries and clanging blades.

When the armies collided at the crest of the hill, Queen Anjine knew the fight was already over, and the soldan-shah must realize it as well. Swords raised, her fighters spread out to face their enemy. As her front lines threw themselves upon the followers of Urec, she shouted, "Urabans, lay down your arms!"

Anjine saw that she had come upon a strange tableau. She easily identified Soldan-Shah Omra, who had planted the crimson Unfurling Fern banner and stood his ground, but she was surprised to see a woman who was obviously Tierran, though dressed in Uraban clothing. The woman faced him, unafraid of a lowered spear he pressed against her. The soldan-shah lifted the sharp point away from her, spoke a sharp comment in Uraban . . . and the Tierran woman moved to stand *beside* him.

A blond-haired man was also with them—a prester, judging by his Fishhook pendant—along with a prominent Urecari priestess. A tall, exotic-looking stranger also stood with them, a man whose race she did not recognize.

On his horse beside Anjine, Mateo looked pained from the rough charge up Arkship Hill. He had loosened his cuirass from discomfort, and she spied blood leaking out from his armor—his wound had opened again. For his sake, if nothing else, Anjine knew she had to end this confrontation without further fighting.

Still looking at the soldan-shah, she said quietly out of the corner of her mouth, "Join me, Mateo. I want you at my side for this." Anjine nudged her horse slowly forward to face the defeated enemy leader. She glared at the Uraban defenders until they let her horse pass so she could approach Omra. "Soldan-Shah, I will accept your surrender! Lay down your arms now, or we will execute all of your soldiers."

The two Tierrans next to the soldan-shah—were they hostages? collaborators?—translated her ultimatum. Omra's face turned ruddy with desperate hatred, and he clutched his spear.

Flicking her gaze away from the Uraban leader, she talked to the man with the Fishhook pendant. "I don't know you, Prester, but tell the soldan-shah that if he wants to keep his head on his shoulders and wants his people to survive this day, then he must surrender Ishalem to me."

Behind her, the Tierran soldiers raised their banners and whooped out a victory cry.

"The ur-sikara and I will be pleased to assist in your discussions, Queen Anjine," said the prester. "But if you have truly read the Book, you know that neither Aiden nor Ondun would want you to slaughter these people."

The Tierran woman next to him spoke up. "I can help you end this war, Majesty. But I won't help you to destroy Omra or the Uraban people."

Anjine was taken aback. "You are clearly Tierrans. This is a day of victory for Aiden! I am your queen."

"And Omra is my husband. My name was Adrea, from Windcatch, but I have lived half of my life in Uraba. If a prester and the ur-sikara can find common ground and discuss peace, then so can the queen and the soldan-shah."

Behind them, a clamor arose from the Pilgrim's Path that led up the opposite side of Arkship Hill. Soot-stained, blood-spattered, and wild-eyed, another group of Tierran soldiers charged to the top of the hill: Destrar Broeck and his nephew Iaros, leading a weary squad they had brought from the Gremurr mines. Anjine felt her heart swell. "There will be no need for negotiation."

The Iborian destrar and his armed fighters saw the queen's banner and rushed forward, cheering. The Uraban defenders, hemmed in by Aidenists now, responded with a ragged, defiant shout for their soldan-shah.

Omra looked trapped and desperate, obviously realizing that all was lost. Anjine waited for him to drop to his knees before her.

But the shaggy black-haired foreigner let out a bellow of laughter and pointed to the sky. Anjine glanced up as a gasp of amazement rippled through her fighters.

Drifting in over the hilltop came fifteen bright balloons attached to sturdy wicker baskets. The baskets were filled with archers—Uraban archers.

Anjine caught her breath, turned her attention away for only a moment, stunned by these incredible reinforcements from the sky. In that instant, Soldan-Shah Omra saw his chance. He lunged toward the exposed queen with his spear, all the years of anger adding momentum to his thrust.

Without a flicker of hesitation, Mateo dove in front of Anjine. Omra rammed the jagged spearpoint with all his might through the gap in Mateo's loosened cuirass, between his ribs, and deep into his chest.

Anjine screamed. The Tierran woman and the prester both cried out in dismay.

With the spear buried in him, Mateo fell to the ground.

Destrar Broeck's roar was louder than a firepowder explosion. "Kill them! Kill them all!" Howling, his warriors hurtled into the Uraban soldiers with redoubled fury, hacking and stabbing.

Even as the unrestrained storm of blades and blood raged around her, Anjine somehow dismounted and dropped to her knees beside Mateo. He lay bleeding . . . dying. With a sob, she pulled off his helm and cradled his head. "No!" She no longer heard the sword clashes that rang across the hilltop.

Destrar Broeck threw himself on the soldan-shah, who fought with equal abandon. Overhead, the shadows of the sand coracles fell over them, and arrows began to rain down from the sky.

Mateo choked, and blood poured out of his mouth. He tried to say something to Anjine, but he died within seconds.

She felt a hurricane of blood gather around her. With ruthless conviction, she decided to have Omra captured, not killed, so that she could have him flayed alive. But even then, she knew in her heart that the violence would not stop there.

She didn't think it would ever stop.

115 *Terravitae*

The towering figure of Ondun, large for a man but with the presence and power of a god, stood before them with a congenial smile.

Criston had seen many astounding things in his life—from Captain Shay and the ghost ships to the terrible Leviathan and the Lighthouse at the End of the World. He had experienced the more personal shocks of discovering his long-lost son and learning that Adrea was still alive. But *this* rendered him speechless.

Ystya gazed at Ondun with a smile. "It's been so long, Father, but we're here at last in Terravitae."

"How you have changed, my daughter! You were a little girl for too long, but your mother simply would not let go." He gave her a wistful smile as though he were any normal man greeting a child after coming home from a long journey. He folded her into a hug and spoke with his face pressed against her shoulder. "You were just an innocent child when I . . . drowned?" His brow furrowed, and a cloudy expression crossed his face. "It was Iyomelka, wasn't it?"

"Yes," said Ystya, swallowing hard.

Ondun gave a sigh. "I always feared she would do something rash. She never could control her passions."

The young woman seemed to be bursting with things she needed to say. "Even after you drowned, the magic from your body infused the spring, and that preserved my mother and me." Criston and the others hardly breathed as they listened.

"It wasn't only my powers, Ystya—it was *you*," Ondun said.

"You are the Key to Creation. When your mother was pregnant with you and fled, our entire race grew weaker in Terravitae. There were so few left. That's why I sent Aiden and Urec to find you, and to find another place for our surviving people. We knew of weaker races on distant continents, much like us, and compatible." He shook his head. "That's why I departed on my own quest. I was the strongest of us, but even I was fading. So many had died off . . ."

Spreading his arms, he leaned his bearded head back and drew a deep breath of the fresh air. "When I found Iyomelka's island and we were reunited, my strength was renewed. I feel it in me now." He raised a large hand and flexed his fingers. "It's very hard to explain. Iyomelka and I had been together for so many centuries in Terravitae. Then, after centuries more on the island . . ." He shook his head. "I suppose it's as much my fault as hers." Ondun looked around, his eyes bright, his expression hopeful as he scanned the awestruck group on the beach. "Your mother—is she here with you? I awoke all alone on the shore."

"She is dead." Ystya lowered her head. "After Saan rescued me from the island, my mother pursued us, wanting to take me back to the island or kill us all." She cast a meaningful, appreciative glance at Saan. "But she was no match for the Leviathan, and it destroyed her."

Ondun was solemn, and he turned away, at a loss for words for a long moment. When he spoke, his voice sounded bleak. "Century after century, that woman put me through the full range of emotions. She loved me, betrayed me, fled from me, even killed me . . . but she also gave me a daughter the whole world needed. And now she is dead." He lowered his gaze. "Is there any hope for our race?"

Ystya said, "Up the shore not far from here, we passed a ruined Arkship, and we found the frozen tomb of Aiden and Urec. They must have returned to Terravitae in their last days, but maybe they or their crews had descendants that still live here."

"I always knew Aiden and Urec would come back home." He stroked his thick gray beard, then brought himself back to the group of explorers who stood on the beach. "What has happened to the world in all this time? For many, many years after I sent my sons on their voyage, I was able to track them from Iyomelka's island, but the world is so vast—too vast even for me to watch the whole thing. I suspect you have a lot to tell me."

Hearing the broad question, Criston realized that every person there had a different set of answers. His mind was filled with so many questions he could barely sort through them all. "We each have our stories to tell, my Lord. We are honored to be in your presence, but I hardly know where to start."

"I know where it ends." Ondun looked at the two captains, the representative sailors from both crews, King Sonhir, the Saedran chartsmen. His face had a knowing expression, as if he recognized them. "You are all here, and I am here. So . . . I take it I was rescued from the well on the island?"

"We retrieved you," Saan explained, "Grigovar and I. But then Iyomelka turned on us and chased my ship across the wide oceans, until we were all nearly destroyed by that sea monster."

Criston said, "The Leviathan is also dead, my Lord."

Ondun looked weary. "Destruction attracts destruction—it is fitting in a way that the Leviathan and Iyomelka were called to each other." He heaved a sigh, then his expression changed. Brightening, swelling large, he spread his arms to welcome them. "But the most important thing is that Ystya survived! And you have brought your friends, from the continents that my sons discovered. We are all returned to the land where we belong—and I feel strong again. A new day has dawned for the world."

Ystya reached out to take Saan's hand, startling him. Her gesture of affection surprised Ondun, but he gave his daughter an indulgent smile. With a respectful bow, Saan said, "Now that we are here, my Lord, we hope to learn the answers to many mysteries. We've read history, from both the descendants of Aiden and Urec, but much doesn't fit with what we know—or what we think we know. I was taught to believe the teachings of Urec's Log, while my father and his sailors from Tierra follow the Book of Aiden. The two accounts are at odds with each other, and much blood has been shed over the differences."

"From what we've seen, neither version is completely accurate," Criston said. He felt hope rise within him. "We've made discoveries on our voyages that simply don't fit with what the presters and sikaras say."

Ondun nodded. "As time passes, stories tend to diverge from the original truth."

Criston bowed. "You are all-seeing and omnipotent, Ondun, and we will trust the answers you provide."

The old man looked embarrassed. "Now, I admit that I am powerful indeed, the strongest of my ancient race, and I could access much of the world's magic, but I never meant to be portrayed as omnipotent."

"You are the creator of all things. We have seen your powers," said Sen Sherufa. "And we've all seen what Ystya can do. You are not merely human."

"Oh no, not human. Simply a member of an elder, more powerful race. Those of us from Terravitae possessed abilities that you would consider incredible, even godlike, I suppose. We could, and did, help shape the world by using our control of the magic that binds all things. But it's quite an exaggeration to say that I single-handedly created everything!"

He stroked his beard again, apparently flustered. "In fact, when my race populated this continent, we had our own beliefs about the deities who fashioned the universe before us, beings that made us look like mice by comparison. They exhibited powers far beyond my own—frost giants, undersea goddesses, wind harpies, lightning sorcerers, the great serpent Bouras. But those titans were mostly extinct before my own race rose to prominence in Terravitae."

Criston thought of the incredible woman with seaweed hair who gathered the ghost ships, and Saan had told him of the ancient ice-locked ship with its frozen crew . . . victims of frost giants? "The titans aren't extinct," he said.

"I believe we've had a brush with them as well," Saan added.

"And you survived? They tend to cause a great deal of trouble." Ondun raised his eyebrows, impressed. "I suppose even they had creation myths and their own gods. We look up to beings who are more powerful than we. It gives us something toward which to strive."

Criston wondered if Prester Hannes or Sikara Fyiri would have debated religion with Ondun Himself.

They stood together on the sun-drenched beach, listening to the waves curl against the black rock outcroppings scattered in the water. The bearded figure seemed to enjoy the beauty of the world around him with a childlike sense of wonder.

He looked out to where the *Dyscovera* and the *Al-Orizin* lay at anchor, far from the rocky shore. Addressing both captains, Ondun said, "Your crews have sailed far across the ocean, with nothing more than rigging and sails and wind. It's remarkable you made it all the way here. Your courage amazes me." He laughed. "There's no need to keep your crews crowded aboard those battered old vessels. Bring them ashore so we can all celebrate."

Criston inhaled a deep breath of the fresh, *new* air that seemed to explode with life and energy. "They would like nothing better, my Lord."

Ondun glanced down at the crystal coffin that had held his body. "I fear Terravitae is empty, but we must search for survivors, settlements." He gave Ystya a warm smile. "Some of our people may yet be alive."

116 Ishalem

The sand coracles appeared like dragons in the sky over Ishalem. Imir and his granddaughters rode in the foremost coracle, along with Khan Jikaris. The other fourteen flying craft were crowded with broad-shouldered Nunghals and all the Missinian archers they had been able to conscript immediately from Desert Harbor. Imir had refused to waste time sending riders back to Arikara.

Each coracle held a large brazier and a generous store of hot-burning coal that could be dampened or stoked to keep the coracles at the best altitude. It took some experimentation, but they discovered an air current that blew west across Missinia, and another northerly current that carried them over Yuarej, Inner Wahilir, and finally to the narrow isthmus that connected the two continents.

The battle for Ishalem was in full swing when they arrived, and Imir saw the collapsed rubble where the Aidenist army had blasted through God's Barricade, smoke rising from burning neighborhoods, and armed enemy soldiers running through the streets, bringing chaos and destruction to the holy city. Blue-and-green Tierran flags now outnumbered the crimson Uraban banners.

To his dismay, Imir saw a large contingent of Tierran soldiers swarming around the base of Arkship Hill, while armed men streamed up the Pilgrim's Path. Another group of Aidenist warriors had ascended the opposite side of the hill to join a furious pitched battle on the broad summit. Tierran and Uraban fighters were locked in mortal combat, hand-to-hand, sword against sword.

Imir felt an ache in his heart, guessing that Omra would be there, making a last stand. The Aidenists looked victorious, about to overwhelm the Urabans.

Adreala turned her sharp eyes toward the flurry of activity on top of the hill. "I think I see Father! How can we save him?"

"The battle isn't over yet," Imir said, anxious to help. "Let's make them doubt their victory today." He pointed to the massed Tierran army at the base of the hill. "There we can cause the most damage. We'll knock the ground from under their feet and send their army reeling."

The bowmen in the sand coracles fired arrows down into the Tierran fighters. Shaft after shaft pelted from the sky, and the enemy soldiers could not protect themselves. Even from such a height, Imir could hear their shouts of surprise and cries of pain.

While the archers continued, Imir lit one of the gourds filled with firepowder, like those he had previously used to bombard the camps of desert bandits. Unexpected explosions erupted among the invaders, sending them scurrying in all directions like panicked beetles running out from under an overturned log. Urabans began hurling explosive gourds from all fifteen coracles.

"If this doesn't turn the tide of the battle, nothing will," he said. "We'll scatter the Aidenist army." He lit another explosive gourd and tossed it out of the basket.

117 *Terravitae*

For the next day, the ships' boats ferried back and forth with load after load of men who fell upon the beach, dug their fingers into the sand, and whooped. They splashed out into the calm waters of the lagoon. At one point, Uraban sailors got into a furious splashing contest with the Tierran crewmen, a reflection of their old rivalries, but this time without rancor.

From the shore, King Sonhir sent out a call, and many mer-Saedrans came out of the water to stand dripping on the beach, where they regarded the majestic old man with expressions of awe. The mer-Saedrans, along with Aldo and Sherufa, told

Ondun their excited tales. Ondun was enthralled to learn how the Saedran continent had sunk beneath the waves and how the people had used their own magic to survive both on land and in the sea.

"Ah, my children, you have done so many interesting things!" He looked meaningfully at Aldo and Sherufa. "I understand you have labored hard to compile your Mappa Mundi? There are many lands and peoples in this world, civilizations that have flourished on their own, other races besides mine—and yours."

"But you have returned, my Lord," Aldo said. "That is why we worked so hard to draw the Map of All Things."

Ondun chuckled. "Your atlas must be wonderful, but I promise you, the world holds lands that you have not even dreamed of. Always horizons to explore, always a new place to see, always something unexpected to discover. That is the true gift of the world."

Ystya waded up to her waist in the calm lagoon, accompanied by Saan. "Everything about this place renews me," she said. "This is where I belong, where my family lived, where my people made their homes."

Saan asked, splashing in the warm water, "What do you expect to find here?"

"Not even my father knows, but if any of our people remain, we'll find them." She lay back and drifted in the sun-dappled water. "Our race was fallow for a long time, but when my mother became pregnant with me, it was a sign of hope, that I would be the start of a new generation." She lifted her head from the water, her pale hair dripping, and reached out to touch Saan's cheek with her wet fingertips.

Three sinuous forms curled through the lagoon toward them. Saan jumped, but Ystya just laughed. The eel-like shapes swam around them, brushing slick, scaly hides against the backs of Saan's legs, and then the small sea serpents rose in front of them.

Their long necks were topped with sharp arrowhead faces and large jaws, and they blasted mist from their blowholes.

Ystya's laughter tinkled like wind chimes. "These are just young ones. They've come to see me."

The sea serpents glided back and forth, and Saan gradually relaxed as he accepted that the creatures were in awe of Ystya and would not harm them. After regarding her with their slitted reptilian eyes, the infant serpents ducked under the water and streaked away out into the ocean, splashing with the tips of their barbed tails.

The sea serpents flashed past two more rowboats that were entering the lagoon. Loaded with crewmen coming ashore, the boats carried few supplies, but Terravitae provided everything they could ask for.

In the rocks at the waterline, the sailors found a wealth of clams, crabs, and oysters that they roasted in large bonfires on the beach. In the fast-running streams, they caught freshwater fish, which tasted far different from the ocean fare they had been eating on their long voyage. Hunters easily found grouse and wild turkeys, as well as fresh eggs in the nests.

Wherever Ystya walked on the new landscape, her very presence as the Key to Creation sparked a fire of verdancy. Thick clusters of berries appeared on vines and bushes. Groves of almond, apple, and pear trees bowed down their lower branches, weighted with a harvest of fruit.

"I suppose it wouldn't be such a bad thing to find ourselves marooned here," Saan said that evening.

But Criston could not stop thinking about Adrea, on the other side of the world, still alive, despite the changes in her life. He said, "I look forward to going home, though I'm not eager for the voyage to get there."

Eager to explore the continent, Ondun led a group up the coast, promising to show Ystya and the visitors where he and his people had lived. "They'll be no more than abandoned ruins now, but it was our home, where Iyomelka and I were once happy, where my sons grew strong . . ."

Both captains accompanied them, along with King Sonhir, both Saedran chartsmen, Kjelnar, and a few handpicked members of each crew, including Grigovar, Yal Dolicar, Javian, and Mia. Though they walked for miles, Criston did not feel weary. Terravitae and its inherent magic seemed to energize his muscles and feet. He turned to look back where they had passed, and saw meadow flowers blooming and grasses growing greener, leaves bursting out from shrubs. Ystya left her mark everywhere.

To the north, Ystya and Ondun took them to the edge of a cliff above rough surf from which they gazed down at the wreck of the Arkship cast up onto the rocks. The skeleton of its hull, piles of split planks, and one toppled mast were all that remained, picked at and pried into pieces by the weather and the waves.

"It appears that Aiden and Urec had barely enough magic left to make it this far," Ondun said. "Let's hope our city is in far better condition."

"If not, we can rebuild it," Ystya suggested.

"Now that you're here with me in Terravitae, daughter, our magic can do just that."

The old man guided them inland, and soon they came upon the ruins of mammoth buildings, villas made out of giant stone blocks, now overgrown with moss and vines. Collapsed marble columns lay like the vertebrae of sea serpents on the ground. In the middle of the largest building, a temple or meeting hall, an immense stone table was canted, one of its legs broken. Saan stared at the arches, the open ceilings, the obelisks and weathered statues. In his imagination, he sketched in the details, painting an incredibly ancient, spectacular city—a home that only gods could have built.

Ondun stepped into the rubble at the perimeter of the assembly hall. "I see we have some fixing up to do." He propped his hands on his hips. His long silvery-gray hair began to twitch and dance in an unseen wind.

"Let me help," Ystya said.

With a rumble and clatter of moving stones, the fallen central structure reassembled itself, as if a huge invisible child were building with toy blocks. The tangled overgrowth of vines acted like pulleys and ropes to lift pillars upright, stacking stones, raising the huge marble table.

Ondun stretched out a hand to indicate the table and the long marble benches that surrounded it. "Let us welcome our new friends with a feast, daughter."

Before long, a greater bounty was spread out before them than they had seen in a long time. Ondun inspected a cluster of fat purple grapes, plucked one, and addressed his guests. "You have all earned a time of relaxation. Who could ask for a better reward, after your arduous journey?" He looked through the pillars of the stone building. "But I am anxious to continue my search of this land, in hopes of finding others."

Looking around himself in wonder, Criston said, "We came to Terravitae expecting to find Holy Joron, my Lord. We found Aiden and Urec entombed in the cave. Will we see Joron here?"

"Alas, no, my third son is long gone from this place. But I hope we will find some descendants of Aiden's and Urec's crew."

Saan looked awkwardly at his father, reluctant to broach the subject that rested like a shadow in the back of his mind. "We came to do more than just explore, my Lord. Our ships set off in search of allies, for the people of Tierra and Uraba are in a desperate war. The *Al-Orizin* was sent to find the Key to Creation and to reach Terravitae in hopes of forming a partnership with Holy Joron against the Tierrans."

Yal Dolicar laughed out loud. "Captain, you would ask *Ondun* to take sides in our war? Now that is funny!"

Criston straightened. "We were both sent on missions to ask for help, my Lord. Tierra has also endured much pain and damage at the hands of Urec's followers. My king asked me to beg Terravitae to fight on our side."

Saan tried again. "And the soldan-shah of Uraba asks your help to protect us against Tierran attacks."

Aldo frowned. "We already saw the prester and the sikara at each other's throats. Hasn't there been enough destruction? We Saedrans bore the brunt of it from both sides."

Javian said, "The divisions between Tierra and Uraba go far too deep to be resolved by any apology. Neither side will easily put their vengeance aside."

"Neither side can forget," Saan said. "Neither side can forgive."

A cloud crossed Ondun's face. "I sent two of my sons to find a fresh land where they could make a new future. I am certain they did not want a war between their descendants."

"Our perspectives have changed," Criston said, looking at his son. "But we still ask for your assistance, my Lord. Our crews have learned to work together, and we survived only because we cooperated. You can help Tierra and Uraba find peace."

Saan grasped at the idea. "This war has gone on so long, I didn't think there was any hope for a solution. But *Ondun* could impose peace on our lands."

The golden ferns growing up from the stone pillars began to rustle and thrash, reflecting Ondun's agitation. He rested his elbows on the stone table. "Aiden's ship found Tierra, and Urec's ship found Uraba." He looked from one captain to the other. "I cannot take sides. Your people must solve their own conflicts."

Ystya's voice was soft and reasonable. "But, Father, you have the power to stop the bloodshed."

Ondun's sparkling white hair was like a mane about his paternal face. "I will not impose my will on one land at the expense of the other."

"They revere you as a god, and the very core of their conflict is how they worship you."

"But I am not—"

Ystya stood from the table. "You are *Ondun*. Shouldn't you use that for the greater good? They will listen to you."

The old man ran a fingertip along his upper lip as he considered. "I am not their 'creator of all things,' but you have renewed my strength." His smile was like a sunrise. "Maybe I can stop the conflict without favoring either side, if I'm careful about it." He flexed his fingers, opening and closing a fist. "Yes, that might be good exercise. It's time for me—in fact, for all of us—to travel to your lands. I should go to Ishalem to see what all the fuss is about." He picked up a round apple, bit into it, and closed his eyes as he savored the taste. "Terravitae can wait while I do this thing for my sons."

Sen Aldo said, "But . . . we come from the other side of the world. Our ships took the better part of a year to get here."

Ondun gave a dismissive wave. "Distance is of no great consequence. I am stronger now than I have been for centuries." The air crackled, and anything *did* seem possible.

Ystya looked at Saan and Criston. "Thank you, Father."

"Very well. Captains, allow your crews another day to rest—I can arrange a banquet for them as well—and then we depart." Ondun found another piece of fruit. "I want to see the lands that my sons discovered. They certainly left their mark on your civilizations."

Criston was perplexed. "My Lord, both Tierra and Uraba have legends of a brother who stayed behind in our lands—but if Aiden and Urec sailed home to Terravitae, who is the Traveler?"

Ondun was surprised by the question. "Why, the Traveler is *Joron*, of course. When his brothers didn't return with the Key to Creation, he set off by himself. That is why he is no longer in Terravitae."

118 Ishalem

The holy city was a scene of chaos. Hordes of Tierran soldiers ran through the streets, recklessly setting fire to homes. The surging tide of the invading army pressed forward, neighborhood after neighborhood. Aidenist slaves escaped from their work camps, turned on their masters, and joined the frenzied battles.

Shopkeepers and family heads tried to defend their property; some used makeshift weapons, ready to die at the doorways, while others huddled with their wives and children in any shelter they could find. Brave or desperate, people tried to extinguish the spreading fires.

An old man walked through the city, cloaked and calm. His step was not hurried. A brown hood covered his face. None of the fighters paid the slightest attention to him. Swordsmen clashed nearby, shield against shield, hacking and screaming and spilling blood while the old man walked past. No one lashed out at him, no one barred his way. With a determined step, he toiled up the steep Pilgrim's Path to the top of Arkship Hill.

As he moved through the Tierran soldiers that marched up to the summit, a vortex of quiet surrounded him. Soldiers stopped fighting. They paused with swords upheld, as if they could not remember why they were there. The combatants blinked at one another, perplexed.

In the air, the fifteen colorful sand coracles hung as if suspended by thin wires in the breeze. The fighters crowded in their baskets shot arrows and threw small explosives down onto the battlefield. But when the hooded man looked up at them, the archers ceased their barrage. No more firepowder bombs dropped.

The old hermit reached the top of the sacred hill. He was not out of breath, he did not speak a word, but the clash died down with his arrival. Destrar Broeck and his fighters paused with their bloody swords in midstroke, then backed away from their Uraban enemies. Soldan-Shah Omra appeared stunned, like a puppet held up only by the last thin threads of his anger, while Queen Anjine cradled the body of Mateo in despair.

Time seemed to stop, like a held breath. Silence descended upon the hilltop. The hermit shrugged back his hood to reveal a contented visage.

Ciarlo gasped. "The Traveler has come back!"

"Yes, I am the one you call the Traveler." His skin began to glow. The air around him crackled with the smell of a thunderstorm, and his figure seemed to fill much more than the space he occupied. "I am also the man you call Holy Joron. And I have come to put an end to this violence."

119 *Terravitae*

Even after the feast in the ruins of Ondun's city, Javian could not embrace the celebration. The secrets he still kept tore at his heart. He had revealed the truth about himself to Prester Hannes, and though the knowledge had died with the prester, the confession had ripped the scab off a wound. Javian had to face his shameful and treacherous heritage. The Teacher had trained him, and all *ra'virs*, to live a lie . . . but Javian was sick of lying.

Encamped in the comfortable seaside forests, the Tierran crew feasted, drank, and sang boisterous ballads in friendly duels with the Urabans from the *Al-Orizin*. They had become close after their tribulations, but for Javian the internal struggle was unbearable. During the entire voyage of the *Dyscovera*, he had been torn between the hatred indoctrinated into him and the kindness he observed in Captain Vora, Mia, and his fellow sailors. And it seemed that the Urabans aboard the *Al-Orizin* displayed an equal range of kindheartedness and brutality. Javian did not want to go back to Tierra—or Uraba—under such terms. He didn't belong in either place anymore.

As he tried to sleep on the soft grass near the crumbled stone ruins, he wrestled with what he had discovered about the world and about himself. The ground felt much more comfortable than his narrow bunk aboard ship, but he battled nightmares. His secrets were like a poison, making him violently ill. Only purging himself of the poison could save his life.

Unable to sleep, he rose, stretched his stiff muscles, and walked among the ancient stone buildings, wanting to draw peace from this empty land. He was startled to see a familiar figure silhouetted in the night—Criston Vora, also contemplating. He hesitated, not sure he was ready for conversation, but the captain turned, noticed him. "I see you can't sleep either, Javian."

"Too much has happened, sir." He moved closer, and they stood together in silence for a long moment. "Are you thinking about your sweetheart?"

Captain Vora sighed. "Yes. I don't need to trust my hope to letters anymore. If Ondun does indeed take us home, then I will find her. We'll be reunited, and I can speak to her face-to-face . . . no matter how much has changed." Moonlight shone on the captain's face as he turned to Javian. "I'd like you to meet her, when everything is settled."

Javian was startled when Mia joined them. "Are you all right, Javian? I worry about you." She had stayed close to him since the death of Prester Hannes, though even she didn't understand the full reason for Javian's distress. The young woman slipped her arm around his waist—possibly the most comforting feeling he'd ever experienced. He was glad to have her there, since she was part of his decision as well.

"Captain, when you return home, I . . . I won't be going with you," Javian said. "I've decided not to sail back to Tierra."

The captain turned in surprise. "What do you mean?"

Mia held him tighter. "Why didn't you talk to me about this? Javian, what's going on?"

The young man gazed past the shadowy pillars and into the darkness of the unexplored continent. "There's no place for me back in Calay. I intend to stay here. Terravitae is what calls to me."

"I can't maroon one of my men here," Captain Vora sputtered.

"Look at how lush and fertile this land is, sir. I won't be an exile—I'll be a pioneer. And you'll be back in a year or two. Ships will probably come from both Uraba and Tierra. Shouldn't somebody be here to greet them?" He hoped they would accept his explanation. He didn't want to reveal that he had been a traitor among them for all this time, a trap waiting to be sprung.

Mia leaned closer to Javian. "Not even my fondest memories of home can match what I've seen in Terravitae." A deep breath. "I'll stay behind with him, Captain. We'll work together, make a home and a life here." She smiled at him. "Where it's all fresh and new. If Javian will have me?"

He was surprised and also thrilled. "Are you sure?"

"I came aboard the *Dyscovera* to get away, remember? There wasn't much left for me back in Tierra, and this new land holds everything I've dreamed of—including you, if you're staying."

"You don't know the truth yet—the main reason I want to stay." He raised his heavy eyes to the captain. "Once you know who I am, you probably won't want me aboard your ship anymore. I'm sorry I betrayed you so . . ."

Captain Vora's brows drew together. "What are you saying?"

Mia was alarmed. "What secret could you possibly have kept from me?"

"I am a *ra'vir*," he said. "Raised by the Urecari and given the sole mission of harming this voyage in any way possible, to sabotage any Aidenist plans. I ruined the Captain's Compass during the mutiny and our fight with the mer-Saedrans. I killed the rest of the *rea* pigeons, so we couldn't send any more messages home." He lowered his head. "But I was wrong. All Aidenists aren't like Prester Hannes . . . and now I know that all Urecari aren't like the Teacher. You changed me, Captain Vora. As did you, Mia."

He continued in a rush as they stared at him in disbelief. "For years I lived a false life among Tierrans, but you finally made me see through the lie. I wrestled with it, but I dishonored a good captain and a good crew. I can't go back to Calay, and I certainly don't want to return to Uraba. This is the only place I can truly start fresh and make a new life—if Ondun will allow it."

Captain Vora looked at him in hard silence for a long, long moment. Mia was unsettled, awkward, and Javian didn't know how much more he could endure. She withdrew from him, stared at him, and didn't answer. It was the longest silence of his life.

At last, the captain changed, like a shifting breeze on the open sea. He drew a deep breath. "If I can find it in my heart to forgive the Urecari after all they have done, if I accept that Tierra and Uraba must let go of their anger to find a lasting peace, then how can I not forgive you, Javian—someone I consider a friend?"

Mia said, "I thought I knew you, Javian. And in a way maybe I *did* know the true you—before you even knew yourself. If I was one of the reasons that you turned away from destruction, I can't abandon you now. I want to stay with you. We should be together, make a new start in a new land."

Javian's throat tightened. Tears stung his eyes, and he breathed heavily to keep himself from crying. "Then there's one last thing I will ask of you, sir, before you go. Since you're the ship's captain, and if Mia agrees . . . would you marry us?"

120 *Terravitae*

The following day, on the sunlit beach by the lagoon with calm waters whispering out to the two anchored ships, Criston stood before Javian and Mia. The crews of the *Dyscovera* and the *Al-Orizin* gathered around, happy to celebrate the fine event.

The sailors were surprised by their decision to stay, but everyone could see the verdant power of the new continent. Even Kjelnar seemed tempted to remain behind on land in Terravitae, but he had already shifted from one world to another, and he was anxious to return to his original home before he gave up anything else.

Criston held the ancient tome they had taken from inside the ice cave, the combined Captains' Log of Aiden and Urec. Considering how their understanding had changed, it no longer seemed appropriate to use just the Book of Aiden to perform the wedding ceremony.

"This is certainly one of the more pleasant duties a ship's captain can have," he said, raising his voice so that all the people could hear, "to join two people in marriage. Javian and Mia, you have chosen to bind your lives together, the way that we bound our two ships, and thus survived our journey. The two of you will now have to rely on each other to set your course, weather the storms, and anchor in calm waters."

Javian looked at Mia with shining eyes, and when Criston called on them to make their mutual vows, the young man stumbled on his words. "Now that we're here in Terravitae, it seems strange to say, 'May the Compass guide you,' for the Compass *has* guided us. Mia, I promise to love you and take care of you. I promise to work with you and make your life as happy as I possibly can. I'll rely on you and support you." After that, Javian didn't know what else to say.

Criston chuckled. Mia spoke her own vows from her heart, and Criston raised his hands and pronounced them wed.

They all looked up to see Ondun and Ystya walking down the grassy slope to the beach. The bearded figure strode up to them, beaming. "And I grant my personal blessing to your union. You will be the first couple of a new generation here in Terravitae, our first settlers, our first pioneers. You have this whole land to roam for now, but I'm sure others will soon come. You may use a dwelling in the old city as your shelter, or build your own homes, if you wish. The climate is mild, and Terravitae has plenty of food."

"Be careful," Saan said, "or you'll convince all of our crewmembers to stay behind."

But that was not the case. Especially with Ondun to guide them, they were all eager to begin the voyage home.

Per Ondun's command, all crewmembers from both battered ships had come ashore, leaving the anchored vessels empty. Together, the Tierran and Uraban sailors followed Ystya and her powerful father to the headlands above the beached Arkship.

When Ondun walked among them, several overawed sailors fell to their knees, and some spoke prayers using whatever words the sikaras or presters had taught them. Offhandedly, the powerful old man blessed them all, because it was expected, but he seemed disconcerted by the worship. "It is time to go end the war in your lands, so that I can return here and search for the rest of my people, if any remain."

From the cliffs above the ocean, Criston was amazed to see the two patchwork vessels drifting up the coast toward the remains of the Arkship, like iron needles drawn by a lodestone. Now they floated in surprisingly calm waters not far from the black rocks and churning surf.

"Ah, I think that's close enough," Ondun said. "I tried to be gentle."

During their long voyages, the *Dyscovera* and the *Al-Orizin* had been battered until they were little more than debris held together with nails and rope.

Beside his father, overlooking the crumbling Arkship, Saan gave a skeptical shake of his head. "I can't see how either ship could hold together for a week, much less all the way back to Ishalem. We barely have any sailcloth, and they'll break apart the moment we hit rough waters."

"I have exactly the same doubts," Criston said, "but I'm curious to see what Ondun intends to do."

The old man pondered. He didn't seem discouraged at all. "Though these ships are damaged, there is enough to work with. From these seeds we will fashion an Arkship." He took his daughter's hand. "Ystya and I have the power." Ondun smiled at her. "Will you work with me now to create a new ship?"

"If you show me how."

Ondun turned to the visitors. "This might be somewhat unsettling, but you will be safe up here."

As he and Ystya concentrated, joining their magic, Criston saw the *Al-Orizin* and the *Dyscovera* sway in the water and begin dismantling themselves. Planks flew apart, waving in the air like living things, and merged. Seasoned boards stretched like the fronds of fast-growing plants. The decks separated, realigned, and clashed together.

At the base of the cliff, the timbers of the broken Arkship thrummed. Hull boards and ribs snapped apart, flew across the water like debris in a hurricane, and fell into the cauldron of ship assembly.

Kjelnar, who had supervised the construction of many ships, stared with wide eyes as three separate vessels fused together, expanding into one gigantic ship.

The bent and splintered masts stood upright of their own accord. Wood shards flew into the air, but instead of scattering they melded into new spars, strung with new rigging ropes. The clack and clatter of a million pieces falling into place at once was deafening.

Ondun and Ystya laughed joyfully all the while.

The tatters of sailcloth stitched themselves together. Swatches of canvas and silk flew up like paper caught in a breeze and swirled around to make a colorful patchwork of new sails.

The vessel rocked in the water, as if undergoing the struggles of birth. The ocean frothed around its hull. Driftwood pulled in by the vortex was smoothed out and incorporated into the new construction. Soon all the remnants of the Arkship were gone, absorbed into the vessel.

As the last components flurried about and fell into place, the gleaming knurled horn of Raathgir the ice dragon drifted to the new bow and settled into a notch left specifically for it, pointing the way back home. The smell of fresh wood, rain, and the open sea filled every breath as Criston watched.

Finally, the transformation was complete, and Ondun drew a deep, satisfied breath. "I trust this new ship meets with your approval, Captains?"

Saan spoke up. "It's a fine vessel and worthy of carrying you and your daughter from Terravitae to the world of mankind."

"I am glad you think so," Ystya said, flushing with pleasure at the compliment.

"Shall we be off, then?" Ondun said.

Criston bowed. "The voyage is yours to command, my Lord."

While the two crews had expected to spend days filling water barrels, harvesting fruit, digging fresh roots and plants, hunting game and preserving the meat for the return trip, Ondun insisted that such measures were unnecessary. "Don't worry—we won't be voyaging long."

Though supplies and equipment had been lost during the recent storms, Criston left Javian and Mia with tools and materials to help them set up their new home in the ancient stone ruins. With the continent's temperate climate and lush bounty, the two would have everything they required. *Pioneers.* Javian and Mia said their farewells to their comrades.

Criston embraced the young man as they stood at the edge of the golden ferns, looking out to sea. "You're sure about this?"

"Absolutely, Captain."

Mia added, "We'll be fine here, sir. It's *Terravitae.*"

Criston was anxious to row back out to the marvelous new Arkship. "We've all had to place our faith and hope in what Ondun told us, and if He's correct, He and Ystya will soon come back here, maybe with other ships. You two won't be alone for long." He smiled. "After all, we know the route now."

Taking the last ship's boat out of the lagoon, Criston looked back to see Javian and Mia waving goodbye, and he was sure they did not doubt their choice.

The new Arkship was ready to sail. Ondun gazed out to sea, as if imagining the far horizon. "Now that Ystya has convinced and inspired me, I find myself in a hurry. I could summon the breezes, but that would not suffice. Let me call up some assistance."

He extended his hands out over the ship's bow and sent a strange call into the depths. Within moments large shapes appeared in the water—the scaly forms of golden sea serpents with heads like seahorses.

"These steeds will pull the Arkship across the world," Ondun said. "They've been waiting a long time for a good run." The golden seahorses let out shrill hoots from their blowholes and swam around the new Arkship, much to the delight of the mer-Saedrans in the water.

Ystya wore an overjoyed smile; her skin and hair glowed with dazzling light. She turned to Saan. "We are so happy we can help.

You've done me a favor, and now I want to show *you* so many things."

He was unable to find words. His deep affection for Ystya, possibly even love, had been overwhelmed by complete awe once he found out who she really was. He shook his head, still disbelieving. "You were such a shy and innocent girl when I took you under my wing. Now . . . I don't know how to act with you."

She found that funny. "I'm no different than I was before."

Using his magic, Ondun uncurled long ropes from piles on the Arkship's deck, and the braided strands gleamed like spun gold. Using the magical rope, Ondun harnessed the five golden serpents to the Arkship's bow, as if they were horses drawing a chariot.

The mer-Saedrans swam astern of the Arkship. King Sonhir floated in the waves, gazing to the high decks. "We will try to keep up with you!"

Ondun called back down, "Easily managed. As this vessel sails, you'll be swept along in her wake. I will pull you with us." He seemed mischievous. "It will be a fast ride, though. We have much distance to cover."

The two captains called for the anchors to be raised, and most of the crew eagerly went to the sides to watch the departure. Ondun's voice boomed like thunder. "We are off!"

The seahorse-monsters lunged forward, pulling the Arkship. Criston turned to gaze one last time at Terravitae. Adjusting his spyglass, he could just make out two small figures—Javian and Mia—waving from the beach.

The land dwindled behind them in only a few minutes, and the hard breeze in Criston's face told him how swiftly they were traveling.

The Arkship's wake frothed and churned, and he saw numerous dolphins bounding in the water. King Sonhir, his daughters, and other mer-Saedrans swam alongside, Kjelnar among them. The big Iborian shipwright waved and shouted, "We're still with you, Captain Vora!"

As they raced along, Ondun stood with Criston and Saan. Ystya's father seemed twice the size of a normal man now, swelled with the power he was using, but when Criston looked more closely, they were about the same height. Ondun flashed a mysterious smile. "For you, Captain Vora, I have asked others to join us. It was a struggle to release them from that woman's greedy clutches, and they'll have to return to her in time. But she isn't much of a fighter. Not this time."

Though the wind whipped in his face and stung his eyes, Criston saw the shadowy outlines of a fleet of spectral ships sailing after them, carried along by ghostly winds. He recognized the *Luminara* in the lead.

"It seemed fitting to bring your lost loved ones," Ondun explained. "So they can see their homes one final time and say farewell."

Criston felt a lump in his throat and he could barely whisper a thank-you. He had already lost Captain Shay and his fellow crewmen once. And he hoped that after he got home, he would be able to find Adrea again. He knew that Saan would help.

"How long will our voyage take, my Lord?" he asked.

Ondun leaned back with a placid look on his face. "Not long. The world is not such a big place, once you know all of it."

121 *Ishalem, Arkship Hill*

With his hood thrown back, Holy Joron—the Traveler—towered like a giant over the armies of Urec and Aiden. After he revealed himself on the top of Arkship Hill, his figure gained stature like a swelling thunderhead, drawing magic out of the earth. Many soldiers dropped their weapons, fell to the trampled dirt, and abased themselves.

Even with the titanic figure looming over them, Anjine clung to Mateo's body and moaned quietly, defeated by her own tragedy rather than the massed enemy army. Facing them, Omra—who had thought his city and world lost—stood tall, his back stiff, shoulders squared, ready to endure anything. He seemed more interested in the smear of fresh blood on the queen's armor than in the return of the Traveler. Asaddan and Istar stayed by the ur-sikara, not daring to speak, waiting for Holy Joron to issue his commands.

While the others were mesmerized, however, Ciarlo was delighted. He tugged on his sister's arm, trying to pull her to meet the towering figure. "This is the *Traveler*, Adrea. I shared my camp with him. He gave me a book of his tales, and he cured my leg. He can help us now." He bowed, smiling. "I cannot thank you enough, sir . . . my Lord."

Joron gave Ciarlo a warm greeting. "It is good to see you again. I enjoyed sharing stories by your campfire."

"My Lord, meeting you changed my life forever. Whatever you wish, I will do." Ciarlo fell to his knees and bowed low.

Joron looked at him with an impatient expression. "Please get up, Ciarlo." Then he gestured to the gathered soldiers, who remained huddled and frightened. "Get up, all of you. If I wanted to be worshiped, would I have stayed *hidden* among you for so long?"

Uncertain, the others stumbled to their feet to stand before him.

Joron's gaze swept across the two armies on the hilltop like a sharp scythe. "Though it seems few people listened to all the advice my brothers and I left you."

Ciarlo got up and glanced at Kuari. "The ur-sikara and I are trying to reach an accord—we still have much to talk about."

"But armies are not quick to consider compromises," Kuari added. "There has been so much hatred and so much pain."

Joron seemed twice as tall as any man now, and his voice had the power of waves crashing against a cliff. "For generations I told my stories. I wrote them down and gave them to your people in every Tierran reach and every Uraban soldanate, because they were meant to be lessons for everyone, not just one land or another. Yet over the years, I have watched you squabble over grassblades and ignore the whole forest."

Listening to the words, Ciarlo didn't think the Traveler was speaking either Uraban or Tierran; the ur-sikara and the soldan-shah's troops seemed to understand him just as well. In the presence of Joron, they could somehow all communicate with one another.

The Traveler raised his voice and let his stern words flow. "How can you all be so passionate about your beliefs, yet understand them so little? The message has never been about trappings and rituals, but about your *humanity*. It is about love and compassion, cooperation and challenge. You must better yourselves by building up, not striking down . . . by exploring new horizons, not building walls and closing doors. Discover, not destroy." Joron looked with great disappointment at the long spear protruding from Mateo's chest. "And yet you persist in killing one another."

While all the others had stood, Queen Anjine remained on the ground, cradling the lifeless body in her lap, her expression wracked with despair and fury. She looked down at Mateo's face—the skin was pale, his eyes closed. She rocked him back and forth so that the protruding spear swayed like a metronome. Blood had stopped soaking into the shirt beneath his armor.

Even with the Traveler standing beside them, she regarded the soldan-shah with pure, raw hatred. Her voice was ragged with cauterizing sobs. "If you are indeed Holy Joron, then strike that man down! He committed countless crimes against God. He . . . he *murdered Mateo*!" The last words were wrenched from her throat.

Omra remained stony, as if he didn't care that the Traveler might strike him down. "You say this, after *you* destroyed the wall? Attacked my people? Soiled the holy streets of Ishalem?"

Before Anjine could escalate the retorts, Ciarlo dropped beside the queen and addressed Joron. "I hear your words, my Lord, and I am ashamed." He touched the spear shaft in Mateo's chest and gazed beseechingly at the Traveler. "Can this not be a time to heal? You fixed the old wound in my leg and let me walk like a young man again. You are the son of Ondun . . . is there anything you can do to save this one man?"

Joron reached out and, seemingly without effort, plucked the spear from Mateo's body and cast it aside. "A difficult wound to be sure, but it can be repaired."

Anjine's voice fluttered with shock and hope. "I'll do anything if you save him."

"Will you?" Joron seemed skeptical. "That remains to be seen. This one life must save many, many more . . . but it can be done. His spark has not gone entirely cold, and Ishalem is a sacred place, a wellspring of magic." He swept a warning gaze around the gathered soldiers. "All of *you*, on the other hand, have much more healing to do."

The Traveler laid his hands across Mateo's body and covered the gaping wound in his side. "He is a good and honorable man. Many like him have died today." Mateo's flesh shimmered as a lambent light built within. Joron closed his large brown eyes and *pushed*. A spark like a lightning bolt surged through him and into the bloody body. The Traveler rocked back and stepped away.

Mateo sucked in a huge breath, like a drowning man coming up for air, and the crowd let out a resounding gasp. Asaddan gave a whistle through the gap in his teeth; Ur-Sikara Kuari muttered an automatic prayer. Omra was rooted in place.

Mateo blinked and sat up, disoriented; he looked at Anjine as if he hadn't seen her in some time. "I've been far . . . far away." The queen wept and held him, swaying back and forth. She kissed his forehead.

But even faced with a miracle, Omra could barely contain his anger. "And now, my Lord, will you heal my soldiers that these Tierran barbarians have slain? Is her grief any greater than mine? You must be fair!"

With tears drying on her cheeks, Anjine was equally incensed. "And all my soldiers that *your* people killed as well! What of all our innocent villagers who died in your raids? All the slaves that died at Gremurr? And what of my little brother Tomas?"

"You are hardly innocent." Omra grimaced and took a step closer. "My brother Tukar, the priestesses at Fashia's Fountain, the thousand victims you beheaded at the wall—"

"*Enough!*" Joron's voice whipped across the hilltop like a tornado. The sound was a physical force that drove Omra back and sent the others reeling.

Ur-Sikara Kuari caught Ciarlo's arm to keep her balance, and he steadied her. "We need to find a different way, Ur-Sikara," Ciarlo said. "Joron is *here*—we cannot lose this opportunity."

Kuari sounded disoriented. "When we first met, I thought you were naïve to suggest that we find common ground and forgive. But now . . ." She gave him a calm, pragmatic smile. "Keeping score of past wrongs cannot help our people—it can only lead to more death."

Neither Queen Anjine nor the soldan-shah backed down. "Holy Joron will punish you," Omra said, as if he could see no one but the queen. "He will stand on the side of the righteous."

"Yes, He will," Anjine said. "And He knows what you have done."

The Traveler regarded the two armies. He sounded drained after healing Mateo, or maybe just discouraged. "Would it be enough if I simply told you all to lay down your arms and make peace?" He crossed his arms over his great chest. "Even now?" An unseen wind continued to blow the Traveler's brown cloak and long hair. As if hearing a distant sound, he cocked his head, glanced up to the sky, and turned to the Oceansea. A genuinely happy smile lit up his face. "Ah, my father approaches! Perhaps you will listen to him."

This announcement caused a great stir. Ciarlo said breathlessly, "*Ondun* is coming?"

Even Omra was taken aback. "He is returning to the world at last?"

Joron's voice held a stern edge. "Yes. Your violence has called him."

122 *The New Arkship*

With a smiling Ondun at the helm, the new Arkship flew across the world's oceans faster than imagination, and the five seahorse-serpents charged forward day and night without rest. The winds of their passage made the rigging ropes hum like the plucked strings on a musical instrument. The Arkship's prow cut a deep gouge in the water and left a wide wake behind them.

Tierran and Uraban sailors crowded on deck, overwhelmed by the cascade of miracles they had witnessed. The ghost ships flanked them, but the spectral vessels kept their distance. The frolicking mer-Saedrans tumbled along in the wake, or sometimes transformed themselves into sleek dolphins to ride the bow waves.

The islands of a previously unknown archipelago came and went with a speed greater than the fastest galloping horse. The skies grew cloudy, and the Arkship dashed into a downpour that drenched them, yet passed as quickly as a splash in a puddle.

Time passed in a blur, and their speed was so great that the night itself lasted only a few hours before the sun rose ahead of them again.

Ystya spent much of her time on deck with him, happy and satisfied. "I don't regret anything, Saan. You did promise you would show me the world—and here it is, all of it."

"I didn't have any idea what I was offering!" Saan vacillated between affection for her and nervousness about who and what she was. He had watched her unleash amazing magic, and he had seen the continent of Terravitae awaken from her very presence. "You were such an innocent girl on your mother's island, helpless, needing to be rescued. I thought I was going to take you away and protect you."

"And love me?" She smiled.

"Yes, and love you. But this isn't like a starstruck romance with a pretty handmaiden. You're the Key to Creation!"

"Yes, but I was always that." She straightened, brushed loose hair out of her face. "Are you afraid to love me now?"

Saan forced a laugh. "Suitors often worry about incurring the displeasure of a girl's father, but in your case that's an altogether different concern. You're *Ondun's* daughter! I hope I never make Him angry at me."

Saan wasn't entirely joking. She chuckled at the idea nevertheless. "So, you're my suitor? Truly?" She flushed, and so did he. She continued in a softer voice, "There's no need for us to rush. It's true that I have a great many new obligations, considering who I am. I never knew how much I could do—and my father needs me. Our magic is stronger together. Once we see your people at Ishalem, he and I will return to Terravitae to search for other survivors of our people."

Spray moistened Saan's face, and he gazed ahead with a wistful smile. Ending this voyage and returning home raised as many uncertainties for him as did the discoveries they had made. Though he longed to stay with Ystya, he also felt a strong pull of

Uraba. "I can't wait to get back home to see my mother, my brothers and sisters, and Soldan-Shah Omra."

And now he also had his real father to consider. . . .

Criston met several times with Saan, anxious to learn more about his mother. Every detail seemed like finding a fleck of gold dust in a stream. "Sadly, you have a great many more stories about her than I do."

"Not necessarily. I know nothing about her life as a young woman, or the village where she lived. She didn't talk much of her past, although she did teach me Tierran." In his son's face, Criston saw hints of his young self—the sailor who had signed aboard the *Luminara* with Captain Shay. He also saw Adrea there.

Though the information was painful to him, Criston listened as Saan described how she had worked for years as a palace slave, how she had saved Omra from an assassination plot, and how she had agreed to marry him to protect her son. "It seems perfectly natural to me now, for I know how well Omra took care of her," Saan said. "She has had a fine life, wealth, respect, but now I can see how hard it must have been for her." His brow furrowed.

"It was a decision she made long ago," Criston forced himself to say. "She can't wish away the last twenty years." Hearing more about Adrea's choice now made him feel as if he were drowning, but he tried not to let Saan see his feelings. At least she was alive. . . .

Finally, the winds died down, the ropes creaked, and the masts seemed to let out a sigh of relief as the strain decreased. Even after pulling the Arkship across half the world, the harnessed seahorse-serpents did not seem exhausted.

Shading his eyes, Aldo could make out the low line of the isthmus ahead. He stood next to Yal Dolicar and Sen Sherufa. "We're here already—we're approaching Ishalem!" The distance they had covered in so short a time seemed impossible. "I've seen so much adventure that all I can think of is getting back to my own family."

Yal Dolicar's grin was infectious. "I feel as if I'm living a wild tale told in a tavern. They'll laugh when I try to convince them what really happened! We've done things so fantastic that even a drunken sailor would never believe them."

"And maybe young and naïve chartsmen wouldn't be fooled either, as I was." Even now, Aldo was embarrassed about how easily he had been duped.

Dolicar gave an embarrassed chuckle and quickly wandered to the other side of the deck.

"I doubt people will accuse us of spinning fantastic stories," Sherufa said. "We have Ondun Himself with us."

The joined crews gathered in the Arkship's broad bow. Ondun raised his head so that the winds blew his gray hair and beard as he regarded the coastline ahead. "So, this is what my sons spotted after their long voyage from Terravitae. The land does look beautiful from here, but I suspect we'll see far too much scarring and bloodshed up close. I'll have to take care of that."

"Is that what our races truly need, my Lord?" Captain Vora asked him, feeling unexpected doubts. "For Ondun Himself to arrive and solve all problems?"

The old man pressed his lips together and pondered for a long time. "Isn't that what the people believe Ondun should do? They've placed me on a very high pedestal, but *imposing* peace and harmony on two continents is beyond any miracle I can perform. Perhaps their own beliefs are strong enough to make them do something positive . . . if I give them the incentive to do it themselves."

By now the Tierrans and Urabans had mixed aboard the Arkship, since the very presence of Ondun facilitated communication. Criston looked at the sailors around him and said, "We're proof that Aidenists and Urecari can work together without rancor, but I fear that once we get back to the battleground, the old wounds will reopen."

Saan felt more optimistic. "Maybe, or maybe not. Without Sikara Fyiri and Prester Hannes to whip us into a frenzy, our crews get along well enough."

The seahorse-serpents pulled toward the coast, and the mer-Saedrans swam alongside the Arkship as escorts. Nearby, the ghost fleet fanned out like a dark navy. Aboard the spectral *Luminara*, Captain Shay raised a blue-and-green Tierran flag high on his mainmast.

As they drew closer to Ishalem, the harbor was in the throes of a fiery battle. Stone emplacements at the harbor mouth held strange black cylinders that roared, spitting fire at Tierran ships that pushed into the port. Peering through his spyglass, Saan saw one of the four overheated tubes explode, spraying metal shards in all directions. Undaunted, the teams at the remaining three weapons kept firing. Saan recognized that they must be using Nunghal fire-powder, but he had never seen such a weapon before.

Even far away, they could hear the faded and tinny sounds of the fray, the clash of metal and screams of men. Ships whose sails bore the Aidenist Fishhook clashed in a free-for-all with an equal number of Uraban warships. The vessels shouldered into one another, hulls grinding against hulls, while grappling hooks and ropes tangled them together. Sailors swarmed back and forth, flailing swords and clubs. At least seven ships were on fire, and flames ran up the rigging ropes as if they were candlewicks.

Ondun scratched his beard, deeply troubled. "I have always considered it best to let humans live their lives and make their decisions, for good or ill. The parent bird must make the fledglings leave the nest and fly on their own." His expression darkened. "But sometimes they need paternal guidance. If we don't put a stop to this, no one will heed the words I have to speak." He loosed the golden harnesses that bound the five seahorse-serpents and shouted to the beasts, "Go and drive those ships apart—stop the fighting!"

Unleashed, the majestic creatures raced into the crowded harbor, rippling the water with the sawblades of their dorsal fins. They leaped and came crashing down, sending a gush of spray in all directions.

The ghost ships also sailed into the fray, nearly outnumbering the embattled navies. The fighters paused to cry out in alarm, sensing the shadow of awe and fear that Captain Shay brought with him as he guided the *Luminara* into the harbor. His vessels were like great sailing ships carved out of thunderclouds.

The silent, eerie fleet cruised expertly into the naval battle. The cannons outside the harbor fired several shots, but the roaring balls caused no damage to the ghost ships. At the head of the shadowy fleet, the *Luminara* shouldered up to the Tierran and Uraban flagships that had been locked in combat. "Cease your fighting!" Shay bellowed. "By the command of Ondun Himself!"

As if the ghost ships hadn't terrified the fighting crewmen enough, the seahorse-serpents rose up between the opposing battleships. The exotic creatures hooted and hissed blasts of steam from their blowholes. The seahorse-serpents rammed Tierran and Uraban vessels alike, snapping the ropes and hooks that bound the ships together. The sailors yelled in terror. While spears and arrows bounced harmlessly off the thick golden scales, the monsters circled, lifting their plated heads high so they sluiced water onto the frightened crewmembers, immediately drenching anyone still engaged in hand-to-hand combat.

The thunderstruck seamen stared as the huge Arkship sailed past them on its way into port. The gigantic vessel towered above the highest mast of the navy flagships. The golden seahorse-serpents cleared a path through the water, like escorts.

When the great ship finally reached the long docks, despite the battle around them, the weary sailors from the *Dyscovera* and *Al-Orizin* cheered, realizing they were back home. Saan stood next to Criston. "I have never seen Ishalem before."

"Neither have I, but I always wanted to." One last cannonball shot into the air, but caused no damage. The ghost ships closed in on the emplacements. Criston shook his head. "This isn't quite how I imagined I would get here, though."

He had meant his comment to be serious, but Saan laughed. "Was *anything* about this voyage what you expected?"

Tears stung Criston's eyes. He reached out to put an arm around his son, the child he had never expected to see. "No, and I'm glad it wasn't."

Even the largest dock was too low to accommodate the Arkship as it came to port, but Ondun created a ramp so He could emerge and step down to the wooden boards. Towering tall, looking like a genuine titan now and filled with power that He drew from Ishalem, Ondun turned to the people on deck, including Ystya. "The rest of you, stay behind for now. There is something I must do." He cocked his head and smiled. "Ah, Joron is already here."

He sniffed the air, seemed to smell the blood and smoke from the battles inside the city. Ondun walked off the pier and set foot in Ishalem at last.

A roar of supernatural thunder rumbled across the sky. Ondun looked up, His eyebrows twitched, and lightning bolts blasted down to strike the tallest buildings, the top of the Urecari church, the turrets that lined the long wall. As He walked forward, the ground beneath his feet trembled, then shook, then lurched from side to side. His robes flapped about in the strong winds that He began to summon.

And He was just getting started. It was going to be a good show. . . .

Part VI

123 *Ishalem, Main Urecari Church*

The stern, dominating Ondun quenched the violence, shut down the battles, and imposed peace.

From the safety of the new Arkship's deck, both crews observed the spectacle of Ondun unleashing the full fury of His powers so as to impress and terrify the two warring sides. Bloody and exhausted, the Tierran and Uraban armies were like two squabbling children forcefully separated from a playground brawl by a stern teacher.

The fighting was over, but the conflict itself was not so easily resolved. The generations-long spiral of hatred went far beyond religious and philosophical differences.

After the ground stopped shaking and the thunderclouds finished pounding and crackling through the sky, Ystya asked Saan to accompany her into Ishalem. "This is your holy city. Show it to me."

From the high deck, Saan looked at the buildings, the immense church of Urec, the docks, the markets and dwellings, even the imposing wall that crossed the isthmus. "I have never seen Ishalem myself."

She took his hand. "Then we'll discover it together."

Disembarking from the Arkship, they walked through the streets and saw the battle damage. Some of the houses had been burned; bloodstains marked the whitewashed walls of buildings; market stalls had been ransacked, fountains toppled.

On a thoroughfare heading toward the center of the city, Saan was delighted to see Ystya's power diffusing into the war-scarred streets: flower boxes began to swell with new pink and yellow blooms; the leaves of mangled shrubs burst into greenery again;

drooping citrus trees straightened and produced clouds of white blossoms. The heady, sweet perfume followed them.

Though the two armies had separated from each other to lick their wounds, catch their breath, and reconsider their hatreds, Ystya found Ondun atop the central hill. The bearded man beside him looked much younger, though he still had a weight of age and power about him.

Ondun waved them closer. "Ah, Ystya—come and meet your brother! Joron has been looking for you a long time."

She brightened and ran forward, while the other man opened his arms to embrace her. Joron rested his chin on the top of Ystya's head. "I was sent out to find you, little sister, and you found me instead."

She looked up at him with her green eyes. "Aiden and Urec are gone, but I'm glad to meet my last brother. It's been a long, hard time."

She introduced Saan, who felt uncharacteristically shy and tongue-tied to be among such powerful beings. "So is the war over then, my Lord?" he asked Ondun.

Ondun wore a wry expression. "The fighting has stopped for a moment, and I've given both sides much to think about. As for the underlying conflict . . . we shall see. My powers of persuasion can do only so much."

While Ystya spent time with her brother and father, Saan headed to the main Uraban army encampment, where he found not only Soldan-Shah Omra but his own mother. Istar saw him first and ran toward Saan, calling out his name. She threw her arms around him and kissed his forehead. "You're back! You're safe! Seeing you is such a bright light in the middle of all this violence and defeat."

Omra looked haggard, but his genuine joy was evident. "The *Al-Orizin* has returned! After so many disappointments, I never expected such good news."

Saan beamed. "I did find the Key to Creation, Father. I brought her here, along with Ondun Himself, although neither is what I anticipated."

Accompanied by Asaddan, his grandfather Imir also trudged up to them, having landed his sand coracles so that his companions could join the camps. The gap-toothed Nunghal grabbed Saan in a bear hug.

"We each have tales enough to tell for years," Imir told him. "There will be time. And . . . Sen Sherufa? Did she return with you?"

Saan laughed. "Yes, she's here, back at the Arkship." Before Saan could say more, his three sisters ran up to welcome him home.

Despite the happy greetings, Saan remained serious. "Both sides here still have much work to do. Our crew and the Tierrans aboard the *Dyscovera* learned to put aside our differences. We worked together, and survived. Uraba and Tierra could do the same. Please think about the future . . . it's a way to save us all."

"I don't know how." Omra looked deflated. So much of his rule of Uraba, and his very existence, had been based on a foundation of hatred against the Aidenists. Now that those props had been taken away, he had to find a new way to balance himself. Tears began to stream down the soldan-shah's face, and he hugged Saan. "But if Ondun commands it, I will have to learn."

When the young man stepped back, Istar was staring at him, intense emotions playing across her face. "And Criston . . . Captain Vora? I read in the journal that you found each other. Did you get my message? Do you know who he is?"

Saan smiled. "He's my father. I know him well enough now, but there is much we still need to say to each other. He's a good man. I can see why you loved him long ago."

Omra turned away as if he could not survive another psychological blow.

"Did he come with you?" Istar asked. "Is he here?"

"Yes, he's safe aboard the ship. Ondun said . . ." Saan paused and shook his head. "There's too much to resolve here first. Don't worry, Mother. You'll see him, I promise."

Ondun granted both sides a day to catch their breath, then He and Holy Joron summoned the leaders of Tierra and Uraba to the new church; the command left no room for argument.

For his entire life Omra had listened to sikaras talk about how Ondun would someday return . . . but it had always been just a story. His father Imir had been taught the same thing, and Soldan-Shah Shieltar before him, and Soldan-Shah Untra before him, all the way back to when Urec and his crew discovered Uraba.

After what he had suffered, after witnessing firsthand the scope of Aidenist barbarity, the soldan-shah had always assumed that when Ondun did come back, He would immediately throw His support to the virtuous side, the Urecari side, and denounce the enemy. Wasn't it obvious that the followers of Urec were right?

And yet in the midst of the climactic battle, Omra had felt like a dog on a leash, bounding toward a hare only to be brought up short. He had watched Holy Joron raise a man from the dead, had watched the towering spectacle of Ondun's return, the thunderclaps and shaking earth, the amazing Arkship that arrived in Ishalem harbor. The titanic figures of Holy Joron and Ondun were exactly as the stories described.

But so much did not make sense. Ondun seemed just as supportive of the Aidenists. He and Holy Joron asked them all to forget the tragedies of the past. Even Ur-Sikara Kuari seemed to be cordial with the itinerant Aidenist prester Ciarlo—Istar's *brother*!

How could the soldan-shah refuse what Ondun Himself requested? How could he not agree to change?

All the parties met in the huge worship hall of the main Urecari church. Soldan Vishkar now wore bandages beneath a clean new olba; he looked haggard after the recent naval battles, and at the other end of the table, his opponent, Comdar Torin Rief, looked just as battered.

The Aidenist military commander sat near a pale Queen Anjine; she seemed just as confused by the turn of events as he himself was. Next to the queen's large chair sat military commander Mateo Bornan, the man she obviously loved—the man Omra had killed with a spear thrust. . . . The man Joron had raised from the dead.

Saan and Istar sat with the soldan-shah and Imir at one end of the long convocation table. Saan insisted on bringing two of his loyal sailors, a reef diver from Lahjar named Grigovar and the shrewd confidence man Yal Dolicar, whose hand Omra had ordered lopped off before sending him aboard the *Al-Orizin*. Asaddan and Khan Jikaris also joined them, representing the Nunghals, though they had remained at the fringes of this war. The Saedrans, including King Sonhir, also sat in the room, apart from either side.

Once all the parties had gathered, Ondun stood, flanked by Holy Joron and Ystya, the Key to Creation. Any one of those beings would have been sufficient to defeat whole armies, and together the three could reshape the world, if they wished. Cowed, Omra and Anjine would listen, knowing the fates of their lands would depend on how they reacted to Ondun's commands.

To make such a change went against the grain of everything Omra had lived for decades . . . and yet he and the Tierran queen would have to do exactly that.

The old man's voice boomed out with the potential to crack stone and bring down the whole church. "My sons Aiden and Urec sailed to these lands to find the Key to Creation, and a new hope. They founded your civilizations before they returned to Terravitae at the end of their lives. My son Joron also came here and spent centuries quietly instructing you through his stories." He shot a lightning-bolt stare at Omra, then at Queen Anjine. "This is not how I expected to return to the world, but neither of your peoples understood the legacy I left. This has gone on long enough."

Ciarlo said to Ur-Sikara Kuari, "If we truly believe, then we have to do as Ondun commands."

Kuari nodded. "Yes, it must be so."

But the soldan-shah was surprised by Ondun's words. Where had He been during the earthquake that leveled Arikara and killed thousands? Why had He not stopped the slaughter of priestesses at Fashia's Fountain? Or the inferno of Olabar harbor? He seemed so . . . innocent. "My Lord, festering wounds live within every Uraban's heart. If you are Ondun, then you know *all* the crimes the Aidenists have committed."

Anjine would not let the matter rest either. "How can I ask my people to ignore the Urecari raids on their villages? The kidnappings? The execution of Prester-Marshall Baine and the workers who came to rebuild Ishalem? And how am I to forgive the man who murdered my brother?"

Omra kept his gaze on Ondun's. "And what about justice for *my* brother Tukar? And for the thousand innocents Tierrans beheaded outside the Ishalem wall?"

"You will both be silent! Are you so stubborn that even miracles won't change your minds?" The whole church trembled, and Ondun's presence swelled so that the chamber no longer seemed large enough to contain Him. He looked like a terrifying vengeful god. "After so much pain and hurt, no one knows how to calculate all the retribution owed to each side, and so I say the balance is paid in full." He looked at them all, as if daring them to challenge Him.

"Both of your faiths know who I am. *I am Ondun*—I can turn your swords to dust. I can flatten your cities into rubble." His eyes were fiery; his hair crackled with static electricity. The walls trembled, and candle flames flickered. "Remember your own stories! If I created the world, do you doubt that I can just as easily destroy it? If you don't cease your fighting, I *will* wipe the slate clean and start again with children who do not disappoint me so much."

When He stopped speaking, the echoing silence in the worship chamber sounded just as thunderous. All those present fell into a terrified awe. The soldan-shah looked at the Tierran queen. She returned his scrutiny, both of them wavering.

Mateo placed a hand on Anjine's arm. "They brought me back for you, Anjine. One miracle should have been enough to change your mind, and they've provided many miracles. You are a strong queen, and you've endured much. But are you strong enough to forgive?"

"It's so much to ask," Anjine rasped.

"Is forgiveness harder than continuing this war? Harder than seeing so many others die needlessly? Do you want this conflict to continue and continue until our child takes the crown? Or would you rather have peace?" Mateo leaned close, and his sad words were for Anjine alone, but in the crystal silence of the great chamber everyone could hear him. "Remember the hurt you felt when I died, Anjine. Remember the pain when you learned of Tomas's death. Each man who died on the battlefield—Tierran or Uraban—left behind someone who hurt as much as you did. Repeated cuts don't make the pain go away."

Unexpectedly, Istar grabbed the ceremonial sword from the soldan-shah's side and threw it to the floor of the church with a great clatter. "It's the decision you know you have to make, Omra."

Anjine closed her eyes, and defeated tears squeezed out as she lifted her own sword and let it fall to the floor as well. "I promised I would do anything to have you back, Mateo."

Watching this, Ondun said, "Good! Now I can return to Terravitae."

*

Saan had witnessed the proceedings with more fascination than fear. He thought he knew Ondun's character; he had even (though he could barely believe it) engaged in genuine conversations with Him. Knowing what he did, the convocation in the main church had seemed like nothing more than a theatrical show. While Ondun delivered a terrifying performance—as he had proved when he quashed the hostilities in Ishalem—Saan couldn't believe that He would carry through on the grave threat of total destruction. It didn't match what the old man had told them, or what Ystya would allow.

Leaving the flurry of confused and intimidated people inside the church, Saan stepped outside. Grigovar and Yal Dolicar joined him under a tall arched entryway above the stone steps.

While in the crowded church, Dolicar had kept his expression studiously unreadable, but when they were alone, a grin spread across his face. "Ondun told us in Terravitae that He *didn't* actually create the world, as the legend says. He said that He doesn't have such tremendous powers, that He believes in a creator far more powerful than Himself—He's just a great sorcerer."

Grigovar was troubled. "Now He claims otherwise. How do we know which is true?"

With a bright smile, Saan looked at his friends. "Ondun used their own beliefs against them. Until now, the absolute certainty of both Aidenists and Urecari drove them to kill each other. Ondun turned their faith into His own weapon and used it to make peace."

Grigovar scratched his dark hair, wrestling with what he now understood. "So Ondun was just . . . bluffing?" He kept his voice low and glanced around, afraid someone had heard him.

Yal Dolicar let out a guffaw. "A wholesale bluff, and He didn't blink once! I recognize a great scheme when I see one."

Saan, however, downplayed the joke. "It doesn't matter whether the threat was real or not. Ondun succeeded in what He needed to do. It's still all about faith. If the followers of Aiden and Urec truly *believe*, then they'll have to find common ground."

124 *Ishalem Harbor*

She longed to see Criston, and she had to face him. He was alive after all these years, yet he seemed to be a ghost in her memory, a wisp of a pleasant dream from long, long ago. Her husband . . . her true husband, in the eyes of Aiden, as she had always believed. Though her heart was torn, Istar quickened her step. She had not told Omra where she was going, but she didn't have to.

The ground had shifted beneath them all, Tierrans and Urabans alike. Istar had seen Queen Anjine struggle with similar shackles of hatred. Over the past day, she had watched Omra reel from so much loss, with the fall of God's Barricade and the defeat of his armies. But worse than any defeat was the obligation to forgive. He was like a man with broken legs learning how to walk again.

The soldan-shah had a land to rule, a people to command, but Istar sensed he was as worried about this Tierran sea captain as about the crises across Uraba. When he saw her depart for the harbor with Saan, he *knew*. She could see it in his eyes: one more crushing loss for him.

But she could not simply toss him aside. Omra was part of her life now, and he had been *most* of her life. Nevertheless, she had to go to the ship. She needed to have a private reunion with Criston Vora; they deserved that chance. Istar swallowed, but her throat remained dry. She could feel her heart pounding in her chest.

"Captain Vora promised to wait for us at the end of the pier," Saan said brightly, startling her tangled thoughts. As they walked along the scarred streets toward the waterfront, the young man spilled his adventures and his excitement about Ystya in a flood of words. He was pleased to accept both of his fathers, and now Omra, Criston, and Istar herself had to deal with that. Ondun had commanded them all to resolve their differences.

The new Arkship dominated the docks of Ishalem harbor, a tall vessel that looked as if it had been carved out of precious metal, far superior to anything a Uraban, Tierran, or Nunghal shipwright could construct.

Istar's legs felt wobbly, and each step seemed mechanical, as if her body was moving of its own accord through a great wind that pulled her forward and pushed her back at the same time.

She looked up. There, at the end of the cobblestone street that ended at the docks, a man stood at the edge of a pier. Though she hadn't seen Criston for more than twenty years, she recognized him instantly. He'd been a young and dream-filled man who sailed off aboard the *Luminara*—her husband, the love of her life, the man to whom she had given her heart so many years before.

Ciarlo told her that dear Criston had waited for her, never forgotten his love, refused to remarry, dutifully written her a letter once a year, cast each bottle into the sea in hopes that the merciful tides would deliver it. . . .

Oh, Criston!

She found herself running without even realizing it, pulling away from Saan, who stood back, grinning. At the dock, Criston perked up like a wilted flower revived by a quenching rain. "Criston!" she cried. "It *is* you!"

He opened his arms and swept her into a great hug. "Adrea, I never thought I'd see you again."

Then they were talking in a rush of words, and she let the warmth of his voice blanket her. It was as if she had crossed over a bridge that led twenty years into the past, and she was barely nineteen again, recently married and madly in love. Because her sailor husband had been so passionate about exploring the world, Adrea had let him go away so that she could keep his heart. When he'd sailed from Calay, heading west, she never guessed it was a nearly permanent farewell. She never had a chance to tell Criston that he had a son. But he and Saan had found each other anyway.

Criston was telling her about the sinking of the *Luminara* and how he had clung to the wreckage, holding on to his memory of her and surviving just so he could get back to Windcatch . . . only to find it burned and devastated, his mother dead, his wife gone.

When Adrea thought back to the raid, nightmare memories returned with the pain and hate she had buried over the years. In those memories, Omra was a monster who killed her friends and relatives, a man who seized Adrea and wrenched her away from her happy life.

She felt the strength of Criston's arms around her, inhaled deeply of the scent of his shirt, his hair. Behind the beard and the weathered skin of his face, she still recognized the young man she had married. The two of them had sworn their vows and linked symbolic fishhooks in the Aidenist kirk, with Prester Fennan blessing them.

That past was like a fireside tale, and she had lived it over and over again in her dreams. But this was no song or story. She had truly lived it—and all those things had indeed been taken from her. She'd been lost and off course for two decades. And now he had come back.

"I know you didn't forget me, Criston," she whispered. "I received one of your letters. It . . . saved me. And I've kept it all these years."

He caught his breath. "One of them made it to you?"

"Yes, and—" She couldn't talk anymore as tears streamed down her face.

Saan came up to them. "Are you two just going to stand there all day?" He glanced at Criston with a mischievous smile. "I thought I told you everything you needed to know about her?"

"Oh no, not by far." He kept holding her. "We have more than twenty years to catch up on."

"Twenty years . . ." she said. "You've met Saan, but I also have daughters. They're here in Ishalem, they came aboard the sand coracles. And . . ." Istar braced herself. "And there is someone else I need you to meet."

The provisional governor's villa in Ishalem had been ransacked during the Tierran army's invasion. Many of the silken hangings had been torn down, the curtains trampled, floor tiles cracked, marble pillars chipped, statues toppled. Soldiers and citizens, including a contingent of uneasy Aidenists that Queen Anjine had assigned to the duty, made quick work of the mess, sweeping away the debris and erasing the most prominent marks of the battle.

When Istar led Criston into the main chamber that the soldan-shah had claimed as his administration office, Omra set aside all of his business and fixed them with his dark eyes.

"So, this is your sea captain—the one you never speak of." Omra looked at her with a mixture of jealousy, sadness, and regret. She actually read *defeat* on his face. She had never seen the man so . . . lost.

Criston tensed, but she drew him along, facing Omra. "I have brought you together for a reason."

"I never pretended that you had forgotten about him," the soldan-shah said. "I'm not that naïve." Not only had his whole world changed with the return of Ondun and the imposed cessation of hostilities between Tierra and Uraba, but now he seemed convinced that he would lose his First Wife as well.

Criston straightened as if drawing strength from the very ground beneath his feet. He had sailed around the world, fought storms and sea monsters, discovered Terravitae, and delivered Ondun to Ishalem. But this challenge seemed even more difficult for him. "You are the man who took Adrea from me. Your raiders burned my village. You killed my mother."

Omra met his gaze and did not deny the accusation. "I did. And you, personally, did nothing to me. Now Ondun says we must all forgive . . . but I have no right to ask it of you."

Criston faced the man, and Istar knew they were both thinking of the decades of life, and love, the soldan-shah had had with her that he didn't deserve. "You also raised and protected my son. You gave him a chance, treated him as your own," Criston said, his voice cracking. "You didn't kill my wife when you could have. Because of what you did, Soldan-Shah Omra, they are alive before me now, however different they may be from what I expected." Tears hung in his blue eyes. "That is far better than weeping by a grave marker on a hill."

Omra rose, looking at Criston with tremendous respect. "I can see why you have loved this man, Istar. I can see that he truly meant all those words he wrote to you."

Istar's cheeks were wet, but she did not wipe the tears away. Suddenly she blinked, startled by what he had said. "You . . . know about the letter?"

Omra nodded. His voice was leaden. "You didn't think I ever found it . . . but I read this man's words years ago. For a long time, I have known who Criston Vora is."

She felt as if the tiled floor had dropped out from beneath her feet. Omra had known all this time?

He lowered his head. "I understand how much you still love this man, and that you only tolerated me. I inflicted terrible harm on your village, and I took you away as a spoil of war. As soldan-shah, I had the power to hold you prisoner in Olabar, but I could never force you to love me." He stepped forward, close to them, and rested a hand on Saan's shoulder, squeezed it, then let go. "Even so, I hope I treated you well enough. I did my best, but how can I compete with your true husband and Saan's true father?" He drew a deep breath and bowed. "Ondun commanded that I wipe the slate clean."

Criston looked at her with surprise and hope, and Adrea—Istar—felt her heart swell. She looked at him, reeled for a moment . . . then turned toward the soldan-shah.

He had been her husband for two decades. Though he was not Saan's biological father, Omra had raised the young man as his own and loved him as much as any father possibly could. And he was the father of Adreala and Istala. She couldn't simply discard her daughters.

Criston was a distant, romantic dream she'd clung to, but Omra had been there for her, year after year. Though he was proud and powerful, he sought her advice, gave her a home and safety. Omra had been her reality, a solid anchor, a man who respected and revered her, even though it caused him many political difficulties.

She stood between the two men now, unconsciously stretching her arms out as if to hold on to both. "You are tearing me apart, both of you."

"Adrea—" Criston began, then stopped, letting his eyes say everything that was in his heart.

She found herself weeping. "Criston, you will always be my first love, and I will always love you. We can imagine the perfect life we would have had." She straightened. "But that didn't happen. To be truly whole and alive, a woman must have dreams, but she must also have reality. Life is life, and it has been twenty years. I have moved on—though not of my own accord, that is the way the currents carried me.

"I spent years with Omra. He protected me, took care of me . . . and, yes, loved me. We have two beautiful daughters and an adopted one." She felt dizzy, but forced herself to go on. "I did not choose this man, but fate gave me a life with him."

She reached out to stroke Criston's cheek. He seemed a mass of despair. "You've lived with the dream of me all this time, but I am more than a few strands of golden hair. Omra has lived with the reality, as have I."

Criston closed his eyes against her words and remained silent for a long moment. "I was . . . ready for this. I understand. I'll always have a part of you in my heart and my imagination—and I still have a few strands of your hair left."

Saan, who had watched his mother struggle with her decision, lifted his chin and spoke loudly. "Well, *I* don't have to choose between you. You've each been my father in your own way, and I accept you both."

125 *Ishalem*

The ghost ships felt the eerie and irresistible call to return to their seaweed purgatory far out at sea. The crews had said their farewells to their former lives. Even Ondun was not keen to arouse anger in the ancient underwater titan, and so Captain Shay took his last leave of Criston. The shadowy ships cruised away from Ishalem harbor, accompanied by clouds and storm winds. . . .

When Ondun was ready to return to Terravitae, crowds gathered on the piers. The followers of both Urec and Aiden had all been chastised into good behavior (for the time being). Before He climbed aboard the huge Arkship, He summoned His golden seahorse-serpents and harnessed the majestic gold-scaled creatures to the vessel. They hooted from their blowholes, restless to be off.

Joron the Traveler walked to the end of the pier where his bearded father stood with the ethereal beauty of Ystya. Joron said, "Though I miss Terravitae, I will remain here, Father. Tierra and

Uraba are my home now—and have been for centuries. I don't know if anyone is left back there."

"That is why Ystya and I must search," Ondun said. "Watch over these people, my son. I don't envy you the task."

Joron simply shook his head. "They will take care of themselves. I'll just become a wandering hermit again and slip quietly among them."

Much to Saan's disappointment, Ystya had decided to return with her father so that she could explore the continent that had been the home of her people. "It's Terravitae, and it's where I belong, Saan. I need to go back . . . just as I understand why you need to stay here, at least for now." Her eyes were filled with longing and difficult decisions.

"I'll miss you, and I want to be with you," Saan said. "You've shown me so much magic that I believe anything is possible now. But there's so much damage that needs to be healed in Uraba . . . and the land of Tierra is also part of me. I can't just sail away again. Not yet."

"I know." Her face shone with contentment now that she had reached her decision. "But it's all right. I'll be around for a long time. I hope you will come to me. The whole world waits for you."

"I'll find a way to return to Terravitae—I promise. Somebody has to lead other ships there."

Beside them, Criston reached out to clap his son on the shoulder. "*We* will. Now that the war is over, think of how much time, energy, and money our two lands can use for exploration."

Saan embraced Ystya, but withdrew awkwardly as he noted Ondun looming over them. Self-conscious, he tried to give her a chaste hug, but Ystya threw her arms around Saan and gave him a passionate kiss. Her lips sparkled, and he felt that she had just placed an entire season of springtime inside his heart. He swayed and almost begged to go with her after all, but he stepped back to stand with his father.

"We know the way now," Criston said. "The Saedrans have their Mappa Mundi, but I kept my own charts. When our lands begin to recover, we can set our course."

"I will see you again, Ystya," Saan said.

Ondun addressed the people who had gathered on the waterfront. "There is much work to do here. Put your own house in order. Once Tierrans and Urabans learn to cooperate and support one another, you will be welcome anywhere in the unexplored world." He lowered his voice, looked directly at Saan and Criston. "I expect to see you soon, Captains."

Ondun strode up the ramp to board the new Arkship, and Ystya blew Saan a kiss before running to join her father.

The seahorse-serpents strained at their filigreed harnesses and pulled the vessel away from the dock and out to sea. The magnificent Arkship sailed away toward the horizon.

126 *Ishalem*

Dust-smeared work teams cleared the rubble at God's Barricade. They dragged splintered timbers from the gate, used levers and ropes to load the debris into carts that were hauled away by weary-looking ponies. Grim volunteers, including Tierrans, retrieved the bodies of those killed in the explosion or slain by the long-range Alamont bows. Every worker wrapped a cloth around his nose and mouth as a meager defense against the increasing stench.

After much discussion and argument, followed by grudging acquiescence, the men did not separate the corpses into Aidenist or Urecari piles. One large funeral pyre would suffice for all the dead.

When the workers uncovered Kel Unwar's body under the stone

blocks, they called Soldan-Shah Omra. He tugged the end of his olba over his face and stood looking down at the corpse. Unwar had been a faithful servant who accomplished great things because his soldan-shah demanded it, and now it tore at Omra's heart to think that the kel had died with the taste of failure on his lips. The last thing Unwar had seen was his wall crashing down and the enemy army surging into the holy city.

Omra stared down at the poor man, shaking his head. "I'm sorry, my friend. I am not disappointed in you. Your canal and this wall are worthy monuments that only history can measure. You proved that my people can indeed achieve anything." He lowered his voice. "You give me hope that I can accomplish something even more difficult—keeping peace with the Aidenists. Now that I think about it, your job might have been easier than mine."

The flames of the large funeral pyre rose high and bright as a signal to departing Ondun that both sides had agreed to do at least this one thing together. Fresh breezes blew the smoke and stench out to sea.

However, Omra did not consider the pyre appropriate for Kel Unwar. He stepped away and shouted an order to his uniformed men. "This was his wall. Bury him here and stack the stones high, so he will always be part of it."

A soldier rushed up, his face ruddy and flushed. "Soldan-Shah, we found another body—you will want to see it."

Omra had already seen enough bodies as he inspected the city, but something about the soldier's expression made him decide to follow. Farther down the wall, he saw a dark-robed figure sprawled among the tumbled stone blocks, and he felt an instinctive chill of fear. "Is it . . . ?"

The soldier moved the hood aside to reveal the polished but now dented silver mask that had struck terror into the hearts of so many *ra'vir* trainees. Omra knelt down.

The enigma of this frightening and mysterious man had filled his mind for two decades, ever since Unwar and the disguised stranger had approached him with the suggestion of turning impressionable Tierran children into saboteurs. Even Omra had never seen the Teacher's face; he wasn't sure he wanted to know. The silver mask was slightly askew on the corpse.

Not wishing the soldiers to notice his hesitation, Omra plucked off the silver mask and gazed into the dead face of a Uraban man with a cleft chin and a swollen lip; a mole stood out high on his left cheek, just below the eye. His shaggy hair needed to be cut.

Omra had no idea who he was.

He straightened. "Take away the mask and robe and destroy them, then add the body to the funeral pyre, just like any other soldier. The Teacher is no more. That is all we need to know."

She entered the main church through the imposing open gates, passed into the worship chamber that had recently held representatives of all factions in the convocation where Ondun had imposed peace.

Alisi could not understand why He had not demanded retribution for the numerous crimes that had been committed upon Uraba. If Ondun was so powerful, if He watched over all humankind, why had He done nothing after she was kidnapped as a young girl, raped, and beaten?

When she fought the Aidenists, she had always known her place. When she unleashed her *ra'virs* to murder and destroy anything the Tierrans loved, she felt satisfied, confident that Ondun would approve. And now . . .

Alisi did not know how to be wrong, but she had given a promise to her brother as his life faded. She could think of only one thing to do.

She had carefully re-dressed the arrow wound in her chest, binding it so that it could heal. There were so many injured in Ishalem that her wounds would draw no attention. She posed as a middle-aged woman who had lost her husband—and Alisi *was* a widow, in the sense that everything she cared about had died. She needed something else.

So she entered the now-empty Urecari church. People would come back to the faith soon enough, searching for how to accept this new reality that redefined their beliefs. When she asked an acolyte if she could speak to Ur-Sikara Kuari, the willowy girl led her to the anteroom.

Alisi bowed for the leader of what remained of the church. "Ur-Sikara, thank you for seeing me. I have a request."

Kuari studied her features and measured her up and down with an even gaze while Alisi averted her eyes out of respect. "All are welcome here in the church. How might I help you?"

"I am lost, and the path of Urec will guide me. I want to become a sikara."

"It is no longer just the path of Urec." Kuari pursed her lips. "Since so many priestesses left the church after Ondun came, I'd be happy to accept you among our recruits for the church of Ondun. But the Golden Fern is a spiral—are you so sure it will take you where you need to go?"

When Alisi straightened, the arrow wound gave her a jolt of pain, but she did not show the twinge. "I am completely convinced, Ur-Sikara. This is exactly what I need to do."

127 Ishalem

Comdar Rief remained in Ishalem with strict instructions to help the Urabans repair the damage the armies had done. He turned his soldiers into engineers, and they labored with the materials at hand to reshape the holy city. The naval crews worked to fix both Tierran and Uraban ships in the harbor; some of the vessels battered by cannon fire had to be scuttled out in the Oceansea, but most were repaired for an eventual return to their home ports.

Across the city, the Aidenist army had pitched their tents and marked out neighborhoods, claiming part of Ishalem as their own. Soldan-Shah Omra had granted them an entire district where they could make their homes, and many freed Tierran prisoners from the work camps chose to stay there as settlers instead of slaves. . . .

At the western mouth of Kel Unwar's great canal, Sherufa and Aldo met King Sonhir's mer-Saedrans as they came ashore to see the city. Kjelnar stood with the undersea people, looking out of place, though the big Iborian would always be one of them.

"I've studied the blockage from underwater," said Kjelnar. "It will take quite an effort to break apart the sunken ironclads and remove the wreckage so ships can sail through the canal again."

"The mer-Saedrans can complete the work much more easily than land-dwellers would," Sonhir said. "Ondun asked us all to work together."

"We are grateful for your help," Aldo said.

Sen Sherufa asked, "It will certainly facilitate trade from the soldanates to the Oceansea . . . but why would you be interested in that?"

Kjelnar laughed, glancing at King Sonhir. "It's not trade we're interested in. With the canal open, the mer-Saedrans can swim through and explore the whole Middlesea! An entirely new territory where they've—where *we've* never been."

"We did hear the words of Ondun," Sonhir added. "Our race has always been content with our sunken continent, but we should explore and discover, too. The Middlesea sounds intriguing."

Sonhir's daughters had been frolicking in the waters of the canal, and they came ashore, dripping, their diaphanous clothes clinging to lissome bodies. Giggling, they circled Aldo. "We showed you our city, Aldo—now you show us yours!"

He fidgeted. "You tried to drown me when you dragged me underwater."

"But we kissed you, and then you were fine." One of the girls startled him by darting forward to kiss him again.

Two more of the mer-king's daughters embraced him, but he stepped back beside Sen Sherufa as if she could protect him. "No more of that! I am close to Calay now. I want to go home to see my wife and children again."

"That's still far away," sniffed one of the young women. "They'll never know."

"Don't spoil the fun!" said another. King Sonhir seemed amused by his daughters' behavior.

Sherufa took pity on her fellow chartsman and said in a placating voice, "Now, I'm not familiar with Ishalem myself, but I can find out what we should see. We'll all go together."

As a group, they walked to the new Urecari church, up the Arkship Hill, along the stone wall of God's Barricade, and to the Saedran District where they saw candlemakers, clock workers, physicians, architects, and scientists.

Sonhir's daughters were at first excited by the exotic sights, but after a few hours they grew footsore and bored. Aldo and Sherufa led them back to the harbor's edge, where the girls sprang into the water and swam about, teasing Aldo to join them, but he remained on the pier. "Thank you, but now that I have solid ground under my feet again, I intend to keep it that way."

King Sonhir swam to meet his daughters, treading lightly on the surface. "Our invitation stands for you to rejoin the mer-Saedrans, and we would welcome you at any time. You two could be the first Saedrans to return where you belong."

"I appreciate the gracious offer," Aldo said, "but I belong here."

After the long voyage aboard the *Al-Orizin* and landing in Ishalem, Sen Sherufa longed to be back in her familiar house in Olabar with her own furniture, her own kitchen, and her own sedentary activities. She wanted to sit and read Saedran books, write descriptions of her travels, jot down her thoughts, talk to her neighbors, go to her temple, and live a contented and fulfilled existence. She had never wanted adventures, yet she had more than enough to last her a lifetime. Exploring the world was for other people . . . and yet she had been forced into it.

Once she made her way back to Olabar, the Saedrans would cheer her return and listen to her stories. All that attention would be embarrassing, and with so much bustle going on all around, her home would not be nearly as quiet as even a cramped cabin aboard the sailing ship. But she would make do.

After her many experiences across the world, Sherufa most looked forward to sharing evenings with the former soldan-shah. Imir was always good company, and she sought him out now.

On her first adventure years ago, she had traveled with him down to Arikara, and flew in a sand coracle across the Great Desert to the Nunghal lands. Imir had kept her company and protected her, and he would be a good traveling companion along civilized roads back to Olabar.

When she reached the large settlement of the Uraban army, she was surprised to see all the tents erected near where the sand coracles had been tied down, their sacks deflated and stored. It reminded her of a Nunghal camp.

She asked other soldiers about the former soldan-shah, and followed their directions to one of the main tents. She called out, "Imir, are you in there?"

She heard movement in the tent, and the flap moved aside. The former soldan-shah stepped out, blinking in the bright light. In one hand he held a platter of pastries and cheese, as if she had caught him in the middle of snacking. When he saw her, he nearly dropped the platter onto the ground, caught it just in time. "Sherufa, my dear, you have returned!"

Standing in front of the tent, Sherufa mused, "I see you find ways to relax, Imir, even after a war and a disaster."

"It's not relaxing, my dear—it's regaining my energy." He looked around for a place to put the platter and finally just set it on the ground. "We've been working without rest for many weeks."

She eyed him up and down. "I can see that. You look much more fit and trim than I remembered."

Despite her teasing tone, Imir's face was serious; his eyes even glistened with tears. "I'm so glad you've come safely back to Uraba."

She embraced him with more warmth than she had intended. Behind Imir, three girls roiled out of the tent, Adreala, Istala, and Cithara. They had been playing a game during midday meal, and now they swarmed around her.

Moments later, Khan Jikaris shouldered them aside, smiling like a starstruck boy. He spoke in clumsy accented Uraban. "The lovely woman comes back to us!" As soon as Sherufa stepped away from the former soldan-shah to acknowledge him, Jikaris swept her into a bear hug and kissed her full on the lips. "You are even more beautiful than I remembered from when you were in my lands."

A flush of embarrassment burned her cheeks, and Imir scowled. "Enough of that, Jikaris. Let the woman breathe."

"Why should she breathe, when I am breathless?" Jikaris laughed at his wordplay. "You come to Ishalem, but I take you back across the Great Desert. We will fly away in sand coracles." He grasped Sherufa's hand and pulled her toward him, though she resisted. "You will join my wives."

"I will do no such thing," she said.

Imir was shocked by the khan's boldness, but the Nunghal was persistent. "We have another month or two before the winds turn. And even then, we're in no hurry." He smiled at Sherufa. "We will go whenever you are ready."

"I didn't say I'd ever be ready."

Imir felt obliged to defend her. He took Sherufa's arm. "You have to wait your turn, Jikaris. I've wanted this fine woman as my wife for years. I have asked her to marry me again and again."

The khan sniffed. "Then you already have your answer."

Imir gazed at Sherufa with great passion. "Now that the khan has raised the question, my dear, why not put an end to this uncertainty once and for all? Choose me, and I will make you happy."

Jikaris was indignant. "I own much more land than this retired old man. I have more buffalo than there are stars in the sky. I have all the plains that we could roam. You must choose me."

Sherufa began to think she should have stayed in Terravitae. This wasn't at all the discussion she had expected.

Imir opened his mouth to continue the argument, but she would tolerate no further questions. She extricated her arm from his grasp and stepped away from both men. "Why does everyone assume I must be married to be happy? I've done quite well all my life." She glared at them both, then softened her voice. "I adore you, Imir. We can be happy together, but I refuse to be your wife, as much as I refuse to be the khan's. Why can't you just leave it at that?"

Imir was taken aback, speechless, and finally gave Sherufa a foolish smile of defeat and acquiescence, as if he had just lost a game of *xaries*. "All right, my dear. I'll just leave it at that."

128 Calay

After a tiring journey north, Queen Anjine led part of the Tierran army back to Calay. At some point, as the two lands took their first steps toward open trade and travel, she would appoint an emissary to the Uraban capital of Olabar.

For now, though, she merely wanted to go home. . . .

For the last leg of the trip, she donned the fine armor that Ammur Sonnen had crafted for her, although her pregnancy would soon prevent her from wearing it. The blue-and-green Tierran banners had been patched so they flew bright and proud again from the staffs of her standard-bearers. She rode beside Mateo, and Jenirod accompanied them, though the queen longed for time alone with the man she loved. Jenirod was neither blind nor a fool, although right now he was being an unintentional pest.

As the group came together up the last hill that overlooked the inlets, bridges, brick buildings, smithies, kirks, marketplaces, and the castle, Anjine paused to drink in the sight. To her tired eyes, Calay was far more beautiful than Ishalem could ever be. "Oh, Mateo, did home always look like this?"

He sat high on his horse and breathed deeply. "Yes, my Queen, it was always like this. But sometimes it takes a new perspective for us to notice what was there all along."

Jenirod said with a laugh, "I have a new perspective, as well. By now, Majesty, you and I might have been married. But that would never have been right. You'd have grown to hate me—or worse, *resent* me. No, this is how it should be." He shifted in his saddle. "Oh, don't feel sorry for me, Majesty. I'll go back to Erietta, where there are more young maidens than I can count. At least one of them should be glad to have me." His voice had a hint of his old smugness.

"No doubt." Anjine's lips quirked in a smile.

The reminder of her ill-advised betrothal was strange to her. She had originally dispatched messengers to Erietta to accept the marriage proposal with Jenirod not because she felt anything for him, but because Tierra needed a queen, and a king, and an heir.

That fact remained unchanged. How she wanted it to be Mateo at her side as she made her decisions. She longed for him to be there to help raise their son or daughter, to think of the people and of Tierra.

"And you two can't fool me." Jenirod looked at her and Mateo. "You haven't fooled many others in the army either. I doubt there's a man among your troops who hasn't seen how you look at each other."

Anjine was embarrassed into silence, but Mateo was serious. He had spoken briefly with her about their future, but it wasn't the heart-to-heart talk they needed. "Anjine, we've been like two people running through the forest with blindfolds on. All the years we've been together, the friendship we've shared—"

She cut him off. "*I* know we belong together, Mateo—you don't have to convince me. We've been through so much. And my baby will need its father in order to be brought up as the next ruler of Tierra."

Mid-swig from his water skin, Jenirod sputtered and spit up in spite of himself. "A child? Well, I suppose that is no surprise either, my Queen. I can be very observant, and now many little things make sense."

Mateo fretted, ignoring the other man. "But you know we cannot marry, Majesty. I am just a soldier, a guard. With the new peace, there are vital political considerations . . . maybe a Uraban soldan would be the best choice. You have to think of Tierra."

She gave a rude snort. "Ondun gave both lands sufficient incentive to get along with each other. I don't need to marry a Uraban to remind myself. If I'm the queen, I can do whatever I like—and marry the man *I* choose."

"By the Fishhook, it's about time you two realized that," Jenirod said.

"How will the people ever accept me as being worthy of the queen?"

Before Anjine could answer, Jenirod made a rude noise. "Why, Mateo Bornan—you've been directly blessed by Holy Joron, saved from death by divine power! Who could possibly suggest you aren't a fitting husband for our queen? And, Majesty, if you believe

Tierrans would object to you two getting married, and for such a silly reason, then—sorry to be blunt—you don't really understand your people at all."

From behind them, the rest of the army ranks streamed past, but the trio sat their horses, gazing down into the city and the harbor. "I do want to be happy, Mateo," she said. "Is that so much to ask?"

Mateo reached out to take her hand. "If you're sure the people will agree?"

"They will agree," Anjine answered.

With a justified smile, Jenirod spurred his horse and rode ahead of them into Calay.

129 *Ishalem, Main Church*

After another month of labor the grand Ondun's Cathedral was finally completed. The work was overseen by Sen Bira na-Lanis, who chose the best craftsmen and artisans, whether they were Urabans, Tierrans, or Saedrans.

Years ago, with Omra's encouragement, Soldan Vishkar had begun the project with high ambitions. Although the final design was not what he had dreamed it would be, the towering church was still a monument to human talent and aspirations. Mosaic artists covered the whitewashed walls with beautiful panoramas of (newly revised) scenes that showed Aiden and Urec sailing back to Terravitae together. Joron had corrected misinformation and provided details, while also granting the artists free rein with their imaginations. Colorful banners hung throughout the church, showing both the golden spiral of the Unfurling Fern and the curved Fishhook.

Among the presters and sikaras, there had been much discussion of eliminating both symbols to start afresh, as Ondun had asked, but neither land wished to erase its culture and history. The important thing, Joron said, was to throw overboard the cargo of hatred and refill the hold with understanding.

The massive new cathedral held an equal number of hook and fern symbols. Each day, the sikaras and presters taught classes to ever-growing crowds. Once they stopped fixating on details, scholars found a surprising amount of common ground in their beliefs, and they learned to respect the brave of the faith, from both sides.

When the Ishalem church was completed with all the gold leaf and brickwork and paintings in place, the tiles laid, roof plates fastened, and bronze domes burnished, the doors were flung open for the great celebration. Ur-Sikara Kuari and Prester Ciarlo gave the initial address to the crowd, though both were intimidated by the presence of Holy Joron inside the worship chamber. The powerful man remained quiet, but certainly not unobtrusive, at the rear of the hall.

After Kuari delivered a brief homily, Ciarlo stepped forward, raising his voice and speaking words he had not planned. "We can celebrate this great structure, but it is not our place to bless it. Joron himself is here—he is the rudder of our church." Ciarlo spread his hands. "We owe this holy place to you, my Lord."

Kuari also spoke to him. "You taught us how to use the strength of our faith to bind us together, rather than tear us apart. Tierrans and Urabans would surely have brought about the end times if you had not helped us steer our course away from the dangers. We owe you our very survival as a race. Let us all sing praises to Holy Joron!"

The Traveler raised his voice and addressed the gathered people who stared at him in awe. "Do not sing my praises. I will not be a god sitting on a throne in this church. I prefer to do what I've done for centuries—I walk among you. I'll watch and observe."

A mutter of conversation rippled through the congregation.

After the devastating span of the long war, the people needed someone to take a firm hand and lead their daily lives, to guide them and stop them from making mistakes. But Joron refused to fill that role.

Now his voice took on a warning tone, and his words echoed off the ornate walls. "As you go about your daily lives, as you interact with one another, always remember that I am here, watching. Do not forget your agreement." Joron seemed larger now, as godlike and powerful as they expected him to be, then he transformed again into a man dressed in hermit's robes. As the people looked in all directions, he somehow vanished into the crowd.

Ciarlo watched from the altar and smiled. Everyone else considered it a miracle, but he had seen the Traveler before. He believed he would encounter the old man again. He had faith.

130 *Iboria Reach*

The frigid wind across the steppes felt wonderful. When Destrar Broeck drew a deep breath, his nostrils burned with the chill. "Ah, so much better than dust and scrub brush, Iaros. Good riddance to Gremurr, I say—this is the weather I prefer."

Each man rode a shaggy mammoth northward into the wasteland dotted with snow, boulders, and low tundra grasses. Iaros twined his fingers in the beast's thick russet fur. "It's good to be home, Uncle. Iboria needs its destrar. All those attacks, the military camp, the prisoners—it wears on a man. I'd rather attend to the business of shipping Iborian lumber south."

Broeck looked ahead to the wide steppes. The mammoths marched ahead, crunching through drifts, and picked up speed as they smelled the redolent peaty marshes they considered home.

"I always feel better after a survival quest," Broeck said. "Relying on myself and my skills, the cold, the endurance—it cleanses a man's mind and heart. We'll both feel whole again, I guarantee it." He self-consciously stroked his naked chin.

Iaros's lips quirked in a smile. "The mustaches are very striking on your face, Uncle. I hope you keep the style."

Broeck snorted. "It leaves my chin cold. There's a reason Ondun put hair on our faces . . . but I'll keep it this way for now." He was amused that the style had indeed begun to catch on across Iboria.

The men had already made plans about how to restore prosperity to Iboria Reach. They planned to increase timber cutting and float large rafts of Iborian pine down the coast of Tierra. In their most ambitious plan, the two men meant to deliver wood in an epic journey through the Ishalem canal all the way to the Middlesea ports. Thanks to Broeck's fiery raid, Olabar harbor was in tremendous need of extra materials, and Soldan-Shah Omra would pay well for the wood and the work (although Broeck would have to dance a fine line about how much he could charge without insulting the Urabans, since he was the one who had burned the city in the first place).

The shaggy beasts trumpeted when they saw a cluster of wild mammoths ahead. They trotted forward, happy to return to the herd. "Time to dismount," Broeck said. "From here, you and I are on our own."

They slid down from the high furry backs, taking their packs, blankets, dried food, and firestarting materials. He and his nephew would live off the land for a time. They carried spears to hunt walrus or seals when they reached the frozen waters to the north and weapons to defend against the great white bears, should they encounter one.

Broeck suspected he might find a camp of nomads following the mammoth herd. The nomads would likely welcome them, share their campfires and food, but he turned away from the wandering beasts and struck out in a different direction. "This way, Iaros." He preferred to be alone.

He shifted the pack on his shoulders, he adjusted the mittens on his hands. "In two days, we'll come upon the ice cliffs. If we're lucky, we might find another ice dragon. A man is fortunate to see Raathgir once in his life . . . but I can dream."

Iaros looked concerned. "You already killed an ice dragon and took its horn. Is it wise to hunt another?"

Broeck laughed. "Not to kill it—just to *find* it. I want to make sure Raathgir is still here to protect the land."

The two men set off into the cold steppes.

131 Peliton, Erietta Reach

Fully settled back home in Erietta, Jenirod stood inside his personal residence and reassessed his most valued possessions. He was not surprised to find that they no longer excited him.

His father, the destrar of Erietta, had a large wooden house with many rooms. Jenirod's little brothers played there, did chores out in the stables (because their father said the work was good for them), and spent their days receiving instruction in mathematics, engineering, agricultural theory, Tierran history, even poetry. The boys learned the basics of the reach's vital industries: animal husbandry, horsecraft, beekeeping, weaving, woodworking, irrigation, and ropemaking.

In previous years, when Destrar Unsul had imposed those classes on his eldest son, Jenirod was scornful of wasting his time. His interests tended toward showy horse cavalcades, breaking spirited stallions, or riding out in the hills. The only thing he knew about garment-making was how to select which outfits made him look the most dashing. He had been rude and disrespectful to his father, convinced that the man understood nothing about the important things a destrar needed to know.

Jenirod had been completely wrong. He realized that now.

Upon coming of age, Jenirod had moved to a separate house in Peliton, where he could do as he wished and not worry about his father's disapproving glances, the disappointed shake of his head. Unsul had stopped trying to reshape his eldest son and devoted his attentions instead to the younger boys, Gart and Pol. Jenirod hadn't even noticed the shift before, but upon returning home he felt ashamed, disappointed in himself.

The main room in his house was a gaudy parade of empty triumphs. Colorful ribbons adorned the walls, pennants from cavalcades he had championed, trophies and cups that proved his prowess as a horseman, polished awards that he barely even remembered. Jenirod had thought such prizes proved his greatness. Now he considered himself little better than a glutton who was proud of the bones from feasts he had eaten.

He grabbed a long green ribbon that dangled from a hook and tore it down. Oh yes, he recalled the day he had won it: gusty winds blowing dust in the horse's eyes and his own . . . his jaunty hat had blown away into the stands, where several young women quarreled over it. When the official presented him with this emerald ribbon, Jenirod had thought his life was complete.

Only one day after his return from Ishalem, Jenirod took an empty crate from one of the storehouses and stuffed the ribbon into it. Then he began pulling one trophy after another off his shelves and throwing them into the crate.

Not so long ago, he had planned to devote a separate room in Calay Castle to his trophies, when he was married to the queen. He had tried to impress Anjine with his supposed accomplishments, and she'd seen right through his façade and found him wanting. How little he had understood! Jenirod realized that he still had a lot of maturing to do before he was ready to become a destrar.

"Are you going to get rid of everything?" His father's voice came from behind him, and Jenirod turned quickly, startled to see Destrar Unsul standing in the room, watching him.

He looked down at the ribbons in his hand. "At first I thought I should burn them, but that's too extreme. I'll keep some . . . but only some."

Buried under several newer ribbons and accolades on a side table, he found a small rosette of hand-stitched ribbon. He picked it up and showed it to his father, who also smiled and said, "I remember that one."

Jenirod's mother had made it for him to wear at his very first show, a lead-line class, where his instructor led the boy securely on a lead rope at a walk. It was a fat sturdy pony, and three-year-old Jenirod's chubby booted legs had stuck out ridiculously in stirrups run all the way up the saddle, barely able to curl over the top of the pony's back. Even then, little Jenirod had done his best to sit tall and correct, to hold the bridle's reins low as his instructor taught him. He hadn't won that first class, but it didn't matter, for his mother had made him the little rosette to wear on his hat.

There were precious few ribbons and awards that meant as much. As he sorted through the bric-a-brac, Jenirod kept the ones he remembered, the ones that mattered. The rest he simply threw into the box.

"Winning a prize won't make me a better destrar. People need to work, to eat, to have homes. I watched them go through great hardships in the war. They suffered and died for their queen and their church. They sacrificed everything." His voice cracked. "Would they do that for me—just because I won a horse show?"

Unsul was a thin man with large eyes, a scholarly figure who liked to experiment and tinker. Jenirod wasn't even sure his father knew how to *ride* a horse, and horses were Erietta's pride. "You'll get no argument from me, son, and I am sorry for what you had to endure in the war."

"No tutor could have taught me that course of lessons. I needed to learn for myself, I see that now. These silly shows are a waste of time, effort, and money better spent elsewhere in the reach." He continued to pile his trophies into the crate, rambling aloud to himself. "We should declare a moratorium on cavalcades and pageants. Tierra has suffered a great blow, and now it's time for us to grow up. We don't have time for frivolous things."

Unsul surprised him, though. "We can't cancel all of them, Jenirod—that would not be wise."

Jenirod lifted a tarnished silver cup with feathery handles. In the past, he had polished it and polished it, though he himself was the only person who ever looked at the trophy. "But what purpose do they serve?"

"The people need *something*, son. It's Eriettan tradition, the foundations of our horse trade and livelihood. Our people are proud, and deservedly so. Forgetting who we are and who we were would be just as great a blow to our hearts as the Urabans dealt us. Our people need their shows, fairs, and festivals to lift their spirits, to give them a brief respite from their toils, to strengthen them as a community. You should ride again yourself. Let them cheer. A destrar must be loved and respected, and you've certainly earned that." Unsul gestured to the remaining awards and ribbons. "We've got to celebrate our prowess, show the world what we do so well, but we need to keep such things in the proper perspective."

"You're a wise man, Father," Jenirod said. "I will also keep this, and this." He chose a large best-of-show trophy from his first cavalcade as a featured rider. "The rest are just hubris."

His father let out a contented sigh. "I am glad to have you back home, Jenirod. I was worried about you—and not just on the battlefield."

Jenirod smiled. "If you'll give me a second chance, Father, I'd like you to teach me the harder parts about ruling. I need to know more than just the fun parts."

A satisfied smile crossed Unsul's face. "Then someday you will be a worthy destrar."

132 Calay

Aldo na-Curic's homecoming was everything he had dreamed of. He came back to Calay with the third wave of soldiers, only to find the city abuzz with preparations for Queen Anjine's impending marriage, due to take place on the upcoming Landing Day. Already banners and ribbons adorned the streets, and everyone seemed giddy with celebrating the end of the war.

After leaving the dusty road into Calay, Aldo crossed the bridge into the Saedran District, hurrying along familiar streets, amazed to see how much had changed. Every detail of the neighborhood was clear in his perfect memory: many of the shops and homes had a patchwork quality of newness, repaired or rebuilt after the recent hurricane; some of the damaged buildings had been torn down entirely. A bakery was gone, replaced by a clockmaker's workshop. He smelled fresh wood and heard the rough huffing of a saw through lumber in a cabinetmaker's shop. He saw two new apothecaries, and an open school in what had been the drafty warehouse of a grain seller.

For him, however, the most important sight was his own home. Aldo had sailed away on the *Dyscovera* nearly a year ago. The last time he'd been gone for so long was because the Urabans had captured him; he had only made it home again through Sen Sherufa's help. He suspected his family would never let him go away again.

When he stood at the front door, though, his hand froze on the latch. Until now, he had thought only of coming home and seeing all the familiar faces . . . but a year was a long time. Children were born, couples got married, people died. The hurricane had obviously caused great damage. Mailes had reassured him, but what if something bad had happened to his family in the meantime? What if his parents were dead or—far worse—one of his children gone? The gray fever? An accident?

For an instant, Aldo clung to the idyllic reality preserved so perfectly in his head, knowing that once he opened the door it would never be the same again. But he could not avoid the truth—waiting like a fool on the doorstep changed nothing. He, Sen Aldo na-Curic had sailed to the edge of the world. He had set foot on Terravitae, spoken with Ondun himself. He could do this.

Aldo pushed open the door and stepped inside.

They were all there.

Because Queen Anjine and the first soldiers had returned weeks earlier, his family was expecting him. He felt like a man facing an unruly stampede as Lanni ran forward squealing with delight, throwing herself on him; then his son and daughter nearly tackled him. His brother, sister, and both his parents crowded around, hugging him, weeping, hurling a storm of questions. He didn't have enough arms to embrace them all at once, but he tried. Tears streamed down his face.

Aldo blocked out the chatter for a minute just so he could hold his wife. Lanni was so beautiful. Her dark eyes sparkled, and the happiness on her face made his heart swell to the bursting point. King Sonhir's daughters had absolutely nothing to compare with this!

Though he tried to be discreet, his arrival had not gone unnoticed in the Saedran District. Within moments, it seemed, people were pounding on the na-Curic door. Aldo wanted time alone with his family, but he had obligations to his fellow Saedrans as well. They would want to know everything. Soon the house was so crowded that there was little room to breathe or move. Neighbors brought food, and the impromptu feast expanded until they had to open the doors and set out tables in the streets.

Then, amid the joy, Aldo realized who was missing. Sen Leo na-Hadra. He looked around as person after person congratulated him. He finally asked Lanni, "Where is your father? I have so much to tell him. We've nearly completed the Mappa Mundi—we've discovered so much!"

But she fell silent and turned her head away. "He was killed, Aldo. *Ra'virs* murdered him and destroyed the model of the *Dyscovera.*"

Aldo felt as if he had received a great blow to the chest. "Oh, Lanni, I'm so sorry." He hugged her tight.

"He tried to protect the ship model, but he couldn't do it."

Aldo felt cold as he thought of how the real *Dyscovera* had also been wrecked, nearly sunk by the Leviathan. The two events must have happened at the same time, inextricably connected.

Lanni took a long breath and clung to his arm, then she straightened. "My father was a great man, Aldo, and he will be remembered and loved. But right now, let us think of happier things. My husband is home, our children have their father again, and we all have a reason to celebrate."

The following day, Aldo and his father entered the Saedran temple and descended to the underground vault. Sen Leo had first showed the young man this place on the day he'd been named a Saedran chartsman . . . so long ago.

Biento na-Curic looked both awed and pleased to hear his son's descriptions. "This is a project that's long needed to be done. You describe, and I will paint."

Aldo let his eyes fall half closed. "I can tell you about the oceans and islands. Thanks to Sen Sherufa na-Oa, now I can give you the Great Desert, the Nunghal lands, the southern sea, even the

Middlesea. And we have sailed across the world, seen wondrous islands, set foot on Terravitae. But given what Ondun said, that is still not all of it."

The Map of All Things had been painted in exquisite detail on the vaulted ceiling and smooth walls of the temple chamber, but many blank spots remained on sections of wall and ceiling. And now Aldo helped fill them in—a broad and colorful panorama of the whole world, including the sunken continent of the original Saedran colony.

Over the hours, while he and his father worked, Saedran elders gathered to observe them. As Biento painted, Aldo marveled to remember all the things he had seen with his own eyes. The whole world . . . or just a small part of it.

He knew that even when his father finished the last brush-stroke here, the Mappa Mundi was not yet complete. In a way, Aldo was glad.

133 *Calay*

After the end of the war and the shift in the world's religions, Queen Anjine had many loose ends to tie up while she and her functionaries also planned for her grand wedding to Mateo Bornan.

Criston Vora insisted that the queen need not trouble herself with the formalities of rewarding him, but she insisted. She sent a royal summons to him and the thirty remaining members of his crew, and they dutifully gathered at Calay Castle, whose turrets had been bedecked with ribbons and streamers. Well-dressed merchants, destrars and representatives from all the five reaches were arriving for the wedding. Even so, Queen Anjine found time to bring Criston and the *Dyscovera* sailors into the throne room.

City guard captain Vorannen had already given each sailor a large purse of coins, twice the payment they were originally promised. In addition, Anjine sent her tailors to see that each crewman had a new set of clothes for the occasion.

The fidgeting and nervous seamen now stood behind their captain, looking up at the throne. Criston bowed to the queen. He had come here many years ago with ship models and plans, proposing to build the *Dyscovera* so he could continue his voyages of exploration. That seemed so long ago, in a different world, and he had been a different person.

"Captain Criston Vora, we welcome you and your crew back to Tierra and give you our gratitude for all the discoveries you have made. This is a most unexpected joy."

He bowed farther. "Thank you, Majesty."

She signaled him to rise. "King Korastine sent you on a quest to find Terravitae. That was his longtime dream, and you accomplished it. I wish he could have lived to see this day." Anjine gave him a bittersweet smile. "You have done everything we asked of you. Name your reward, Captain, and as queen of Tierra I will grant it. What do you desire most—a chest full of gold coins? Lands? A title?"

Criston had not considered any reward beyond the generous payment she had already given him. In a very real sense, the *Dyscovera* and his quest had brought him back to life, saved him from the emptiness that had smothered him for years. He straightened, though, as the answer occurred to him. "What would please me most, Majesty, is another ship."

During the weeks of the queen's wedding preparations, Soldan-Shah Omra dispatched emissaries from Ishalem, whom Anjine welcomed. Ur-Sikara Kuari herself accompanied Prester Ciarlo to the great city of Calay. Ciarlo had already been designated the next prester-marshall—after all, the Traveler himself had befriended him.

He and Kuari preached in the square before the main Aidenist kirk, then walked through the streets of Calay in a great procession, spreading the word. By order of the soldan-shah, and following the wishes of Urec as spoken by the ur-sikara herself, they addressed any remaining *ra'virs* who still hid among the Tierrans. Kuari raised her voice and spoke to all the Tierran faces in the crowds, telling them to put aside their training, relinquish their missions, and plan no more harm to Calay or any other Tierran city.

"That time is past," Kuari shouted in the main square. "The Teacher is no more. You served Urec in the best way you thought possible, but Ondun Himself has given you a new mission. Live your lives as who you are, with no more secrets, no more retribution."

When she delivered the message, Ciarlo didn't expect indoctrinated young men and women to appear out of the crowd and reveal themselves as *ra'virs* who had lived in Calay all this time. He hoped, at least, that the hidden saboteurs would quietly go about their true lives, and no one need be the wiser.

Nevertheless, the ur-sikara's words were powerful and compelling; to Ciarlo, they demonstrated that the world had changed in a fundamental way.

By the queen's order, the wedding itself took place with a minimum of confusion and contradictions. The event would be like salve on a painful wound for the people of Tierra—and then the healing could begin.

Enifir fussed over Anjine for hours on the day of the wedding, primping the queen's dress and hair, coloring her lips and eyelids, adding a wreath of flowers instead of a crown. "The people need this as much as you do, Majesty. Please be patient." She tucked an imagined loose strand of Anjine's hair under the floral wreath.

Anjine had heard that a bride-to-be was supposed to be nervous on her wedding day, but she was entirely content. With or without her handmaiden's fussing, she had to admit that she felt beautiful and, beyond that, truly happy. She felt the baby inside her, strong and growing.

Loud bells rang out from the highest tower of the main kirk, accompanied by the brassy songs of bells in the other kirks throughout Calay.

When she and her procession made their way to the kirk, walking through the main doors and marching down the grand aisle, Anjine looked ahead to the altar. The split horn of Raathgir had been restored to its stand, but she concentrated only on the dashing and handsome figure of Mateo waiting for her.

Fully healed now, he wore a formal military uniform without rank insignia or medals. His service was well respected, as was that of all the soldiers of Tierra, but the provocative glories of the long and bloody war were best kept safely locked away. Mateo grinned at her just as he had as a young boy.

The people in the crowded kirk rose to their feet as the queen passed. Anjine saw Ammur Sonnen in the front row, his eyes filled with tears and a wistful smile on his face. The big blacksmith showed no anger or resentment, only a genuine pleasure to see the queen and Mateo being wed.

Prester Ciarlo and ur-Sikara Kuari stood together at the altar, with the ancient leather-bound book between them, the Captains' Log, the new Book of Aiden and Urec that Captain Vora had retrieved from Terravitae. They had opened the tome to passages with which they were only just now becoming familiar. The two had agreed on verses that would be appropriate for the queen's wedding ceremony.

When Anjine and Mateo stepped up to the altar together, the two religious leaders held out the silver-and-gold chains, interlocked fishhooks and fern spirals, one linked to another. Ammur Sonnen himself had crafted the intricate new chains of their wedding bond, following the special new design that Kuari and Ciarlo had created.

Amid the background noise of fanfare and applause, Anjine heard Mateo mutter just for her, "I hope they don't go on too long. I am very anxious to be married to you."

She smiled at him. "I gave them explicit instructions to be brief."

Ciarlo and Kuari opened the ceremony by each reading a verse from the new book, then they directed Anjine and Mateo to link their delicate chains, fishhook and fern.

The couple spoke the sincere vows they had crafted together, but from that point, it was all just words, for in their hearts, Anjine and Mateo had been married for a very long time.

134 *Ishalem*

Before leaving Ishalem to return to his capital city, Omra went with Istar to the cathedral's highest minaret. From that vantage, they could look across the beautiful holy city. The soldan-shah inhaled the fresh salty air and felt its healing strength. "It's good to be a *ruler* again, Istar, instead of a military commander," he said. "I want to meet with emissaries from all five of my soldanates to discuss the future of Uraba. We have so much work to do."

Istar leaned closer to him, and Omra slipped his arm around her waist and held her there. He knew this woman belonged at his side. "I am glad you decided to stay with me. I need you."

"It was the right choice." Her voice grew wistful. "Someday, though, I'd like to return to Windcatch and see my old home. Would you go with me?"

His throat went dry. "I doubt that would be a good idea, considering the circumstances the last time I was there."

"But it might be a necessary step . . . after the other wounds heal."

"If that's what you ask of me, how can I do anything less?"

Their quiet moment was broken when Naori joined them, accompanied by Omra's two boisterous young sons. "Oh! The view is beautiful from up here." The boys bounded to the open windows, eager to see.

Omra looked at the two women and mused, "My father set up a separate residence for his wife Asha here in Ishalem, while his other wives remained in Olabar." He glanced from Naori to Istar. "Would you like me to do the same for you? If we're at peace now, you will both be safe wherever you are."

Naori answered immediately, "No. Why would we want that?"

Istar laughed. "We're happy together, Omra. Naori and I help each other."

The older boy, Zarif Omirr, interrupted them, pointing vigorously. "Look, are those the Saedrans?"

From the minaret, they could observe the canal across the isthmus. The mer-Saedrans had labored hard to clear away the sunken ironclads, and the waterway was finally open again. As Omra and his family gathered to look, they spotted a group of swimmers frolicking and laughing in the water.

"The one in the lead is King Sonhir, I think," Omra said.

"Where are they going?" the zarif asked.

"Wherever they like."

Together, they watched the mer-Saedrans swim through the canal, all of them heading out to the Middlesea and new waters to explore.

135 *Ishalem Harbor*

After a year, it was time to sail away again.

Criston Vora and Saan drew funding from the coffers of Ishalem. With money donated by Soldan-Shah Omra as well as the Saedran treasury, and many materials delivered directly from Tierra with the blessings of Queen Anjine, the two captains had begun their plans just months after watching Ondun sail away in the great Arkship.

Ystya haunted Saan's dreams, and he could not stop thinking of her. After six months helping with the rebuilding in Ishalem and then Olabar, he was ready to set off for the far horizon once more.

For himself, Criston no longer felt at home on land or in a city, even one as glorious as Ishalem. Though his decades-long quest to find Adrea was over, he would always be a man of the seas. After many tribulations, he had lost the love of his life, but at least he knew she was safe, even happy. After he met her three daughters, he understood that she had built a vast part of her life—a happy life—without him.

Saan introduced his sisters to Criston, who quickly saw how much Adrea loved her daughters. He accepted her decision to stay; how could he have torn that family apart? She could never have been happy if she surrendered her daughters for him. Criston would have been taking her away from that life just as much as Omra had taken her from Windcatch so many years earlier.

And in spite of the painful losses, Criston had unexpectedly gained a son—a son very much like himself. He and Saan worked together for months to prepare for this voyage. Queen Anjine and Soldan-Shah Omra had agreed that the two captains could take any vessel they chose for their next expedition to Terravitae.

Criston and Saan spent weeks studying the Tierran and Uraban ships that remained in the harbor—the hulls, the masts, the lines—and talking with their captains. They knew the true extent of the voyage they were undertaking, and in their individual logbooks they had two alternate routes to Terravitae. And beyond those routes lay half a world of unexplored water.

Having designed many vessels himself, Criston was very

particular. In the end, he and Saan chose a sturdy two-masted Uraban warship with a broad beam and spacious hull—the largest of the vessels Soldan Vishkar had rounded up for defending Ishalem. Saan convinced his father that such a design would be best suited for the long voyage back to Terravitae.

While the mer-Saedrans continued to travel back and forth through the canal, spreading out into the Middlesea before returning to the great waters to the west, Kjelnar rejoined his captain, offering his services. "I hear you plan to undertake another voyage, Captain Vora. I would like to be part of it, if you'll have me. I could be of some help."

Criston clapped the big Iborian on the shoulders. "You are always welcome on my ship, Kjelnar. There could be quite an advantage to having someone with your underwater skills among my crew, but right now we need your skills as a shipwright." He stretched out his arm to indicate the Uraban warship. "This is the vessel we'll take. Can you make her strong enough to withstand another trip around the world?"

"That I can, Captain."

Saan put out a call throughout Ishalem, and Criston sent messengers up the Tierran coast to recruit only the best sailors willing to undertake a long and arduous voyage. Grigovar and Yal Dolicar were two of the first to sign up, and Saan accepted them gladly. He even paid for a set of newly crafted hand attachments so that Dolicar had plenty of tools for his wrist.

By the heart of the following summer, after weeks of unbroken good weather, the new exploration vessel was finished, loaded with supplies, rigged, and ready to sail. The glorious ship was christened the *Infinita*, for her exploration of the world would not be limited by the earth, the seas, or the stars.

On the day of their departure, as the crew crowded aboard and waved farewell, Criston stood with Saan on the dock. Adrea came all the way from Olabar to see them off, dressed in the finest Yuarej silk robes to denote her rank, yet she had removed her head scarf to let her blond Tierran hair blow free.

Saan embraced his mother. "I'll be back again, I promise."

"I know you two will keep each other safe."

Criston stepped very close to her and felt love welling up within him, but his dreams were different now. Adrea touched his cheek, and he kissed her farewell. "I have to chase the horizon now, but I promise to keep sending you letters."

"Then you'll need this." Adrea teased out a thick lock of her golden hair, took a jeweled knife from her sash, sliced off the lock, and gave it to him. Criston smiled and cried at the same time, squeezing the soft strands as if the lock was the most precious substance he'd ever held, before tucking it securely into a pocket of his vest.

Saan pointed out, "We're bringing another sympathetic logbook. That's the fastest way for us to keep in touch."

"We'll use both," Criston said. He looked at Adrea, gazed around the city of Ishalem, and realized that the beautiful, graceful *Infinita* called him more than staying here did. Deep in his heart, he knew he had to go back to Terravitae . . . and from there to anyplace else in the world that remained to be explored. He knew Saan felt the same way.

After a last round of goodbyes, they boarded the *Infinita*, cast off, and set sail for the open sea.

Glossary

ABILAN one of the soldanates of Uraba.

ADREA wife of Criston Vora, captured by Urecari raiders; now named Istar.

ADREALA first daughter of Adrea by Omra.

AIDEN one of the two brothers who sailed from Terravitae to discover the world. The descendants of his crew populated Tierra.

AIDENIST follower of the Book of Aiden.

AIDEN'S COMPASS ancient relic whose needle will point back toward Terravitae.

AIDEN'S LIGHTHOUSE tall lighthouse on the western side of Ishalem, now controlled by Urabans.

AIZARA Uraban driftwood reader.

ALAMONT one of the five reaches of Tierra, rich agricultural land led by Destrar Shenro.

ALDO NA-CURIC, SEN Saedran chartsman aboard the *Dyscovera.*

ALISI sister of Unwar, kidnapped by Tierran traders.

AL-ORIZIN Uraban exploration ship sent off to find the Key to Creation.

AMMUR SONNEN blacksmith who runs the largest smithy in Calay, father of Vicka.

ANDOUK soldan of Yuarej, father of Cliaparia.

ANJINE queen of Tierra, daughter of King Korastine.

ANTOS captain of Soldan Vishkar's flagship in the Uraban fleet.

ARDAN subcomdar of the Tierran navy.

ARIKARA capital city of Missinia.

ARKSHIP ancient vessel wrecked in Ishalem, believed to be the original vessel belonging either to Aiden or Urec.

ASADDAN Nunghal refugee who crossed the Great Desert to Missinia.

ASHA second wife of Soldan-Shah Imir, murdered by Prester Hannes.

BAINE, PRESTER-MARSHALL former prester-marshall of the Aidenist church, martyred with his followers in the ruins of Ishalem.

BELLUC captain of the slave galley *Moray*.

BIENTO NA-CURIC Saedran painter, Aldo's father.

BOOK OF AIDEN Aidenist holy book.

BORA'S BASTION capital city of Alamont Reach.

BOURAS legendary Father of All Serpents, supposedly girdles the world.

BROECK destrar of Iboria Reach, father of Ilrida, grandfather of Tomas.

BURIAN NA-COWAY Saedran model-maker.

BURILO the son of the Missinia soldan, Omra's cousin.

CALAVIK capital city of Iboria Reach.

CALAY capital city of Tierra.

CAPTAIN'S COMPASS a compass that always points home.

CHARTSMAN a Saedran navigator possessing perfect memory.

CIARLO brother of Adrea, lame in one leg, prester of the town of Windcatch.

CINDON VORA father of Criston, a fisherman lost at sea.

CITHARA daughter of Cliaparia and Omra, now raised by Istar.

CLIAPARIA Omra's second wife.

COMDAR leader of Tierran army and navy.

CORAG one of the five reaches of Tierra, a mountainous region led by Destrar Siescu.

CRISTON VORA captain of the *Dyscovera*, survivor of the *Luminara* expedition. Criston is married to Adrea (Istar), who was lost in a Urecari raid.

DESERT HARBOR new settlement on the edge of the Great Desert, from which sand coracles launch, devastated in bandit raid.

DESTRAR the leader of one of the five Tierran reaches.

DOLICAR, YAL confidence man who moves back and forth from Uraba to Tierra.

DRIFTWOOD READER a fortune teller who can determine the future by studying the whorls in a piece of driftwood.

DYSCOVERA Tierran ship built to explore the seas and find Terravitae, captained by Criston Vora.

EDICT LINE the boundary agreed to by the leaders of Tierra and Uraba, dividing the world in half.

ENIFIR Anjine's handmaiden, wife of Guard-Marshall Vorannen.

ENOCH DEY crewman aboard the *Dyscovera*.

ERIETTA one of the five reaches of Tierra, mainly rangeland, led by Destrar Unsul.

ERIMA ur-sikara from Lahjar, successor to Lukai.

EYE OF UREC symbol painted on the sails of Uraban ships.

FASHIA'S FOUNTAIN important shrine to Urecari faith.

FENNAN prester in the village of Windcatch.

FIRUN old Aidenist slave at Gremurr mines, household servant to Tukar.

FISHHOOK symbol of the Aidenist church.

FROST GIANTS legendary titans who live in the cold, can bring winter with a breath.

FYIRI prominent sikara aboard the *Al-Orizin*.

GART young son of Destrar Unsul.

GOLDEN FERN fern with mythic properties, supposedly planted by Urec before he became the Traveler. Anyone who finds the fern is destined for greatness.

GOLDEN FERN first ironclad warship in Uraban navy.
GREAT DESERT arid wasteland in the south of Uraba.
GREMURR secret Uraban mines on the northern coast of the Middlesea, in Tierran territory.
GRIGOVAR member of the *Al-Orizin*'s crew, former reef diver from Lahjar.
HANNES prester serving aboard the *Dyscovera*, once saved by Criston Vora. Years earlier, he also lived in Ishalem as a spy learning about the Urecari faith.
HIST subcomdar of the Tierran army.
HUTTAN soldan of Inner Wahilir, husband of Kuari, charged with building a large church in Ishalem.
IAROS nephew of Destrar Broeck, heir apparent of Iboria.
IBORIA one of the five reaches of Tierra, the region to the far north, led by Destrar Broeck.
ILRIDA daughter of Destrar Broeck, second wife of King Korastine and mother of Prince Tomas; she died of tetanus.
IMIR former soldan-shah of the Urabans, father of Omra, now retired.
INFINITA sturdy sailing ship designed for a voyage to Terravitae.
INNER WAHILIR one of the soldanates of Uraba.
ISHALEM the holy city considered the center of both the Aidenist and Urecari religions, burned in a great fire and now reclaimed by Uraba.
ISTALA second daughter of Adrea by Omra.
ISTAR (1) young wife of Zarif Omra, died in childbirth.
ISTAR (2) First Wife of Soldan-Shah Omra, mother of Saan, Adreala, and Istala; formerly Adrea, wife of Criston Vora.
IYOMELKA mysterious woman living on an isolated island, mother of Ystya.
JAVIAN cabin boy aboard the *Dyscovera*.
JENIROD eldest son of Destrar Unsul of Erietta.
JERARD old prester aboard the *Luminara*, killed by a sea serpent.

JIKARIS khan of the Nunghal-Ari.
JORON third son of Ondun, who remained behind in Terravitae when Aiden and Urec sailed away.
KEL rank of captain in the soldan-shah's palace guards.
KEY TO CREATION mysterious powerful object sought by Urec and Aiden.
KHALIG Uraban merchant, chosen by Kel Unwar as a messenger to Calay to deliver Tomas's head.
KHENARA port city on Oceansea coast of Uraba.
KIRK Aidenist church.
KJELNAR Iborian shipwright, builder of *Dyscovera* and her first mate.
KORASTINE king of Tierra, father of Anjine and Tomas.
KRAKEN enormous monster from the depths of the sea.
KUARI First Wife of Soldan Huttan from Inner Wahilir.
LAHJAR port city on Oceansea coast of Uraba, the farthest settlement south.
LANDING DAY Aidenist festival commemorating the landing of Aiden's Arkship.
LANNI wife of Sen Aldo na-Curic.
LEO NA-HADRA, SEN old Saedran scholar, adviser of King Korastine, teacher of Aldo na-Curic.
LEVIATHAN terrible sea monster that destroyed the *Luminara.*
LIGHTHOUSE AT THE END OF THE WORLD isolated outpost where Mailes watches the rest of the world through a magical lens.
LITHIO First Wife of Soldan-Shah Imir, mother of Omra.
LUKAI former ur-sikara of the Urecari church, killed after a plot to poison Omra.
LUMINARA magnificent exploration vessel dispatched from Tierra to discover the world, sunk by the Leviathan.
MAILES keeper of the Lighthouse at the End of the World, exiled by Ondun and cursed to remain there.

MATEO BORNAN childhood friend of Anjine, now subcomdar in the Tierran army, liaison to the throne.
MIA sailor aboard the *Dyscovera.*
MIDDLESEA vast sea to the east of Ishalem.
MISSINIA one of the soldanates of Uraba.
MORAY slave galley in the Middlesea, captained by Belluc.
NAORI second wife of Soldan-Shah Omra, mother of his sons.
NIKOL NA-FENDA, SEN Saedran chartsman on the *Luminara.*
NUNGHAL race inhabiting the Uraban continent to the south of the Great Desert. They are composed of two branches, the nomadic Nunghal-Ari and the seafaring Nunghal-Su.
NUNGHAL-ARI nomadic branch of the Nunghals.
NUNGHAL-SU seafaring branch of the Nunghals.
OCEANSEA vast sea to the west of Ishalem.
OLABAR capital city of Uraba.
OLA NA-TEN, SEN Saedran physician.
OLBA turbanlike head covering, usually white, worn by Urecari men.
OMIRR Soldan-Shah Omra's eldest son, by his second wife Naori; the zarif of Uraba.
ONDUN creator of the world; father of three sons, Aiden, Urec, and Joron.
OUTER WAHILIR one of the soldanates of Uraba.
PELITON capital city of Erietta Reach.
PILGRIM'S PATH processional path up the hill to the Arkship in Ishalem.
POL young son of Destrar Unsul.
PRESTER an Aidenist priest.
PRESTER-MARSHALL leader of the Aidenist church.
QUANAS captain of the *Sacred Scroll.*
RAATHGIR name of the Iborian ice dragon, whose horn is said to be a talisman to ward off sea serpents.
RAATHGIR ironclad ship from Gremurr, captained by Iaros.

RAGA VAR mountain scout in Corag.

RA'VIR Tierran children raised by Urecari to become spies and saboteurs, named after an opportunistic bird that lays its eggs in other birds' nests.

REEFSPUR Tierran coastal fishing village.

ROVIK kel of the soldan-shah's palace guards.

RUAD outcast of the Nunghal-Su.

RUDIO former prester-marshall of Aidenist church, killed by a sea serpent.

SAAN son of Criston and Adrea.

SACRED SCROLL Tierran trading ship where Alisi was held captive.

SAEDRANS "Ondun's Stepchildren," independent people not descended from either Aiden or Urec. Saedrans serve as chartsmen, engineers, doctors, apothecaries, and other scientific professions.

SAPIER grandson of Aiden, founder of Aidenist church. In a legend, he caught a sea serpent with a fishhook and rode it to safe waters.

SAPIER'S GLORY flagship of Tierran navy.

SAPIER'S LIGHTHOUSE one of two lighthouses at the mouth of Calay harbor.

SAZAR leader of a clan of rivermen; he calls himself the "river destrar."

SEN term of respect and accomplishment for Saedrans.

SHARIQUE wife of Yuarej soldan Andouk, mother of Cliaparia.

SHAY, CAPTAIN ANDON captain of the *Luminara*, killed by the Leviathan.

SHENRO destrar of Alamont Reach.

SHERUFA NA-OA, SEN Saedran scholar in Olabar.

SHIELTAR former soldan-shah, grandfather of Omra.

SHIPKHAN captain's title among the Nunghals.

SIESCU destrar of Corag Reach.

SIKARA priestess in the Urecari church.
SILAM HENNER crewman aboard the *Dyscovera*.
SIOARA port on the Middlesea, capital of Inner Wahilir.
SOELAND one of the five reaches of Tierra, a group of islands.
SOLDAN leader of one of the regions of Uraba.
SOLDAN-SHAH the soldan of soldans, leader of all Uraba.
SONHIR leader of the undersea people of the sunken Saedran continent.
STONEHOLM capital city of Corag Reach.
TAVISHEL former destrar of Soeland Reach, killed in naval attack of Ishalem.
TEACHER mysterious hooded figure in charge of Omra's *ra'vir* program.
TERRAVITAE the original land where Ondun created his people, from which Aiden and Urec departed on their voyage.
TIERRA the northern continent, composed of five reaches; its population follows the Aidenist religion.
TOLLI name used by Anjine as her alternate childhood identity.
TOMAS son of King Korastine and Ilrida, brother of Anjine, grandson of Destrar Broeck, murdered by Kel Unwar.
TRAVELER wandering old man who leaves tales of his travels, rumored to be either Aiden or Urec.
TYCHO name used by Mateo as his alternate childhood identity; also, a cat raised by Queen Anjine.
UNFURLING FERN symbol of the Urecari church.
UNSUL destrar of Erietta Reach.
UNTRA former soldan-shah, grandfather of Imir.
UNWAR kel in the Uraban military, captain of the horse soldiers.
URABA the southern continent, composed of five reaches; its population follows the Urecari religion.
UREC one of the two brothers who sailed from Terravitae to discover the world. The descendants of his crew populated Uraba.
URECARI follower of Urec's Log.

UREC'S LOG Urecari holy book.
UR-SIKARA lead sikara of the Urecari church.
VICKA SONNEN daughter of Calay blacksmith Ammur Sonnen.
VILLIKI third wife of Soldan-Shah Imir, mother of Tukar.
VORANNEN marshall of the Calay city guard, married to Enifir.
WEN NA-CURIC younger brother of Aldo.
WILKA wife of Destrar Broeck, lost in a snowstorm.
WILKA ironclad flagship from Gremurr, captained by Destrar Broeck.
WINDCATCH small Tierran fishing village on the Oceansea coast, original home of Criston Vora.
XARIES a Uraban board game similar to chess.
XIVIR soldan of Missinia, father of Burilo.
YSTYA beautiful young woman living on an isolated island, daughter of Iyomelka.
YUAREJ one of the soldanates of Uraba.
YURA NA-CURIC Aldo's mother.
ZADAR workmaster in the Gremurr mines.
ZARIF Uraban title of prince.

Acknowledgments

The Terra Incognita trilogy has been an epic undertaking, both the story itself and all the behind-the-scenes work. Special thanks to my editor Darren Nash and publisher Tim Holman at Orbit Books, and agent John Silbersack at Trident Media Group.

Richard Ware creates the excellent maps of the Terra Incognita world. Lee Gibbons produced three magnificent covers that perfectly capture the feel of the series. The "Roswell Six" team did an amazing job interpreting the story and characters in rock music: composers Henning Pauly and Erik Norlander; vocalists Michael Sadler, Steve Walsh, James LaBrie, Sass Jordan, John Payne, Lana Lane, Nick Storr, Arjen Lucassen, Alex Froese, and Juan Roos; musicians Gary Wehrkamp, Kurt Barabas, Chris Brown, Chris Quirarte, Martin Orford, David Ragsdale, and Mike Alvarez.

My typist Mary Thomson kept up with me, transcribing the chapters as quickly as I sent her the audio files, and she also offered her expertise in horses. My hardworking test readers went over drafts of this novel with sharp eyes and sharp pencils, adding their input, insights, and ideas to make this a stronger story—Deb Ray, Diane Jones, Louis Moesta, and of course my wife, Rebecca Moesta.

About the Author

Kevin J. Anderson has written forty-six national and international bestsellers and has over twenty million books in print worldwide in thirty languages. He has been nominated for the Nebula Award, the Bram Stoker Award, and the *SFX* Readers' Choice Award. Find out more about Kevin J. Anderson at www.wordfire.com

Find out more about Kevin J. Anderson and other Orbit authors by registering for the free monthly newsletter at www.orbitbooks.net